ONCE IN A LIFETIME,

YOU GET TO LIVE THE FANTASY

With Joe Scarlatti on the watch, reclusive financial genius Rowena Willow may finally have to let down her hair....

Archaeologist Chelsey Mallon will be stunned by Alex Duport's ability to grant her three special, life-changing wishes....

And Caron Carlisle, accustomed to spinning straw into gold for her curmudgeonly client, must find a billion-dollar baby through a man who had long ago broken her heart.

Close your eyes,
and make a wish, with

CARLA NEGGERS
MARGARET ST. GEORGE
AND LEANDRA LOGAN

Carla Neggers, now a *New York Times* bestselling author, began her fiction writing career at the age of twenty-four, when she was a magna cum laude graduate of Boston University—her newborn baby learned to sleep to the pecking of her mother's rented typewriter. Most of her nearly forty books have appeared on national romance bestseller lists; she is a four-time *Romantic Times* award winner, and a Romance Writers of America RITA Award finalist. She is proud to note that she can claim over eight million copies of her books in print worldwide. The daughter of a Dutch sailor and a Southerner, Carla grew up in New England, and lives in Vermont with her husband and two children.

Margaret St. George is the talented author of over thirty novels, in categories ranging from historical to mystery to romantic romp. In addition to her very popular Harlequin American Romance novels, she has contributed to several special limited Harlequin series, such as Weddings by DeWilde and Delta Justice, and has also written a number of novellas for anthology collections, of which *The Arrangement* is the most recent. Maggie brings a wealth of life experience to her writing, having served as a flight attendant for United Airlines, as well as the national president of Romance Writers of America. She has received numerous awards for her work, and lives in her home state of Colorado with her husband, George.

Leandra Logan has written a total of twenty-six novels for adults and teenagers over her thirteen-year writing career. She is an award winner, and her name frequently appears on Waldenbooks and B. Dalton bestseller lists. Her next Harlequin Temptation novel, #725, *Just for the Night,* will appear next month as a featured title in Temptation's Bachelor Auction miniseries, celebrating Harlequin's fiftieth anniversary. A lifelong resident of Minnesota, Leandra makes her home in a St. Paul suburb with her husband, Gene, and children, Cindy and Tom.

ONCE UPON A TIME

CARLA NEGGERS
MARGARET ST. GEORGE
LEANDRA LOGAN

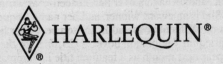

HARLEQUIN®

TORONTO • NEW YORK • LONDON
AMSTERDAM • PARIS • SYDNEY • HAMBURG
STOCKHOLM • ATHENS • TOKYO • MILAN • MADRID
PRAGUE • WARSAW • BUDAPEST • AUCKLAND

If you purchased this book without a cover you should be aware that this book is stolen property. It was reported as "unsold and destroyed" to the publisher, and neither the author nor the publisher has received any payment for this "stripped book."

HARLEQUIN BOOKS

by Request—ONCE UPON A TIME...

Copyright © 1999 by Harlequin Books S.A.

ISBN 0-373-20159-1

The publisher acknowledges the copyright holders of the individual works as follows:
NIGHT WATCH
Copyright © 1993 by Carla Neggers
A WISH...AND A KISS
Copyright © 1993 by Margaret St. George
THE MISSING HEIR
Copyright © 1993 by Mary Schultz

This edition published by arrangement with Harlequin Books S.A.

All rights reserved. Except for use in any review, the reproduction or utilization of this work in whole or in part in any form by any electronic, mechanical or other means, now known or hereafter invented, including xerography, photocopying and recording, or in any information storage or retrieval system, is forbidden without the written permission of the publisher, Harlequin Enterprises Limited, 225 Duncan Mill Road, Don Mills, Ontario, Canada M3B 3K9.

All characters in this book have no existence outside the imagination of the author and have no relation whatsoever to anyone bearing the same name or names. They are not even distantly inspired by any individual known or unknown to the author, and all incidents are pure invention.

® and TM are trademarks of the publisher. Trademarks indicated with ® are registered in the United States Patent and Trademark Office, the Canadian Trade Marks Office and in other countries.

Printed in U.S.A.

CONTENTS

NIGHT WATCH

by Carla Neggers

Prologue

JOE SCARLATTI had a book and a beer and figured to ride out the fourth straight day of San Francisco fog in his booth at Mario's Bar & Grill.

His cousin ran the waterfront place. Joe had a couple of rooms upstairs. It hadn't always been that way, but it was that way now. And it wasn't a bad life. After close to six months, Joe had almost gotten to the point where he enjoyed it.

Almost.

He spotted Hank Ryan making his way through the swirling, milky fog outside the window and put down his book. Hank was a fellow cop. A *working* cop. He believed Joe should be working, too. He stopped by about once a week to tell him so.

Joe felt the dampness of the fog when Hank opened the door. It was midafternoon and the place was quiet, just Joe with his book, a few stragglers, Mario clanking around in the kitchen.

The tourists and cheap-eats types had yet to discover Mario's Bar & Grill. It was not a fancy place. Booths, a long bar of dark, aged oak, a worn hardwood floor, a jukebox and a couple of video games in back—that was it. Mario's had been known for good food and fair prices since Joe and his cousin's grandfather—Mario, Sr.—had started the place the week after Prohibition ended.

Hank plopped into the booth across from Joe, uninvited. Hank was a big man. Bigger than Joe, African-American, smart. Cops didn't come any smarter than Hank Ryan. He knew the law, but more than that he knew people. He was a sergeant with the potential of being a captain.

Joe was a sergeant, too. Technically.

"*Moby Dick?*" Hank shook his head. "You are in bad shape, Scarlatti."

"It's 'a damp, drizzly November in my soul,'" Joe quoted dryly. "Now I know what Ishmael meant when he said that. Something wrong with reading?"

"No, but *Moby Dick?* Why the hell don't you read something fun?"

"*Moby Dick* is fun."

Hank shook his head again, regarding Joe with the mix of despair and disgust he usually reserved for repeat offenders.

"You want something to drink?" Joe asked, knowing Hank stayed away from alcohol.

"No. You look like hell, Joe. I'm surprised Mario hasn't thrown you out."

"He does periodically, but he always lets me back in. I'm family and I pay my rent on time. And I don't look *that* bad, Hank. You're just jerking my chain."

Hank sighed. "That's why your family and friends are always on your case—so you won't burn out totally. There's no escaping us, Scarlatti. But I know there's no talking to you when you're in this mood. Look, I've got some news I thought might interest you—Eliot Tyhurst is out of prison."

Immediately Joe felt a twist of pain and anger deep within him. "He wasn't in long enough."

"I know it. Woman who put him there is still in San Francisco. Rowena Willow." Hank pulled a crumpled scrap of paper from a pocket and shoved it across the scarred wooden table. "That's her address."

Joe looked at the scrawled name of the Telegraph Hill street, and right away he knew what Hank wanted. But he said, "What the hell kind of name is Rowena Willow, anyway? You ever wonder that?"

"Frankly, no."

"Bet she made it up. Probably born a 'Debbie' and figured it was too ordinary and changed it."

"It's for real."

"Who'd do that to a kid?"

Hank shrugged. "Her parents were kind of eccentric."

"Kind of?"

"They're dead now. Died when Rowena was eight. She moved in with an aunt even weirder than the parents. The aunt died right before Rowena nabbed Tyhurst. Now she lives alone in the aunt's house. I hear it's quite a place. I've been by it but not inside. It's right out of *Ivanhoe*. A regular castle. I'm surprised it doesn't have a moat. You've probably seen it."

"Maybe," Joe said. "I don't make a point of checking out architectural wonders. How do you know all this stuff about this Rowena character?"

"There was a lot of gossip about her during Tyhurst's trial, and I've kept track of her since, on and off. No big deal."

Hank was silent a moment. Then he said, "Tyhurst will come after her, Joe. You know he will."

"It's not my problem." The words were automatic, born less of conviction than of necessity. Nearly six months on voluntary leave hadn't convinced Joe that he belonged back on active duty. He still didn't trust himself. He pushed his empty beer bottle—only his

first of the day—to one side and opened *Moby Dick*.
"Count me out."

Hank didn't react. He looked around the dark, atmospheric bar. Joe Scarlatti's home. Hell of a life.

"What am I supposed to do?" Hank asked.

"What do you mean? Tyhurst has served his time.
Nothing you can do."

"I've got a feeling about this one."

"Hank, the bastard's never made any threats
against her that we know about. We've got no cause,
can't order a watch on her."

Hank leaned forward, his gaze hard and knowing.
"I was in the courtroom when the jury brought in the
verdict. Rowena Willow was sitting in the same row
as me. Tyhurst's eyes never left her, even when the
foreman read the verdict. I've never seen such cold
eyes."

Joe flipped a page in *Moby Dick*, but he wasn't reading.

"He's not going to forgive and forget, Joe. He's not
the type. He's going to make Rowena Willow pay."

"No guilt trips," Joe reminded him. When he'd
gone on leave, Hank had promised he wouldn't stoop
to guilt trips to get Joe back on the job.

"This isn't a guilt trip, Joe. You're Rowena Willow's last chance. Maybe her only chance."

"According to your gut."

"Yeah."

Joe blew out a breath and drummed the bar with
his forefinger, and Hank let him think. Mario had
emerged from the kitchen and was polishing the mirror their grandfather had installed behind the bar.
People, old grandpa said, should have a good look at
themselves when drinking. Maybe that was why Joe

had taken a booth. He didn't want to look at himself. He hadn't shaved in a couple of days, combed his hair, bothered with anything dressier than jeans and polo shirts. He knew there were dark circles under his red-streaked eyes. But for his endless walks, filling up the hours when his cousin ran him out, he would have gone to flab by now. Six months. It seemed like an eternity. He had taken a leave of absence only because he had promised his grandmother he wouldn't just up and quit. Sofia Scarlatti had suffered enough.

She and her late husband—the founder of Mario's Bar & Grill—had been among Eliot Tyhurst's victims.

Something Hank Ryan knew all too well.

"If this Rowena Willow lives on Telegraph Hill," Joe said, "she can afford to hire her own damned bodyguard."

"Yeah, but she won't. Doesn't think like that. Even if I encouraged her to hire someone, she'd just tell me I was overreacting. She lives alone, works alone, seldom if ever goes out. Hates distractions of any kind. Rowena Willow likes to keep to herself, Joe. She assumes people won't bother her if she doesn't bother them."

"Even a man she put in prison?"

"Yeah."

Hank would know. He had answered Rowena Willow's call when she'd announced to the police she had captured a bank robber. She hadn't mentioned that "captured" to her had meant that, with the help of her computer, she'd nailed him to the wall. Hank had called in the feds and the white-collar criminal guys, but he'd kept track of the case.

An ordinary bank robber—the kind he and Joe dealt with—would have done a couple of decades'

time for stealing not one percent of what Eliot Tyhurst had stolen. But Tyhurst was a unique case.
Once a prominent San Francisco banker, he hadn't
used a gun to get what he wanted. Instead, he had
used the trust people had put in him.

"He'll come after her," Hank repeated, without
drama. "I saw it in his eyes three years ago. One way
or another, Eliot Tyhurst is going to make Rowena
Willow pay for finding him out. You know it, Joe, and
I know it."

"But she doesn't."

"She doesn't think that way."

Just what way did Rowena Willow think? Joe remembered reading about the brilliant financial analyst who had unraveled Tyhurst's nefarious schemes
on her own time, apparently for her own amusement.
He tried to picture her and found he couldn't. "I
haven't met her, have I?"

"You'd remember if you had."

Joe assumed it was because he had a good memory
for faces.

"I doubt she's even aware Tyhurst is getting out,"
Hank added.

Joe sighed. It didn't sound good. "What is she,
some kind of dingbat?"

"An eccentric genius."

"Hell. Sounds peachy. You going to talk to her?"

"Nope. I think it's best we keep our plans to ourselves."

"Hank, there is no 'we.' I haven't agreed to take
this case."

"It shouldn't be tough work, you know. All you
have to do is keep an eye on her place, make sure Ty-

hurst doesn't contact her. She doesn't even have to know you're there."

It still didn't sound good.

"Rowena Willow ruined Tyhurst, Joe. His reputation, his career. Cost him millions in fines and fees, a few years in prison."

"It wasn't enough," Joe repeated.

"No," Hank conceded. He settled back against the tall wooden booth. "Catch Tyhurst coming after Rowena Willow to exact a little revenge and we can put him away for the good, long stretch he deserves."

"Why me?"

Hank looked him straight in the eye. "You need to work, Joe."

Without responding, Joe snatched up the crumpled scrap of paper bearing Rowena Willow's name and address and slid out of the booth. He didn't look back. He walked straight to the door and into the San Francisco fog, letting it envelop him, his soul.

Behind him Hank called Mario for a cola, asked him how he was doing. He would know that Joe needed to be alone right now, just as he had known that six months was a hell of a long time for a cop to be off the streets. Just as he'd known that Joe needed to work.

Maybe this job would save him from the abyss of regret and despair he'd fallen into. Then again, maybe nothing could. Maybe it was too damned late.

BLEARY-EYED from a marathon session at her computer, Rowena Willow found herself stumbling into walls on the way down from her third-floor office to the kitchen. It was an enormous, drafty room with modern appliances that had been installed during her Great-Aunt Adelaide's reluctant remodeling twenty years ago, right after Rowena had come to live with her. She remembered her aunt tearfully selling a painting from an upstairs bedroom to pay for the job. Aunt Adelaide had never had any real money of her own. Rowena had vowed never to repeat the sweet but rather eccentric old woman's fate.

Or her parents' fate, she thought. But before she could probe the thought further, she dismissed it, willed it back to the far recesses of her mind. She didn't like to think too much about her parents' fate.

She put on the kettle for tea and fed her two cats, Mega and Byte. For her, romantic names. Then she did some stretches and her hand exercises, trying to work out the increasingly worrisome tingling and numbness in her fingers. She couldn't come down with carpal tunnel syndrome or any of the other repetitive-motion disorders associated with keyboard use. How would she work? What would she do with herself if she had to stay off her computer?

The kettle whistled, and she poured a little of the

boiling water into her simple white porcelain two-cup pot, swirled it around to warm the pot, then dumped it into the sink. She added two heaping spoonfuls of loose-leaf English breakfast tea and filled the pot to the brim, setting it on a teak serving tray. While the brew steeped, she chose a china cup and saucer from her collection in a glass-fronted cupboard—the forget-me-not pattern, she decided. She filled a tiny white pitcher with a dollop of milk, got out the tea strainer and placed one fat honey-butter cookie on a delicate, pale blue paper napkin. Perhaps Aunt Adelaide hadn't known how to make a living, but she did teach Rowena how to do a wonderful tea.

Already feeling better, Rowena carried the tray up to her tower sunroom, not far from her office on the third floor. It jutted out from the main body of the house and had floor-to-ceiling windows on three sides with spectacular views of San Francisco. The sunwashed city glistened below her. Sailboats dotted the bay, so blue under the cloudless sky. Or maybe everything seemed brighter and clearer after the days and days of fog. Rowena opened the windows and let in the breeze, half tempted to take her tea into the courtyard behind the house.

But in the courtyard, she wouldn't have a view of the street.

After Aunt Adelaide's death, Rowena had removed from the sunroom the clunky Victorian furniture her aunt favored, replacing it with dozens of pillows of every imaginable size and shape. She could plop down wherever she wanted to on the thick Persian carpet and look out at the world, a relief at the end of a long, harrowing day working at her computer and dealing with clients. Sometimes it seemed more fun, more of a fantasy, safer, just to look out at the world rather than to go out into it.

Today she leaned back against a giant, overstuffed, tapestry pillow and set her tea tray on the floor at her side. She stretched out her legs in front of her, not on pillows, as generally would have been the case, but on the thick Persian carpet. She wanted nothing—not even her toes—to obstruct her view.

Her view not of the skyline or San Francisco Bay, but of her street.

She poured her tea through the strainer set carefully over her cup. As she set the pot down, her eyes scanned the cars crammed into coveted spaces up and down her steep, quiet, expensive street.

What kind of car would he be driving today? Yesterday it had been a modest two-door black sedan. The day before a red German sports car. The day before that a tan minivan.

She added a few drops of milk to her tea. Three days in a row he had been out there, on her street, in front of her home.

He parked in different spaces and drove different cars. Sometimes he read the newspaper and sometimes a book. Most of the time, however, he seemed just to sit there doing nothing. She didn't know if he stayed there all day; she had to work. But he was *always* there at teatime. Rowena meant to check the street first thing in the morning but she kept forgetting. With the three-hour time difference between San Francisco and Wall Street, she liked to get an early start. And once on her computer, she concentrated only on the job at hand. Her work demanded her full attention and received it without quarrel. She had no intention of ending up like Aunt Adelaide, selling off paintings to survive.

And of course she wouldn't end up like her parents. They had been a disastrous match, feeding each other's worst instincts. Yes, they'd been happy, but they'd died young and broke.

Willing them to the back of her mind once more, Rowena set her cup back on its saucer and did a few neck rolls to ease out the stiffness, her eyes still narrowed on the street. Her hair—the color of spun gold, friends had told her—was piled up on her head, expertly pinned, not one strand errant. She wondered if its weight contributed to the stiffness in her neck. She couldn't recall when she'd last had her hair cut. It was quite long, at least to her waist, thick and naturally wavy—not that she ever wore it down. She always pinned up her hair first thing in the morning, even before brushing her teeth or checking her computer, which she kept on at all times. It was one of the ways she exacted control over her life.

Maybe he's finished what he came to do, she thought. *Maybe he's never coming back.*

She was surprised at the rush of disappointment she felt, but she didn't have a chance to examine its source.

She spotted him.

He was settled behind the wheel of a rusting, dented gray pickup truck directly beneath her window. Rolling up onto her knees, Rowena peered down through the center window, suddenly irritated by its dozens of tiny panes. She wished he would step out of the truck so she could get a good look at him. Her powers of observation and her prodigious memory were her greatest weapon. She would remember if she had seen him before. Perhaps she would be able to make an educated guess as to whether he was a thug, an undercover cop on a stakeout or a private investigator. She had already dismissed a whole host of other possibilities, including a drug dealer. A drug dealer, she reasoned, wouldn't eat powdered doughnuts in such a disreputable-looking truck; he would stick to the German sports car.

If she could see him, she knew she would be certain.

Who, she wondered, was he watching? She considered her various neighbors on the street, so many of whom she had never met, although she had lived there since she was eight years old. Any likely suspects? She supposed he could be waiting for something scheduled to happen *on* her street, but not involving anyone who actually lived there. She couldn't deny her interest: She seldom got to unravel a mystery that involved human beings rather than numbers.

The truck door opened.

Rowena held her breath, waiting.

He climbed out.

A cop. *Definitely* a cop. There was no doubt in her mind.

Nothing specific eliminated his being a thug or a private investigator. Nothing specific, even, blared police. But Rowena knew. She just knew.

Down on the street, his back to her, he stretched his arms above his head, then turned and drummed his fingers on the roof of his truck. He looked impatient and irritable. He was, Rowena saw, a thickly built man with very dark—almost black—hair and a face that was more striking than handsome, the nose crooked, the mouth rather severe. She expected that up close she would see scars. Suddenly she wanted to see him smile. What would he look like if he smiled? Would she change her mind about him? Would he have bad teeth, look goofy, menacing, dishonest?

No, she thought. A smile wouldn't erase the gravity and the stubborn sadness that seemed to cling to him.

From her position, she could see the gray sweatshirt that was stretched across his broad chest. A pair of jeans went with it. Close-fitting jeans. He would, she imagined, have muscular legs, particularly his thighs. His was a sprinter's build; he would use speed and power in a physical encounter. Any kind of physical encounter.

Heat rushed to her cheeks at the unexpected, unruly thought.

What was she thinking?

He took a deep breath, pounded the truck roof with the flat of his hand and climbed back in the driver's seat as if he'd had enough for one day. Three floors up, Rowena heard the engine race and watched him drive away.

She finished her tea, in no particular hurry.

Then she looked up the main number for the San Francisco police department. She used her cordless telephone and took it into the sunroom, where she stood in front of the windows above the now-empty parking space and made the call. She identified herself to the woman who answered and said she would like to speak to the person in charge of the undercover officer staked out on her Telegraph Hill street. She gave the name of her street and the number of her house and spelled her name. She was put on hold. In another minute a man picked up. She repeated what she wanted. He said, "You've got to be kidding," and put her on hold, and in a moment another man picked up.

"Good afternoon," she said, "my name is Rowena Willow and I—"

"I know who you are, Ms. Willow. I'm Sergeant Ryan. Hank Ryan. What's up?"

She recognized the name at once. He was the policeman who had investigated her report on Eliot Tyhurst. He had come to her house to make sure she wasn't some kind of lunatic; she wasn't sure that he hadn't decided she wasn't. But he *had* taken her findings to higher authorities. Ultimately Tyhurst had been arrested and convicted.

She wondered if she'd been handed off to him just because she was a known eccentric and he'd dealt with her before.

The thought made her angry, if not defensive. She had almost grown accustomed to people's stereotypes of her.

"Well," she said coolly, "I've spotted your man on Telegraph Hill—"

"Excuse me?"

"Your man. I spotted him. I was afraid since I spotted him, someone else might have as well. I'm particularly concerned that the subject he's watching might have seen him. I wouldn't want anything untoward to happen simply because those of you in authority didn't realize your man isn't very...subtle."

"I see."

There was a note of caution in his tone. She bit the corner of her mouth, hoping she didn't sound weird;

sometimes she just didn't know. "I don't mean to be insulting."

Hank Ryan cleared his throat. "You're saying that since you made our man, some bad guy he's after might have made him, too."

"That's correct."

"What makes you think he's a cop?"

"Oh, that's obvious."

She thought she heard Ryan chuckle. She remembered him as a competent, rigorous individual who had made no derogatory remarks about her, her lifestyle or her work. He said, "Thanks for the tip."

Rowena bristled at being dismissed. "Check him out. He's approximately five feet ten inches tall, thickly built. He has near-black hair cut in no particular style. He doesn't shave every day. I would say his nose has been broken once or twice. My guess is a Mediterranean ethnic background, probably Italian."

Hank Ryan was silent.

"He has driven four different vehicles." She described them in detail and recited their license plate numbers which, she explained, she had memorized. "I'm observant but not suspicious by nature. Someone up to something illegal is likely to be both observant *and* suspicious and...well, I'm sure you don't want your officer stumbling into a situation in which he's dangerously over his head."

"I'm afraid he already has," the sergeant grumbled under his breath. "I'll see who we've got out there and warn him. Thanks."

She hung up wondering if she would ever see the dark-haired man again.

ROWENA WILLOW had one hell of a boring life, so far as Joe could see. Four days now and the only glimpse he'd had of her was in that damned tower room above the street. He had to crane his neck, so it was never much of a glimpse. She showed up every afternoon promptly at five-ten. What she did there he had no idea. Water plants? But he couldn't make out any plants.

He sat at Mario's bar, waiting for hot pastrami on rye. He already had his beer. Ah, reality.

Mario, a balding, good-humored man ten years Joe's senior, shoved the sandwich in front of him. "Working, Joe?"

"Doing a favor for a friend, keeping an eye out on a crazy woman." He decided not to tell him it was Rowena Willow, the financial genius who had put Eliot Tyhurst in jail.

"Pretty?"

"Doubtful. I haven't seen her yet, though."

"How can you keep an eye on her if you haven't seen her?"

Joe shook his head. "She doesn't lead a normal life, that's how. She's weird, Mario. Weird, weird, weird. So far as I can tell, she never leaves her house."

"Where's she live?"

"Telegraph Hill."

Mario paused to greet a regular customer and slide him a beer, not waiting for his order. "Fancy neighborhood."

"Yeah. It's quite a place. She has her groceries delivered, works there, doesn't seem to have any friends—and this house, Mario. Put a full moon in the background and we're talking bats and vampires. She probably has her own torture chamber."

His cousin laughed. "Maybe after this job, police work will look good again."

Joe wondered if it would.

In the mirror across from him, he saw Hank Ryan walk grim-faced into the bar. Without a word he sat down on the stool next to Joe. Mario poured him a ginger ale and Hank took a sip. Then he looked at Joe. "She made you the first day."

At first Joe didn't know what he was talking about. "Who?"

"Rowena Willow. She spotted you, Joe."

"The hell she did!"

Hank nodded. "The hell she did." He nibbled on a pretzel and repeated his bizarre telephone conversation.

Down the bar, Mario was laughing with a customer, demanding to see the I.D. of another, acknowledging the designated driver of another group—all, it seemed, at the same time. Or maybe, Joe thought, his brain was jumbled from his strange assignment. He didn't want to think about crazy ladies who lived in strange houses.

In his twelve years as a cop, five working undercover, Joe Scarlatti had never—not once—been made.

He glanced sideways at Hank, who looked tired, still in his uniform. Joe hadn't asked about Hank's day and wouldn't. "She had the license plate numbers of all four vehicles?"

"Yep. Memorized them. Said she didn't write them down because she thought she was just being paranoid." Hank's mouth twitched. "Must be a hobby of hers, memorizing license plate numbers of suspicious characters like you."

"Hell, she just made up those numbers. You know damned well she—"

Hank withdrew another of his infamous crumpled scraps of paper from a pocket and laid it on the bar. Joe took a bite of his sandwich and had a look. One, two, three, four sets of numbers.

"Are they correct?" Hank asked.

"How would I know? You don't think *I* have nothing better to do than memorize license plate numbers?"

"She got the one on your truck right. I checked with motor vehicles."

The one on his brother's Porsche, too, Joe thought, and probably the other two—Mario's wife's minivan and another friend's econo-box.

"Do you realize," he said to his fellow cop, "how incredibly dull her life must be if she takes the time to memorize license plate numbers? She must think staring at parked cars is high entertainment." He swallowed a mouthful of beer. "What a weirdo."

"You're just ticked because she made you."

"I'm not."

"Your pride is wounded."

"Hank, my pride is not wounded. Name me one cop a woman like that wouldn't have made."

Hank was damned close to grinning. "Admit it, Scarlatti, you underestimated her."

"Okay. I'll admit I underestimated the sick life she leads."

"Beware of stereotyping, my friend. Any sign of Tyhurst yet?"

Joe sighed. "Not a peep."

"He'll show, Joe. My gut says so. I've got reports he's in San Francisco."

"Where's he staying?"

"Don't know—I'm trying to find out. Like I say, he's a free man. He's served his time, says he's reformed."

"Maybe he has."

Hank didn't comment. He didn't need to. He would know Joe didn't believe his own words. Eliot Tyhurst had been born an arrogant, slippery con man and would die an arrogant, slippery con man.

"Rowena Willow put him away for a while," Hank reminded him. "Think about that before you leave her to the bastard. Tyhurst has had three years and then some to figure out a way to pay her back."

Joe slid off the bar stool and started out, but double-backed for his sandwich. He muttered a goodbye to Hank.

"Joe, where are you going?"

"Obviously," he ground out, "the indirect approach isn't going to work with Ms. Weirdo Willow."

Hank looked worried. "What are you going to do?"

"Try the direct approach."

2

THE NEXT MORNING Rowena remembered to check her street for the undercover cop. She took her tea and the three daily newspapers she received into her third-floor sunroom and arranged a bunch of pillows close to a tall window. Her hair was pinned up, but she was still in her silk bathrobe and had yet to shower and dress.

She scanned the street even before checking the newspaper headlines.

Nothing unusual caught her eye. There was no un-identified vehicle. No glimpse of a dark, solid male figure. Just empty, ordinary parked cars.

Rowena acknowledged a sense of disappointment and wondered at it. What was wrong with her? She wasn't looking for any excitement! Certainly none in-volving undercover policemen and criminals. She had had enough of that sort of thing three years ago with Eliot Tyhurst.

"I wonder what kind of criminals the police are af-ter up here," she mused aloud to no one. Even Mega and Byte weren't present. Her short-haired tabbies seldom ventured all the way up to the sunroom.

What if her telephone call yesterday had prompted the police to assign someone else to the case? Some-one more competent, who wouldn't be so easily spot-ted by a resident?

Someone, Rowena thought uncomfortably, who wouldn't intrigue her as much.

Dissatisfied with her train of thought, she jumped up and went back downstairs to her kitchen. She popped a fresh peach whole wheat scone into the microwave, her one addition since Aunt Adelaide's day; she'd ordered it from a catalog. She put the scone on a small plate, added a small pat of butter and headed back up to the sunroom, feeling calmer.

Down on the street, a neighbor was buckling her toddler into a car seat. A car was waiting to take her spot. The driver was an elderly man.

Rowena situated herself among her pillows, making herself comfortable, and while the butter melted on her scone, she opened her first newspaper of the morning, the *San Francisco Chronicle*. Her heart stopped. Every muscle in her body tensed. She didn't move. She had no idea how long she stared at the headline.

Tyhurst Returns to San Francisco. In smaller headline print: *Out of prison, mastermind of multimillion-dollar bank fraud say he's reformed.* She couldn't read the article, not until her eyes could focus and her heart had resumed its normal beat. Eliot Tyhurst was out of prison. She hadn't kept track, hadn't known. Hadn't *wanted* to know. After three years, she had finally come to the point where she didn't think about the brilliant, handsome, scheming financial operator she had put in prison. Now he was back.

But Eliot Tyhurst had put *himself* in prison. He was responsible for his actions, not she. She had only unraveled his tangled, corrupt financial system and reported her extraordinary findings to the authorities.

Her mind flashed back to the image of the crowded

courtroom when the jury had brought in the guilty verdict. The defendant, formerly one of San Francisco's most prominent and trusted savings and loan owners, had looked at only one person: Rowena Willow. She would never forget how his blue eyes had bored through her. He hadn't said a word. But she knew. He would never forget who had ruined his life.

Now he was a free man.

Reformed, he said. *Rowena Willow, the brilliant financial analyst who brought Tyhurst down*, the newspaper account continued, *couldn't be reached for comment about his release.*

Of course not. Her number was unlisted and if someone rang her doorbell during the day, it was unlikely that she would even hear it. Her concentration was that intense while working. A reporter would have to be intrepid to reach her, and reaching her, it seemed, hadn't been that important. Eliot Tyhurst, she realized, was old news. His return to San Francisco merited a front-page mention only because it was a slow day.

Well, he was bound to be released sometime, she reasoned. And San Francisco was his home. It was logical that he would return to the city. If he had indeed reformed, he had a right to return, start over, mend fences…*but I don't want anything to do with him.*

She ate her scone and finished her tea, then had another look out at her street.

Nothing.

Was it possible Hank Ryan had ordered her house watched in the aftermath of Tyhurst's release from prison?

It was. The police had put her through to Ryan

when she had called in her warning about the under-cover policeman on her street.

Was he worried about her? About any intentions Tyhurst might have toward her?

"No," she said aloud, firmly, reining in her increasingly wild thoughts. "He would have had to tell me."

Surely that was true. She reminded herself that her undercover cop was nowhere to be seen this morning.

She calmed down. Eliot Tyhurst was a footnote in America's financial history; he had served his prison sentence. The police wouldn't—couldn't—spend the time and money worrying about him, about whether he would come after the woman who had put him in jail and cost him millions. They were yesterday's news.

Well, she thought, that would teach her to jump to conclusions based on nothing more than "gut feeling." She had learned the hard way to rely on logic, experience, facts—to always remain in control of her feelings.

Even feelings that insisted against all logic and fact—as hers did now, again—that she had not seen the last of her undercover cop.

JOE COULD HEAR the doorbell to Rowena Willow's mausoleum of a house groan and echo, probably reaching every corner of the bizarre stone building. Hank was right, it looked like a minicastle. The facade was stone, the windows heavily paned and leaded and draped, the door something for a bunch of knights with a battering ram. Weird stuff. He half expected Lurch to open up.

But no one did.

He rang twice more. Rowena Willow, the recluse, had to be home. Where the hell else would she be?

When there was still no response, he pounded on the solid door with his fist in case she just couldn't hear her booming doorbell. At least she would know he meant business.

Not that he gave a damn about Rowena Willow or even, really, this damned job Hank had put him on. It just bugged him that a dingbat like her had spotted him. As Hank had guessed, his pride was wounded. But if his old cop-friend thought that meant Joe was back in the game, he was wrong.

Not a sound came from the castle.

"Hell," Joe muttered through gritted teeth, wondering why he was even bothering. Why not just go on back to Mario's for a beer and burritos?

He went out to the wide sidewalk and glared up at the three-story building, looking for a cracked window, a moving shadow, anything that hinted where she might be. Then he could throw a rock or something and get her attention.

"Hey," he yelled, "anybody home?"

As if Rowena Willow would be anywhere else.

Still nothing.

Joe exhaled in disgust and went back to the massive front door and rang the bell three times in succession, not waiting between rings. He was considering tear gas through a second-floor window when he heard what sounded like someone pounding down a flight of stairs.

He peeked into a narrow side window.

There was a whirling flash of blue, the clicking of locks being thrown free, then the creak of the door as it was drawn open.

Rowena Willow—he assumed it was her—stood before him, breathing hard. She was a hundred times prettier and a thousand times sexier than Joe in four days' watching her had expected.

He was stunned.

He didn't like being stunned. It reduced his sense of control over himself. Even as Rowena Willow's gorgeous, wild, smart blue eyes narrowed on him, he could feel himself putting up mental barriers around himself.

"Don't you answer your door?" he asked.

She looked annoyed. "I just did."

"It took six rings."

"No, only three. I counted."

Her and numbers. "Nope. Six. *I* did the ringing."

She frowned. "I must not have heard…" She trailed off, pursing her lips, apparently deciding what she had heard and hadn't heard was none of his business. "What do you want?"

Joe hooked a thumb on a belt loop of his jeans and tried to look as if he dealt with eccentric geniuses every day. *Beautiful* eccentric geniuses. Funny how Hank had neglected to mention Rowena Willow's looks in his briefing.

"Is this how you always treat visitors?" he asked.

"Yes."

Ask a question, he thought, get an answer. "I'm—"

"You're the police officer who has been on a stake-out on my street for the past four days. I spoke to your boss yesterday."

"Hank's not my boss," Joe said, maintaining his good humor despite how much it rankled him that she'd spotted him. He had underestimated Rowena

Willow. "And I wasn't on a 'stakeout.' Mind if I come in a minute?"

She sighed, not pleased. "Since you've already blown my concentration—it'll take me hours to get back to where I was—" She stopped herself again, and breathed, "I still need to see some identification."

"Some I.D.," he repeated. "What, when you're not in front of a computer, are you in front of a TV?"

Her lips pursed, and she didn't answer. Her hair, a rich, deep, unusual gold color, was piled up on her head; Joe counted three cloisonné combs and a half-dozen bobby pins at least. Her skin was smooth, flawless, pale. He wondered if it had ever been exposed to the sun. She had a straight nose and those incredible eyes, and a chin that maybe was too strong to put her on a magazine cover. Otherwise she was a classic beauty, tall—almost as tall as he was—and slender. She had on a flowing, azure caftan over cropped black leggings and little tapestry flats.

Joe produced his badge and said, "Name's Scarlatti. Sergeant Joe Scarlatti."

"You're a sergeant?" She sounded dubious. "I would have thought a sergeant would have been more circumspect."

Rub it in, toots, Joe thought. *Go right ahead.* He was a pro. He could take her contempt. What did he care if Rowena Willow figured she was smarter than he was? Hell, it might be something he could use later on.

She gestured for him to go in ahead of her, which he did. The temperature dropped and the light dimmed; the enormous entry was downright medieval. An open staircase of some dark wood zigzagged up all three floors; a person could fall a long way. The walls were done in some kind of straw matting, and the floor was a dark hardwood with a patterned deep red Persian runner that was so long it would run right out of Joe's place above Mario's Bar & Grill.

A nasty-looking suit of medieval armor complete with spear stood in one corner and an armless statue of some poor bastard stood in another.

"A regular house of horrors," Joe muttered. He should bring Hank for a look-see; maybe he'd quit worrying about what Eliot Tyhurst would do to helpless Rowena Willow.

"We'll talk in the drawing room," she said, opening a set of double doors across the entry from the stairs. "I would offer you something to drink, but five minutes doesn't give us enough time."

Joe started through the door. "What do you have in here," he said, "poison darts and a couple of mummies?"

"I beg your pardon?"

"Never mind."

There was no point, he realized as he crossed the threshold. She wouldn't get his sardonic humor. She'd just take his question seriously, tell him the poison darts and mummies were in another room. *This* room was reserved for stuffed animals. Not the cute, cuddly kind grandmas and grandpas bought for their little grandkids, either. Rowena Willow's stuffed animals—there were dozens of them—had been alive at one time.

"Quaint," Joe said. He walked over to a curio cabinet of stuffed birds, some ordinary, some rare. There were other cabinets and stands and shelves of larger animals—a raccoon, weasel, gopher, red fox. A few

heads—deer, antelope, buffalo—adorned the walls.
"Is this what you do with your old boyfriends?"

Rowena Willow eyed him from the middle of the
room. "Sergeant, I fail to see your humor."

"Now why doesn't that surprise me?"

"My great-grandfather was a noted taxidermist."

And you, Joe thought, *deliberately use this room to
scare off unwanted company.*

"You're wasting your five minutes on trivialities,"
she pointed out coolly.

He wondered how long her hair was. Midback at
least. Did she ever get the urge to pull out all the pins
and combs and shake it loose?

"Sergeant," she prompted.

Probably not.

"Just Joe is fine. I'm not here on official business."

That got her interest. She stood next to a small table
displaying a single, brightly plumed dead bird.
"You're not?"

"Nope. A friend asked me to keep an eye on you in
case Eliot Tyhurst decides to exact a little revenge."

It only took a few seconds for his words to sink in.
"This friend—you mean Sergeant Ryan?"

Joe shrugged, letting her come to her own conclusions. He didn't want to lie, but he didn't want to rat
out Hank, not that his friend didn't deserve it.

"Why would anyone care?" She paused and
twisted her fingers together—a gesture of frustration,
Joe suspected. He noted the fat sapphire ring on her
right hand. There was no engagement ring, no wedding band. "Eliot Tyhurst has made no threats
against me. He's served his prison sentence. I don't
qualify for police protection."

"Hence, yours truly. I'm on leave from the department—"

"Why?"

A direct woman, but Joe didn't squirm. He pushed back the creeping self-hatred, the memories he had been fighting for too many long months. "Personal reasons."

He waited a moment, giving her a chance to challenge him, press for a better answer, but she didn't, just twisted those fingers together. He had no idea if she understood that he'd said all he planned to say on the subject or if that straight-A mind of hers had figured out that his leave of absence had nothing to do with her case.

"My friend's a good cop," he went on. "He operates a lot on instinct, and his instinct says there could be trouble between you and Tyhurst. He asked me to keep watch, just in case. I've been out here every day for the past four days. I'm not on a twenty-four-hour watch at this point, but I'd guess nothing's happened. Am I right? Tyhurst hasn't been in touch?"

She nodded tightly, then inhaled, tossing her head back, fastening those gorgeous blue eyes on him. Joe let himself notice the soft swell of her breasts under the satiny fabric of her caftan, the pulse beating in her pale throat. Her sensuality was unexpected, overpowering. So was his reaction to it. He had to turn his head, focus on the snarl of the stuffed red fox on a stand beside him. There wasn't a sound in the room. They might have been on the moon, not in the heart of a busy city, atop Telegraph Hill, one of San Francisco's most prestigious and picturesque neighborhoods.

"I gather," Rowena Willow said in a steady voice, "no one thought to ask me what *I* wanted."

"Like I said, it was all very unofficial."

Acknowledging his words with a curt nod, she folded her arms under her breasts and walked slowly over to an enormous window, hung with dark, heavy drapes right out of a Vincent Price movie. With her back to him, she drew the drapes aside and looked out at the street. "You're parked in front of a fire hydrant."

"The privileges of the badge. I'll move if there's a fire, trust me."

"It's your truck—you own it. The other vehicles were borrowed."

"Yep. Hank said you memorized the license plate numbers."

"I wouldn't say I deliberately memorized them. I just made a point of remembering them."

Horsefeathers. She was just trying to intimidate him. "Go ahead," Joe said, "impress me."

She looked around at him, frowning, not one hair out of place.

His attention to every physical detail about her bothered and surprised him. It wasn't professional. It wasn't objective. It wasn't clinical. He didn't do this sort of thing with every woman he met.

"I will do no such thing," she replied stonily.

"Can't remember 'em, huh?" He was being obnoxious and he knew it—but, he told himself, the cop that was still rooted somewhere deep inside him needed to see how Rowena Willow would react.

Not very well. She said calmly, "Your five minutes are up, Sergeant Scarlatti. Have a good morning."

"We didn't finish."

"But we did."

"I haven't gotten to the part about my moving into your little house of horrors here and keeping an eye out on your behalf. It'd be a hell of a lot easier on both of us. I'd have a comfortable place to sit, a kitchen and a bathroom handy. You wouldn't have to stare at parked cars and try to figure out which one's mine."

Color flashed in her milky cheeks. So, he thought, Ms. Weirdo Willow's veins ran with real blood, not ice water. "We don't need to get to that part, Sergeant."

"Are you rejecting my services, ma'am?"

If his sarcasm registered, he couldn't see it. She said, "I don't ever want to see you on this street again unless I call 911 and you're required to come."

"What'll you do if I ignore your wishes?"

"I'll—" She pursed her lips, apparently a habit with her. He wondered if she realized that it made him think about kissing her. Probably not. Not that he *would* kiss her or even wanted to be thinking about doing such a thing, but there it was.

She recovered and went on, "I'll report you to your superiors."

"That'll be fun. You know what they'll tell you?"

"Sergeant—"

"They'll tell you I've got an authority problem. Besides, I don't think I have any superiors. I don't listen to anyone. And like I said, I'm not on active duty." He headed toward the double doors. "You decide you need me, give me a buzz at Mario's Bar & Grill on the waterfront."

"I *won't* need you."

She said it through clenched teeth. Joe grinned. He *had* gotten to her.

"I'll let myself out." He glanced back at her, standing rigid and deliciously beautiful, and nodded to the taxidermy display. "Bet you're wishing these critters could bite. Nice meeting you, Ms. Willow. Mario's Bar & Grill. Got it? Or don't you ever need anything repeated?"

She refused to answer.

Stubborn. But stubbornness—and a distaste for authority—could sometimes get in the way of good judgment. It could even get a person killed, Joe thought. And not always just yourself. He pushed the thought aside as the heavy door thudded behind him. Now wasn't the time for dwelling on past mistakes but considering how the hell not to make new ones.

He was afraid he already had.

ONLY ONCE BEFORE had Rowena been too distracted to work. It was the day Eliot Tyhurst's case had gone to the jury for a verdict. She had wandered and paced in her house until she could stand the tension no longer and had gone down to the courthouse.

Now it was the thought—just the very notion—that *she* had been the target of Sergeant Scarlatti's stakeout that had her too rattled to work. He had been watching her. Protecting her. For four days. Such a prospect had never even occurred to her, even after she had learned Eliot Tyhurst was back in San Francisco.

She felt as if Joe Scarlatti had outwitted her just by knowing something she didn't know. It was, she thought, how *he* would think.

How much did he know about her life?

About her?

She felt the rushing heat of embarrassment—and pure, unadulterated, unwelcome sexual awareness. It was elemental, primitive, surprising, a challenge to her self-control as well as her concentration. And it was unavoidable. Joe Scarlatti was a thickset, compact, physical man who radiated sexuality. Wouldn't any reasonable woman be attracted to him? She knew he'd been attracted to her, if only fleetingly. His appraisal of her had not been from the point of view of a professional, but from that of a man. Had he wondered what she was like in bed? Speculated on her love life?

Her office long abandoned, she heated a bowl of canned vegetable soup—she rarely bothered with lunch—and ate it standing up in the kitchen, trying to regroup.

Would Joe Scarlatti take no for an answer?

No, he wouldn't. He was someone who couldn't resist defying the odds. It was entirely possible she had only succeeded in ensuring he would stay on her case, watching her, *waiting* for something to happen.

But nothing would, she told herself.

Who, she wondered, was she trying to convince?

Her telephone rang, startling her so severely she jumped, spilling a few drops of hot soup onto her hand. She set the bowl down on the counter, still shaking. It was always like that when she was disturbed while she was concentrating—even if on the wrong things. She would be so damned unaware of what was going on around her.

She almost let her machine take the call, as was her general practice during the day, but at the last possible moment she snatched up the wall phone in the kitchen. "Yes?"

"Rowena Willow," a man's silken voice, oddly familiar, said. "Did I get you up from your infamous computer?"

"Who is this?"

"I'm sorry, I thought you might recognize my voice. It's Eliot, Rowena. Eliot Tyhurst."

She forced an inner calm over herself. She couldn't allow a tremor or tightness in her voice to betray her apprehension. "I read that you were in San Francisco. I wish you well, Mr. Tyhurst. Now if you'll excuse me—"

"I'd like to come by and see you."

"I'm very busy."

"I want to thank you, Rowena. Without you, I wouldn't be the man I am today. I wouldn't have seen I was on the wrong path. I grew and changed because of you. I'm a better person because of your courage."

He sounded so sincere. She remembered how polished and deceptively handsome he'd been. Had prison changed him?

"There's no need to thank me," she said quickly. Her stomach had begun to hurt. "I wish you the best, that's all."

"Let me take you to dinner tonight."

"No, I couldn't—"

"Rowena, I *need* to thank you. I need you to believe me. It's important to my total recuperation, my redemption."

She bit down on her lower lip, feeling her rising tension, knowing he would sense it. "Mr. Tyhurst, please understand how difficult this is for me. I don't want to see you."

"I do understand. That's the whole point. And call me Eliot, please. Rowena, how can I convince you I'm a new man? How can I convince *anyone* if not you?"

Rowena twisted the phone cord, wondering what Joe Scarlatti would have her do if he were here. Turn the phone over to him? Let him handle Eliot Tyhurst?

She handled her own life, her own problems. It had *always* been that way for her.

Her hesitation provided the former banker his opening. "Then you do understand. I'll pick you up at seven." And he added matter-of-factly, "I know where you live."

JOE SCARLATTI MET Hank for a hot dog and soda at a street vendor's in front of Eliot Tyhurst's old savings and loan downtown. It was located in a flashy modern building famous on San Francisco's skyline.

"I want everything we've got on that SOB," Joe said. "Whatever you can get me, I want."

"Will do."

"Unofficially."

"Sure."

"And I'm not saying I'm really on this case."

"There is no case," Hank said.

"Right." Joe squirted mustard over his sauerkraut. "One more thing."

Hank, the turncoat, was grinning, having sucked Joe Scarlatti back into the world he had been trying for six months to leave behind. "What's that, Joe?"

"I'm going to stay on Rowena Willow," he said, "and if she catches me this time, I'll turn in my badge for good and become partners with Mario and serve drinks and greasy sandwiches for the next forty years."

"I won't hold you to that."

"What, you have no faith in me?"

"No, Joe, I've got all the faith in the world in you,

but Rowena Willow—she rooted out Tyhurst, didn't she? What makes you think she won't root out a burnt-out cop she's met, decided she doesn't like, doesn't trust and wants out of her life?"

Joe stuffed a few strands of loose sauerkraut back into his hot-dog bun. "You just watch me."

3

TWO HOURS AFTER Eliot Tyhurst had called, Rowena ducked through her back door and courtyard and slipped through a wrought-iron gate to a side alley, her usual shortcut around the block. The scent of roses lingered. Aunt Adelaide had planted scores of them in the little courtyard, and Rowena felt a rush of nostalgia and pain. Her aunt had done her best in difficult circumstances, raising a child long, long after she herself had chosen to have no children. If Rowena's parents had lived...if Aunt Adelaide had been less eccentric, more social, even understood the basic needs of an extraordinarily bright, lonely, grieving little girl...if Rowena had been less inwardly drawn herself...

But that was all in the past. Aunt Adelaide was gone, and her parents were gone. Rowena had forgiven her, and them, and even herself.

Did she now owe Eliot Tyhurst her forgiveness?

Was it hers to offer? He hadn't fleeced her of a single cent, and she believed people deserved a second chance. A judicial system couldn't work properly if society didn't allow ex-convicts an opportunity for a fresh start.

And yet that was so much easier to believe in principle than to act upon in real life.

She walked quickly down Telegraph Hill, toward

the water, enjoying the feel of the warm sunshine. It was a clear, glorious October day. She had changed into knee-length walking shorts, a cropped top and walking shoes. Given the sensitivity of her skin to the sun, she'd put on a big floppy hat that hid most of her face. Her jaunts through the city, although relatively infrequent lately given the mountains of projects she'd agreed to undertake, were always welcome. She loved San Francisco's steep hills and stunning architecture, the clanging of its streetcars, the blaring of its foghorns. Everywhere there was another incredible, breathless view of the bay, the ocean, the Golden Gate Bridge.

Enjoying the scenery, however, did nothing to distract Rowena from thinking about Eliot Tyhurst and Sergeants Hank Ryan and Joe Scarlatti. They presented a knotty problem indeed, not the sort she was accustomed to solving. She was comfortable among numbers and complex financial systems, analyzing companies and trends and markets for her business clients. She had never claimed ease among the male of the human species.

She walked and walked, trying to focus on the scenery, trying to tell herself she wasn't headed where she knew full well she was headed. But soon she could feel the dampness of the waterfront in the air, feel the cool breeze off the bay on her face. The wind grew stronger, and she had to hold on to her hat. Automatically, because this was her city and she knew every street and alley of it, and because she had called up the address on her computer, she turned down the street where Mario's Bar & Grill was located.

It was in an older, Victorian-style building with a simple sign giving its name.

Rowena hesitated, wishing she'd opted for an outfit that would give her a more commanding presence. Or hadn't come at all.

But she had come.

She went through the door—oak and frosted glass—and immediately fought a rush of emotion at the smell of popcorn and sourdough bread, at the sound of laughter and soft jazz, of a life she didn't lead. She squared her shoulders and approached the gleaming bar. The place wasn't crowded; it was between lunch and dinner. A plump man in a dark green apron was polishing beer glasses with a clean white cloth.

"Help you?" he asked.

"I'm looking for Joe Scarlatti."

The man set down his cloth and eyed her. "Won't he kick himself for not being around for once. Do I know you?"

"My name's Rowena Willow."

"You're the one put that slime-mold Tyhurst in jail. Yeah, I know you. Joe didn't tell me—"

"Eliot Tyhurst put himself in jail," she corrected.

"Right, right. Mario Scarlatti." He put out a hand, which Rowena shook briefly across the bar. "Joe's cousin. Go out the door and holler for him. He probably followed you down here."

Rowena felt a surge of heat. "But I told him—he's not supposed to follow me."

"Mistake number one. Never tell Joe Scarlatti what to do. His mama gave up when he was two years old."

"It wasn't his choice—"

"All the more reason not to do what you said."

"Did he tell you—are you sure—" She stopped, disgusted with her sputtering, and marched over to the door, kicking it open with one foot.

Joe Scarlatti was tying the laces of his beat-up running shoe on the top step of the landing. He grinned up at her. "Well, well, if it isn't our eccentric genius. Care for an afternoon beer, Ms. Willow?"

"Did you follow me?" she demanded.

"You're the one who knows everything. You tell me."

"You have no right—"

"Mario tell you I followed you? Don't believe everything he says. He's trying to get me into trouble because he's sick of me hanging around." Scarlatti finished tying his shoe and straightened up. "What're you doing, checking up on me?"

"No, I..."

"You what?"

She felt ridiculous. And angry. Scarlatti must have followed her. What was more, her reaction to him was just as violently sensual as it had been that morning—as it had been since she'd spotted him five days ago and had only *imagined* him. In person, up close, for real, he was even more overpowering than glimpsed, half-imagined, from her third-floor sunroom.

"I've got to go," she mumbled, starting past him.

He grabbed her upper arm, effectively stopping her in her tracks. His grip was strong, but not harsh. A terrible, wanting ache spread through her at the feel of it. Her mouth went dry. She would never respond this way to Eliot Tyhurst, reformed or not, but it was he, not Sergeant Joe Scarlatti, who had invited her to dinner. But Joe Scarlatti, she thought, represented a greater threat to her personal security—her sense of control over her life—than Eliot Tyhurst ever could. She knew that now. It was why her attraction bothered her. A man like Scarlatti could make her forget her purpose in life, her responsibilities, the unintended lessons her parents' destructive love for each other had taught her.

"At least have something to drink first," Scarlatti said.

Rowena found herself nodding. Acquiescing. She didn't know why, except that she *was* thirsty, and it was a long way back up to Telegraph Hill—and she somehow felt she should be here. She had learned to trust her intuition. No one, least of all her, could explain the unique blend of intuition, memory and raw intelligence that permitted her to know things the way she did. Even if she didn't yet completely understand why, she'd had to come here.

Mario had a beer waiting on the bar for Scarlatti. Rowena could see the questions in the older man's eyes, but he said nothing to his cousin. She asked for mineral water with a twist of lime.

"Will you take seltzer?" Mario asked. "Same thing, my opinion, just not as fancy a name."

It wasn't the same, but Rowena didn't argue. "That's fine."

The younger, more fit Scarlatti slid onto the bar stool. Rowena noticed that his leg muscles were as thick and solid as she'd imagined yesterday when he'd climbed out of his truck. She didn't sit down. The sergeant frowned at her and told her to sit.

"Thank you, I'll stand."

"If I told you to stand, would you sit?"

"I'm not being obstinate."

"Then you're being self-conscious. Sit down, for Pete's sake. You're making me nervous."

She very much doubted that, but she eased halfway onto the bar stool, somewhere between sitting and standing. Mario brought out her seltzer with lime, and a fake-wood bowl of pretzels and mixed nuts.

"Finished computing for the day?" Joe asked.

"I never really got started. There were too many interruptions."

"What, one little visit from a cop blows your whole day?"

"Coupled with an unsettling phone call, yes."

Scarlatti was silent. His eyes, however, were dark and alert, ready to seize upon anything she dared give away.

"I'm having dinner with Eliot Tyhurst tonight," Rowena said quietly.

"The hell you are."

"It's his way of making peace with what he did. He says he's reformed. He needs to have me accept his new self. I was a party to his downfall. I might not owe him a second chance, but I owe society—"

"What kind of garbage is that? Tyhurst can get his second chance without having dinner with you."

She thrust her jaw out stubbornly. Scarlatti's domineering attitude was just the push she needed to convince herself to go ahead with the dinner. "I can't *not* have dinner with him."

"Yeah, you can." He was not succeeding in dissuading her. He drank some of his beer and told her arrogantly, "You call him up, you tell him you've made other plans and you make sure you're not home tonight in case he doesn't listen." Scarlatti set his beer firmly on the worn, smooth bar. "Better yet, *I'll* call him."

She sipped her seltzer, which was refreshing if not good. It gave her something to do besides stare at this intriguing, infuriating man and acknowledge how easily he could get to her. "I don't have his number."

"You found millions of dollars he'd stashed away. You can find his number."

Rowena stiffened. "You're not my keeper, Sergeant Scarlatti."

"And you're a romantic, Rowena Willow, if you believe Eliot Tyhurst has changed. You live up in your castle tower and don't know squat about the real world."

"I'd rather be a bit of a romantic than a cynic. Someone who has paid his debt to society deserves a chance to prove he's rehabilitated. Society cannot function if that person isn't given that chance."

Scarlatti didn't even look at her. "You breathe real air up in that ivory tower of yours?"

Rowena was insulted. She refused to say a word until he looked at her. When he did, she almost wanted to look away, so powerful was his pull on her. But she forced herself to fasten her gaze on him. She set her jaw.

He didn't flinch.

"I will make my own decisions," she told him.

As she started up, she placed her hand lightly on the lip of the bar for support. Scarlatti covered it with his, holding her steady. "Why tell me about Tyhurst if you're not going to listen to my advice?"

"Was that advice? It sounded more like an order to me. I came, Sergeant," she said icily, "as a simple courtesy to you and Sergeant Ryan. You anticipated

Eliot Tyhurst would contact me, and he has. I believed it my duty to inform you, just as I believe it my
duty to have dinner with Mr. Tyhurst this evening.''

Scarlatti still hadn't released her. His hand was
warm and strong, and she could feel the calluses. In a
sudden, totally out-of-place thought, she wondered
what his hands would feel like on her breasts, the
curve of her hip.

She *must* be going out of her mind. Perhaps she
needed a vacation. Or more work. Lots more work, to
keep her mind productively occupied.

"You could have called the department and left a
message for me,'' he said, watching her closely. His
eyes narrowed. "Something wrong?''

"No!''

She dismissed the vivid, paralyzing thought of him
making love to her. She was in shock. How could her
mind be so treacherous? It wasn't that she was sexu-
ally repressed or considered attraction to a man un-
healthy, just that she considered her attraction to *this*
man out of proportion and potentially dangerous. He
was a detective on leave from the San Francisco police
department. She was a financial whiz. They had nothing in common. It wasn't sensible to respond so heatedly to a man so clearly not right for her, and she had
vowed to herself that she would be sensible not only
in matters of finance, but of the heart.

With tremendous self-discipline—which she hoped
he couldn't detect—she tossed her head back haugh-
tily. "Why should I waste the police's time with something unofficial—'' she eyed him significantly "—and
so *trivial?*''

"Cute, Ms. Willow.'' He let her go, and she could
breathe again. "Real cute.''

This time when she left, he didn't stop her.

Until she reached the door.

"What time is Tyhurst picking you up?"

"Seven. Do *not* interfere, Sergeant."

His grin was intentionally sexy, challenging. "Sweetheart, you won't even know I'm there."

ROWENA SENSED Joe Scarlatti's presence the rest of the afternoon and into the evening.

She sensed it when she was putting on a slim chocolate brown skirt and cream-colored silk blouse. She sensed it when she slipped on her stockings and combed her hair and repinned it and clipped on sapphire earrings. She sensed it when she paced in the entry before seven o'clock, hearing only the sounds of her footsteps echoing in the cavernous house.

She'd checked the street periodically, but there was no sign of Scarlatti.

Yet he was out there, somewhere. She knew it.

Could *feel* it.

Aunt Adelaide's suit of armor stood silent, almost like an old friend. Rowena hadn't yet bothered redecorating the first two floors of the house since her aunt's death. She wasn't sure why: she could certainly afford it. She loathed the taxidermy room. She planned eventually to donate its displays to a museum, although the room came in handy to discourage certain kinds of visitors. After all, she could have taken Joe Scarlatti out to the courtyard to talk.

The doorbell rang. She answered it at once.

Scarlatti strode into the entry. He had on a black pullover and black canvas pants, worn and loose. Burnt-out or not, he looked very tough and competent. And annoyed. "How come you answer on the first ring when you think it's Eliot Tyhurst and it took me six rings to rouse you this morning?"

"I was working and you were uninvited," Rowena replied coolly, "just as you are now. What are you doing here?"

"Just seeing if you were going through with dinner with this ex-con who bilked the American people out of millions."

"He served his time."

"He'd have gotten more time if he'd held up a gas station."

"I have no control over the criminal justice system."

"Yeah, well." He left it at that and gave her a long, deliberately obvious head-to-toe once-over that finished at her face. "My, my. Makeup, even. Eliot Tyhurst gets the full treatment and I get sensible shoes and a floppy hat."

"It's after dark now, and I burn easily, and we won't be walking. Not that I have to justify myself to you."

"How old are you?"

His non sequitur caught her off guard. "What does that have to do with anything?"

"You're young for an eccentric genius, aren't you?"

"Eliot Tyhurst will be arriving any minute. I would prefer not to have to introduce you as my bodyguard."

"I'm not a bodyguard, sweetheart." He moved toward her, across the invisible line that marked the boundary to her space, invading it with his primitive heat. "You couldn't afford to pay me what I'd charge to protect you, even if you sold off every stuffed bird and horror-house trinket in this place and raided every mutual fund you own. I'm a cop. I'm not in this for you."

She believed him. Joe Scarlatti, she thought, was a hard and complex man, and she dared not underestimate him. The only way to deal with him was on a basic, elemental level.

She raised her chin slightly and peered into his eyes, which were hot and dark and challenging. She kept hers cool and objective. "I stand corrected. Nevertheless, you're not here in an official capacity and I have a right to ask you to leave. Please do so."

He didn't back off a millimeter. "Call off your dinner, Rowena."

"Is that an order?"

"A suggestion."

"Are you going to follow me?"

He shook his head. "Can't risk it. You're on your own tonight."

"Fine."

"Dammit—"

"I'm choosing the restaurant. He doesn't know that yet, but I am. We'll be at the Meridien. I didn't want anything too small and intimate."

"More chance someone will recognize him."

"Precisely why I chose such a public spot. If his motives are suspect, he'll have a hard time acting on them with witnesses who not only can provide a description of him, but his name, too."

"What about transportation?"

"I'm driving."

Scarlatti couldn't hide his surprise. "You have a car?"

"I intend to drive his," she said. "Look, he's going

to be here. Duck into the drawing room until I'm gone, then let yourself out."

He gave her a nasty, sexy smile. "Is that an order?"

She smiled back, just as nastily, maybe not so sexily, and refused to act on the urge to step away from him. "Give it up, Sergeant. You care about Tyhurst seeing you more than I do. You know why? You're not interested in protecting me from him. Neither is Sergeant Ryan. You're after Tyhurst for reasons that have nothing to do with me personally."

Something—she didn't know what—made his eyes flash. "Tell me, do you ever doubt one of your own opinions or are you always so obnoxiously sure of yourself?"

"My only question," she continued, as if he hadn't spoken, "is *why* an ordinary cop like you would want Tyhurst so much."

"Lady, I'm a lot of things, but ordinary isn't one of them."

She ignored the implication of his words. Or pretended to. She was intensely aware of every millimeter of him. "I'll find out," she promised.

The doorbell rang, and Scarlatti quietly—if not obediently—slipped into the drawing room.

JOE FELT hundreds of beady glass eyes on him in the dark, overly populated drawing room. Rowena Willow was much more of a handful than he had anticipated. He had almost lost her this afternoon when she took off to Mario's. He should have checked right in the beginning for a back exit from her mausoleum. And he should have guessed someone so independent, so damned alone, would jump all over a dinner invitation from an ex-con she'd helped nail. She was giving him a second chance. She owed society. Hell. The lady was bored out of her mind.

And out to show him.

That had been a mistake, he thought. He shouldn't have got her goat the way he had. She certainly wasn't acquiescent.

And she suspected his motives for watching her weren't entirely unselfish.

Joe *had* taken the case because of Tyhurst and not because of any real concern for Rowena Willow. But Rowena didn't have to know that. It was none of her business that his grandparents weren't financial geniuses, that Tyhurst had been able to rob them blind.

For a reclusive workaholic, she had a way of stirring things up.

Admit it, Scarlatti. You haven't felt this alive in months.

He wasn't admitting anything.

He pressed his ear to the thick double doors and listened.

"Rowena—my heavens, you look lovely."

Joe felt bile rise in his throat at the sound of the bastard's smooth voice. But he had to agree with Tyhurst on that one point—Rowena did look damned attractive. He hoped, however, the crooked banker was responding to her in a more objective, clinical, calculated manner than Joe himself did. Rowena Willow made him think about sex. It was that damned simple and probably would surprise the hell out of her if she knew. And maybe scare her into being less confrontational. Maybe if he *were* on official business his professionalism would have kicked into gear.

He silently cursed Hank Ryan for getting him into this mess, although he knew if he hadn't been on leave, he wouldn't have been free to take the crazy case of Rowena Willow and the banker. His leave of absence was his own choice. What else could a man do who blamed himself for his partner and best friend's death? After almost a year, it still ate at him, day and night. He would never forgive himself, never be the man he was before Matt's death.

He couldn't let anyone else trust him the way Matt Lee had come to trust him. Matt had trusted him with his life, and Joe had failed him. There were no two ways about it. That was the plain, raw truth.

Joe heard Rowena awkwardly thank Tyhurst, obviously unaccustomed to getting compliments on her appearance. She needed to get out more, he thought. She'd get used to it fast if she did. "I thought the Meridien would be nice tonight," she said.

Tyhurst laughed softly. "No, no, I have a special place all picked out."

Joe stiffened, placed a hand on the door latch. He shoved thoughts of Matt and the past deep to the back of his mind. He was ready to act.

"Where?" Rowena asked.

Good, Joe thought, but he didn't for a minute think she'd asked on his account, so he would be able to follow. She was asking because she wanted to know.

But Eliot Tyhurst said, "On the water—you'll love it."

Argue with him, Joe urged silently. *Argue with him the way you do with me.* She didn't say a word, and the front door creaked.

Joe raced across the dark drawing room to the windows. Standing to one side, he carefully pulled back the drapes and peered out at the quiet, pretty street.

Eliot Tyhurst had one hand on Rowena's elbow. She shook loose, subtly. He was a tall, lean, handsome bastard. His suit alone would set Joe back a month's rent with Mario. Tyhurst was educated and sophisticated, just the kind of man for Rowena Willow, if he weren't also a crook.

Joe saw her glance back toward the drawing room window. Her smile was forced, her face pale and tight in the harsh streetlight. Joe reminded himself that Tyhurst was a white-collar criminal, not the armed-and-dangerous variety Joe dealt with on the streets. It was unlikely Rowena was in any physical danger.

Then Tyhurst opened the passenger door, and she got in.

They weren't going to the Meridien. She wasn't driving.

Joe got out the keys to his truck.

The hell she was on her own.

4

ROWENA SAT STIFFLY beside Eliot Tyhurst. He seemed unchanged, at least outwardly, by his prison experience, but she reminded herself he was a newly released convict. She shouldn't be fooled by the scent of his expensive cologne, by the sleek cut of his suit, by the neatness of his tawny-colored hair. He seemed as pulled together and sophisticated as he had at his trial, before conviction and prison. Rowena was uncertain why she'd climbed into his car, why she'd let him take control of their destination. Impulse? Curiosity? A way of getting back at Joe Scarlatti for doubting her ability to handle herself? She just didn't know.

She hardly spoke until they were on the Golden Gate Bridge. "We're going to Marin?" she asked.

"Yes, is that all right? I thought it would be quieter, less chance for either of us to be recognized."

"It's fine. I haven't been out this way in a long time."

Tyhurst nodded as if he understood. Other than completely ignoring her wishes for the evening, whether or not he had done so deliberately, he was behaving like a perfect gentleman. Of course, his smooth manner had contributed to his ability to bilk hundreds of people out of their life savings. They had entrusted their money to him with the same blind faith that had led Rowena into his car. Nothing would

happen to her, she told herself. She wasn't afraid of
Eliot Tyhurst. At worst he was a con man. A computer criminal. A slick white-collar operator. It wasn't
as if she were trapped in a car with a sociopathic
killer.

And at the time, she had to admit, climbing into his
car with him had seemed preferable to crying out to
Joe Scarlatti for help. Already she regretted her plain-
tive look back toward the house. How had he interpreted it? *Surely* he had been watching from the
drawing room window.

Well, she thought, *now you're on your own.*

Wasn't that what she wanted? It certainly was what
she was accustomed to. What she'd worked for,
struggled for. She had learned at a young age to rely
on her own wits and abilities.

Tyhurst wound the small, comfortable car—nothing as ostentatious as what he probably used to
drive—into the picturesque village of Sausalito and
parked at a restaurant that offered a spectacular view
of San Francisco across the bay. Rowena forgot her
uneasiness as she got out of the car. She absorbed the
beauty of the skyline glittering in the distance, the
freshness of the wind in her face, the freedom of being
away from her house and computer.

Eliot Tyhurst materialized beside her. "Stunning,
isn't it?"

He was, indeed, a handsome man, she thought. Re-
fined, polished. And there was a sadness in his eyes
that intrigued her. Yet she felt no rush of sensual heat
the way she did with the police sergeant.

She smiled. "Yes, it is."

"I requested a table by the window. Shall we?"

He put out his arm, and short of being rude, Rowena had little choice but to take it. She was mildly surprised by his obvious strength. Had he taken up pumping iron in prison? She felt self-conscious. All she needed now was an astute news photographer to jump out of the shrubs and snap their picture.

The restaurant was intimate and elegant, with a small bar and no more than a dozen tables arranged in front of huge floor-to-ceiling windows overlooking the bay. Rowena stood back while Tyhurst took over, suave and at ease with himself and his surroundings. He chatted with the maître d' without any of the awkwardness she might have expected from a man fresh out of prison.

He pulled out Rowena's chair for her at their candlelit table. "Thank you for being here," he whispered in her ear. "Not everyone would have trusted me."

Rowena licked her lips as he sat across from her. "I did encounter opposition from one friend who—who suggested you could be out for revenge." She'd managed not to trip over her description of Joe Scarlatti as a friend.

Tyhurst nodded grimly, the sadness drifting from his eyes to his mouth. In the soft light of the restaurant she saw now that lines had formed at the corners of his eyes and etched into his forehead. The cockiness he'd displayed during his trial was gone. Maybe he had changed. "That friend doesn't understand what you did for me. I'm not a bad person, Rowena. I admit I resented you for a long time. I wanted desperately to believe you and you alone were responsible for my downfall. I kept telling myself that if you hadn't interfered, nothing would have happened. If you'd just left me alone, I believed I would have been able to keep my clients' money safe—that in the end everything would have worked out."

"Is that what you still believe?"

"No!" His eyes widened, appalled. "Oh, no. I finally came to understand that I and I alone was responsible for my own downfall. If I'd been left alone, I only would have destroyed more people. I had an inflated view of my ability to make things work out. I refused for a long time to see the true nature of my activities. Arrogance and overconfidence led me to use my clients' money for my own gain. It was wrong of me not to fully inform them, even if I never really intended them to suffer."

"You broke the law," Rowena reminded him.

"That, too."

"What do you want now?"

He looked at her. He seemed weary, filled with regrets. His shoulders sagged. "A fresh start."

She opened her mouth to answer but a movement near the bar drew her eye.

Joe Scarlatti had climbed onto a bar stool. The bartender was sliding him a tall glass of what looked like beer. Rowena felt her heart thump wildly in her chest.

"Is something wrong?" Tyhurst asked, concerned.

"What? Oh—oh, I'm sorry. No, nothing's wrong. I'm just not used to being out in the evening. It's nothing you said."

But she watched as Scarlatti turned in his seat, his back to the black-wood bar. His eyes sought out hers. Deliberately. Overpoweringly. She had to fight to pull her gaze away.

Why had he followed her?

How?

That look she'd given him. He had interpreted it as helpless and frightened. In need of him.

Eliot Tyhurst was frowning. "Rowena?"

She made herself smile. He didn't know about her unofficial protector. She had nothing to worry about.

Except for Joe Scarlatti himself. She had no idea what he would do. None. His actions were completely unpredictable. She didn't like things—including people—she couldn't predict.

Mercifully their waiter intervened, and she ordered a glass of champagne. "To celebrate," she said, almost as smoothly as Tyhurst himself. And she smiled at him. "To celebrate new beginnings."

Relief and pleasure washed over his face, and instead of opting for a second glass, he asked the waiter to bring a bottle of champagne. Their discussion of what vintages were available gave Rowena the opportunity to pull herself together. Scarlatti was going to make an evening of it. He'd sit there all through dinner, an immense distraction.

Suddenly she wished she had stayed home and played solitaire on her computer.

She noticed Eliot's eyes on her and quickly opened her menu. "Have you been here before?" she asked.

"No, but I understand the menu's limited but very good—everything's fresh."

And probably will taste terrific after months of prison food. What did she think she was doing out with an ex-con?

From the look of him, Scarlatti was wondering the same thing. As if she couldn't be trusted to be out on her own. She knew he thought she was too reclusive, too naive, too *weird*.

Tyhurst's eyes got a faraway look, and as if he had

read her thoughts, he said, "But don't expect me to be a good judge—what I consider acceptable cuisine after my ordeal would surprise you."

If not for his easy manner, his almost self-deprecating tone and his soft, warm eyes, Rowena might have winced. Yet his words seemed without edge or self-pity.

She snuck a peek at Scarlatti. He had turned back to the bar and was engaged in conversation with the bartender. He looked comfortable there. His casual attire didn't even seem out of place, despite the more formal dress of those who had come for dinner.

Did he know more about the Eliot Tyhursts of the world than Rowena did?

He assumed he did. Tyhurst had been to prison. Ergo, Scarlatti knew more about him.

Their champagne came, and they ordered—Tyhurst the grilled salmon, Rowena a pasta dish—and toasted to knew beginnings. Finally he said, "Tell me about yourself, Rowena. I know so very little."

Awkwardness inundated her, and she looked quickly out the window, noting the lights of boats bobbing on the choppy water. She didn't know what to say. Although introspective by nature, she was not self-absorbed. And she didn't know how much she wanted Eliot Tyhurst to know about her. What should she tell him?

"My work is going very well," she said. "I recently received a complicated assignment from a New England company that looks interesting—"

Tyhurst stopped her, shaking his head indulgently. "I want to know about *you*. What makes Rowena Willow tick?"

Nothing came to her. Absolutely nothing. Was it

because Sergeant Scarlatti was just yards away? Had his nearness left her tongue-tied? "That's not an easy question to answer."

"You don't trust me."

"It's not that. Mr. Tyhurst—"

"Eliot. Please call me Eliot."

"Eliot—" she tried to smile when she said it "—to be truthful, I don't know whether I should trust you or not. I don't know you well enough. You're making a new beginning for yourself. I wouldn't presume to judge you. It's simply not my place."

The hurt look vanished from his handsome face. "That's a start."

A start toward what?

Toward giving him the second chance he needed, she told herself. Nothing more.

"I'm afraid," she went on, "that if I can't talk about my work, I never know what to say when someone asks about me. My Aunt Adelaide—she raised me— taught me not to talk too much about myself, not just because it's vain but because Willows aren't always understood. I—well, I come from an eccentric family."

"So I've heard," Eliot said gently. "Suppose you just start with the basics and we'll go from there."

She smiled, relaxing. "I have two cats, and I live alone."

"You have an interesting house," he said, almost as if he were coaching her. He sipped his champagne. She did likewise.

"Oh, yes. My great-grandfather, Cedric Willow, built it. Some people say I'm a lot like him and..." She couldn't go on, and it had nothing to do with any reluctance to talk about herself. Her stomach was twisted with tension, and it was all because Scarlatti was there at the bar, watching her again, and she couldn't stop thinking about him. "Excuse me a moment, won't you?"

Tyhurst's face clouded again, but he said smoothly, "Of course."

She rushed toward the ladies' room, right past Scarlatti, stifling an impulse to mutter something to him.

The ladies' room was small and scented with potpourri, papered with tiny roses. Rowena patted her face with cold water, careful not to smear her makeup. Her eyes looked huge, her cheeks flushed, her lips full. She was out of her element. Cops and ex-cons—the closest she usually came to them was on a computer game, or reading about them in the papers, or in a book. She didn't have *dinner* with them. She didn't have them *spying* on her.

This wasn't her life. Not tonight.

What she had to do, she decided, was get through dinner with Eliot Tyhurst and thus show Joe Scarlatti her judgment was sound and she didn't need him following her around, and in the morning she'd get her life back.

It was a good, simple, solid plan.

Resolved to follow it, she swept out of the ladies' room.

And almost landed in Joe Scarlatti's arms.

He had the receiver of a wall pay phone in one hand. "You've been talking a blue streak," he said to her, his eyes dark, penetrating, angry. "You telling the guy your life story? Eat up and go home."

"He's trying to get me to talk about myself," she said, "and I am not 'talking a blue streak.'"

"What's he need to know?"

"He says everything. Maybe he's just being courteous."

Scarlatti slammed the phone down and swung back around at her. "And maybe he's a goddamned crook."

She set her jaw. "You can go home now, Sergeant."

"Did I ever say I was working for you?"

"I'll have you arrested for harassment."

He gave a low, arrogant laugh.

"I can take care of myself," she said.

"Yeah," he said, "that's why you drove and that's why you're at the Meridien. Or don't you *know* where the hell you are?"

"If we were anywhere else," she said through clenched teeth, "I would slap you across the face."

He didn't back off. "You'll have your chance."

"Go home."

She started off, but his hand shot out, grabbing her by the wrist, spinning her around to his chest. If Eliot Tyhurst decided to go to the men's room, he would see them, and yet Rowena's head spun with the thrill of the risk she was taking, of the masculine smell of the hard cop whose breath she could feel hot on her face.

"Let me take you out of here," he said in a low, tight voice. "Now."

"I can't—"

His mouth came down on hers with such sudden fierceness Rowena didn't have a chance to let out a cry of surprise, only to open her lips. He took full advantage. His tongue plunged into her mouth, tasting her, warning her. She felt herself sinking against him, responding. An agonizing desire spread through her.

He pulled away as fiercely as he'd come to her. His gaze swept over her. Then he straightened. He seemed at the very edge of his self-control. "You'd better hit the ladies' room again before you head back."

And he stalked down the short hall and around the corner into the restaurant.

This time Rowena did as he advised. Looking at her reflection in the mirror, she knew what he'd meant. Her nipples were visibly hard under her filmy blouse, her eyes dusky with pent-up desire, her lipstick smudged. The taste of him was still on her tongue.

What if she'd asked him to drive her home?

They would never have got that far. They'd have had to stop somewhere and make love.

It was that way between them.

She quickly redid her lipstick and hoped the restaurant's dim light would prevent her dinner date from noticing any other evidence of what she'd been doing on her trip to the ladies' room.

Passing Joe Scarlatti was no mean feat. His smoky gaze settled on her, told her that he wanted her—that he would have her. She felt its searing heat as she wove through the tables, now crowded with diners, back to Eliot Tyhurst.

"Is everything all right?" he asked.

"Yes, fine."

Their dinner arrived, and Rowena, grateful for the distraction, raved perhaps more than was necessary. Tyhurst seemed pleased. But before he could resume asking her about herself, she said, "What do you plan to do now that you've served your sentence?"

He shrugged. "I'm not sure. I'm thinking over my options." He had, she recalled, declared himself bankrupt three years ago. "I'll find something to do. Something positive, I hope."

Rowena wanted to believe him. Part of her *did* believe him. "With your talents," she said, "you have a whole host of positive opportunities to choose from."

"Do I?"

"Of course."

He smiled sadly. "You're so naive, Rowena—or maybe I'm too jaded. I hope…" He paused, looking pained. "I hope I'll find other people as willing to forgive and forget as you are."

"I know you're barred from certain financial activities for life, but I should think if you've served your sentence and take a little time to prove your good intentions, someone will give you a second chance."

"Let's hope so."

There was an edge to his words this time. She wondered if it had more to do with his fear of the future than his regrets about the past. But he launched into a discussion of how San Francisco had changed in the three years he'd been away, and Rowena was grateful he didn't insist on having her talk about herself. Still, she ate her pasta as quickly as she could, telling herself she wasn't taking the sergeant's advice.

He was still at the bar, his back to her. Every time she stole a look at him, she could taste his mouth on hers, feel the hot probing of his tongue. Was his kiss deliberate? Impulsive?

Did she dare trust him any more than Eliot Tyhurst?

It didn't matter. Whatever he was after, *she* wanted a chance to kiss him. To leave him as distracted and taken aback and aching as she was.

After she and Tyhurst had finished their main

courses, Rowena agreed to a cup of coffee, but refused dessert. And she insisted on paying for her own
dinner. This time she didn't just go along with him as
she had with his choice of restaurant and decision to
drive. There'd be no more impulsive behavior, no
more indulging curiosity or a ridiculous need not to
show weakness to a burnt-out San Francisco cop.

When she got up to leave, she saw that Joe Scarlatti
had vacated his seat at the bar.

Where was he?

There was no sign of his battered truck out in the
parking lot, or of him. Rowena wondered fleetingly if
he'd taken her advice and had gone home. *You're on
your own again,* she thought, but quickly reminded
herself that she'd always been on her own. A few
days of Joe Scarlatti in her life hadn't changed a thing.

She spoke little on their way back across the
Golden Gate Bridge, into the view that had so transfixed her from the other side of the bay. Glancing at
Tyhurst, she tried to imagine what it would be like to
pick up the pieces of her life after a prison sentence,
however brief. Would she fare any better than Eliot
Tyhurst? Could she be as magnanimous to the person
who had put her there? *If* that was what he was being.

She couldn't tell. She was no judge of people, and
Eliot Tyhurst was particularly hard to read. She
watched him as he drove with both hands on the
wheel, his eyes narrowed on the road like a teenager
just learning to drive. It had been a while, she realized, since he had driven a car. *Thanks to me.* No,
thanks to himself.

"Would you like me to walk you to your door?" he
asked when he pulled up to her house. It did look like
a dreary old castle at night.

"No, thanks. I can manage."

She pushed open the car door and started out.

He leaned toward her, touched her shoulder. "Is there anyone special in your life, Rowena?"

A chill ran up her spine. She turned to look at him. She had one foot out on the pavement. "Lots of people."

"I lost my wife over this ordeal. She was horrified at my—how did she put it? My 'unconscionable behavior.' As if I were a mass murderer." He sighed, letting his hand fall away. "It's not easy being alone."

She climbed out of his car and looked around at him, feeling a small surge of sympathy. "I guess it's not so hard when it's all you've known."

In a few moments, she was on her doorstep and Eliot Tyhurst was gone.

The door echoed in the cavernous entry when she shut it behind her. She peeked outside. There was no sign of Joe Scarlatti or his truck. Was he more competent than she'd given him credit for? Or just less interested, less concerned about her safety?

Mega and Byte floated down the carpeted stairs and rubbed against her leg, welcoming her back.

"Ahh, kitties," she said, "you don't know how good it is to be home."

But she froze, hearing the loud rumble of an old truck engine outside her door. Looking through the window, she saw Joe Scarlatti's battered truck parallel-parking in a space that was clearly insufficient for its bulk. He didn't give up. He just parked it at a sharp angle—a thorough eyesore on her attractive, upmarket street—and climbed out with a big bundle tucked under one muscular arm.

A sleeping bag.

Rowena had the door open by the time he reached it. "You can't be serious," she said.

"I'll take any room but the morgue in there."

"Sergeant, you aren't invited to spend the night." It was an outrageous thought. How could he mean to spend the night after their kiss? "I—I don't *need* you here."

"I'll bet the hell you don't," he said sardonically.

She wouldn't let him get to her. She just wouldn't. "Eliot Tyhurst and I had a pleasant, innocuous dinner. He made no mention of wanting to see me again." She threw up her hands when all Joe Scarlatti did was stand there waiting for her to let him in. "This is absurd. I assure you, Tyhurst is finished with me."

Scarlatti shook his head, every inch of him the pro now, not the hothead who'd risked kissing her. "He went around the corner after dropping you off, parked, got out and walked a few yards to where he'd have a view of your ivory tower up there. Maybe he was contemplating the stars, but I don't believe it."

"And what of it?"

"He's not finished with you yet, that's what of it. The bastard's just getting started."

5

SHE GAVE HIM a little room off the kitchen that had a studio couch with a mattress that must have been stuffed with dried sticks. Joe didn't know what the hell it was doing there because pretty soon he discovered that the musty, earthy smell that was keeping him awake emanated from a thirty-pound bag of potatoes. He was in the damned pantry! The gall of the woman! He was looking after her miserable hide and she'd stuck him in with the potatoes!

He slid himself down deep into his sleeping bag and gritted his teeth. His whole body was tense. He should be unwinding at Mario's with a couple of beers, a little chitchat with some friends, maybe a little hanky-panky with an attractive and willing woman.

Hell. He should be upstairs making love to Rowena Willow.

It was what she was afraid would happen if she gave him a room any closer to hers. He was sure of it. He'd gotten the pantry because she had responded to his kiss in the restaurant in a way that scared the hell out of her.

And him, too. Her hunger had stirred not just his body but his sense of responsibility. He had to *think* dammit, not just act. When he'd gone on leave, he'd promised himself he would use the six months to try to pull himself together. He had no business encouraging Rowena Willow to fall for an emotional wreck like himself.

Not that she would. And not that he really felt like such a wreck anymore. The fog of his soul was lifting. Was it because he was working again—or was it because of Rowena?

Two cats jumped up onto his chest and pawed his sleeping bag. He had visions of them using him for a litter box or settling in for the night, so he bounced them unceremoniously back onto the floor. Cats were all right, but not in his bed and not in this quaint little house of horrors.

Their yellow eyes shone as they looked back at him in the darkness. If he weren't a big tough cop, Joe told himself, he'd probably get the willies.

All in all he figured it'd be a long night.

IT WAS.

He awoke stiff and sore. He didn't require the usual couple of seconds to shake off sleep and remember where he was: he knew *exactly* where he was. What he needed time to remember was *why* he was there. What did a sensible cop such as himself expect to accomplish sleeping in the pantry of a weirdo like Rowena Willow? How the hell could he keep an eye on her? The house was so damned huge, an entire SWAT team could slip inside and make off with her without his knowing.

Well, he thought, staying over must have seemed like a good idea last night or he wouldn't have done it.

Then again, Joe Scarlatti was known for being impulsive. He bent rules, took risks. He acted fast when he needed to, relying on the instincts and reflexes born of training and experience. Thinking too much could get a cop into trouble.

But not thinking at all...

He shook off his introspective mood. It would lead him down a path he did not want to go, not this morning. Instead, he climbed out of bed, pulled on his pants and headed into the kitchen.

The only signs of Rowena Willow were the still-hot kettle and the two cats stuffing their faces at their dishes over by the door to the courtyard. Presumably they hadn't got their food out themselves.

He searched the cupboards for something resembling coffee and came up with a dozen different kinds of teas and finally, way back behind a plastic bag labeled Chamomile, a small jar of instant coffee. It took some muscle to open. There were a couple of spoonfuls of grounds caked at the bottom of the jar. He had to scrape them out. Even then, they came out in clumps that he hoped boiling water would dissolve.

An old-tasting, bad cup of coffee was preferable, he reasoned, to no coffee at all. So long as the stuff didn't poison him.

The cats finished feasting and wandered off, ignoring him.

Joe checked the front of the refrigerator, the table and the counters for a note from Ms. Rowena telling him what the hell she might be up to this morning. There wasn't one.

Guess I'm on my own. Apparently she didn't own a coffee mug, either. Then he found a freestanding cupboard holding about two dozen china cups and saucers, each one different, none of a variety that had ever worked its way into his life. He chose a design with a black-and-gold band on the rim; it looked more masculine than forget-me-nots.

"You're a sick man, Scarlatti," he muttered to himself, "to worry about such things."

He scooped out the few grounds that refused to dissolve and drank the coffee black. It wasn't as bad as some he'd had, but it wasn't good. Fortunately he wasn't hungry. He hadn't seen anything he considered suitable for a quick breakfast in his search through her cupboards. He was not about to spend the next twenty minutes cooking hand-cut oats.

Coffee in hand, he wandered down the hall to the front entry, figuring Rowena would hear him and give a yell. The morning sun was filtered through sheers on the panel windows next to the door, but instead of cheering up the place, it only made it seem lonelier. Joe peeked into the drawing room.

"Hi, guys," he said to the stuffed animals.

They just stared back at him.

He patted the suit of armor in the entry on the shoulder as if it could commiserate with his plight and sipped his coffee, trying to figure out a way to get a decent hold on the damned cup. His fingers were too thick.

Probably, he thought, he should just go home, call Hank Ryan, tell him he was out, done, *fini*, Rowena Willow could damned well handle Eliot Tyhurst herself. He wouldn't mention that he'd kissed her.

But he started up the sweeping stairs.

Sombre paintings and old photographs hung on dark Victorian wallpaper. Where the stairs curved, there was a window seat made of polished wood, no cushion, no pillows. Heavy drapes were drawn over

the window above it. Even the cats wouldn't hang
around there.

On the second-floor landing the doors to what
rooms he could see were all shut. There were more
forbidding paintings—portraits of dour men and
women and eerie forest landscapes—and more dark
wallpaper. Joe decided he was just as glad he'd had
the pantry.

He paused and listened.

Tap-tap-tap . . .

The sound, barely audible, was coming from the
third floor. He finished off his coffee in one big swallow and headed up, not skipping steps lest he trip
and break his neck, but moving quickly, with a re-
newed sense of energy.

Rowena Willow at work.

That would be something to see.

He came to the third floor and was struck immediately by the sunlight streaming in through the bright
clear glass of tall windows unfettered by drapes and
sheers. The walls were painted a warm, ultrapale
peach. Underfoot was a simple runner in a soft neu-
tral color. A window seat was cushioned in a peach-
flowered fabric and piled with pillows. Everything
was bright, clean, simple.

Rowena, Rowena, Joe thought. *I haven't even begun to
figure you out.*

Not that figuring her out was necessary to keeping
Tyhurst from hurting her, he told himself. *Pull back,
my man, pull back. You don't belong in her world.*

The tapping sound had stopped. Joe figured she
must have heard him. He walked down the hall and
turned left through an open doorway, into a large,
airy, cheerful state-of-the-art office. A computer and

fax machine and copier hummed, but the place smelled faintly of cinnamon; he spotted a bowl of pot-pourri on the edge of one of four long desks.

Rowena sat at one of them in the middle of the room, her back to him, staring at a bunch of numbers on a computer screen. Her hair was pinned up, not a strand hanging loose, and she had on a russet-colored jumpsuit and no shoes.

She did not look around at him. Joe figured she was either pretending she didn't know he was there or didn't, in fact, know he was there.

He cleared his throat.

She screamed and jumped right up off her chair, which backed out from under her. When she came down, she caught just the edge of the chair and slipped onto the floor. A thick lock of hair fell down one cheek. She was shaking. She got up on her knees and turned, holding on to the seat of her chair as her big blue eyes focused on the intruder.

Joe smiled. "Morning."

She glared at him.

"Guess I startled you."

She didn't seem too thrilled. Tucking the errant lock of hair back where it belonged, she climbed to her feet and rearranged her jumpsuit, which had gotten twisted in her tumble to the floor. Joe tried not to let his gaze linger on the soft swell of her breasts, but it was one of those things that, by the time you try not to do it, you've already done it. Rowena glared at him some more. Her cheeks, however, were flushed. Again he realized that despite her bizarre life-style and genius, Rowena Willow was not unaware of the needs of the flesh, her own included.

"I thought you would be gone by now," she said, barely recovered.

"I'm not."

"Why not?"

"Just got up. Haven't even had my morning hand-cut oats. How long you been at it?"

"Since five. I like to get an early start. I..." She licked her lips, clearly embarrassed at having jumped out of her skin. "My concentration—when I work, I'm often unaware of other...I don't hear things. I jump when the phone rings, a fax comes in, Mega or Byte show up." She smiled feebly. "One of the hazards of the job, I guess."

"As hazards go," Joe said, "it could be worse."

She nodded, and the flush receded, the eyes lost some of their angry embarrassment. She licked her lips again. It was about as distracting as the twisted jumpsuit had been. But then she said, "Yes, I understand you've faced a number of hazards in your career with the San Francisco police."

He frowned. "How would you know?"

With a small gesture, she indicated her computer. "I looked you up. I'm tied into a number of..." She paused, probably thinking of the right way to explain it to a nontechnical type. "A number of networks. I typed in 'SCARLATTI, JOE' more or less for my own peace of mind and—well, I got quite a lot."

Joe stiffened. "Such as?"

"I would think you would already know."

Joe did indeed.

"If you can spy on me, know things about me, sleep in my house, I see no reason why I shouldn't find out what I can about you." Her tone was cool but not judgmental and a nervous look had come into her big blues. "I'm sorry if it's awkward for you."

"Yeah," he said, and headed for the door.

"Where are you going?"

His jaw was clenched tight, his body tense with the pain of being reminded of why he had time to keep an eye on her. Of Matt Lee's death. Of his own role in it. He didn't bother turning around. "I'll let you know."

"If you stay—" she hesitated, then blundered on "—please don't scare me again."

He looked around at her, saw how smart and independent and yet vulnerable she was, felt a surge of something he couldn't identify—something between attraction and protectiveness—and nodded curtly, knowing he had to get the hell out of there, and fast. He had to get himself under control. He remembered last night's promise to himself: to think before he acted.

Not thinking before he acted had gotten Matt killed.

FOR ONCE in her life, the numbers on her computer screen made no sense to Rowena. They were a jumble of high-resolution dots on her color monitor. They might just as well have been baseball scores. She couldn't focus. She couldn't concentrate. Maybe she needed a break.

She pushed back her chair, blinked her eyes several times and raised her arms above her head to stretch. Tension and stiffness had penetrated her muscles; her wrists ached. She'd been at her computer for four hours straight and it was only nine in the morning.

But that wasn't anything out of the ordinary and certainly not the reason she couldn't concentrate.

Joe Scarlatti's presence in her house, however, *was* out of the ordinary.

Dammit, I won't think about him!

She clicked to the next screen of the file she was examining, hoping it would make more sense or at least jog her back into action. She was supposed to be unraveling the tangled financial network of a private winery. A prospective buyer wanted to be certain he knew all there was to know about the company from an objective—and respected—source. Namely herself.

But still she stared blankly at the screen.

Instead of seeing financial clues, she saw her tough San Francisco cop's dark, searching eyes. His rugged face. His thick thighs. Instead of thinking about the future of the mercurial wine business, she thought about the intriguing nature of Joe Scarlatti. His grit and determination. His wit and unusual sense of humor.

And his past. The last year in particular. She thought about that a lot.

A burnt-out cop.

And for her a potentially dangerous man.

Even before he'd come up to her office earlier this morning, she had known he was still in her house. She knew he was there now. She could feel his presence. He hadn't left.

Banging keys, she quickly exited the file and returned to the C-prompt.

Her hands were trembling.

"This is absurd," she said under her breath.

Before she knew what she was doing, Rowena suddenly flew to her feet and raced down the two flights of stairs, nearly running into Joe Scarlatti in her front entry. He appeared to be in a staring contest with her suit of armor. He looked around at her, but said nothing. She wondered if he knew how close she'd come to plowing into him as she had in the restaurant. Would he have caught her up in his arms again?

I have to stop this sort of thinking! We would be a disaster together!

Like her parents...

"We should talk," she said, hating the way her voice croaked.

"About what? You're the genius." His mood was obviously still sour over what he clearly perceived to have been an invasion of his privacy. "You must know everything there is to know about me by now."

"Only what's in public records I have access to through my computer."

A corner of his mouth twitched. "That's about everything."

"Sergeant—"

"Joe," he said. "You know that much about me, you get to call me Joe." There was no humor in his tone, none in his eyes.

Rowena was unintimidated. "So it's okay for you to know everything about me, but I'm to know nothing about you."

"I doubt I know everything about you, Rowena. I doubt anyone does. I only know what I need to know to do my job."

"A job I didn't ask you to do. Suppose I need to know about you in order to trust you?"

"Then you should have asked me."

"Would you have told me?"

He didn't hesitate. "No."

"I didn't figure you would." She backed up a step. "I'm sorry about your partner, Matt Lee. He—"

"You don't need to tell me his name. I remember."

She accepted the criticism without comment. She had no experience talking to cops who blamed themselves for their partner's death. She noticed his rigid stance, the cold pain in his eyes, and she asked softly, "He's why you're on leave of absence, isn't he?"

"And available to keep an eye out on a pretty, blue-eyed genius? Yep, he's why. Get a kick out of it, too, Matt would." But Joe Scarlatti wasn't getting a kick out of anything; his whole demeanor was without humor. He was angry and sarcastic, but Rowena wasn't fooled—his pain was nearly palpable. "Anything else you want to tell me about myself?"

She inhaled, still not intimidated, not afraid of him. "You're angry."

He shoved his hands into his jean pockets. "Let's just say I don't appreciate your sneaking around in your computer like goddamned Big Brother."

She swallowed and made herself meet his gaze with all the courage and directness she could muster. "I can understand that. I also understand that a computer search can't give the full measure of a human being. The newspaper accounts I accessed—I'm sure they didn't tell everything. But I'm not apologizing, Sergeant. You've invaded my life. I have a right to know the background of a man who purports to want to protect me—"

"I'm not protecting you, sister. I'm using you to find out if Tyhurst is as reformed as he says he is. That's all."

Rowena chose not to respond to his nasty remark. She could see that he was definitely angry. Hurt and pained and haunted by his partner's death, but also truly annoyed that she had looked into his background without his say-so.

He raked a hand through his hair, still unruly from his night in the pantry, and she thought she saw a flash of regret in his dark eyes. He started toward the door. "I've got to get out of here, get my bearings. Tyhurst gets in touch, call me at Mario's. Number's in the book."

"Sergeant—"

He glanced around at her one final time. "Or just look it up on your computer."

BY TEATIME Rowena stood in the kitchen disgusted with herself and furious with Joe Scarlatti. She had given up an entire day to him. Not that he'd come back, not that he'd called, not that she'd spotted him on her street. She'd simply allowed him to disrupt her concentration for hours on end. Never, never had she had so much trouble zeroing in on her work without permitting anything else to intrude.

Of course, there'd never been anything quite as distracting as Sergeant Joe Scarlatti.

As she brought her tea tray up to the sunroom, she wondered if she'd driven him away by prying into his background. It wouldn't be the first time her adeptness with a computer had driven off a man. Aunt Adelaide had warned her that many men couldn't handle an intelligent, driven woman, never mind an eccentric Willow. Rowena had never pretended to be less intelligent than she was; she had never pretended that she didn't know things, didn't have a natural ability with numbers. She had always simply been herself, around men and women. And she *had* met men who were attracted to her; she'd even dated a few. But she was very, very careful about romance, and that had precious little to do with her high I.Q. It had to do with the experience of a little girl whose parents' insane love for each other had robbed her of them too young.

Scarlatti, she reminded herself, was a cop on a case. He wanted Eliot Tyhurst. As far as Scarlatti was concerned, she was just a financial whiz, and a tad strange—and nosy—at that.

Kissing her last night had been a spur of the moment thing. Because she was there and he'd wanted to make a point. Probably had been a knee-jerk reaction for him. It meant nothing. She arranged her pillows close to the windows and stared down at the street. Her heartbeat, she noticed, had quickened as if in anticipation.

"Of what?" she snorted, disgusted with herself.

Squinting, she examined each vehicle parked on the street below her just as she had before she had come face-to-face with Joe Scarlatti. She recalled her first good look at him, climbing out of his truck, stretching, irritated and impatient.

In spite of herself, she imagined what it would be like to go to bed with him. He would be an experienced lover. He would know what pleased him, what pleased a woman. Possibly he would even—

"*Stop!*"

Tea splashed onto her front, but she hardly felt its heat. She didn't finish it, but returned the tray to the kitchen, dumped the rest down the drain, and wiped her shirt. She played with Mega and Byte for a while, throwing a catnip toy down the hall toward the suit of armor. One or the other would bring it back for her to throw again, like a couple of dogs playing fetch. They were good cats—pretty, predictable, decent company.

Why now, more than ever before, did she feel the crushing silence of Aunt Adelaide's peculiar house?

The doorbell rang, startling her, although not nearly as much as when Joe Scarlatti had snuck into her office.

Checking through the side window, she saw not a tough cop, but Eliot Tyhurst, looking so deceptively correct in his conservative gray suit. She opened the door.

"Hello, Rowena. I hope I'm not disturbing you." He had a Burberry raincoat draped over his shoulders against a light but persistent drizzle; it made him look even more competent and powerful. Less of an ex-convict. "May I come in?"

"Why?" she asked, not rudely.

If he took offense it didn't register on his handsome face. "I want to make you a proposition."

What if *he* wanted to go to bed with her? She almost laughed out loud. Really, she was thinking nutty thoughts. She had better make herself another pot of tea and get herself back under control before she started thinking every man in San Francisco wanted her.

Then, as if to prove what an idiot she was turning into, Tyhurst said formally, "I want to hire you."

6

TWO DAYS AFTER Joe had stormed out of Rowena Willow's Telegraph Hill monstrosity, he sat at Mario's Bar & Grill nursing a cold beer and taking occasional bites of a black bean enchilada. The spicy sauce was enough to make his eyes tear. He accused his cousin of deliberately adding more jalapeños to his plate.

"Wished I thought of it," Mario said, wiping up after a customer, "but I didn't. You going to hang around here all day?"

"Maybe." He probably should have sat at his booth, out of Mario's immediate range, but he'd wanted some company, some distractions.

"What about Rowena Willow?" Mario asked. "Aren't you supposed to be watching her?"

"'Supposed to' implies I've got orders. I don't. Not from the department, not from her and not from you."

Mario took no notice of his cousin's surly tone. "She turned Tyhurst in."

"Yeah."

"Figure we owe her."

"*We*, Gunga Din?"

Mario grunted. "The SOB decides to come after her, somebody better be there."

"Lady can take care of herself. You've seen her. She keeps a spear in the front hall."

"You scared of her or what?"

Joe gave him a look of disgust and tried another bite of the enchilada. Hotter'n hell. He didn't believe Mario about not trying to char his esophagus. "You wouldn't serve something this hot to customers."

"Some people like their food extra-spicy. Thought you did."

"I do, but this is—do I have flames coming out of my ears?"

Mario scoffed. "Can't have a fire in a vacuum."

"Funny, funny."

"Hank Ryan called again. You going to call him back?"

"Maybe."

His cousin tossed his rag onto his shoulder with a hard snap and glared at Joe with growing impatience. His expression reminded Joe of their grandfather. The younger Mario Scarlatti was easygoing in comparison. He said, "Finish your lunch and get the hell out of here for a while. I'm sick of looking at you."

"One thing I can say, Mario, I always know where I stand with you."

But he'd already stomped back to the kitchen, muttering to himself about how *some* people tested his sense of family loyalty beyond endurance, only he had a way of putting it that was even spicier than his enchilada sauce. Not ones to cross, the Scarlattis. But Eliot Tyhurst had, and Mario, Sr. hadn't fought back. He'd just given up and died a broken man. If his grandson and namesake hadn't been able to take over the bar, he'd have had to sell it.

Joe finished off his beer and knew he'd need something more to drink if he was going to eat the last of his enchilada. Or maybe he ought to dump the damn thing down the drain and ruin Mario's plumbing for him. He was still arguing with himself when Hank Ryan wandered in.

His fellow cop was clearly annoyed. "How the hell tough is it for you to pick up the damned phone and call me?"

"Hey, Hank."

He plopped on the stool beside Joe. "You drunk?"

"Nope. Too early."

Hank scowled. "You'd be better off watching Rowena Willow and Eliot Tyhurst than wasting away in here all damned day."

"I'm not wasting away. Mario wouldn't let me. And I don't get drunk. As for Ms. Willow and Mr. Tyhurst—I don't want to have a harassment charge laid on my doorstep."

"Harassment for what? You haven't done enough." Joe eyed him and shrugged.

Mario came out of the kitchen and pointed a thick finger at Hank. "You," he said, "get him—" he redirected the finger to Joe "—out of here."

"I'm trying," Hank said.

"Try harder," Mario said and stomped back to the kitchen.

Hank sighed. "See, Joe, you're bugging everybody. A man like you needs to be doing something, not sitting around licking his wounds."

"What would you say if I told you I've been keeping an eye on our two financial types, only I've been especially subtle about it?"

"I don't know." Hank looked dubious. "Would you be lying?"

Joe grinned, and for a second he forgot about the

extra-hot enchilada sauce and took too big a bite. It burned all the way down and continued to burn in his stomach. It was a distraction, anyway, from the way he burned for Rowena Willow.

"What," Hank said, "Mario trying to kill you?" He laughed. "I knew I liked that guy. Look, I just wanted to check in, keep in touch. You know you haven't been yourself for a hell of a long time. I don't want this thing to—it's supposed to help, not hurt."

"If he's up to something—and I'm not saying he is—Tyhurst isn't going to be easy to nail this time."

"He wasn't easy last time." Hank glanced at Joe. "Think maybe he's a new man after all?"

Joe didn't hesitate. "No."

"One more thing. I'm going to be talking to a guy Tyhurst knew in prison. He says he has some information on him. He's a real lowlife himself so I'm not holding my breath. I'll let you know if anything pans out."

"Yeah."

After Hank left, Joe gave up on his enchilada and got himself a large cola and returned to his bar stool, staring out at the passersby and the milky mist. What the hell was he going to do about Rowena Willow?

Not about her, he thought. About himself and his loss of objectivity. He had worked for six months to shut down his feelings, to keep them under control, keep them from hurting anyone else. Now he couldn't stop thinking about Rowena Willow.

Then she was there beside him and for a second he thought he'd just conjured her up, but he was stone-cold sober and there was no denying her presence. The light scent of her perfume. The cool mist clinging to her hair. She had it in some kind of prim-looking twist. It was becoming, but again he found himself imagining it down, imagining his hands in it.

He sipped his soda and said nothing. Neither did she.

She wore no makeup, had on leggings and a huge San Francisco Giants shirt, and still she looked gorgeous. Her body was trim and fit and feminine, but there was something tentative about her as she shifted on the stool, twisted her hands together on the smooth surface of the bar. She seemed not so much self-conscious or awkward as just unsure of what to do, what to say, why she'd even come. She was out of her element, no buttons to push, no numbers to analyze. Joe figured she'd gotten out more in the past few days than she had in months.

Finally he said, "You want something to drink?"

She ignored his question, her black-lashed eyes narrowing on him. "You haven't been watching my place."

"You sure about that?"

He could see she wasn't. She untwisted her hands and ran her fingertips along the edge of the bar. "I wanted to talk to you."

"About what?"

"I—first I have to say I'm sorry about prying into your past. I thought I had a right."

He wished she hadn't brought it up. "Maybe you did."

It seemed enough of an answer for her. "Are you still interested in Eliot Tyhurst?"

"Depends."

"I mean, I know your interest is unofficial, that Hank Ryan put you up to watching me...my place in case Tyhurst tried anything. Technically you're still on leave of absence, aren't you?"

"Yes."

"So anything..." She swallowed, inhaled and started again. "If Tyhurst does anything suspicious or outright fraudulent, if anything really did happen, or does happen, I should go to the police, not to you."

Joe's entire body went rigid. "Rowena, what's going on?"

She gave an audible sigh, her dark eyebrows knitted together. Her convoluted speech, he realized, wasn't tentativeness or uncertainty or awkwardness. She was an eccentric genius who sometimes came across as a dingbat because her mind worked faster than her mouth.

"Eliot—Tyhurst—came to my house after you left the other day."

"What, does he want me to chaperon another dinner between you two?"

She frowned. Either his wit passed her by or she was deliberately ignoring it. The woman's one-track mind wasn't on a track that included kidding. "He doesn't know about you."

Joe kept quiet, not wanting to scare her off. He wanted her to talk to him. A sudden pain in his gut told him he more than wanted it; he needed it. He needed her trust.

"He wanted to talk about hiring me," she said.

"And you told him to go soak his head."

"No."

Again that deadly serious tone. Joe said, "Uh-huh. Go on."

"I told him I would meet him this morning."

This morning. "Nice of you to come to me after you

let the horse out of the barn. Did you meet in a well lit, well populated location?"

"In my drawing room."

"With the dead animals looking on. Terrific. Some protection."

"I didn't think I needed protection," she said in that cool, I'm-smarter-than-you voice. Joe was beginning to think it was a cover-up, that he'd jumped to some wrong conclusions about Rowena Willow of Telegraph Hill.

"Did Tyhurst get the creeps?" he asked sarcastically.

Rowena blinked at him as if she didn't have the faintest idea what he was talking about. "Is that a joke?"

"You should have called me before you had Tyhurst to your house alone."

"I thought you might be—" she licked her lips, an immense distraction "—out on the street."

"And you not know it? My, my. I'm surprised it even occurred to you I might be able to outwit you."

Her big eyes seemed to reach for his; he could feel them drawing him toward her. "Did you?"

It pained him, but honesty was generally one of his habits and he had to shake his head. "I was here."

"I see." Her shoulders drew back slightly, as if in reaction to some kind of realization that she was on her own. It didn't seem to be an unfamiliar state of affairs. "Well, nothing happened. Fortunately for me. I suppose it doesn't make any difference to you whether anything happened or not." There wasn't an ounce of self-pity in her tone; she was just stating the facts. "Excuse me."

She whipped to her feet, every hair in her twist

staying right where it was. She was a woman, Joe thought, who kept her emotions under tight rein. She *was* upset that he'd left her on her own. Only she'd never admit it, maybe not even to herself.

"You knew where to find me," Joe said quietly. "You could have called."

Her answer was a haughty toss of the head, about as phony as the uppity tone, as she marched toward the door.

He leaned back against the bar, noting what a slim behind she had. Hardly any hips at all. Nice legs. Probably would bug the hell out of her if she knew he was giving her the once-over. She'd tell him he was a worm and probably he'd have to agree.

"Rowena," he said, keeping his voice calm, no hint of the downright primitive urges he was fighting. "What does Tyhurst want to hire you to do?"

She pretended not to hear him and in two seconds flat was out the door.

Joe swore under his breath.

Mario appeared behind the bar. "Go after her, give yourself something to do and get out of my hair at the same time."

"She's trouble, Mario."

His cousin grinned. "Yeah. Way I look at it, you need some real trouble so you'll quit dwelling on trouble that's over and done with."

"Getting philosophical in your old age?"

"Out."

Joe took his advice, or followed his orders, or maybe just did what he'd have done anyway. He only knew that he was heading across the bar, through the door, and then standing in the heavy fog and persistent drizzle. He looked up the street and down, toward the waterfront.

If he were a recluse, where would he go?

Simple. Home.

ROWENA GOT as far as an ancient drugstore on the corner before she had to stop and pull herself together. She was shaking, close to hyperventilating. She couldn't see straight. Her head was spinning. She knew she'd been putting in too many hours at her computer, poring over financial newsletters and periodicals, reading every line of the *Wall Street Journal*. Trying to get her life back under *her* control.

Trying to exorcise Joe Scarlatti from her mind.

Trying not to think about her reckless plan to meet with Eliot Tyhurst again tomorrow morning.

She removed her earrings and clutched them so hard they pricked her palm. Even before Aunt Adelaide's death, she had felt alone in the world. She had learned to rely on herself. Trust herself. Now she wondered if she had just been fooling herself. Maybe she couldn't handle the real world. Couldn't survive on her own.

But you always have.

No. She had survived by cutting herself off from the so-called real world. She had isolated herself—maybe not as much as Joe Scarlatti thought, but more than other people did. Other *normal* people.

Backing out of the way of a customer going into the drugstore, she leaned against the dirty plate-glass window and felt the fog swirling all around her. She could smell the salt in the air. Exhaust fumes. She could hear the distant clanging of streetcars and the roar of a faulty engine of a passing delivery truck. She was out of her element. This was Joe Scarlatti's world, not hers.

My world is just as real as his. I have friends…

It was true. She did have friends. She did have a life. She went to movies and restaurants and took walks in the park. She was just careful about when and with whom, and about how often. Yet ever since Joe Scarlatti had penetrated her existence, she had felt more isolated and alone—as if she'd been missing out on something deep, worthwhile, necessary to her being, something her friends and clients and work couldn't provide.

Had she been missing, simply, him?

She shut her eyes and concentrated on her breathing. One breath at a time. In through the mouth, expand the diaphragm, keep the chest still, fill the lower lungs, then the upper lungs. Slowly, methodically. Exhale through the mouth to the count of ten.

One…two…three…four…

"Don't tell me you do yoga, too."

Her eyes popped open.

Joe Scarlatti scowled at her. "I could have knocked you on the head and made off with your purse."

"I'm not carrying a purse."

"Okay. I could have knocked you on the head and made off with *you*."

She managed to tell him, "I'm capable of taking care of myself."

"Never said you weren't. It's just that doing yoga breathing in public in this neighborhood—which I know and you don't—can lead to trouble."

"Stumbling around out of control would lead me into deeper trouble, I would think."

His dark eyes narrowed on her, and she immediately realized her mistake. "Why were you out of control?"

She should have risked stumbling home. She never should have stopped. "I didn't say I was."

Scarlatti looked dubious, but said nothing. His presence was making it even more difficult for her to pull herself together. His hard body, his too-knowing eyes, the mist collecting on his dark hair. He was too real.

"It seems to me, Sergeant—"

"Joe," he corrected.

"It seems to me you can say anything you want to me no matter how probing or insulting but I can say nothing to you."

He tilted back on his heels, studying her through half-closed eyes. What he was thinking, seeing, Rowena couldn't guess, didn't want to guess. Finally he said, "Point to the blonde."

"I'm more than just the color of my hair." Why, she wondered, was she being so testy?

"Okay, point to the eccentric genius of Telegraph Hill."

She didn't like that any better. She was a human being. A woman. "Don't inflict your stereotypes on me."

"And you haven't judged me based on your stereotypes of a burnt-out cop?" he asked calmly.

She sighed. "You try a person's patience, Joe Scarlatti."

"Talk to my captain," he said, grinning. "Look, let's go back to Mario's and start over. We'll both be nice. We can talk upstairs."

"What's upstairs?"

"My place."

He walked fast down the block, but Rowena, with her long legs, had no trouble keeping up. And her breathing exercises *had* helped. Or was it just Joe Scarlatti's presence—his coming after her—that had her back in sync?

Scarlatti unlocked a side entrance and led her up a flight of uncarpeted stairs badly in need of a good sweeping. Rowena, who had help with the cleaning, made no comment—not that if their positions were reversed and *her* stairs needed sweeping would Joe Scarlatti resist. He seemed to have absolutely no verbal-impulse control.

At the top of the stairs he unlocked another door, which he pushed open and motioned for Rowena to enter.

She stood on the threshold in wonder.

Henceforth, she thought, he would have nothing to say about how *she* lived.

His apartment consisted of a small living room, a galley kitchen, a small bedroom and a minuscule bathroom, all within view of the front entrance. The appliances were decades old, the furnishings spare and unremarkable, a plant dying in a window. Things were fairly tidy, though. The bed was made, the dishes were done, a tattered afghan was smoothed across the back of the couch instead of in a heap. On the other hand, an overturned orange crate, which served as a coffee table, was strewn with dog-eared paperback books, and the morning newspaper was plopped on the floor beside a scarred oak captain's chair.

"All in all," Rowena said, "I guess you don't have to worry about anything falling down on top of you in an earthquake. Everything's pretty much already down."

"Only if it were the whole damned building," Joe said, walking past her into the living room. "Mario says it can take eight on the Richter scale, but I think he was lucky the place didn't come down in the quake of 1990. You in town for that one?"

She nodded. "Aunt Adelaide was alive then. She was terrified. She remembered the 1906 earthquake, the fires, the deaths. She was only a child."

"As my grandmother would say, life isn't for the fainthearted. I'd like to hear more about this Aunt Adelaide. You want something to drink?"

She noticed the empty beer bottles lined up on the kitchen counter. There had to be a dozen. She said, "Anything nonalcoholic. And I'm not sure I want to talk about my aunt. She did her best, but she wasn't cut out to raise a child. She was an agoraphobic."

"Never left the house?"

"Almost never."

"Must have been a hell of an upbringing."

"It had its moments."

He glanced over his shoulder at her, squinted a moment as if trying to decide if she was patronizing him, but said nothing as he went into the kitchen. She remained standing in the middle of the living room, watching him pull open the old refrigerator. The door, she saw with surprise, was covered with a variety of magnets: fish, butterflies, dolphins, birds, Betty Grable in a swimsuit.

"Iced tea okay?" he asked.

"Is it herbal?"

He pulled his head out of the refrigerator and looked at her.

"A glass of water would be fine," she said. "I don't drink caffeine."

Without comment, he got out an old orange juice bottle he kept filled with water and poured a glass while Rowena remained standing, glancing around the very lived-in yet simple apartment.

Her eyes fell on a framed picture on an end table. It featured two grinning young men in San Francisco police uniforms. Both were in their early twenties. One was Japanese-American. The other was Joe Scarlatti. They looked ready to take on the world.

He materialized beside her with her glass of water. She tore her gaze from the photograph, but it was too late: Joe had followed her eyes. His mouth was a grim line. Rowena sipped her water and said quietly, "That's Matt Lee, isn't it?"

Joe sighed, his dark eyes fixed on the old photograph, his emotions hidden, buried, under rigid control. "Matt and I went through the academy together. I was married to his sister for a couple years way back when; it didn't work out. A husband and a brother who were cops—it was too much. Just as well considering what happened."

"The internal investigation of his death found you were not at fault," Rowena said softly.

"Legally, technically—no, I wasn't at fault. Morally..." He twisted open the beer he had brought with him, took a swallow. She noticed a slight tremble to his hand; otherwise there was no visible indication of the pain he must be feeling. "We were after a couple of drug dealers, real heavies. Matt was so sure they'd left town. The warehouse where they'd set up shop was empty—he was just so sure. My instincts told me he was wrong. I should have acted on them, made him listen."

"He made the decision to go into the warehouse the way he did. It was his mistake, not yours."

"We were partners. His mistakes were my mistakes. If Matt was reckless, so was I."

Rowena drank more of her water, feeling awkward, out of her element. But it wasn't just being away from home. Even if they'd been in her drawing room, Joe Scarlatti would make her feel self-conscious, intensely aware of herself. The personal agony he was trying so desperately to conceal from her stirred her emotions all the more.

"I didn't mean to get off on this subject," he said briskly, motioning toward the couch. She admired his control and resented it at the same time, wishing he could articulate his pain to her. "Have a seat, tell me about Tyhurst."

She chose the captain's chair instead.

Joe leaned over her so suddenly it almost took her breath away. "Don't want to risk getting too close, huh?"

"Sergeant—"

He held up his hand, stopping her. "Don't start. Just sit where you're comfortable and talk."

She watched him plop down on the couch, its tan plaid cover badly in need of replacement. His jeans stretched taut over the well developed muscles in his thighs. No fat fell over his belt buckle. She decided not to push him about his partner's death. She said, "First I need to know if you're still on my case."

His eyes shot up and bored through her with a heat that was primitive and very physical. Rowena felt her mouth go dry, felt the awareness rocket through her.

"Yeah," he said thickly, "I'm still on your case."

"You've kept an eye on my place?" She wished the heat would dissipate; instead, it just surged into her breasts, and lower, impossible to ignore.

"On and off. I missed Tyhurst's visit." He didn't seem too pleased about that. "If anything had happened—"

"It wouldn't have been your fault, it would have been Eliot Tyhurst's. And mine. I made the decision to let him into my house. I based that decision on the absence of any violence in his transgressions. He's a white-collar criminal, a thief. He never physically assaulted anyone." At the intense look in his eyes, Rowena felt a rush of panic. She pressed her water glass to her lips, tilted it back, sucked in the last few drops. She was burning up!

"Something wrong?" Scarlatti asked.

"No, nothing." But he knew, she could tell he knew. "I just was thirstier than I'd thought. I'm fine now. As I was saying, I take responsibility for my own actions and decisions. You can't control everything in your world, Sergeant Scarlatti. You can't make everything turn out right."

"Chaos reigns outside the castle, huh?"

She let his jibe at her house go. "Often inside the castle, too."

"What about Tyhurst?"

Getting a grip on herself, Rowena crossed her ankles and tucked them to one side the way Aunt Adelaide had taught her "proper ladies" sat. She made herself meet Scarlatti's gaze. His eyes were as dark as any she'd ever seen. What did they see? She felt raw and exposed, totally open to his penetration.

"I want to hire you," she said, hearing the hoarseness—the heavy desire—in her voice. "I want to pay you for your work on my behalf. I would feel better about it if I did."

Joe shook his head without hesitation. "I wouldn't."

"But—"

"No deal. I'm not a licensed private investigator. I'm still a member of the San Francisco police department—I can't take clients. Let's just keep this arrangement unofficial."

She frowned. "That leaves me with little control over you."

Again his gaze probed and seared and thoroughly aroused her. Was it deliberate? Did he *know* what he was doing to her? Or was it just her, her reaction to him?

"You hold that thought," he told her finally.

His voice was quiet and determined, as if he knew he had her close to melting. Before his words had fully registered, she was on her feet, striding toward the kitchen. She set her glass in the sink, wishing she could splash her face with cold water. But that would be too obvious.

Joe was behind her.

"I'm sure we're overstating Tyhurst's threat," she said crisply. "He's not out for revenge. He just wants my brain. That—that's what everyone wants from me."

"I don't."

He put his hands on her waist, his touch more gentle than she ever would have imagined possible for a man so hotheaded, so shaped by a violent world.

"Rowena."

She could feel his breath on the back of her neck; she didn't know what to do.

He said again, "Rowena," and she turned, sandwiched between his hard, taut body and the cold counter. She raised her eyes with a look of challenge, but she saw that she was too late, he had already seen, felt, sensed the longing that had her head spinning, her body aching. Now there'd be no denying it.

With one finger she touched the uncompromising line of his jaw. For her it was a bold move.

"Rowena."

It was a hoarse whisper this time, and he caught her hand up in his, placed it on his abdomen; she could feel the iron wall of muscle. She let her fingertips drift downward, over his hips, down to the hardness of his thigh. Suddenly she wanted to probe farther, to feel every inch of this mesmerizing man, but she kept her hand where it was.

He traced the outline of her lips with his thumb. "Say my name, Rowena."

Her mouth was too dry, her throat too tight from the impact of that brief touch, his closeness.

"Say it."

It wasn't an order but a plea. She started to lick her lips but touched the callused skin of his thumb instead; she almost sank to her knees. She closed her eyes and whispered, "Joe."

His mouth came down onto hers, hot, hungry, determined, his tongue outlining her lips just the way his thumb had. She heard herself moan, felt herself falling back against the counter. He pressed himself into her. Her hand was still between them and dropped lower, brushing against the hardness between his legs.

His tongue plunged deeper into her mouth, its rhythm as primitive as the heat that surged through her.

She felt bold and sexy, wanted.

He lifted her sweatshirt, his hands cool against her overheated skin, his tongue still probing, thrusting. His palms coursed up her sides and without warning covered her breasts that strained against the flimsy bra, the nipples as hard as stones. Her knees went weak.

"Do you want me to stop?" he asked, his breathing labored, tortured.

"No!"

It was out before common sense could intrude.

He raised her sweatshirt to her shoulders and gazed at her breasts and flat stomach. "You're so beautiful," he murmured, fumbling at the front clasp of her bra and freeing her breasts. She could feel the cool air and the searing heat of his gaze, and then the aching wetness of his tongue, the erotic pleasure of his teeth. She groaned wildly and pushed her hand against his hardness, stroking, telling him as words couldn't that she wanted more of him, all of him, that she was desperate to return the pleasure he was giving her.

Nothing could stop them.

Absolutely nothing.

He lifted the sweatshirt over her head. She shook her arms and let her bra drop to the floor. Her clingy leggings seemed like no cover at all. She realized that her breathing was ragged, strands of hair had loosened from their pins and combs.

He tore off his shirt, unsnapped his jeans.

"I've never..." He couldn't finish, but swept her

into his arms, her breasts responding at once to the feel of his warm skin against them, the prickly feel of his chest hairs, the thrill of their near nakedness.

Taking her hand, he put it back between his legs. She could feel the tremble in her fingers. But she unzipped his jeans, took his hot, thrusting maleness into her palm. She had never felt such abandon.

He kissed her, languidly, erotically, his fingers slipping her leggings and underpants down over her hips, lower, cupping the smooth skin of her bottom. Her senses were overpowered. For a wild, panicked moment she thought she would just short-circuit, go catatonic, die before she had experienced the wild, thrilling passion of this man.

But he said her name, whispered it gently, and she came back, her eyes meeting his as his fingertips reached the throbbing center between her legs. He stroked her. She stroked him.

"I want you, Rowena."

"We need…I need…" She almost laughed. "I can hardly talk!"

"It's okay. We don't need to talk."

"But I…it's been…I've never…"

"What?"

"I never thought…I never thought I'd lose my virginity in a cop's kitchen."

His hand went rigid and stopped. His eyes darkened.

She released him and bit her lip. "It's not a disease, you know. I assumed you—you didn't guess?"

"No. I didn't guess."

Up went her underpants, up went her leggings. He scooped up her bra and sweatshirt and thrust them against her exposed breasts. He zipped up his jeans, snapped them and grabbed his shirt.

"Joe, it's all right. I'm more than ready—"

"It's not all right. I'm sorry. I—" He raked a hand through his hair. "Get dressed."

He took his shirt into the bedroom and shut the door.

Rowena got dressed.

Using a scratch pad and stubby pencil by the wall phone in the kitchen, she scrawled him a note in a shaky hand.

Tyhurst is meeting me at my house at eleven o'clock tomorrow morning. What you do is your choice. You can always hide in Aunt Adelaide's suit of armor.

                                                    R

She wondered if he would get the underlying meaning of her note. Because he hadn't rejected her. She knew that. He had exercised supreme control in an act of nobility she found frustrating but endearing—one didn't make love to a virgin on the kitchen floor.

Her knight in shining armor.

She didn't say goodbye when she left, and his bedroom door remained shut.

7

JOE ROLLED out of bed, literally, the next morning with the worst hangover he'd had in months. He lay on his back on the prickly wool rug. Hank's wife had given it to him because she thought his life was so damned pitiful.

She was right.

He placed his palms on his ears and waited for the world to stop spinning. Blood pounded behind his eyes. Maybe I'll just lie here, he thought, until someone takes me out on a stretcher.

He could hear footsteps pounding up his stairs. "Joe? Joe, you up?" his cousin Mario yelled.

Then there was a pounding on his door. And a worse pounding in his head.

Joe groaned. *"Arghh!"*

"That you, Joe?"

"Leave me alone, you damned sadist!"

His head threatened to burst. He squeezed it tighter between his palms.

Mario banged on his door once more. "You dead or what?"

Just wishing he were. He rolled onto his stomach and tried to get up on all fours, felt a wave of nausea and flopped back down like a dying salmon.

"Ah, hell," Mario grumbled, and Joe could hear the rattle of keys, the turning of the lock, the creaking of the door, Mario's heavy footsteps across his living room. He appeared in the bedroom doorway. "Naw, you ain't dead—you're still twitching."

"Funny, Mario."

"What you need is a little hair of the dog."

Joe had learned the hard way that Mario used "hair of the dog" to mean anything from an experimental drink to drain cleaner. In this case, it probably meant one of his posthangover milkshakes. He put tofu, yogurt, fruit and honey together in a blender with a lot of ice, poured the contents into a tall glass and made his victim drink up in his presence.

They were a huge incentive to stay sober.

"Go away."

"Nope. Last night while you were tying one on, you told me to come drag your miserable carcass out of bed if you didn't come down by ten in the a.m. I gave you 'til 10:02."

Ten o'clock in the morning. What the hell did Joe have to do at ten? He was on leave of absence. He didn't have to go into the station.

"You want a swift kick or ice water?"

Joe made his entire body relax and lay still. His head pulsed. His stomach churned. A kick or ice water—would he feel either?

Mario sighed, impatient. "Why don't I just drag you to the damned window and toss you out on the street by your heels?"

"Fine with me."

"Well, it's 10:10 and whatever you've got going you're going to miss if you don't drag your miserable butt up off the floor and get moving." Mario made a sound of unadulterated disgust. "What Rowena Willow sees in you I don't know. Saw her flying out of here yesterday afternoon. That why you're such a pitiful hunk of flesh this morning?''

Rowena…

Yesterday afternoon. In the kitchen. Soft, pink-tipped breasts. Milky skin. Wide, passion-filled blue eyes. Moans of wanting, hands of unbelievable temptation, of sweet torture.

Joe bolted up onto his knees. The blood drained out of his head too fast and for a second he thought he'd pass out, which would no doubt prompt Mario Scarlatti to opt for a swift kick. Possibly two or three.

"Rowena…"

Mario responded with another sigh, this one of resignation. He walked into the bedroom and put out a beefy hand. Joe accepted it and let his cousin help him to his feet.

"I'll be downstairs in five minutes," Joe said.

"You okay?"

Joe didn't dare nod. He couldn't have his head exploding when he had work to do. He just looked at his cousin and said, "Yeah. Thanks. I was waking up, but there's no telling if I'd have come to in time."

"I'll have a shake waiting."

Moving as fast as he could, Joe put on a clean shirt and pair of jeans and slipped on his running shoes, opting to tie them later. He just couldn't bend down that long. He stumbled into the bathroom, filled the washbasin with cold water and stuck his face in it. He held his breath for as long as he could, blew some bubbles and held it a few seconds longer.

"Be a hell of a thing if you drowned yourself," he muttered, examining his reflection in the cracked medicine cabinet mirror.

Bad. Real bad. Bloodshot eyes. Bags. Dark circles.

Enough beard growth to look scruffy but not sexy. Breath that would wipe out entire populations.

He brushed his teeth and gargled with his least favorite, most powerful mouthwash.

"Gotta stay away from eccentric geniuses, Joe m'boy."

So what was he doing half killing himself to race to her rescue? Probably wouldn't need him. Could manage on her own, thank you very much.

Virgin that she was.

Damned knight in shining armor that he was. He could have avoided this hangover if he'd made love to her right there on the kitchen floor, just the way she'd wanted. The way *he'd* wanted.

They'd come so close.

Another two seconds and he would have been inside her. Making love to her. Trying his damnedest to let her body consume his pent-up desire for her. He would have made love to her all afternoon, all night if he'd had to.

He had a hell of a lot of pent-up desire for her. Still did.

"Arghh!"

He grabbed a towel and rubbed his face hard, then made himself tie his shoes. Better to think about his aching head than aching other parts of his body. He hadn't felt so rotten in months.

He hadn't, he thought, felt so alive.

Mario had a mud-colored shake and a thermos of coffee waiting on the bar for him. Joe knew better than to go for the coffee first. His cousin, his white butcher's apron stretched tight across his ample abdomen, watched from behind the bar until Joe had drunk every last drop.

A little hair of the dog.

"If I don't throw up now," Joe said, "I won't. Do I want to know what kind of fruit you used?"

"Didn't have any. Used a few drops of vanilla instead."

"Vanilla, huh?"

"It's ten-thirty."

"You're lucky I don't have time to kill you. You ever drink this swill yourself?"

His cousin just grinned. "Ever seen *me* with a hangover?"

Joe took the thermos to his truck and headed for Rowena Willow's house of horror on Telegraph Hill.

ROWENA LET him in. If she was embarrassed about yesterday, she gave no sign of it. If she even *remembered* yesterday, she gave no sign. Joe knew he himself still looked like hell. He could see her noticing, wondered if she could guess why he hadn't shaved, why his eyes were bloodshot, why he had a thermos of hot coffee hanging from his thumb. Wondered if she could tell that he could carry her upstairs and make love to her right now. Could even take her into the drawing room and make love to her with her beady-eyed stuffed animals looking on.

It wasn't going to go away of its own accord, this hunger he had for her. He realized that now. Like hunger for food, like a vitamin deficiency, a thirst, it wouldn't go away until it had been satisfied. He had to have her in his arms again. And even then the desire would still be there.

He gritted his teeth. Such professional thinking.

Rowena did not look like hell. She had on a sleek tropical-weight wool pantsuit in a warm, rich brown that made her skin seem even creamier, even more touchable. Her hair was pinned up, as tight and formal as she was pretending to be. The schoolmarm, the ice princess.

The untouchable virgin.

"Good morning, Sergeant," she said, her voice cool, calm, professional. But her eyes didn't linger on his, and he could see the faint color high in her cheeks, as close to a betrayal of her awareness of him as he would get. She glanced at the thick-banded watch on her slender wrist. "It's almost eleven. Mr. Tyhurst will be here at any moment. Might I suggest the drawing room?"

Joe felt himself beginning to relax. What an act. He decided to go along with it. "For him or me?"

She pursed her lips; she had a luscious, sexy mouth. "You. Mr. Tyhurst and I will conduct our meeting in the parlor across the hall." With a slight nod she indicated the room through the archway to her left; it looked friendlier than the one she had in mind for him.

He shrugged. "I won't be able to listen in."

"Do you need to?"

"Afraid I won't understand what you two are talking about?"

The lips pursed again; he saw they were highlighted with a blackberry-colored lipstick. Very appealing. He could almost taste it. She said, "That's a highly defensive remark, Sergeant."

"It wasn't a remark—it was a question."

"My point is, if I need you, I'll call." A half smile. "If I'm in any danger, you'll have no trouble hearing me."

"If I sense you're in any danger, sweetheart," he

said, sexy, deliberately cocky, "you won't have a chance to yell. I'll be there first."

She tilted back on her heels, her arms folded on her breasts. "So sure of yourself, aren't you?"

"Of many things, no. Of that, yes."

And he turned on his heels and headed into the morgue.

"Hey, guys," he said cheerfully as Rowena Willow snapped the sliding pocket doors shut behind him in a huff.

Teach her to pretend he hadn't had her naked in his arms less than twenty-four hours ago.

Or was she teaching him?

He frowned and looked for somewhere to sit and have a cup of coffee. The only furnishings built to accommodate living, human rear ends were a couple of stiff-backed antique chairs. Their red-cushioned seats might have been out of a bordello from San Francisco's early, less chichi days.

A weird family, the Willows.

The doorbell rang, and Joe tensed as he listened to Rowena greet Eliot Tyhurst and usher him into the parlor. The lying bastard sounded ready to do anything she asked.

Joe hated being reduced to peeking through keyholes, but there he was on his hands and knees doing his best to see into the entry.

Nothing. They'd already gone.

He got up and paced for a full two minutes, careful not to make any noise. His audience of dead animals seemed to be mocking him. *So, Joe, does she know more about police work and the likes of Eliot Tyhurst than you do? Going to stand on your head and spit nickels if she asks you, Joe?*

"The hell with it," he growled under his breath.

He went through a single door at the back of the drawing room into a smaller sitting room of some kind—an unbelievably dreary place—and out it into the hall near the kitchen, through the kitchen, through a butler's pantry, through the dining room and into yet another short hall.

How the hell many rooms did one woman need?

And all, he noted, were as dark and forbidding and spooky as every other room he'd ventured into in the peculiar house, except for Rowena's office on the third floor. He had a sudden urge to see the tower room she'd visited every afternoon at five while he'd watched her from the street, thinking he was unseen. A mistake where eccentric geniuses were concerned, he now realized. He had been as arrogant as charged.

He came to the library and slowed, hearing voices. Hers, Tyhurst's.

His instincts and training taking over, he walked softly across the thick Persian carpet, making no sound in the darkened, eerie library. A stuffed owl watched him from a tall stand. He half expected it to spread its wings and swoop down after him, wondered what would come to Rowena's mind if Mario started talking to *her* about a little hair of the dog. Probably not milkshakes or experimental drinks.

The connecting door to the parlor was shut tight. Joe pressed his ear to it. *You're a pro,* he assured himself, *not a sneak.*

Tyhurst and Rowena were talking numbers and stuff. The ex-convict understood her jargon. They spoke each other's language.

If Tyhurst was running a new scam, Joe would need Rowena to decipher for him what the hell the two of them had talked about. But if Tyhurst was out for revenge against the woman who'd put him in prison, Joe wouldn't need anyone's help. He'd damned well know what was going on. And he'd know what to do about it.

Skewer the SOB.

"I'd like your analysis," Tyhurst was saying. Just the sound of his voice irritated Joe. "I know you have no reason to trust me—I appreciate your even agreeing to see me again. I had no right even to hope that you would go out for dinner with me, never mind entertain the prospect of taking me on as a client."

Joe made a face. *Laying it on a little thick, Tyhurst.*

Rowena didn't seem to think so. "I have no grudge against you, Eliot."

Eliot?

"Then you'll help me?"

"I can't work for you." She was using her cool, high-IQ tone. "It would be unethical on my part after having…given our past."

There was a short, pained silence. *Eliot* said, "I understand, but I'd like you to think over my proposition. I'm only trying to do the right thing. I will never, never repeat the mistakes I made. I know that even if no one else does."

"I'm sure people will realize that, given time."

Like hell; Joe wouldn't.

"I just want to be absolutely certain," Tyhurst went on, "that I don't tread even close to the line the authorities drew for me. You know I'm banned from certain financial activities. I don't want to touch anything that might raise suspicions, however incorrect they may be. I know in my own heart I'm reformed."

Damned con man, Joe thought. But he had to give

the bastard credit; he certainly was slick. Even a small part of Joe wanted to believe him.

Tyhurst went on in that vein for a few more minutes. Apparently Rowena was supposed to do some financial analysis for him on a new venture he was undertaking and make sure he didn't cross any lines, get into anything, not just from which he was barred by law, but that would raise eyebrows. One would think the bastard would know, Joe thought.

Which was more or less what Rowena told him, except she was more polite and long-winded about it.

She'd dismissed him and as far as Joe could tell was showing him the door when Tyhurst—*Eliot*—abruptly said, "Rowena, I want to see you again."

And Joe heard it in his voice. Knew in his gut that the man had precious little interest in Rowena Willow's impressive capabilities with matters financial.

Eliot Tyhurst wanted to get her into bed. Whether as part of a revenge scheme or just because he'd been in prison for a long time and she was a beautiful woman, Joe couldn't say. But he knew.

He went rigid, ready to tear through the door—*on what grounds? And to do what?* Hell if he knew. Ring the bastard's neck. *And how are you any better? As if you haven't thought about getting her into bed yourself.*

As if he hadn't almost done it.

Hell, they'd never have even made the bed.

He shoved his hands into his pockets and forced himself to stay put.

"I'll call you after I've given your proposal some thought," Rowena said. "I don't have your number—"

"Let me call you instead."

A beat. Then, coolly, "Fine."

And he was gone.

Joe heard her mutter something under her breath that he didn't quite catch. Then she yanked apart the library's elegant pocket doors and caught him red-handed spying on her.

She glared at him, hands planted firmly on her slim hips as he rose up straight. "It's a wonder Eliot didn't hear you."

"You did? You knew I was here?"

"Of course! I heard you prowling through the downstairs working your way in here."

Somehow Joe was neither intimidated nor insulted. "That's just because you're used to this tomb. You hear every damned creak and groan—unless you're working at your computer. Tyhurst was too preoccupied gazing into your pretty blue eyes to pay any attention to a few odd noises."

"He didn't *once* look at my eyes."

"So," Joe said casually, "what did he look at?"

Her cheeks reddened. She whirled past him and the stuffed owl. "It's a wonder you've ever caught any criminals. Your incompetence and audacity must constantly get in your way."

That phony I'm-smarter-than-you tone again. Joe tilted back on his heels. "Tough to be incompetent and audacious at the same time, don't you think?"

She was at the hall door. "No, I don't, not since I've met you."

And then she was through the door.

"Hey, Rowena." His voice was calm, unperturbed, mostly because he sensed her anger had more to do with the sheer fact of his presence than his professional abilities. Having him this close got to her. He didn't think he was jumping to conclusions: he just knew.

He waited until she turned back toward him, reluctantly, angrily. Her eyes were a smoky blue. Watching him. Wanting him. *Pretend you don't notice*, he warned himself. *Stick to your job.*

"Is the bastard up to something?" Joe asked.

The breath went out of her, the anger, the frustration. "Give me an hour and I'll give you my best guess."

AFTER TWO HOURS Joe ventured up to the third floor. This time he made sure he didn't make a sound. He didn't want to give her a heart attack. He edged into the doorway.

The place was humming.

Her back to him, she tapped madly at her computer. Lights were flashing, numbers blinking, papers flying out of the fax machine, printing out on the laser printer. Magazines and financial newsletters and spreadsheets were scattered on the floor all around her. Not one hair was out of place.

Joe could feel her concentration. She was completely unaware of his presence. He was reminded of what, before Matt's death, he'd been like when he was deep into a case. Nothing could distract him. He'd given his work everything he had.

Maybe he and Rowena Willow weren't so different after all.

The thought disturbed him, told him that his attraction to her went beyond the physical, and he withdrew silently, heading back down to the kitchen with the cats. He scrounged up a muffin that looked like something a horse would just love and zapped it in the microwave, pouring a cup of coffee from Mario's thermos while he settled in and waited.

AFTER A TOTAL of four hours, Rowena stumbled down to the kitchen where Joe Scarlatti was warning Mega and Byte that he wasn't a scratching post. Bleary-eyed and stiff, she glanced at her watch and winced. "I'm sorry, I didn't realize the time. Why didn't you just leave?"

He shrugged. "Rough night. I needed a lazy day. You find out anything?"

"Nothing concrete."

His eyes clouded. "Or just nothing you think I'd understand?"

"There you go inflicting your stereotypes on me again. I don't know what you'd understand. I don't worry about that sort of thing. I just don't have enough information yet to be sure what he's up to, if anything." She rolled her shoulders a few times to loosen up the muscles. "I'm not sure exactly what he's after."

"You for starters."

"Me?"

"Yeah. Ol' Eliot's got the hots for you."

She blinked at him. He was seated at her kitchen table, right at the point where her eyes couldn't seem to focus properly. Probably it was just as well she couldn't see him clearly, given what had transpired in *his* kitchen yesterday afternoon. She made a look of distaste. "Even if that's true—and I doubt it is—it's irrelevant. Eliot Tyhurst wants my approval, I think. If he can convince me he's reformed, he can convince others. I'm not sure why that's so important to him except—'' She stopped abruptly. "Why are you shaking your head?"

"Because you're wrong," Joe said.

She bristled. "Just because *you're*…physically attracted to me doesn't mean Eliot Tyhurst is."

Joe was watching her very closely. "When's the first time you realized I was 'physically attracted' to you?"

"When you—when we—"

He grinned. "See? You don't know. Rowena, I knew I wanted to go to bed with you the minute I laid eyes on you."

"That's not true."

"Want to make a bet?"

She refused to show her discomfort. "You're just saying that so you can win this argument. You want to prove I'm naive about men and can't be trusted to know when one's attracted to me or not." She cleared her throat. "Just because I haven't had sex with a man doesn't mean I'm naive or repressed or—or mentally ill. I consider my decision to wait until I was ready an act of independence and self-knowledge, not desperation or insecurity."

"Uh-huh," he said.

"I—I've never allowed myself to get carried away before."

"Why not?"

"It's irresponsible."

"And what made you so responsible, Rowena Willow?" he asked quietly.

She licked her lips. "My parents. They—they were very much in love, but they brought out the worst in each other. They had me when they were far too young—"

"Says who?"

"They were barely into their twenties. They did everything on impulse. Mother would make an off hand comment about wanting to take an Alaskan cruise and the next thing she knew, Father would have the tickets. Father would make an off hand comment about starting his own business and the next thing he knew, Mother was encouraging him to quit his job. They did everything on impulse, they lived totally for the moment. They spent everything they had and died virtually penniless." She kept her gaze on Joe. "They were killed when their car ran off the road up in the Marin hills. It was pitch-dark. They didn't have a good reason for being up there. They'd just wanted to see the stars."

"And they left you alone to be raised by a weird aunt."

Rowena smiled suddenly, remembering Aunt Adelaide. "But she knew she was weird, and she tried very hard to give me a normal life. It's true, though, she only left this house a half-dozen or so times that I can remember in all the years I knew her. Anyway, she did teach me to be comfortable with myself, to know what I want and don't want."

"To be responsible," Joe said. He stretched out his muscular legs, looking very relaxed. "Then how come you were ready to jump into the sack with me the first chance you got?"

"Because I had been thinking about it for several days and had decided if the opportunity arose, I would seize it."

"Seize it you did," he said wryly.

She tossed her head back in an attempt not at haughtiness but at maintaining dignity. "You're being deliberately crude just to get me flustered. It won't work. You're operating on the assumption that I was somehow out of my head yesterday and that you're the first man who ever provided me the opportunity of a physical relationship."

"You always talk like that? Sounds like a report on a corporate takeover, not two people who got caught up in the moment and almost overdid things."

"*I* didn't get caught up in the moment—"

"Oh, no?" he said, amused.

She swallowed. "Well, I did, but as I said, I'd contemplated that moment before."

If she felt awkward and exposed, Joe Scarlatti seemed perfectly at ease with their conversation. Entertained, even. He folded his hands on his flat abdomen, watching her. "Okay, Rowena. Confess."

"What do you mean, 'confess'? I have nothing to confess. I've told you everything."

"You haven't told me when you started speculating on what we might be like in bed together."

She pursed her lips. *How* had she gotten herself into this mess? She said quickly, "Before I met you."

One of Scarlatti's thick eyebrows went up. "Before, huh? That's about impossible to top."

"It was just imagining on my part. I was anticipating what you might be like."

"Were you close?"

She nodded, her mouth dry. "Very close. But I didn't know for sure until I'd actually met you that I definitely—that you were…" She cleared her throat once more, a dead giveaway of the difficulty she was having with this level of intimacy. "You were as tough, arrogant and sexy as I'd imagined. It was a…purely a physical reaction on my part."

"I see."

She could see he had no idea if she was telling him the truth or putting him on so she could win the argument—provided she could remember what they were arguing about. Something to do with Eliot Tyhurst's supposed attraction to her. She made herself tell Joe, "I would have no regrets if we had finished what we started yesterday. I hope you ended it for your own sake, not mine."

He was on his feet, moving toward her with an efficient, masculine grace that she'd come to recognize as distinctly, uniquely Scarlatti. Yesterday's near lovemaking hadn't cooled her desire for him, she realized. It had only made her want him more. He brushed a knuckle across her jaw, then let it skim her breasts. She had removed her suit coat and could feel the immediate response of her nipples beneath the silk fabric of her blouse.

"Would you have any regrets," he said languidly, "if we finished what we started now?"

And he caught her by the wrists, holding her arms at her sides, keeping her tantalizing inches from him. He kissed her without allowing their bodies to touch. Desire ran up her spine like a hot wire. His tongue plunged between her parted lips, explored, tasted, probed with a primitive rhythm that made her moan into him with a longing deeper and more demanding than she'd thought possible. "I don't know if I'd have regrets," she answered as the kiss ended.

He pulled back. His eyes were darker than she'd ever seen them, aching with a passion she recognized in herself, but he gave a small smile of satisfaction. "I didn't think so."

But could he guess the reason? That yesterday she

had wanted to make love to a sexy, thrilling man and to hell with where it led, it just didn't matter—that she had consciously decided to seize the moment. Joe Scarlatti could be her once-in-a-lifetime chance to experience a physical relationship with an exciting man who also, if only for a time, was attracted to her. It had been of no consequence if *he'd* had any regrets. She had only wanted to know the feel of a man's body—*his* body—throbbing inside her. Wanting her. Satisfying her as she'd never been satisfied.

Today she still wanted to make love to him, to have him make love to her. That hadn't changed. It couldn't. But today she also wanted to know him, to hear him laugh, to meet his friends, to talk to him about everything, not just the dangers Eliot Tyhurst might present to her and society. Maybe this emotional attraction to him had always been there, too, and she simply hadn't wanted to admit to it.

She still didn't. She still knew that she and Joe Scarlatti were the same kind of disastrous combination her parents had been. Driven to act on the moment. On impulse. On desire rather than thought, logic, facts.

But her emotions were increasingly difficult to ignore.

Was she falling in love with a burnt-out cop?

This wasn't the life she'd imagined for herself. She'd imagined she'd end up more like Aunt Adelaide than her parents.

"I—I need a cup of tea."

He raked a hand through his hair. "Yeah, I'll bet."

She stumbled toward the stove, feeling his eyes on her. "Would you care to join me?"

"You've been trapped in this mausoleum all day. Don't you want to get out of here?"

"Out?" She looked over her shoulder at him, perplexed.

"Yeah, out. Outside in the great big wide world."

"And do what?"

"Nothing. Unwind."

"That's why I was going to have a cup of tea."

He sighed. "Okay, we'll find a tea shop."

"Do you know any?"

"No."

"Then how can you propose—"

"Come on, Rowena." His voice was teasing, but without mockery. "For once in your life let your hair down."

8

THEY WALKED.

Rowena had changed into an oversize multicolored chenille sweater—it was chilly—and black leggings. The fog had receded from the hills but continued to swirl in low pockets and still completely obliterated the Golden Gate Bridge from view. She didn't mind. She liked foggy San Francisco days almost as much as the sunny ones. They were eerie, isolating, romantic. The fog seemed to make the pastel-colored buildings and the flower boxes and small gardens stand out even more, give even more pleasure than they did in the sunlight.

Or maybe she was so agreeable toward the fog because Joe Scarlatti was at her side.

He walked fast, as she did, but his powerful legs ate up pavement where she tended to glide along. In the sunlight his face seemed even more ravaged. The man needed a shave, a bath, sleep.

Or not, she thought uncomfortably. There was a roguish masculinity about him that suggested all he physically needed was to finish making love to her.

She shrugged off her discomfort. Was it so bad having Joe Scarlatti want her?

They didn't touch as they descended a steep hill into the fog. Rowena tried to picture them as hand-holding tourists. They could take a cable car and kiss under lampposts. Wander into shops—expensive and tacky alike—that catered to tourists.

But the picture didn't quite form. In both appearance and attitude, Joe Scarlatti was too much the tough, cynical cop; she too much the eccentric genius. They made too bizarre a pair. Sexual attraction was one thing. Becoming a couple was very much another.

For one thing, it took a man who would talk. Since they'd left her house, Joe hadn't said a word, just squinted his eyes against the glare of the sun and now the fog and kept walking. Rowena wondered what he was thinking. Cop thoughts? Romantic thoughts?

Or was he just plotting to get her into bed?

She almost asked him, but they'd turned a corner and he suddenly nodded to a shop topped with a pink awning. "There," he said. "Tea."

They went inside a small, attractive shop with glass counters filled with pastries, shelves lined with glass jars of coffee beans and loose-leaf teas and about a dozen small round marble-topped tables. There were stained-glass lamps, rose wallpaper, pink napkins, flowered teapots.

Rowena suddenly smiled to herself.

Joe narrowed his eyes at her. "What's so funny?"

"I was just thinking about bulls in china shops."

His eyes smiled back at her. "You saying I don't fit in here?"

"I'm saying I'm grateful that you agreed to come here with me. I know Mario's is more your style."

"Hey, I'm not a slug," he said with a grin.

They sat at a table by the window overlooking the street, and Rowena ordered Earl Grey tea and currant scones with clotted cream from a young waitress.

"Clotted cream?" Joe asked.

"It's a lot like butter—it's very soft, perfect with scones."

"I'm sure. Okay, I give in." He looked at the waitress. "Bring me coffee—black—and a scone with clotted cream. Can I get my scone without currants?"

"Sorry, no."

He gave the waitress a devastating smile. "Leave the currants in, then."

When the waitress had retreated, Rowena said, "You're quite the charmer, Sergeant. I suppose you have no trouble with women." She smiled suddenly. "Or should I say *too much* trouble?"

He laughed. "Got me figured out, do you?"

"No, I would just think you aren't…inexperienced."

"Depends what you mean by inexperienced." He stared out at the street. "Yeah, I've been around. Was married a couple years. There've been women to share a night on the town when I wanted—but not many real relationships. And my 'experience' doesn't mean I don't want what other people want." His eyes, dark and unreadable, drifted to her. "Maybe I'm just more pessimistic about getting it."

"Because of what you've seen on your job?"

"Because of who I am, Rowena. What I've seen, what I've done, what I know. I don't like reflecting on all this stuff. It's easier for me just to shut down. What I don't think about, I don't think about. Six months off the job is an eternity, though, I can tell you that."

"I can't imagine what I would do without my work," Rowena said pensively.

"You're more outgoing than I ever thought you were."

"Am I? I spend a lot of time alone—my work requires it. I certainly get out more than my reputation would suggest."

The waitress brought their pots of tea and coffee—his was white, hers pink-flowered—and their scones and two tiny pink-flowered dishes of clotted cream. Joe examined his with some skepticism. He dipped his spoon in, smelled, then sampled the creamy white delicacy. "Tastes like something between whipped cream and butter."

"Good, isn't it?"

Rowena split her scone and slathered it with the clotted cream, wanting to resume their conversation about his leave of absence and its consequences. But she could see he'd drawn the curtain on that subject and said all he'd planned to say—probably more than he'd planned. She sensed him pulling back, retreating from introspection. Despite being a man of action, Joe Scarlatti felt his own and others' pain deeply. It wouldn't be a simple matter for him to confront the consequences of his mistakes. But confront them he would.

"I have a feeling," she said, "that no one's harder on you than you are on yourself."

He looked at her. "And on what do you base this judgment?"

"It's not a judgment at all. I'm just speculating."

"I see."

Her scone was soft and fresh, lighter than her usual whole wheat, no-sugar fare—a real treat. A Mozart sonata played quietly in the background. People continuously wandered in and out of the small, popular shop. Couples, elderly tourists, students, an old man who sat in the back with a book of poetry and a pot of tea, a young woman with two small children who couldn't make up their minds over which cookie they wanted. "The one with the sprinkles…no, no, the chocolate cookies…oh, wait—wait, I want *that* one!"

Rowena shook off a sudden longing for more normalcy and companionship in her own life.

"What's wrong?" Joe asked.

"Is it so obvious or are you just that observant? I guess my marathon session at the computer is having an effect."

She wanted to leave it at that, but Joe urged her on. "What kind of an effect?"

She shrugged. "I'm usually very optimistic about my life. Satisfied. I accepted a long time ago that I'm different, that my life would have its own peculiar limits. I have no parents, no siblings, no cousins. I was raised by an elderly, eccentric aunt. I have a gift for numbers. For understanding and unraveling complex financial systems. I am who I am. I can't suddenly stop being who I am because sometimes it gets in the way of living like other people live. Aunt Adelaide taught me not to worry about things like that but to accept who I am."

"She sounds all right after all, your Aunt Adelaide."

Rowena smiled and nodded, suddenly missing the old woman who'd tried so hard. "She meant well. I might have had an easier time if she'd been more sociable, but then again I might not be as comfortable with myself. None of us can change the past."

"No," Joe said heavily.

"You can't pretend you don't know, haven't seen, the things you know and have seen on the streets."

"Yeah, I guess. How's your scone?"

He wasn't going to talk more. She didn't push him, but smiled instead; if she wanted him to accept her, she had to accept him. "It's very good. Yours?"

"Fine. I could do without the currants, though. Coffee's great." He narrowed his eyes a moment, studying her. "Takes a while for you to come down after a long day, doesn't it?"

She nodded. "That's why I usually have tea in the tower."

"Sounds ominous—'the tower.' But I know what you mean. After a long day on the streets—yeah, it takes some time to unwind. Are you still processing what you learned about Tyhurst on your computer? Coming up with new ideas?"

Tyhurst. Of course. Eliot Tyhurst, she must remember, was the reason Joe Scarlatti was in her life.

She shook her head, sipping her now-lukewarm tea. She added more hot tea from the pot. "Nothing new. Why do you care so much about Tyhurst?"

He frowned as if he didn't like her question, but he said amiably, "I have my reasons. Hank Ryan got me involved unofficially. He was at Tyhurst's trial, doesn't believe he's reformed. I guess the man's done his time and is due a chance to go straight, but if he's up to something, tries to exact a little revenge on you, I'll be there."

But Rowena sensed he wasn't telling her the complete truth and wondered why. "It's not your usual sort of case."

"Nope. I don't usually take on cases of white-collar crime. But then it's not usual for me to be on leave, either."

She drank her tea and ate her scone, wondering if the Joe Scarlatti she had met and was so attracted to, however much against her better judgment, was anything like the Joe Scarlatti his colleagues in the police department knew.

When it came time to pay, their tea and coffee and scones consumed, Rowena realized she hadn't brought a nickel with her and felt like a fool. "And you know so much about money," Joe teased, tossing a handful of bills onto the table. "Tut-tut."

Outside, the fog had receded even more, and instead of turning back up toward Telegraph Hill, they continued along the narrow streets toward the waterfront. They had no purpose, no direction. They were just walking. Rowena couldn't remember feeling so free.

"You like just walking the streets?" Joe asked.

"Yes, it's wonderful. But I have to admit it's not something I do on a regular basis."

He glanced sideways at her.

She laughed. "You're wondering if I'm just fooling you and if I ever get out at all."

"Well…"

"I do, Joe. Trust me. Not often, and when I do, I like to know where I'm going, when I'll be back—I suppose it's a control thing."

"But you do have friends," he said dubiously.

"Of course I have friends. Some I've never met—we communicate over the computer—but I have a few here in the city. Not tons and tons—I'm not that type. But I've been extra-busy lately—I owe people visits and phone calls."

"How lately is lately?"

"What do you mean?"

"Have you been extra-busy for a month, six months, a year?"

"I'm always busy. But the past six months have been particularly rough. I bit off more than I could reasonably chew, you could say, which means I haven't been out very much at all."

"And Tyhurst and I are distractions?"

She smiled over at him. "Big distractions."

"Do I hear a 'but' in your tone?" he asked not so much hopefully as confidently.

"Well, I don't know about Tyhurst, but you're—I suppose you're proving not as bad a distraction as I'd first envisioned."

"'Not as bad' a distraction doesn't mean I'm a welcome one." Again that bantering tone, as if he knew damned well just what kind of distraction he was. And liked it.

"Let's just say you're a *unique* distraction and leave it at that."

"If that's what you want."

"I'm enjoying myself right now, Joe. I feel a little as if I've been in a cave for the past six months and now I've ventured into the sunlight—like a bear coming out of hibernation, I guess."

He laughed. "Bad analogy. If there's one thing you don't look like, it's a bear."

She laughed, too, feeling relaxed, unworried, more open and ready to take on the world. The Joe Scarlatti effect. And why not let her guard down for a little while? What harm could come to her?

They continued along in silence. Rowena didn't feel as if Joe was leading and she was following, but more that they weren't really headed anywhere specific, just enjoying the coming of evening in their beautiful city. She couldn't remember having gone so long without any purpose in mind.

Somehow they ended up within a couple of blocks of Mario's Bar & Grill.

"We can walk on back to Telegraph Hill," Joe said, "or we can have dinner at Mario's."

"Does he…what kind of food does he serve?"

They had stopped on a breezy corner. Joe looked cold and tired…and so sexy, so physical and alive and real, it took Rowena's breath away.

A corner of his mouth twitched. "Not clotted cream, for sure. No tofu, either, unless you got a hangover. And no brown rice."

"Italian?"

"Sure."

She smiled and in a fun-filled gesture, hooked her arm into his. "I love Italian."

"Italian what?"

"Italian food."

"Oh."

EVEN WITH Mario's more eclectic dinner crowd, Rowena Willow stuck out. Her flushed cheeks against otherwise milky white skin. Her thick, shiny golden hair piled up on her head with pins and bronze combs. Her dazzling smile. Her wide blue fascinating—and fascinated—eyes. They set her out if not apart, said in so many ways she was from a different world than was Joe Scarlatti, old Mario's cop grandson, the reckless one, the one anchored in the real world. She could visit his world; he could visit hers. Joe thought of her cats and lonely house, the hum of her computer, her scones and tea and clotted cream. Could either of them live in the other's world?

He hadn't thought about the future in a long, long time. It felt good.

Maybe too good.

Mario had pulled up a chair to their booth in the corner and he and Rowena were having an animated discussion about Italian cuisine. Something about olive oil. Roasted peppers crept into the conversation. Wood-fired ovens. Whole-milk ricotta versus part-skim. Italian wines versus California wines. Rowena was drinking a California red wine from Sonoma Valley.

Joe sipped his beer, satisfied to catch snatches of what the two of them were talking about. To watch Rowena's mouth on the thin rim of her glass. He wasn't picky about food himself, but a woman's mouth—that was something to be a connoisseur of. He noticed the fullness of her lower lip, the way her tongue would sneak out and lick the wine off her mouth after she drank.

She was good with people, he thought. Better than he ever would have expected sitting out on her street those first days, watching her *Ivanhoe* house. He wondered if she needed to be around people more than she could let herself admit.

Finally Mario heaved himself up. It was still early for dinner and he wasn't as pressed in the kitchen, where he had help at night anyway. "I'll fix you up a nice eggplant parmesan—light on the oil, fresh rotelli on the side, splash of red wine in the sauce. You'll love it." He glanced down at Joe. "You look a sight better than you did this morning. But next time shave before you come to dinner."

"You sound like Grandma," Joe said.

"Yeah, go see her when you look like that and she'll shave you with a butcher knife." Mario turned back to Rowena, his expression softening. "I'll fix you a nice salad, too, tossed with just a teaspoon of my special Italian dressing. How's that sound?"

She was beaming under the attention. "Wonderful."

After Mario had gone, Joe settled back in his seat and eyed Rowena. "Eggplant parmesan isn't on the menu."

"It isn't?"

"No. Mario's probably sending a busboy out to the grocery now for an eggplant."

Her cheeks colored. "Well, I never suggested—"

"You didn't have to. He likes you. First woman I've ever brought around he's done anything more than grunt at." In spite of himself, Joe was pleased. "Not that I give a damn what Cousin Mario thinks."

"He seems like a nice man," Rowena said judiciously.

Joe laughed. "You should have seen him this morning. He offered to throw me out the window feet first."

"And what did you do to deserve such a threat?"

"Who says I deserved it?"

"I can't imagine a charmer like Mario making such a threat unless it was warranted."

"You've known him half an hour!"

She sniffed. "I make quick judgments."

"Yeah, well, you may have a genius IQ but that doesn't mean you know my cousin better than I do. That snake has been on my case for six months. Runs me out of here every chance he gets." Joe grunted. "Charmer my hind end."

Rowena, he saw, was grinning, her blue eyes gleaming in the dim light of the bar. "You take me far too seriously, Joe Scarlatti. And probably your cousin

Mario, too. Probably life in general. Despite your wit and sense of humor, you are at root a very serious man."

He leaned forward, his forearm pressed against the edge of the scarred pine table. "You're bluffing, Rowena Willow. You haven't come close to figuring me out. You don't know what I am at root."

She sipped her wine and said over the rim of the glass, "Don't I?"

"Dammit, woman—"

"Oh, so it's 'woman' now?" She set her glass down and tossed her head back; if her hair were down, it would have been a sexy gesture. "I rather like the way you say Rowena."

He squinted at her, intrigued by this glimpse he was getting of a looser Rowena Willow. "How much wine have you had?"

"Not much. I'm—how did you put it? Letting my hair down. Yes, that was it."

"Then let it down," he said.

"What?"

"Pull out a few pins and combs, Rowena. Let it down all the way."

"I always wear my hair up."

"Even in bed?" he asked in a husky voice.

But she was spared answering by the unexpected arrival of Hank Ryan. He did a double take on Rowena. "Whoa," he said, "didn't expect to find you here."

She graced him with a polite smile. "Hello, Sergeant Ryan. Would you care to join us?"

He slid into the booth next to Joe. "I can only stay a minute. How're things going?"

Joe couldn't tell whether the question was directed

at him or at Rowena, but she answered, "Very well, thank you. So far Mr. Tyhurst has done nothing to justify your concern. You *did* twist Sergeant Scarlatti's arm so that he would keep an eye on me? I don't believe I've ever gotten a straight answer to that question."

Hank frowned. "It didn't take much twisting."

"Why not?"

"Beg pardon?"

"White-collar crime isn't his area of expertise. We'd never met. He didn't know me. And he had no personal or professional interest in taking on this case."

She was sounding like a damned detective, Joe thought, refusing to squirm.

Hank shifted in his chair, looking as if he wished he'd snuck back out once he'd seen Joe with Rowena. "He needed the work," Hank said finally. "He knew it, and I knew it."

"So." Rowena pushed her lips up, then took another swallow of wine. Joe could see her computer-mind at work. He knew he'd have to get around to telling her about his grandparents. It just wasn't an easy topic to bring up to a woman who made her living keeping people from making financial mistakes. "What you're saying is that I was a convenient excuse to try to renew Joe Scarlatti's interest in his work. You were worried about him?"

With a sideways glance at Joe that said he felt like a fly on a light bulb, Hank said, "A lot of us were worried about Joe."

"I see. And presumably you were more interested—and still are—in catching Eliot Tyhurst if he's up to no good than in actually protecting me from harm."

"Ms. Willow—"

"That wasn't a question. It requires no answer. What I'm saying," she went on icily, "is that I'm a pawn in your game to find out if Tyhurst truly has reformed and to get Joe Scarlatti back in uniform."

"He doesn't really wear a uniform, he's plainclothes—"

Her gaze shut him up. "That's splitting hairs, Sergeant Ryan. You know perfectly well what I mean."

Joe stretched out his legs and cleared his throat. "Mind if Joe Scarlatti says a few words?"

His colleague and—what the hell *was* Rowena Willow to him? Not a client. Not even a lover. An almost lover? She didn't look much like she wanted to go to bed with him at the moment. Whatever she was, she and Hank turned their attention to him as if just remembering he was there.

Joe said, "First of all, Tyhurst is a snake, whether we end up locking him up again or not. Second, I'm riding out the end of a six-month leave of absence and will make my own decision about what to do when the time comes. Third, if I have to protect you, Rowena, from physical harm, I will."

"I'm under no threat whatsoever of—"

He silenced her by holding up a hand and talking louder than she was. "And if Tyhurst is trying to run something on you—meaning he's pulling some kind of financial scam on you—I can't help you. In fact, I should wish the poor bastard good luck because you're smarter than he is, you can spend more time at a computer than most human beings and you'll catch him and hang him out to dry. By the time you get through with him, Tyhurst would be glad to see the police."

Hank looked more relaxed, in his element. "Think that's what he's up to, trying to suck Rowena into some kind of financial scam he's running? Get his revenge and get back into the game at the same time?"

"It's possible," Joe said. He could see that Rowena was fuming now that *she* was being referred to in the third person.

"But you don't think so," Hank said thoughtfully.

Joe shook his head. "I think he's out for revenge, straight and simple. *Physical* revenge."

Hank raised up in his seat. "Anything I can take to the captain, get a twenty-four-hour watch on her?"

"No," Rowena said sharply, "there isn't."

But Hank was looking to Joe for an answer. "She's right," he admitted. "Tyhurst hasn't made any overt threats. I'm just going on gut. I listened in on the two of them meeting this morning. He's attracted to her, wants to woo her, then…" He lifted his shoulders, trying to deny the tension he was feeling as he imagined what Tyhurst would do. But he couldn't maintain objectivity, not where Rowena was concerned. "Then he'll make his move. And he'll cover his tracks."

"What meeting?" Hank asked, his concern knitting his eyebrows together.

Joe filled him in, deliberately using police jargon that Rowena, given how much she knew about everything else, probably could translate. But it would remind her that he was a professional. He was a cop, and whatever else had erupted between them, his first and primary obligation to her—his *only* obligation, dammit—was as a cop.

And what the hell, it would tell her that he knew a few things she didn't know.

When he finished, Hank let out a long breath. "You know, the bastard could be on the up-and-up."

"Could be," Joe agreed. "But he's sounding just too clean to me. He was a model prisoner, and now he's going to be a model ex-con? I don't buy it. The SOB stole millions of dollars and lost it because of a plucky financial whiz—a fluke."

Rowena's fingers were stiff on her wineglass. "I hate that word, 'plucky.' It's so condescending. Do you ever hear a man being called plucky?"

Hank didn't seem to have heard her. "He's got to have a lot of pent-up anger toward her. I saw it seething when he was on trial. I don't buy it that he's romancing her. Just doesn't work for me."

Wanting to go to bed with her, Joe thought, and romancing her were two different things.

He winced. Was he just as bad as Eliot Tyhurst after all?

As if Hank were reading his thoughts, he said, "Going to bed with her, yeah, maybe I could swallow him wanting to do that—but only in the context of exacting revenge."

Rowena reddened. Set down her glass hard. Swept to her feet. "I'm leaving," she announced.

Joe caught her by the wrist and held her still.

Hank looked embarrassed. "No, wait, I'll leave. I'm sorry, I should have been more subtle. I didn't mean to upset you."

"I'm not upset. You have every right—every duty—to discuss Mr. Tyhurst's intentions. That doesn't bother me. I'm annoyed, however, that you pretend I'm not even here, that *my* opinion of his intentions doesn't count. I've spent more time with him than either of you." She was so mad she was shaking. "I've—I've probed his finances."

Hank raised an eyebrow and looked at Joe.

"That's tough to beat," Joe said, straight-faced.

Rowena would have thrown the rest of her wine at him if she weren't so repressed. Lord knew he deserved it. Wouldn't bother Mario, either. He'd probably applaud. But instead she satisfied herself with an ice-cold look at the two cops.

Hank pushed back his chair, contrite. "Keep me posted. I'm—you remember what we discussed the other day?"

The possible snitch, Joe thought. He remembered, and nodded.

"I'll be in touch," Hank said. He mumbled a goodbye to Rowena and beat a path to the door before she could wrest herself from Joe's hold and follow him out.

"Let me go," she said in a low voice.

"You going to run away?"

"I'm going to leave. That's not running away."

Joe loosened his grip, stroking the inside of her wrist with his thumb. He saw her bite her lower lip. So, she wasn't unaffected. But she wasn't about to sit on his lap and run her fingers through his hair, either. "What about Mario's eggplant parmesan?" he asked.

"I'm sure he knows how trying you can be."

"He'll be disappointed if you leave."

"But he would understand."

"You'd walk back to your castle by yourself?"

"I could call a cab," she said.

"And pay him with what?"

"I—" She glared at him. "I could make him wait on

the curb, run inside, get some money and pay him. I have options, Sergeant, besides you."

"Sit down, Rowena. Have another glass of wine. Here, I'll flag Mario and have him bring out a basket of bread." Still holding on to her wrist, Joe got up halfway from his seat at the booth and yelled, "Hey, Mario, how 'bout some of your special garlic bread?"

Ordinarily Mario would have told him to go to hell or get it himself, but tonight Joe was with Rowena Willow and his cousin was smitten. He called from behind the bar, "Sure, coming right up."

"Never," Joe said to her, "be rude to a man who makes garlic bread with fresh garlic and real butter."

Rowena raised an eyebrow.

"It's out of this world. Beats a currant scone with clotted cream hands down."

"We'll see about that," she said, deliberately haughty, not ready to give up. But she did sit down, and Joe released her.

AFTER DINNER, they took a direct route back to Telegraph Hill. It was mostly uphill, and by the time they reached her door, Rowena's legs ached along with her mind.

Joe Scarlatti was the most enigmatic man she had ever met. More elusive than the most complicated financial network she had ever unraveled. More frustrating.

Certainly more alive. Indeed, he made *her* feel alive.

How, she wondered, did she make him feel? She knew he'd tried to shut down his feelings as a result of his partner's death. But he had too many friends, too close a family—they would keep him from closing himself up completely. Besides, he was a man who felt and felt deeply, no matter how hard he tried not to or how much he tried to deny it.

He hadn't, as Rowena had half expected, invited her upstairs to his apartment after dinner but instead had offered to walk her home. She'd retorted that she could walk herself home. He'd remarked in turn that she knew damned well what he meant and if she wanted to walk all the way back to her mausoleum by herself, then *fine*. Did she have to pick apart every damned word he said? Lord, he muttered, but she was stubborn. Besides which, he had to fetch his truck.

She'd relented, admitting to herself if not to him that she was glad for his company. It would have been a lonely walk without him.

Until meeting him, she had not thought much about being lonely. Alone, yes. But not lonely. It was a fine, but important, distinction.

He lingered on her doorstep while she fumbled for a key hidden in some exterior scrollwork. She noticed his frown in the lamplight. "What's wrong?" she asked.

"You should take your keys with you."

"Usually I do, but I didn't want to be encumbered by a handbag or hip-pack—"

"Someone could see you out here and help themselves to the place one day when you're not home." His gaze hardened. "Or when you are."

"I change my hiding place frequently."

"Doesn't matter. They know a key's hidden, they'll find it."

She shivered at his ominous words. "How unpleasant. You're dampening my optimistic view of human nature."

"I'm not a pessimist or a cynic, Rowena."

"Just a realist?"

He said, "Yeah, just a realist."

She stuck her key in the door. "I'll remember your advice. Thank you." She hesitated. "Are you going home now?"

He nodded curtly, his hands shoved deep into the pockets of the charcoal-colored sweater he'd grabbed from Mario's kitchen, his cousin griping at him about what in hell it was doing there. "Good night, Rowena," he said softly. "I enjoyed this evening."

"I did, too."

And she was inside, the door echoing as she shut it firmly behind her. She could hear Mega and Byte padding down the stairs to greet her, could hear the hissing of the old heating system as it struggled against the dropping temperature. Could hear her own ragged breathing.

Tears sprang hot in her eyes.

Joe Scarlatti had pulled back from her. He had decided that he had to be noble. Going to bed with a virgin, a woman who knew numbers and money and business, wasn't his style. He wouldn't use her and drop her.

She had never been the kind of woman men came to for short-term liaisons. For one- or two-night stands. For sex. She had always been proud of not jumping into bed just to please a man. She had decided long ago that she would rather wait until she was ready than to get involved in a physical relationship just because a man expected or demanded it of

her. A man who made such demands, she'd told herself, wasn't worth the risks.

Not that many had.

But it had never occurred to her that when she was,
in some unspecified, unpredictable future, ready, that
the man she wanted wouldn't, in turn, want her.

But Joe Scarlatti *did* want her. She was sure of it!
Then why weren't they upstairs together?

Was he trying to shove her out of his life because of
his own problems? Because he didn't *want* to feel
again?

She frowned, heading slowly upstairs. She would
take a long bath scented with relaxing bath salts and
tell herself that Joe had gone home tonight because
the man was dead on his feet. She would tell herself
over and over again, until finally she believed it.

JOE WAITED in the shadows just beyond the corner of
Aunt Adelaide's castle and watched Eliot Tyhurst finally emerge from his car and approach Rowena's
front door. She hadn't, Joe was sure, spotted Tyhurst
on their way down their street. But Joe had. It had
meant not inviting himself in, not even kissing her
good-night. He had thought he'd seen a flash of disappointment in her big eyes, but couldn't dwell on
that possibility now.

Tyhurst was ringing her doorbell.

After a full thirty seconds, Rowena still hadn't answered her door. Tyhurst rang again.

Then the door opened, and Joe's heart nearly
stopped when he heard Rowena's voice. "Joe?" But
she recovered quickly—he couldn't see her, but could
hear her recovery, her easy confidence. "Oh, Eliot!
What a nice surprise."

"Yes, I'm sure." His tone was cold, even unfriendly. Joe tensed. "I saw you with your...friend."

"Did you? He and I are working on a project together—simultaneously, I should say. He's an accountant."

A bloody accountant!

"His name's Joe. Would you like to come in?"

"No, I—" Uncertainty had slipped underneath his voice, as if he'd just realized he didn't have Rowena Willow all figured out after all. *Good luck, pal,* Joe thought. *You're not alone on that one.* Tyhurst went on, "I was feeling rather alone tonight and thought I'd ask you out for a drink. But if you've just come in..." He trailed off, leaving her to fill in the blanks.

She did. "You're right, I don't feel like going out again. But would you like to come inside? I have a bottle of wine. I'd be happy to have a drink with you."

Tyhurst was beaming. "Thanks, that'd be great. You're sure I'm not intruding?"

"Not at all. I've been thinking about your proposition. I have a few ideas I'd like to contribute."

"Another time," Tyhurst said, walking into the house of the woman who had cost him millions, his reputation and, for a while, his freedom. She had changed his life, and not for the better. "I'd like to keep this informal."

The heavy front door shut with a thud.

And Joe Scarlatti let out a string of curses that prompted a well dressed couple out walking their poodle to cross to the other side of the street. Now what the hell was he going to do?

"Whatever it takes, my friend," he muttered to himself. "Whatever it takes."

9

"Is THERE something wrong?" Eliot Tyhurst asked, sipping his glass of wine.

"No, nothing." Realizing she must seem preoccupied, Rowena forced a smile. She had not, wisely, she thought, poured herself a glass of wine. She had consumed quite enough at Mario's. "I've concentrated so hard for so many hours today that I just feel a little spacy."

"I understand."

She wondered if he did. If anyone did—if anyone could. Maybe it was asking too much.

He stood in front of the ornate rosewood fireplace in the parlor. She didn't know why she persisted in bringing him in there instead of in the more bizarre—and off-putting—drawing room. Tyhurst turned back to her, his expression impossible to read. "So, you've considered my proposition."

"I've been giving it serious thought, yes."

"And have you decided, Rowena?" he asked softly, taking a step toward her. "Will you work for me?"

She hesitated. She had no intention of actually working for him—that would be improper in her view—but if she put him off too soon, he might walk out of her life for good. That had a certain appeal on the one hand. On the other she wouldn't be privy to any additional information that could lead her to understand more fully what his future plans were. He could be up to no good or he could genuinely be trying to give himself a fresh start. The idea that he was out for revenge seemed very farfetched. He'd had ample opportunity to go after her if he meant to.

She did *not* need the protection of an action-oriented cop who specialized in violent crime. So what if Joe Scarlatti had gone home? Eliot Tyhurst wasn't about to lay a hand on her.

Finally she said, "I need more information."

He frowned. "Rowena, you must realize I can't give you everything until we have an agreement. That would be too risky on my part. I trust you, but—"

"I understand," she said quickly. "I'm also concerned…well, it's not entirely clear to me you can afford my services so soon out of…after your ordeal." Her words came out in a rush, and she suddenly wished she hadn't had so much wine at dinner—and so much of Joe Scarlatti all day.

"You mean you need to know if my troubles completely cleaned me out. You need to know I'm not broke."

There was a note of self-deprecation mixed with bitterness, which seemed to Rowena directed at himself rather than at her, the woman who had brought his financial machinations to the attention of the authorities.

He let out a long exhalation. "Well, I admit I'm not as well off as I was in the past. And I know a lot of people in San Francisco think I should be on the streets, living in shelters and eating in soup kitchens. But I have some resources left." He paused just a moment. Nothing in his tone or manner indicated any animosity toward her. "I can afford to hire you."

Rowena decided to confront him directly. "Eliot, do you hold a grudge against me?"

"No, of course not." He seemed taken aback but not offended. "I thought I'd made that clear already. If I hold a grudge against anyone, Rowena, it's myself. But I'm trying to leave the past behind. It's something I can't change."

"But I'm part of your past. Why hire me? Why even return to San Francisco?"

He moved toward her, everything about him radiating confidence, sensitivity, trust. He was handsome in a classic way, one that bespoke intelligence and power; Rowena could well understand how people had believed in him. She remembered how some, even with the evidence of his abuses before them, had resisted damning him for the thief and con man he was. But she felt no sparks when she was around him, none of the wild energy and thrilling tension she experienced when Joe Scarlatti was in the room.

"San Francisco is my home," he said simply. "It's a part of me. Every day when I was in prison, I pictured its hills, the Golden Gate—" he smiled "—even the fog. It feels damned good to be back. If I have to go somewhere else to begin fresh—if I can't be accepted here—then okay, I'll do it."

"But you feel you have to try here first," she said.

"That's right. And as for you…" His smile faded, his blue eyes growing intense, and he stood just inches from her. "Rowena, I don't think of you as just a part of my past. I like to think of you as a part of my present…and future."

"You mean on a professional basis."

"Maybe it could be more."

Rowena shook her head. "Don't. I want to believe you've changed, and I'm willing to give you a chance to prove yourself if that's what you want. But that's all I can offer. I can't let you think—"

"I understand. It's much too soon for such talk." His words were quiet and stiff, and she sensed his loneliness. He set his wineglass on a coaster. "I'd better be going. Good night, Rowena. Thank you for the wine, and the company."

"You're welcome."

She saw him to the door. Never the most sympathetic of women, Aunt Adelaide would have said the man had made his own bed; now he could lie in it. Rowena had to agree that she couldn't take charge of his life. She couldn't erase his past or take responsibility for it.

And she couldn't feign a romantic interest in him just to make him feel better.

His languid eyes searched hers for a moment as he stood on her front stoop. Then he said curtly, "We'll be in touch. Sleep well."

Rowena shut the door very firmly behind him and belatedly questioned her sense in having invited him inside to begin with. She hoped she hadn't done it to get back at Joe for beating a path home, barely saying good-night to her. But that wasn't her style. She might be eccentric, but she wasn't self-destructive. She had invited Eliot Tyhurst in because she had wanted to know more about his true reasons for having looked her up so soon after his release from prison. And because she didn't consider him a physical danger.

She took the stairs two at a time up to her tower

sunroom, feeling her self-control slipping. She was out of her element with Tyhurst and Scarlatti.

Stumbling over pillows in the dark, she made her way to the windows overlooking the street and stood so close her breath fogged up a circle on the glass.

Her eyes, tired and strained, searched the dark street. She could see Eliot Tyhurst climbing into his high-priced foreign sedan, probably rented, halfway down the block. She felt neither sympathy nor revulsion, only a matter-of-fact sense of wonder at how he had changed her life: He had brought Joe Scarlatti into it.

The expensive car, the streetlights reflected in its shiny exterior, pulled out into the quiet street. Rowena continued scanning, squinting through the fog of fatigue, wine and confusion. Was this what really living did to a woman?

Suddenly she gasped. She stood very still and resisted the urge to back away from the windows. Joe's battered truck was still parked where he'd left it that morning.

Had he gone home without it? Or was he still out there somewhere in the dark? Doing what?

Rowena swallowed in a tight, dry throat. He was there. She could feel his presence. Feel his eyes on her.

Then she saw him.

Slouched against a telephone pole in the shadows across the street a few yards down from his truck. Looking so confident and sexy and masculine.

Watching her.

Automatically, instinctively, Rowena took a step back from the windows. Could he see her? Was he just looking up at her tower, but unaware she was there?

Tyhurst's car disappeared down the street. Rowena supposed Joe would be next. He must have spotted Tyhurst and delayed his departure. Now surely he would climb into his truck and head back down to Mario's Bar & Grill. Things would still be hopping there, not dead and silent as it was in the Willow house.

She watched him walk back to his truck. But he didn't climb in right away. Instead, he thumped the flat of his hand on the roof as if in impatience. With himself? Her?

You think too much, Rowena. Ask too many questions. Just go with the moment, wait and see.

He crossed the street in long strides, without looking.

Rowena flew down the stairs, was on the second-floor landing when she heard the doorbell ring. She jumped the last three steps, landing lightly. But before opening the door, she forced herself to take a moment to catch her breath and push locks of hair that had fallen from their pins back behind her ears.

Joe inhaled sharply at the sight of her. Rowena felt self-conscious, deeply aware of his eyes on her, but also strangely exhilarated. She wondered how wild-eyed she looked, how out of control, how alive. But he only said, in a tone that was curtly professional, "I figured I should spend the night."

"You saw Eliot?"

A single nod.

"He wasn't threatening in any way. I'm sure he won't be back tonight."

"Do you want to take that chance?"

She licked her lips. "It's not much of a chance. I don't believe he poses a *physical* threat to me. If he is out for revenge, it'll be in the form of trying to ruin my reputation, my livelihood, just as I did his—but he's given no indication of planning to do that. He says he's responsible for what happened to him, not me."

Joe didn't seem to be listening. He said, "Then you want me to leave?"

"No!" It was out before she could stop it. She spun around out of the doorway, heard him coming inside, shutting the door behind him. "There's a bedroom on the second floor you can use. It's more comfortable than the pantry, unless you want to remain on the first floor to watch for bogeymen."

"Rowena," he said.

"What?"

He sighed, apparently abandoning what he had intended to say. "If I'm going to stay, I need to run back to my place and pick up a few things. I'll be back in twenty, thirty minutes."

"I'll be here." She thought, *Where else would I be?*

THE BEDROOM Rowena offered Joe was almost normal.

There was a thick line, however, between almost normal and normal. Joe dropped his bag onto a hand-hooked rug featuring a huge red amaryllis and took in the ornate brass double bed, the empty Victorian bird cage on a stand in one corner, the huge, carved wardrobe. Cream-colored lace hung on the windows and covered the bed, and the wallpaper was an over-powering design of red flowers.

A little much, perhaps, but nothing too weird.

The artwork was what just about crossed the line for Joe. He nodded to a painting above the bird cage that showed a half-dozen wolves prowling through snowy woods. "What's that for, in case a guest might be prone to sweet dreams?"

Rowena seemed to notice it for the first time. "It is rather vicious-looking, isn't it?"

"Not real restful." He pointed to the portrait above the bed of a bearded, dour, beady-eyed old man in a turn-of-the-century suit. "And who's that sourpuss? Be tough to thrash around in the bedsheets with him looking on."

Rowena glanced at him quickly, then carefully cleared her throat. "That's my great-grandfather— my Aunt Adelaide's grandfather, Cedric Willow."

"Was he weird, too?"

"He made quite a lot of money in railroads. He was quite the adventurer. He hunted buffalo and ventured to Alaska, the Far East. He built this house."

Joe grunted. "Enough said."

"Aunt Adelaide was a good-hearted woman," Rowena went on, without prompting, "but she didn't have a normal upbringing. She lost her only brother, my grandfather, when she was still a little girl. He was much older, already married with a child of his own."

"That child was your father?"

She nodded. Her eyes seemed even bigger in the dim light, her cheekbones more prominent. Joe acknowledged his desire to pull the pins from her hair, to stroke it, feel its softness beneath his fingers, but he fought against the urge. He had sensed Rowena's wariness upon his return from Mario's with his overnight bag—not of him so much as of herself and her own feelings. He thought he understood.

"This was an unusual place to grow up, I now re-

alize," she said without resentment. She accepted—if
didn't approve of—her odd upbringing. "Aunt Adelaide did her best to provide me with a happy childhood. She had her quirks, and money was always a
struggle because she refused to sell this place. But I'm
afraid I'm a lot like him." She gestured to old Cedric.

"In what way?" Joe asked. "You sure as hell don't
look like him."

She smiled. "He had a gift for remembering things
as well. Not many of his contemporaries understood
him, but that was all right with him. He had his
friends, and even if they were few in number, they
were very close. But never mind. I'm sure you're
tired. There's a bathroom down the hall, second door
on the left. If you need anything, just give a yell up
the stairs."

"The third floor's all yours, is it?"

She glanced back over her shoulder at him, on her
way to the door. "The whole house is mine, Sergeant.
Good night."

He could have let her have the last word.

But he wasn't the type.

He said, "Rowena," and was behind her in two
long steps, and when she spun around, she came
within inches of barreling into his chest. He said
again, more softly, controlling the heat surging
through him, "Rowena," and touched her hair. It was
as soft and silken as he had imagined. It fired not only
his body but his soul. He traced her mouth with his
thumb, then followed with his lips. Just his lips. He
felt the shudder go through her but kept himself from
deepening the kiss. He needed to show restraint—not
just for her sake, but for his—when making love to
Rowena Willow.

Because he would. One day very soon he would.
Now.

No. Not now.

He pulled himself away from her softness, saw the want in her eyes. He wanted more than a chaste kiss, so much more. But he heard himself say, "Good night, Rowena."

She said nothing in return. She retreated quickly, quietly, and in a few seconds Joe could hear her padding softly up to the top floor of her bizarre castle.

He checked out the bathroom down the hall. It was elegant but old-fashioned, straight out of the 1930s. Pale yellow Egyptian cotton bathsheets hung on a free-standing rack, and there was a porcelain dish of oatmeal soap. Even the woman's damned soap was made of oatmeal.

Joe got cleaned up and returned to his room.

He wasn't sleepy. Didn't feel like reading. Couldn't pace around the big drafty house in his underwear. Didn't even have a radio in his room. Damned place was quiet as a tomb. Hell, he thought, recalling the drawing room, it *was* a tomb.

He pulled back the bedcovers and lay down flat on his back on the soft, cool sheets.

Nobility was for the birds. Every fiber of his being wanted to be on the third floor with Rowena Willow. He wanted to see her smile, hear her laugh, feel her wanting him again.

He physically ached.

His only consolation was that he was positive—beyond the realm of doubt—that she was upstairs suffering just as much as he was.

So why the hell don't you march on up there and make love to her? Because you can't. You promised yourself.

He had indeed. Rowena had to be ready. He wasn't going to let her off the hook by making the first move, capitalizing on the electricity between them. He wasn't going to create the moment for them to get carried away with. Nope. No way. Uh-uh. It was her turn.

If he just wanted to satisfy his physical desire for her, he would leap up to the third floor in a single bound. But he wasn't interested only in taking from Rowena. He wanted to give to her as well.

Give her what?

He was a burnt-out cop. He lived in a crummy two-room apartment above a bar. He blamed himself for his partner and best friend's death. He didn't know numbers, and he hated computers. All he could give Rowena Willow, he thought, was one hell of a night in bed.

Maybe that was all she wanted from him.

He stared at the ceiling and tried to imagine making love to Rowena and then walking out of her life forever.

He couldn't.

AT PRECISELY four o'clock in the morning, Rowena gave up on getting back to sleep. She had watched three o'clock and three-thirty come and go on her clock radio and couldn't stand tossing and turning another minute.

She jumped out of bed and pulled on a hotel-weight white terry cloth robe over her filmy nightgown and crept downstairs. She fought an urge to peek in on Joe, just as for the past hour she had fought images of having him in bed with her. She had more success stopping herself from turning down the hall to his room than she had had stopping the images that had her wide-awake and on her way down to the kitchen for a cup of hot herbal tea.

Mega and Byte materialized beside her as she filled the kettle. To her surprise she had dropped off to sleep without incident, the wine, excitement and exhaustion having caught up with her. But she hadn't stayed asleep. Awakening, she'd found herself incapable of getting back to sleep, only of thinking about her houseguest.

Her entire house seemed to pulsate with Joe's presence.

"Up kind of early even by your standards, aren't you?"

His rough, deep voice caught her by surprise, and she whirled around, seeing him slouched against the door frame. He wore nothing but a pair of jeans. His arms were folded on his chest, a muscular wall of muscles and dark, sexy hair. She noticed a thick scar on his lower right side, a reminder of the dangerous work he did. He didn't look relaxed, either. His dark eyes were half-closed, watching her; his hair was tousled, as if he'd run his hands through it in frustration too many times.

How could she have fallen for a man so unpredictable and earthy?

But she had.

"Yes," she said, annoyed at how her voice cracked, "I am up a bit earlier than usual. Did I wake you?"

"No."

She didn't think she had. "Would you like a cup of tea?"

"No, thanks."

His tone didn't change. It sounded as if someone had dragged his vocal cords through sand.

Rowena's eyes drifted down to his bare feet. "I have hot water for coffee."

"Too early."

"Sergeant—"

"It's Joe. At four o'clock in the morning, Rowena, it's Joe." His eyes held hers. "Say it."

She swallowed. "Joe."

A smile softened his hard features, instantly relaxed her. "It's an easy name, isn't it?"

"Yes. Not like Rowena."

"Rowena's a pretty name—different." He straightened and glanced around the kitchen. "Kind of chilly down here, isn't it?"

"I was thinking about having tea upstairs in my sunroom."

"Mind if I tag along?"

Her hesitation only lasted a moment. She wondered if he even noticed. "Of course not."

She fixed her tea tray, using her big white porcelain teapot and two plain white cups and saucers, the only two she had that matched, and brought it upstairs. Joe followed. Rowena could hear his footsteps echoing in the stairwell. Her own hardly made a sound.

Neither spoke.

Finally, as they approached the third floor in the murky darkness, Joe murmured, "We could use some creepy music, don't you think?"

A week ago she would have been highly offended at such a remark. She would have gone on the defensive. Now she smiled to herself at Joe's wry tone. One couldn't take oneself too seriously with him around.

"A big tough cop like you," she said, "scared of an atmospheric house."

"Atmospheric, huh?"

"Yes."

They came to the landing, and she led them down the twisting hall and up the narrow stairs into her tower sunroom. It wasn't quite light enough yet that they could do without the overhead, and she flipped it on as Joe walked past her, in among the pillows.

"My, my," he said.

"The pillows are my doing." She set the tea tray on the floor near the side wall. "This room was much like the other rooms in the house—even worse—when Aunt Adelaide died. I got rid of the furniture and replaced it with pillows."

"Why pillows?"

She shrugged. "They're fun. I collect them."

"Something to do, I guess."

But she could see from his expression that he thought her room, her pillows, were just as weird as the drawing room display of her great-grandfather's taxidermy collection. Just weird in a different way.

"I had only myself to consider. I could do whatever struck my fancy. My friends never come up here. I wanted something comfortable and informal—totally different from the rest of the house. I didn't want any furniture, any machines, nothing to come between me and the view." She looked out at the nightlit skyline. "Beautiful, isn't it? Sometimes it feels like I'm floating over the city."

Joe moved beside her. "I can understand now how you managed to spot me."

"The ever-practical Joe Scarlatti. You know, you do stand out in this neighborhood."

"I guess so."

She plopped a fat tapestry pillow against the wall and sat down with her knees drawn up. Joe remained on his feet. She poured the tea. Her hand, she noticed, had a slight tremble. She blamed lack of sleep.

But Joe could have stopped in his room and put on a damned shirt.

From his narrowed eyes she guessed that he'd noticed her trembling hands, her sudden awkwardness. He was a man trained and conditioned to notice everything about his immediate surroundings. He was anchored in the present. In contrast, an hour could pass in which Rowena would be totally unaware of her surroundings.

"You're sure you don't want some tea?" she asked.

"Why not? I'll have it with milk and sugar since I don't usually drink the stuff."

She handed him a cup and saucer, his fingertips brushing hers as he took it. The tea was hot and slightly strong, just what she needed just before dawn with a shirtless man in her tower sunroom.

"I used to play up here as a little girl. I think I read *Little Women* and *Anne of Green Gables* a half-dozen times each in Aunt Adelaide's horrid old chaise lounge. Sometimes I liked to dream I was a princess."

Joe turned from the window and looked down at her. "A handsome prince would scale the walls to your tower?"

"Mmm."

She met his gaze. He wasn't handsome. He wasn't a prince. He hadn't forced his way to her tower. There were no dragons to slay, no witches to outwit, no evil stepmothers to undo. He had asked if he could come up and she had said yes.

"What do you want now, Rowena?" he asked. His voice had lost its teasing quality; there was an edge to it that hadn't been there before.

"What other people want..."

"I mean *now*, at this moment. What do you want?"

She didn't answer right away.

He turned his back to her and stared out at San Francisco as if to give her space to think. But instead she noticed the jagged scar just above the waistband of his jeans, the breadth of his back, the taut muscles, the narrow hips. Instead she wondered how fast he could run and how high he could jump and how far he would go to keep her from harm.

She would go a long, long way, she thought suddenly, to banish the pain from his eyes, to keep him from hurting.

But she knew what she wanted. Right now, at this moment. She knew. And she was willing to admit it. She said, "I want to finish what we started yesterday in your kitchen."

10

"AND WHAT was it we started?"

Joe hadn't turned from the windows. Rowena felt her mouth go dry. She set her cup and saucer back on the tray; tea sloshed out onto a delicate paper napkin. He hadn't touched her and already she was responding to him. She saw the rigidness of the muscles in his arms and knew he was holding himself under tight control. He also was not oblivious to their being alone together just before dawn, to the simple fact of their physical attraction to each other.

It seemed almost easier, Rowena thought, to comprehend a handsome prince wanting her than this cop who had seen too much of the dark side of human nature.

But she took the plunge.

She said, "We started to make love. That's what I want. Here. In this tower room. *Now*."

"In spite of where it could lead you?"

"Because of where it could lead *us*. I'm not worried. We'll take the proper physical precautions and let what comes tomorrow come."

"That's not your usual way," Joe said, without condemnation, simply stating the obvious.

"No, it's not."

Joe turned around. Then, very deliberately, she tugged pins and combs from her hair, one after the other, quickly and expertly, dropping them on the floor.

He never took his eyes from her.

Long, thick, shiny locks tumbled down her back.

There, she thought, *I've let my hair down.*

"I'm not caught up in the impulse of the moment, Joe, and I'm not planning for the next century, either. But you asked what I want, and I've answered you."

Joe's response wasn't what she expected.

He exhaled heavily and took three strides toward the door. She thought for sure he was gone. Common sense had returned. Whatever it was that kept pushing him away from her had prevailed. She would remain untouched. Maybe even untouchable.

But he stopped at the door and looked back at her. He raked her with his eyes. She felt exposed, more than just physically naked. Her breasts strained against the silken fabric of her nightgown. She was hot inside the robe, intensely aware of the few inches of leg it didn't cover, even of her bare toes.

"Pull the drapes," he said.

In a moment the lights of San Francisco were obliterated and it was just the two of them in the small room, amongst the pillows. Rowena didn't hesitate as she turned from the windows. Joe's eyes were still on her.

Without blushing, she let her robe drop to her feet. Then she pulled the spaghetti straps of her gown over her shoulders and let it, too, fall.

He gazed at her for a long time, not moving from the doorway.

"Joe," she whispered, "come to me."

He was there in an instant. She didn't think she'd seen him move. He swept her up into his arms, mur-

muring things she couldn't make out but understood
in the deepest part of her being. He laid her down on
her sea of pillows and kissed her. It was a long, sweet,
aching kiss that told her how much he wanted her,
how easily he could fall in love with her. His passion
and emotion left her delirious with desire.

But she didn't touch him. She started to, but he
said, "Let me love you first..."

He started with her throat, touching her only with
his lips and tongue. She felt the rest of her aching for
their heat. He moved lower. He tasted the soft flesh of
her breast, the pebble-hardness of her nipples. She
balled her hands into fists at her sides so that she
wouldn't grab hold of him. He moved lower, down
the flat muscles of her abdomen, over her hips, licking
and tasting, leaving in his wake a trail of fire.

At last he came to the smoothness of her inner
thighs.

"I don't know what to do," Rowena murmured,
quaking. "I want you so much."

"You've done your thinking. Don't think anymore.
Just do what your body wants you to do." His voice
was ragged with his own longing. "Show me what
you want."

She wanted his lips and tongue to do to the hot center of her what they'd done to her breasts, her stomach, her thighs. She wanted that blazing heat *there*.
Then it was. She hadn't even realized she'd opened
her legs. Her hands flew out to her sides and clenched
two small pillows as the heat mounted. It didn't stop.
She'd expected it to stop. How could it not stop? But
every time she thought she had the heat under control, he would reclaim it.

She stopped thinking. There was no controlling this

heat, this man. She gave herself up to it, and it remained, consuming her, even when he drew back long enough to discard his jeans. He came back to her all hard and naked and thoroughly, thoroughly male, and there was no hesitation on her part. He joined their bodies with a single, sweeping thrust that made her cry out with a sweet blending of pain and joy and physical pleasure that she'd never known. He cried out her name, and the heat overtook them both.

When they fell apart, exhausted and spent, Rowena felt not even the faintest hint of embarrassment. She ran one hand up the hard length of his hip. "One day I want to do to you what you just did to me."

His smile reached the dark depths of his eyes. "Do you have that kind of self-control?"

She remembered how he had never touched her with anything but his lips and tongue. "You'll just have to wait and find out."

But he didn't have to wait long. Before sunup he found out just how much self-control she had...and, in a different way, how much he had.

Later they opened the drapes and showered and changed.

It was a new day.

HANK RYAN STUDIED Joe from the other side of his booth at Mario's Bar & Grill. "What's eating you?"

"Nothing's eating me." But Joe could hear the impatience in his own voice.

"Something is," Hank said, unruffled by his friend's foul mood. "Is having something to do getting to you or is it Rowena Willow?"

"It's your imagination."

Joe wondered at his own gruffness. What was

wrong with him? He had started his day making love to a beautiful woman. An enigmatic woman. A woman he suddenly couldn't imagine not having in his life.

Still, it was one thing to make love to Rowena Willow. It was quite another to fall in love with her. And he was afraid that was just what was happening.

He drank some of the beer Mario had reluctantly brought him. *Was* that what was happening—had he fallen for Rowena? Even the question made him shift in his seat. Falling for Rowena Willow could be damned dangerous. Not for him. He didn't give a damn about himself. For Rowena. How the hell could she imagine what his life was really like? How could he dare feel so damned alive with her in his arms?

"Scarlatti?"

He sighed. "I'm still the same man I was before I got mixed up with Rowena Willow."

But it wasn't true, and he knew it.

So did Hank. "You two have something going," his friend said. It wasn't a question.

Joe just scowled at him. Mario had said much the same thing when Joe had stumbled in two hours earlier. Must have something printed on his forehead.

"You're crazy, you know that?" Hank was shaking his head in despair. "You two have nothing in common. Nothing."

"We're survivors, Hank, each in our own way. I didn't see that at first. I just saw her as a weirdo who memorized license plate numbers. But I see it now."

"You're a cop, Joe. You're on a job—"

"Unofficially."

"What you're doing is unethical."

"What am I doing, Hank?"

Hank pointed a finger at him. "You're sleeping with her."

Only once, Joe thought. Only once. Well, twice if he counted how many times they'd made love. But it was only one...well, event, he thought. Just that predawn collapse of his common sense.

And arousal of all his other senses.

"Hell," he said under his breath.

"Don't lose your edge, Scarlatti." Hank had leaned forward over the table, his expression turning professional. "Just because Tyhurst hasn't made his move yet doesn't mean he won't. I've got news. It's not good."

Joe's cop-instincts immediately clicked into gear. "Your snitch?"

Hank nodded, without pleasure or satisfaction. "He checks out. He had access to Tyhurst in prison. Says our boy Eliot is a cold-blooded bastard who's out for just one thing—to see Rowena Willow suffer. He's out for revenge. Period."

Joe felt a stab of cold in the small of his back. He clenched his beer bottle in one hand but took no drink. "You believe this snitch?"

"I don't know. He wants to ingratiate himself, see what's in it for him. I wouldn't be surprised if he's telling us what he thinks we want to hear."

"What's his story?"

"He says Tyhurst kept track of Rowena's goings-on while he was in prison. He didn't actually tell anyone he was planning revenge, but our fellow says it was obvious he wanted to make someone pay for his downfall and that someone is Rowena Willow."

"You have enough, Hank. Put someone on her."

He shook his head. "No evidence. Tyhurst hasn't

made any threats. No one else says he's out for revenge. Our tattletale doesn't have a good track record."

"Then Tyhurst could be what he says he is—a man who wants a fresh start."

"That's right."

"But you don't think so."

Hank didn't respond right away. "No," he said finally, "I don't think so."

"I don't, either."

"Stay sharp." Hank climbed heavily to his feet. "I trust you, Scarlatti. Just be sure you trust yourself before you put Rowena Willow's life in your hands."

ELIOT TYHURST came to Rowena's house while Joe was out for the afternoon, having left a perfunctory note on her refrigerator. She immediately suspected Tyhurst's presence, and Joe's absence wasn't a coincidence, something the former banker confirmed. "I saw your boyfriend leave," he told her tightly on her front stoop.

"My what?"

He gave a small shake of the head, as if indulging a recalcitrant toddler. "I know who he is and what he is, Rowena."

"And obviously you've jumped to some unkind conclusion," she said coolly.

"He's a San Francisco cop, a detective sergeant. He's on leave of absence from the department over the death of his partner. He's a real head case. He has a short fuse, he thinks everyone in the world is a criminal. He's a cynic."

She had to remember that Eliot Tyhurst was not a man to underestimate. "Look, Eliot—"

"He'll do anything to get what he wants. He risked the life of his partner and best friend to arrest some two-bit drug dealers." Tyhurst breathed out slowly, his tension visibly easing. He opened his hands from the fists he had them clenched into. His tone softened. "And he's done his damnedest to get an isolated, brilliant and beautiful woman to fall for him. Another feather in his cap, I suppose. A notch on his gun, whatever. I can't say I know how such a man really thinks."

Rowena suppressed an urge to slam the door in his face and run upstairs to her office, bury herself in her work. She said stiffly, "Unkind conclusions indeed. And fairly extraordinary ones, Eliot."

"Extraordinary perhaps, but I don't think unkind, and I don't think incorrect." His eyes narrowed, but he looked more frightened than intimidating. Rowena noticed that he had cut himself shaving, that his tie was poorly knotted. "The truth is, Joe Scarlatti is after me. He wants me back in prison and he'll do anything to get me there."

"What makes you think that?"

"I'm not stupid, Rowena." He sounded almost sad.

"No, you're not. But the truth is something a bit different from what you apparently think." She debated inviting him inside, then quickly decided against it. His state of mind was just too volatile. "I haven't told you this sooner because I don't believe it's been my place to do so. However, since you've seen Sergeant Scarlatti and have your own ideas about why he was here, I see no reason not to tell you. A friend of his on the force—Sergeant Hank Ryan, remember him?"

Eliot Tyhurst nodded without interrupting.

"He put Scarlatti up to watching here unofficially in case you decided to come after me for purposes of revenge. Ryan wanted him to get back to work. He was afraid Sergeant Scarlatti was sliding into some kind of funk, that he wouldn't return to the force when his leave of absence ended." She swallowed. It was strange referring to a man she had made love to just hours ago in so clinical a fashion. "I'm afraid I don't know all the details."

"No," Tyhurst said coldly, unmoved by her explanation, "you clearly don't."

She blinked at him, waiting for him to continue, trying not to acknowledge her growing uneasiness that he just might be right.

"Rowena, Joe Scarlatti has a *personal* vendetta against me."

He sounded confident. Certain of the veracity of his statement. Rowena shivered not with cold—it was a warm, sunny November afternoon—but with the uncomfortable thought that Eliot Tyhurst might know something about Joe Scarlatti that she didn't know.

There was a lot about Joe Scarlatti, she thought, that she didn't know.

"But why would he?" she asked. "He doesn't know you."

Tyhurst smirked. "I see he hasn't told you."

Rowena began to shake. "Told me what?"

"Come to my hotel tonight. Without him. Have dinner with me." He stepped forward, his eyes pleading, filled with anguish. "I'll tell you more about why I need you, Rowena."

There was an obvious double meaning to his words. She bit down on her lower lip and cleared her throat, no longer certain of what she should be thinking or even feeling. She said, "I can't…"

"Please. Just have dinner. I'll tell you everything. Then you can decide what you want to do."

"I—I don't want you to pick me up. I'll meet you."

"All right. My hotel's restaurant is very good." He smiled sadly. "And it's generally crowded. You don't have to worry about that."

"Don't assume I don't believe you've reformed. It's not my place to judge you."

"But you've been hanging around with Joe Scarlatti. Falling for him, I daresay. His cynicism has washed off onto you. He's convinced you I can't change."

She stiffened at his accusation. "I said I'm willing to give you a chance."

Some of the tension seemed to go out of his body. "Seven o'clock, then?"

"I'll be there."

JOE CAUGHT UP with Eliot Tyhurst in the bar of the downtown hotel where he was staying, a tidbit provided by Hank Ryan. It was time, Joe had decided, for him and the ex-con to have a few words.

"Your average bank robber fresh out of prison couldn't afford a place like this," he said, taking in the elegant lobby with an exaggerated sweeping glance.

Tyhurst gave him a supercilious look. "I'm not an average bank robber, Sergeant."

"So you know who I am. Figured as much. No, you're well above average. You stole millions instead of a few grand. But you got caught."

"And I served my time. This is harassment."

"Nope. This is fair warning. I'm rattling your cage,

Eliot. You're out for revenge. Rowena Willow ruined you and you're going to make her pay. I don't know how and I don't know when you plan to make your move, but I promise you, I'll be there."

Tyhurst shook his head. Joe had to admire the guy's control. "I've done nothing."

"Go on your way, Tyhurst. Leave Rowena alone. Get out of her life and stay out."

"For your sake?"

"For yours. I'm watching you."

"And I'm watching you." Tyhurst spoke through his teeth, the only indication he gave that Joe had gotten to him at all. Otherwise he looked like an honest banker out for a drink after a long day. "One wrong step, Sergeant Scarlatti, and I'll see you removed from the force."

Joe shrugged. "That doesn't worry me, you know."

"I suppose it wouldn't." His nostrils flared as if he smelled something bad. "Your only worry these days is Rowena Willow. Well, she has nothing to fear from me. I suggest," he went on arrogantly, "that she has far more to fear from you, Sergeant Scarlatti."

It was a fair point, Joe thought. The bastard just might be right. But he didn't budge. "Watch yourself, Tyhurst."

Tyhurst responded with a downright disdainful smile. "I intend to. Good evening to you, Sergeant."

WHEN ROWENA ripped open her front door for him, Joe immediately noticed two things. One, her hair was down. Tangled and shining and unbelievably gorgeous.

Two, she was ripsnorting mad. At least by her standards. She wasn't the type to kick and scream and throw things, but when she saw him, she whirled around in the entry, hair flying, and marched back and forth in front of her auntie's medieval suit of armor.

"Going to borrow our pal's spear here and run me through?"

She cut her eyes, gleaming and mad, around at him. "It's a thought."

"I had that feeling. What's up? Am I late?"

"*Late?* Late for what?" She seemed to have no idea that he'd said the first thing that had popped into his head just to get her to open up. It wasn't a question meant to be dissected. "You left a note saying that you were going out and would be back later. How could you possibly be late if you gave no specific time of return?"

"Not the possessive type, I see."

She scowled at him. "Don't try to soften me with your sarcastic wit, Sergeant Scarlatti. I'm very annoyed with you."

Very annoyed? A comment worthy of inciting his sarcastic wit, but Joe resisted. The woman was angry and didn't deserve to have him patronize her. "Rowena," he said seriously, "do you want to talk?"

She nodded stiffly, unmollified, and gestured toward the drawing room, a sure sign that she was in a truly foul mood. Joe went in and stood next to the curio cabinet of dead birds. Rowena's footsteps clicked on the shiny hardwood floor, then grew muffled as she marched across the thick Persian carpet. She was dressed casually in leggings and an oversize top, but her natural elegance shone through. Joe remembered his fingers in her hair, remembered it splayed across his chest.

"Okay," he said. He could see that she wanted herself to do the talking and him the listening. At least for starters. "Tell me what's wrong."

She had her back to him as she gazed either out the window or at the buffalo's head, Joe couldn't tell which. Maybe she was thinking about what *his* head would look like mounted on her wall.

What had he done?

You made love to her, my friend. You took her virginity.

Then she said, "Your grandparents, Mario and Sofia Scarlatti, lost their life savings as a result of Eliot Tyhurst's financial machinations."

Hell, he thought. So she'd found out on her own. He'd always known she could do it. She'd unraveled Eliot Tyhurst's little scheme, hadn't she? But he hadn't thought she would find out about his grandparents, at least not before he got around to swallowing his pride and telling her his own connection to their pal the ex-con.

"I guess it won't do any good to say I was planning to tell you," he said.

She didn't turn around. "You should have told me the day you met me."

"Maybe. My grandfather was a proud man, and he made a mistake. I didn't want you thinking less of him for it."

Her eyes didn't soften. "You should never even have taken on this case. Sergeant Ryan never should have asked you."

"Why?"

She whirled around at him. "Because you're biased! You have an agenda. *You* want revenge."

"Rowena—"

"I thought you were objective. I thought you were

a professional. I believed your advice was uncolored by personal motives."

"Rowena—"

"I *trusted* you!"

"Rowena, what happened to my grandparents and how I feel about Tyhurst has nothing to do with us." Not that she'd said it had, but he was taking a wild stab it had crossed her mind and was one reason she was so mad. "You're right. I should have told you sooner."

"The day we met, Scarlatti. The damned day we met you should have told me."

"Well, I could argue that I wasn't planning on making love to you the day we met. Not that the thought didn't cross my mind. The point is, I owed you the full story and I should have given it to you before now. I just didn't feel it was my place to expose my grandparents' financial mistakes to someone like you."

It wasn't the right thing to say. "And just what is 'someone like me'?"

"You're hard on people who die broke, Rowena."

She drew in a deep breath, stalked past him, said, "You're a snake," and kept on going.

A woman who spoke her mind, Rowena Willow was.

Joe accepted that she had a right to be angry. He accepted that he had been a moron for not having told a woman with a computer-mind like hers much, much sooner that his grandparents had been among Tyhurst's victims. She was bound to figure it out all by herself.

How had she figured it out? Tyhurst had had hun-

dreds of anonymous, innocent victims like Mario and
Sofia Scarlatti.

Joe went into the entry and yelled upstairs, "Tyhurst tip you off?" A door clicked shut somewhere in
the upper stories of the cavernous house. Rowena
wasn't the door-slamming type, either.

He turned to the suit of armor. "Tyhurst tipped her
off."

One point to the ex-con. Joe sighed. Then it occurred to him that he wasn't particularly bothered by
Rowena's anger. He regretted his role in it. He hated
seeing her feel bad. But he wasn't *bothered*. He didn't
feel defensive or hurt or angry.

He wasn't bothered, he thought, because he knew,
deep down, that this was just the first time he had really and truly pissed her off. There would be more
times. And times when she would really and truly
piss *him* off.

"Ah, hell," he muttered.

All the woman needed now was to have him falling
in love with her.

11

By the time she reached Eliot Tyhurst's hotel, Rowena felt wrung out. She was drained of any anger. She doubted she'd ever gotten so mad at anyone in her entire life. Joe Scarlatti had a way of getting to her.

His words kept ringing in her ears. *Was* she hard on people who died broke? She prided herself on not judging the financial mistakes of others. She'd made her own, although none as disastrous as her parents', and she'd never been so stubborn about money as Aunt Adelaide.

But they'd died broke, her parents and Aunt Adelaide. In trying not to repeat their mistakes, had she judged them too harshly?

Tyhurst was waiting for her in the lobby. He was handsomely dressed in an elegant evening suit and greeted her warmly, murmuring something complimentary about her appearance. She couldn't quite make out all the words. She'd put her hair back up into a severe twist and had on very little makeup, and a flowing, comfortable dress in a fabric two shades darker than her hair. She imagined herself out on the town with Joe. He wouldn't wear a suit anything like the former banker's. Yet he would go anywhere, feel at ease anywhere. He put on absolutely no airs.

But he had lied to her. How could she stand here imagining ever again doing anything with him?

It hadn't been an outright lie, she reminded herself. It had been an omission of an important fact.

Wasn't that worse?

He had been in the kitchen playing with Mega and Byte when she'd left. Aunt Adelaide's training had gotten the better of her and she'd said a tight good-bye.

He'd told her to have a good time. That was it: have a good time. Nothing more.

What did she expect?

"Rowena, is everything all right?" Tyhurst touched her shoulder with apparent concern. "You look a bit tired."

She attempted a smile. "I'm fine. It's just been a long day."

They entered the quiet dining room, where Tyhurst had reserved a table in a dimly lit corner. Rowena immediately ordered a bottle of mineral water with a twist of lime. Her throat was dry from nervousness and now-spent anger. Maybe she should have let loose and yelled at Joe instead of controlling herself as she had.

Tyhurst ordered scotch and watched her from across the table.

"You don't have to tell me about Joe Scarlatti's grandparents," she said abruptly. "I know."

"He didn't tell you," Tyhurst said knowingly.

His unexpected insight grated on her already-raw nerves. She hadn't had enough sleep. Her routines were shattered. She had made love last night for the first time in her life. That was plenty for anyone to tackle without having to face a man whom she had helped send to prison.

"No," she said, "he didn't tell me. I did some research on my own."

"You and your computer." He laughed.

Rowena couldn't come up with an answering smile. Indeed, her and her computer. "Mario Scarlatti died two years ago."

Tyhurst's eyes clouded; she couldn't read his expression. "I'm sorry."

She looked at him. "I wonder if you are."

"Do you doubt me?" There was no bitterness in his voice—he wanted to know.

"What I think doesn't matter. Eliot, I can't work for you. It wouldn't be proper. You're entitled to your fresh start, but I can't be a part of it. I wish you well." Their drinks arrived. She didn't touch hers. "If you want me to leave now I will."

"No—no, don't leave. I've changed in so many ways thanks to you." He raised his glass of scotch to her, as if in a toast. "I owe you, Rowena Willow."

THEY FINISHED dinner early. It wasn't so much unfriendly as awkward, their relationship finally, Rowena felt, coming to an end. Eliot Tyhurst promised to keep in touch. She assured him she was glad he had paid her a visit upon his release from prison and once again wished him well.

She grabbed a taxi outside the hotel and asked the driver to take her to Sofia Scarlatti's apartment a block from Mario's Bar & Grill on the waterfront. She had looked up the address in her telephone book and, of course, remembered it.

Sometimes she wondered if she remembered too damned much.

A sudden fog had descended over the city. Rowena

shut her eyes and breathed in its dampness. It wasn't even nine o'clock; Joe's widowed grandmother might still be up. Rowena would make up her mind whether to bother her when she got there.

"Here you go," the driver said.

She paid him and climbed out onto the curb. So close to the water, the fog was thicker, enveloping her in its silence. She went up the short walk to the main entrance of the three-story stucco building. About a half-dozen rosebushes were tangled together on a wooden fence, their riot of color penetrating the gray fog.

Rowena hesitated at the front door. There was a light on inside, but she didn't know if Sofia Scarlatti had the first-floor apartment. The upper two floors were dark. Would she only frighten the old woman, banging on her door uninvited?

"Go on up," Joe Scarlatti said behind her.

She spun around in surprise, stopped just short of screaming. She could tell nothing from his expression, whether he was angry at having her there, shocked, saddened. Her own expression, she was sure, betrayed her uncontrolled reaction to his overpowering sensuality. Every fiber of her being wanted to touch him again, to feel him inside her again and again.

It was madness.

He said matter-of-factly, "My grandmother's a night owl."

"Did you follow me?"

"Yep."

"All along? I mean, you followed me to the hotel, then here?"

"Right again."

"But I…" She remembered her anger and straightened her shoulders. "Never mind."

Joe grinned. "You were going to say you never saw me, weren't you? I'm pretty good at what I do once I know what I'm up against." His gaze darkened. "And I wasn't going to leave you to Tyhurst no matter how mad you were at me."

"Are, Scarlatti. I'm still mad."

He moved toward her. "No you're not."

She wasn't. She knew she wasn't. "I want to be."

"Yeah. That I can understand." An outside light came on. Joe grinned. "Uh-oh, Granny's on the prowl. She doesn't miss a trick. You go on in. I'll wait out here." He trotted up the steps as a tiny elderly woman pulled open the door. "Grandma," he said lovingly, giving her a kiss on the cheek and a quick hug. "Somebody here to see you, a friend of mine."

Sofia Scarlatti answered him in Italian. He answered her back. Then she shoved him aside and gave Rowena a wide, friendly smile. "Come in, come in, don't stand out there in the rain." Her smile broadened. "We'll let Joe do that!"

He shot Rowena a look that she realized was a warning not to point out to her grandmother that it wasn't raining. One, she could see, did not contradict Sofia Scarlatti.

Joe settled down on the top step, just under an overhang.

Rowena went inside.

"My, my, you're all dressed up," the old woman said, eyeing her guest's flowing, expensive dress as she led her down a short, narrow hall.

"I've been out to dinner—"

"Not with Joe," she said. It wasn't a question.

"No, I—"

"I'd skin him alive if he went out wearing those holey jeans with a pretty woman. I don't know how often I've told him I'd mend them." Like her grandson, Sofia Scarlatti, Rowena noticed, didn't have a trace of an Italian accent, yet she spoke the language of her ancestors fluently. "Come in, sit down. Would you like a nice glass of brandy?"

"That would be lovely, yes. Mrs. Scarlatti, my name is Rowena Willow—"

"I know. Joe told me, but he didn't need to. I'd have remembered you from the trial."

"Eliot Tyhurst's trial," Rowena said unnecessarily. "Yes."

There was a note of finality to Mrs. Scarlatti's tone, as if they were talking about something very much over and done with. Already Rowena could see that Sofia Scarlatti was not a woman who dwelled in the past; she lived in the present. They went into a brightly lit, simple kitchen, much in need of remodeling, and she seated her guest at a small table covered with an attractive, if worn, cloth splashed with grapevines.

In the light, Rowena guessed that Joe's grandmother was closer to eighty than seventy and not over five feet tall, her hair snow white, her face heavily lined. But her movements and smile were quick, and her dark eyes—her grandson's eyes—missed nothing.

She filled two glasses with brandy and set them on the table. "I wished I'd never heard of Eliot Tyhurst," she said, sitting down. "We were too complacent, my Mario and I. We believed a man like that wouldn't rob two old people. And he didn't. He robbed hundreds of old people!"

"He abused your trust in him. It could happen to anyone."

"To you?"

Rowena shrugged, remembering Joe's earlier words. "We all have financial setbacks, even catastrophes. We try to know the risks but we can't always. That's what was so terrible about what Tyhurst did— he didn't give you the information you needed to make your decision. He didn't inform you of the true risks."

"We didn't ask enough questions."

"Buyer beware? That doesn't always save you from deceit. Tyhurst was an expert. You're no more at fault than if you'd been robbed on the street at gunpoint."

Sofia Scarlatti wrinkled her nose. "I'd have been at fault if I'd been stupid enough to carry everything I own in my pockets! Ten, twenty dollars, you let it go—but everything? No, that's my fault." Her tone was matter-of-fact. She seemed more embarrassed by her ordeal than embittered.

"I really do think you're being hard on yourself, Mrs. Scarlatti," Rowena said. She tried her brandy; it was strong but smooth, and more welcome than she wanted to admit. She pushed aside an image of Joe on his grandmother's front stoop. "I'm very good with this sort of thing and it took me a long time to unravel Tyhurst's scheme. If someone put a little grass or dirt in your lasagna you'd know it, wouldn't you?"

"I should think so," Sofia Scarlatti said.

"But what if they mashed the grass so thoroughly you couldn't detect it? What if they carefully mixed the dirt with the meat? You might know something's wrong but you might not figure it out right away. Someone who doesn't know lasagna might not even realize anything was wrong. Is that their fault?"

"You're saying you know money. I know lasagna."

"I'm saying we all have our areas of expertise and that Eliot Tyhurst deliberately used his against the very people who put their trust in him. It would be like you putting ingredients you know are bad into your lasagna and then feeding it to your own children."

Mrs. Scarlatti leaned back in her chair and regarded Rowena thoughtfully. "I see your point. I can tell you, though, I'd never make the same mistake with the likes of Eliot Tyhurst again. But I won't get that chance. I have no money left to invest."

"Others learned from your 'mistake.' It won't be so easy for the Eliot Tyhursts of the world to get away with such larceny in the future."

"I suppose it's something, serving as an example," Sofia Scarlatti said, a surprising twinkle in her alert eyes, "but I'd rather have my money!"

Rowena smiled. "I'm sure you would."

"My Joe, he thinks his grandfather died a broken man, but I want you to know he didn't. He died of a heart attack. He'd had a bad heart for years. He was angry with himself, yes, for trusting Tyhurst, but he'd survived much worse hardships in his life than losing his money." She sipped her brandy, studying Rowena. "You know, my Joe needs a good woman in his life."

"I can't cook lasagna."

"Who cares? You know money."

JOE REALIZED he was probably going to go through life being periodically mystified by Rowena Willow.

All she said upon leaving his grandmother's apartment was, "I found the grass, but I haven't even looked for the dirt."

He didn't bother trying to figure that one out.

He got her into the car he'd borrowed from a friend for the express purpose of tracking her. It was one she hadn't seen before and therefore her computer-mind wouldn't remember.

She didn't even comment on it. She just climbed into the front seat and stared straight ahead.

Joe started the engine and glanced sideways at her. Strands of hair had come out of her twist and fallen down her forehead and the back of her neck. Very sexy. Most of her lipstick had come off during dinner, and she'd never bothered to apply a fresh coat. Even sexier. And her dress—

But the woman was thinking about grass and dirt.

"How'd your dinner with Tyhurst go?" he asked.

Nothing. Just that glassy-eyed stare out the window.

"My grandmother liked you. I could tell because she gave you the good brandy. She's got some rotgut you wouldn't believe. Keeps it around for the landlord." She'd been carrying her glass when she saw Rowena to the door and thrust a helping of some leftovers wrapped in aluminum foil at Joe. He could never leave empty-handed, even if he hadn't actually gone inside for a visit. "I don't know what's in the foil but it's probably good. Granny's a hell of a cook. She does great Italian, of course, but also Mexican. Makes a terrific dish she created, sort of a taco lasagna."

He was talking to himself. He knew it. Rowena's mind was occupied in some realm he couldn't access.

Back on Telegraph Hill, he had to hunt for a parking place. If Hank Ryan hadn't told him about the prison-mate who claimed Eliot Tyhurst was a cold-blooded bastard out for revenge, Joe might have let Rowena off at her front door. As it was, he didn't plan to let her out of his sight.

Not that she noticed.

Joe pulled into a tight parking space, turned off the engine and unlocked his door.

Rowena just sat there.

"We're here," he said.

She might have been catatonic.

He touched her shoulder. "Rowena."

She screamed and jerked up, looking as if he'd jumped her in a dark alley. More hair escaped from its pins. Catching her breath, she looked around at him, her eyes wide and faraway. "I'm sorry, I'm thinking..."

And she was out of the car and on her way, turning right when she needed to turn left even though this was her own neighborhood. She might as well have been on the damned moon for all she was aware of her surroundings. Joe caught up with her and took her by the shoulders and pointed her in the right direction. Not only did she not look embarrassed, she didn't even look *aware* he'd touched her.

Unlike last night, he thought.

"Eccentric geniuses," he muttered. "Who can figure?"

He fell in behind her, observing as she unlocked her door and pushed it open and dropped her purse and turned on lights and headed upstairs, on automatic pilot. She was oblivious to what was around her, lost in her world of thought.

Joe assumed he was in for a long night and headed back to the kitchen to find the cats, Mega and Byte. Hell of a couple of names for two not-so-bad cats. He liked them because they could play fetch, almost like dogs except they had sharper claws.

"Hey, kitties," he said when they didn't pad out to greet him. "Mega? Byte?"

He called them a few more times, whistling and clapping his hands, but they didn't show up. He checked their dishes. Rowena, still in full snit, had fed them before she'd left for her dinner with Eliot Tyhurst.

The cats had hardly touched a bite.

Joe's cop instincts kicked into gear. Every part of him went on high alert. He stopped calling the cats. He backed up toward the kitchen wall and listened.

Something was wrong.

Then he heard a scratching at the pantry door. He opened it, and Mega and Byte wandered out. They were genius's cats, he knew, but cats, he didn't care how smart, couldn't close themselves up in pantries like that.

And then he heard Rowena scream.

"DON'T SCREAM," Eliot Tyhurst said.

Rowena stepped backward toward her computer desk, trying to control her terror. "You startled me."

"You were so intent on destroying me, you just didn't hear me." He nodded at her blank monitor. "Find anything?"

She licked her lips. Her heart was beating much too fast. He had interrupted her high level of concentration, scared the proverbial living daylights out of her. He must have used the key Joe had warned her not to keep outside to get into her house. He must have hidden while she and Joe were at his grandmother's.

Although she'd gotten over his startling her, her heart rate hadn't diminished, and her fear had only grown. She felt nothing but dread.

Eliot Tyhurst, she thought, hadn't reformed. Joe was right.

"You know what I found," she told him. "The dirt in the lasagna—a personal account, very well hidden, containing a half-million dollars you neglected to mention to the authorities was yours. You're not broke, Eliot. You never were."

"No." He smiled coldly, taking a step toward her. "I never was."

Any facade of gentlemanly demeanor had vanished. His eyes were blue ice. His hair was standing on end. His shirt was half-untucked, his tie askew. Spittle had collected at the corners of his mouth. There was blood on his lower lip where he must have bit down too hard.

Rowena had never seen anyone so consumed by hatred.

Hatred of *her*. It was very specific, and very vicious.

She wondered if Joe had heard her scream. Wondered if she should hope he had—or hope, for his sake, that he hadn't. She needed to think and get out of this one herself.

"You never wanted to hire me," she said. "You only wanted to make sure I didn't uncover your secret account."

"You're wrong, Rowena." If possible, his eyes became even icier. "You didn't know about that account three years ago. I fooled you then. I thought I could fool you again. What you don't realize is that I have an even greater purpose in contacting you after all this time."

He reached behind him, into the waistband of his elegant suit pants, and withdrew a gun. It was small and silver, and he pointed it at Rowena.

"Even with a half-million dollars, there's no way I can stay in the United States. I have to leave the country." He sounded aggrieved, as if he were the one who had endured the greater wrong, not the people he'd duped. He went on, "It's all planned. Once I knew I'd have to act tonight, I purchased tickets to South America. I'll be out of here for good in another hour." He smiled. *"With* my money."

"Why didn't you just go? Why risk coming here?"

"Revenge, Rowena. You ruined me. You *destroyed* me. I have no family, no friends, no country, no *life* thanks to you. Do you think I could just vanish without repaying you in kind for what you did to me?"

"So you're going to shoot me." She hated how her voice cracked, but she knew she needed to keep him talking, needed to give Joe a chance to act. "Your revenge is to shoot me."

He shook his head sadly, looking hurt. "I could never shoot you, unless, of course, you leave me no other option."

With his free hand, he removed a length of twine from his suit coat pocket and ordered her to cross her wrists at the small of her back and turn around. She did so. She had no choice.

He tied her wrists fast and hard, squeezing off the blood supply to her hands.

"I've dreamed of this moment for three years," he

said harshly, his breath hot and foul on the side of her face. "It feels even better than I imagined."

"And you've fallen even further than I'd ever imagined possible. I feel sorry for you, Eliot."

"You arrogant bitch."

He caught her twisted hair into his hand and pulled hard. Tears sprung into her eyes at the pain. He shoved her down onto the floor, and without ceremony, he snatched up her feet, binding them together with another length of twine.

Where the hell was Scarlatti when she needed him?

Tyhurst kicked her in the thigh, pushing her under her desk. "You can die under your damned computer."

Then he was gone.

And in a moment she smelled smoke.

Ignoring the pain in her hands and feet, Rowena inched backward out from under her desk. Smoke was everywhere above her. She could hear the crackle of flames. Smell the gasoline Tyhurst had used to start the fire.

She flipped over onto her bottom and sat up, her nostrils and mouth filling with smoke. She coughed. "Joe!" she yelled.

There was no answer.

"Scarlatti, where are you? The bastard's got a gun!"

Smoke billowed in from the hall where Tyhurst had obviously started the fire. Rowena grasped a filing drawer with her numb fingers and pulled herself to her feet, into the deadly smoke. She kept an artist's knife in her mug of pens and pencils. Coughing, perspiring, she got it out with her mouth and dropped back down to the floor, tucking her knees up under her chin and immediately getting to work on her bound ankles. If she could get free, she could break a window, climb out onto the rickety, ancient fire-escape ladder.

If only Joe Scarlatti had sense enough not to brave an armed man and a fire to get to her. But that was his job.

The smoke was thickening, stinging her eyes, making her work nearly impossible. She didn't stop. She sawed relentlessly at the twine. It was around her ankles in four layers. If she could get through two, surely the other two would be loose enough to permit her to work them free, or at least to walk.

One layer snapped.

She started immediately on the next one. She could no longer see through her tears and could barely hold on to the knife in her mouth with her coughing, but it didn't matter. She had her rhythm down. And she had to get out, find Joe.

Don't let Tyhurst be his undoing. Please don't let it, if not for my sake, for his grandmother's sake...

Somewhere from beyond the flames she heard a shot.

"No!"

The second layer snapped.

With a sudden burst of energy, she forced her ankles apart, oblivious to the pain of the twine bearing into her skin.

She was free.

"Joe," she yelled, "I'm all right. I'll go out the fire escape!"

How, she thought, with her hands still bound?

She had to find a way. She had to!

Then his voice came to her over the roar of the

flames that were consuming Aunt Adelaide's house. "Rowena!"

And he was there, coming through the flames and the smoke, hair and clothes singed, smoldering. Blood poured down his arm. Rowena stumbled toward him. Her feet ached as circulation returned and blood rushed through them.

"Rowena," he said again, "thank God."

"Tyhurst?"

"Threw him off the second-floor landing. Probably didn't kill him. We gotta get out of here."

"I know, there's a fire escape, if you can manage to cut my hands free—"

She stopped, and time seemed suspended. Something was terribly wrong about the way he was looking at her. "Joe?"

"You'll have to give me a knife or a pair of scissors and I'll get you free. Come on, hurry."

"Joe—"

His face was filled with grime and pain. He blinked, and she knew.

He touched her arm. "It's okay, love, but I can't see."

12

ROWENA PACED outside Joe's hospital room.

It was late, after midnight. Hank Ryan had come, Sofia Scarlatti, Mario. Joe was holding his own, the doctors had said. The bullet had only skimmed his left upper arm. The effect on him of smoke inhalation wasn't as severe as they'd first anticipated. His burns were all first-degree.

But he still couldn't see. Smoke, a blow to the head, heat—even the doctors weren't yet sure what had caused his blindness.

Hank put a big hand on her shoulder. "You sure you don't want to have a doctor look at you? Place is crawling with them."

"No, I'm fine." Even to herself her voice sounded faraway. She rubbed her raw wrists. Blinded and bleeding, Joe had managed to cut her free. And she had managed to get him down the fire escape. "I'll just be coughing up smoke and stuff for a few days."

Hank nodded. She had given him her statement. She didn't know what Joe had told him. A neighbor had called the police and the fire department. Eliot Tyhurst was in custody, being treated not too far from Joe Scarlatti for, as Hank had put it, the thrashing of his life. He would be charged with attempted murder.

The fire department had put out the fire on the third floor of Cedric Willow's strange house before it had spread to any of the other floors. She'd rescued her cats. A neighbor had offered to take them in.

"Do you have a place to stay?" Hank asked.

"I haven't thought that far ahead."

"My wife and I would be happy to have you."

"I'll keep that in mind. Thank you."

He sighed, dropping his hand from her shoulder. "I'm getting you a cup of strong coffee. You need it."

"But I don't drink coffee."

"How could you be in love with Joe Scarlatti and not drink coffee?" He managed a soft laugh, laced with concern for his wounded friend. "I always told him the woman who'd get him would surprise the hell out of everyone, including him. You break the molds, Rowena Willow. Give me five minutes. If I can find you tea, I'll do it. Otherwise it's coffee."

She made herself meet his eyes. They were so dark, so filled with pain for a fellow policeman, a friend. "Thank you."

"Yeah."

A moment later Sofia Scarlatti joined her. "He'll be fine, my Joe. I've seen him in lots worse shape."

"What about his sight?" Rowena asked softly.

She patted Rowena's hand. "We'll just have to wait and see."

Hank returned with a cup of coffee that tasted surprisingly good to Rowena. "You ready to head out?" he asked.

She shook her head. "I'd like to see Joe one more time."

"I'll be out here."

The doctors and nurses had retreated for the time being, and Joe was dozing in his dimly lit room. Rowena leaned over him and realized she was crying only when she saw her tears glistening on his cheek. His eyes were bandaged, his wounded arm, his burns treated. He wasn't in danger of dying. He *would* recover.

But would he see again?

He stirred, and found her hand, squeezed it gently. "You still here?"

"Always."

"I smell coffee. Someone with you?"

"No, it's mine. Hank brought me a cup."

"Life is full of surprises," he said, startling her with his undampered humor.

"I don't know, it tastes all right to me, not that I'd know the difference. Maybe the smoke killed my taste buds."

"You're okay?"

"I'm fine. You?"

He stroked the top of her hand with his thumb. "Go on and get some rest, Rowena. You don't need to stick around."

"I can't leave. Joe, I owe you so much—"

"You don't owe me anything," he said sharply, cutting her off. He dropped her hand. "I was just doing my job."

Her one consolation was that he couldn't see the hurt that washed over her. But she knew what he was doing. He was pushing her away because he was injured, blinded, and his future was uncertain. He didn't want to burden her.

It wasn't going to work.

SHE ENDED UP staying in Joe's apartment above Mario's Bar & Grill because his cousin insisted it was what Joe would want if he were in any frame of mind to articulate what he wanted. As it was, Joe said he thought Rowena should stay with a friend or get a room at a hotel, charge her insurance company.

"Ignore him," was Mario's advice.

Hank Ryan and his wife had her over for dinner. Sofia Scarlatti loaded up the refrigerator and cupboards and checked her grandson's apartment for "vermin," pronouncing it habitable after a close inspection. Mario prepared her low-fat eggplant parmesan and low-fat bean chili and bought a case of mineral water to keep on hand.

Her life was changing, had changed, and although so much of that change was out of her control, Rowena was surprised and delighted. And amazed at how good it felt to rely on other people, not just herself.

Her own friends came to her assistance without prodding and provided her with technical and personal support in salvaging, repairing and restoring her office, damaged by smoke and water. The fire itself hadn't got that far. She would be back in business soon.

But where? And under what circumstances?

Right now, however, for once, she wasn't preoccupied with the future.

She spent as much time as she could every day with Joe, staying until he or the doctors kicked her out. He was clearly trying to keep his distance. She didn't press, but they found themselves talking about their lives, their hopes, their regrets. They exchanged funny stories, and some sad ones.

They became friends.

Away from the hospital, Rowena discovered that Joe Scarlatti led a life filled with people. She enjoyed the coziness of his apartment, the constant presence of family, friends, perfect strangers. She got to know his neighborhood. And she realized that she couldn't go back to her old life, to its relative isolation. Instead, she found that she wanted things she'd long thought she was too different, too odd, to have—a little house, a garden, a yard. She wanted to give parties.

She wanted to have children.

She wanted to have a husband.

Joe Scarlatti had changed her perspective on her life and her future. Loving him had changed *her*.

On a cool, bright morning a week after their ordeal with Eliot Tyhurst, she was nursing a pot of tea and going over a report for a client at what she'd come to know as Joe's booth at Mario's Bar & Grill.

Mario burst out of the kitchen. "The hospital just called. Joe's getting sprung today, Row." He always called her Row now. "He can see."

JOE GRINNED when Rowena came into his room. "Aren't you a sight for sore eyes."

He meant it. He had never seen her look so alive and beautiful. After two weeks of darkness, he drank in the sight of her. Her eyes were as blue as the California sky. Her gleaming spun-gold hair hung down her back in a thick French braid. And she had on jeans. Rowena Willow in jeans. It was a sight to see.

He couldn't stop smiling.

"I've come to take you home," she said, and tears sprang into her eyes. "I'm so glad, Joe…I couldn't…if I'd been responsible for your losing your sight…"

He touched her cheek, gently brushed away a tear with his knuckle. "You wouldn't have been responsible."

She held her breath. "I never thought I'd hear those words from you, Joe Scarlatti."

"I know it. I've had a lot of time to think these past few days in a way I haven't let myself think in months. You weren't responsible for what happened to me any more—" for a moment, he choked on his words "—any more than I was responsible for Matt's death. I miss the crazy bastard—I guess I always will. But it wasn't my fault."

Rowena smiled through her tears and kissed him about a quarter-inch from his right eye. "You look terrific."

Desire shot through him, hot and electric. If she'd kissed him on the mouth, he'd have hauled her down onto his hospital bed and made love to her. As it was, it was all he could do to finish buttoning his shirt. He already had on his jeans. All he had to do now was put on his sneakers and be gone.

"So," he said, "are we taking a bus back?"

"Nope."

"You're driving?"

"Uh-huh. You're in for a surprise, Sergeant Scarlatti."

He suspected this wouldn't be an uncommon event. But he was sure about one important thing—how he felt about her. "You don't own a car."

"I've got your truck." And she reached into her jeans pocket and withdrew his keys, dangling them in front of him.

"You're going to drive my truck—"

She grinned at him. "I've *been* driving it."

"Mario gave you the keys?"

She nodded without a hint of guilt. Her eyes were

sparkling the way Joe had imagined them for the past week.

"What else haven't you told me?" he asked.

"Well, your grandmother has started to teach me how to knit and crochet and says she's going to teach me how to make lasagna, but I don't know—she puts sausage in her lasagna. And Mario taught me how to pour beer. I helped Hank and his wife put up a new swing set for his kids—you should see the thing, it's even got a tent." She licked her lips. "And I've been staying at your apartment."

He just stared at her. She seemed very pleased with herself. Smug, even. Like she'd outwitted him just as she had that very first day when she'd spotted him out on her street. It seemed so damned long ago. What had his life been like before Rowena Willow came into it?

"My apartment," he repeated.

"Yep. I'd have told you except I thought picturing me sleeping alone in your bed might inhibit your recovery."

She was out of the room and into the corridor before he could grab her.

"By the way," she told him on their way out to the parking lot, "I had the oil in your truck changed. It needed it."

"You *had* it changed?"

She glanced sideways at him. "I don't do oil, Sergeant."

"I'll remember that."

"I did vacuum and clean the interior. I found an old doughnut under the seat. I called the Smithsonian to see if they were interested—"

"Very funny. I hope you didn't touch any of my guns."

She shook her head. "Guns make me nervous."

She fell silent and Joe reached out to touch her arm.

"I was scared," she said suddenly, in a quiet voice. "When Tyhurst pulled out that gun and tied me up..."

"Should you have been anything else but scared?"

"I don't know. Sometimes I think I was pretty cowardly, complying with him the way I did."

"Rowena, if you hadn't done as he asked, he would have shot you."

They headed out into the bright day, and Joe inhaled the cool air, relishing his freedom. The doctors had given his eyes a clean bill of health. Told him to take it easy for a few days.

"Were you scared?" she asked as they crossed the parking lot.

"Yeah. Scared and madder than hell. I thought the bastard had killed you." He hesitated, then decided he might as well tell her the rest of it. "I didn't care what happened to me. I saw those cats and knew he was there, then heard you scream—it was all I could do not to barrel up the stairs and have at him. But I kept my cool."

"Your training took over," Rowena said. "Your instincts. You trusted yourself."

He shrugged. "I wasn't thinking about that. I was just thinking about wringing Tyhurst's neck. He figured he'd be as good with a gun as he is with a con, but he wasn't. I took him by surprise—or at least enough by surprise that he only got off that one shot." Joe's eyes darkened suddenly. "I had him hanging over the stairs, Rowena. I could have flipped him over the side, killed him."

"You're not an Eliot Tyhurst," Rowena said.

"No, I'm not." He shook off his gloom and grinned at her. "A cop 'til the bitter end, Rowena. That's what I am."

His truck was cleaner than he'd seen it in months, and impeccably parked between two white lines. "What'd you do, get out a ruler and *measure?*"

"Parking crooked is so discourteous in tight quarters like this."

Discourteous? Joe climbed in the front seat and waited while she climbed in behind the wheel, her long braid flopped down her front. "You do that when you're self-conscious, you know—talk in that prim way. I've had a week just of listening to you, without the distraction of seeing you. I've noticed."

She scowled. "I am who I am."

"Yeah. You are. It's been fun to figure out just who you are."

"And you have that figured out?"

"Working on it."

She used more gas than he would have to start the engine. He went to warn her about how fickle reverse could be, but she seemed to know already and jammed the gearshift down hard, so it wouldn't jump out, just as he would have. He watched her maneuver the finicky old truck out of the parking space and out to the street.

"Not bad," he said.

"It can be exasperating on the hills. I almost rolled into a car a few times when I had to keep stopping and going. An automatic transmission is definitely easier in San Francisco, in my opinion. Have you ever considered trading this thing in?"

"No."

She smiled. "You didn't even hesitate. Well, I've found I enjoy driving. I might have to invest in my own car."

On that first day when he'd rung her doorbell, Joe would have asked her why someone who didn't go anywhere needed a car. But in their long talks over the past week, he had heard in her a pent-up longing to go, to do, to see. Rowena Willow had a zest for adventure he'd never have guessed possible when he'd watched her arrive in her tower sunroom just after five every afternoon.

He noticed she wasn't taking the most direct route back to Mario's Bar & Grill. Maybe she didn't know it. "Rowena, where are we going?"

"Telegraph Hill," she said.

"Why?"

"I want—I need to show you something."

When they came to her quiet, exclusive street, Joe saw nothing unusual, nothing changed. The fire damage was restricted to the interior. From the outside, Rowena Willow's little castle looked as weird as ever.

Except there *was* a group of people milling about outside. About a half-dozen. They were well dressed, gesturing and talking excitedly.

"Looks like a committee meeting," Joe said.

"It is. Before I tell you about it, however, I need to get a few things straight with you."

"Okay."

She'd double-parked in front of her house. Joe didn't point out that that was more "discourteous" than being a little crooked within a parking space.

"First of all," she said, still gripping the wheel with both hands, "you weren't just 'doing your job' last week with Tyhurst. If you will recall, you weren't on duty. You were—and are—still on leave of absence from the department. Our association was unofficial."

She glanced at him, apparently to see if he had any comment, and he said, "Are those my jeans you're wearing?"

He almost got a smile. "You're impossible, you know that? I'm trying to have a serious conversation. Will you allow that you weren't just doing your job?"

"I'm a cop, Rowena. It's who I am."

"Yes, I know that." She pursed her lips. "But you don't—um—make love to all the citizens of San Francisco, do you?"

A corner of his mouth twitched. "Not all."

She sighed, exercising supreme patience. "You stayed in my house with me. After you were hurt, I stayed at your apartment."

"Without my knowledge," he observed. "You know, I think those *are* my jeans."

This time she just ignored him. "Your family and friends took me under their wing. I've visited you every day. I've been driving your truck all around town." She looked over at him, her eyes huge and luminous. "I'm wearing your jeans."

"Dammit, I knew they were mine!"

"I think I have longer legs than you do."

Joe didn't know why he didn't just drag her out of the truck and cart her upstairs to one of Aunt Adelaide's strange rooms.

"And I certainly have a smaller waist," she said.

Hell, he'd even make love to her in with the critters.

"My point is," she went on crisply, "that you can't just push me out of your life when bad things happen."

Joe grew serious. "Rowena, falling for a man like me is dangerous."

"I'm not falling for a man like you. I'm falling for *you*. Have fallen, I should say. Your profession carries with it certain risks. I accept that. Life's a risky business. And retreating from it doesn't lessen the risks. I was just sitting in my office minding my own business when something about Eliot Tyhurst's financial activities caught my eye. Look how dangerous that proved to be."

Joe digested her words, raking a hand through his hair and staring out at the people on the sidewalk. One was pointing to Rowena's tower room. "Tell me about the committee," he said.

She hesitated. He knew that what she'd just told him, how she'd just exposed herself, hadn't been easy for her. He understood, even if he hadn't yet acknowledged it to her.

"They're from the historical society. I contacted them a few days ago. It turns out they've had their eye on the Willow house for a long time—I had no idea. When I told them that Aunt Adelaide had made very few changes from Cedric's day, and I very few changes from her day, they were ecstatic."

Joe turned in time to see her run her tongue along the bottom of her lip, then bite down with her top teeth. She still had the steering wheel in her grip.

She went on, "But when I told them I would consider donating the house and its entire contents to them, they were speechless."

"So am I," Joe said.

She smiled at him. "You're never speechless, Sergeant Scarlatti."

"It's a valuable piece of property. The fire damage was confined to the third floor. You'd be giving up a fortune."

"I make a good living doing what I do," she said. "And I want to be free. I want my own house, my own furnishings, my own garden."

"You won't keep anything?"

"Just a few personal things Aunt Adelaide gave me, and any Willow family pictures and papers. Not Cedric's portrait, though." She nodded to the house her great-grandfather had built. "It belongs here."

"I see," Joe said.

"I just wanted you to know."

She pried one hand loose from the wheel, turned the key in the ignition and started back down Telegraph Hill.

For a long time Joe didn't say anything. He had to process what Rowena had just done.

Finally, he said, "You're not even keeping one dead bird?"

"Not one."

"Good. I did kind of like the owl in the library, but I'd probably get the heebie-jeebies having a beady-eyed thing like that hanging around my place."

"*Your* place?"

"Our place, then."

"Scarlatti—"

"There is one thing I'm going to arm-wrestle the historical society for, though—Sir Lancelot in the front hall. I figure the only way I'm going to be a valiant prince is to have a suit of armor kicking around for the right occasion."

"Aunt Adelaide purchased it." She was going along with him, he could tell, showing him she understood what he was trying to say. "I suppose I could speak to the committee."

"I figure it can be payment for my having saved your ass."

"Mine! I saved yours! You'd have been burned alive if I hadn't got you down that fire escape."

"Naw, I'd have found my way out. You, on the other hand, would never have gotten out of there if I hadn't freed your wrists."

"No way. If you'd have managed blind, I'd have managed bound."

"You're stubborn, Rowena," he said, enjoying himself, "and you're wrong."

"I'm not wrong."

He grinned at her. "Quite the shrinking violet, aren't you? Well, I warn you, I'm not one to back down from a good fight. I'm not easy to live with."

"Neither am I," she said.

"Oh, I already know that."

"You'll always be this honest?"

"Always."

"We're not a disaster together, Joe, are we?"

"Depends on your point of view, I guess. From mine, no, we're far, far from a disaster together. What about yours?"

She smiled. "No."

He sat back. "Great. Now, do I get the armor?"

Epilogue

JOE GOT the armor.

The historical society considered it a small price to pay for a valuable historic house on Telegraph Hill, built by one of San Francisco's true rich eccentrics. He tried setting it up in Mario's, but his cousin came after him with a carving knife and Joe carted it upstairs to his apartment.

Rowena had been out looking at office space in a real office building. When she came back, she found Joe kneeling over the damned thing. "It won't fit in here standing upright," he said, not looking at her. "Ceilings are too low. Guess we're going to have to get busy finding a place of our own."

"Your grandmother will be thrilled. She's been clipping ads."

Finally, he looked at her. And his jaw, literally, dropped. She realized he was as close to speechless as he probably would ever get. "Rowena," he managed to say.

She ran both hands through her hair, still getting used to its new length. "I stopped by a hair salon on impulse. Do you know, I'd never been to one? It was quite an experience. I thought they were going to throw me out because I didn't have an appointment, but—"

"But once they saw your hair, they couldn't let you out of there."

"I told them to take off a good eighteen inches."

Joe climbed to his feet, never taking his eyes from her.

She liked the feel of her freshly cut hair. It was still long—below her shoulders—but she relished its bounce, its lightness. She felt free.

He was in front of her now, touching it. "It's beautiful."

She smiled. "I might never wear it up again."

ONLY DAYS LATER—when they had a house all picked out and Mario already had a couple hundred meatballs in the freezer for their wedding—did Joe discover the little surprise Rowena had in store for him when he was sorting through a bunch of junk in his bedroom closet.

He damned well almost screamed. Him, a tough cop. He'd returned to the force a week ago, ending his self-imposed leave of absence. It felt good to be back. Still, who the hell wouldn't be shocked by a pair of beady eyes staring from inside a dark closet?

"*Rowena!*"

She materialized behind him. "Oh, I see you've found Arnold."

"Arnold? It's a goddamned dead bird!"

"It was my great-grandfather's favorite."

Joe stepped back so the overhead light could angle in and he could see better. Yep, it was the stuffed owl from the library. He looked around at Rowena, all gorgeous from her haircut, as free and loose as he had ever imagined her. His heart seemed ready to burst with loving her. How had he survived those horrible six months on leave, before he'd met her? He didn't think he'd ever felt this alive.

And something became clear to him now, with the damned stuffed owl staring down at him, that hadn't been clear before.

"You know something, Ms. Willow?"

"I know a lot of things, Sergeant Scarlatti."

"Yeah, you're an eccentric genius. You know a hell of a lot of things. Did you know that you didn't rescue me?"

"Yes, I did."

He shook his head. "Nope." He wrapped her in his arms and pulled her close. "We rescued each other."

A WISH...AND A KISS

by Margaret St. George

Chapter One

"I have come to do your bidding, mistress."

"Great," Chelsey said, looking up from the long wooden table with a distracted smile. She had been so absorbed in cleaning a tarnished silver cup lamp she hadn't heard anyone enter the workroom. "I'm Dr. Chelsey Mallon, assistant dean of archaeology. But I guess the personnel office must have told you who I was and where to find me."

The rag with which she tried to clean her hands only deposited more grime on them. Chelsey made a face and shrugged.

"Guess we'll save a handshake for later." She examined the only applicant who had shown up for what had to be the worst summer job on campus—helping her inventory a huge building crammed with forty years' worth of archaeological artifacts, most of which had been forgotten by whichever professor had collected them.

The one and only applicant was about her age, Chelsey guessed, thirtyish, which wasn't surprising with so many older students returning to college. He wore the same uniform as younger students: running shoes, faded jeans and a gray sweatshirt with the sleeves cut off. Straight dark hair fell to his shoulders, longer than was fashionable, but it softened the angles of his roughly hewn face.

The first thing Chelsey noticed, though, was how great-looking he was. In fact, ''great-looking'' didn't do him justice. This man was drop-dead handsome. At least he was if you were the type of woman who was attracted to a brooding, smoldering, keep-your-distance type of guy.

Chelsey gazed into his face, concentrating, and tried to recall if she had ever observed eyes of that particular, almost translucent, shade of blue green, or eyes as deeply fringed with curling black lashes.

When she realized she was staring, she cleared her throat with a self-conscious sound, then ran her hands down the thighs of her work jeans, leaving black streaks across the faded denim.

''Okay, here's the program,'' she said. He stood before her, muscled arms crossed over his chest, studying her with an unblinking expression that contained the faintest hint of hostility. She didn't blame him. The job she was about to offer expected too much and paid too little.

''There's no way we're going to finish inventorying this building before the fall semester begins. We'll accomplish a miracle if we complete one floor.'' She glanced around the cavernous workroom, at the rows and racks of shelves and drawers receding into the afternoon shadows. The task ahead was daunting. There were half a dozen work-rooms as large as this one, plus a rabbit warren of storage rooms stuffed to the rafters with boxes and cartons containing heaven only knew what. And the university had agreed to give her only one assistant.

''Most of this stuff has been here so long that no one remembers what it is. The good news is we might uncover a surprise or two, maybe a treasure. Archaeologically speaking, of course.''

He didn't say a word; he just watched her and listened. In fact, Chelsey didn't even notice him blink. His intense blue-green eyes bored into her as if he had heard the rumors about her and believed every slanderous word. The only movement he made was the small motion of rubbing a fold of his sweatshirt between his thumb and forefinger.

"For instance," she continued, irritated that lately she felt driven to fill any conversational silence, "you see this little cup lamp? This is the only example I've ever seen made out of silver. I discovered it almost by accident inside an unlabeled drawer over there on..."

Chelsey recognized boredom when she saw it. The man standing before her was utterly indifferent to the unusual silver cup lamp.

"Never mind," she said finally, tucking a strand of ginger-colored hair into the blue bandanna she wore against the dust that seemed as much a part of Wickem Hall as the wooden floors and tiers of shelving. "The hours are long and the pay is lousy. But the job is yours if you want it."

"I am yours to command, oh learned mistress." Bending at the waist, he leaned into a bow. Actually it was more of a salaam as he touched his fingertips to waist, chest and forehead, ending with a flourish.

It was a cute bit, the stuff about being here to do her bidding, being hers to command, except the routine didn't quite work. Cutesy didn't suit him. He was more gothic.

"I assume that means you accept the job," Chelsey said after a minute. "So, what's your name?"

"I am your genie, Mistress Mallon. You may address me however you prefer." His second deep bow was the tiniest bit mocking, with a touch of irony in the motions, but he performed the salaam with grace and finesse.

Still, Chelsey decided he was just too ruggedly masculine to pull off this kind of silliness. Certainly she wasn't the right type to play along and keep the joke going. When men turned cute on her, Chelsey turned tail. She found herself tongue-tied, annoyed and desperate to escape.

"Seriously," she said in a level voice, "what's your name?"

"You wish to know my Christian name?"

Oh, brother. Maybe this I'm-your-genie/I'm-yours-to-command routine had coeds eating out of his palm, but Chelsey was rapidly finding it tiresome. Not for the first time, she decided there must be a cosmic rule that stated really good-looking guys had to be jerks.

"I'm afraid I don't have much patience for games," she said sharply, not bothering to disguise her irritation. "Unless there's some reason for keeping your name secret...."

There was something about really good-looking men with perfect bodies that brought out the worst in her. She turned brisk and irritable, impatient and critical.

"My name is not a secret." His voice startled her, but it fit the rest of him—attractive, deeply pitched and taut with annoyance. "No one has asked my name in a very long time."

"Probably not since you left the campus personnel office about an hour ago, right?"

"Not in two centuries."

Chelsey shook her head and rolled her eyes. "Look, a dozen experts couldn't finish this inventory if they had a year to do it. You and I have this summer, that's all. The point I hope I'm making is that we don't have time to waste on foolishness."

She gave him her famous do-I-make-myself-clear look, polite but dripping ice.

"Alexandre Duport." The name emerged grudgingly, as if Chelsey had dragged forth a deep, dark secret.

"That wasn't too painful, was it?" Carefully, she packed the pottery cup lamps back into the drawer she had cleaned and freshly labeled. "Do I detect a faint accent?"

Her instinct was to guess France, but his accent wasn't quite French. Close, but…

She closed her eyes to focus on the nuances of his pronunciation, and when she opened them again, she found him standing directly in front of her worktable, studying her with those intense blue-green eyes. For a moment Chelsey held his gaze, unaccountably feeling her heartbeat accelerate. She wondered if Alexandre Duport knew how damned sexy he was when he wasn't acting cutesy. What was she thinking? Of course he knew.

"Never mind the accent," Chelsey said when it became obvious that her new assistant balked at personal questions. Next to him, Marcel Marceau was a chatterbox. But that was okay. She wasn't looking for a personal relationship. All she wanted was an assistant.

She capped the jar of silver polish and returned it to the supply box before she wrapped the little silver cup lamp in chamois cloth. The artifact, now polished to a gleaming finish, had blown her away with its beauty. It seemed a shame to place such an amazing find in a drawer with pottery lamps where it might remain forgotten for another forty years.

"You may leave the lamp here or take it with you. It is no longer important," Alexandre Duport said. Leaning forward, he ran his palm across the worktable as if admiring the smooth touch of old wood.

"I beg your pardon?" Chelsey's voice turned shrill and suspicious. Was he suggesting that she steal the cup lamp?

"The lamp belongs to all and to none. It will vanish after your third wish."

"After my— Oh, I get it. We're back to the genie thing." Alexandre must have noticed her polishing the silver cup lamp when he entered the workroom and that's where the genie business originated. "The lamp is university property—it stays here," she said sharply, placing the chamois cloth in the drawer with the other cup lamps.

She looked behind her for her purse, stalling a little. Then came the moment of truth, the moment that in some way altered and defined all her relationships with men, even a relationship as tenuous as this one was and would remain.

"Alex—may I call you Alex?—would you do me a favor and bring me my cane? I believe I left it over there, near the south door."

Bending, Chelsey reached for her briefcase, not waiting to observe the startled look she knew would cross his face. By now the sequence of reactions was well-known to her.

First he would look surprised. He might even murmur, "I hadn't realized…" Then he would feel a little embarrassed. After he saw her walk with the cane, he'd feel compelled make some remark, some acknowledgment that he wasn't ignoring her circumstance. Maybe he would comment on the cane itself, ask what wood it was made from or something inane like that. Or maybe he would flatter her, try to persuade her that she looked chic carrying a walking stick.

"Your cane, Mistress Mallon."

This time it was Chelsey who was startled. She hadn't heard him walk across the wooden floor, didn't think enough time had passed in any case. But he stood beside her with her cane in his hand.

"Thank you." Briefly she met his gaze, brought up

short when she realized he didn't display a flicker of curiosity. Which only made her want to explain.

"I had polio as a child," she said in a casual voice as she adjusted her purse strap over her shoulder. "One leg is about two inches shorter than the other. I wear special shoes, so usually it's not a problem." After collecting her notebook, she walked toward the door. Because she knew he was watching, she felt acutely self-conscious. "Unless I'm especially tired, I don't really need the cane." After waving Alex through the door, she flipped off the lights and stepped into the hallway. "But on days like today— when I've climbed up and down a dozen flights of stairs— it's nice to have it." Her calf muscles were on fire and aching.

"I know."

She stopped and looked at him, abruptly aware of how tall he was. Chelsey was five foot nine in her stocking feet, but Alex Duport stood a full head taller than she. "You know?"

"I know everything about you."

"Is that right?" She stared at him. "Whom did you speak to in personnel? And exactly what did he tell you?" Then he knew about last summer and the rumors, she thought. A rush of paranoia brought a bitter taste to her mouth, and she closed her eyes and swallowed.

When she opened her eyes again, she gasped and her muscles jumped.

It was the damnedest thing. They were standing in front of Wickem Hall—but Chelsey had no memory of walking down two flights of stairs, crossing the tiled lobby or exiting the building. She dropped her briefcase and threw out a hand to steady herself, grabbing Alex's arm and looking around with wide, startled eyes.

Nothing else seemed out of the ordinary. From where

she stood at the side entrance, Chelsey could see groups of summer-session students strolling along the walkways between buildings or sitting on the grass, chatting together or reading. No one glanced in their direction.

Alex lifted his face to the late-afternoon sun. "The warmth of sunshine," he murmured softly. "The scent of grass and leaves and summer air. No feat of memory or imagination can reproduce this, these scents or—" He noticed her stricken expression and frowned. "Are you well, mistress?"

Immediately Chelsey snatched her hand away from the hard muscles rising on his warm bare arm. "This is really weird. I don't remember… This is so…"

Never in her life had Chelsey Mallon experienced a blackout, and it was hard to accept that she had done so now. But the memory of walking through Wickem Hall and exiting the door was simply…not there. It was as if she had closed the workroom door, turned around and was instantly outside, standing on the flagstone floor of the west terrace.

"Did I lock the building?" she wondered, staring back at the door and striving to remember. She had no memory of that, either.

"If you wish the building locked, mistress, then it is locked."

"Look, knock off that genie crap and stop calling me mistress." Instantly she felt mean-spirited for taking out her confusion on him. She drew a deep breath. "I'm sorry," she said in a softer voice. "I've had some problems and…well, I've got a lot on my mind. I'm in no mood for games. The genie thing was cute in the beginning, but you're overdoing it. I've tried to tell you nicely, now I'm telling you bluntly. Stop acting like a genie, okay?"

The humorless smile twisting his lips contained an edge of bitterness that Chelsey didn't attempt to understand. "Believe me, Mistress Mallon, if I could, I would."

"Just do it," Chelsey said between her teeth. "And don't call me Mistress Mallon. Mistress Mallon sounds like something you'd name a dominatrix or whatever they call those women who dress up in leather and chains and slap men around. Call me doctor or professor or call me Chelsey if you like. But no more mistress, okay?" She leaned on her cane for a moment, steadying herself then descended the terrace steps onto the walkway that led across campus. "Bye. See you Monday morning at eight o'clock sharp," she called over her shoulder.

She hadn't taken three steps before Alex Duport appeared beside her. "Would you like me to carry your briefcase?"

His dark hair was sleek and shiny in the afternoon sunlight. It swung across his shoulders when he looked down at her. Now that Chelsey saw him in bright light instead of the dusty gloom of the workroom, she noticed his jeans fit like a glove and the gray sleeveless sweatshirt molded his heavy chest and upper-arm muscles. More than one coed watched him pass with a predatory gleam in her eye.

"Thank you, but I doubt we're going in the same direction."

His dark eyebrows slashed together in a frown. "I don't know how to interpret much of what you say. It's annoying."

Chelsey stopped dead to level an incredulous stare. "Excuse me? *I'm* annoying?"

"It should be obvious that I must go where you go. I must remain within the sound of your voice. I have no choice—that is the rule."

"What the hell are you talking about?"

"You summoned me, oh confusing mistress." The words were mild enough, but his blue-green eyes glittered like winter ice. "But you spoke for a time as if you wished me to *choose* to serve you. You made it plain—at least, I think you made it plain—that you wish the contents of Wickem Hall inventoried, but you suggest the task cannot be accomplished. Very confusing. You pry into my past but seem furious that I know of yours."

"All I did was ask your name, for heaven's sake!"

He raked his fingers through his hair, then spread his hands in frustration. "Finally you walk away with a word of farewell as if our business is concluded and seem surprised when I follow after you. Yet you have not stated your wishes, nor have I yet presented the coins!"

A few students cast curious glances in their direction as they squared off and faced each other on the sidewalk, both speaking in voices pitched louder than normal. Chelsey realized they were in fact creating a small, angry scene. Ordinarily, she would have crawled over lava rather than embroil herself in a public confrontation. But this situation was far from ordinary.

As she listened to the sincerity beneath his tone, a dawning suspicion gripped Chelsey's thoughts. She deliberately placed her hand on Alex's arm and patted him in what she hoped was a calming gesture. She drew a breath and gazed into his eyes. Did one just come right out and inquire if a person was seeing a therapist?

Actually, there was no doubt in her mind that Alex Duport was seriously disturbed. The only surprise was that she hadn't identified the problem earlier. She was grateful he believed he was a genie instead of Charles Manson or Jeffrey Dahmer. Better to serve someone than carve them into fish food.

"I'm sorry I didn't understand sooner," she said, patting his arm. From the corner of her eye she searched the quad for a campus policeman. "Alex, what is your doctor's name?"

He glared down at her. "What?"

"Maybe you think of him as the genie master. The head genie." She gave him a bright, encouraging smile. "The genie master will want to know if you served anyone today. Don't you think we should phone him and tell him how well you did?"

Alex pulled back from her, staring at her as though it was Chelsey who was deranged. Chelsey attempted a different approach. "Do you know your address? I think you should go home now, Alex. Don't you? I'm sure someone is getting very worried about how long you've been gone."

"You think I'm insane." Incredulity thickened his voice "You don't believe I am who I say I am. You think I'm crazy."

"Not at all." Where the hell were the campus police? She didn't really believe Alex was dangerous, but when it came right down to it, she didn't know diddly about him. It seemed prudent to humor him. Chelsey patted his arm and arranged a reassuring smile on her lips. "Of course I believe you're a genie. I was just testing to see if *you* believed it."

He lifted her hand off his arm and moved backward a step before he spread his arms in a frustrated gesture. "What do I have to do to prove to you that I'm a genie?"

A couple of frat boys walked around them, swinging tennis racquets at their sides. They grinned and gave Alex a thumbs-up. "Hey, baby, we can vouch for him. The guy's definitely a genie. He can show you some magic that you won't believe. Right, dude?" They fell against each other, laughing.

"Fun-ny," Chelsey muttered, glaring at them.

If Alex noticed the frat boys or heard their comments, he gave no sign. He continued to glare at Chelsey. "I appeared before your eyes when you summoned me by rubbing the silver lamp. Your cane materialized in my hand when you requested it. To spare your leg I moved you from the workroom outside to the terrace in the blink of an eye. Your inventory is finished." Knots rose along his jawline when he clenched his teeth. "What else must I do to convince you, oh stubborn mistress?"

Chelsey froze. Her mind raced backward.

She had indeed rubbed the little silver cup lamp—had, in fact, been concentrating so hard on polishing it to a high gloss that Alex could very well have materialized in front of her without her being aware—

She couldn't believe she was actually thinking this!

But she recalled noting at the time that she had not heard him walk to the door to get her cane. And he'd handed it to her almost instantly.

Then there was the craziness of turning around from the door of the workroom and discovering she was standing on the flagstone terrace in front of Wickem Hall.

"No, I don't believe this," she whispered, staring up at him with eyes the size of drachmas. She tried to swallow but her throat was too dry. "I'm an educated woman. I hold a doctorate. I've traveled. I've studied history. I don't believe in genies."

"You will."

Chelsey's thoughts felt like physical objects, bouncing off the inside of her skull. "Uh, Alex. You said—at least, I thought you said—that the inventory was finished." It couldn't be. That wasn't possible. Not even remotely. Not in a million years. She was allowing her imagination to run away with her, allowing a couple of peculiar unexplained incidents to bend her mind. "Uh, what did you mean by that?"

He nodded impatiently toward Wickem Hall behind her. "Every item in every room is described in detail as to its location and the known history of the item."

Chelsey turned toward the building and leaned on her cane. "Wickem Hall has five stories and two basement levels."

"Each item is cross-referenced as to date of expedition, site of expedition, leader of the expedition, type of artifact and the known age of the artifact. Is that sufficient?"

Chelsey turned her head and looked him squarely in the eyes. "What you're claiming is absolutely impossible," she stated in a low, firm voice. "To accomplish what you just described would require a team of at least two dozen people working ten hours a day every day for at least three years. I'm not convinced it could be done even then." They held each other's gaze as students hurried around them on the sidewalk, heading for dorm lines or local eateries. "Where are the inventory lists?"

"Twenty-eight notebooks are lying on your worktable."

There was a simple way to conquer the crazy thoughts buzzing around her head: she turned on her heel and started walking back toward Wickem Hall. Part of her mind reared back in astonishment that she actually meant to waste her time verifying Alex's ridiculous claim.

"You wait here," she called to him. She didn't want to find herself alone in an empty building with a muscle-bound stranger who had just been proven a certifiable nut case.

"I must remain within the sound of your voice. That is the rule."

"Really? And just who makes the genie rules?" Chelsey asked, turning back to him. "I'd really like to know the head genie's name, Alex."

She gasped and sucked in a hard deep breath.

They were no longer on the sidewalk beyond the Wickem Hall terrace. They were inside Chelsey's workroom on the third floor.

And the neon lights above her long worktable shone down on twenty-eight neatly stacked and labeled notebooks.

Chelsey stared at the notebooks and listened to her heart slam against her rib cage. When she thought she could speak, she lifted a bone-white face to Alex. "I don't believe this," she said in a husky whisper. "We're inside Wickem Hall, aren't we? I thought so. You teleported us here. Or whatever it is you call bipping people around in time and space. But you did this, didn't you? You used some kind of magic to bring us here."

The suggestion of a smile hovered at the corners of his lips. He managed not to look smug, but Chelsey could see it was a struggle.

"My God! I'm not dreaming this…?"

"No, mistress."

Dust tickled her nose. The wooden floor was solid beneath her feet. She knew this room as well as she knew her name. This experience was real. "And those are the notebooks you told me about. The inventory. Right? You inventoried and cross-referenced every item on five floors and the two basement levels." Reaching a shaking hand, she opened one of the notebooks. It was everything Alex had claimed. In fact, he had neglected to mention the illustrations. Which were breathtaking. "And you did this in about, oh, sixty seconds, maybe."

"Yes, mistress."

"I see," Chelsey murmured, feeling her eyes start to

cross. The inventory that couldn't be done was finished. In fabulous detail. A genie had done it.

"Nice job," she whispered.

Then she fainted dead away, falling backward across a damask-covered chaise lounge that hadn't been there a split second before.

Chapter Two

Alex transported the chaise lounge and Chelsey Mallon to her rented house on Pleasant Avenue. The house was small and modestly furnished, but that would change. She would spend her first wish to accumulate great wealth; they all did. A month from now Chelsey Mallon would be living in a palatial mansion staffed by a half-dozen servants.

He sipped a glass of wine and glanced at her. Unconscious, she didn't look as stubborn or feisty, not as self-absorbed with her own selfish world. At this moment she looked innocent and childlike. He could almost believe this mistress would be different.

But he had fallen into that trap before. By now he knew better than to expect anything but the worst from human nature. Like all the others, Chelsey Mallon would be greedy, selfish, ambitious. She would wish for wealth, power, maybe revenge.

It didn't matter anymore. He no longer took much interest in his masters or mistresses, didn't care if they sensed his indifference or contempt. He deeply resented pandering to the worst in human nature, but his resentment was seldom noticed. His masters were too absorbed in gloating over their newfound riches.

Rolling the wine on his tongue and inhaling the fragrance of a lilac he had plucked from the bush outside the door, he examined the items on the mantelpiece while he waited for her to regain consciousness.

Prominently featured was a family photograph taken a week before the avalanche that killed her parents. The photograph was flanked by pottery shards that were mementos of her first archaeological dig. The items interested him only to the extent that he wondered if Chelsey Mallon understood how fortunate she was to be surrounded by reality and fresh memories, by life with all its varying textures and richness. Nothing he could give her would equal what she already had.

When the energy changed in the room, he knew she was awake. Turning, he watched as she swung her feet off the chaise lounge and stumbled to her own faded plaid sofa, staring at the chaise as if it might attack her. As the chaise had served its purpose, he dispensed with it. The small room was crowded enough.

She screamed and collapsed backward on the sofa. "Don't *do* that!"

"Don't do what?" he asked, frowning. She was the most contrary mistress he had encountered in over two centuries.

"That silent magic stuff! If you're going to do magic tricks, at least give me some warning. Clap your hands or point a finger or wink or say 'shazam.' But do or say something so I'll have a second to prepare myself!"

"As you wish, mistress." Holding his wineglass to one side, he performed a deep, showy salaam. As always, he resented the gesture of servitude demanded by his role. "May I serve you a glass of malmsey?" She still looked white and shaken.

In times past, no one had fainted at his appearance or

made him prove his identity. Previous masters and mistresses had accepted him at once and proceeded immediately to the wishes. On the other hand, the aggravation of dealing with Chelsey Mallon's disbelief was balanced by the extra time in the reality plane.

Chelsey flattened her shaking palms on the thighs of her jeans and frowned. "You look real," she said slowly. "Are you real? Or am I imagining you?" A distracted look appeared in her eyes, and Alex wasn't certain if she was addressing him or talking to herself. "I can see the hair on your arms. I can see muscles shifting when you move. I can see you breathe. Can I really be imagining all that?"

"I assure you that I am real." It irritated him to deal with this type of nonsense. In the brief time allotted him, he'd rather taste and touch and experience all he could.

"I believe I'll accept your offer of a glass of wine," Chelsey whispered. "What did you say you were drinking?"

"Malmsey. It's a sweet white wine from Greece." He glanced at the coffee table in front of her. A glass of wine appeared.

She gasped and a tremor raced through her body. "Shazam, remember?" She gave her head a violent shake. "I'm seeing this, but I still can't accept it."

He made the wine disappear. "Shazam," he said flatly. The chilled glass reappeared. Perhaps that would be enough proof. Part of him longed to prolong his time in the reality plane but another part of him, disillusioned with humanity, simply wanted to complete his business and be gone.

"Thank you," she said in a tight voice, tasting the wine. When she placed it on the coffee table, the glass was full again. A sigh dropped her shoulders. "I guess you know I have a thousand questions,'' she said after a minute.

Her comment surprised him. He turned away from stroking a begonia leaf between his fingers to look at her directly. After today he doubted that she would ever again wear work jeans, an old shirt and a dusty bandanna. He noticed that her left leg was trembling slightly.

"You summoned me by polishing the silver lamp. I am here to grant you three wishes. Once your wishes are granted, I will leave you," he said impatiently. "Does that answer your questions?"

"Look, I'm sorry if my skepticism irritates you," she said. "You're probably accustomed to materializing out of thin air and offering people their dreams on a platter, but this is the first time something this fantastic has happened to me. Until this minute I've always assumed genies were flights of the imagination or inventions concocted to spice up children's stories. Not in my wildest, most whimsical dreams did I for one minute imagine that genies actually existed. I apologize if that offends you, but that's why I'm having trouble accepting you. I see the magic, but I'm having great difficulty believing."

"You will believe after your first wish is granted," he said, not interested in the conversation.

He moved around her small living room, running his palm over chair backs and tabletops, breaking the leaves of her houseplants and holding them to his nose, lifting and stroking the books scattered around in piles. He knew better than to believe he could store the sensations in his fingertips, but he always tried. While his new mistress had been unconscious, he had opened the windows and the French doors leading to a small patio. The mingled scents of lilac, honeysuckle and summer grass permeated the

room, the fragrance so real and heady he felt almost in-
toxicated by it.

"So. What happens next?" Chelsey asked, interrupting
his examination of an arrowhead. He closed his fist around
the flint wedge, wanting to sample the sharp edges. Pain
was a sensation he had not experienced for longer than
he could remember.

"On the table before you are three gold coins." He
opened his hand to examine the red marks left by the
arrowhead. The flint edges hadn't cut his palm, but he had
felt the possibility.

The three gold coins glowed against the glass tabletop,
about the size of silver dollars. Chelsey lifted one and
centered it in her trembling palm. No date was stamped
on the coin; it betrayed no hint of its origin. The only
marking was an impression of a scimitar.

"Each time you make a wish, you must surrender one
of the coins," he explained. Alex had presented this
speech more times than he cared to recall. It was necessary but uninteresting. "The rule is, I cannot grant your
wishes unless they benefit you directly."

Chelsey didn't feel faint anymore but she still wasn't
functioning on all burners. Despite the accumulating evidence, her mind balked at the thought that she was talking to a genie. "I never imagined a genie would look like
you."

This wasn't surprising as she had never tried to imagine
a genie at all. If she had, she felt reasonably certain that
she would not have imagined a genie dressed in sexy tight
jeans, a cutoff sweatshirt and Nikes. "Wouldn't it be easier to convince people that you are who you claim you
are if you looked more like genies are supposed to look?"

A grimace tugged her lips. Those were probably the
dumbest two statements she had ever uttered. She rolled

her eyes and reached for the wineglass, wishing she hadn't said anything.

"How do you imagine genies are supposed to look?"

She laughed and spread her hands. "I guess you should be big and blue and sound like Robin Williams."

"I beg your pardon," he asked, staring at her.

"I don't know. Something exotic, I guess." Her only experience with genies came from old reruns of "I Dream of Jeannie," and Disney stories of Aladdin and the magic lamp.

"Would you find something like this more convincing?"

In the span of a heartbeat he stood before her clad in the damnedest outfit Chelsey had seen. Red silk pantaloons ballooned above green slippers with long, upward-curving toes. His golden chest was bare, exposing a thatch of dark hair and swelling muscles. Gold bracelets enclosed his wrists and heavy upper arms. Gold links circled his neck, and he wore a jeweled hoop in one ear. A red-and-green silk turban hid his hair. He crossed his arms over his chest and glared at her, obviously irritated.

"Is this what you expected?"

Chelsey drew a quick involuntary breath and held it. Alex Duport was the most flawless, most exciting male specimen she was ever likely to observe.

He was magnificent. Perfectly proportioned, a sensual exhibit of muscle and sinew. Smooth golden skin. Taut, hard flesh. He was truly a beautiful, thrilling and consummate man.

His shoulders were broad, squared and rippling with muscles. His torso narrowed in a classic wedge shape to a hard flat belly framed by washboard ridges. Through the red silk pantaloons, she glimpsed heavy tapered thighs and well-shaped calves. The sight of his male perfection made her feel funny inside, as if someone were pouring warm honey through her body.

"Okay, you've made your point," she said finally, wrenching her gaze away from the arrow of dark hair pointing down his chest toward the red pantaloons. "I was wrong. If you'd popped up looking like that I would have called the men in white coats to haul you away."

She sensed the outlandish costume was intended to make her feel foolish, and it did. Also, seeing him half-naked was oddly arousing, which embarrassed her. "Let's go back to the jeans and sweatshirt."

"As you wish, mistress." Instantly he returned to his original choice.

Chelsey twitched. "Shazam, remember? Or clap your hands. Something." Creating that costume fantasy had been unnecessary and had displayed an element of contempt. What struck Chelsey as curious was her impression that Alex's contempt was directed at himself as much as at her.

"I have an idea that you're not too wild about being a genie," she commented. He gave her a steady look that revealed nothing. "And I'm getting the impression that you don't like me very much."

God, where had that come from? Embarrassment flamed on her cheeks. Why should she care if he liked her or not? For all she knew, they weren't even part of the same species. Certainly this was not going to be a long-term association.

Alex chose not to address either of her statements. Keeping his features expressionless, he replied carefully, "If my demeanor offends you, mistress, I apologize. You have only to state what annoys you and I shall cease that action immediately."

The words were conciliatory, but the tone was off. His

tone suggested he had nothing for which to apologize and he did so solely to appease her and thus get on with the job at hand.

Chelsey folded her arms over her chest and scowled. "You're a genie with a bad attitude, do you know that?"

Alex's gaze narrowed into slits of blue-green and his mouth tightened. For a moment Chelsey thought he would respond to her own rude comment, but he didn't. "If you are prepared to make your first wish…" Staring at her, he inclined his dark head toward the gold coins.

"You want me to get on with it, right?" Chelsey said, glancing down at the coins. She still couldn't believe this was actually happening. "I'll make my wishes and then you can return to wherever you came from and I'll stagger off and have a nice little nervous breakdown." She glanced up at him. "That was a joke. Don't you ever smile?"

He ignored her question. "Your first wish…" Lifting his wineglass, he took a sip and held it on his tongue.

"Okay," Chelsey said, directing her attention away from him and toward the gold coins glowing on the coffee table. After drawing a deep breath, she touched a fingertip to one of the coins and pushed it forward. Despite the evidence she had already seen, she didn't wholly believe that Alex Duport could truly grant her three wishes. Such an incredible event was just too fantastic, too good to be true.

But she couldn't help thinking: What if it was true?

"Okay. I'm ready." She closed her eyes, flexed her arms, then drew another deep breath. "I wish for a cure for AIDS." She thought a moment, then opened her eyes and pushed forward the second coin. "I wish for lasting world peace." The coins felt unusually warm and smooth beneath her fingertips. "And I wish for an end to world hunger."

Alex stepped forward to stand in front of the coffee table. He crossed his arms over his chest and scowled down at the coins, then raised his eyes to Chelsey.

"There," she said, dusting her hands briskly. "We're finished. So. Aren't you supposed to take the coins and disappear?"

This thought caused her an unexpected pang of regret. Alex Duport was surly and cool, enigmatic and distant. But he was a genie, and there were dozens of questions she would have liked to ask him. He was also the best-looking man Chelsey had ever spent time with, and she found herself strongly attracted to him. She wanted to know what lay behind that brooding exterior.

"I thought I explained the rules." His scowl deepened. "Each wish must benefit you directly."

"You can't grant any of my wishes?" Maybe this whole genie thing was a hoax, Chelsey thought. Then she remembered Alex saying so before—the wishes had to benefit *her.* "Wait a minute," she said, working it out. "This rule means the wishes must be entirely selfish. No wonder you don't seem to hold a high opinion of human nature."

A shrug moved the sweatshirt across his shoulders. "They usually are."

"Mine weren't," Chelsey reminded him.

His eyes widened slightly in surprise. "I don't recall a master or mistress who spent their wishes on anything noble or selfless as you tried to do. Usually it isn't necessary to mention the wishes must directly benefit the wisher. That is the master's first inclination."

Chelsey tilted her head. "How many times have you granted someone three wishes?"

"Why do you ask such questions?" Annoyance drew his brow.

"I'm a curious person. Is there some rule that prevents you from talking about yourself?"

"Not that I know of." Again he looked surprised. He fixed his eyes on her. "Most masters or mistresses are far more interested in the wishes than in he who grants them." After a brief hesitation during which he watched her with an expression of curiosity, he added, "I have had hundreds, maybe thousands, of masters and mistresses."

Chelsey considered. "And all those thousands of wishes satisfied selfish desires." She leaned back against the sofa cushions and focused a long look on this incredible man. "Tell me something. Are you human or are genies a different species? Were you born a genie? And how old are you? You speak of centuries like I might speak of years."

He stiffened, and the surly attitude she disliked returned along with his scowl. "What difference do those things make? What is your first wish, mistress?"

"I'd like to know something about the man who is going to make all my selfish dreams come true." Chelsey wasn't sure if she was trying to lighten a tense moment or if she was delaying her first wish. She held her wineglass up to the flare of sunset glowing in the window. The undrainable glass fascinated her.

"Indulge me for a minute," she said. "I'm trying to figure this out. You've done a lot of razzle-dazzle in the last couple of hours, performed several feats that are magical to me. What I don't understand is how completing the Wickem Hall inventory differs from the wishes attached to the coins."

Alex leaned back against the mantelpiece and turned his head toward the scent of lilacs drifting through the open French doors. "The wishes attached to the coins originate with you," he explained, rocking back on the heels of his Nikes. "Any other magic originates with me. Do you understand?"

"No." She watched him search for the patience to answer a question he didn't consider relevant.

"My obligation is to serve you, mistress. If serving you best means cushioning your faint with a chaise, I may choose to do so. I may choose to offer wine or food. I may choose to complete your inventory."

"Or you may choose not to do those things?"

"Yes," he said slowly. "In which case you would have found it necessary to expend a coin to complete your inventory."

Chelsey felt absurdly pleased. He could have let her crash to the floor when she fainted but he had chosen not to. "I'm grateful to have the inventory finished, but I wouldn't have used a coin to wish for it. In fact, that inventory is going to cause a problem. How on earth am I going to explain to the university that I've already finished a project they expect will take three to five years to complete?"

Alex was more interested in her porcelain candy bowl than in Chelsey's problems. He sampled a lemon drop, then ran his fingertips over the smooth surface of the candy bowl with a poorly concealed expression of pleasure.

Chelsey lifted a puzzled eyebrow. "I've never met anyone as touchy-feely as you. What's that all about?"

"It's been sixty years since I was last summoned. And my time here is limited," Alex said softly, stroking his thumb over the smooth contours of the bowl. "One forgets the rich scents and tastes, the different textures..." His hair moved across his shoulders as his head snapped up. Back came the frown, as if he were angered at revealing part of himself. "Your wishes, mistress, what will they be?" He replaced the porcelain bowl on the table beside Chelsey's favorite chair, then moved to stand before her, a look of purpose stiffening his expression. "Do you wish for wealth? For revenge? Power? Love?"

Chelsey imagined that his intense blue-green eyes bored into her brain and examined her darkest desires. "Can you read my mind?" she inquired uneasily.

"No." Unless she imagined it, a ghost of a smile touched his firm lips. So he wasn't entirely humorless, after all. "You will have to state your wishes aloud."

"Okay." Chelsey licked her lips and twisted her hands together in her lap. "This is it." She contemplated the sunset glow captured by the gold coins while myriad possibilities sped through her mind.

She could wish for fame. And fortune. She could wish for her own fully funded expedition to search for Ebrum, a city lost in the far mists of antiquity. For years she had fantasized that she would be the archaeologist to finally unearth Ebrum; she could make that fantasy a reality simply by wishing it. Or she could wish for the return of the marble busts. For the restoration of her professional reputation. She could wish for a dream laboratory with state-of-the-art dating equipment. Or maybe a home of her own with a working fireplace and no stairs to climb. Maybe she could wish for someone to love who would love her back....

The choices overwhelmed her. "You know, this isn't as easy as I thought it would be," she said, glancing up at Alex. A puzzled frown deepened the lines framing his mouth. "Did your other masters experience any difficulty deciding what to wish for?"

"Never." His frown deepened.

She thought for a moment. "Look, is there a time limit on this? I mean, do I have to make my three wishes now, right this minute?"

"You don't know what you want to wish for?" He looked incredulous.

"If you really are who you claim to be—and I think I'm beginning to believe that you are—and if you really and truly are going to grant me three wishes, then I don't want to rush into this and make a hasty decision." She leaned forward, speaking earnestly, thinking as she spoke. "I guess it isn't necessary to tell you that this is a once in a lifetime opportunity. I don't want to make a wrong choice that I'll regret for the rest of my life. So, would it be acceptable to you if I thought this over for a couple of days?"

"A couple of days?" he repeated. His eyebrows soared like dark wings.

After a moment the incredulity fled his features, replaced by an expression of dawning joy. Clearly Alex's surprise was so great that he didn't realize how mobile and transparent his expression had become. The hostile, almost gothic resentment vanished, transforming his face. Chelsey had thought he was handsome before; now, with eagerness leaping in his eyes and with his body suddenly taut and vibrantly alive, the brooding suggestion of mockery gone, he simply took her breath away. An unconscious sigh flowed past her lips.

"By all means, mistress, take as much time as you like!" For the first time, his concern for her well-being seemed genuine.

"I take it the idea pleases you," Chelsey said dryly, stating the obvious. The startling change in him made her smile.

"More than you could possibly know." Now he

stopped pacing and relaxed into the chair facing her. When he looked at her, his face was softer somehow, the tense lines eased. Chelsey suspected she might actually see him smile before this was over. The transformation pleased her enormously.

"The coins! They're gone." Had she forfeited her wishes?

Hastening to reassure her, Alex lifted a hand that was surprisingly elegant considering the rest of him was so large and ruggedly masculine. "You have only to say 'I wish,' and a coin will appear in your palm."

Another first occurred. Alex gazed at her with a flicker of puzzled interest, as if he were seeing her for the first time. For a long moment their eyes held, then, when Chelsey felt her heartbeat accelerating, she cleared her throat and glanced at the grandfather clock standing near the dining room door.

She started. "Damn, I forgot. Betty will be here any minute. We planned to grab a pizza, then see a screening of *Robin Hood: Prince of Thieves*." Chelsey looked down at herself in dismay. "I have to shower and change and I don't have time for any of it. And how am I going to explain *you?*"

Alex actually smiled, a stunning smile that revealed white, white teeth. And sent Chelsey into a state of momentary paralysis. "Shazam."

Instantly the paralysis broke. A light, tingly feeling rose on her skin as if she had just stepped out of a shower. The faint scent of her favorite soap surrounded her. Chelsey raised a tentative hand to her hair and found it curled and clean to the touch, arranged in the wild, curly style she had worn in the photograph on the mantelpiece. When she looked down, she was wearing a black silk cocktail dress, dark nylons and sequined high-heeled pumps.

The nerve-racking part was that she hadn't felt a thing. But she reacted violently to the aftermath. Her heart flew around inside her chest, knocking painfully against her ribs. She felt her pulse slamming against her wrists, throat and temples. When she could speak, she swallowed hard and gave him a wobbly smile.

"Thanks. I'm grateful for the assistance, but the evening isn't this formal. And I never wear skirts," she added in a level voice, meeting his eyes. Skirts made her feel self-conscious of her leg. "If you're going to dress me, I'd prefer my white slacks and the red cotton sweater, if you wouldn't mind. And my own white shoes." Which were constructed to compensate for one leg being shorter than the other.

"Shazam."

She closed her eyes and gritted her teeth, but she didn't feel anything this time, either. When she opened one eye and looked down, she saw that she was dressed as she had requested. Falling backward on the sofa, Chelsey passed a hand over her face, then tried again to drain the undrainable wineglass.

"I'm beginning to wonder how I could ever have doubted you." She gave him a critical look. "You might consider an upgrade for yourself while we're dressing for the evening."

Actually she wasn't concerned about Alex's clothing. She was wondering if there had been a split second, a microinstant that only genies could glimpse, when she had been naked as he was dressing and undressing her. The possibility made her feel annoyingly warm and tingly.

He didn't say "Shazam" this time, but she was expecting an altered appearance when she looked up again. Now he was wearing khaki slacks and a shirt that almost matched the remarkable color of his eyes. Tasseled loafers completed his outfit. "More appropriate?" he asked. To Chelsey's astonishment, an unmistakable suggestion of humor twinkled in his eyes. "I've never been skilled in the sartorial arts."

She would have assured him that he looked fine, but the doorbell rang and she felt a stab of panic. Jumping to her feet, Chelsey glanced toward the front door, then looked back at Alex. "Look, we'll say you're a colleague, okay? We met…in…in college. Right! Your accent… Okay, we'll say you're from France. You are from France, aren't you? Originally?"

God only knew when originally had been. And maybe he wasn't French at all. Maybe genies spoke some kind of genie language which gave them an accent that sounded vaguely like archaic French.

"Whatever you wish, mistress."

She stopped with her hand on the doorknob and hissed back at him, "For God's sake, don't call me mistress! Call me Chelsey. And listen—no magic! None. That's key, Alex. No magic in front of other people."

Before she pulled the door open, she paused and drew a deep breath, then squared her shoulders. How was she going to get through this evening without Betty noticing something weird? She could wrest a promise from Alex but she wasn't confident he would comply. Or that he could even if he wanted to. Magic seemed automatic to him, an habitual response that required no special thought or effort.

"Hi, come in," she said, opening the door. "You look great tonight, but you always look great. Do you like my new hairstyle?" Which was about four inches longer than it had been mere minutes ago. "I used to wear it this way. Hey, there's someone I want you to meet." Babbling, ignoring Betty's surprised expression, she prodded her into the living room. "I should have called and canceled but I didn't think of it until too late. You see, an old and dear friend of mine is in town for a few days and—" She stopped, made herself breathe, then waved a hand. "This is Alex Duport. From France. We met at Cornell. He's, uh, a professor back east. Alex, this is my best friend, Betty Windell. She's a computer whiz who specializes in setting up programs for businesses small and large. What she does is so complicated that no one but her understands it. All I can say is that she's the best there is at whatever it is she does."

Betty, a vivacious brunette with large, intelligent dark eyes, stared at Chelsey with a quizzical look that managed to ask, "What's the matter with you tonight, and why have you been hiding this hunk for so long?" She turned to Alex and extended her hand.

"You've known Alex since college?" she asked, gazing into his eyes with frank interest.

Chelsey hoped Alex had provided her with a good genie deodorant after her genie shower; this was going to be a nervous-perspiration night. She drew a deep breath, then waved her fingers in a dismissive gesture.

"I've mentioned Alex before, dozens of times. You've just forgotten. I'm sure I told you about running into Alex last summer in Istanbul." One of the problems with lying lay in knowing when to stop. A person could lie themselves right into a pit as Chelsey was doing now. She cast Alex an imploring look that begged him to intercede and make her stop prattling.

"I'm afraid I don't know much about computers," he said smoothly, offering Betty the glass of wine that appeared in his hand. Chelsey leaned against the wall and closed her eyes. "But I'm fascinated by the idea of them."

Betty touched her chic hairdo and gave him a flirtatious smile. She tasted the wine. "Umm. This is good. Don't tell me you write papers and keep notes in longhand."

Before Betty could notice the level in her wineglass did not recede, Chelsey pasted a bright smile on her lips and spoke in an overly loud voice. "Look, maybe we should take a rain check for tonight," she hinted, giving Betty a long, penetrating look. "It seems like a lifetime since I've seen Alex.…" She and Betty had been friends for enough years that Betty should have picked up the obvious message. Betty chose to ignore it.

"Nonsense. We're all here, we all have to eat. We might as well go," Betty said, cutting a smile toward Alex. "Are you a Kevin Costner fan?" Turning, she linked arms with Alex and started toward the door. "Frankly, I'm glad you're visiting Chelsey," she said in a conspiratorial tone. "Maybe you're just the tonic she needs. Certainly she could use some cheering up. If you were in Istanbul last summer, then you know how hard it's been for her since. All her friends are worried about her."

Chelsey rolled her eyes and cast Betty a look of exasperated affection. The friends Betty referred to had dwindled to a precious few. But Betty had loyally stuck by her, dismissing the rumors and the professional and personal slurs as outrageous and beneath notice. If there was anyone in the world in whom she might have confided about Alex, it was Betty.

But Chelsey couldn't bring herself to do it. Even a friend as steadfast and nonjudgmental as Betty would find it hard to believe that she had found a genie.

"WHATEVER HAPPENED in Istanbul must have happened after I left," Alex said evenly, studying Chelsey across the restaurant table. "I'd like to hear about it."

"What? My mind was drifting."

Chelsey was having trouble adjusting to the difference in Alex. From the moment she had requested a delay before making her wishes, Alex Duport had become a different person. The angry lines around his mouth and between his eyes had eased. Although he continued to touch everything around him, and he ate prodigious amounts of pizza, he almost seemed relaxed. Clearly he was enjoying himself, and he had actually smiled several times during dinner.

Betty looked stricken. "Did I put my foot in my mouth? I assumed Alex knew about last summer."

Fascinated and appalled, Chelsey watched Betty take a slice of pizza from the tray. Immediately the empty slot filled and the pizza was whole again. The regenerating pizza was making Chelsey's nerves stand on end.

"I thought you knew everything about me," she said in a distracted tone.

"I know the basics. What happened in Istanbul last summer?"

Chelsey gave herself a mental shake, dragging her gaze away from the pitcher of Coors that remained full no matter how many glasses were poured from it. Alex was watching her closely, waiting for an answer.

Raising her arm, she pushed back the sleeve of her red sweater and made a show of consulting her watch. "We'd better go or we'll miss the start of the film."

"The film will begin when you wish it to begin, mistress."

Betty looked at the slice of pizza in her hand, then at the tray. "You know...something really weird is happen-

ing with the pizza. And the beer, too. I could swear
that—''

Chelsey jumped to her feet. ''Time to go,'' she said,
pulling Betty out of her chair.

Biting her lip, she glanced at Alex's smile and experienced a sinking feeling that things were only going to get
worse.

Chapter Three

While Alex settled the bill, Betty dragged Chelsey outside the door of the restaurant. "You're having an affair! Why didn't you tell me? I thought you were still seeing Howard Webber."

"I am still seeing Howard," Chelsey said, irritated. She might have guessed something like this would happen. "I'm not having an affair with Alex."

"Oh, come on. He referred to you as his mistress right in front of me." One of Betty's eyebrows soared in a skeptical arch. "I know what I heard."

Thrusting her hands deep in her pants pockets, Chelsey leaned toward the restaurant window and glared at Alex inside. "I wish I could explain this, but I can't."

Inside the restaurant, Alex instantly stiffened and turned sharply to face her. He started toward the door as a warm, round object appeared in Chelsey's hand. One of the gold coins. Good God, she had said "I wish." Frantically, she shook her head and waved Alex back. The coin vanished from her palm.

Feeling her legs shaking, Chelsey leaned against the outside wall of the restaurant and held her breath for a moment. She began to see how easy it would be to blow this opportunity. Now the coin system made sense. It permitted a brief interval to correct an error or allow for second thoughts.

"Are you all right?" Betty asked, concerned.

"I am *not* Alex's mistress!" Betty's insistence was painting erotic mental pictures that made Chelsey feel fluttery inside, sort of overheated, tense and nervous.

"Methinks the lady doth protest too much." Betty studied her with a thoughtful expression. "The only reason I can think of to explain why you want to keep this affair a secret is that Alex is married."

"Believe me, that isn't the reason. There is no affair."

"Well, is he? Married?"

Chelsey threw out her hands. "I don't know, okay? I haven't asked him."

"You're having an affair with an old friend and you haven't bothered to ask if he's gotten married since you saw him last?" Betty looked appalled. "Listen, Chelsey, you have the right to know! My opinion of Howard Webber is no secret. You know I think he's small, petty and a pompous ass. And no one in their right mind would choose Howard over a gorgeous hunk like Alex. But at least Howard isn't married!"

Chelsey tried to calm herself by taking a long, deep breath and holding it for a count of five. "Look, this is simply a misunderstanding that's getting out of hand. It doesn't matter whether Alex is married, because I am not—repeat, *not*—having a fling with him!" The only good thing about this conversation was that Betty had been diverted from thinking about the regenerating pizza and beer pitcher.

A flash of anger and hurt jumped in Betty's dark eyes. "I'm not blind. I saw how the two of you looked at each other over dinner! Look, if you don't think you can trust me with your secret...well, okay. It's none of my business, anyway."

Chelsey groaned. She took Betty's hands in hers and spoke in an anxious voice. "It isn't like that. You know I trust you absolutely! It's just...it's just that..."

Betty's eyes widened. "I just figured it out! You suspect he's married, but you're not sure so you're keeping the relationship a secret. Chelsey Mallon! You're *afraid* to ask him, aren't you? You're afraid of the answer!"

Suddenly Chelsey felt weak. If Alex had been real and she had been having an affair with him... Well, maybe Betty's claim came too close to the truth.

"I left my cane in the car," she muttered, looking for an escape.

"Well, *I'm* not afraid to ask him!" Betty said firmly. A grimly protective expression tightened her mouth. Shoulders squared, eyes suspicious, she stepped up to Alex as he pushed through the restaurant door. "Are you married or not? And don't lie—we can check it out!"

"I beg your pardon?" Alex's eyebrows lifted, and he shot a questioning look toward Chelsey.

Chelsey sighed and threw out her hands. "This is your fault. I asked you not to call me mistress."

"Quit stalling. Do you have a wife?" Betty demanded. It didn't matter to her that people were moving around the island they created in the restaurant doorway. She sensed a friend in danger, and that possibility was enough to send her on the warpath.

Alex fixed his eyes on her flushed face, judging the extent of her indignation. "I had a wife," he said finally. "It was a very long time ago."

"Then you're divorced?" Betty wasn't letting the subject drop until all ambiguities were cleared.

"My wife is dead." No hint of emotion altered Alex's tone. He stated the fact in a flat, even voice.

Betty visibly relaxed. She looked pleased with her triumph before she arranged her features into an expression of sympathy. "I'm sorry your wife died," she said to Alex in a softer tone, patting his arm. "I hope you understand why I had to ask. Chelsey has been through a lot. I don't want her to get hurt."

"I fail to grasp how my marital status could hurt Dr. Mallon," Alex said, frowning. He lifted his gaze to Chelsey, making certain she noticed his emphasis on *Dr.* Mallon. "I assure you I would never injure Chelsey— I'm here to grant her wishes. My services will be a direct benefit to her."

"Jeez, what an ego." Betty rolled her eyes, then laughed as they walked toward the car. "You're going to grant Chelsey's fondest wish, huh? And going to bed with you will be a big benefit to her." She shook her head and slid into the car. "I'll say this for you, Alex. You have to be a real stud to make a claim like that. You're giving yourself a lot to live up to." She met Chelsey's eyes in the rearview mirror. "Lucky girl," she murmured with a grin.

Chelsey gripped the steering wheel and stared straight ahead, feeling wildly exasperated. She had lied about Alex to her best friend who was now convinced that Chelsey was having a secret affair with an ego-driven sex machine. A long, frustrated sigh escaped her lips. She slid a narrowed look toward Alex in the seat next to her. He was running his fingertips over the plush seat covers and sniffing the night air with oblivious pleasure, unaware of Betty's misconceptions.

What next? she thought as she turned the key in the ignition, then drove down Broadway toward the Campus

Theater. An evening with a genie, she decided uncomfortably, was like playing hopscotch on a mine field.

THE MOVIE THEATER was jammed with marvelous sensory impressions, and Alex was eager to sample them all. The smells in particular delighted him, blending a rich mixture of women's perfume, men's cologne, carpet shampoo, candy and other scents he couldn't readily identify. Above it all drifted the pervading enticement of the popcorn machine, a seductive hot buttery smell that made his mouth water.

"But we just finished eating a mountain of pizza!" Chelsey protested when he insisted on buying buckets of popcorn, soft drinks and boxes of chocolate-coated candy.

"I've never tasted these things," he explained.

"Where have you been?" Betty inquired. "In outer Siberia?"

Foods had altered dramatically since his day. Variety and taste were vastly improved. Ordinarily Alex didn't spend enough time in the reality plane to sample much of anything. He was determined not to waste this rare opportunity to taste, touch and inhale everything there was to taste, touch and inhale. A century might elapse before he was offered another chance like this one.

Once they were settled in the dimly lit theater, Chelsey leaned against his shoulder and whispered curiously, "Have you been to a movie before?"

She wasn't wearing perfume but her natural scent was clean and fresh, distracting enough that Alex had to forcefully remind himself of her question. "I know about movies, of course, but I haven't actually sat in a theater and watched one, no," he said finally. Being reminded of his lack of actual experience pained him.

Resentment diminished his pleasure in the scent of

Chelsey's skin and in the crunchy taste of the popcorn. Only after the lights dimmed and the screen flared did he set aside a bitter roster of grievances and focus his concentration on the experience at hand.

Instantly Alex forgot the concerns of a moment ago. The opening scenes of *Robin Hood: Prince of Thieves* stunned his mind into shocked attention. Chelsey had explained that this was a film about a thief who robbed from the rich and gave to the poor. Nothing had prepared him for a depiction of the Crusades. Leaning forward in the theater seat, he scanned the screen intently, feeling a deep and building anger at the superficial portrayal of the pivotal event in his life. What he watched on screen was a tidied-up, prettified depiction that was far from what the Crusades had actually been. Where were the horrific battle scenes? The screams of dying men, the smell of blood and urine and rotting flesh? Where were the mountains of bones and amputated limbs, the exhaustion and disillusion, the cries to heaven?

No, he thought, it hadn't been like what he was watching on the screen; it had been like this…. Totally absorbed, he shifted the image on the screen to a scene immediately following the battle at Baldaz. This is what it had been. Ragged thieves scavenging a scorched field littered by mutilated and dying men, plundering the men's valuables even as they pleaded for a scrap of shade or a sip of water to ease their last thirst. And dazed, vacant-eyed men, stripped of youth and illusions, stumbling over fallen comrades, shock, horror and exhaustion carving their bloody faces.

Not wanting to see, but unable to resist, Alex shifted the scene to the south of the battlefield, near the city walls, and examined himself astride the white stallion that had belonged to his liege lord. His bloodied sword hung limp in his hand. His tunic was filthy and stained, hanging in tatters. Tangled hair—matted with dust and another man's blood—obscured his vision.

Isabel rode pillion behind him. She leaned against his back, her arms clasped around his waist. Her flaxen hair, her vanity, had swirled loose from her braids; her eyes were as colorless and blank as his own as they silently skirted the carnage of a battle inexplicably lost.

Curling his hands into fists, Alex leaned forward in the theater seat and stared. Isabel. Once her name had sung to him. How could he have forgotten how young she was? Shock clenched his stomach as he realized she was plain of face and sharp featured. To him she had been beautiful, a prize among women. Emotion had thrown a veil across the slyness in her slanted eyes, the deceitful twist of a mouth too thin and cunning.

"How odd. I don't remember any of this," Chelsey murmured, staring up at the screen.

"I'd forgotten how bloody and gritty the opening is," Betty murmured in agreement. "These scenes are so real they make me squirm. When does Costner show up?"

Alex didn't hear. His gaze remained riveted to the screen, his memories whirling backward across centuries. He passed swiftly over his capture and his anguish as Isabel was dragged screaming from the stallion. The scene leapt forward to those last searing moments in Selidim's palace.

Yes, there was the small curtained room where he had been tortured and beaten, exactly as he remembered, authentic in every detail. Torment in the midst of silken opulence. And there was Selidim and his hawk-nosed vizier, Mehmed. Alex let the vision of Selidim grow to fill the screen as hatred blackened and scalded his mind.

Selidim, magnificent in snowy robes, his turban encrusted with a king's fortune in jewels. Selidim, mystical prince, victorious general, husband to a thousand wives. Selidim, philosopher, scholar, conjurer. Selidim, magician, tormentor, guardian of dark secrets.

Selidim's heavy lips curved in a poisonous smile. "Where is your God now, Crusader, the God you would impose on us?" His smile thinned. "It appears that you, who would force your wishes on others, now stand deserted, at the mercy of an infidel's pleasure." Cold flame flickered in eyes as black as the void.

"His punishment, oh Magnificent One..." Like an ancient bird, Mehmed hopped from one slippered foot to the other.

Selidim leaned so near that Alex could see the grid of veins reddening his eyes, the pockmarks pitting his handsome dark face, could smell the scent of honey and almonds floating on his breath. "Two were captured. One shall live. You decide, Crusader. Do you live...or does the woman?"

"Kill me." Alex barely recognized the croak issuing past his cracked lips. "You have no quarrel with the woman. Let her live."

"Such nobility, such innocence. Such devotion to chivalrous ideals, yes, Crusader?" Selidim's black eyes narrowed in chill amusement accompanied by a grudging flicker of respect which Alex had not identified at the time. "Do you truly suppose the woman worthy of your sacrifice? You are a fool, Crusader. You forfeit your life in tribute to a false God and false philosophy."

"She is worthy. Let her live." Alex heard the depth of conviction in his shattered voice, the blind and unquestioning faith in the goodness of his beloved, his Isabel, his wife.

Selidim clapped his jeweled hands. At once there was

movement behind the curtain as someone was led into the room at Alex's back. Selidim leaned near him again, his whisper a long, malignant hiss. "You inflict your wishes at the point of a sword, Crusader. You claim your religion, your philosophy, your ideas and ideals are superior to all others and you would impose them through blood and subjugation. I say to you, listen and hear the destruction of one dream, one ideal, then ask if all your ideals are equally as false."

The vizier shoved a silk scarf into Alex's mouth, then bowed to Selidim and drew the curtain aside that Selidim might enter the next room. Alex stiffened and his heart leapt as he heard Isabel's frightened cry.

Selidim murmured softly to her, then spoke in a voice Alex was intended to overhear. "Two were captured. One shall live. You decide, little jewel. Will you offer your life so the Crusader may live? Or will you stand by my side and watch your Crusader die?"

"Take him," Isabel whispered. "I will make you happy, sire. Kill him, not me. I beg of you. Not me. Not me."

An elbow shoved Alex to the far side of his theater seat, intruding on the remembered anguish which had blackened to hatred, then eventually to indifference, as slow centuries passed. After scrubbing a hand across his face, Alex turned his head to look into Chelsey's indignant stare.

"Stop screwing around," she whispered fiercely. "Put the Robin Hood movie back on the screen!"

"I don't remember *any* of this." Betty's hand had frozen in midair above her box of popcorn. "You know...if that actor wasn't so bloody and beat-up, he'd look a little like Alex."

"Shhh!" An irritated chorus erupted from the seats behind them.

Alex stared, watching Selidim return through the curtain, his black eyes burning with triumph. He could not bear to hear Selidim's pronouncement of punishment. The scene flickered and faded, then Kevin Costner's boyish smile jumped onto the screen.

"Wait a minute," someone whispered behind them. "What happened to that other guy?"

Alex stumbled to his feet, spilling his bucket of popcorn. He grabbed Chelsey's hand and strode up the darkened aisle, pulling her behind him. In the lobby he bent over the drinking fountain and splashed cool water on his face.

It had all happened over a thousand years ago, yet for a moment the memories had come crashing back, still painfully vivid, still possessing the power to carve him into little slices.

The poison that circulated through his spirit was the knowledge that Selidim had been right. Alex had been a fool to dream noble dreams. Self-interest ruled the world, not self-sacrifice or lofty principles. Nobility of spirit was a false conceit. Love was only as strong as its first selfish challenge.

Chelsey grabbed his arm and spun him to face her. "How could you! You promised you wouldn't do anything weird, then you did that stuff at dinner and now you're rewriting movie scripts to amuse yourself! Damn it, Alex!"

She stared up at him. And the anger abruptly drained from her expression. She stumbled backward a step and her fingers flew to her mouth.

"Oh my God. That Crusader didn't just resemble you—it *was* you! Alex...that was your story!"

"I need a drink," he said roughly. "Something stronger than that pale weasel piss you people call beer." He knew it would annoy her, but right now he didn't care. A flagon of strong dark ale appeared in his hand and he drank steadily until beads of sweat rose on his brow and his lungs screamed for air. He tossed the flagon toward the ceiling where it disappeared, then wiped the back of his hand across his mouth. "I apologize," he said finally, avoiding her wide, stunned gaze. "I didn't intend to alter the film. But they depicted it falsely, and I just…" He stared across the lobby at the popcorn jumping inside the machine. "The past…it overwhelmed me."

"In living color," Chelsey added softly, pressing her hand against the muscles twitching in his arm. "I'm sorry, Alex." She drew a breath. "Isabel looked very young. I'm sure she loved you, but she was frightened, and a long way from home."

"In those days seventeen was a ripe age. Isabel was a widow when I married her."

His arm was rock-hard beneath Chelsey's fingertips, as hard as his expression. Not thinking, Chelsey reached a hand to his face, wanting to comfort him for a loss that right now seemed as fresh to him as yesterday.

The instant she touched his face, all her inner systems stopped, as if they had received an electric jolt. The past dropped from his eyes and he stared down at her with a gaze so focused and intense that Chelsey's mouth went dry.

Hastily she pulled her hand away and wet her lips. "What happened to you? Did Selidim kill you?" She waved a hand, unable to meet his steady stare. "Well, of course he must not have killed you, but—"

Betty popped out of the theater doors and walked toward them, shaking her head. "I must be getting old. I've seen that movie twice but I don't remember half of what we've seen so far.'' She made a face. ''Early senility. I wonder how many outfits I've forgotten at the cleaners?''

Chelsey examined Alex's face. ''Betty, would you mind terribly if we deserted you? It's been a long, very strange day. I think Alex and I need to talk.''

''Talk? Or make a few wishes come true?'' Betty winked. ''Go ahead. Don't worry about me, I'll hook a ride home with Professor Markley and his wife.''

''Thanks.'' Chelsey gave her a hug.

When she turned to take Alex's arm, she noted the far-away look in his eyes and understood his thoughts had turned backward again.

And she was feeling jealous of a woman who had been dead for over a thousand years.

CHELSEY AND ALEX DIDN'T speak during the drive back to Chelsey's rented house but both were aware of the strong physical current that flowed between them, enhanced by the close confines of the small car. It was as if a magnetic tug had leapt between them, creating an invisible attraction they both tried to ignore.

Once Chelsey started to speak, but noticed his hands were clenched into fists on his thighs and changed her mind. She wondered if the differences between their lives and experiences made her seem as exotic to him as he was to her. Perhaps that explained her strange heightened awareness of his slightest move. Or perhaps it was a primal recognition of male and female that originated deep in the cells. Whatever was happening, it made her nervous and uneasy.

Neither reached for the door handle after Chelsey switched off the ignition in her driveway. They sat together in the summer darkness, listening to the ticking sound made by the engine as it cooled.

It was a pleasant Colorado evening. The sky was clear and velvety dark, spangled by distant stars. The night air had cooled enough that Chelsey's sweater felt good against her skin. Insects strummed love songs from the safety of dark trees and bushes. The scent of lilac and cut grass was strong and poignant. From the house next door came the muffled gaiety of the "Tonight Show."

"What happened to Isabel?" Chelsey asked quietly, dropping her hands from the steering wheel.

Alex leaned his elbow out the window, drummed his fingertips against the roof of the car. Chelsey had the feeling she was sitting beside a coiled spring. His memories upset him, but she sensed something else running beneath the obvious. A powerful and perhaps dangerous awareness had been released when she touched his face in the theater lobby. For both of them.

"Selidim..." he said in a harsh voice. Stopping, he waited, then began again. "Selidim decided Isabel was disruptive, an influence he did not wish for his harem. Less than a year after the scene you witnessed, Selidim ordered her drowned in the seraglio pool as an example to his wives and concubines."

Chelsey nodded, familiar with the ruthless cruelty of Alex's period. She heard him rub a hand over his face, but she didn't embarrass him by watching his anguish. Instead she stared at the summer moths batting themselves against the porch light globe. "I'm sorry."

"Why?" he asked after a moment, shifting in his seat to look at her. Chelsey felt a bolt of lightning shoot through her body when he met her eyes. "It happened over eleven hundred years ago."

"It happened. Obviously it still upsets you," she said,

looking away from him and rubbing her arms. What was happening here? She felt hot and cold, nervous inside. The realization that if she moved only a little she would be touching him made her feel apprehensive and thrillingly aware of his maleness.

"It's odd," he said softly, looking at her mouth. "I haven't thought about Isabel in centuries."

Chelsey hesitated. "Did you love her very much?"

A bitter laugh scraped the back of his throat. "Love is the grandest of all illusions and the easiest to puncture. Self-interest is the only true reality. Self-interest will conquer love in any contest."

"I don't believe that."

"Then you have never experienced a conflict between self-interest and the illusion of love."

Stung by the implication, Chelsey's chin lifted defensively. "If you're suggesting that I've never been in love, you're wrong. I'll admit it wasn't a grand passion, but it was real enough." The pain had certainly been real when it ended.

"I said only that your love has not yet been tested against self-interest."

"Perhaps not," Chelsey conceded, trying to be fair. Heat rose in her cheeks. "But I know in my heart that I would not have made the same choice as Isabel."

"With all respect, Mistress Mallon, I suggest you're speaking with the haste of idealism rather than the logic of reality. Until you have actually faced a similar choice, you cannot state with true certainty how you would choose." His voice and expression softened. "Chelsey, do you honestly believe Isabel made the wrong choice? Self-interest and selfishness are protective mechanisms. Isabel's instinct for preservation gave her ten months of life that she would not otherwise have enjoyed. Can you condemn her for wanting to live?''

''That wasn't your choice,'' Chelsey bluntly reminded him.

''I was a fool.''

''I don't think so.''

Chelsey surprised herself by wanting very much to stroke his hand resting on the car seat beside her. Learning of Alex's story had softened her perception of him. She knew she was responding strongly to his personal tragedy and to the intimacy her new knowledge imparted. Her impulse was to extend that warmth into something greater that she couldn't put a name to. Or didn't want to name. Still, she resisted touching his hand because her instincts also sensed danger. She shied from the explosive power of a single compassionate touch.

''Alex, before we go inside, there's something I want to say.'' She paused to gather her thoughts, pushing aside the images of bubbling sexuality that impressed her as wildly hopeless and inappropriate. ''I greatly admire your capacity to forgive. Regardless of your generosity toward Isabel's memory, she betrayed you. Isabel betrayed the ideals you believed in, she betrayed your faith in her and your loyalty. She betrayed all that the two of you meant to each other. And she betrayed your love for her. Yet somehow you found a way to forgive and make her choice seem logical and acceptable in your mind. I don't think many men could do that.''

The glow from the porch light illuminated his smile. ''Most men don't have eleven hundred years to work it out. I'd like to believe I deserve your praise, but I don't.''

''What's wrong with this picture?'' Chelsey asked. His smile made her skin feel taut and tingly. ''My surly swaggering genie with the belligerent attitude is suddenly modest? I don't believe it. And I don't believe it required eleven hundred years to forgive her. You forgave her almost immediately, didn't you?''

"Perhaps," he said after a minute. "You leg is tired, isn't it?''

"You're trying to change the subject." But it was his story. She had no right to press. "Yes, my leg is throbbing and achy." It surprised her that they could mention her bum leg so easily, without Alex looking uncomfortable and without her feeling acutely self-conscious or apologetic.

"What I'm longing for right now is a long, soaky bath and a good night's sleep." When she thought back to arriving at Wickem Hall this morning—was it only this morning?—it seemed like an event that had occurred in another lifetime to a different person. So much had happened since. Chelsey suspected she wouldn't be— couldn't be—the same person she had been before Alex whirled into her life. Shaking her head, she reached for the door handle. "On second thought, I doubt I'll get much sleep tonight. I'll probably be awake until dawn, thinking about wishes."

"Shazam."

Her fingers closed around air. Instantly they were standing in the upstairs hallway outside her bedroom door. Senses reeling, Chelsey flung out a hand and steadied herself against the papered wall. Her cane dropped from suddenly boneless fingers.

"God! That's...really hard to get used to!" The abrupt transition sent her heartbeat flying into overdrive. She clapped a hand over her breast, feeling the rapid pounding against her palm. When she realized the gesture had drawn Alex's intense interest to her breasts, she felt her cheeks heat and made herself drop her hand. Her cane lifted of its own accord from the carpet and nudged her hand until she grasped the curved handle.

"Thanks," she said in a voice that emerged sounding higher than her own. "I hate to sound ungrateful," she added with a wobbly smile, "but did you put the car in the garage and lock the downstairs door?"

"Shazam," he said, returning her smile. Chelsey wondered why she had ever thought Alex incapable of good humor. He had a gorgeous smile, and when he was relaxed he smiled often.

Performing a graceful flourish with his fingertips, he dipped into a salaam. For the first time, the gesture was light and easy, free of resentment or shades of mockery. "Your car is in your garage, mistress. Your house is secured for the night."

"Thank you. I—" Her remark was interrupted by the sound of running water. Alex was filling the bathtub for her. The fragrance of jasmine-scented bath oil floated into the hallway. "You know," she said with a sigh of genuine pleasure, "you're spoiling me. I think I could get used to having a genie around."

"I could get used to being around."

They gazed into each other's eyes and smiled. Gradually Chelsey's pounding heart called her attention to how close together they were standing. Near enough that she could inspect at close range the thick fringe of dark eyelashes framing his remarkable eyes. Close enough to warm herself within the male heat radiating from his large, sexy body. Because Alex was lean and magnificently proportioned, she tended to forget how big he was and how overwhelming his height and size could be.

Ordinarily Chelsey resisted any situation that might make her feel fragile or in need of protection or assistance. But Alex's height and solid muscled torso made her feel fragile by comparison. His male heat and swelling masculine power made her feel suddenly helpless against the magnetism that drew her hand upward toward his face.

Embarrassed, she straightened abruptly and dropped her hand. After clearing her throat with a self-conscious sound, she hastily stepped backward. "Well," she said, sounding overly brisk and cheerful. "It's a bath and bed for me. I suppose you'll be going into your lamp."

"I beg your pardon?" His thick eyebrows moved together in a puzzled frown.

"The silver cup lamp," Chelsey repeated, suddenly uncertain. "Won't you be using it tonight?"

"Chelsey, I'm sorry but I don't have the faintest idea what you're talking about."

Silently, she cursed the late night reruns of "I Dream of Jeannie." Although Chelsey had a sudden awful suspicion that she was going to sound like an idiot, there was nothing to do but blunder forward. And who could tell? Maybe there was an outside chance that she was right. She fervently hoped so.

She fiddled with her cane, not looking at him. "You live and sleep in the silver cup lamp, don't you?"

He stared down at the top of her head. "Let me see if I understand what you're saying. Is it possible that you believe something this size," he waved a hand down the length of his body, "will fit into something the size of the silver cup lamp? Which I could carry in my pocket?"

Chelsey had guessed right the first time. She was an idiot.

"Let us assume for a moment that I could indeed shrink myself to the size of your little fingernail. Why would I then want to go inside the cup lamp?" His frown deepened. "Do you imagine there's a miniature inn concealed within the lamp? With stamp-sized beds? Is that it?"

Embarrassment flamed upward from Chelsey's throat. "All right, so I don't know where genies sleep. Pardon me, I must have dozed off during Genie Lore 101."

An effort toward patience puckered his brow. "The silver cup lamp is merely a summoning device." He thought a moment. "Think of the lamp as a garage-door opener. The device opens the door, that's all. Your garage-door device does not power your car, nor can you park your car in it. It does one thing and one thing only. It opens the door. The silver cup lamp does one thing and one thing only. It summons your genie." A broad grin split his lower jaw. Amusement twinkled in his eyes. "Did you honestly imagine I lived in the lamp? That I could shrink or enlarge myself at will?"

Bright crimson fired Chelsey's cheeks. "Look, twenty-four hours ago I would have sworn there was no such thing as a genie! How am I supposed to know where you sleep?"

"How was this sleep-in-the-lamp idea supposed to work?" His eyes were sparkling brightly now, dancing with humor. Chelsey suspected he held back a shout of laughter. "Was I supposed to hunker over the lamp, say shazam, then hope I dropped into the opening when I suddenly shrank? Did any fanfare accompany this feat? Maybe a burst of flashing lights or colored smoke? The clash of tiny cymbals? Or do I shrink myself, then depend on my master or mistress to pick me up with a pair of tweezers and lower me into the lamp? Frankly, that sounds perilous."

"All right," Chelsey said, narrowing her eyes and lifting her chin. "You've made your point." She spun on her heel and walked down the hallway. Halting in front of the guest-room door, she pressed the handle and stepped inside. "You can sleep here. There's an extra pillow in the closet if you want it."

He walked around the room, running his palm along the bureau top, leaning to glance out the window, testing the pillow. Finally he walked to the door and leaned his head out, judging the distance to Chelsey's bedroom door.

"This won't be acceptable."

Now it was Chelsey's turn to strive for patience. "Why not?"

When he looked at her, his smile had vanished. "I must remain within the sound of your voice. That is the rule."

"Alex, I sleep like the dead. I promise I'm not going to wake up at three in the morning, snap my fingers and make a wish. You can sleep here in perfect confidence that I'm not going to be making any middle-of-the-night wishes!"

"The rule cannot be broken. I must remain within the sound of your voice."

She hadn't mistaken the stubbornness hinted in the strong angle of his jawline. He spoke firmly in a voice that allowed her no argument or persuasion.

Chelsey stepped into the hallway and eyed it uncertainly. The hallway was short, narrow and uninviting. "Well, you can't sleep on the floor. I think we're stuck. I don't know where you can sleep and still adhere to this idiotic rule."

"I'll stay in your room, of course. With you."

Chapter Four

Because Alex suspected Chelsey would vigorously protest if he stated his intentions, he didn't seek her consent before gently easing her into a natural sleep. Had he not assisted, he suspected she wouldn't have slept a wink. He sensed her nervousness and racing thoughts, and she was obviously uncomfortable about trying to relax in bed while a strange man watched from a chair not three feet away.

Alex considered assuring her that he was a man of honor and had never violated a woman or taken advantage of a woman's vulnerability.

But that wasn't entirely true. In fact, as Alex stood in the darkness at the foot of Chelsey's bed and studied her sleeping form, he knew he was violating her trust by gazing at her as she slept. But he could not help himself.

She was so beautiful. In sleep her defensiveness dropped away like a shadow from a rose, as did the brisk, businesslike manner she adopted to hold people at a distance. She looked younger, softer, more womanly.

A moment ago she had kicked aside the sheets, and Alex noticed her ankle-length summer nightgown had traveled upward to a point about an inch above her knees.

The neckline had dropped to expose one smooth shoulder and the tops of her breasts.

He sucked in a hard deep breath. When he opened his eyes again, Alex made himself focus on her legs instead of her lush breasts. Her right leg was long and sensually curved, tapering to a slender ankle, so perfect that he yearned to trace the contours with his palm. As her two legs did not lie close together, the shortness of the left was not apparent. But her left leg was thinner, not as beautifully shaped or curved. That she insisted on wearing nothing but slacks and chose ankle-length nightgowns suggested that, regardless of her professional accomplishments, and no matter how strenuously she might object to his conclusion, Dr. Chelsey Mallon defined herself in terms of her body.

It was unfortunate that her definition was negative, because Alex thought her body was magnificent, beginning with her heart-shaped face, translucent skin, and her intelligent eyes, whose color reminded him of rich dark earth. A halo of ginger tendrils fanned across her pillow, framing twin crescents of lashes that shadowed her cheeks and her slightly parted lips.

When she softly sighed and shifted on her side, he let his narrowed gaze travel slowly down her body. The seductive arch of her hip had lifted and folds of her light nightgown settled into the curving valley of her waist. For a long moment Alex stared at the sweet promise of hip and waist and the glimpse of pale thigh beneath. Finally he raised his eyes to the full rounded globes of her breasts. His hands clenched by his sides. He ached to discover if her breasts were as firm yet as soft as they appeared. If her nipples were pink or brown; if they rose like tiny thrusting pebbles to greet a man's caress.

His arousal was swift and powerful, almost painful in

intensity. Silently turning on the balls of his feet, he ground his teeth together and faced away from her, trying to recall when he had last bedded a woman.

Over the centuries he had encountered mistresses who had invited him into their beds, had commanded him. He was a man; he had accepted their invitations. He had done his best to give them a night to remember, a night of fantasy and rapture.

But each time, the summons from a mistress came as a surprise, not as a result of his own instigation or calculation. Never had he gazed at a mistress and thought of her as a woman first, nor had he speculated how it would feel to hold and stroke her or make love to her. When invited into a mistress's bed, her sex had aroused him, not the woman herself.

Until now. Chelsey Mallon was different.

She was the first woman in centuries whom he had begun to regard as more than an object to serve. Because of his extended time with her, Alex was beginning to view Chelsey Mallon not only as his mistress but as a woman, a very desirable woman, and as a person who intrigued his interest.

Such an occurrence had not happened in a very, very long time. If ever.

When Alex attempted to recall the masters and mistresses he had served, they emerged as nameless, faceless links on a long dark chain. Part of their anonymity was the result of preference. Largely their anonymity resulted from the brief span of time he spent in their company. They passed uneventfully through his consciousness, blurring into obscurity.

Until this emergence with Chelsey Mallon, the longest he had spent in the reality plane had been twelve hours. Unlike Chelsey Mallon, most of his masters and mistresses knew at once how they would spend their three wishes. Seldom did the process require more than two, possibly three hours.

Because Chelsey had given him the gift of extended experience, he knew he would never forget her. She would not become another obscure link in the long chain.

She would remain unique in his grateful mind because of the time she had granted him, because of her beauty, and because he physically wanted her as he had wanted no other woman.

After gazing at her with hungry, smoldering eyes, Alex forced himself to move away from her. He walked into the hallway and cocked his head, listening to the silence that had settled over the house. Because it was a quiet night, he discovered he could move farther from her than he would ordinarily have been able to. If he strayed beyond the range of a master's voice, the air around him thickened, became almost tangible and pressed him back. An unpleasant urgency built in his nerve endings, nearly painful, until he returned to the prescribed range.

But tonight's stillness permitted him to explore most of her small house except the kitchen, adding to his knowledge about her. She liked plants and books, especially textbooks, history books and books about people who had overcome adversity. Few of the objects in her room had been chosen for display, but rather for comfort. He assumed that sentimental attachment accounted for a collection of stones, the composition of which indicated widely varying origins. Pottery shards of no value suggested mementos of digs that had been important to her. Her doctorate was framed and given a place of honor on the dining room wall. A basket of yarn and knitting needles waited on the floor beside a well-worn chair. He could approach the kitchen near enough to glimpse a flower press on the end of the counter.

There were no signs of a man either past or present.

That pleased him.

"DID YOU SLEEP WELL?" Chelsey asked, mounding her pillows behind her back, then examining the breakfast tray that had appeared above her lap. There were eggs Benedict, blueberry crepes, croissants, a pot of steaming hot chocolate and a vase holding the most perfect red rose she had ever seen. She combed her fingers through her hair and hoped she didn't look as disheveled as she usually did in the mornings.

"I dozed for about thirty minutes."

"That's all? Don't genies need sleep?"

Her question made him smile. "Yesterday I would have said no. But now I'm not as sure. I was surprised that I slept for thirty minutes."

"You don't know if you need sleep?"

"I've never been in the reality plane long enough to find out."

Chelsey considered his answer for a minute, then decided to forgo further questions until she was more awake.

"So what did you do all night?" Averting her face, she spread butter and jam over a croissant. She could not believe she had actually managed to fall asleep with Alex sitting next to her in the dark. It had been the weirdest and most uncomfortable sensation. She, wearing a thin nightgown with nothing underneath; Alex, fully dressed beside her. She had listened to his quiet breath, remembering his naked chest and the look of his smooth hard skin. Wondering. Then wondering some more.

He shrugged. "Once the house quieted, I discovered I

could move farther from you than I originally thought. I spent most of the night downstairs in the living room.''

"Really? Doing what? Did you watch TV? Read?"

A light shudder of distaste tracked down his spine. ''No. During the eighteenth century I developed an interest in fencing, so I practiced lunges and parries for a while. Then I arranged a banquet based around menus I found in one of your magazines. I spent most of the night grooming a horse.'' He related these activities in a matter-of-fact tone, as if there was nothing unusual about them. ''I miss riding, but more than riding, I miss caring for a horse. It's a deeply satisfying set of tasks. Unless grooming a horse is something you have experienced and enjoyed, the pleasure is impossible to describe.''

Chelsey closed her mouth and slowly lowered the croissant to the tray. She concentrated on keeping her voice level. ''Alex—you're saying you had a *horse* in my living room?''

''I grasp your concern. Let me assure you that I restored everything exactly as it was before. To see your living room now, you would never guess that last night it briefly served as a fencing gymnasium or as stables.''

She nodded slowly, staring at him. ''What would my landlord have seen if... No, I don't want to know.'' She blinked and fought beyond the idea of a horse prancing around her living room. ''Then you gave yourself a banquet. Seriously, Alex, how can you eat as much as you do? Why don't you gain four hundred pounds?''

His smile dazzled her. ''Actually, I don't need to eat at all. I've forgotten what hunger feels like.''

''But—''

''Don't ask me to explain—I can't. But food isn't necessary. Eating is, however, a great pleasure. The taste, the different textures and flavors. I can indulge that pleasure without feeling full or sated, and without changing weight.''

''Lucky you,'' Chelsey murmured enviously.

He watched her sample the items on the tray, then inquired, ''Have you made any decisions about making a wish?''

''Is there a rush?''

''Absolutely not.'' The swiftness with which he assured her made Chelsey suspect that he was in no hurry, either.

''Actually,'' she said, feeling excitement rise in her eyes, ''I've decided on my first wish.''

Alex sat straighter, and his expression instantly sobered. He inclined his head. ''I await your command, mistress.''

Chelsey pushed back a lock of hair, then moved the breakfast tray aside. Happiness competed with the excitement sparkling in her dark eyes. ''It's a perfect wish. But it would be easier to explain if I showed you. Give me a few minutes to shower and pull myself together, then we'll take a short drive. No,'' she added quickly raising a hand. ''No help this time. I want a real shower.'' She studied him a minute. ''I just had a thought. Would you like a shower?'' The intimacy of the invitation brought a rush of pink to her face. Her uncharacteristic shyness deepened as she recognized the smoky look smoldering in his suddenly speculative eyes. ''I don't mean with me,'' she explained, sounding more snappish than she had intended. ''I meant by yourself. You keep talking about wanting to experience physical sensations. I just thought…''

''I would appreciate the opportunity to feel water running over my skin more than I can tell you. Thank you.'' The smoky look still glowed in his eyes, not as intense as a moment ago, but intense enough that Chelsey felt her cheeks heat and her heartbeat quicken.

"Uh, look. Why don't you go first." Now that the image of showers and nakedness flickered in her mind—and possibly in his—Chelsey felt too self-conscious to slide out of bed in her nightgown in front of him. "There are extra towels on the shelf over the commode."

Excitement danced in Alex's eyes, and he darted an eager look toward the bathroom door. "You don't mind if I go first? You're sure about this?"

"Go." Would that all men were as easy to please, she thought, smiling at his enthusiasm. She reached for the tray. "I'll finish breakfast."

But she couldn't swallow a bite. Alex left the bathroom door open so he would hear if she uttered an unexpected wish. Before the mirror fogged, Chelsey caught an arousing glimpse of firm, rounded buttocks and heavy male thighs. A deep valley ran down his spine, bordered by thick ridges of muscle. She stared, then made herself look down at the breakfast tray, swallowing hard.

The image of Alex's naked backside was so powerful and disturbing that Chelsey didn't hear the doorbell. When she finally became aware of the persistent ringing, she started, then leapt out of bed and threw on a light robe, wondering how long someone had been standing on her porch before she heard the sound of the bell. Grabbing her cane, she hurried down the staircase and pulled open the front door.

Her landlady and next-door neighbor gave Chelsey an uncertain smile. Marge was in her mid-fifties, plump, and spent most of her time worrying about things that never happened. When she couldn't nibble to accompany her worrying, she twisted a tissue between her fingers as she was doing now.

"I'm sorry to bother you," Marge said, looking at Chelsey's robe, "but—and I know this is going to sound strange—it's just... Well, you see, it's Marvin.'' She drew a long breath and shifted her gaze to a spot somewhere beyond Chelsey's right ear. ''Last night Marvin swore he saw your car vanish into thin air.'' She steadfastly refused to meet Chelsey's eyes. ''I know that sounds nuts, and I guess it is, but the thought of a car vanishing kept bothering Marvin. I mean, he was so sure it had happened. Anyway, he kept worrying about it, so he finally gave up trying to sleep, got up about one o'clock, put on his robe and came over here to look inside your garage windows to see if your car was there or if it had really vanished.''

''My car is in the garage, Marge.''

Marge nodded. The tissue began to shred between her fingers. ''Marvin said the front of the house had changed. It was larger. Much larger. And I know this sounds insane, but Marvin swears on his mother's grave that he heard horses inside. He made me swear that I'd come over here as soon as you were awake and ask you about it. He's absolutely positive you had a horse in your house last night.'' She looked down at the tissue in her hands. ''This is really embarrassing, but...''

Chelsey opened the door wide so Marge could see inside. She phrased her answer carefully. ''If there was a horse in here last night, he managed not to break a single item or overturn a thing. He didn't damage the floor or walls. Would you like to step inside and check for yourself?''

''Mistress Mallon!'' An angry shout roared from the staircase. ''If I've told you once, I've told you a dozen times that I must stay within the sound of your voice! Damn it, Chelsey!''

Marge stared over Chelsey's shoulder. Her eyes widened and her mouth dropped open. Chelsey spun to see Alex striding down the staircase, his hair dripping wet

above a furious expression. But that wasn't the worst of
it.

He was stark-naked.

And there was something about Alex's perfect, powerful body that made him seem more naked than any other
naked man Chelsey had ever seen. He was totally, incredibly, so damned *naked*.

His dark hair was slicked back and dripping. Tiny bubbles of soap slid down his shoulders as if his skin were
lightly oiled. His wet body glistened and flexed in the
morning sun, the statue of an angry Greek god come to
life.

But what drew Chelsey's helpless glance was the arrow
of dark soapy hair that streaked across his muscled chest
and pointed down to… She blinked hard, then looked
again. "Good God," she whispered. He was large and
powerful all over. She couldn't help staring any more than
Marge could. Behind her, Marge released a long, choked
sigh.

Alex seemed oblivious to their shock. He stood in the
middle of the staircase, glaring furiously, splendid in his
certainty that he was in the right, waiting impatiently for
Chelsey to explain or apologize. Tiny rainbow droplets
ran a zigzag course through the dark hair adorning his
thighs, legs and arms. His naked skin caught the morning
light and gleamed with male power and beauty. He was
absolutely magnificent.

Chelsey couldn't tear her eyes away from him. She
wasn't sure whether to laugh or cry or throw off her robe
and chase him back upstairs. A hysterical bubble lodged
in her throat. She touched her fingertips to her eyelids and
wondered frantically what she would say to Marge. Finally she did the only thing she could think to do. She
brazened it out.

"Alex, I'd like you to meet my neighbor and landlady, Marge Craddock. Marge, this is Alex Duport, my...my friend." Brazenness wasn't her style. Chelsey fervently wished the floor would open and swallow her. "I hope you'll pardon us for being a little underdressed," she said, giving Alex a furious glare. She wondered if the hysteria in her voice was as obvious to Marge as it was to her. "We're getting a late start this morning."

When she dared a peek between her fingers, Alex was moving down the staircase, arranging a charming smile on his lips. He now wore white chinos and a blue chambray shirt. Only his feet were bare.

"How do you do, Mrs. Craddock," he said, bending to take Marge's hand in his. Marge looked thunderstruck. He raised her limp fingertips to his lips. "It's a pleasure to make your acquaintance."

Marge's eyes had dilated. She looked to be in shock. Maybe it was having a blindingly handsome man with a foreign accent kiss her hand. Maybe it was seeing a naked man with a physique like an Olympian god. Maybe it was the fact that one minute Alex had been standing before them naked and furious and the next instant he was dry, dressed and smiling at her.

The instant Alex moved away from them and stepped into the living room, Marge swallowed and whispered. "He...he was buck naked, then just like that he was dressed! I saw it but I don't believe it."

"I beg your pardon? Did you say Alex was naked?" Chelsey couldn't think of any other way to handle this situation. She was desperate. "You think Alex was... Oh my." She tried to look surprised, shocked and amazed that Marge could even imagine such a thing.

"He was!" Marge hesitated, her mind telling her that what she had seen was impossible. "Wasn't he?" A flicker of uncertainty appeared in her eyes as she studied Chelsey's carefully questioning expression.

Chelsey hated herself for doing this. She frowned, striving for a look of concern, then placed her hand on Marge's sleeve. "Marge, are you and Marvin taking any kind of medication? Something where hallucinations might be a side effect?"

Confusion pinched her landlady's face. The tissue she'd been holding drifted to the porch in a spray of confetti. "I'm taking estrogen. And Marvin is taking those new megavitamins...." Her voice trailed. She peered through the door at Alex who smiled back at her with perfect innocence. "No," Marge whispered. "It isn't possible. I must be... But it was so *real*."

"Perhaps you and Marvin should have a checkup," Chelsey suggested, easing the door shut.

When Marge had gone, shaking her head and muttering, Chelsey collapsed against the closed door and breathed deeply for a full minute. When she opened her eyes, she stared at Alex.

"I can't believe I tried to make Marge think that she was hallucinating." Her stare deepened. "And I wouldn't have believed how much one person—you—could screw up another person's life—mine—in so short a time."

The smile Alex had manufactured for Marge vanished, replaced by the arrogant scowl Chelsey had observed when he first arrived. "If anyone is to blame, it is not me. How many times must I explain the rules?"

"Are you suggesting that what just happened is *my* fault?"

"It was you who wandered off while I was in the shower!"

Chelsey charged forward until she stood toe-to-toe with him, her chin jutting. "Look, you, I didn't ask to have a genie pop up and complicate my life. I was just doing my work, plugging along, not expecting or asking for anything.'' Thrusting her hand in front of his face, she started ticking down her fingers. ''Since you arrived, I've got a completed inventory that I can't begin to explain, I've lied to my best friend who now believes I'm having a secret affair, about three hundred people are going to swear they saw movie scenes that don't exist, my landlord and landlady think they're losing their minds, and you're running through the house buckass naked, causing me enormous embarrassment. So far all I've gotten out of this deal is breakfast and a whole lot of complications!''

He leaned over her. ''It was your suggestion that I take a shower.''

Chelsey refused to be intimidated. Rising on her tiptoes, she returned his angry stare. ''Let's get something straight right now. I don't mind not getting something for nothing. If you bipped back to never-never land right now, it wouldn't cause me a minute's regret. I was getting along just fine before you showed up and I'll get along fine after you leave. But I mind like hell the problems you're creating that I'm going to have to deal with! What do your insufferable rules have to say about *that?* About the problems you're creating!''

His scowl loomed over her. ''Most people are happy to have a genie at their disposal.''

''Maybe when I start seeing some wishes granted, I'll be happy, too. But right now, Alexandre Duport, you're nothing but trouble and a pain in the neck, one giant headache!''

He spoke through his teeth, bending closer until their noses almost touched. ''Naturally my fondest desire is to provide for your happiness, Mistress Mallon. So let us proceed to your first wish.''

"Excellent! Good! Let us do that." Chelsey pulled back from him. "Forget what I said earlier. Do your magic stuff and give me one of those instant showers and shampoos. I'd like my beige linen slacks and silk blouse, please, and—" When she looked down she was dressed as requested except for her shoes. "You may be enamored of high heels, but I'm not," she snapped. "Give me my own built-up sandals. And say shazam, damn it."

"Shazam, damn it."

She glared at him. But now she was wearing her own specially constructed shoes. "Thank you," she said between her teeth as she passed him on her way to the kitchen for her purse and car keys.

"You don't have to drive," he said, following her. "I can just—"

"And tip a dozen old people into heart attacks when they see two people materialize out of thin air? No, thank you! We'll travel by conventional means." She saw him eyeing her car keys with avid interest. "Forget it. No, never, not a chance, not in this lifetime! God knows what you might do to my car. It's a clunker but it's paid for. I don't want some guy from another century experimenting with my car, and that's that."

THEY ONLY HAD TO TRAVEL a few blocks to reach McKenzie's Nursing Home, but it was a hair-raising ride.

Alex slammed to a halt in front of the low flagstone building, taking up two parking spaces. He cut the engine and leaned back. "Driving isn't as easy as it looked."

Chelsey willed her hands to stop shaking. Amazement trembled in her voice. "I can't believe I let you talk me into this." She closed her eyes and dropped her head against the seat back. "When you smashed that woman's fender, I wanted to kill you."

"I repaired the damage to both cars," Alex said in a tight voice.

Chelsey covered her face with her fingers. "It was… Did you see her face when she realized her car had healed itself?"

She couldn't help it. Suddenly she was laughing so hard that her sides ached and tears ran from her eyes. Alex frowned, then he was laughing, too.

When Chelsey had composed herself, she opened the car door and slid outside, looking at him over the top of her newly mended and painted car. "Seriously, Alex. No more funny stuff, okay? We go inside, you grant my wish, and that's all. We leave, and no one's the wiser. No extra magic. Right?"

"Right." He studied the neat, low building and the landscaping. A mischievous glint sparkled in his eyes. "Tell me, don't you think those flower beds would look more appealing if the flowers were all blooming?"

Chelsey halted on the path and gave him an appalled glare. "I mean it, Alex. Don't you dare do anything to those flowers!"

"I was joking."

She studied his dancing eyes. "I knew that," she lied, feeling vastly relieved.

"What is this place?" he asked, opening the door for her. Chelsey prayed that no one noticed the door open by itself. Her shoulders dropped. Alex was a hopeless case. Even when he tried not to use magic, he couldn't help himself. It was second nature.

"McKenzie's is a home for elderly people who can no longer manage on their own." She gripped her cane, then strode toward a receptionist seated behind a desk overlooking a large, comfortably furnished lawn terrace. "We're here to visit Dr. Florence Harding."

The receptionist, a blue-haired woman in her early sixties, gave Alex the once-over, ending with a coy fluttering of darkened lashes. "Dr. Harding is in the crafts room. I'll show you where it is."

"I've been here many times," Chelsey said. "I can find the way."

She led Alex down a carpeted corridor, past an exercise class and a music class, to a large, sunny room that smelled pleasantly of paint and glue. Touching Alex's arm, she paused in the doorway.

"Do you see the white-haired woman wearing a gray skirt and print blouse?"

Alex looked puzzled. "The handsome woman sitting beside the window?"

"Dr. Harding was the first person to believe in me. No," Chelsey amended after a moment's thought, "that isn't right. Dr. Harding was the first person to help me believe in myself. I met Dr. Harding when I was in high school. High school was a difficult time." She shook the memories away. "Dr. Harding took me out of myself by introducing me to history and archaeology. I'll never forget...she took our class on a field trip to help excavate some dinosaur bones in the foothills. After a couple of hours of kneeling on rock, my leg hurt like hell and I wanted to quit. Dr. Harding wasn't having any. She fixed me with one of her famous looks and said briskly that I could be bitter or better—which was it going to be? Before I could answer, she stated firmly that in her opinion, I was more than just one leg, I was her best student and she expected great things from me. Wasn't it time that I started expecting something from myself?"

Chelsey smiled affectionately at the woman across the room. "She told me I could concentrate on my mind or on my leg. It was my choice. If I allowed my leg to make my decisions, I would live a very narrow life indeed. Dr. Harding changed my way of thinking and changed my life. I stopped being just a leg and became a person.''

"Did you really, Chelsey?" Alex asked gently.

She hesitated, feeling the pink rise in her cheeks, then she brushed his question aside. "I think so. At least, for the most part. Anyway, Dr. Harding was a brilliant, compassionate woman who changed the lives of many people, not just mine. Her paper on Roman concrete is still the definitive work on the subject." She turned to look directly at Alex. "She's eighty years old. Until last year she was sharp as a tack. Now she has Alzheimer's disease. She doesn't recognize me, she..." Chelsey bit her lip and stopped speaking. She couldn't bear to list the depressing symptoms.

But the symptoms didn't matter anymore. They were about to vanish. Excitement grew and replaced the depression that always accompanied a visit to McKenzie's Nursing Home. She drew a long, deep breath, preparing herself.

"I'm ready, Alex. Pay attention. I wish..." A gold coin appeared between her fingers, growing unnaturally warm. "I wish that Dr. Harding's Alzheimer's would disappear and her mind would be as sharp as it has always been." Eyes shining, she gazed up at Alex and extended the coin. "Take it."

"Chelsey, I cannot grant your wish."

"No, listen," she said urgently. "I've thought this out. You're going to claim this wish does not benefit me. But, Alex, you're wrong. Nothing would make me happier than to see Dr. Harding sharp and alert like she used to be. If being happy doesn't benefit me, then I don't know what does. Happiness is a legitimate benefit. You have to grant this wish!''

"The rule is specific. It doesn't say you must benefit. The rule states that you must benefit *directly*. Curing Dr. Harding's Alzheimer's would directly benefit Dr. Harding—you would receive only a fleeting secondary benefit."

"Alex, please." Chelsey gripped his arm, pleading with him. "I beg you. Grant me this wish. You can have the other two wishes back, all I want is this one. Please. Please, Alex. I know you can grant this wish if you only would."

Alex stared at her in frank amazement. Nothing like this had ever occurred before. No master or mistress had ever begged to waste a wish for the sole benefit of another person. But her earnestness and sincerity could not be doubted. He looked into Chelsey Mallon's pleading eyes and felt cracks shoot through his philosophy regarding human selfishness.

"Chelsey, if I could do this for you," he said slowly, "I would. But I can't."

Her fingers dug into his arm. "Look at her. She was one of the most brilliant minds in archaeology. She loved to read and work puzzles. She was an amateur artist. Now she can't even remember her own name. She can't read or paint anymore. She just sits there, confused and in mental pain. You can help her, I know you can! Please, Alex. I'm begging you!"

He clasped her shoulders as tears brimmed in her eyes, then spilled over her cheeks. "Chelsey, listen to me. I admire you more than I can say for wanting to help Dr. Harding, but I can't accept this wish. The rule states—"

Jerking backward, she twisted out from under his hands. "The hell with the rules! If you won't grant this wish, then...then I want to speak to your supervisor or the head genie or whoever it is who made up these stupid damned rules! Do you hear me, Alex? I want to speak to the boss genie and I want to speak to him now!''

"There is no such person." His mind raced. Since this problem had not arisen before, he didn't actually know if the rule could be bent. "Give me the coin," he said finally. "I don't think it's possible, but I'll try to grant your wish."

"Thank you!" Immediately she thrust the gold coin into his hand and held her breath expectantly, her face blazing with hope.

"This is not in your best interest," he said, looking at her. "You understand that."

"Just do it!"

He studied her expression for a moment, then flexed his shoulders and turned, clearing his mind. He stared hard at Dr. Harding. Concentration narrowed his eyes, his body tensed. He willed forth the indefinable burst of energy that signified a wish had been granted.

Nothing happened. The sensation of forces gathering in his mind and body did not occur; he felt no alteration of his energy level. Dr. Harding continued to gaze out the window with vacant, uncomprehending eyes.

Silently, he turned to Chelsey and gently dropped the coin into the pocket of her slacks where it promptly disappeared. "I'm genuinely sorry."

Angrily she dashed the tears from her eyes. "What good is it to have a genie if you won't grant any of my wishes? This isn't fair!"

"Chelsey—"

But she didn't wait. Furious, she spun on her heel and ran out of the building. For the first time, she looked awkward to Alex. The sight of her trying to run and manage her cane unexpectedly squeezed his heart.

This was a unique and puzzling woman. She was defiant one moment, stunningly generous the next. Running away from him, she looked achingly vulnerable. But she could also be stubbornly fierce. He sensed she was intrigued by him, possibly drawn to him, yet she pushed him away. He didn't recall meeting anyone like her.

He reached the curb in time to watch her jump into her car and speed away from McKenzie's with the intention of leaving him behind.

Striving for patience, he appeared in the passenger seat beside her. "As I've explained several times, the only wishes I can grant are those—"

She ground her teeth and edged her body away from him. "Don't tell me again. In fact, don't even talk to me! I have nothing to say to you."

"I didn't make the rules. I only—"

"The thing is, I let my hopes and expectations build, I *believed* in you, that you could do it, then you trot out some insane rule and blandly announce you can't grant my wish. How would *you* feel if someone made extravagant promises, but when it came time to deliver, they wouldn't do it?"

"You're in the wrong lane. There's a car coming straight at us." Driving and riding in an automobile were nerve-racking experiences, exhilarating but perilous. It amazed him that the streets were not littered with crashed cars and broken bodies.

"Don't try to change the subject, damn it," Chelsey snapped, jerking on the steering wheel. "I'm furious, okay? I'm trying to think of a word that wraps together frustration, fury, disappointment, impatience and a dozen other depressing terms. This just is not fair! You're supposed to serve me, right? You're supposed to make my dreams come true, right? Well, let me tell you something,

Alex. You aren't doing it! As far as I'm concerned, I drew a dud genie!''

What she was saying stung his pride. He hated being a genie, despised catering to humanity's base desires, resented his perpetual servitude and loathed to the depths of his soul being deprived of life and reality. But no one—not one single master or mistress during the course of eleven hundred years—had *ever* so much as hinted that he had failed them. Or suggested that he was shirking his duty. Not once had a master or mistress accused him of betraying their trust.

Chelsey sped into her driveway, stamped on the brake inches from the garage door, got out, slammed the car door behind her, then threw up the garage door and shot the car inside, braking a hair's width from the back wall. Alex realized his fingers were digging into the upholstery.

''I need to calm down,'' she whispered, gripping the steering wheel. She drew several long, deep breaths. ''You do whatever you want to. I'm going to dig in the yard until I feel human again.''

''I am trying to serve you, mistress,'' he said stiffly, staring at the back wall of the garage. It was infuriating that she blamed him for rules that he hadn't made and had no choice about obeying. ''It would benefit us both if you would accept and adhere to the rules.''

''I mean it. Don't talk to me.'' She narrowed her eyes. ''I have a big date tonight, Alex. An important date. I'm warning you right now. If you do anything—and I mean *anything*—to mess up my date with Howard, I'll…I'll… I don't know what I'll do, but it will be drastic. So don't mess with me. Right now I'm more upset than I've been in a very long time. Don't make things worse.''

His jaw clenched and his eyes narrowed. ''My only

desire is to serve you and make you happy, oh wise mistress.''

''Don't give me that genie gibberish. What you say and what you do are two different things. I want your promise that you will not interfere with my date with Howard. That you won't do any weird magic stuff while he's here. That you won't embarrass me or do anything awkward that I'll have to invent a lie to explain. Promise me, Alex.''

He ground his teeth together, furious that she assumed the worst of him. ''I desire nothing but your happiness and pleasure,'' he said tersely. ''I exist to serve you.''

''That is a promise you had damned well better keep!'' she said sharply, getting out of the car and slamming the door.

He followed her inside, placing as much distance between them as it was possible for him to do. She was too angry to notice that he had not promised a damned thing, and he didn't intend to. Regardless of what she thought about his job performance, he couldn't disobey the rules.

Entering the back door, he gave one of the kitchen chairs a kick.

Who the hell was Howard?

Chapter Five

"How do I look?" Chelsey inquired nervously, smoothing her palms over the hips of a black silk pantsuit. A glitter belt hugged her waist. Her silk camisole was the same tawny ginger as her hair. As she liked the loose, wild curls that Alex had given her yesterday, she had kept the style, dressing it up for tonight by brushing back one side and securing it with a glitter comb.

"You instructed me not to speak to you."

She looked across the living room. "I'm still mad at you. But not as much."

Working in the yard had eased Chelsey's anger, but had increased her nervousness. While she planted geraniums along the back fence, Alex had knelt near the porch and experimented with flowers he wanted to remember. At one point her entire backyard, except for a circle around her, was filled with rye plants. When Chelsey jumped to her feet, pointing at the two-story houses overlooking her backyard, Alex had apologized and explained that peasants had grown rye around the village where he grew up north of Paris. He wanted to see and smell the rye fields again.

Aside from that moment and the moment when Chelsey

had tersely announced she was going upstairs to take a long, relaxing bath, they had not spoken.

"You look beautiful," Alex said in a husky voice. His smoldering gaze lingered over the ginger-and-black silk that molded the curves of her body. Finally his gaze returned to hers. "May I offer you a glass of wine?"

"Thank you." Blushing at his close inspection, Chelsey turned toward the grandfather clock. Howard was never late.

Hastily she reviewed a mental checklist. Toothpaste, makeup, mouthwash, a change of lingerie for tomorrow. It all fit inside a large purse. She preferred the purse to an overnight bag, in case she had misunderstood Howard's intentions. Chelsey didn't think she had, but it was better to be on the safe side than risk embarrassment.

"Who is Howard Webber?" Alex asked, crossing his ankles on top of the ottoman.

Now she noticed Alex was dressed more formally than she had previously seen him. He wore a lightweight cream-colored turtleneck beneath a charcoal jacket that made his eyes seem more blue than blue-green. Navy slacks and shoes completed the outfit.

"You look nice tonight, too," Chelsey commented, trying not to stare. Alex looked gorgeous, like a male model. "This wine is very good. What is it?"

"It's a Spanish vintage. It was a great favorite during the late eighteenth century."

Chelsey checked the clock again. She tried to convince herself that she wasn't feeling apprehensive about going to bed with Howard. They were friends. He already knew she didn't have a perfect body. There would be an awkward moment or two, then everything would be fine. Maybe it would even be wonderful.

"We'll tell Howard the same story we told Betty, okay?

You're an old friend from back east, we met in college, blah, blah, blah.'' She gave Alex a slightly narrowed look. ''It's crucial that you don't slip and call me mistress. And please, no magic while Howard is here.''

Alex moved to stand beside her, studying her fingers playing nervously with the wineglass. ''Are you in love with this Howard person?''

She bit her lip and gazed into the amber wine, feeling uneasy that Alex stood so close. He wore cologne tonight, a fragrance she didn't recognize. The faintly musky scent made her think of rumpled sheets and bodies twined together.

She moved backward a step. ''The relationship seems to be moving in that direction.'' A frown puckered her brow. ''It's too soon to tell if it's love.'' Maybe after tonight.

''But Howard Webber is important to you.''

She inhaled Alex's cologne and thought about feverish whispers and exploring hands. If the sofa hadn't hit the back of her knees, she would have moved backward another step. She swallowed and tried to recall what they were discussing. Howard.

''Howard's been a good friend at a time when I need all the friends I can get. When the university regents met to discuss…what happened last summer, Howard appealed to them on my behalf.'' Her eyes dropped to Alex's firm, wide mouth. When she realized she was staring, she made herself turn toward the front window. What was keeping Howard? ''He's been very supportive during a difficult period.''

''You aren't talking yourself into something, are you? Perhaps mistaking gratitude for something else?'' Alex asked gently. His glance traveled slowly down her body. ''Your blouse is the same silky color as your hair.''

"It is?" she asked weakly, meeting his eyes. His eyes were as deep and blue-green as the Mediterranean. She could drown in those eyes.

Chelsey straightened abruptly and gave herself a shake. What on earth was she doing? Fantasizing about one man minutes before she planned to go off to spend the night with another.

Frowning, she tasted her wine, then lifted her chin. "I think Howard and I are developing a relationship that's important to both of us." Alex was temporary; Howard would always be there for her. She needed to keep that distinction uppermost in her mind. "Howard cares about me. Does it really matter if my feelings began with gratitude? Of course I'm grateful to him." She paused, trying to focus. "A lot depends on tonight." She thought about the items in her purse, then darted a look at Alex. "Look, are you absolutely sure that you can't read people's minds?"

"I sense things," he answered, smiling. "But I can't read minds, no."

"What kind of things do you sense?" Chelsey demanded.

He shrugged. "I know if a person is good or evil, if his or her intentions are beneficial or malignant. I can usually tell if a person is lying. Occasionally the knowledge is specific—usually it's more of a general impression."

Chelsey thought about that. Anxiety overwhelmed her better judgment. "What do you sense about me?"

Could he tell that his cologne reeled through her senses and made her feel hot all over? Did he know that the rich timbre of his voice occasionally sent a thrill up her spine? Was he aware of how often she recalled him standing naked on the staircase? A warm blush tinted her throat as she waved a hand. "Never mind, I don't want to know."

Stepping forward, he cupped her chin in one hand and looked deeply into her eyes. His touch paralyzed her, made her nerves fizz like the end of a frayed cord. "You are a genuinely good person, Chelsey," he said quietly. "Something troubles you deeply, something I don't know yet. And you don't have the confidence in yourself that you should have."

His gaze dropped to her mouth. Staring at her as if mesmerized, he ran his thumb across her lips. Time seemed to stop. Chelsey's breath halted in her chest, and her eyes widened helplessly. She could not have stepped away from him even if she had wanted to. His fingertips were light on her skin, but they possessed her, drew her closer to the hard heat of his body. She stared at his mouth, absorbed by the contours of rough promise, and felt her own lips part in expectation. The wineglass trembled in her fingers.

The doorbell rang.

For an instant neither of them moved. They continued to stare into each other's eyes, drawing the moment out.

Finally, her heart pounding, Chelsey made herself step past him, careful not to brush against his body. She had the absurd idea that if her body touched him, something explosive and earthshaking would happen.

"Saved by the bell," she said lightly, hearing the quaver in her voice. Howard, she reminded herself firmly. Howard is your future. Not Alex; not a genie. She glanced toward the front door, drew a breath, then whispered, "Remember…you gave your word. You promised not to mess this up for me."

After straightening her shoulders and arranging a smile on her lips, trying to behave as if she were sophisticated enough to leave an intense moment with one man and go off with another, sophisticated enough that dinner followed by a night in a hotel was nothing extraordinary, Chelsey stepped to the door.

"Howard! On time as usual. Please come inside, there's someone I want you to meet."

A slight pucker of annoyance dimmed Howard's smile, and he made a point of consulting his pocket watch. "Our dinner reservations are for eight, and it's a forty-minute drive...."

"This will only take a minute. I'd like you to meet an old college friend. Alex has an archaeology grant from Harvard." Each time she told the lie, it rolled from her tongue a little easier. There was something depressing in that. "Alex, this is Howard Webber. Howard heads Colorado University's English department."

Chelsey watched as the two men shook hands, warily taking each other's measure. Her heart sank. Standing next to Alex, Howard looked short, bland and uninteresting. His sandy hair was thinning on top, something Chelsey hadn't previously permitted herself to notice. Nor had she taken note of the smug quirk of his thin lips or noticed how small his eyes were. Although it was a warm night, Howard wore a wool tweed jacket with suede patches on the sleeves. The stem of a pipe poked out of his pocket. He held himself like a man utterly convinced of his own importance, a man infinitely superior to his peers.

Chelsey gave herself a sharp mental shake. Howard might not resemble a film star and he might be a bit pretentious and overbearing, but he was her friend. After tonight, he would be much more. Howard had stood by her when others had not. He had defended her to the university regents. Did it really matter that he liked to quote Hegel, Kierkegaard and Nietzsche in everyday conversation? Or that he preferred Chelsey to leave her cane at home when they went out? Howard cared about her.

She could see that he and Alex had taken an instant dislike to each other. As Chelsey anxiously watched, they examined one another like prizefighters sizing up an opponent.

"Well," Chelsey said, summoning a cheerful tone. "I'll just get my purse, and we'll be on our way." She hesitated, then chose her brass-handled cane, the one she preferred for evening. She hoped the cane wouldn't embarrass Howard too much, but her leg was aching from kneeling all afternoon in the garden. She had been too angry at Alex to plan ahead.

Taking Howard's arm, she let him hasten her to the front door. "Don't wait up," she called to Alex. Then she cast an uneasy look at Howard, trying to guess his thoughts. "We'll be late. Very late."

"Is Duport staying here, with you?" Howard asked in a low voice. When Chelsey nodded, his thick eyebrows clamped into a frown of disapproval. Chelsey suspected she would hear more about this later. Howard paused, then turned at the door to glare back at Alex. His arm tightened around Chelsey's in a proprietary gesture. He had to tilt his head back slightly, but he met Alex's steady eyes. "We'll be back after brunch tomorrow. I'm sure you understand."

A silent sigh dropped Chelsey's shoulders. On the one hand, she was secretly pleased and a little surprised to discover Howard's jealousy and possessiveness. On the other, she would have preferred not to reveal their plans so pointedly. Especially not to Alex.

Alex returned Howard's stare. "It makes no difference to me when we return," he said.

"Good," Chelsey said, stepping forward and reaching

for the door handle. She froze. Surely Alex had not said *we*. Turning slowly, she leveled a long, now-hear-this stare. "There are leftovers in the fridge," she said evenly. "For your dinner. I'm sure you'll find plenty to do this evening, to occupy yourself while you're here. Alone. Do you understand?"

"I understand perfectly." He was so tall and so handsome and so damned sure of himself.

"Good," Chelsey said, holding his gaze. "Goodbye then," she called before she closed the door firmly behind her, feeling vastly relieved to escape before something went wrong. But she spoke too soon. She and Howard had not taken three steps before Alex spoke from directly behind her. Chelsey and Howard both jumped and whirled around.

"I believe you know the rule," Alex continued in a pleasant voice, speaking as if their conversation had not been interrupted.

"What rule?" Howard asked. He stared at Alex. "How did you get outside?"

Angry crimson flared upward from Chelsey's throat. She removed her hand from Howard's arm. "You go ahead. I'll be right behind you. I need to have a word with Alex." Her smile was grim.

Still staring at Alex with a puzzled expression, Howard pulled out his pocket watch and tapped a finger against the glass, reminding Chelsey that time was passing and they were running late. He looked as if he wanted to add something, but changed his mind and did as Chelsey asked. Each step signaled annoyance as he walked toward a green Ford parked at the curb.

When Howard was out of earshot, Chelsey whirled. "What do you think you're doing?" she asked furiously, speaking between her teeth.

Alex pushed his hands in his pockets and gazed down at her with a bland expression. "We're going out to dinner. Isn't that correct?"

"Don't play innocent with me! As you perfectly well know, that is not correct. Howard and I are going out to dinner. You are staying here. You are not invited." She stared at him. "Alex, don't take advantage of a weak moment. I'm not sure what happened between you and me a few minutes ago, but it changed nothing. Howard may be my future. I could fall in love with him. Now, don't mess this up!"

"As I have explained numerous times, oh forgetful mistress, I must remain within the sound of your voice."

"Not this time. This is a date, Alex, an important date. Tonight… Well, just take my word for it that tonight is very special. I thought I made that abundantly clear. Howard and I need to be alone."

"We have no choice." Alex spoke in a polite but firm voice. He glanced at Howard, who was standing beside the car, glaring at his watch. Alex's eyes twinkled and danced. "If it distresses you to have me ride inside with you, I'm willing to ride outside. I could still hear your voice if I sat on top of the car."

"Fun-ny," Chelsey snapped. She glanced at Howard, aware that his irritation increased by the second. Howard hated to wait, hated to be late. He was not a patient man. "I swear on all I hold dear that I will not be making any wishes tonight! Alex, you *cannot* come along!"

"My obligation is to remain by your side at all times." A twinkle of infuriating amusement accompanied his stubbornness.

Angry and starting to feel frantic, Chelsey clutched his lapels and gave him a shake. "Listen to me. What do I have to say to make you agree to remain here and leave us alone tonight?"

"There is nothing you can say, mistress. Where you go, I go."

Frustrated beyond reason, Chelsey stamped her cane on the walk. "Alex, this is crazy! You can't come with me on a date!"

"I regret to say the point is not negotiable."

Like hell he regretted it. He was enjoying the trouble he was creating. Before Chelsey exploded, Howard called to her, "We're going to be late!"

"I know, I know. I'll just be a minute." Leaning forward, she glared up into Alex's eyes and begged him. But it was hopeless. Chelsey recognized the unyielding truth in his gaze and in his posture. He was polite, he regretted everything, he was oh, so sorry. But he wasn't going to budge. "Damn it!" She could plead and argue from now until the next ice age and it wouldn't do any good. Alex's holy rules would not be broken; he would not yield an inch. Chelsey swore beneath her breath. "I hate this! Wait here," she said furiously, jabbing him in the chest with her finger. Leaning heavily on her cane, her thoughts racing, she stormed down the sidewalk toward Howard.

"Exactly what is going on here?" Howard demanded, scowling up the walkway to where Alex stood with his arms crossed over his chest. Alex wore a knowing smile that was designed to infuriate Howard. "Who is that bozo, anyway? And why is he staying at your place? Hasn't he heard of hotels?"

"Howard, we have a little problem." Reaching, Chelsey smoothed her hand down his jacket lapel. "You see…" As she had been doing since Alex popped into her life, she searched frantically for a plausible lie, hating the necessity. "The thing is, Alex is going through a rough time right now.'' She drew a long deep breath. ''His wife died, and…well, I don't think he should be left alone.''

''If he's so damned broken up, then why is the bastard smiling? And why does he look at you like he's undressing you in his mind? Is something going on between you two?''

Chelsey threw a venomous glance over her shoulder. Howard was right. Alex was smiling as if he knew a secret that Howard didn't. In another age a smile that insulting, that challenging, would h<u>a</u>ve called for swords and the naming of seconds.

She spoke through clenched teeth. ''Alex is an old friend, that's all.''

''Then why haven't I heard you mention him before?''

''He may be smiling on the outside, but he's mourning on the inside.'' Chelsey fought the desire to dash up the walk and assault Alex with her cane. She and Howard weren't even out of the driveway and already the evening was turning sour. They were both in dark moods which Chelsey was about to worsen. She made herself do it because she could see no other choice. ''Howard, I think it would be a nice gesture if we invited Alex to join us for dinner. He really shouldn't be alone.''

''What?'' Howard's mouth dropped open, then snapped shut. ''Chelsey, I've been planning this particular evening practically since the day I met you!'' Howard's gaze skimmed her lips, dropped suggestively to her breast. ''I thought you understood. I also thought you shared my feelings.…''

''I do!'' At least, she thought she did. She wanted to. Chelsey bit her lip hard. ''It's just that… Look, wait here. I'll talk to Alex again. There has to be a way to work this out.''

"If he's nothing but an old friend, as you claim—" Howard drew back and raised a suspicious eyebrow "—then he'll understand that we want to be alone. He won't make a problem."

Chelsey winced. She understood Howard was challenging her to prove that she and Alex were only friends. He was sensing something fishy.

Leaving Howard standing beside the car frowning at his watch, she hurried up the walkway and gripped Alex's arm. Desperation darkened her eyes.

"Alex, listen to me. Are you absolutely, positively sure there is no way I can go on this date without you tagging along?"

"None," he confirmed, smiling pleasantly. Chelsey was beginning to detest the reasonableness in his smile.

"I'd hoped it wouldn't come to this, but…there is a way around this problem. I just thought of it. All I have to do is use my wishes."

His smile vanished and he frowned. "Chelsey—"

"Here's my first wish," she said, speaking rapidly and urgently. "I wish you had never appeared in my life. Are you listening?" A coin came into her hand. "I wish you would go back to your lamp or wherever you came from. I wish you would disappear and let me get on with my life. Adieu, Monsieur Duport, it's been fun. Goodbye." She stared into the amusement dancing in his eyes, and waited for him to vanish. When he didn't, she sighed. "Okay, Alex. Why are you still here?"

"Wishing your genie away is not in your best interests. It does not benefit you."

Behind her Howard began drumming his fingertips on the roof of the car. Chelsey could feel his stare and his growing anger.

"Okay, we'll try again. I wish for a diamond ring, I

wish for great hair, I wish for a long, wonderful, uninterrupted evening alone with Howard. Those are my three
wishes, here are the coins.'' Grabbing Alex's hand, she
closed his fingers around the coins. ''Grant me the wishes
quickly, then take a hike while I still have a prayer of
salvaging this mess. Better luck on your next mistress or
master. Adieu. Adios. Goodbye and farewell.''

He smiled down at her, clinking the coins in his hand.

''Damn it!'' She cast a nervous glance back at Howard.
''Why aren't you gone?''

''It does not benefit you to squander your wishes on a
hasty impulse.''

''I am so frustrated I could scream!'' She stamped her
cane on the walk, then shoved back a lock of hair. ''I
plain don't believe this! Are you saying you won't grant
three bona fide, legitimate wishes? You can't do that!
Where do I go to file a complaint?''

''You're making a mistake, Chelsey. Are you aware
that Webber plans to seduce you? The bastard has it all
planned. The restaurant he's taking you to is located in a
hotel.''

''Augusta's is one of Denver's finest restaurants! And
we're going to forfeit our reservations because of you!''

''After dinner Webber plans to take you upstairs to a
hotel suite he has already rented. He plans to seduce
you.''

''Alex, I'm begging you. It's been a year and a half
since I was last seduced. Can you understand what I'm
saying? I *want* to be seduced. I can't wait to be seduced.
I'm dying to be seduced! So get the hell out of the way
and let it happen!''

''Howard Webber is not worthy of you. He's dung on
a camel's tail.''

Chelsey hastily checked her own watch. If Howard

stepped on the gas and they made all the lights, they would only be fifteen minutes late for their dinner reservation. "Howard may not be a paragon of virtues, but neither am I. Alex, I'm begging you. Grant my wishes and let me go."

He bristled, swelling up before her eyes. "You are indeed a person of virtue, mistress. You are a beautiful woman with many fine qualities. Any man would be proud to call you his own." His dark head lifted to glare at Howard. "It pains me more deeply than you can guess that you wish to surrender yourself to a piece of camel dung like Howard Webber. But if that is your preference, then so be it." Inclining his head, he dropped into a deep salaam. "I shall make myself invisible. You will not be aware that I am present."

"Chelsey?" Howard's voice spiraled toward a shout. "This is getting ridiculous!"

"That won't work!" Chelsey's voice was as wild as her eyes. "I don't want you in the hotel room with Howard and me even if you're invisible! I'd feel— I don't want you there at all!" She pressed a hand against her forehead. "This is hopeless. Please, Alex," she whispered, her voice a plea. "Don't do this. Please let me have this night alone with Howard. Howard is the first man in a long time who… Please, I'm begging you not to ruin tonight."

He touched the back of his hand to her cheek, his touch gentle, almost sympathetic. Almost. "Dear mistress, the rules must be obeyed."

"You and your crazy rules are ruining my life!" And there was no way out, no acceptable solution. "This isn't going to work, is it?" Conceding the obvious and not waiting for an answer, Chelsey walked slowly back to Howard's car. Her purse strap hung heavy on her shoul-

der. Now she felt foolish about the items inside, the toothpaste and lingerie. The plans and hopes.

"Well, are you satisfied?" Howard asked angrily.
"We've missed our dinner reservations."

"I'm sorry, Howard, but I think we'll have to postpone
our special evening."

"I beg your pardon?" He stared at her. "Are you telling me that you're choosing him over me?"

"That isn't true. But it is true that I can't leave him
right now." At some point between pacing back and forth
between the two men, Chelsey had dropped her cane. Her
leg was throbbing. With surprise she noticed twilight had
faded to full darkness. "Believe me, I wish I could leave
Alex behind. You'll never know how much I wish it. But
I can't. It's impossible."

"I was right. There is something going on between you
two!"

Alex moved up behind her, then stood in front of Howard, placing Howard at a distinct disadvantage. Alex was
taller and leaner. More handsome, better dressed. His
smile was cold and didn't reach his eyes.

"Allow me to explain," he said, speaking to Howard.
Contempt flickered behind his hard gaze. "I am not permitted to leave my mistress's side until I have made her
most secret desires come true."

"You bastard!" Howard said between his teeth.

"Alex, you are absolutely wrecking my life," Chelsey
groaned. His choice of words and the look he gave her
were deliberately sensual, deliberately intended to pro-
voke. She closed her eyes in despair and her hands curled
into fists. "Why are you doing this?"

Alex continued to stare a challenge at Howard. "I am
obligated to remain within reach of my mistress's most

tender whisper. Should her sweet lips murmur a wish, I must be near enough to hear it.''

A dark plum color infused Howard's cheeks. He glared an accusation at Chelsey. ''If you wanted to break it off, all you had to do was say so. You didn't have to humiliate me!''

''Howard, please! It isn't like that! I can explain everything if you'll just—''

''Forget it!'' Outrage stiffened Howard's frame. His lips pressed together so tightly they disappeared. ''I've heard all I need to hear.''

''Howard, please listen.'' Despair pinched Chelsey's features. ''I know how unbelievable this is going to sound, but Alex is—''

''You picked your moment, didn't you? You let me think we were going to have a 'special evening.' I'll bet you and your 'friend' had a lot of laughs planning this!''

Horrified by what Howard was saying, by what was happening, Chelsey watched helplessly as he marched around his car to the driver's side. She started to follow, but Howard shot her an icy smile across the roof of the car.

''Well, don't flatter yourself, Chelsey honey. I planned to dump you after tonight. You didn't really believe I'd settle for a cripple, did you? I can do a lot better than you.''

Chelsey's head jerked as if he had slapped her. Shock froze her in place as Howard slid into his car and sped into the darkness. She stood on the curb, pressing her hand against the pain that filled her chest then expanded to fill her body.

''Revenge is a valid direct benefit,'' Alex said sharply, stepping up beside her. Anger shook his large frame. ''You have only to wish it, and Howard Webber will suffer a fatal accident. He will never insult you or anyone else again."

A second wave of shock shot down Chelsey's spine. She stared up at him with wide, damp eyes. "I don't understand you. You're willing to murder a man if I wish it...but you wouldn't permit me to enjoy a romantic evening that would have harmed no one. What kind of monster are you?"

"You heard what Webber said. He intended to use you, then abandon you."

"He was speaking in anger! He thinks you and I are lovers, that we were deliberately toying with him, making a fool of him."

"He was also speaking the truth. He's small, petty and cruel. I knew everything about Howard Webber the instant I shook his hand."

"Stop it! I don't want to hear this." Bending, Chelsey found her cane in the grass, then, moving with as much dignity as her aching leg and devastated pride would permit, she returned to the house. By now she knew a locked door was no defense against a genie, but it made her feel marginally better to slam the door.

"You're far better off without Webber," Alex said, appearing beside her. "You deserve better."

"Do I?" Chelsey shouted, spinning to face him. "Howard was right. I am a cripple!"

That Alex had witnessed her humiliation devastated her. Alex, who was making a shambles of her life.

Tears sprang into her eyes and spilled down her cheeks, adding one more embarrassment to an evening overflowing with humiliation. Mortified, Chelsey grabbed the banister and fled up the staircase.

"Leave me alone!"

All she wanted was to wash her face, put on her oldest,

most comfortable bathrobe and curl into a solitary ball on her bed. She hadn't felt this wretched since her mother made her attend her high school prom. Watching the others dance while she sat on the sidelines had driven a dagger into her heart. She felt the same humiliation now, the same hideous embarrassment of being publicly rejected.

Holding back the tears, she slammed her bedroom door behind her.

ALEX PACED IN THE HALLWAY outside her door, seething with jealously and righteous indignation.

How dare that self-centered, puffed-up, malicious little bastard even think of putting his hands on Chelsey.... The thought of it enraged him.

It wasn't enough merely to thwart Howard Webber's intentions. He wanted to punish Howard Webber and punish him decisively. As he recalled the deliberate cruelty of Webber's parting comments, Alex's jaw clenched and the blood pounded in his head. Watching Chelsey return to the house, holding her head high with quiet, painful dignity, was enough to make him shake with the need for revenge.

Pacing back and forth, he tried to think of a way to compensate Chelsey for her undeserved pain and her failed expectations for this evening. Although he detested sharing anything in common with Howard Webber, Alex conceded that he was as much to blame for Chelsey's pain as Howard was. If it had not been for Alex and the rules that bound him, Howard would not have deliberately insulted and wounded his mistress.

His obligation was to serve, not to agitate. To gratify, not to anger. But all he had accomplished so far was to upset Chelsey and disappoint her.

The admission made him feel wild inside. He wanted

to blot out her bad experience with Webber. He wanted to restore her self-image and make her smile again. Damn it, he wanted her to be happy.

Somehow Chelsey Mallon was different from all the others. She had gotten under his skin and stirred something inside.

When he'd first met her, Alex had thought she was pretty and attractive, but he didn't recall thinking of her as stunningly beautiful. This omission now seemed incredible to him. When she was happy, Chelsey Mallon was the most beautiful creature he had ever observed. She took his breath away. Her smile could have launched the thousand ships attributed to Helen of Troy. Her sparkling eyes captured the sunlight with twin flames. No one observing her vivacious smile could resist smiling in return.

And there was much more. She possessed a quiet bravery and a generous heart. She combined spirit and vulnerability. Temper and compassion.

"Chelsey?" He knocked on her bedroom door.

"Go away!"

Had he remembered to list pride and stubbornness when he listed her unique qualities? The obstinate tilt of her chin was justified. She didn't capitulate easily, he thought, smiling. But then, neither did he. Their battle of wills was well matched.

"Chelsey, come here, please. I'm not going to stop knocking on your door until you come out."

"I mean it. Go away and leave me alone!"

"I have a surprise for you."

"I don't want a surprise! Give me a break, Alex. Just go away."

He rapped his knuckles on her door. "Chelsey?"

A long silence ensued during which he called to her

again. Finally he heard her swear. A moment later the
sound of angry footsteps approached the door.

''Shazam,'' he muttered, straightening his tie.

She flung open the door, her face furious. She wore an
old bathrobe and her feet were bare. ''This better be important, Alex, because—'' Her angry words ended on a
gasp and her eyes flared wide with astonishment. ''Good
God,'' she whispered, staring past him. ''What happened
to the hallway? Where did it go? Alex...where are we?''

Chapter Six

They stood on the marble terrace of an Italian villa that had once belonged to a friend of Alex's, a fellow crusader. Soaring stone arches framed ribbons of moonlight glistening across the Mediterranean Sea. A warm night breeze floated off the waves, stirring the bougainvillea that dripped like crimson lace from huge terra-cotta urns.

"Since Roman antiquities are your specialty, I thought..." Here and there he had scattered marble pedestals topped by Roman artifacts. The air of Southern Italy shimmered with the luminous quality he had discovered nowhere else. Italy seemed a logical choice for her.

The delight in Chelsey's wide eyes told him that he had guessed correctly. His surprise had succeeded.

Lustrous marble tiles, stone balustrades and a warm moonlit sea were as romantic a vision as he could conjure. And he had not forgotten that Chelsey had missed her dinner. Positioned in the center of a high curving archway facing the sea was a long, lace-draped table. Paper-thin china and heavy silver gleamed beneath the soft radiance of scented candles.

"You shall have your romantic dinner," he announced firmly. Stepping forward, he took her hand and wrapped it around his arm, leading her forward.

"But, Alex…" She wet her lips then spoke in another whisper. "I'm not dressed for—"

"Shazam."

In an instant her terry bathrobe vanished. He dressed her in Grecian gauze, a petal-draped hem reaching to her ankles as he knew she would prefer. He gave her gold sandals and a gold bracelet that circled her upper arm. The low neckline and filmy material drew his gaze to her breasts, and he sucked in a low, hard breath. She was so beautiful. It required enormous willpower not to pull her into his arms and ravage that trembling mouth.

Chelsey didn't notice the hard intensity of his narrowed gaze. She peered down at herself with pleasure and wonder, then held the gown out from her body, letting the material slip through her fingertips like cobwebs. She raised a quick, self-conscious hand to her hair. Before she could speak, Alex dressed her hair in a tumbled upsweep, restraining the springy ginger curls with a gold circlet that rested at the top of her forehead. A few unruly tendrils escaped the circlet and curled beside her cheeks and at the nape of her slender neck.

"This is… It's… I don't know what to say," she murmured. She tried to smile, the effort self-conscious. "Did you give me the right makeup to go with this splendor?"

"Yes." But he hadn't. Her heart-shaped face required no artifice beyond a slight darkening of the lashes. Her skin was smooth and lovely, her mouth naturally rosy.

Raising the hem of the gown, she examined the gold sandals and thin straps that crisscrossed her calves. For a moment Alex believed she would protest his choice. She started to speak, but changed her mind. Instead, she took his arm again and allowed him to escort her to the table.

Alex could easily have provided a built-up shoe like she usually wore, but he deliberately decided against it.

When she emerged barefoot from the bedroom, he had instantly noticed the shorter leg gave her a provocative, slightly rolling gait that he found wildly seductive. His eyes had been riveted to her undulating hips and sexy walk.

Swallowing, he mounted a heroic effort not to dwell on those perfect curving hips and fought to ignore the yielding softness of her breast brushing his arm. Concentrating, he made himself focus on the scents of the food and the perfumed fragrance of the air instead of the sweet apple scent rising from her skin and hair.

After holding out her chair, he stepped backward away from temptation. "Is everything to your liking, mistress?" The array of serving dishes marching down the long table included everything he had imagined she might enjoy.

"Oh yes," she answered softly, gazing toward the moonlight shimmering on the sea. Silver-capped waves whispered up a pebbled beach and foamed around a rock outcropping. A swollen moon filled the sky like a plump lemon resting on black velvet. "Alex…" She touched her fingertips to her throat and gazed up at him, her eyes as soft as her voice. "Is this real? Or am I dreaming?"

He smiled, hungering to kiss her. "It is real."

"I don't know how to thank you for all this." Her hands rose, then fluttered back to her lap. "It's just… It's magical. The sea, the flowers, the moonlight shining on the marble, all this…." A gesture indicated the table and candelabra, the urns and stone arches, the scented air, her gown.

"It isn't necessary to say anything," he said, pleased by her dazed reaction. Clearly she was not thinking about that bastard, Howard Webber. "Enjoy your dinner, mistress." Inclining his head, he stepped backward, hoping to fade into the shadows. But he was unable to take his eyes off of her.

Candlelight alternately disclosed then shadowed her face and the tops of her breasts, softly illuminating her skin, enhancing the satiny glow of strawberry and pale ivory tones. Her eyes were fringed pools of dark liquid. The warm night breeze toyed with loose curls framing her graceful throat. Hungrily, Alex stared at her beauty and felt his stomach tighten sharply.

For several minutes she sat very still, gazing out at the waves and moonlight. Once she lowered her head and raised her fingertips to her eyes. At length she reached for her wine and returned her attention to the table. But Alex didn't begin to relax until he watched the tension drain from her shoulders and thought he glimpsed a smile.

"Alex?"

In an instant he was at her side, worried that he had overlooked some crucial element. "Mistress?"

A flash of exasperation compressed her features. "What is it going to take to break you of that habit? Please don't call me mistress! It's causing me no end of problems."

"For which I apologize," he murmured, bowing to conceal a smile. "How may I serve you?"

"Everything you've done is wonderful—enchanting, in fact—and I'm deeply grateful."

"But…?" A frown drew his heavy eyebrows.

She smiled, and at once he relaxed, thinking how absolutely lovely she was. He wondered if she guessed how wildly desirable she was. He suspected she had no idea.

"There's something missing. Usually a romantic dinner is more successful if two people are present, don't you agree?" A twinkle of humor returned to her wonderful dark eyes. "Dinner for one sort of defeats the whole idea. Will you join me?"

"I would be delighted." Being uncertain of her mood, he hadn't anticipated that she would welcome company. Especially his. It flattered and pleased him that she did.

"No, don't sit way down there. Sit here beside me so we can talk." Tilting her head, she squinted down the length of the table. "I've seen tables like this in films and I always thought it was a lonely arrangement."

He took the seat to her right and draped a snowy napkin across his dinner jacket and slacks. "Will you have mushrooms or shrimp or escargot?" he inquired.

"The mushrooms, I think." She watched him serve the mushrooms, then shrimp for himself. "Why did you look so surprised when I asked you to join me?"

"I assumed you were still furious with me. And rightly so."

"Alex…" She dropped her head and frowned at the lace cloth. "About tonight…"

"I'm deeply sorry for my role."

A sigh lifted her magnificent breasts, and he almost spilled the shrimp platter. "You were only following your rules."

"Chelsey, is it necessary to discuss this? I'd hoped to help you forget it."

"There are a few things that need to be said." She drew another full breath that molded the gauzy material of the gown around her full breasts. Alex stared. He could almost see her nipples through the filmy material.

"I was wrong to get so angry, and I apologize. I'm still learning about genies. It sounds stupid now, but I didn't think your rules would apply to a date. I know," she added, raising a hand. "You've made it clear that you have no control over the rules—they must be obeyed. I didn't think the situation through. I should have verified

my assumptions. Then, when they proved wrong, I should
have phoned Howard and postponed our evening.''

''Postponed?'' he asked, searching her eyes. ''Or canceled?'' He was doing it again. Intruding in her life.

She turned to face the night sea, gripping her napkin in
her hands. Circles of pink bloomed on her cheeks. ''I was
trying so hard to convince myself that I could fall in love
with Howard. Trying so hard to be the person Howard
wanted that I didn't ask myself if Howard was what I
wanted.'' She turned and met his eyes with a clear gaze.
''Obviously, he isn't.''

''I'm glad to hear it.''

''Everyone I know will be.'' A suggestion of regret
hovered around a half smile. She shook her head, then
sampled one of the mushrooms before she leaned forward
to steal a shrimp off his plate. Her unconscious theft
charmed him as much as the sudden, breathtaking glimpse
of her cleavage.

''Howard is a closed chapter, and I have you to thank.
I guess I always knew he was a mistake. But after he
defended me to the regents...'' She shrugged. ''He kept
pushing for a relationship, and I coasted along, letting it
happen. I was grateful, plus he didn't seem to mind
that...'' The color deepened in her cheeks. ''That isn't
important anymore.''

Alex refilled their champagne flutes. ''What happened
last summer in Istanbul? Why was it necessary for Howard, or anyone, to defend you?''

When she tilted her head back, the breeze caught the
tendrils at her neck and teased them across her smooth,
bare shoulders. ''I wish I didn't have to tell you about
Istanbul.'' Hastily she lowered her head and raised her
palm. ''That's rhetorical, not a real wish. But I have decided on my first real wish, and it's connected to what

happened last summer. So I guess I'll have to tell you."
A plea appeared in her eyes. "But not now, not tonight.
Alex, this moment is too magical to spoil. We'll talk about
Istanbul tomorrow, okay?"

"As you prefer." Someone besides Webber had hurt
her. He saw the pain and embarrassment in her eyes before she looked away.

During dinner they restricted their conversation to safe
topics that carried no emotional charge. Both shared an
interest in history, and Alex listened avidly to Chelsey's
anecdotes about digs and historical finds. He contributed
a few anecdotes of his own, delighted when he made her
laugh. They traded memories of traveling in Italy, Greece,
and the Middle East. They discussed art and music. Alex
told his camel story; Chelsey told her train story. They
talked about interesting people they had met or known,
compared their favorite foods.

After dinner, Chelsey gave him a smile that electrified
his skin. She gazed into his eyes. For a minute, all Alex
could think about was sweeping her into his arms and
molding her womanly heat against his hard body. She
looked pliant and yielding, soft eyed and moist lipped.
His body ached from wanting her.

"Tell me about you," she said softly, folding her arms
on the cleared table and giving him an attentive, speculative look that required another effort of will not to mis-
understand. Such seductively intent gazes had undone
many a man. "I know you were a crusader. Once you had
a wife. Now you're a genie. Tell me more about the man
who is going to make my wishes come true."

He shrugged, glancing away from her feathery long
lashes, soft lips and the glowing skin he wanted to stroke
and caress.

"Alex?"

"There isn't much to tell. My father was a blacksmith, my mother raised eight children of which three survived to adulthood. I was the second-oldest son. My family lived in a cottage in a farm village about sixty miles north of Paris. It might as well have been a million miles. I knew only one man who had traveled more than fifteen miles outside the village, our liege lord, Baron Duvoux. When Duvoux called for men to join his Crusade, I was among the first to appear at the fortress."

"Were you a religious man? Was that why you were eager to enlist in a Crusade?"

"I wasn't especially religious," he answered. "But Duvoux was, and I believed in Baron Duvoux and in his philosophy and ideals. Duvoux took an interest in me—I was educated at the manor with his sons. What I wanted was to discover what existed beyond the perimeters of the rye fields. I wanted to see and know the world. I wanted to experience all that life could offer a man with no wealth and few prospects." He smiled at the memory.

"Ah," Chelsey said, returning his smile. "The second-son syndrome."

"In my day only the first son could inherit. Not that there was much to inherit in my family. The prospects were uncertain for Jean and dismal for myself and my younger brother. There were many who joined the Crusades in search of adventure, glory, or, like myself, a future."

She touched his hand and gazed into his eyes, speaking softly. "It was Selidim who made you into a genie, wasn't it?"

He nodded, idly lacing his fingers through hers. Her hand combined strength and softness, another of the contradictions that fascinated him.

"Mehmed argued for having me drawn and quartered,

but Selidim possessed a more subtle hatred. He sought a punishment worse than death—he wanted disillusionment and his own form of justice. To Selidim, I represented all the crusaders who arrived in waves to subjugate his people, to impose a foreign philosophy upon him and his subjects. He turned the tables by deciding that I would spend eternity bound in servitude to others, granting wishes instead of imposing them.'' His grim smile did not reach his eyes. ''To Selidim, this was punishment founded in basic justice. There is a certain ironic elegance to his reasoning.''

''Selidim possessed the power or the magic to do such a thing?'' Chelsey whispered. ''Obviously he did, but...?''

''I can't explain how it was done. I don't know. But yes, the dark arts exist, and Selidim had mastered them.''

Her eyes were so intent, so large and dark and filled with sympathy, that Alex felt as if he were drowning in soft brown velvet. His thighs tensed and his jaw tightened. He wanted her with an urgency that was becoming physical pain.

''What happens when you are not serving a master or mistress? Where do you go?''

''I can't explain, at least not the physical place,'' he said, frowning at her lips. ''I don't know. It's like being submerged in a floating dream state.'' He looked away from the distraction of seductive lips and eyes, seeking words to describe the indescribable. ''I dream the world as it's happening. I saw Columbus land in the New World, observed Napoleon's march to Moscow, witnessed the ovens at Dachau. I observed the triumphs of Washington, Jefferson, Lincoln, Kennedy.... I watched it all as if in a dream. The wars and broken treaties. The inventions, the industry, the progress. I dreamed it.''

After a pause, she asked, "Is that why you seem so modern and up-to-date? It isn't that you're out of touch with the world—you're aware of all that occurs. But you only dream it?"

"The frustration of the dream state is the lack of sensation. I observe and hear, but I cannot taste or smell or touch. It's as if—" he searched for an adequate comparison "—as if you lived within your television set. The figures are negatives. They have no weight or substance, no compelling reality. You can observe and learn, but you can experience nothing sensory, can affect nothing. After a time, you begin to question reality itself. What is it? Does it exist? In the dream state there is no pain, no pleasure. No sense of time passing. No hunger, no weariness, no comfort or discomfort. There are no sensations beyond the inadequate facilities of memory."

Shock knit her brows. "I can't imagine existing like that."

"If the dream state were all there could be or would be, perhaps such an existence would be tolerable. But there are moments of emergence into the reality plane, two or three hours when I'm summoned to a reminder of all the richness of experience that I can no longer enjoy. This world—" he flexed his shoulders and spread his hands "—is so bright and noisy and ripe with scents and tastes and textures. It's so raw and splendid and *alive!*"

For a long moment, she sat looking at him without speaking. "It must be terrible to return to the dreaming."

"Returning is agony," he admitted simply. There was no bid for pity in his voice. "I promise myself I will remember the scent of a wood fire or the fragrance of a rose or the earthy good smell of a horse's sweat. I think it's not possible to forget the sweetness of summer wine or the rich tang of Greek olives and cheese. Or the taste of bread. I'm certain I will recall the difference between a dog's warm fur and the silky hair of a child. Always I am wrong. There is no memory more elusive than that of a scent or a taste or a touch. They tantalize but evaporate and cannot be retrieved.''

"I'm sorry." Her sympathy filled his vision. The scent of her skin reminded him of apples on a summer day. Her hand gripped his. "How long must this punishment endure? When will Selidim release you?"

A harsh laugh shattered fantasies of kissing her until she grew dizzy in his arms. "Selidim has been moldering in his tomb for centuries. He was not fool enough to wish eternity for himself. Eternity is a punishment."

"I don't understand," Chelsey said, frowning. "If Selidim is dead, then who imposes your rules?"

"The rules simply are. They were never explained, yet I knew them." He stroked his thumb across the back of her hand. "This experience with you, this prolonged stay in the reality plane, has been enlightening. I'm learning new rules."

"Heaven help us," she said, smiling and rolling her eyes.

He returned her smile. "For instance, I didn't know I required sleep."

"Thirty minutes isn't sleep. It's a catnap."

"And I've discovered I can eat without feeling sated."

A deep, smoky look appeared behind his eyes, and Chelsey's heartbeat quickened. She imagined him wondering if there were other things he could do without feeling sated.

Dropping her head, she caught a breath and studied their clasped hands. His hands were large and strong, yet the fingers were tapered and elegant. A few silky dark hairs showed between his wrist and cuff. "How long can you stay in the reality plane? Are there rules governing that?''

''The problem hasn't risen before.'' He gazed at her, hoping to memorize her lovely face. Her hair formed a slight peak at her forehead, enhancing the heart shape of her face. ''I'll know if a governing rule emerges. I'll feel an inner pressure.''

One delicate, ginger-colored eyebrow lifted, and she laughed, her eyes soft and shining in the candlelight. ''You must have thought I was an idiot when I mentioned that nonsense about you sleeping in the cup lamp.''

''Not an idiot.'' He paused, then grinned. ''But you have to admit it was a peculiar idea.'' She was so lovely that he couldn't look away from her.

''No one has ever made that suggestion before?''

''I've never been in the reality plane long enough that where I slept or if I slept was a concern. Moreover, past ages have been more willing to accept a genie than this age seems to be. There were fewer questions.''

When she smiled, her entire face lit from within. ''You could search the world over and I doubt you'd find three people who would admit to actually believing in genies.''

Returning her smile, he lifted her hand and pressed her palm over his heart. ''As you can see, genies are very real.''

Their eyes met and held. An aeon passed and worlds collided while two people gazed into each other's eyes and glimpsed dark whirlpools of promise.

That's how it felt to Chelsey as she pressed her hand against the rock-solid warmth of his hard chest. As if time had stopped to allow this moment to expand and expand until she thought the growing tension between them would cause her to fly apart inside. In self-defense, she finally cleared her throat self-consciously and gently withdrew her hand. She lowered her gaze and laid aside her napkin. "Thank you for tonight, Alex. This was absolutely lovely. Most of all, I appreciate what you were trying to do."

"Did I overlook anything?" He was still staring at her with those blazing blue-green eyes that asked so many questions and promised so much.

She glanced at the sea beyond the urns of flowers and released a sigh. "This is so perfect. The only thing missing was music." A teasing twinkle enlivened her lovely dark eyes, lightening the moment. "Frankly, the conversation was so interesting that I didn't notice until now."

"Shazam," he said, humoring her with the nonsense word.

A forty-piece orchestra appeared on a dais at the far end of the terrace. Chelsey laughed out loud and clapped her hands as the haunting strains of a Viennese waltz reached them across the expanse of moonlit marble tiles.

"Wonderful!"

Taking her fingertips, Alex drew her to her feet and led her to the stone balustrade overlooking the sea. He should have remembered music. Music and dancing were an integral part of a romantic evening. Of course she would expect music.

Turning her to face him in the moonlight, he paused for an instant to look at her, then gently guided her into his arms, intending to dance. But the stunning warmth of her woman's body momentarily paralyzed him. This, above all things, was impossible to remember in the dream state—the yielding softness of a beautiful woman's curves, her warm seductive scent, the quickening of breast and breath, the explosive passion hinted in shining eyes and parted lips.

He held her firmly against his body, against his hard

instant arousal, while tides of erotic sensation rocked his senses.

The instant Alex guided her into his arms, Chelsey experienced the force of a lightning strike. She, too, felt paralyzed. His hand seared through her gown as if the gauzy material had fallen away, and his fingertips explored her naked skin. Her blood heated and raced through her body with a tingling sensation. A deep hot tremor began in the pit of her stomach and thrilled through her limbs. With her trembling hands on his shoulders, she gazed into Alex's smoldering eyes, and her mouth went dry as she read his desire. Something stunningly physical was happening that had never happened to her before.

She could feel each single fingertip on her back, gentle yet masterful, sensitive yet mapping the feel and heat of her, sending earthquake tremors through her nervous system.

Standing hip to hip with him, she could feel his body hard against hers, as taut and urgent as the physical hunger blazing in his eyes. An answering passion swept through Chelsey's body like a soaring flood tide. Because she could not help herself, because suddenly she desperately needed to touch him, Chelsey lifted a shaking hand and stroked her fingertips across his jawline, then traced his lips, surprised to discover the firm contours disguised a softness she had not expected. Her touch sent a shudder down his body and he groaned softly.

"Alex, I feel..."

Gazing into his eyes sent the world spinning around her. His personal magic electrified the air and his eyes and hands and body, and it electrified Chelsey, as well. She felt his restrained power, felt as if her nerve endings were fizzing and throwing off sparks. She gazed into his smoldering eyes and trembled with wanting to taste his kiss.

Alex's intense gaze held hers as he lifted a hand and gently raised her chin. Not looking away from her, he lowered his head until his mouth almost touched her lips, until their breath mingled and tension crackled between them. Then he paused, a pause that sent her nerves into a frenzy, and one dark eyebrow lifted.

"Yes," she whispered when she understood. "Yes."

Finally his lips softly brushed hers, teasingly, tentatively, as if he expected her to resist and pull away from him. When she offered no resistance—could not resist— Alex's arms tightened around her and he kissed her again. This time he pulled her tightly, almost roughly, against his tall hard body. This time his mouth was not soft, but demanding, hot and eager on hers, claiming her, possessing her.

Chelsey could not have resisted him if her life had depended upon it. Never had she been kissed like this. Never. Alex's kiss, increasingly hard and insistent, shot a burning brand through Chelsey's body, scorched across her nervous system. Her knees weakened and she swayed dizzily against him, gripping his shoulders for support. Then his tongue parted her lips, and she gasped as he plundered the sweetness within.

When they drew apart to gaze into each other's eyes, Alex tightened his arms and held her so close she could feel his heartbeat pounding against her breast, could feel his powerful arousal. He pressed his face into her hair with a low groan.

"If you only knew how long it's been since I've wanted a woman as much as I want you...."

Chelsey felt weak from the force of a sudden explosive passion. Never had a man's kiss or a man's touch affected her as Alex's kiss had. Never had she experienced this kind of erotic urgency, this passionate blend of confusion and desire, this melting dizziness at a man's caress. Only his powerful hands on her waist kept her from falling—that and the strength of her growing desire.

"Alex," she whispered, "Alex," needing to say his name aloud, hearing it emerge as a soft moan of yearning and wonder. "Alex." There was urgency and discovery in her whisper, surprise and desire.

This time when he kissed her, there was no hint of holding back. His mouth was as hard and demanding as his body, possessive on hers. His large hands molded her hips, forming her body tightly against his. Her arms wound around his neck, her fingers twisted through his hair. She could not think, could not breathe, she could only feel the hot wild sensations flooding her secret places. The sea and sky fell away and nothing existed but Alex. Alex. His mouth, his eyes, his large hands exploring her body and her own breathless response and burning desire.

Chelsey had never before felt this sudden volatile need and flooding passion, this sensitivity to a man's slightest nuance and to the contrast of his hard masculine body crushing her feminine softness. The yin and yang of oneness. Never had she been so powerfully aware of her own physical desires.

Kissing, frantically touching each other, swaying to the music, they clung together, fingers flying, stroking and discovering, lost in the magical wonder of what was happening to them.

It seemed so natural when Alex's hand slipped around Chelsey's waist, when he cradled her hand close to his chest and stepped forward as the music swelled and enveloped them.

Chelsey stumbled.

Cold reality washed over her. She returned to her senses as abruptly as if she had been splashed with a bucket of ice water. Shock and repugnance trembled down her body.

Alex wanted to *dance*.

White-faced and shaking, she flattened her palms against his chest and sharply pushed him away from her. The gesture was automatic and involuntary. She could not have prevented it even if she'd wanted to.

"I don't dance!" she snapped furiously, her voice a choked whisper.

That Alex would expect her to dance devastated her with a force as painful as Howard's comments. With her shorter leg and without her special shoes, she couldn't possibly dance. She would be graceless and awkward, stumbling after him in a clumsy parody. An object for ridicule and laughter.

"I don't know how to dance. I can't."

It was so obvious that he should have guessed, should have known. Feeling betrayed and confused, Chelsey spun and hurried toward the nearest door, knowing she looked clumsy and ridiculous, praying that the door led back to her bedroom.

When she saw her old bathrobe folded across her spread, she dashed inside and slammed the door behind her. Leaning against the door, she drew a long, shuddering breath that ended on a sob. Throwing herself on the bed, she curled into a ball and pressed her palms against the hot tears stinging her eyes.

If only. Damn it…if only.

Her traitorous imagination revealed what it might have been like. Alex, tall and handsome, holding her, his attention focused intently on her. Chelsey, willowy and fluid in his arms, her gauzy hem floating behind as he whirled her around and around the marble terrace. Moving together in faultless harmony, a poem of symmetry and grace. It would have been an enchanted waltz to end a perfect evening.

So lovely. So impossible.

"Chelsey?" Alex rapped on her bedroom door. "Chelsey, I'm sorry. It didn't occur to me that you don't dance. I'll teach you."

What kind of fool did he think she was? Did Alex believe she was a masochist who enjoyed humiliating herself? That she welcomed fresh opportunities to look clumsy and awkward?

A dozen angry retorts sprang to Chelsey's tongue. But what was the point of sarcasm? Would it change anything to reveal that she would rather be tortured than go lurching around a dance floor?

"Forget it," she said in a dulled voice. She was too upset, too beat down, too lacking in energy to fight any more battles tonight. She hoped he wouldn't argue.

"There's no reason why you can't—"

"I'm tired, Alex," she snapped, cutting him off. "Thank you for dinner and for trying to help. Right now I just want to go to sleep." She couldn't believe that Alex was cruel, wouldn't allow herself to consider such a possibility. He had committed a thoughtless error, that was all.

After a long pause, he called softly through the door. "Good night, Chelsey." A current of disappointment flowed beneath his voice. That was what Chelsey heard the loudest. And that hurt the most. She had not lived up to his expectations.

Hot color flooded her cheeks. Alex had no right to expect anything from her. She didn't care what he thought about her. Alex Duport would only be a brief interlude in her life; that's all he could be. Tomorrow Chelsey would make her first legitimate wish, and soon her genie would disappear. A year from now she would look back and wonder if she had imagined all of this.

Chelsey's chest tightened and she bit her lip sharply. She lay in the darkness, staring up at the ceiling and remembering the exciting thrill of his large hands exploring her body, the passionate brandy-tasting kisses. No man had ever made her feel so utterly desirable. Already she understood that for the rest of her life she would compare all other men to Alex.

And none would be his equal.

Chapter Seven

The Flatirons were Boulder's most distinctive feature. The vertical slabs of reddish limestone reared into the Western sky like jagged, giant lengths of sidewalk set on end. When Chelsey needed a quiet place in which to ponder a problem, she headed for the mountain meadows rolling back from the top of the Flatirons.

She clenched her jaw and shifted down, not looking at Alex. They had hardly exchanged three words this morning. Last night he had been a charming, attentive companion, wildly sexy. This morning he was still wildly sexy, but he'd gone gothic on her. Chelsey imagined she could see a chip on his shoulder, could definitely see the wariness in his brooding eyes. Distance and a hint of hostility had returned to his posture and voice.

Okay, maybe he was right to be angry. He had tried to do something nice for her and she had ended up spoiling the evening. But there was more than the dancing incident and their continuing misunderstandings to make them both edgy and tense today.

There was the second thing: the memory of deep, feverish kisses and frantic touches.

From the corner of her eyes, Chelsey could see Alex's hands and long legs. He wore bleached jeans and a white shirt opened at the collar wide enough that she could glimpse a few curls of crisp dark hair. Occasionally, taut muscles jumped along his neck and shoulders, and she was aware that his gaze frequently returned to her own jeans-clad thighs.

Her fingers tightened on the steering wheel. There had been one stunning moment last night when she knew she would surrender to him. She had, in fact, expected the evening would end in rapturous lovemaking, and she had wanted it to end that way. She'd had a narrow escape.

In the bright light of day, logic kicked in. Making love to Alex would have been a mistake, a crazy lapse of judgment. Alex was a genie, for heaven's sake. There could be no commitment from his side, no tomorrow, no future. All he could offer was pure sex.

Which, she thought, sliding a glance toward his thighs, wasn't all that bad. This uncharacteristic thought shocked her, and a long sigh escaped her chest.

They didn't speak until they had almost reached the meadow that Chelsey thought of as her own. She cleared her throat and cut a sidelong look toward the passenger seat, deciding she might as well get the apologies over with. Alex sat beside her with his eyes closed, inhaling the clean, cool scent of pine and fir. The breeze tumbled his longish hair. He looked as if his thoughts were a million miles away. And he was heart-achingly handsome.

Chelsey drew a long breath and released it slowly, pushing away thoughts of his kisses and her own breathless response. "Look, Alex, I'm sorry about last night. You're feeling angry and unappreciated, and you have every right to feel that way. You did something lovely for me and I responded by ruining everything."

"I am here to serve you, mistress," he said without opening his eyes. "The fault was entirely mine. I failed to anticipate correctly. You have no need to apologize for anything.''

''Yes, I do.'' She kept her gaze on the road, trying to sort through the stew of frustration and regret that bubbled in her thoughts. The important thing about last night was the hungry passion that had exploded between them. Even now Chelsey couldn't help responding to Alex's sheer physical impact. Seeing his heavy thighs from the corner of her eyes make her feel weak and hot inside, shaky and a little unsure of herself. But she sensed they wouldn't talk about that. They would talk about the other important thing—her bad behavior.

Her hands tightened on the wheel, and she didn't look at him. ''I had no right to suppose you'd know that even the thought of dancing is painful and embarrassing for me. I guess I assumed you knew that being unable to dance is the limitation I most regret.'' When he said nothing, she stumbled on. ''Slow dancing looks so dreamy and graceful. Fast dancing looks like great fun.'' Still he didn't speak. ''I tried it once. I was awkward, graceless. Let's just say I avoid dance floors as if they were poison. I guess you didn't know, Alex, I'm sincerely sorry that I exploded. It's just that the evening was so perfect, so wonderful. Then… And it shocked me. I reacted very badly and I apologize.''

He opened his eyes and studied the pink on her cheeks. ''I'm only a genie, Chelsey, not a mind reader. Before I appear to a new master or mistress there's a brief span of cognizance in which I see the new master's life in very broad strokes. I knew you were an orphan with no surviving family. I knew you were a professor of archaeology at the university and had published three respected papers. I understood that you'd suffered a childhood illness which left you feeling crippled.''

Chelsey winced and pressed her lips together.

"I'm sorry, but that's how you see yourself. The point is, I don't know the details of your life or your emotions unless you choose to share that information. Sometimes it seems you ignore your handicap entirely, refusing to give in to discomfort or pain. Other times you impose limitations that don't seem logical to me. If I offended you, all I can do is apologize."

Instantly Chelsey bristled. Her knuckles turned white on the wheel. "All my limbs are functional and I'm not in a wheelchair, but I *am* disadvantaged. There *are* things I can't do or things I prefer not to do because I'd look like a clumsy fool and open myself to ridicule. But I'm the one with the bum leg, Alex. It's up to me which challenges I choose to tackle and which I don't. Those choices don't have to be logical to you or anyone else!"

"Look, Chelsey, before this gets out of hand, let me say that I admire all you've overcome. It isn't easy being alone in the world. You've had to fight for everything you've achieved and you haven't had much outside help. You've managed to overcome physical discomfort and accomplish goals that must have seemed daunting in the beginning." She felt his stare. "All I'm suggesting is that you may have a few blind spots. It's possible that you impose a few false limitations on yourself."

"Really?" she snapped, jerking the wheel through a hairpin curve. She didn't like the direction this conversation had taken. "I doubt Howard Webber would agree that a person with one short leg has no limitations."

"Chelsey, I never said—"

"And Howard never made me feel like a coward because I wouldn't humiliate myself by trying to dance!"

"You know that was never my intention," he said

coldly. "But if you believe it is, then again—I apologize."

An icy silence pushed against the warm air rushing in the windows. Chelsey let the silence continue until she couldn't stand it another minute.

"All right, damn it. I'm sorry," she said angrily, confused by a tangle of emotions. "Somehow I feel I've been maneuvered into arguing in favor of being regarded as severely handicapped, an image I've resented and fought against all my life." A humorless smile tightened her lips. "How did that happen?"

"You tell me."

"I can't." She shoved back a lock of hair that had tumbled across her forehead. "What I can tell you is that I've never in my life had as much trouble communicating with someone as I do with you. It's so frustrating! All I've done since you popped into my life is apologize for one thing after another. And when I'm not apologizing— then you are. I don't understand this, and I hate it! What's going on here?"

He was silent, swaying with the motion of the car as the tires bumped over rocks that had fallen into the rutted fire road.

"I'm probably to blame," he said finally.

"Please." Chelsey took her eyes from the road long enough to scowl at him. "I hate it when you go into the genie routine that insists the customer is always right. Sorry, Alex. That isn't honest and that isn't how it works in the real world. It takes two to argue, two to have a misunderstanding. I'm right in here, doing my part to screw things up. We're not going to find a solution to our communication problems if you insist on taking the blame. Especially when you don't really believe you're at fault. You're just accepting the blame to smooth things over.''

It was a long speech, and she paused for breath and a chance to get her emotions back in control. But it made her angry when Alex patronized her by acting like a genie. Which, she realized, was about as reasonable as getting angry at a dog for barking.

For the first time today, Alex smiled. ''This time I'm not just smoothing things over.''

Chelsey rolled her eyes and muttered.

''Hear me out. It's genuinely possible that I'm the source of the communication problem. I don't have occasion to use communication skills very often. Frankly, there's a lot I've forgotten about the turmoil of human emotions, the confusion, uncertainty and ambiguity. The frustration of trying to please someone and understand them is something I don't deal with on a frequent basis. Believe me, granting wishes is a snap compared to negotiating the battlefield of simple conversation.''

''Okay,'' Chelsey conceded, somewhat mollified. ''That makes a certain amount of sense. And I guess it would help if I'd quit making assumptions. If we both do. At least we can try. Deal?''

''It's a bargain.''

The worst of it was over, Chelsey thought with relief. With the apologies behind them, they could go on without the cool silences that were making her acutely uncomfortable. Already she sensed a thawing from Alex's side of the car.

For her part, her traitorous mind suddenly conjured the memory of Alex standing naked on her staircase. She swallowed hard and thrust away the image of long lean lines, of tight muscles and buttocks. She had a depressing suspicion that all her life she would wonder what it would have been like to make love to him.

But Alex wasn't the only person with rules; she had a few of her own. Chelsey Mallon had never had a one-night stand in her life and that was a rule she didn't intend to change. Sex was not casual to her. Sex meant commitment. Sex was the beginning of forever and happily ever after. Unfortunately, Alex could never make a commitment to a woman. And certainly no sane woman would commit to a genie. At best Alex could be only a fleeting passion. And that didn't work for Chelsey.

"I'm going to fill in a few of those details you mentioned," she said, concentrating on the twisting, rutted road. "It's time to explain last summer." And it was definitely time to change the direction of her thoughts. "I know what I want to wish for. But I keep wondering if I've made the wisest choice. There are so many possibilities that it's difficult to decide. I'm about to spend one, probably two, of my wishes. And suddenly I'm having second thoughts."

Immediately Alex sat up straight and shifted in the seat to look at her directly. "Are you ready to make a wish, mistress?"

"Soon. Within the hour."

"Excellent."

Chelsey noticed he kept his voice carefully emotionless. She didn't have a clue as to what he might be thinking. Did he regret that he was soon to be one wish closer to his return to the dream state? He had to be thinking that.

Frowning, she eased the tires over a pile of rocks in the road, then stepped on the gas to urge the car over the next rise. The last wish was going to be very difficult to make, knowing that it would condemn Alex to leave the reality he so obviously craved and loved.

And she would miss him when he left her. A lot. The admission surprised Chelsey although it shouldn't have. Her association with Alex had been brief and often confusing, but it was also intense and highly emotional. Their unusual circumstance was forging a bond that bypassed ordinary conventions. Also, Chelsey could think of no other person who could have the impact on her life that Alex was exerting. There were the wishes, of course. And the awakening of physical desire. And because of Alex she would never again dismiss unlikely claims as silly or impossible. Maybe there really were UFOs and alien visitors. A week ago she would have scoffed; now she wasn't sure.

Yes, Chelsey, there is a Santa Claus.

She smiled, her smile fading as her thoughts returned to the wishes. "There's something I was wondering about." A blush heated her cheeks and she couldn't bring herself to look at him. "If I... Could I wish for someone to love me?" The color in her cheeks flamed to a bright, embarrassed scarlet. And it was Alex's fault, she thought defensively. It was he who had reminded her so sharply of physical and, yes, emotional needs. He who had awakened dormant yearnings.

"I'd suggest you make the wish specific." Alex spoke in the same carefully expressionless voice. She couldn't guess what he was thinking. "I suggest you phrase your wish along these lines—I wish that Mr. John Smith would love me until I die."

"And Mr. John Smith would then love me forever? He wouldn't have a choice about it?"

"John Smith would love you for as long as you specify in your wish. He would have no choice. He would love you regardless of whatever you said or did."

"That's what I was afraid of," Chelsey said grimly,

driving the car onto the meadow. She cut the engine, then sat a moment, gripping the steering wheel and looking out the windshield. Wild iris bloomed near a stand of aspens, tiny purple daisies sprang up in clumps on the mountainside. Lush meadow grass rippled beneath a light breeze, growing nearly as tall as her calves.

"Is that your first wish? For someone to love you?"

Although Alex tried to disguise any hint of emotion, Chelsey identified an appalled undertone. She turned to examine the concern darkening his eyes and laughed out loud.

"No, I'm not thinking of Howard. I'm not thinking about anyone, in fact. It's just that wishing for love seemed like a legitimate wish. However, I don't want someone who's forced to love me because a genie cast a spell on him. I want to love and be loved—like everyone else—but I want it to be honest. It has to happen naturally. If you made some poor guy love me, I'd always wonder if he would have loved me without the spell."

Alex stared at her. "You amaze me."

"Really? Why is that?" she asked, sliding out of the car and drawing a deep breath of clear air that was free from the smoke and smells of the city.

Alex closed his car door and walked around to stand beside her. "What difference would it make why the man loved you? Being loved would feel the same, wouldn't it?"

"I don't think so. Unconditional love is wrong. Love ought to be conditional on both people trying to be lovable." Bending, Chelsey reached into the back seat and removed an old blanket and a picnic basket. She pushed the basket into Alex's hands, then picked up her cane and set off across the meadow toward a spot where aspens and firs grew in a large semicircle.

After she spread the blanket and poured coffee from the thermos, she beckoned Alex toward the edge of the rocks.

"We're standing almost on top of one of the Flatiron formations," she explained, smiling softly. "Isn't it lovely?"

Behind them, the Rocky Mountains soared, some still white-capped from late-winter snows. The plains stretched in front of them, a flat patchwork quilt that extended as far as the eye could see, eventually blurring into a distant bluish haze.

"That's Kansas," Chelsey said, pointing east with her cane. "I'm sure we can see it. And there's Utah," she said, nodding to the west. "Ahead of us is Wyoming. This spot is our own Olympus. From here we can see the whole world, but it can't see us."

"Really?" he asked, smiling.

"Probably not, but I like to think it." She sipped her coffee, gazing toward the far horizon. "Up here, with this vastness in front of me, my problems seem very, very small and not terribly important. Coming here puts things in perspective."

Her mouth tightened with dread as she walked back to the aspens and firs and sat down on the blanket. She hated telling him about her problem. She hated talking about last summer with anyone, but especially with Alex. From the first, she had experienced an odd desire for Alex's good opinion. She wanted him to like and admire her, but her story wasn't very admirable.

"I'm listening," he prompted, stretching out on the meadow grass instead of choosing the blanket. His long fingers probed the dirt, and he chewed on a stem of grass. His eyes narrowed against the thin sunlight, almost translucent, and she felt his steady gaze on her lowered face.

Chelsey drew her knees up and wrapped her arms around them, looking toward Wyoming. She held her breath a moment, then began.

"Last spring, I received a letter from Dr. Julian Porozzi inviting me to be his assistant at a dig outside Istanbul. I was thrilled to be selected since I'd had a serious case of hero worship for Dr. Porozzi. On the down side, the dig itself wasn't interesting, even though it was Roman. A dozen or more teams have excavated the site over the years—there was virtually no possibility of finding anything interesting. Our team would only be taking measurements. Very dull stuff."

Alex rummaged in the picnic basket until he found a chicken leg. Chelsey frowned, remembering she had packed chicken salad but not fried chicken.

"In the end, the opportunity to work with Dr. Porozzi outweighed the disappointment of reworking a finished site. Porozzi's name would add prestige to my résumé, and the university was willing to offer a sabbatical for however long I required…." She shrugged. "At the time, accepting the offer seemed like a sound decision."

"But…?" he asked, watching her face over the chicken leg.

"Nothing worked out like I thought it would." She managed a glum smile. "Julian wanted the money from the grant and the sponsors, but he wanted to stay in Istanbul and play footsie with his new lover. He didn't care about the dig. He knew it was worked out. All he wanted from me was to supervise a crew of students whom he'd hired at dirt wages to satisfy the minimum requirements of the grant. He dumped us in the desert, told his men to unload our supplies, and that was the extent of his involvement."

Alex dug a hole in the ground with his finger and buried

the chicken bones. He offered Chelsey a chicken-salad sandwich and found a large slice of chocolate cake for himself, which Chelsey hadn't packed either.

"I put the students to work measuring the foundations," she said, turning the sandwich between her fingers. "All except a bright kid named Scott Markem. Scott and I kept from going nutty by excavating what looked like the stones of an alley floor. It wasn't exciting work, but it was a damned sight more interesting than standing in a boiling sun holding a tape measure. And there was the possibility that we might find some pottery that had been overlooked."

"What happened?"

"By the middle of the fifth week, Scott and I had uncovered about three, maybe four feet of the alley floor. At that point the length of floor caved in. It wasn't a floor at all, it was a ceiling."

Interest flared in Alex's eyes. "Something important was in the room below?"

Chelsey nodded, setting aside her untouched sandwich. "It was a major find," she explained in a dulled voice. "Inside the storeroom were four marble busts in such prime condition that much of the original paint still remained. Unquestionably they were from Nero's period and were later confirmed as the work of Aristes Marcellus, one of the most gifted and celebrated sculptors of his period. Complete surviving works are exceedingly rare and highly prized. On the private market, a genuine Marcellus is worth a king's ransom. And we found four of them."

"Let me guess," Alex said, sitting up. "Dr. Porozzi returned to the scene."

"Oh yes," Chelsey said, frowning, trying to soften the bitterness thinning her voice. "I phoned him at once, so excited I could hardly speak. He advised me to sit tight.

Tell no one else. No media, no announcements, no publicity until he had personally verified the find.'' She paused, frowning down at her hands. "He arrived with a half-dozen international news teams."

"I see this coming," Alex said quietly. "I'm sorry, Chelsey."

"Porozzi knew the busts came from a period that was my specialty. He didn't doubt the busts were authentic—he didn't need outside experts to verify them. The delay he requested, and which I fell for, was so he could notify the world press and take credit for the find. Scott Markem vanished from the account. For the most part, so did I. I stood on the sidelines, stunned, and listened as Dr. Porozzi told the press how he had suspected the existence of the busts, how he had relentlessly pursued the search, and how he had finally uncovered them."

In the ensuing silence, a deer peeked out of the firs, blinked at them, then silently vanished. "The press loved the story, and Dr. Porozzi's fame grew by leaps and bounds. You couldn't pick up a major newspaper or turn on CNN without seeing a photo of Julian standing in front of the busts. His story grew also. He claimed he had been searching for these particular busts for twenty years. Had narrowed the search to Ballan. Blah, blah and blah."

"So that's what happened. Some bastard took credit for your work."

"I wish that was all there was to it. And it wasn't really my work. It was a lucky accident that was as much to Scott's credit as mine." Chelsey continued to stare at her hands, biting her lip. She would have given anything to end the story right here. "There's more. It gets worse."

"Chelsey, if you—"

"I don't want to tell you any of this! But I have to so you'll understand my wish." She drew a breath, frowned, and stared at her twisting hands. "All four busts vanished."

"Vanished?" Alex folded his long legs beneath him and hunched forward, his eyes fixed on her face. For once, he wasn't touching or stroking something while they talked.

"Like a puff of smoke. One day the busts were in the Caraki Museum, awaiting a special private showing, and the next day all four were just...gone."

"What happened to them?"

She bit her lip so hard that she tasted blood beneath her teeth. "Someone stole them. There was another flurry of press coverage. Only this time Dr. Julian Porozzi was not smiling. He gave the world cameras a steely-eyed look and pointed out that only four people had a key to the Caraki Museum. The curator, a trusted assistant named Mustafa, himself...and me."

"Oh."

"Yeah." Chelsey let her head fall backward and stared at the cloudless sky. "Logic says the curator didn't steal the busts. Why should he? He already had them. And Porozzi was the one who discovered the theft. So it came down to Mustafa or me. I was everyone's favorite suspect."

"Why?"

"Why?" She shrugged. "First of all, Mustafa had an ironclad alibi for the night the busts were stolen. In fact, everyone had an alibi for that night except me. Plus, rumor had it that I was angry and hurt at not being given more credit for the find. The tabloids hinted that Dr. Porozzi and I had an ugly falling out. I guess the prevailing theory was that I wanted to embarrass Porozzi and enrich myself. The bottom line is...my reputation is ruined. There's no proof that I stole the busts, but just about everyone assumes that I did. I'll never receive another professional grant. No trade journal will publish my papers. I'm damned lucky I wasn't fired from the university. The decision to keep me came down to one vote. Only the intervention of people like Howard Webber and Betty Windell saved my job. They argued that nothing was proved, that I was innocent until proven guilty, all of that. But I've lost all credibility. That's why I'm doing inventories this summer instead of doing what I love best—working on a dig. You'd have to search far and wide to find anyone more persona non grata than I am.''

Alex stared at her. ''You didn't steal those busts,'' he stated flatly.

Tears sprang into her eyes and she ducked her head. ''Thanks,'' Chelsey whispered. ''I wish my colleagues had as much faith in my integrity as you do.''

''They're fools and they are dead wrong.''

''They don't think so. And you have to admit it looks bad.''

Pushing to her feet, Chelsey approached the edge of the rocks and leaned on her cane, staring at the seemingly endless plains. There were thousands and thousands of people out there who had never heard of Chelsey Mallon or the stolen Roman busts. It was good to be reminded of that. When she had regained a measure of composure, she called to Alex over her shoulder. ''Alex, if I asked that my reputation be restored…would that be a legitimate wish, and could you grant it?''

His large warm hands framed her shoulders, startling her. For an instant Chelsey resisted, then she leaned back against his solid chest, accepting the comfort he offered. She rested her chin on his arms when they came around her. With Alex holding her, she could almost believe that everything would be all right.

"Does the opinion of other people matter that much to you?" he asked gently, speaking against her ear.

"If I don't have my good name," she answered quietly, "then I have nothing."

"Your wish is legitimate and I can grant it." He paused for a moment. "I cannot alter history, so I can't go back and prevent the busts from being stolen. But I can grant a wish that the busts be found and the thief exposed. I can ensure you a public apology and vindication. Is that your wish?"

"Yes." Chelsey hesitated. "And no."

Turning her in his arms, Alex smiled down at her. "I've never had a master or mistress who struggled so hard to make three wishes."

"I don't want to make a mistake," she said, looking at his mouth. A melting feeling stole over her as if his touch were transforming her to hot, bubbling liquid. Gently she extricated herself from his arms. "Alex, I need to think this through. Give me a few minutes alone, will you? It's quiet here, you'll hear me call when I'm ready."

Lifting a hand, he smoothed a strand of hair back behind her ear. He looked as if he wanted to deliver a speech, but all he said was, "As you wish," before he walked away from her.

CHELSEY SAT on the meadow floor, her arms clasped tightly around her raised knees, watching Alex and the black mare. The sunlight was hot on her bare head. The scent of pine and crushed grass surrounded her, along with the lulling drone of insects.

As always when she came to this meadow, her inner turmoil had diminished and she felt in balance again. Watching Alex helped, too. She had never met anyone as aware of small sensory pleasures as Alex Duport, and his appreciation heightened her own.

To him the warm sunshine that Chelsey took for granted was a tangible joy to gather around himself. The pines and firs and tiny spring flowers were not scenery to Alex, but living things deserving of all the awe that life and beauty inspired. Each twig, each blade of grass, had something unique to offer, was singular in texture and structure and in its place within the universe. Eagerly Alex tried to touch and taste and experience all of reality's bounty.

She watched him now, standing in the middle of the meadow, leaning against the black mare, stroking his large hand along her neck. Chelsey could hear his soothing murmur, the deep richness of his voice, but the words were indistinguishable.

As she watched, Alex swung up on the mare's broad back, the motion so natural and graceful it appeared almost liquid. When he twisted his fingers in the mare's dark mane and bent over her neck, the elation on his face was so transfiguring that Chelsey made herself look away, embarrassed to intrude on a moment so private and intensely joyful.

When she looked up again, Alex and the black mare were flying across the meadow grass, moving through air and sunlight as if man and horse were one. The sight was so beautiful, so natural and right, that it took Chelsey's breath away. He rode leaning forward, his hair streaming behind him, his powerful thighs clasping the mare's back. Tears filled Chelsey's eyes. Never had she witnessed anything so magnificent, so utterly harmonious and moving as this splendid blending of illusion and reality.

She didn't know how long she sat transfixed, her mind empty of all but the erotic beauty of man and horse cantering across the meadow grass. She might have sat there all day, hardly daring to breathe lest she shatter the image rushing toward her.

Alex drew up beside her, his face flushed with exhilaration, his eyes joyful and triumphant. The mare pranced and tossed her head before coming to heel in front of Chelsey. The sensual scent of horse flesh and male sweat rose in Chelsey's nostrils, stirred something primal and raw in her stomach.

She was acutely aware of the sexuality of man and beast, the power of fusion and flying hoofbeats that pounded the earth like her own heartbeats.

Alex swept her body with those smoldering brooding eyes as she slowly rose to her feet in front of the mare's tossing head. His gaze challenged as he wordlessly extended his hand to her.

Chelsey had never ridden a horse before, let alone bareback, but she didn't hesitate. As if in a trance, she stepped forward and gripped Alex's hand. Instantly she found herself seated in front of him, her buttocks snugged tight against his crotch.

"Relax," he said in a husky voice, his arms coming around her. "Lean against me." His solid warmth enclosed her, and strong elegant fingers twisted in the mare's mane. Chelsey closed her eyes, listening to her heart thunder in her ears, feeling his hard body cupped around her.

Alex made a sound beneath his tongue, and she felt his thighs tense. Then they were racing like the wind across the meadow, which seemed to expand and lengthen. She, too, gripped the mare's flying mane as wave after wave of exhilaration swept over her and the pounding hoofbeats drummed in her ears and heart and brain.

It was wonderful, thrilling and wildly arousing. The warm breeze rushed past her face and hair. Alex's solid heat wrapped around her. Massive muscle flowed beneath her body and his. She felt Alex's breath on her cheek followed by the flame brush of his lips. His powerful legs clasped the horse as his hands slipped from the mare's mane to frame Chelsey's waist then slid upward. His large, hot hands cupped Chelsey's breasts and pulled her back against his chest.

As if at a signal, the mare slowed to a walk, then halted beside the blanket. And Chelsey surrendered to the chaos erupting inside her as Alex's hands gently kneaded and stroked her aching breasts. His breath flowed hot against her temple. She felt his hardness against her buttocks where he held her tightly against him.

And she wanted him even if it could be nothing more than raw, urgent sex. Regrets be damned. The passion pounding in her temples and at the base of her throat could not be denied.

Alex slipped from the mare's broad back and extended his arms to her. Wordlessly, Chelsey let him lift her from the horse and slide her down the long, hard length of his body. Her arms wound around his neck, and she strained against him as his mouth came down hard to cover hers.

"Yes," she moaned, her voice husky with need. "Yes, Alex."

He tangled his hand in her ginger hair and pulled her head back to look deeply into her eyes as if judging the depth and honesty of her desire.

Then he swung her up into his arms, his mouth hungry on hers, and he carried her to the blanket and laid her across it. Not taking his burning gaze from hers, he reached for her shirt, his fingers shaking slightly as he opened the buttons then flung her shirt aside before he reached for the snap on her jeans.

Chelsey's hands knocked against his as she reached for

the buttons of his shirt, frantic in her eagerness. They both laughed, then their smiles faded and they hastily flung aside the rest of their clothing.

Finally, finally, they were both naked beneath the warm morning sun. Chelsey looked up at Alex's magnificent rampant body and sucked in a deep moan. A thrill partly of fear, partly of pleasure, rocked through her body. He was so large and powerfully built, so hard and splendid and beautiful that she didn't at first realize that he was staring at her with the same awestruck look as she stared at him.

"You are so beautiful!" he whispered in a thick voice. Kneeling in front of her, he extended his hands and gently, almost reverently, cupped her breasts, drawing his thumbs across the quivering tips. "So utterly and wonderfully beautiful!"

The sun burnished his body to a rich golden color, gleamed in the thicket of dark hair covering his chest, shone in the tousled strands falling across his forehead. Chelsey raised trembling hands and pressed them flat on his chest, thrilling to the swell of muscle that flexed taut at her touch. Her breath caught in her throat, sounding almost like a sob, when he leaned forward to kiss her breasts and tease his tongue around and around the nipple until the almost painful pleasure of his teasing made her want to scream and pull him on top of her.

"Lie back," he whispered, his hands supporting her weight as he eased her down on the blanket. "Let me make love to you."

But if she lay flat, he would see her bare leg. She tried to protest, tried to sit up suddenly, but Alex hushed her with a kiss and pressed her down on the blanket. He spread a sheet of fiery kisses down her body, moving lower and lower until he was kneeling on the end of the blanket near her feet.

Chelsey waited for that inevitable little pause. Her heart thudded painfully against her rib cage and she didn't open her eyes, not wanting to see his face. And then…and then she felt his fingertips caressing her left leg, raising her ankle to his lips. He kissed her toes; his warm, gentle hand stroked the withered calf. And he murmured words of praise for her beauty, for the perfection he imagined he saw.

Tears slipped from beneath her lids and her heart swelled so full she thought it would burst. "Oh, Alex," she whispered. Blindly, she reached for him, pulling him down on top of her and covering his face with frenzied kisses of gratitude and desire.

But this was not her realm to dominate. Alex returned her frantic kisses roughly, with force and passion, but his restraint was greater than hers. He would not come to her until he decided the moment, until she could not wait another second, another instant, not until she was thrashing and quivering and pleading with him to take her.

Pressing her back on the blanket, he moved slowly over every inch of her body, doing things with his tongue and hands that Chelsey had never dared imagine. When finally he returned his attentions to her thrusting, swelling breasts, she was drenched in perspiration and her heart was pounding in her chest like a mad drummer.

"Alex, please!" she gasped, reaching for him. But it was too late. An orgasm tore through Chelsey's body like a riptide, and her body arched beneath his hands, lifting to his mouth and fingers. Her plea drowned in moans of rapture and release that left her shaking and feeling faint.

Then and only then, when the recurring waves of intense pleasure had begun to recede, did Alex press his knee between her damp legs, gently guiding them open. He kissed her deeply, then thrust his hips forward, and Chelsey gasped as his powerful fullness entered and filled her. Her eyes closed and her sated body reawakened and arched to meet each possessive thrust. Again and again he rocked into her, taking her higher and higher with the magic of his powerful male body until a scream burst from her lips and a profound shudder rippled through her being. Only then did he satisfy himself, exploding into her with long, deep strokes before his damp head fell forward on her shoulder.

"My God," she said softly when she could speak. "I never dreamed sex could be like that." She pressed her face into his naked shoulder, inhaling the musky male scent of his perspiration. Never before had she been so uninhibited. The memory brought a rush of scarlet to her throat and cheeks. "It really and truly does not matter to you, does it?" she asked softly.

"What?" One hand lazily stroked her shoulder, the other rested on the curve of her hip. She heard the hint of drowsiness in his voice.

"My leg," she whispered.

Gently Alex turned her in his arms until she faced him. "You are one of the most beautiful women I have ever known. Beauty is more than the curve of an ankle or the shape of a leg. It's more than silky skin or sparkling eyes. Beauty is that rare combination of form and spirit. It's warmth and courage and a tilt of the chin. It's a blend of sensuality and intellect, a mix of laughter and loveliness. You are these things."

Because she didn't want him to see the sudden tears brimming in her eyes, Chelsey pressed her face into the crease at his neck until she could control an outpouring of emotional gratitude.

"Did you do something magic to me, or was what we just experienced honest and real?"

His laugh carried across the meadow. "The only magic came from you," he said, kissing the top of her head. "And, Chelsey, you were magic. I will never forget you."

"In your case, never is a very long time," she said, smiling against his chest.

In her case, never wouldn't be as long, but Chelsey knew she would never forget him. For Alex, she had broken her most stringent rule. But she didn't regret it. It would have been tragic to go through life without fully knowing or understanding the depth of pleasure a man and a woman could enjoy together.

The problem lay not in breaking her rule, but in what followed after. Already Chelsey felt the stirrings of a crazy commitment to Alex. Already she felt the strengthening of bonds.

Which, she thought with a tiny sigh, was merely a high-handed way of saying that she was falling in love with him. And falling in love with a genie was a dead-end road.

Alex caressed her damp curls and smiled down at her. A mock sigh lifted his chest. "I hope neither of us is going to apologize for making love."

Chelsey laughed and kissed the dark hair glistening on his naked chest. "Nope, no apologies. Not for something as wonderful as this was."

Sitting up, she tilted her face to the sun and smiled. The last time she had exposed her naked body—or more accurately, her seminaked body—to the sun had been in junior high school.

She looked down at her body stretched out beside Alex's on the blanket. His long legs were golden, covered with thick, silky dark hair. Her legs were milky white.

"You should get out in the sun more," he teased, following her gaze.

"Mmm." For the first time in her life she had not ended a session of lovemaking filled with embarrassing questions she couldn't bring herself to ask. Alex thought she was beautiful. He had said so, and she had seen his belief in his eyes.

"Oh, Alex," she said softly. "You will never know what you've done for me today."

"I haven't done it yet," he said, misunderstanding. Sitting up, he reached for his jeans. "Then you're ready to make your first wish?"

Chelsey laughed and shook her ginger curls in disbelief. She had forgotten about the wish.

"Yes," she said, feeling reluctant to dress, exhilarated by the unique feeling of sunlight warming her bare limbs. Regretting the necessity, she slowly dressed, pleased to notice that Alex watched her with an expression of pleasure.

Finally she was ready. Sitting cross-legged on the blanket, she faced Alex and drew a breath, trying to focus on wishes instead of kisses and naked bodies. "Do we have to do anything special? Are there any rules or procedures about making the wishes?"

"No," he answered softly, his eyes on her face. "Merely state your wish. Be precise."

Chelsey drew another long breath and concentrated. A sense of unreality fizzed around her, making her feel strange inside.

"I wish…"

Chapter Eight

A gold coin appeared between Chelsey's fingers, catching the sunlight. The longer she held the coin, the warmer it felt against her skin.

Alex sat on the blanket in front of her, his muscled arms crossed over his chest, his intent blue-green eyes fixed on her face. This was not her lover of a moment ago. This was the powerful gothic man who had appeared in her workshop at Wickem Hall, an exotic visitor from a faraway place lost in the mists of time. The man before her was mystical and foreign, a stranger to Chelsey and to her world. His intensity awed her and frightened her a little.

"I await your command, mistress. State your wish specifically."

Chelsey swallowed hard, feeling slightly foolish.

"I wish to know the present location of the four marble busts sculpted by Aristes Marcellus which Scott Markem and I found in the ruined Roman city of Ballan about twenty miles outside of Istanbul." She thrust the coin forward as if it had begun to burn her fingers, an eventuality Chelsey thought was definitely possible. The coin glowed hot to the touch. It would be uncomfortable to hold much longer.

Alex glanced at the coin, but he did not take it from
her. Instead his eyebrows soared like dark wings and he
stared at her with a frown. "I need to be very certain this
is the wish you want to make. Once the wish is granted,
I cannot change it. I thought you intended to wish for the
restoration of your reputation."

Chelsey placed the coin on the blanket between them,
then gripped the handle of her cane, too nervous to leave
her hands idle. "Someone set me up, Alex. I want that
someone exposed, but not by magical means. I want him
caught fair and square. And I want to play a role in clearing my name. Can you understand that?"

"No."

"I couldn't control the theft of the busts or the rumors
that circulated afterward. I couldn't control the innuendos
the journalists chose to print or what my colleagues believed. I couldn't control the university's reaction." She
gave him a pleading look. "Is it so hard to understand
that I want—no, I *need*—to have some control in solving
this mess?"

"If you wish it, I can reveal the thief's name."

Chelsey shook her head. "I want to discover the thief
myself. Someone did this to me. I want to be there when
he's exposed. I want to look him in the eye. Don't waffle
on me, Alex, not this time." Her sudden panic sounded
like anger. She gave him her most piercing, most threatening stare, the stare that brought students and salesmen
to their knees. "Knowing the whereabouts of the marble
busts is the first step toward reconstructing what happened
and restoring my reputation. I want that more than anything."

Alex hesitated then he inclined his head. "As you wish,
mistress." Leaning forward, he accepted the coin.

Locking his gaze to hers, Alex raised his palm to the

level of his chin. The gold coin gleamed and flashed in the sunlight. It appeared to pulse briefly, then burst into flames so hot and bright that Chelsey gasped and closed her eyes against the fiery glare. When she opened them again the coin was gone. There was no residue of molten gold, no burn mark on Alex's palm.

"Impressive," she murmured weakly. "Real genie stuff."

And very sobering. It was all too easy to forget that Alex was not a man like other men, that he was something unique and strange, a man not of this world.

"If you liked that," he murmured, his smile not reaching his steady eyes, "wait until you see this. But watch carefully, because I can do this only once."

"The rules," she guessed, her voice still small and whispery with an awed sense of discomfort.

"Yes. To repeat the showing will require another wish. So take all the time you require, be thorough in your inspection."

"Wait a minute." She flexed her shoulders and her fingers, then blinked hard and rubbed her eyes. "Okay, I'm ready. You're going to show me the present exact location of the marble busts."

Alex flattened his palms on top of the knees of his crossed legs and closed his eyes. His chest swelled and his upper arms bulged. The sunlight seemed to gather and coalesce around him until Chelsey could have sworn he glowed and became radiant. She had a crazy idea that he was exaggerating, performing a little razzle-dazzle for her benefit. She gave her head a shake, sending her secret smile flying, then she blinked hard to clear her thoughts.

At the same instant, Alex opened his eyes, and frowning, concentrated on the empty space between them. The air shimmered and appeared to thicken, assuming color and form.

A three-dimensional image formed into a hologram that hovered, then steadied, above the blanket. Chelsey pressed her hands together to stop them from shaking and leaned forward. The hologram image revealed two finely sculpted busts displayed on marble pedestals.

"Yes," she whispered, feeling a rush of excitement rise in the back of her throat. The busts flanked a velvet-curtained archway. "Those are two of the Marcellus busts. Where are they?"

The hologram collapsed, then reformed to reveal the imposing colonnades fronting a three-story building. Even before Chelsey read the name etched in marble above the entrance, she recognized the building. "It's the Lupberger Athenaeum," she murmured. "I know it well. It's a privately owned museum located in New York City, a block off Fifth Avenue near Central Park East."

"Take your time. Once we leave this vision, we cannot return to it."

"Go to the next," Chelsey instructed him eagerly, staring at the hologram.

The third bust shimmered into view. It, too, appeared to be in a museum. The bust rested on a marble shelf in a place of honor, dominating two other busts of lesser value which had not been created by Aristes Marcellus.

"Yes," Chelsey whispered. "Pull back to the outside of the building."

At once she recognized the London Museum of Roman Antiquities, which surprised her.

Both the Lupberger and the London Museum were noted for stringent standards. Both had impeccable reputations. To the best of Chelsey's knowledge, neither museum had endured a single breath of scandal. This suggested a brilliantly forged provenance had accompanied the Marcellus busts.

"Go to the last bust," she said, staring at the hologram so hard that her eyes burned and stung.

At first Chelsey didn't spot the final bust. The hologram revealed a small, dark storeroom crammed with items that appeared to be household cast-offs. She saw a sagging chair with exposed springs, a torn lamp shade, battered cardboard boxes and a leaning stack of old clothing. It wasn't until an invisible hand pulled away the sheet covering the bust that she saw it.

When she was absolutely certain that she was indeed looking at the final Marcellus bust, she nodded. "Go on. Let's see the outside of the building."

The hologram shifted in a swirl of colour, then resettled into a depiction of a narrow two-story white house with a red tile roof. Other houses just like it crowded in at the sides. The front door opened onto the street. Judging from the rooftops behind, the row of houses sat on a street that ran downhill. There were no markings on the house, no street numbers or anything to identify the building.

"I need more," Chelsey said uneasily, daring a quick look at Alex. "Can you show me a street name? And a city name?"

"I'm sorry."

Chelsey's heart sank. In a flash she identified the flaw lurking behind her three wishes. A genie could grant a wish, but only the wish as stated. He could provide neither more nor less than what was contained in the statement of the wish. He could not make assumptions as to what the master or mistress intended to accomplish with his or her wish. Alex had told her this by warning her to be specific, and Chelsey had tried. But she saw now that she had not been specific enough. It was sheer dumb luck that she had been able to identify the first two sites. Had all four busts been hidden in the storeroom of the house she was studying now, she would have wasted her wish.

"Do you recognize this house?" she asked Alex, hoping against hope that somehow he did.

"No."

"Istanbul? Egypt? Iraq?" The house could have been located in just about any warm climate in the world. Frustration wrinkled her brow. Her hands clenched into fists. "Think," Chelsey muttered, talking to herself. "Where could this house be? Is there anything unique about it?"

Staring until her eyes began to sting and water, she searched the hologram scene for clues. After rubbing her eyes, she tried again. But there was simply no hint of the greater location. There was nothing unique about the house. She had seen a thousand just like it in various parts of the world.

Frustrated and bitterly disappointed, she finally shoved back her mop of ginger curls and nodded to Alex. "That's it. I could stare at this house until I was ninety and still not guess where it's located."

The hologram flared, then faded away.

Chelsey struck the ground with a fist. "I see what you mean about phrasing the wish specifically. I screwed up, didn't I? Why didn't you tell me?"

He shrugged and spread his hands. "You said you wanted to know the exact location of the busts and that's what you were shown. You did not say you wanted to know the addresses of those locations. I've already told you, I'm not a mind reader."

She sighed. "You're right, of course," she admitted after a minute, trying to swallow her disappointment and focus on the locations she did recognize instead of the one she did not.

For some reason, Chelsey had expected Alex to look tired and drained after producing the hologram and granting her wish, but he didn't. He looked alert and curious, concerned about her.

"Did you see anything that was helpful?" he asked.

She turned her face toward the vast expanse of plains basking in the noon sunshine. "Yes. I know the location of three of the busts. That's more than I knew an hour ago. It's a beginning. I hope it's enough."

After a moment, she opened the thermos and poured them both fresh cups of coffee.

Actually she was glad she had the marble busts to occupy her thoughts. Without the marble busts to worry about, Chelsey suspected she might have drowned in the blue-green depths of Alex's concern. She wouldn't have been able to think about anything except the wild passion they had shared. Or how glad she was that they were still two wishes away from the moment when they had to say goodbye. She didn't want to think about that.

Standing, she leaned on her cane a moment, then walked to the edge of the rocks where she had a clear, unobstructed view of forever.

"What happens next?" Alex inquired, coming up behind her.

"We fly to New York and speak to the curator at the Lupberger Athenaeum," Chelsey answered absently. She was thinking about the concept of forever and how meaningless it was. Maybe for some people, forever could be compressed into a few days. She found herself hoping so. "We track the Lupberger's two busts back to their origination point. Once we've accomplished that, we'll find some answers."

"Shazam."

ALEX CAUGHT CHELSEY'S arm when she flung it near his face, steadied her, then bent to pick up her cane from the sidewalk.

He admired her, respected her, and God knew he desired her. But he didn't understand her. It would have been a relatively simple matter to resolve the theft of the marble busts and expose the culprit. He could have assisted her in phrasing a wish specific enough to accomplish the return of the busts and the restoration of her reputation. He only partially understood her desire to be personally involved in the denouement. She frustrated him, fascinated him and kept him continually feeling slightly off balance.

"Where are we?" she gasped, clutching his arm and staring around her with wild eyes.

"We're in New York City, standing on the sidewalk in front of Fifth Avenue." It surprised him that she didn't immediately recognize the site. Where else would she see so much traffic, both pedestrian and vehicular? Where else did the air seem tangible with the scents of humanity and excitement? Where each street was a canyon flanked by cliffs of glass and stone? "The Lupberger Athenaeum is across the street and a few doors up."

Chelsey looked so shocked that he immediately decided she needed a moment to orient herself. Taking her arm, Alex led her toward one of the park benches set back from the sidewalk. They passed a woman who had frozen in place at the sight of them, and was staring with huge eyes.

She gripped a shopping cart which seemed out of place alongside Fifth Avenue and the park. But the shopping cart and the peculiar assortment of items inside didn't surprise Alex as much as the layers and layers of clothing she wore. It was hotter on the pavements of New York City than it had been in the mountain meadow. He couldn't think why anyone would wear three dresses and two coats when waves of heat shimmered around the tires of the vehicles charging up and down the avenue.

"Sit here for a minute," he suggested to Chelsey, indicating a park bench. "Would you like something cool to drink?"

"Yes. A lemonade, I think," she answered in a whisper, glancing toward the striped awning of a hot-dog stand on the corner. "God, Alex. I wish you'd give me more warning when you intend to fling out your magic carpet! No, no," she said, raising a hand. "That's not a *real* wish. But I can't tell you how disconcerting it is to suddenly be transported somewhere unexpected! My heart is pounding like crazy."

He offered her a crystal tumbler filled with ice and lemonade. Instantly her eyes flared then narrowed, and she swiftly looked around her at the people on nearby benches and passing on the sidewalk.

"Don't *do* that!" she said sharply. "Someone will see." She passed a hand over her forehead. "Maybe genies have outlived their time. I'm not sure the modern world is prepared for you guys."

It occurred to Alex that perhaps she was correct. Certainly he hadn't experienced this kind of reaction in the past. His previous masters and mistresses had readily accepted his magic, had delighted in it to the extent that they wished him to demonstrate his magical powers for friends and acquaintances. It gave them pleasure to command a magician. He couldn't grasp why the same was not true for Chelsey, or that times had changed so greatly that magic was no longer valued. Did this mean that *he* was not valued? Magic was now as much a part of him as his arms and legs. He used it automatically, without much thought.

Disturbed but striving to please, he made the crystal tumbler disappear from her fingers.

"Oh God," she groaned.

"Chelsey. Do you want the lemonade or don't you?" he asked, hoping he didn't sound as exasperated as he felt.

"I want the lemonade," she admitted as the tumbler reappeared in her hand. She closed her eyes and made a choking sound. "But I wanted you to buy it. I don't want anyone to see things appearing and disappearing. Alex, we're surrounded by people. Someone is certain to see. I'm amazed that no one has gone crazy over us popping out of thin air!"

"No one is paying us any attention," he said reasonably.

This was true. Except for the overdressed woman with the shopping cart. She continued to watch them intently, still frozen in place. The shredded feather atop her red hat pointed toward them like a rusting sword.

"See?" Chelsey whispered. "That poor bag lady probably thinks she's hallucinating."

Alex wasn't interested in the bag lady. He was, in fact, paying scant attention to a discussion he considered irrelevant. Instead, he watched the dappled sunlight that filtered through the trees overhead and played across Chelsey's heart-shaped face. Sunlight and shadow heightened the angles of her features, making her seem alternately strong then soft, but lovely in both cases.

She was taller than Isabel had been, but small boned and delicately formed. Isabel had affected fragility because fragility was in fashion, but in truth Isabel had been a sturdy woman, big boned, and as strong and ruthless as a man. In contrast, Chelsey Mallon had perfected her distancing stares and a proud posture that projected confi-

dence and self-reliance, but at her core lay an unexpected
and genuine fragility that gripped his heart and twisted his
emotions.

Already Alex knew that leaving her would crush something inside of him. Because no one had ever impacted
his emotions as this woman did. She exasperated him,
fascinated him, engaged his admiration, made him angry,
drove him wild with desire. It would require centuries to
recover from her, if ever he did.

She placed her hand on his arm and looked up at him.
"Alex, thank you for trying to expedite things, but this
won't work. This isn't the way to proceed."

Frowning, he gazed down at her. She was so intense
and lovely that it was difficult to keep his mind on what
she was saying. Her face looked now almost as it had
when he began to make love to her. Anxious but eager,
hinting of apology. Wanting to go forward, afraid to go
forward.

The bag lady wheeled her cart closer to them, halting
at a safe distance. "Hey there. How did you do that?"

"Don't you see," Chelsey continued, glancing at the
bag lady, then back at him. "If I'm going to clear my
name, there can't be any questionable circumstances. Like
popping up suddenly in New York City. Finding the busts
and exposing the thief is going to cause a stir. In case
some journalist wants to check our involvement, we have
to leave a paper trail."

"Such as?"

The bag lady edged closer. "Are you aliens?" The
shredded feather atop her hat quivered with cautious interest. "What do you want with earth? Why are you here
and what are your plans?"

Chelsey lifted her cane and stood up. "We're not
aliens." She glared at Alex.

"What kind of paper trail are you talking about?" he asked.

"Airline tickets, passport stamps, hotel and food receipts. That kind of thing. And the times have to work out. There can't be any mysterious gaps. I'm trying to restore my credibility, not compromise it further."

The bag lady's eyes narrowed shrewdly. "Well, I wouldn't expect you to admit it, now would I? You're going to take over the world, aren't you! Well, that's all right with me. I say go ahead and take it over. Can I ride in your spaceship?"

"What are we going to do?" Chelsey asked helplessly. "She saw us appear out of nowhere, and she's not going away."

Alex bowed and gave the bag lady his most charming smile. "Madam, I assure you that we have no interest in taking over the world."·

"Who are you?"

"I'm a genie, and this is my mistress." His explanation seemed simple enough. He was genuinely surprised when the bag lady hooted with disbelief.

"Alex, the minute she turns around, get us out of here. Please?"

Alex smiled at the shaking feather, then he gently turned the bag lady to face the street, sensing her resistance in his mind. She knew something invisible was turning her against her will. "Shazam."

There was an instant before they reappeared on the blanket in the meadow, and in that instant he glimpsed Chelsey's look of yearning as she glanced toward the Lupberger Athenaeum. He understood then how difficult it was for her to follow her own procedures. In her heart, she longed to dash across the street and confront the curator at once. But a stubborn sense of integrity would not allow an impulsive move that might compromise her goal.

He caught her as she stumbled on a rock hidden beneath the blanket and held her tightly against him. Instantly he felt their chemistry ignite, responded to his powerful need for her. Tilting her face upward, he kissed her roughly, possessing her with his lips and tongue.

"I'M TURNING INTO a shameless hussy," Chelsey said, smiling softly and buttoning her shirt. She suspected she wore a slightly dazed and dreamy expression. After not making love for over a year and a half, she'd done it twice today. In broad daylight. It was enough to leave anyone feeling a little dazed and dazzled.

"Should I apologize?"

She laughed and planted a kiss on Alex's wide shoulder. "If you do, I'll be offended."

Leaning forward, Alex cupped her face between his large hands. His gaze traveled slowly over her face before meeting her eyes. "I can't get enough of you. You smile and I want you. You speak and I want you. You look at me and all I can think about is the silky touch of your naked skin against mine."

"Plus, you're storing up physical impressions," she said, teasing him to lighten the seriousness in his eyes.

He drew back. "Is that why you think I made love to you? Merely to experience the physical sensations?"

"Now, don't sound so offended. That's why most people make love. To experience the physical sensations." While he thought about that, Chelsey finished dressing, noticing that her body was still warmed by a rosy glow. Without intending it, her movements were almost seductive. For the first time ever, she didn't feel embarrassed or uncomfortable dressing in front of a man.

In fact, she felt content and happy, desirable and beautiful. She couldn't recall feeling anything like this in a very long time. If ever. And it was all because of Alex. She wished she knew who to thank for sending him to her. He was changing her life and her image of herself in subtle ways she would still be discovering long after he had gone.

"Making love to you is more than just wanting to experience the physical sensations. Although that's part of it," he added grudgingly.

Chelsey tossed his shirt to him and grinned. "Feeling a little defensive, are we?"

She felt wicked about taking pleasure in Alex's sulky expression, but he deserved a bit of discomfort. After all, he'd turned her life upside-down. Take today for instance. Today she had ridden a horse, made love twice, and she'd been to New York City and back. And it wasn't even dinnertime yet. If Alex felt a little off balance, well, he had it coming.

"It's you, Chelsey. I want to make love to you."

The smoky, speculative look in his eyes made her want him again. A blush stole up from her throat, and she turned her face away. She was becoming shameless. A wanton. The image secretly pleased her. She could just imagine what her students would think if they could eavesdrop on her thoughts. The ice queen as a wanton? No way.

"I think this is an area we'd do better not to examine too closely," she suggested, seeing that Alex was disturbed. "Some things should just be enjoyed, not analyzed. We'll drive ourselves crazy if we think about this too much. I'll start feeling guilty about sexual relationships that can't go anywhere, and you'll start feeling bitter about all you're missing in the dream state. We'll mess up the time we have left together, and I don't want that to happen. I want to enjoy every minute I have with you.''

''I just don't want you to think that making love to you falls into the same category as grooming a horse or smelling a rye field, or—''

Chelsey burst into laughter. She was too happy to take offense at anything he said. Her eyes sparkled. ''It never occurred to me that you might compare me to a horse.''

''Damn it, that isn't what I said!''

''Come on,'' she called, heading toward the car. ''We're going home. We have plans to make.''

He spread his hands and tilted his head back to scowl at the sky. ''Is it all women in general? Or just this particular one?''

''This particular one is going to leave you standing there without your pants if you don't hurry up,'' she called over her shoulder, laughing because it was a wonderful day, a sunshiny summer day, an Alex day. And she knew where the stolen busts were. It was a fine, fine day, indeed.

''What sort of plans are we making?'' he asked, appearing in the passenger seat beside her, stuffing his shirttail into his pants.

''We need to make airline and hotel reservations.'' She swung the car in a circle, then pointed it down the fire road. ''I have to stop by the bank.'' That thought gave her pause. After a minute she continued. ''And we have to think of a way to explain you to the Lupberger curator. A colleague, I think. Which means we need a paper trail for you. We need to create a history for you that can be checked if necessary.''

''Such as?''

''Such as everything. Birth certificate, high school and college records, social security number, driver's license, passport, job history. You know…everything. A history, and all the usual papers that everyone carries who isn't a genie.''

He shrugged, stretched his arm across the seat back and played with the loose tendrils fluttering around her neck. ''It's done. Anyone who cares to check will discover Alex Duport, archaeologist and all-around ordinary person, colleague of Dr. Chelsey Mallon.'' He touched his back pocket. ''Complete with wallet stuffed with the usual papers.''

''Good.'' God, what his fingers did to her. Tiny electric thrills chased up and down her spine. ''Money is going to be the big problem in all of this. We may have to return to Istanbul. That's going to be expensive.''

''Most masters wish for wealth.''

''I could think about this more efficiently if you'd keep your hands to yourself.''

He laughed and pulled his arm back, turning his face to the air rushing in the window.

WITH A GENIE IN RESIDENCE, there was no need to leave the house. Chelsey wanted grilled salmon for dinner but felt too lazy to drive to the grocery store. It had been a long, eventful day and her left leg ached. Before she finished phrasing a shy request, a beautiful salmon had appeared on the kitchen counter.

''Thanks,'' she said, toasting Alex with the ever-full glass of French wine that he had also provided. ''If you'll put this on the grill, I'll pop some potatoes in the microwave and put together a salad.''

''I could—''

''No,'' she said, waving aside his offer. ''We'll use conventional means. I don't want to get spoiled.'' Then she smiled and tilted her head. ''But you could whip up something low-fat and wonderful for dessert, if you like.''

By now she knew Alex enjoyed performing everyday tasks like grilling the salmon. He would baste the fish with his fingers, test the heat of the charcoal and stand over the grill, inhaling the scent of the cooking salmon. Chelsey also realized she enjoyed watching him, and enjoyed pretending they were doing normal things that any couple might do—small, homey, insignificant things that mattered only to the couple involved.

Except they were not an ordinary couple. And the fish had appeared by magic. As had the wine. And Alex could not wander farther than the sound of her voice. And she was about to make her second wish, an event that would move them closer to saying goodbye.

The thought jolted her and diminished her pleasure. The threat of depression nibbled at the edge of her mind. She couldn't bear the thought of saying goodbye to Alex.

She was falling in love with him. The realization exhilarated her and scared her to death.

''Why so quiet?'' Alex asked midway through their candlelit dinner on the small outside patio. ''Is something the matter?''

Chelsey gazed at him across the table, her heart in her eyes. Sunset rays painted red highlights through his long, straight hair and sharpened his chiseled profile. This was one of those moments when she looked at him and saw the crusader in his proud posture and the stubborn angle of his chin.

''I was thinking about the next wish,'' she said, turning the lie into fact. ''I checked my bank balances and I don't have enough money to cover too many unexpected expenses. Such as a trip for two to Istanbul.'' Pushing aside her plate, Chelsey reached into her apron pocket and produced a list. She totaled the figures again in her mind. ''I think I'd be more comfortable if I had about two thousand dollars more than I do. I'm thinking I should wish for it.''

Alex stared at her. ''That's not sensible. If you're going to use your second wish for money, then wish for wealth, not two thousand dollars.''

Chelsey shifted in her chair. ''I don't know. Doesn't that sound...well, greedy?''

He threw up his hands. ''Chelsey, I'm not judging you. No one is. The wish is yours to use for your direct benefit.''

''Selidim had this all figured out,'' she observed softly. ''The wishes seem like a boon, but there's a subtle corruption involved. For you, it's a corruption of ideals. For me, it's a corruption of what I thought I was and what I thought I believed in. I didn't think I was a greedy person. But here I am secretly agreeing with you. I only need two thousand or so, but if I'm really honest with myself, I'd like to wish for a million.''

''Wish for five million. Ten million. What difference does it make? It's your wish and you can use it however you like.''

She met his eyes, then looked away. ''This is going to sound idiotic, but I don't like having you know that I'm secretly lusting for a million dollars. It sounds so rapacious. But I guess I am. Whenever I think about it, I picture a house of my own, a new car, the possibility of financing a dig or an expedition. I get a little crazy with the idea.''

Reaching across the table, Alex took her hand. ''Look at me, Chelsey. Don't let what's happening to us get in the way of using your wishes to the fullest benefit for you.'' Something like pain flickered behind his eyes. ''Soon I'll have to leave you. If you spend your wishes

based on what you think I may or may not approve…you'll have nothing but regret when I go.''

Chelsey heard nothing after *Soon I'll have to leave you.*
The words struck her like a dagger in the heart. It wasn't
fair. All her life she had waited for and dreamed about a
man like Alex. A man whom she could love and respect.
A man who might love her, too, and make her heart feel
whole. At last fate had given her such a man, but fate
would snatch him away again.

''Oh, Alex,'' she said softly. Sudden tears swam in her
eyes. ''Don't you think I'll regret it when you go?'' His
image blurred. ''This time with you has been the most
exciting, the most wonderful time in my life.''

He came around the table and gently pulled her to her
feet, taking her into his arms. ''Chelsey…''

The warmth of his thumb brushing away her tears made
a shudder of longing race through her body.

His strong hands brushed the hair from her cheeks and
cupped her face, tilting her mouth up to his. For a long
moment he stared into her eyes. The intensity of his gaze
seemed to reach deep inside her.

''If only…'' he whispered. Then he kissed her, and it
seemed to Chelsey that their passion and need for each
other caused the universe to tremble.

Chapter Nine

"I never thought I was the type of person to whom money mattered," Chelsey said. "But suddenly I'm thinking what a relief it would be not to worry about paying the bills."

Full darkness had descended, but they continued to sit outside on the patio. Alex examined Chelsey's face in the light of the candle flame. She appeared to be trying to justify or apologize for a wish made by one hundred percent of his masters and mistresses.

This woman astonished him. First she tried to give away her wishes by spending them for the benefit of others. Now she was struggling with the personal morality of making a wish that was universal in scope. Alex was not sure what was expected of him. Did she want him to persuade her in favor of wishing for money?

"If you're concerned about needing two thousand dollars to follow the trail of the busts," he said carefully, testing the water, "that is an amount I can produce as the expenses arise. But if we're addressing financial security, that's a different thing and a larger amount. That will require a wish."

Circles of pink bloomed in her cheeks. "Would you think less of me if we were talking about a million dollars?'' At once she raised a hand to the pink deepening on her throat. "No, don't answer that. All right, financial security is the issue here. And Alex, I don't want you to pay the two thousand dollars. Running off to New York City and possibly overseas is my idea, not yours.''

He resisted an urge to roll his eyes. "Chelsey, it isn't as if the money were coming out of my personal account. I don't have a personal account. The money just appears when I need it. Besides, the idea of a quest is appealing.''

His last comment was an understatement. Alex was a man who understood quests. Once he had grasped that Chelsey would not be deterred from tracking down the missing busts and that he would have the opportunity to participate, he found himself impatient to begin. First, the money question had to be settled.

Her chin jutted and a defensive look entered her eyes. "This is my quest and I should handle the expenses.'' A sheepish look stole across her expression. "The problem is, I can't pay without wiping out my accounts. So…'' She drew a deep breath and met his eyes. "I'd just wish for the two thousand, but that seems a bit shortsighted. It seems that as long as I'm doing this, I should wish for a million. That's what everyone else does, right? I mean, it just seems sensible.''

"But…?'' He was becoming adept at spotting that inevitable but. He read it in the crease between her eyes and in the way she continued to move the wineglass in agitated circles.

"But there's a problem. And I can't see a way around it.''

"The money won't appear in a heap on the floor, if that's what you're worrying about. It will appear in your bank or investment account, however you specify. All paperwork will support the figures. You'll experience no suspicion or scrutiny from anyone.''

Once upon a time the actual coins would indeed have appeared in a pile on the carpet. He recalled masters and mistresses gathering coins from the floor before hiding them away. But those days were long gone. The world was more sophisticated now, and so were banking procedures. The paper trail Chelsey had mentioned earlier was doubly important in financial matters. The money had to be accounted for. Which was easy enough to do.

''If I suddenly turn up with a fortune that I didn't have yesterday, how will that look?'' She pushed aside her wineglass and dropped her hands into her lap. ''It will look as if I really did steal the Marcellus busts then sold them. I don't have any way to explain the money.''

''There's no need for concern.'' He smiled and shrugged. ''We'll structure the wish in such a way that you inherited ten million dollars five years ago. An impeccable paper trail will support that premise.''

''Ten million?'' Chelsey blinked, then stared at him. ''Alex, let's not get crazy here. One million will do nicely. Besides, if I'm so rich, why didn't I mention my wealth last summer when rumors were flying that I stole the busts to enrich myself.''

He grinned, enjoying the discussion. ''The suggestion was so ridiculous that you didn't dignify the rumors with a response.''

''Not bad,'' she said, nodding her head. ''If we leak the information about my wealth, it could work in my favor.''

''If you want wealth, I'd advise you to consider at least five million.'' When she started to protest, he leaned forward, pushing the candle out of the way. ''If you want to finance your own dig, that's an expensive undertaking.''

It astonished Alex that he, who had scorned the greed of humanity, was arguing strenuously for an amount higher than his mistress would have chosen if left to her own inclinations. But it was important to him that Chelsey be financially self-sufficient and not dependent on a job she retained through the grace of one vote. He didn't want to think of her ever wanting something she could not afford. When he thought about it, he realized he wanted her to have the life he would have moved the earth to give her if he had had the chance.

This realization brought him up short. His chest constricted painfully. For a brief instant he cursed the fate that had brought him to Chelsey Mallon. He cared for her; he cared deeply. More so with every hour that he spent in her company. His reward would be nothing but pain.

With a jolt he realized that Chelsey would also suffer if he continued along this course. He had only to look at the radiance shining in her eyes, needed only to recall the eagerness of her lovemaking to know that she was beginning to care for him as strongly as he cared for her.

Had they been any other two people, the knowledge that they teetered on the sweet edge of love would have made him want to shout with joy. But he was a genie. He could offer her no commitment, no future. He had no right to love a woman; it would be an act of cruelty to allow Chelsey to fall in love with him.

For a brief moment he closed his eyes, feeling a twist of pain deep inside. "Are we agreed on the amount of money you will wish for?" he asked tersely.

As hard as it would be, as much as he wished it could be otherwise, he had to ease back, had to reestablish a distance between them. He had to protect Chelsey from falling in love with him; he had to shield her from a hopeless love that could bring her nothing but disappointment and pain. This was the kindest, most loving gift he could give to her.

"I'll cede to your judgment," Chelsey said after a moment's consideration. "It appears you know about financial matters and I don't."

Her trust strengthened his resolve. She deserved better from him than a broken heart. Looking away from her lovely face, he concentrated on securing her finances.

"We'll frame your wish for five million dollars and we'll structure the paperwork to reflect the money was inherited five years ago." He explained how he thought the money should be invested. Chelsey shrugged and agreed. "I suggest you hire a financial advisor. Your portfolio will be in order, but a financial advisor familiar with today's markets and investments will undoubtedly prefer to make some changes. Plus you'll want ongoing management of your affairs."

The dazed look returned to her expression as if she were having difficulty making the high figure seem real. "You know, this is going to feel funny. I've never had to think about investments before." She smiled at him. "But it's going to be a nice problem. Much better than worrying about the utility bill. Will you help me word the wish so I don't overlook anything? I don't want to screw up again."

They worked it out together, scribbling across a notepad that Chelsey fetched from the kitchen.

"I think we're ready," she said finally, studying the written wish. "I wish..." A gold coin appeared in her hand.

Alex accepted the coin and watched it blaze in his palm. Personal magic required no effort on his part. But fulfilling the wishes required that he concentrate and tap into something outside of himself. There was no name for the something he tapped into; he thought of it as an omnipotent presence. Occasionally, when in the dream state, he pondered the thing or being that granted the wishes, sensing that granting wishes was merely a fraction of its purpose. It frustrated him that his mind was too small, too mired in the human state, to comprehend more.

"It is done," he said, opening his eyes.

"Really?" She looked doubtful. "Wait here a minute."

Three minutes later she returned with her checkbook and a thick portfolio that she'd found on top of her desk. "Look at this!" Excitement swirled in her brown eyes. "My checking-account balance is now thirty-two thousand dollars! And this portfolio! Alex, I'm rich! Rich!" She threw out her arms and spun on the toes of her right foot. "I can buy a CD player."

He laughed out loud. His inclination was to take her into his arms and dance her across the patio, sharing in her excitement. But her remembered how she felt about dancing, and more importantly he remembered his vow to withdraw from her. Clenching his teeth, he remained in his seat.

But he could watch her. When Chelsey Mallon was happy, there was no more beautiful woman on earth. It made him feel sick inside to think of leaving her or to think about another man touching her. It caused him despair to realize that caressing her or kissing her were acts of teasing and cruelty if he did so knowing his caresses would bring her only pain in the end.

"IS SOMETHING WRONG?" Chelsey asked after they had turned out the lights in her bedroom.

"Why do you ask?" The answer was evasive and sounded moody even to his own ears.

She sat up in bed and clasped her hands on top of the

sheets. In the soft glow of the moonlight, he saw a flush of discomfort heat her cheeks. "I thought…well, doesn't it seem a little silly for you to sit over there in a chair? We could share the same bed. After all, we…" She ended by biting her lip and making a small confused motion with her hands.

"I'd only keep you awake. I won't sleep for more than an hour." That startled him. When had it become an hour? And what did it mean that his requirement for sleep, a surprise to begin with, had lengthened? "Once you fall asleep I thought I'd go downstairs and view your portfolio. Maybe practice my fencing."

She nodded and pushed back a wave of the ginger-colored curls. "I'm sensing that something isn't right between us, that something has changed.…"

"Why would you think that?" he asked, stalling. It was his task to be sensitive to the moods of others. Chelsey was the first person he had met who was sensitive to his. It left him feeling exposed and more vulnerable than he was comfortable with.

She shrugged and one strap of her thin summer nightgown dropped off her shoulder. Alex ground his teeth together, trying to ignore moonlight gleaming on satin. "You seem different somehow. More like you were when I first met you."

"And how is that?" God, but she was lovely. The moonlight polished her skin to a pearly glow. She was an inviting combination of shadow and warmth, moisture and promise. His stomach tightened and he wanted her again.

"I'm not sure. Distant and brooding. Far away. Did I say or do something that offended you?"

"No! Not at all." He ran a hand through his hair. How could he tell her that he couldn't look at her without wanting to take her in his arms and kiss her until she was dizzy and moaning his name? How could he admit that he was falling in love with her, but knew love could only bring pain to them both? He had no right to declare his feelings to her. No right to take pleasure in the affection he saw growing in her eyes and in her expression when she looked at him. The last thing he wanted for Chelsey was pain or regret.

"Then what?"

He wanted to shout and storm and brandish his crusaders' sword at the cruelties of fate. He wanted to smash and ruin, to rampage and scream his frustration. Bitterness flooded his mouth with a dark taste. After centuries of loneliness he had found a woman—his woman. And he had been given a glimpse of what their life together might have been like.

But he could not have her. Not now, not ever. He was one slender wish away from the dream state, from oblivion. Life in all its richness would rush away and continue without him. He would lose her and everything they might have shared together.

He turned a hard face to the moonlight filtering past the gauzy curtains. Knots rose like stones along his jawline.

"Go to sleep," he said finally.

CHELSEY STRUGGLED with the question of whether to inform the university that she was leaving Boulder for a while. In the end she decided against it. No one would miss her. And if she were challenged later, she had the completed inventory to offer in her defense.

She did phone Marge, her landlady, who seemed relieved that she was leaving town for a week or so. And she phoned Betty to cancel lunch and tell her not to worry if she didn't hear from her for a while.

"Is Alex still visiting you?" Betty asked, trying to sound casual. "Are you two running off together? Is that what this mysterious absence is all about?"

"It isn't mysterious. I've received a tip about the Marcellus busts. Alex and I are going to check it out."

"What happened? Did you win the lottery? Or is Alex paying? Don't tell me a guy that gorgeous is rich, too!"

"I don't have to worry about money since…since my inheritance." This was the hardest part. Deceiving friends.

"What inheritance?"

"You know I don't like to talk about money. Listen, there is something I want to clear up with you." She leaned against the wall next to the phone. "You were right about Alex and me."

"I knew it! So what should I buy you for a wedding present?"

"It's not like that," Chelsey said, closing her eyes. Feeling the pain of wishing. "It won't last, Betty. We're geographically incompatible." Which had to be the understatement of the century. "I live here, and Alex lives…very far away." In genie-land. But she still couldn't bring herself to tell Betty the whole truth. "There's no way to work it out, so don't start offering suggestions. I'm okay with it. All I can do is just enjoy this while it lasts."

Next she phoned United Airlines, then a hotel near Central Park South. Even though their flight was booked for the following day, she packed a battered suitcase that had accompanied her around the world and was pasted over with peeling stickers.

And through it all, she worried about Alex. He followed her without speaking, his hands thrust into his pants pockets, his expression angry and brooding. It worried her most of all that he wasn't touching and stroking every-thing that came within his reach.

And he hadn't made love to her this morning even though she had brazenly left the bathroom door ajar when she took her shower.

"THIS IS A WASTE of time," Alex muttered once the plane was airborne and there was nothing to do but sit and wait.

"I know you'd rather travel by magic carpet and you'd rather spend your time doing something more interesting than riding in a plane for several hours, but we have to do this by conventional and traceable means," Chelsey told him for the fourth time. She suspected she sounded more stubborn than understanding.

Leaning forward, she rummaged in the seat pocket in front of her and withdrew a copy of the *Enquirer* that a previous passenger had left behind. She shook it open across her lap, the pages making a firm snap.

"Oh my God!" After reading the headlines a second time, she stared at the accompanying picture, then burst out laughing. "Look," she said when Alex turned to her with a raised eyebrow.

The headline read, Aliens Invade Fifth Avenue. There was a photograph of the bag lady, complete with shapeless hat and indignant feather.

Chelsey dropped her head into her hands and continued to laugh helplessly. "It's not just *my* life that you've turned upside down. You're having a weird effect on a lot of people's lives."

After he read the article, he gave her a sheepish grin. "I don't know what to say."

Chelsey leaned her head against the seat back and turned to face him. "Tell me why you're behaving so strangely," she said softly. "What's wrong between us?"

"Do we have to talk about this?"

"Believe me, this isn't easy. In the past, when I've sensed something amiss in a relationship, I haven't confronted it. I've stiffened my pride and walked away." She frowned. "But Alex, your rules won't let us walk away from each other. So let's talk. We agreed to communicate."

She hated it that she blushed so easily. Chelsey considered herself a brisk no-nonsense type of woman. That's how she conducted her classes; that's how she ran her life. But let a man enter the picture, and she turned vulnerable and squishy inside. Her emotions turned pink and flamed in her cheeks. It made her furious.

Alex looked past her at the clouds drifting beneath them. "All right," he agreed finally. Chelsey suspected that his acquiescence was a genie thing and had more to do with pleasing his mistress than his own preference.

"So, talk," she said quietly.

"Look, Chelsey. We made love because that was what both of us wanted." When he paused, Chelsey tried to think about pale cool cheeks and snowy throats, hoping the blush pulsing in her cheeks would recede. "But there's no future here. I must leave you after your next wish. I don't want you to get hurt."

She drew back, feeling stung and defensive. Obviously he thought she was becoming emotionally involved and he didn't return her feelings. If he had, he would have mentioned the possibility of getting hurt himself.

"Wait a minute. For your information, I'm not the type of woman who falls in love with someone I've only known for a few days. So if you think I'm going to be hurt when you hop on your magic carpet and fly back to never-never land, you can put that idea right out of your head."

Chelsey wasn't lying. She wouldn't be hurt—she was going to feel as though she'd lost a limb when he left her.

"I know our relationship is temporary," she went on, feigning courage. "I know it doesn't really mean anything except the chemistry is right. I'm not looking for happily-ever-after, Alex. Not this time—not with you. Happily-ever-after is impossible in our situation. All I'm doing is taking it a minute at a time and enjoying what we do have. I thought you were, too."

"I'm starting to feel foolish," he said in a quiet voice. "I thought you were beginning to…"

She placed her hand on his arm. "Even if I were becoming emotionally involved, don't you think I've figured out there is nothing but loss and hurt at the end of the ride?" Stating it aloud darkened her eyes with anticipated pain. "If I ran away from every situation that might end badly, nothing good would ever happen, either. Look, Alex, I'm a big girl. I'm going into this with my eyes open. I care about you, yes. But it isn't love. This isn't the grand passion of my life."

Pride was speaking, not truth. Chelsey knew there would never be another man in her life like Alex. And it wasn't just that he was a genie. What she felt for Alex reached beyond mere emotions. It was a primal passion that originated in a cellular recognition. This was the man who completed her. This was the man she needed in order to feel whole.

In a peculiar way it didn't matter if Alex returned her feelings. She could almost believe that it was enough just to experience an all-consuming passion once in her life. To know what it was like. To know that she would live her life having experienced the chaos and joy of a grand passion that transcended time and space. Not to have experienced this would have been a tragedy; she saw that clearly. And it could so easily have happened that way.

"So," she finished softly, gazing into his intent eyes, "don't pull away thinking you're doing what's best for me. I'll decide what's best for me. And I'll deal with the consequences. In the meantime, let's enjoy the time we have together. Let's enjoy each other to the fullest."

His blue-green eyes seemed to bore into her brain. Chelsey suspected he sensed she was not being straight with him.

"All right," she admitted after a minute, turning her face away. "Forget what I said a minute ago." Her shoulders stiffened and her chin lifted. The hated pink flamed on her cheeks. "I will be hurt when you leave. Terribly. If you're pulling inside yourself in order to spare me from hurting when you leave…it's too late. I'm emotionally involved. The damage is done."

She felt his presence beside her, the hard warmth of his shoulder pressing against hers, the tension mounting in his silence.

"For God's sake, Alex. Say something."

His arms came around her and, none too gently, he turned her to face him again. The armrest gouged into Chelsey's side as he pulled her toward him. Then his mouth came down on hers, hot and passionate. His large hand cupped the back of her head, holding her mouth to his as he parted her lips with his tongue.

Chelsey was glad she had booked first-class tickets, glad there was no one sharing their row of seats.

When his palm slipped to her breasts, she reluctantly pushed him away. "Not here," she said weakly, managing a small smile. Her heart was pumping wildly. It was hard to remember what they had been talking about.

His hands slid upward to frame her face. "Listen to

me. The last thing I want is to hurt you or cause you pain. But I forgot how brave you are and how clear-sighted. For that, I apologize.''

He kissed her again, and all thought rushed out of her mind, replaced by rapturous sensation. His hands, tightening on her shoulders, his firm hard lips claiming hers. She heard her pulse pounding in her ears and felt the quickening breath lifting her breast.

Before the possibility of rational thought went up in flames, Chelsey eased back from him and let her head fall against the seat back. Lifting a hand, she pressed it against her thudding heart. Never before had she indulged in such a spectacle in public. Oddly, it didn't bother her as much as she would have thought. There was something wildly appealing about a man without inhibitions, a man who took what he wanted when he wanted it and the rest of the world be damned.

''Do we have this settled?'' she asked, unable to speak above a whisper. His face was classically beautiful and perfect.

The back of his hand stroked down her cheek and throat. His eyes made love to her mouth. Finally he smiled, sending her nervous system into overdrive.

''Being together may end painfully, but consequences will be dealt with when they arise. In the meantime, we'll follow our inclinations. Would you agree that's an accurate statement of our situation?''

''I'd say so.'' Chelsey gazed at him with a soft expression. His dark hair curled on his collar. His eyes were the shining color of the Mediterranean. Needing to reassure herself that this splendid man was real, she raised trembling fingertips and touched his jaw.

''You need a shave,'' she murmured, smiling, trailing her fingertips across his cheek and chin.

"I do?" Surprise lifted his eyebrows, and he touched his face. "I do." A frown sobered his expression. "How odd."

"Don't you shave?" Now that she thought about it, Chelsey didn't recall seeing him shave. But that didn't mean anything. He could have disposed of his whiskers through magic.

"I'm sleeping longer. I haven't shaved since Seli-dim.…"

Chelsey could almost see his mind working. She straightened in her seat. "Alex, why does this upset you? What does it mean?"

"I don't know." They stared into each other's eyes. He touched her hair. "Maybe…it means our time together is growing short."

The instant they stepped off the plane at La Guardia, Chelsey turned to him, speaking quietly. "The airport is crowded. Maybe no one will notice." Right now she didn't care if anyone saw them vanish. She was willing to throw caution to the winds because his suggestion about time growing short had shaken her badly. "Take us to the street outside the hotel. I don't want to waste another minute."

Alex pulled her into his arms and kissed her deeply, spreading hot fire through her veins. He didn't care that other passengers had to walk around them and neither did Chelsey. All she cared about was having Alex's arms around her. When Chelsey pulled back, feeling weak-kneed and shaky, they were standing on the sidewalk in front of the St. Moritz Hotel.

"Hurry," she whispered. They raced through registration, ran to their room and tore off each other's clothing.

In the back of their minds they were both aware that

somewhere a clock was ticking, counting down their time together.

IN THE MORNING, happily tired from a night of enthusiastic lovemaking, Chelsey shifted in bed and drew a finger down Alex's naked muscular shoulder. "You know," she said, "the busts will keep. They aren't going anywhere. I could follow up later. We could just—"

He stopped her words with a kiss, then pulled her down on the pillow so he could look in her eyes.

"No. I want to be with you through as much of this as I can. Certainly it must have occurred to you that tracing the thief could be dangerous."

She smiled, seeing the eagerness behind his eyes. "The danger appeals to you, doesn't it?"

Naturally she had considered that tracing the thief might be dangerous, but she hadn't allowed herself to examine the possibility too closely. There had been Alex to think of, and their growing passion. Besides, if her quest turned dangerous or frightening, she could quit.

She must have spoken aloud, because Alex rose on an elbow to look down at her. "If you abandon the quest, then you will have wasted your first wish. Restoring your reputation is important to you, and we'll follow the trail to the end. Or as close to the end as time allows us."

So he was worried, too.

After propping up the pillows, Chelsey remained in bed and watched through the open bathroom door as Alex shaved with a strap and straight razor he produced out of thin air.

She didn't know how she was going to bear it when he left her. His departure would be like a hand crushing her heart and leaving it as withered as her leg.

The good news, and she tried to focus on the good

news, was that she could exert some control over the situation. She would not make her third and final wish until Alex told her the time had come when she must.

"The sleeping and the shaving...are you becoming more—I'm not sure how to say this—more human the longer you stay in the reality plane?"

"I don't know." He frowned at his image in the mirror, and Chelsey realized he was wrestling with the same question. "I honestly don't think that is possible."

Chelsey sat up in bed. "Alex...will you know when you have to return to the dream state? I mean, you won't just vanish, will you?" Although she tried to keep any hint of panic out of her voice, the sudden panic was there. Surely there would be time for goodbyes and final words.

"I think I'll know when the time arrives," he said, speaking slowly, his frown deepening. He met her eyes in the mirror when she stepped up behind him. "It's tied to the third wish. I know you're delaying the last wish and I'm grateful. But there may come a moment when I tell you that you must make the last wish or lose it."

Chelsey wrapped her arms around his waist and rested her cheek against his smooth, satiny back. The smell of shaving soap and clean warm skin rose in her nostrils.

"We'll cross that bridge when we come to it," she said finally.

He put down the razor and spoke in a gruff voice. "What time is our appointment with the curator? Maybe you'd like some company in your shower?"

Laughing, Chelsey threw off her nightgown. She had a moment to think how strange and wonderful it was that she no longer felt embarrassed to stand naked in front of him.

Then he stepped into the shower and molded her against his rampant body. He groaned and ran his hands over her naked eagerness, soaping her body until she was covered with glistening bubbles and laughing at the designs he drew through the bubbles with his fingertip.

"Oh, Alex," she whispered, wrapping her arms around his neck. "I didn't know sex could be fun. I always thought it was so serious."

She had been wrong about so many things.

Chapter Ten

"I assure you the provenances for the Lupberger's Marcellus busts are beyond reproach. The Lupberger would never traffic in stolen artifacts! The suggestion is preposterous!"

"Perhaps not knowingly," Chelsey agreed, watching Albert Petre, the curator at the Lupberger Athenaeum. He sat behind an ornate Louis XV desk, twisting his hands together. When Chelsey looked at him, she saw circles. A round face, round nostrils, round wire-rimmed spectacles and a round pursed mouth.

She drew a breath and leaned forward. "Mr. Petre, I've inspected the busts flanking the Roman room and I'll stake what remains of my reputation that you have two of the missing Marcellus busts." She kept her expression blank. "I'm sure you're aware that it's illegal to remove antiquities from Turkey."

Mr. Petre tugged at his collar. A glisten of perspiration appeared in the gray hair at his temples. "It is simply not possible that the Lupberger's Marcellus busts were stolen."

"Obviously the provenances are forgeries," Alex snapped.

Without having discussed it previously, Chelsey and

Alex fell into the good-cop/bad-cop routine. Chelsey kept her voice and expression quiet and sympathetic. Alex stared at Petre as if the man were a confessed ax murderer.

"Mr. Petre, if I can prove to you that your busts are the same busts that vanished from the Caraki, will you tell us where and how you acquired them?"

Mr. Petre mopped his brow with a snowy handkerchief. He started to rise behind the desk. "I'm sorry, Dr. Mallon, but I think I must terminate this appointment at once. We have nothing further to say to one another."

"My colleague's request seems reasonable," Alex growled. His eyes were glacial. "Dr. Mallon believes she can prove to your satisfaction that your busts are stolen. If Dr. Mallon is wrong, she will apologize and we will leave. If she is correct—"

Chelsey interrupted. "Then naturally you'll want to return the busts to the Turkish authorities and correct an unfortunate error."

Petre's voice spiraled upward into a squeak. "Do you know how much the Lupberger paid for those busts? The trustees will…" He sat down heavily and rubbed his handkerchief across his forehead. "Dr. Mallon, these cannot be the busts you helped discover."

"I'm certain you believed that when you acquired the busts for the Lupberger," she said generously. "Surely you want to know for certain."

"Of course he does," Alex said, standing. His posture was vaguely threatening.

Petre also stood, and Chelsey suspected he hadn't done so of his own volition, but was helped along by magical prodding.

"Shall we go to the Roman room and allow Dr. Mallon the opportunity to present her proof?" Alex continued.

"This will ruin me," Petre muttered as he led the way

through the halls of the museum. "I don't know why I'm doing this. Our Marcellus busts are not the stolen Turkish busts. I would never purchase stolen antiquities."

Before approaching Petre, Chelsey and Alex had visited the Roman room to inspect the busts. They were magnificent, so beautiful that Chelsey couldn't view them without feeling the heat of appreciative tears behind her eyes. She didn't blame Alex for stroking his fingers over the marble faces—they seemed so real.

"I think it would be prudent to have other witnesses present," she suggested, casting a meaningful look at Alex. At once, two museum guards appeared, along with a woman who had been viewing the Roman exhibit.

Chelsey gazed at Petre, who wore an expression of deepening despair, then she studied the busts. "If you tip the busts to expose their bases, the bust on the right side of the archway will have a Roman numeral II carved into the underside. The bust on the left will have a Roman numeral IV carved on the base. These are original markings, and I can't imagine they were effaced. If these are the stolen busts, both will have a tiny *M* in a circle next to the Roman numerals. That is my own mark."

Under Alex's steady stare, Petre mopped his forehead, then nodded at the two guards. "Raise the bust on the right and tilt the base toward us." His instructions emerged in a whisper.

Chelsey didn't have to look; she knew what the base would reveal. "There's the Roman numeral II and there's the *M* within a circle."

Petre covered his face. Turning on his heel, he walked back to his office and collapsed into his chair. His eyes seemed to shrink behind the magnifying lens of his glasses. "This is going to be terrible," he said quietly. "The Lupberger's reputation will be destroyed."

"Not necessarily," Chelsey offered. "You might turn this to your advantage if you make a splash about returning the stolen items. The Lupberger's integrity and all that."

"Possibly," he murmured.

Chelsey drew a breath. "From whom did you purchase those busts, Mr. Petre?" When he hesitated, she added, "You might as well tell us. You must know the story is going to come out."

He sighed, then removed a file folder from the cabinet behind him. "I purchased the busts from the Burgeson Import House. This is the first time we've done business with them." He pushed the file across his desk toward her. "I've been with the Lupberger for twenty-eight years, Dr. Mallon." He spread his hands in a helpless gesture. "The Marcellus busts were just so beautiful."

Chelsey felt sorry for him. "I know," she said softly.

"I DON'T LIKE THIS," Alex said, frowning at the dilapidated warehouse in front of them. Harbor gulls dived overhead. The area smelled of decay and rotting garbage.

"It's not the location I would have expected for a reputable import house," Chelsey agreed with an uneasy expression, watching their cab depart. Speaking in understatement was getting to be a habit. "But this is the address on the invoice Mr. Petre gave us." Unconsciously, she stepped closer to Alex and squared her shoulders. "I hope Mr. Burgeson is in. I'm not crazy about having to come here again."

Maurice Burgeson was in, and he granted them an audience, looking surprised that he did so. Chelsey followed his scowl into a shabbily furnished office above the warehouse, sliding a look of gratitude toward Alex. She almost stumbled when she saw him.

Alex's hair was slicked back in the wet look favored by Hollywood mobsters. His lightweight summer suit had vanished, replaced by dark silk, a crisp white shirt and a black tie. Only someone who knew him well could have identified the twinkle of enjoyment in his eyes. Anyone else would have seen an aggressively hostile man who projected a silent threat of physical force.

Maurice Burgeson hunched down behind his desk, puffing on a cigar while Chelsey explained the purpose of their visit. Occasionally he glanced at her. For the most part, he kept his cold gaze fixed on Alex.

"So?" he asked when she finished.

"So it appears you sold the Lupberger Athenaeum two stolen Marcellus busts," Chelsey repeated uncomfortably. Burgeson was a large man running toward fat. Diamond rings flashed on his fingers. Power and ruthlessness flattened his eyes. His stare made Chelsey's nerves jump, and she gripped the handle of her cane with shaking hands.

"How was I supposed to know the busts were stolen?" Burgeson offered in a bored voice, measuring Alex's unblinking stare.

"I'm sure you didn't," Chelsey said, not believing it for a minute. "We'd like to know where you acquired the busts. From whom."

"Are you cops?" Burgeson inquired, exhaling a stream of smoke in Chelsey's direction. Cigar smoke stacked in blue layers above the cardboard cartons surrounding his desk.

"It's a fair assumption that you'll be hearing from the NYPD in the next few days. But no, we're not with the police."

"What's it going to take to make you people go away and forget about this?"

Chelsey looked into his flat, icy eyes. She felt as if there wasn't enough air in the room. "Information. How did you acquire the Marcellus busts?"

The cigar glowed cherry red, then he grinned, exposing a gold tooth. "Nice try. But this interview is over, honey."

The blood rose in her cheeks. "All I'm asking is—"

"We can do this the easy way or the hard way. You walk your gorgeous butt out of here right now, or I'll sic my henchmen on your henchman." He inclined his head toward Alex, not looking away from her. "You're outnumbered, Doc." He dropped a hand under his desk. "Now what's it gonna be? Do I call my boys?"

She gave him her most scathing stare. "I'm not leaving until I discover who sold you the Marcellus busts." Her most scathing stare only amused him. Chelsey wasn't sure she would have been so courageous and foolhardy if she hadn't had a genie in her corner.

Burgeson's grin widened. "Forget it. Trust me on this one, babe. You don't want to know. We're talking some nasty people here. Real nasty. I'm doing you a favor to kick you out of here."

"Dr. Mallon asked you a question," Alex said, his voice a menacing rumble. Chelsey shifted to stare at him. His French accent had altered into something more rough and threatening. "Answer the lady."

Maurice Burgeson's heavy brow clamped into a frown as he leaned to inspect the button he was pushing without effect. A handful of thugs should have responded to his summons.

"Your pretty boy don't scare me, Doc." He smiled at the idea. "We'll see if you can say the same." Rising behind his desk, he looked expectantly toward the door of his office.

Invisible hands flung him against the middle of his office wall. His arms and legs spread in an X shape. He looked as if he were stuck to the wall with universal-strength Velcro. Burgeson's mouth fell open and the cigar dropped to the floor as Alex stalked forward. "Tell Dr. Mallon what she wants to know."

Chelsey gasped. She couldn't guess what this turn of events was doing to Maurice Burgeson's nervous system, but she knew what it was doing to hers. Her pulse raced at a million miles a minute. Her eyes were as wide as pie plates. This was a side of Alex that she hadn't seen before. All traces of playfulness had disappeared from his gaze, assuming any playfulness had existed to begin with. Chelsey wondered if she had only imagined it. She stared at him.

The man whose intent gaze pinned Burgeson to the office wall was the angry crusader, a man infuriated by humanity's baser side, a knight protecting his lady. Alex looked coldly furious. His hands opened and closed at his sides as if he wanted to do more than merely stick Burgeson to the wall.

"Jeez!" Burgeson breathed, looking down at himself in disbelief before he raised his head to stare at Alex. "Who the hell *are* you?" Sweat poured down his reddened face. He tried to pull his arms free but couldn't.

"Who sold you the Marcellus busts?" Alex demanded.

Burgeson studied Alex's face, then answered promptly. "Sami Kahd. The information you want is in the file cabinet. The key is in my desk."

They didn't need a key. The file drawers along the east wall burst open and files began pouring out onto the floor like a paper river. One of the files floated across the room and hovered in front of Chelsey until she grasped it in her shaking fingers.

"Thank you," she whispered, not certain if she was

thanking Burgeson or Alex. She just wanted to get the hell out of there.

Burgeson was splayed against the wall like a grotesque doll, his weight beginning to sag. He stared at Alex. "Whatever she's paying you, I'll triple it."

"Do you have everything you need?" Alex asked.

"I think so," Chelsey answered, swiftly scanning the contents of the file. "I'll need copies for the police and for Eric Fry."

The copies instantly appeared. Her plan was to add this file to the file Petre had copied for her, scribble a note about locating two of the stolen busts, then send the package to Eric Fry, an Istanbul stringer for CNN who had spearheaded the story about the busts' discovery and their subsequent theft. Eric had been the first to report Julian Porozzi's innuendo that Chelsey was the thief. Chelsey didn't hold the revelations against Eric. He was only doing his job.

Once Eric received Chelsey's package, he would guess what she was doing. When the time came, Chelsey hoped she could count on him to devote as much space to clearing her name as he had devoted to besmirching it. She hoped she wasn't wrong about him.

"Let's get out of here," she said to Alex, stuffing the file into her oversize purse. She glanced at Maurice Burgeson. "I trust you won't mention our visit to your friend Sami Kahd."

"If you do," Alex snarled, "I'll have to pay you another visit. And I won't be in a good mood."

Burgeson just muttered, his eyes bulging as he watched the files pouring out of his cabinet, the papers piling on the floor.

Once they closed Burgeson's office door behind them, Chelsey bent forward at the waist and breathed deeply,.

trying to calm herself. "That got a little scary," she whispered when she could breathe. "How long will he stay stuck to the wall?"

Alex shrugged. When she looked at him again, he was dressed in faded jeans and a blue shirt, the sleeves rolled to the elbows. This was the Alex she knew.

"I think we'll leave him there for a while," he said, grinning down at her.

"You enjoyed every minute of that, didn't you!" Chelsey wished she knew if she was amused or furious. Her emotions swung somewhere in between.

Taking her arm, Alex led her out of the building and onto the street, where he turned her to face him. "I hope you've noticed that the people we're encountering on this quest are getting progressively nastier." His expression had sobered.

"Thank heaven I have a genie on my side." She didn't know how the interview with Burgeson would have ended it Alex hadn't been present. She suspected the outcome wouldn't have been good. Certainly she would not have obtained the information she needed.

"If I have to leave you before this is finished...I want you to promise that you'll end the quest at once. It stops that minute."

Chelsey considered his request. "I'm sorry, but I can't make that promise," she said finally.

He gave her a shake and his hands tightened on her arms until she winced. "Don't be a fool, Chelsey."

She eased out of his grasp, straightened her jacket, then leaned on her cane and eased the weight off of her leg. "Look, Burgeson scared the hell out of me, and this Sami Kahd sounds even worse."

"All right, then."

"But without my good name, I have no future. I have to go as far with this investigation as I can, Alex."

Alex thrust his hand through his hair and swore heatedly.

Leaning on her cane, Chelsey waited until he fell silent and glared at her. She straightened her shoulders and shoved her pride aside. "But I'm willing to do a little backpedaling." Willing? After Burgeson, she was ready to jump at the chance to reconsider. "I'm starting to believe archaeologists should restrict their sleuthing to the ancient past. What I'm saying is, maybe the procedure isn't important, after all. I've reconsidered and I'm willing to do this the easy way." She drew a breath. "So, okay. Let's use your magic to jump ahead to the end of the quest. Tell me who the thief is and we'll go confront him."

"Shazam."

Chelsey gasped and flung out her hand, steadying herself against the top of a chair. They were back in their suite at the St. Moritz. "Damn it, Alex. Do we really need more stories about aliens teleporting themselves around New York City?"

"I can't tell you the name of the person who stole the bust out of the Caraki Museum. I can't tap into that information without you spending another wish."

"The final wish," Chelsey whispered. They stared at each other across the bedroom suite. Turning abruptly, she took off her suit jacket and hung it in the closet, then fluffed out her hair and smoothed her palms over her slacks. "Well then, we'll proceed as we planned."

"That works as long as I'm with you. But suppose time runs out before the quest ends? I saw Burgeson's file, Chelsey. Sami Kahd, the next step in the chain, is in Munich, Germany. Since you insist on traveling by conventional means, we're talking about a twelve-hour flight, maybe a day or so to track down Kahd, then on to the next step. Time is passing. I don't know how much time I have left. I think we should discuss the advisability of using the final wish to end this quest and ensure your safety. We can structure the wish to expose the thief, reveal the remaining busts and restore your reputation.''

''Is that what you want?''

Their eyes held. ''What I want is unimportant. I'm only making a suggestion.''

''I'll decide what's best for me. And the answer is no, I'm not ready to spend my last wish.'' She could hardly bear to think about it.

''Sometimes you irritate the hell out of me,'' he said, striding forward to glare out the window at Central Park.

''And sometimes you irritate the hell out of me,'' she said, frowning at his profile. ''I think that's called a relationship. Maybe it's a by-product of spending every waking hour with the same person.'' She thought about that a minute. Other than Alex, Chelsey couldn't think of a single person with whom she could have spent this much uninterrupted time without being bored silly or going crazy. But every minute with him was fresh and exciting and wonderful. And sometimes irritating.

''You're a practical woman. So why can't you be sensible now? Each step of this quest becomes more and more dangerous. If I wasn't here—''

''But you are here,'' Chelsey pointed out in a reasonable tone. She sat on the edge of the bed and opened Maurice Burgeson's file on Sami Kahd. Leaning forward, she studied the papers in the file.

''You know,'' she said, examining the information, ''I think we've stumbled onto a smuggling ring. If the information in this file is correct, Burgeson has been buying stolen artifacts from Kahd for at least three years. He's sold them to museums all across the United States.''

Her gaze settled on the telephone. Her instinct was to give the files to the police and let them complete the investigation. But there were problems with that scenario.

First was time. An official investigation would eat up weeks. And how would she explain her role? The police would demand to know how she had learned the two Marcellus busts were in the Lupberger. Okay, she could claim an anonymous tip. But how could she hope to explain what had happened in Burgeson's office? A two-hundred-pound man stuck to the wall? Files magically pouring out of a file cabinet? And what if the police insisted that she produce Alex for questioning?

There was nothing to do but go forward. She would mail the files to the NYPD. By the time the police had deciphered the contents or Eric Fry broke the story, maybe she would think of some answers that sounded plausible.

''Does the file explain who Sami Kahd is?'' Alex asked from his position beside the window.

It always surprised her to realize there were things Alex didn't know. ''The paperwork involving Kahd shows the address of a Munich gallery. It's probably a clearing house of some kind for artifacts smuggled out of Turkey. And other parts of the world.''

''We can speed this process by—''

''No, Alex. We still need that paper trail. Now more than ever. If you want to help, phone Lufthansa and make airline reservations for us.'' He glanced at the phone with an unhappy expression. ''I'll make it up to you,'' Chelsey promised softly.

As she reached for the tiny pearl buttons running down her blouse, Chelsey kept remembering how he had jumped to her defense. She recalled the look on his face, and a tiny shiver traveled down her spine. There was something powerfully arousing about the image of a man leaping into battle for his lady, a subtle seduction within emotional fury.

"Come here, crusader," she said in a husky whisper.

THEY WALKED IN THE PARK and took a carriage ride, then explored Fifth Avenue, window-shopping until it was time to dress for dinner. Chelsey's leg throbbed with fatigue, and she would have preferred to order dinner in their suite, but she said nothing. Alex had made reservations in the Mirage Room. She suspected he was still trying to make up for the special dinner she had missed with Howard Webber.

Howard now seemed like an unpleasant memory from a different life. Whenever Chelsey thought about him, which wasn't often, she felt embarrassed and appalled. If it hadn't been for Alex, she would have made a hideous mistake. She might actually have gone to bed with Howard, an error of judgment she would have regretted for the rest of her days.

"I'm so glad you came into my life," she said softly, looking at Alex in the mirror as she spritzed perfume on her wrists and behind her ears.

"So am I," he said, coming up behind her. His arms wrapped around her waist, and he buried his face in her upswept curls. "You smell like apples."

Chelsey laughed. "Like apples?"

"And you look beautiful," he said, gazing at her in the mirror. She wore a silk slack suit, the color of which almost exactly matched Alex's eyes.

"So do you."

For a moment she gazed into the mirror and saw them as a couple. No wonder people stared. Alex was tall and handsome; his air of confidence and curiosity was commanding. As for her, it surprised Chelsey to recognize how pretty and happy she looked. There was a radiant vibrancy to her skin and features that she didn't recall noticing before. And tonight she didn't consider her cane ugly and detracting. She could almost convince herself that it was somewhat elegant and made her look interesting. Not quite, but almost.

Throughout a lavish candlelight dinner they leaned toward each other in the banquette and spoke of ordinary things. If they touched too often or gazed too deeply into each other's eyes, if observers smiled and recognized them as lovers, they didn't notice. They delighted in pretending they were an ordinary couple enjoying a special evening in an ordinary way.

It wasn't until the dessert cart had come and gone and the waiter had served coffee and brandy snifters that Chelsey returned the conversation to an earlier subject.

"Alex, did I understand you correctly?" she asked, discreetly massaging her left calf under the table. She had overdone it today. Her leg throbbed and ached and felt hot beneath the skin. "Are you suggesting that I use my final wish to conclude our quest?"

"That's one possibility," he said cautiously, watching the candlelight reflecting in her dark eyes. "I know how important restoring your reputation is to you. But it isn't my place to suggest how you use your wish."

"Without a good reputation, I might as well retire from archaeology and find a job checking groceries." She saw his grin, then laughed aloud. "I keep forgetting that I'm rich now. But you know what I mean. Archaeology is my passion. It's the only thing I've ever wanted to do. And in this field, reputation is all."

The music began.

Only now did Chelsey notice the raised stand at the front of the Mirage Room and the musicians who had assembled there. They began the evening's repertoire with a lively cha-cha. A half-dozen couples moved through the tables toward a small polished dance floor, facing each other with smiles before they floated into the rhythm.

Falling silent, her buoyant mood fading, Chelsey watched the dancers with longing in her eyes.

Over the years, and without really being aware of what she was doing, she had focused all the bitterness, disappointment and frustration about her withered leg on dancing. Dancing embodied all of her limitations. She would never be graceful. Would never be fluid or lithe. She would never move without thought, without considering her next step. She would never be symmetrical, would never be fully harmonious within herself.

Suddenly her image of herself as a radiantly desirable woman evaporated. It was nothing but self-deception. Had she approached the dance floor, everyone would have seen her as she really was.

"I'm tired," she said in a tight, thin voice. "I'd like to return to our room."

Alex followed her gaze from the dancers to the hands twisting in her lap. "Is it the dancing?"

She tried to see past the curve of the banquette. "Where's our waiter? We need our bill."

"Wait a minute." He stared at her. "Something just occurred to me."

"Please, Alex." She averted her face from the dancers, unable to glance at them without feeling the shame of white-hot envy. "It's time to leave."

"My God," he said softly. "You really don't know, do you?"

"Know what?" Something very like panic was squeezing her chest. She felt an irrational compulsion to rush out of the room, away from the music and away from the dancers flowing smoothly into something slow and achingly romantic.

"Chelsey." Leaning forward, he caught her hand and clasped it tightly between his. "Chelsey, I can fix your leg. I can make your left leg as strong and perfect as your right."

Her head snapped up and the blood drained from her cheeks. She stared at him as if she had never seen him before. "What?" The word was no louder than a breath.

"All you have to do is wish it."

She continued to stare at him, hardly daring to breathe. Her heart slammed around inside her chest, and she couldn't hear over the pounding in her ears. "That isn't possible," she whispered. "You couldn't cure Dr. Harding's Alzheimer's."

"Oh my God." Alex closed his eyes, then leaned toward her, cradling her hand against his chest. "Restoring your friend's health was not a direct benefit to you. Repairing your leg *is.* I thought you understood that."

"But history—you said you couldn't alter history."

"If I repair your leg, nothing in your past history will change. What changes is the future. It will be as if you had an operation at the time of the wish."

Chelsey wet her lips and clung to the edge of the table for support. She felt dizzy, almost sick to her stomach from the sudden surge of blinding hope. "The best doctors in the United States couldn't do anything for my leg. They tried."

"I can. If you wish it."

She released the table edge and clutched both of his hands. Hope exploded inside her chest and flamed into excitement so intense that she was on fire with it, hurting inside with it. She could hardly breathe. "Alex…is it really true? Please don't promise this unless you're very, very certain. Could you really…?"

"Yes."

"Oh God. Oh dear heaven!" She closed her eyes and fell backward against the banquette. "If you only knew how much I…" Tears sprang into her eyes, shining on her lashes when she opened her eyes and looked at him. "Oh, Alex, I could wear skirts! Short skirts! Skirts that split up the side. I could run if I wanted to! Kneel for hours on a dig like everyone else. I could swim or ski without being afraid I was making a fool of myself. And Alex! Oh, Alex." She turned shining, wet eyes toward the dance floor. "I could dance!"

Alex held her hand so tightly against his chest that she could feel his heartbeat. "I know you won't believe this," he said quietly, "but I love it when you forget your special shoes. You have a slightly rolling gait that is wildly seductive and provocative."

"A rolling gait," she repeated with a shudder of revulsion. She hunched her shoulders as if hiding from the image. Then she grabbed his hands again. "Oh, Alex. Thank you, thank you, thank you! You can't possibly know what this means to me! It's a miracle! A miracle!" Tears ran down her cheeks, but her eyes were radiant and blazing. "I don't know what to say. There aren't enough words to express my gratitude. This will change my life! I'll be a whole person again!"

He straightened beside her. His voice was low and somber. "Is this your wish, mistress?"

"Yes. Yes!" She didn't understand the sadness in his eyes. He raised his hand to her face, and she felt a tremble in his fingertips. Grasping his hand, she pressed it against her cheek. "Be happy for me. Please, Alex, be happy for me. I've dreamed of this, ached for this! But I never imagined it could really happen. Will I feel anything? Will it hurt? No, don't tell me. I don't care. Just do it. Oh do it, Alex, right now! I wish…''

The last gold coin appeared in her hand, caught the glow of the candlelight and grew warm against her palm.

"I wish…"

Chapter Eleven

"Oh my God!"

Chelsey snatched her hands back, horror darkening her eyes. Not breathing, she watched the gold coin fall to the tablecloth and wobble to a stop against the base of her brandy snifter.

She raised large, stunned eyes to Alex. A tremor began in the pit of her stomach and rocked through her body, leaving her trembling as if she'd been gripped by a violent seizure.

Collapsing against the banquette, she buried her face in her hands. "Oh my God," she whispered again. "I almost...I... It was so close!"

Turning blindly, she pressed against Alex's chest, wishing she could crawl inside of him. His arms came around her. He stroked her hair, caressed her shaking back. Soothing murmurs rumbled deep in his throat.

When she could breathe again, Chelsey lifted wet eyes to his face. "Why didn't you stop me?"

"The rules state—"

"Your stupid damned rules!" Anger fueled by the deep fear of almost losing him shot through her body. "One blindingly selfish minute almost sent you back to oblivion! And you couldn't say anything? Not a word? Not

'Do we have to do this now?' Not 'Goodbye'? Or 'Hey, it's been fun'?'' She couldn't stop shaking.

Alex gripped her shoulders and lowered his face close to hers. "Listen to me. There is nothing wrong with wanting a perfect leg! You never complain, but I know your leg hurts sometimes and pains you. I don't agree with the way you see yourself, but I know nothing I say will change your opinion. Your image is valid for you. But is it selfish to want something for yourself? Is it selfish to wish for a dream come true? No. Chelsey, Selidim forced the wishes to be selfish. They can't be anything else. So don't flog yourself for wanting something wonderful that you can have simply by wishing it."

"But not now, not yet!" Accepting his handkerchief, she wiped her eyes, then blinked at the smudges of mascara. She felt like someone who had leaned too far over the edge of an abyss and was snatched back a split second before plunging down. She couldn't breathe and her nerves continued to jump and twitch. Her stomach rolled in long, slow loops. She didn't start to feel better until the gold coin shimmered briefly, then disappeared.

A waiter appeared to refill their coffee cups, sliding a quick, curious glance toward Chelsey.

"I can't believe that you couldn't have said something," Chelsey snapped after the waiter had moved to the next table. "Don't you care?" She stared into Alex's steady blue-green eyes, trying to read his expression. "Are you ready to return? Is that it? Are you tired of me, Alex?"

His fingers tightened on her shoulders so powerfully that she winced. "If I thought it would make a difference, I'd cut off my right arm to stay here with you. Every little thing you say or do delights me. You fascinate, irritate and excite me. I couldn't grow tired of you if we had a thousand years together.''

''But...'' Confusion drained the color from her face.

''Chelsey, listen to me. The third wish must come. It will happen. I won't allow you to forfeit your wish. I want you to have it, to have your reputation restored or a perfect leg or whatever you decide. Then I must leave you. We've both known from the beginning that's how it will end. Nothing can change that. Your final wish may come tonight or two weeks from now. But it *will* happen. We can delay it, but the moment will come.''

''Alex—''

''There may not be time to say goodbye or to tell you how much it has meant to me being with you in the reality plane. The wish could overwhelm you again as it nearly did tonight. Swiftly, emotionally, joyfully. If that should happen, then I want you never, never to look back with regret. You know I care about you, and I know you care about me. And we both know our time together is measured. Enjoy your wish. Exalt in it. Don't castigate yourself that you claimed your wish at my expense. You have no choice. And please, my dearest, dearest mistress, please know that wherever I am, I'll be sharing your joy.''

Chelsey dissolved in tears. ''Use your magic and take us out of here. Right now I don't care if anyone sees. Hold me, Alex. I need you.''

Standing he threw some bills on the table, then swept her into his arms.

And they vanished.

THEY MADE LOVE frantically, hurriedly, straining to get closer, closer. Their hands flew over each other's bodies, stroking, caressing, reassuring. They rolled off the bed to the floor but neither of them noticed or cared. All that mattered was melting into one another, becoming one entity, one being. All that mattered was the urgency of finding each other and, in the discovery, finding themselves.

Later, lying side by side in blissful exhaustion, they sipped chilled wine from crystal goblets and murmured words lovers have murmured since man first stood upright. And because it was their words and their moment, the sentiments seemed fresh and new and wonderfully unique to them. Only gradually did their whispers bend toward more ordinary conversation.

Alex cushioned her head on his shoulder and brushed his fingertips over the wet tendrils clinging to her forehead and cheeks.

"It isn't fair," Chelsey said softly, feeling a prick of tears. "I've looked for you all of my life. I thought you didn't exist. Now I find you, but only for a brief moment."

Alex's arms tightened around her in a gesture of possessiveness that was a mockery given their circumstances. "I thank the powers that be that I've had this time with you," he said gruffly. "Never to have had this, never to have known you..."

Turning her in his arms, he kissed her, long and deep, trying to tell her with his mouth and hands what he could not put into words.

This time when they made love, the frantic urgency had abated. They touched each other with tenderness and gentle delight, marveling in the differences between them. His hardness; her softness. The silkiness of her hair; the scratchy coarseness of his whiskers. The golden bronze of his skin; the milky whiteness of hers. The jigsaw compatibility of male and female.

And when he kissed her withered leg, tears of love,

gratitude and excruciating loss slipped from the corners of her eyes.

ALTHOUGH ALEX FIDGETED, the twelve-hour flight to Munich passed in the blink of an eye for Chelsey. She dozed once or twice, but her mind was too active to permit a deep sleep. She couldn't concentrate on the new Anne Tyler novel.

Finally she gave up and let her mind wander freely among the possibilities offered by the final wish.

Alex was right. The time would come when the final wish could be delayed no longer. She needed to push her mind beyond the devastation of losing him and decide what she would wish for so she would be ready when the moment came.

Last night she would have stated emphatically that her final wish would be for a perfect left leg. There was no real choice to make.

But upon reflection, Chelsey experienced a disturbing nibble of doubt even though her idea of herself was linked intrinsically with her leg, her cane and her limitations. To a large extent her personality had been shaped by these things. But at the same time her idea of herself was also tightly bound to her profession. Archaeology was how she defined herself, her accomplishments, how she measured herself.

But unless the timing worked out exactly right, she would have to choose between restoring her professional reputation, thus preserving her identity as an archaeologist, or repairing her leg and that part of her psyche that was as damaged as her withered muscles.

It was a terrible, impossible choice. Like trying to decide whether to relinquish her heart or her soul.

Shifting, Chelsey turned to gaze at Alex, who was trying unsuccessfully to doze. Long, curling lashes rested on his cheeks. His arms were crossed over his chest in an effort to squeeze himself into a seat too small for a man his size.

A dark hint shadowed his jaw and upper lip; already he needed to shave again. She decided he could also use a haircut. Last night he had slept a full two hours. And he had perspired during their lovemaking, which had surprised him. She wondered if Alex had realized yet that he'd stopped eating anything and everything for the taste and tactile pleasure and had become selective in his choices, stopping at almost the same point at which an ordinary man would. This change indicated he was experiencing hunger and satiation.

Chelsey didn't fool herself that these physical changes meant Alex was becoming less of a genie and more of an ordinary man. They had discussed the possibility several times and had reluctantly dismissed it as wishful thinking. His magic was as strong and effective as it had ever been and as readily available. Had he been undergoing a transformation from genie to man, the magic would have diminished correspondingly.

The physical changes were a result of his prolonged sojourn in the reality plane. An indication that his time here was growing short.

"A penny for your thoughts," he said softly, and she realized he was watching her.

"I was thinking about whiskers and perspiration and haircuts," she said, looking down at her hands. "Selfish things."

He understood as she had known he would. "You're worrying that I'll have to return before we conclude the quest."

And worrying about terrible choices. "How will it happen, Alex? How will you know it's time to return?"

The dream state had assumed an aura of horror for her. Chelsey couldn't imagine the unthinkable frustration of drifting through time in a dream, unable to touch or feel, unable to reach out and experience.

"I think the process has already begun," Alex admitted quietly, rubbing his fingers across his jaw. "The physical changes are a signal."

She closed her eyes and lowered her head, swallowing a cry of the heart. "What happens next?"

"I don't know. I've never stayed in the reality plane this long before." He frowned and looked past her shoulder at the wing of the plane. "I think a pressure will begin to build. And continue building until it becomes almost unbearable. Something like what happens when I wander too far from your voice, only a hundred times more intense. The knowing will come. I'll know you must make your final wish immediately or agree to forfeit."

"Has it begun?" she whispered. "Do you feel the pressure?"

His hand dropped to his chest, the movement involuntary. "Not yet. But it's there, Chelsey. I sense it gathering."

Heaven help her, so did she. She felt like a person trapped in the bottom of an hourglass, watching helplessly as the unstoppable grains of sand poured down on her. Burying her, choking her.

"I don't want you to forfeit your final wish."

She made a helpless gesture with her hands. "Without a reputation for integrity, I might as well give up my profession. And that would be like giving up breathing. But I want a perfect leg, too. I've dreamed that impossible dream for over a decade."

He took her hand. "Maybe you won't have to make that choice."

But the pace had accelerated in their race against time.

THE HILTON INTERNATIONAL was located on Am Tuckerpark, a scenic avenue between the Isar River and the Englischer Garten. As their suite wasn't made up yet, they walked in the Englischer Garten, passing beneath ancient oaks and elms, birches and fir.

The long flight had left her leg feeling cramped and tight, and Chelsey relied heavily on her cane.

"There's a bench. Would you like to rest a minute?"

Chelsey hesitated, pride warring against fatigue, then she nodded gratefully. Ordinarily she would have vigorously denied an urge to rest her throbbing leg. But knowing that very soon she would be able to walk for miles and miles without tiring made it acceptable to give in now.

"It's beautiful here," she said, admiring the banks of summer flowers surrounding the bench. A hundred yards to Chelsey's left, a naked couple reclined in the grass, casually embracing. She smiled, wondering if Americans would ever be comfortable with the less inhibited mores of an older culture.

Alex offered her a frosty stein of strong German ale, and she accepted it with pleasure. They sipped ale and listened to music drifting toward them from a nearby beer garden.

"Does the music upset you?" Alex asked.

"Why would you ask that? Oh. No, music has never upset me. I love music, all kinds except jazz. I don't understand jazz—it sounds like noise to me." She smiled, then fingered the handle of her cane. "It's dancing that upsets me."

But not for much longer. Tilting her head back, she gazed at a leafy overhang of thick branches and leaves so dense they smothered the morning sunshine.

The one man in the universe with whom she longed to float around and around a dance floor would be gone. She and Alex would never dance together.

"While you were freshening up, I phoned Kahd's gallery," Alex informed her. "It's located on Prannerstrasse, a few blocks from the National Theater. Are you familiar with the area?"

Chelsey frowned, trying to remember. "I haven't been in Munich since the year after I graduated from college, and then it was only for a few days. But I think that's a good area." Which surprised her. She had expected Sami Kahd to have located his gallery and/or clearing house for stolen antiquities in a spot as seedy and out of the way as that chosen by Maurice Burgeson. She gazed at Alex over the foam capping her stein. "Did you make an appointment for us?"

"Kahd wasn't in. But his secretary recognized our names. She said Sami Kahd would see us at four-thirty this afternoon. Is that too soon? Would tomorrow have been better for you?"

Chelsey met his eyes. In the back of her mind she listened to a clock ticking. "The sooner the better." A full minute elapsed before she spoke again. "What does it mean that Kahd expected our call and granted us an immediate appointment?"

Alex stretched his arms across the back of the bench and gazed forward. "It means our friend Maurice phoned ahead."

"Then why did Kahd agree to see us? Did you use your magic to make him agree?"

Alex shrugged and shook his head. "Who knows?

Maybe Kahd's curious to meet the people who stuck Burgeson to his office wall. Maybe he wants to discover how much we know about his operation. Or maybe he thinks we're Tupperware salespeople and he's in the market for a lettuce crisper.''

His last remark was so unexpected that Chelsey burst into laughter, spilling foam and ale across her slacks. ''Sometimes you know things that I'd never imagine you would know. Other times you don't know things that any self-respecting genie ought to know. Where did you learn about Tupperware? No woman worthy of the name can run a kitchen without it.''

''What do you do with all those little plastic bowls?'' he asked, offering his arm. They headed back toward the Hilton.

''Contrary to the genie method, most women can't consign leftovers to a cosmic black hole. We save them in airtight plastic bowls.''

''Why?''

''Because we can't bear to throw food away until it's green and fuzzy.'' She started laughing again. ''The longer the period between usable and green and fuzzy, the better we feel.''

By the time they reached the Hilton, tears of laughter rolled down their faces. Part of the silliness was due to the fatigue of jet lag, but part was a release of the tension they felt about meeting Sami Kahd in a few short hours. The mention of Kahd's name had caused Maurice Burgeson's lips to pale. It wasn't going to be a pleasant experience.

THEY ASKED THE CAB DRIVER to circle the block so they could examine Sami Kahd's gallery and the building that housed it. Although the building was large, the gallery portion appeared unusually small. A glimpse of the alley-way revealed unmarked trucks unloading crates into the building's warehouse entrance.

"My guess is the gallery is mainly a cover," Chelsey suggested, leaning from the cab window to peer up. Even the windows on the third and fourth floors were protected by thick iron bars. "I'll bet most of Kahd's pieces are moved in and out of the back without ever appearing in the gallery."

They entered the deserted gallery and confirmed Chelsey's guess. Inside were two rooms crammed with indifferent items of little interest or value. An overlay of fine dust coated pieces that would have disappointed even a novice collector.

At the sound of their footsteps against the hardwood floor, an unsmiling older woman appeared from the gloom shadowing the end wall of the second room. After inspecting Chelsey's cane, then sweeping a glance over Alex, she gave them a short nod. "Follow me, *bitte.*" Turning sharply, she led them through a door at the back of the gallery, locked it behind them, then indicated an elevator at the end of a dim hallway.

After giving each other a glance, Chelsey and Alex rode the elevator upward in silence, stepping off on the fourth floor. Here the corridors were carpeted in thick, rich plush. The walls were a deep plum color. Here and there urns and marble busts rested on ornate pedestals. Skillfully lit paintings lined the hallways.

"Good Lord," Chelsey breathed. "That's a Rubens! And there's a Titian!" She tried to calculate what the paintings in this corridor were worth. So many zeros made her eyes glaze.

The woman led them to carved double doors at the end of the corridor. Without a word, she turned and departed the way they had come. Alex waited until they heard the hum of the elevator, then he raised an eyebrow at Chelsey and pushed open the doors.

Inside was a lavishly appointed reception area. The antique chairs and settees were worth a king's ransom. Many of the paintings and artifacts were simply priceless. Chelsey recognized a magnificent jeweled cross that had vanished four years ago in a bold daylight theft from a museum in Seville.

Two secretary desks faced the doors, both deserted. Directly ahead was a second set of double doors. These doors were open and a massive, custom-made desk faced them from inside the room beyond. The man behind the desk, Sami Kahd, examined them with eyes the color of black ink.

His hair was black; his Italian silk suit was black. A hawk nose jutted from the middle of a swarthy complexion. If it were true that a man's eyes offered windows to his soul, then this man had no soul. Not a flicker of emotion stirred behind Kahd's icy black stare.

"Oh boy," Chelsey murmured. Her heart flip-flopped in her chest, then sank. She thanked God that Alex was beside her. Placing each reluctant step with care, she summoned a whisper of courage and walked into Kahd's office.

Before she could sort out what was occurring, five men sprang from behind the doors and jerked her away from Alex. Rough hands pinned her arms behind her; a huge man stood in front of her, aiming a gun at her breast. On the other side of the door two men subdued Alex. A third thrust a gun against his jaw. It all happened in less than a minute.

Sami Kahd walked around his desk. "We're going to discover why you're so interested in the Marcellus busts.

Then we're going to kill you.'' He spoke in a bored voice, neither pleasant nor unpleasant, glancing at a medieval clock as if he resented time lost on interrogation, torture and killing.

A gathering noise rumbled across the room like an angry wind.

The guns flew out of the hands of Kahd's men, burst from shoulder and leg holsters, out of a desk drawer and a wall safe that banged open. Two or three knives ripped up out of jackets or pants. The weapons whirled in the air near the high ceiling like strange blue-black birds, then vanished.

The men stared, their jaws slack. One of them swore. ''You said Burgeson was lying!''

Lengths of rope and thin chain poured out of the ceiling. It happened so swiftly there was no time to react. The rope and chain sought Kahd's thugs and wound around them with a faint hissing sound. Once they were bound, a giant invisible hand hurled them across the room against the back wall. They slid to the floor like limp rag dolls. Dark hoods materialized in the air above them and dropped over their heads. Aside from a single moan, no one made a sound. None dared move a muscle.

''Did the bastards hurt you?'' Alex gripped Chelsey's shoulders and scowled into her face.

''No,'' she whispered, dragging her gaze from the pile of bound men. Her heart was galloping a mile a minute and her nerves were raw, but she wasn't harmed. Only frightened and more than a little awestruck. She wasn't sure she had the nerves for this kind of thing. Pressing a hand to her forehead, Chelsey leaned against the wall and fought to compose herself.

When she opened her eyes, she noticed a tiny kernel of interest growing across Kahd's bored expression. ''It seems I erred. I didn't believe Burgeson." Ignoring his men, he studied Alex. "Who are you and what do you want?"

"Dr. Mallon wishes to know who sold you the Marcellus busts."

Kahd's dead eyes shifted to Chelsey. His accent was faint, but suggested Turkish origin. "I'd think you would know, Dr. Mallon, as you stole the busts in the first place."

"No," Chelsey said, her face hot.

"Oh?" A thin smile made his face look grotesque. His eyes remained removed and empty. "Whatever your motivation, the trail ends here." His smile held. "You—or any officials you may think to involve—will find nothing here to suggest stolen artifacts. No evidence leads to this gallery."

Chelsey leaned forward. "Maurice Burgeson—"

"It seems Mr. Burgeson has vanished. I doubt he will reappear. Last night his warehouse and all his records burned to the ground." His gaze returned to Alex. "None of your theatrics impress me, Mr. Duport. Nor would a further display induce me to jeopardize a lucrative venture. So, I'll wish you good day and advise you to forget the Marcellus busts." His smile tightened. "Perhaps we'll meet again."

He started to turn away, but the invisible hand returned and slammed him into a straight-backed chair that appeared in the center of the room. After a brief struggle to rise, Kahd relaxed and lifted an eyebrow at Alex.

"An interesting parlor trick. I confess a curiosity as to how you accomplish these feats. But you're wasting your time. Perhaps I should mention that I once spent two years in a Turkish prison. Are you familiar with Turkish prisons, Mr. Duport?" The glacial smile returned. "Turkish prisons are the most brutal in the world. There is nothing you can do that has not been done to me before. I did not speak then, either."

"Chelsey, I want you to leave the room." Alex walked around Kahd's chair, watching and circling. The muscle and tendon stood out on his arms like cords of cable. "Leave the doors open so I can hear if you call. Under no circumstances are you to look inside this room. No matter what you hear or think you hear, you are not to enter this room or look inside it."

"Alex…I don't know about this." Chelsey wet her lips. She glanced at the bound and hooded men lying against the back wall, then back at Sami Kahd, stuck to a chair in the center of his lavish office. Although Kahd's complexion had paled and his darting eyes no longer seemed as lifeless, he effected a relaxed and arrogantly confident posture. Actually it was Alex who worried her most. Chelsey no longer knew him. He looked large and ruthlessly powerful. Icily furious and frightening.

"Go."

There was no room for argument in that growled command. No mercy. No yielding. Chelsey picked up her cane and went.

Standing well outside Kahd's office doors, Chelsey pressed her back flat against the paneling and wondered what in the hell she had gotten them into. It frightened and appalled her to think of the destruction that had followed the discovery of the Marcellus busts. Lives had been altered. Reputations had been destroyed. Now someone had died.

If Alex hadn't employed his magical powers, he and Chelsey might also have been dead by now.

She shuddered, straining to hear the murmur of voices from the room behind her, unable to decipher more than a few isolated words. The voices rose to shouts, followed by a period of thick taut silence.

Then Sami Kahd began to scream.

There were words within the screams, and pleas, but Chelsey didn't hear them. She heard only the shocking sound of a man's screams. The screams clawed across her nerve endings. Rocking mindlessly, she clapped her hands over her ears and chewed her lips until they bled. She reminded herself that Sami Kahd had intended to have her and Alex murdered. It didn't help. The horror and pain in Kahd's screams made Chelsey sick to her stomach. She had never heard anything like this and prayed she never would again.

She spun toward the doors, hoping she wouldn't vomit or faint before she stopped the torture in the other room, but she had to stop it or go insane herself. She took two steps before Alex appeared, closing the doors firmly behind him.

"We're leaving now," he said calmly. He opened a humidor on one of the secretary's desks, removed a thin dark cigar and lit it, sucking the smoke deep into his lungs.

"I didn't know you smoked," Chelsey whispered inanely. Her nerves jangled. Her body shook and her skin twitched. She thought it possible that she was about to throw up.

"I need to cut the taste in my mouth." After drawing deeply on the cigar, he tossed it aside, then led Chelsey out of the reception area.

Kahd's screams followed them into the corridor.

The screams didn't end until Alex dropped his arm around her waist and said, "Shazam." They materialized in their suite at the Hilton.

Chelsey collapsed into the chair near the window,

pitched forward and covered her face in her hands. "Oh my God, Alex! What did you do to him?"

"One of Kahd's men put his hands on you."

"You tortured him, didn't you?"

"In a manner of speaking." Anticipating her needs, he materialized a frosty pitcher of ice water and poured a glass. He also produced a cold wet cloth which Chelsey accepted and pressed against her forehead.

When she had stopped shaking enough to speak again, Chelsey looked up at him with a white face. "What exactly did you do? Please, Alex. I have to know."

Alex sat on the edge of the bed, watching her. "Every man has secret fears, his own brand of terror and hellish nightmares. I showed Kahd his fears and nightmares in a hologram much as I used to show you the location of the Marcellus busts. But I let his terrors and his nightmares escape the hologram. They crawled over his body and into his eyes. They entered his mind."

Chelsey tried to imagine the horror of what he was describing. She couldn't. "What were Kahd's nightmares?"

"No," he said quietly, looking away from her. Now she noticed how pale his lips were. "That I won't tell you."

Standing abruptly, Chelsey wordlessly threw off her clothing. When she was naked, she walked into the bathroom and stood under as hot a shower as she could stand. It was a long time before she felt clean and safe again.

THEY ORDERED DINNER in their suite, but neither had an appetite. After making a pretense of eating, Chelsey gave it up. She carried a china cup of rich dark coffee out onto their small balcony. Her hair was still damp from her shower and she wore the thick, plush bathrobe provided by the hotel.

She pushed back the terry sleeves and leaned on the balcony railing, gazing out at the dark Englischer Garten. Somewhere far below, an oompah band played German drinking songs. The night air was pleasantly cool. Clouds obscured the stars.

When Alex joined her, leaning his elbows on the railing beside her, she rested her head against his shoulder, suddenly so tired she thought she might collapse.

"Kahd ordered Burgeson killed, didn't he?" she murmured, closing her eyes.

"Yes."

"I wish I'd never started this." She glanced at the gold coin that appeared in her fingers, then tossed it off the balcony. "I want to set the record straight and restore my reputation, but…" It occurred to her that even Sami Kahd had believed she was responsible for the theft of the busts. Maybe Albert Petre had believed so, too. And Maurice Burgeson. People all over the world believed Dr. Chelsey Mallon was a thief. "Did you learn anything from Sami Kahd?"

"Kahd masterminds a very large, very profitable operation dealing in priceless antiques and artifacts." Alex moved behind her. His large hands massaged the tight knots that had turned her shoulders to stone. "These items, all stolen, are smuggled into Munich from Europe, the Middle East, and the Orient. Kahd's organization creates new provenances for the antiquities and notifies a hundred outlets like Maurice Burgeson's. It doesn't take long to locate a buyer, even for items known to be stolen. The highest bidder is selected, then the items are shipped from Kahd's gallery to a middleman like Burgeson."

"You make it sound simple," Chelsey murmured, closing her eyes and leaning into his hands.

"The Marcellus busts came to Munich through Bulgaria. Kahd's deal was with two shopkeepers in Istanbul, two brothers named Achmed and Ish Hamish. I have their shop address."

"So," Chelsey whispered, looking at the dark sky, "Istanbul is next." They had been moving toward Istanbul from the beginning.

"There's something else. Kahd purchased three of the Marcellus busts. Not four. Two went to the Lupberger Athenaeum, one to the London Museum of Roman Antiquities. He knew nothing of the whereabouts of the fourth bust."

"The bust in the storeroom," Chelsey remembered, frowning. "I thought about that on the plane. I think the thief still has the fourth bust. Maybe he can't bear to part with it. Or maybe he's waiting for the price to rise. If we find that bust, we'll find the person who stole them all."

"I phoned Pan Am while you were in the shower. We have reservations on the morning flight to Istanbul."

That's where Chelsey's nightmare had begun. That's where it would end. Along with the greatest joy she had ever experienced.

She had wanted events to move rapidly so she wouldn't have to choose between restoring her reputation or her leg. Now that the end was in sight and speeding toward her more swiftly than she had dreamed possible, she wanted to throw up a barrier and hold back time.

That Alex had phoned Pan Am without any prodding from her told Chelsey the dream state was stirring. Alex had begun to feel not a vague sense of impending pressure, but the pressure itself.

Blindly she turned toward him. "Hold me, Alex. Hold

me like none of this is happening, like you'll never let me go.''

He caught her in his arms and buried his face in her damp curls.

Chapter Twelve

Chelsey and Alex flew into Yesilköy Airport, then took a cab to Pera Heights, crossing the Golden Horn to reach Beyoglu north of Stamboul, the old walled city. Although still referred to as the "new" city, Beyoglu had housed foreigners since the tenth century. Now the hills of old were flattened, crowned by luxury hotels and restaurants, theaters and consulates.

"Is this where you stayed last summer?" Alex asked as they registered into the Topkapi Hotel, which was almost as ornate as Topkapi Palace but nowhere near it. The palace commanded the tip of the promontory fortifying the old city.

Chelsey laughed. "Not hardly. I spent a few days in a run-down place outside Kanlica. Then weeks camping in the desert."

While the bellman explained their water supply would be erratic because the rivers were running dry earlier this year than last, Chelsey wandered outside onto a tiny balcony.

What she loved most about Istanbul were the domes, minarets and fountains. The multitude of minarets reminded her of spears challenging the sky. And, of course, she couldn't think of Istanbul without the Bosporus, an incredibly crowded waterway that sustained the city like a brown artery. Docks and wharves jutted from every available piece of waterfront.

Today the wind was from the southwest, blowing the exotic scents of the old walled city to the heights. The pungent smell of packed humanity invaded every breath, as did the stench of burning rubbish and automobile emissions. Riding atop the breeze was the sweet smoke of a hundred different varieties of incense. No city smelled quite like Istanbul, Chelsey thought. It smelled of people and food and religion and history.

There was also a dark side to the city's beauty. Secrets flourished here. Every imaginable vice had a price tag and a vendor. Human life was cheap. Nothing was quite what it seemed on the surface.

"Have you been here before?" Chelsey murmured as Alex came up behind her and wrapped his arms around her waist.

"I've dreamed of Constantinople. I watched the armies of the Fourth Crusade sack the old city."

"A disgrace, if I remember correctly. The gentlemen, and I use the term loosely, of the Fourth Crusade behaved abominably."

They stood close, gazing out at the sun-bright domes and minarets. Wistfully, Chelsey wished they were visiting as tourists with nothing more pressing to do but enjoy historical tours and pleasure excursions.

"Do we have a plan?" Alex murmured against her ear. His large hands slid up to gently cup her breasts and pull her back against his chest.

"Only to find Achmed and Ish," she said, closing her eyes.

The realization that their time together had dwindled to a matter of days increased their hunger for each other.

They had to compress a lifetime of memories into a few spare hours.

"The Hamish brothers can wait," Alex said hoarsely, turning her in his arms. His eyes smoldered down into hers.

Chelsey unbuttoned his shirt and ran her palms over his powerful chest, anticipating the timeless delirium of his hands on her thighs, her belly, her breasts.

Truly he was magic.

THE CAB LET THEM OUT on Mevlanakapi Street near a side street that veered into a labyrinth of twisting alleyways. From here they proceeded on foot through unpaved alleys overhung by dilapidated wooden houses and laundry lines. The smells were strong and unpleasant. The heat trapped in the alleyways was intense, but no sunlight penetrated the overhang. The residents of this dismal section lived in perpetual gloom.

Chelsey blotted perspiration from her forehead, then edged closer to Alex and took his arm, aware that hidden eyes watched. Few tourists ventured into these mean streets.

"There are moments when I'm damned glad you're a genie," Chelsey whispered, sensing hostility from the dark forms who slid past them in the alleyway.

"Only moments?" he asked. His arm beneath her fingertips was taut and tense. He scanned the alleyway in front of them.

"This is one of them."

At length the gloom opened into a noisy square that housed a local bazaar. Chelsey eyed the rabbit warren of aisles that twisted and turned in a confusing maze. The sound of animal bleatings and human haggling pounded against her skull, as did the high whine of Turkish music, which she had never learned to appreciate. A biting blend of incense, roasting lamb and other less pleasant smells assaulted her nostrils.

"Is this where we'll find the Hamish brothers?" she asked in a faint voice.

"Over there."

Following Alex's gaze, Chelsey was relieved to see they would not have to plunge into the chaos of the bazaar. Achmed and Ish's shop was a permanent structure located on the corner of one of the alleyways spilling people into the bazaar.

"Good God!" Chelsey breathed, gripping Alex's arm. "Do you see that man entering the Hamish brothers' shop? He's carrying a bronze amphora that must have come from Gilmach! I read in the trade journals that Dr. Robinson uncovered a stunning cache." Shock darkened her eyes almost to black. "He isn't even trying to conceal it! The Hamish brothers are so damned brazen they're trafficking in stolen antiquities in broad daylight in front of a thousand people!"

"Do we confront them or not?" Alex inquired, watching her face, protecting her from the jostling of the crowds.

She hesitated. "We need to think about this."

It occurred to Chelsey that Achmed and Ish Hamish were not likely to be any more forthcoming than Burgeson or Sami Kahd. Alex would again have to intervene. But in this instance, Alex's persuasion would be conducted in an open-front shop before hundreds of people. Chelsey doubted that performing before an audience would inhibit Alex, but the idea horrified her.

"We're so close," she said, thinking aloud. Sliding a look toward Alex, she added, "Maybe it's time to involve the authorities."

"It's your call," Alex said reluctantly. He cast a final glance at the Hamish brothers' shop, impatience hardening his eyes, then he led her back through the maze of alleyways.

They returned to the Topkapi Hotel and ordered a late lunch in their suite. While Chelsey made one frustrating telephone call after another, Alex expanded the room and replicated a Roman ruin. The carpet disappeared beneath packed sand and tufts of salt grass. Patiently, Alex applied himself to excavating the cornerstone of what he told her was a Roman temple.

"I want to understand what you do," he explained.

Trying to ignore the sand dunes behind her, Chelsey telephoned the official who had investigated the theft of the Marcellus busts from the Caraki Museum. After several attempts, it became clear he would not accept her calls.

"All right, we'll do this the hard way," she muttered with a sigh. She began the tedious process of wending her way through the leviathan bureaucracy of the Turkish government.

IT WASN'T UNTIL the next morning that she discovered Harry Sahok and convinced Sahok to give her and Alex an appointment.

On the positive side, Harry Sahok headed a department whose purpose it was to stem the flood tide of antiquities leaving Turkey. Chelsey hadn't realized there was such a department. The bad news was that Sahok's department was ridiculously understaffed and underfunded.

When Chelsey finished explaining the route of the stolen Marcellus busts, Sahok leaned back in his desk chair and studied her with sympathetic dark eyes. He was a handsome man approaching forty, Chelsey guessed, but his eyes were much older. Lines of fatigue bracketed his mouth and carved railroad tracks across a broad forehead. His office was no larger than a cubicle. His cluttered desk was made of scarred metal.

"The Hamish brothers buy stolen antiquities and smuggle them out of the country almost before we know about the theft." Sahok leaned forward and folded his hands on his desk top. "Their father ran the operation before them, their grandfather before that. But prove it?" He shrugged, glancing at an overhead fan that wheezed, then coughed to a stop.

"The Hamish brothers aren't making any effort to hide what they're doing," Chelsey insisted. "A thousand people must know they're trafficking in stolen antiquities."

"But will any of those thousands of people testify?" Sahok passed a hand over his eyes. "People who threaten the Hamish brothers have a nasty way of disappearing. If I could help you, I would. But unless I can catch Achmed and Ish in the act...my hands are tied."

"But you *know* they're shipping stolen antiquities to Sami Kahd in Munich!"

"I know it but I can't prove it, and I don't have the resources to protect witnesses if I had any. I don't have the manpower or the finances to conduct a full-scale investigation." He spread his hands, indicating his cubicle and shabby furnishings. "Turkey has problems more pressing than preserving antiquities, Dr. Mallon. Here, Roman ruins are as ubiquitous as mosques. If a few artifacts get smuggled out of the country, there are more where those came from."

Chelsey stared. "Do you believe that, Mr. Sahok?"

"That's the official attitude. Every country has priorities. Maybe someday...but for the present my department is near the bottom of the funding list." He studied her.

"I'm sorry about what happened to you. For what it's worth, I never believed you stole the Marcellus busts. I figured the curator, maybe Porozzi."

Chelsey spread her hands in frustration. "Is there anything I can say to—"

"I'm sorry. There's nothing I can do."

Desperate, she searched her mind. "Will you agree to this much? If I can set up a sting, will you put some official weight behind it? Will you arrest Achmed and Ish? And cooperate on an international level to shut down Sami Kahd's operation?"

Harry Sahok glanced at Alex.

"This is Dr. Mallon's show," Alex said. "I support however she wants to handle the situation."

Sahok nodded and looked back at Chelsey. "If you can arrange something where I can catch Achmed and Ish red-handed, I'll slap the handcuffs on. But I don't have the hours or the manpower to get involved before your sting is about to unfold."

"Fair enough. I'll let you know when we're ready." She shook his hand. "It'll be very soon."

"A sting?" Alex asked, raising an eyebrow when they were back on the hot, teeming street.

"I'm so frustrated I could scream," Chelsey said, banging the tip of her cane against the pavement. "We're this close, but time is speeding by and no one gives a damn!"

Alex took her arm and flagged a cab. "Sahok's a good man, but tired and overworked. He'll be there when the time comes."

"The problem is, I don't know when that will be." Chelsey slid into an air-conditioned cab with a sigh of relief. She leaned forward to massage her throbbing leg. "I don't have a plan, worse luck. Can you think of something?"

"Suppose we make Achmed and Ish an offer," Alex suggested after a minute, his blue-green eyes twinkling. "Suppose we offer to buy the fourth bust..."

"Wait a minute. Yes!" Chelsey sat bolt upright and stared at him, excitement building in her chest. "Achmed and Ish will have to contact the thief to relay our offer. We follow and—bingo—we discover the thief's identity! We'll phone the Hamish brothers first thing in the morning and set it up"

"Or maybe we arrange to meet the thief and make the buy on our terms. But let's phone the Hamish brothers now, Chelsey. Perhaps we can arrange a meeting for tonight."

"So soon?"

Chelsey met his gaze, and her expression instantly sobered. She caught a ragged breath and held it, wishing she could hold time as easily. Suddenly there were a million things she wanted to say to him. A million questions she needed to ask.

But all she said was "There's a pay phone at the university. It's not far from here."

THE FORCES GATHERING around Alex began as a vague sense of unease and gradually deepened toward discomfort. The mounting pressure made him restless and irritable. He found himself particularly impatient with delays. Chelsey's insistence on rail and cabs drove him wild. Magic could have lessened the time required to resolve their quest, time he didn't have to spare.

The physical changes were the most worrisome. Last night he had slept three hours. When he woke, he left Chelsey in their bed and slipped into the bathroom where he trimmed his hair, shaved, and clipped his finger-and toenails, frowning while he did so. He had not performed these ablutions in centuries.

There were other signs. His physical acuity was not as intense as it had been when he had first arrived in the reality plane. It was as different as stroking a red-hot stove top or one that was merely warm. During his first hour in the reality plane, he could feel print on a page. Now it felt as if his genie's body were going numb. He perceived the world more as he imagined an ordinary man would. The change was not unpleasant, merely different. But the implications alarmed him.

Time was his enemy.

Leaving Chelsey waiting in the cab, he hurried into the administration building at the university of Istanbul and found a pay phone. Achmed Hamish answered on the eighth ring.

"What happened?" Chelsey asked anxiously when Alex returned a few moments later and slid onto the seat beside her.

"The Hamish brothers agreed to see us tonight at nine o'clock. They'll phone our hotel at eight-thirty and tell us where to meet them."

Chelsey nodded, her eyes large. "What did you say to them?"

"They recognized our names. Achmed had spoken to Sami Kahd."

"And he still agreed to meet with us?" Amazement shot her eyebrows toward her heart-shaped hairline.

"I suggested it would be worth his while."

"Magic?"

"They sniff money." Leaning forward, he signaled the cabby. "Take us to the Hagia Sophia. We may as well do a little sightseeing." The restlessness building inside him required movement.

THE HAMISH BROTHERS chose a small, smoky coffeehouse located near Mavlana Gate. The coffeehouse was reasonably accessible, being near the old-city walls and the railway that ran along the far side of an ancient moat. But it was in an area that only a very brave and very foolish foreigner would enter.

Alex swept aside Chelsey's objections and arrived at the coffeehouse by uttering "shazam." Even at nine o'clock, the unpaved alley was stiflingly hot and jammed with thick crowds. Chelsey glanced around, then pressed next to his body as they entered the coffee shop.

Inside, the dense air was gray with cigar and cigarette smoke and sickening sweet clouds of opium. A sharp-faced boy caught the end of Chelsey's cane and tugged them to a small banquette almost hidden at the back of the room. A double string of beads provided a thin curtain of privacy.

At first glance Achmed Hamish reminded Alex of Mehmed, Selidim's vizier. He was small and wizened, blackened by the sun. Mehmed's ancient, cunning eyes darted about Achmed's swarthy face. Ish appeared simple by comparison, but it would have been a mistake to disregard him. Ish Hamish was not cunning or shrewd like his brother, but he was the more impulsively dangerous of the two. Alex examined Ish's face and sensed the man preferred to kill first and consider later. Ruthless violence was his talent and his pleasure.

"Dr. Mallon and I own three of the Marcellus busts," Alex began.

The Hamish brothers flicked expressionless eyes across Chelsey, sweeping her ginger curls, her anxious face, the wedge of pale skin at her collar. They returned to Alex.

"It is our understanding that you can help us obtain the fourth bust."

"Perhaps. What's in it for us?" Achmed asked. He spoke perfect English with the merest trace of an accent.

"Nothing. Unless you have access to the fourth bust."

Ish made a grunting sound, rolled a dark, pungent-smelling Turkish cigarette between his thumb and forefinger. "Kahd didn't mention anything about you being buyers."

Alex's gaze narrowed. He felt Chelsey's fingers gripping his thigh beneath the table. "We prefer to deal direct. We're not willing to pay a dozen middlemen. Can you produce the bust or not?"

Achmed considered the surface of his coffee. He offered none to Chelsey or Alex. No waiter disturbed them. "Let us suppose for a moment that we know how and where to obtain the fourth bust...." One thick eyebrow lifted. Waiting.

"Naturally we would pay a commission for your assistance in arranging a sale." Alex dropped his hand beside the beads and lifted a suitcase which he placed on the table. He opened it to reveal stacks of banded hundred-dollar bills. The Hamish brothers stared at the cash, their black eyes glittering until Alex closed the lid and replaced the suitcase at his side.

"There's a condition," Chelsey said quietly. She continued to grip Alex's thigh under the table as if anchoring herself to reality. "We wish to purchase the bust directly from the present owner. If he won't meet with us, the deal is off."

"That is not possible," Achmed said flatly.

"I'm sorry we wasted your time," Alex said, gripping the suitcase. The bead curtain rattled like old bones as he parted it, and he and Chelsey started to rise.

"Is this point negotiable?" Achmed asked, making a motion with his hands.

"No," Alex said coldly. Beside him, Chelsey shook her head.

Achmed studied his coffee again. In the dim, filtered light it looked like mud. "How much are you willing to pay for the bust?"

Alex and Chelsey sat back down. "Name a price."

A silent dialogue ensued between the Hamish brothers. "Seven hundred thousand dollars American," Achmed said finally. Ish nodded. "Our commission for setting it up is ten percent."

"Agreed."

A tiny flutter of surprise disturbed Achmed's eyelids. Greed spun in his brain. Since the foreigners had not protested, he grasped that he should have named a higher price. Ish saw it, too, and was irritated. Alex read Achmed's thoughts as easily as if they were printed on his forehead.

"How soon can you set up the buy?"

A shrug. A swift glance at Ish. "A week from tonight."

"Make it two days—no longer," Alex said firmly. "We're leaving Friday morning with or without the bust."

"We'll decide where the exchange will take place," Chelsey interjected. When the Hamish brothers balked, she continued. "The spot will offer no advantage to either side."

A long silence ensued before another invisible signal passed between the two brothers. Achmed glanced toward the suitcase beside Alex. "We will phone you"

"We're staying at—"

"We know where you're staying." Ish produced an ornately handled knife and ran the blade across his thumb.

Alex laughed aloud. Grinning at Ish's murderous scowl, he took Chelsey's arm and led her out of the coffeehouse.

WHILE CHELSEY SLEPT, Alex stepped out onto the balcony and inspected the night sky. There were no stars overhead, at least none that he could see. The French couple next door had finally stopped arguing and now the night was silent except for distant city noises.

The pressure inside his chest continued to build.

He experienced a compelling urge to wake Chelsey and tell her that she must make her final wish. It was this urgency that had propelled him to the balcony and away from her. The push toward the final wish originated outside himself, it was not something Alex wanted. Right now he could still control whether or not he acted on the pressure filling his chest. He didn't know how much longer his control would hold.

The unwanted possibility of leaving her now, as events were coming together, flooded his mouth with a dark, brackish taste. He knew Achmed and Ish. He had dreamed their kind throughout the centuries. The Hamish brothers were masters of the double cross. And he had seen their eyes on Chelsey. He knew what they were capable of doing to her. She would beg them to kill her long before they did.

It was imperative that he remain in the reality plane until the sting was over. He wanted Chelsey to have her perfect leg without the anguish of having to choose between it and her reputation and future.

Until she had her perfect leg, she would not allow a man to fully love her. He had understood this from the beginning.

He wanted her last wish to bring her joy and fulfillment. That would be his gift to her.

Returning to the hot, darkened bedroom, he stood at the foot of the bed, listening to the drone of the overhead fan and watching Chelsey sleep. Leaving her would be the worst punishment of his life. If ghosts could laugh, Selidim was enjoying his revenge.

She loved him.

The knowledge of Chelsey's love sliced through Alex like the blade of Ish's knife, leaving a wound that almost doubled him over. He saw her love in her clear, shining eyes, felt it in her caress and in her touch. He heard her love in the softness of her voice, read it in the morning smile that was for him alone.

He clenched his fists, wanting to rage and shout and bellow at the injustice, at the sweet cruel pain of being loved.

He had never expected to find love again. Nor had he tortured himself by hoping for, or even thinking about, love. He had thrust such thoughts out of his mind, believing that that part of his humanity was long dead.

But along with his growing hair and beard, along with his increased need for sleep and diminished sensitivity to objects, his humanity had returned with human needs and desires. He needed Chelsey Mallon, needed her deep in his spirit. He needed her more than he needed reality, more than he needed life itself. His need for her roared through his blood and brain.

This was Selidim's cruelest revenge, not the lonely centuries that had preceded this moment. Selidim's revenge lay in obstructing the miracle of being loved, the intense wonder and joy of it. Selidim's revenge lay in the hopeless anguish of Alex's knowledge that he would betray Chelsey's love by abandoning her. To allow Alex to find love, then force him to betray it—that was Selidim's greatest revenge.

WHEN THE CALL CAME, Chelsey handed the telephone to Alex and listened to his side of the conversation with a worried expression. His manner was strange and erratic.

One moment he couldn't keep from touching her, holding her. The next moment he seemed almost hostile, striding away from her with a moody expression. He couldn't sit still. He'd started stroking things again, but this time with a frown, as if his fingertips no longer provided the sensation he sought. She thought he was trying to store physical impressions in his memory but the physical impressions disappointed him somehow.

Except for their lovemaking. Their lovemaking remained magical and wonderful, something Chelsey would never forget. A tiny shiver passed through her body. No man had ever made love to her so deliberately or so thoroughly. No man had ever made her feel so desirable and cherished. Their lovemaking truly was magical—enchanted moments they had created for themselves.

"No," Alex said sharply, speaking into the telephone. He paced the length of the cord to look out the balcony doors. "Not tomorrow. It has to be tonight."

Chelsey's heart lurched, and she swallowed hard, then looked away from him. Tonight was too soon. But she had only to glance at him to know further delay was perilous. Alex looked like a man in physical pain, a man with something dark consuming him from the inside.

"If that's what it takes, then tell your man we'll pay a million." He stared toward the waterfront. "In cash. But only if the exchange takes place tonight. For a million dollars, your seller can rearrange his schedule and be there." Finally he looked at Chelsey, his eyes almost translucent in the sunshine streaming past the balcony doors. "Tell your seller to bring the Marcellus bust to the Ballan dig site at nine o'clock. You know where it is."

A hint of a smile brushed his lips. "Naturally we'll expect you and your brother to be present, as well."

After he broke the connection, Alex handed the telephone to Chelsey. "We're on for tonight," he said. "Whoever has the bust didn't want to meet in person, but he finally agreed. Achmed believes upping the ante will make our thief happier about exposing himself. It's time to call Harry Sahok and arrange the big finish."

"And Eric Fry, the CNN stringer," Chelsey added, taking the phone. "Alex...are you all right? Are you in pain?"

She could swear he had lost weight even since yesterday. His face was pale and drawn. There were new lines beside his mouth. He paced the hotel room as if he had to keep moving or explode.

"I'm fine," he snapped.

"No you're not."

"Please, Chelsey. Just make your calls."

Harry Sahok eagerly agreed to meet them at the Ballan dig site and to bring Eric Fry with him.

"If this works," Sahok said into the phone, "it will be a career capper. I'll owe you a big one, Dr. Mallon."

"All I ask is that you help me clear my name, Mr. Sahok."

"Count on it. You hand me the thief and the Hamish brothers, and I'll sing your praises to the skies!"

Eric Fry expected her call. "Where have you been?" he demanded, his voice crackling in her ear. "I've received your package of information and I have a million questions! But first, did you know that Burgeson's warehouse was torched? Yesterday Burgeson himself washed up in the East River. You don't want to know what was done to him. Dr. Mallon, I never believed you stole the Marcellus busts. I was just doing my job, you know?"

"I know," Chelsey said, covering her eyes with her hand. She sat down and nodded gratefully to Alex when a pot of café au lait appeared on the table in front of her. "I want you to do your job again, Mr. Fry. I want you to clear my name."

"Where are you and what have you got?"

"I'm here in Istanbul. With a colleague." Chelsey drew a breath and told him almost everything, editing out the genie parts. "That's the story. Can you be there tonight?"

"Are you kidding? Murder? An international smuggling ring? The recovery of the Marcellus busts?" A short bark of laughter came over the phone line. "I'd be there if I had to crawl on bleeding stumps! Can I bring a photographer?"

"You can ride out to the site with Harry Sahok. He'll fill you in on the back story. But bring your own camera instead of a photographer. It's going to be difficult enough to hide you and Sahok's men while we're waiting to spring the trap. We don't need another person to worry about."

After Chelsey hung up the phone, she studied Alex's expression, then dropped her head in her hands and quietly wept.

It was almost over.

How did one say goodbye to a genie? To one's own heart?

Always before, Chelsey had held something back in relationships. Maybe her wait-and-see attitude had contributed to the relationships falling apart. But not this time. This time she had held nothing back. She had given all she had to give and had taken all that Alex offered. Consequently, she was now dying inside at the thought of losing him.

And his urgency communicated itself to her. "It's time,

isn't it?'' she whispered in despair, wiping at hot tears. ''Do I have to make the wish now?'' No, she couldn't do it. She would rather forfeit the wish than have him vanish from her life. Thinking about a future without Alex caused a physical pain behind her heart.

''Not yet.'' Kneeling in front of her, Alex smoothed his hand down her white face. She could see the effort it cost him to smile. ''You need me there tonight. Unless you have a suitcase full of cash that I don't know about.''

She hurt too much to return his smile. ''Alex…will you be here when I wake up tomorrow morning?''

Gently he guided her into his arms and held her so close that she could feel his heart beating against her breast. Her tears ran into his collar.

''I don't think so, Chelsey.'' He buried his face in her hair. ''You need to decide on your final wish. I'll ask you for it the instant tonight's business is finished.''

''Oh God! Alex—'' Her pain and frustration were so great that she wanted to scream and shout and hit something over and over.

''No, my darling mistress, don't cry. Smile for me. Tomorrow you'll have your perfect leg. Be happy, Chelsey. I beg you. Be happy.'' He caught her hands and held them tightly. ''Please be happy.''

''I am,'' she whispered. But she cried even harder.

Chapter Thirteen

Although the night air was warm, a chill of dread and anticipation passed through Chelsey's body. She leaned against Alex's warmth. The Ballan site was as she remembered it, a windswept grid of crumbling stone foundations stretching away from her in the moonlight. Once these ruins had teemed with life. And someone had concealed four busts in an underground storeroom.

Chelsey turned away from the shadowy ruins. Twenty miles to the west she could see the glow of Istanbul against the sky. Two solitary headlights approached across the desert.

"That will be Achmed and Ish," she said. She didn't speculate on the identity of the seller. She was too preoccupied with Alex. Their time together was nearly over. It was all she could think about. She clasped his hand so hard that she was afraid the bones in her fingers would crack.

Stepping up beside Chelsey and Alex, Harry Şahok watched the headlights approaching in the distance. "Malmud and I will be behind that low wall," he said, nodding toward the ruins. He patted his shoulder holster, the gesture unconscious. "We've planted microphones there and there," he continued, pointing. "The instant they accept the suitcase and you get the marble bust, it's over. All you do is get out of the way. Understand?''

Chelsey blinked back the tears in her eyes and tried to concentrate on what Sahok was saying. She was shocked that he had only brought one man to assist. Although both Sahok and Malmud were professionals, hard and capable, she would have preferred a squadron.

Eric Fry, the journalist, crushed a cigarette under his heel and fiddled with his camera. "Early tomorrow morning we sit down for a full exclusive interview, right?"

"Right," she agreed, wetting her lips. The headlights were almost upon them. Sahok prodded Malmud and Fry to the Roman wall. They ducked out of sight. Alex scanned the sand dunes that flowed away from the site like tall, moon-washed waves.

He pressed her arm against his side and examined her face. "Are you all right?"

"None of this is important," she whispered. "I thought it was, but it isn't. Oh, Alex. I can't stand knowing it's almost over." Raising her hands, she pressed the heels of her palms against her eyes.

"I know," he said in a strained voice. He hugged her close to him. There were no words of comfort, nothing either of them could say.

Headlights swept the ruins, then flashed off. An engine died and car doors opened. Achmed and Ish emerged. And Dr. Julian Porozzi, struggling with the weight of the fourth Marcellus bust.

Sadness filled Chelsey's dark eyes. "I hoped I was wrong," she said softly, mourning the loss of heroes.

She hadn't remembered how defeated Julian Porozzi looked, or how stooped and small. Once she had believed that he stood as a giant among mortals.

Porozzi followed Achmed and Ish to where she and

Alex waited. "You're young, Chelsey, and full of ideals. You don't know what it feels like to watch others make the big finds and garner the fame and the accolades. And the money." He passed a hand over his eyes. "I deserve something for thirty years of being an also-ran."

She stared at him. Moonlight fingered his white hair, deepened the wrinkles drawing his cheeks. "Why did you make everyone think it was me? I didn't deserve that, Julian. You ruined my reputation! Archaeology is the only career I ever wanted and you took it away—or tried to."

"Let's get on with this," Ish snapped. "Where's the money?"

"Aren't you afraid I'll expose you?" Chelsey asked Porozzi while Alex knelt to open the suitcase on the sand.

"My security rests on the fact that we're all at risk. Expose me and you expose yourself. I may be selling a stolen artifact, but you're buying one." His eyes flicked up to Chelsey, then returned to the suitcase. "May I inquire where you got this much money?"

"Hold it," Sahok's voice shouted. He and Malmud popped up behind the low wall, then stepped over it. "You're under arrest. Don't anybody move." Eric Fry ran up to the group standing around the suitcase. A flashbulb exploded.

The flashbulb momentarily blinded Chelsey. Gripping Alex's arm in confusion, she blinked hard and strained to identify a sudden burst of unexpected sounds. There were shouts, and the sound of hoofbeats. Then rifle shots.

Alex shoved her to the ground, and she heard him run forward.

Blinking frantically, Chelsey pushed up on her elbows. Her vision cleared in time to see a half-dozen men circling them on horseback. She screamed as blossoms of fire exploded from the men's rifles.

Horrified, she watched Harry Sahok, Malmud, Eric Fry and Julian Porozzi reel backward, then fall sprawling in the sand.

And Alex.

It seemed to happen in slow motion. Staring in shock and disbelief, Chelsey watched Alex grab his chest and fall.

''Oh God, no!''

No one was left standing except Achmed and Ish. They rushed through the milling horses and men toward the cash and the Marcellus bust.

''No!'' Chelsey screamed. Blinded by tears, frantic, she crawled on hands and knees toward Alex. ''No, this can't be happening!'' He couldn't be dead. Not Alex! No! Desperately, she searched for a pulse beneath his ear.

''I want the woman,'' Achmed shouted.

One of the horsemen leaned from his mount and grabbed Chelsey, flinging her facedown across the front of his saddle before he galloped back toward the sand dunes. In a frenzy of grief and despair, Chelsey dashed the tears from her eyes and strained for a final glimpse of Alex. He lay sprawled and lifeless in the moonlight near the others.

Alex was dead. The only man she would ever love was dead.

Chelsey went limp, her head dropping. It didn't matter what they did to her, she thought dully. Alex was dead. As she might as well be. Without Alex, she had no life. Sobbing, she surrendered to a black hell of devastating grief.

THE IMPACT OF A DIRECT hit dazed Alex and knocked him to the ground. But, of course, no mortal can kill a genie.

Mortals can, however, irritate genies and make them dangerously furious. Enraged, Alex jumped to his feet.

One by one the other men slowly sat up and gingerly touched their chests. Disbelief and amazement stunned their expressions.

Sahok exchanged a blank look with Malmud. "I don't remember putting on a bulletproof vest. Do you?"

Jerking open his blasted shirt, Eric Fry stared down at himself with huge, frightened eyes. "I don't even own one. But I'm wearing one. What the hell is going on here?"

When Alex roared "Shazam," they all swiveled to look up at him. Their mouths dropped open.

Alex stood wide-legged and raging. Heat lightning crackled around his body. His dark silhouette impressed the others as enormous and terrifying.

Flinging out a hand, he pointed to a spot on the sand, his eyes blazing. A white Arabian stallion caparisoned with silver fittings appeared before their astonished eyes, snorting and pawing the earth.

"Shazam!" Alex's jeans and white shirt vanished. He swelled before his stunned audience, garbed in the flowing black robes of a desert sheik, swinging a scimitar in his large hand.

"My God," Harry Sahok breathed. His eyes bulged.

Alex glanced at him, almost smiling for an instant. "I'm going to miss this," he said, giving Sahok a wink. Then he ran toward the prancing white stallion.

He leapt on the stallion's back and raised the scimitar against the starlit sky as the animal reared. Then his robes flew out behind him as he galloped across the dunes in pursuit of his lady.

Eric Fry fainted.

THE SADDLE DUG INTO Chelsey's stomach and her head banged against the man's rifle butt. Sand flew up in her face.

It didn't matter; with Alex dead, nothing mattered. She didn't feel the pain of her jolting body. The pain in her mind was so much worse. Each time she remembered Alex lying dead on the sand, her breath felt like hot razors in her throat. She was sick to her stomach. Her grief was so intense she didn't think she could bear it.

The blackness clawing at her mind parted enough to allow a dim awareness of something soft and wispy blowing against her wet cheeks.

Soft and wispy? Chelsey opened her eyes and dashed at the tears. Then she blinked uncomprehendingly at a length of scarlet chiffon flapping against her face. *Scarlet chiffon?*

Confused, she raised a hand and tracked the chiffon to her head. She was wearing a filmy headdress. A contorted glance over her shoulder, then down at her breasts, revealed she was also wearing a wildly imaginative harem outfit. A gold sequined bikini top covered her breasts. Gold sequins flew past her face, torn from where the saddle rubbed against her hips. Her arms were heavy with gold slave bracelets. More chiffon fluttered against her legs.

Alex? Alex!

Grabbing her abductor's knee, she used it as a lever and pulled upward to peer behind the horsemen, slapping the streaming chiffon out of her face. Hope flared in her wet eyes. It had to be Alex. It had to be.

A white stallion flew over the dunes. On the stallion's back, a dark rider bent forward, his desert robes billowing behind him. Moonlight flashed across the blade of the biggest scimitar Chelsey had ever seen.

Thank God, thank God! He was alive! Fresh tears of elation flooded her eyes, and relief drained the strength from her bones. She flopped limp across the bouncing saddle, then pulled herself up again. A strangled sound rasped her throat, partly a sob, partly a laugh, a combination of joy, fear and exasperation. Chelsey Mallon roared back to life.

"Alex," she screamed, cupping her hands around her mouth, slapping at the clingy chiffon. "Damn it, Alex, stop screwing around! These men are killers. Use your magic!"

But no. Magic would have been too easy. He was too furious and he was enjoying himself too much to use magic. He had to do this the hard way. Chelsey threw up a hand and swore. She jerked on the sleeve of her abductor and pointed back at Alex.

"You can't kill him, you oaf. He's a genie, understand? And he's coming after you!"

The horsemen had already spotted him. Their leader shouted, and they all twisted in their saddles and raised their rifles. Except their rifles had turned into scimitars. They stared at the scimitars in fear and horror. Chelsey understood just enough dialect to identify a few excited words. Demon. Magic. Something from the bowels of hell.

The men reined abruptly, milling in frightened confusion as they watched the fury bearing down on them. The man carrying Chelsey drew back from her, pointing to her harem costume, speaking in a rapid terrified voice.

The leader shouted, and Chelsey's abductor threw her off his horse as if he had discovered a viper in his lap. Screaming, the men dug their heels into their horse's flanks and galloped hard across the dunes, riding as if Satan pursued them.

The ground thundered beneath Chelsey's palms as she pushed to her feet and shook sand out of her hair. As the white stallion swept past her, a powerful arm scooped her up. Suddenly she was part of the man and the horse flying across the moonlit dunes. Alex held her tightly against him, his robes billowing around her harem costume.

Chelsey flung her arms around his neck. "Stop!" she shouted. "Let them go!"

Gradually the fury drained from his glittering eyes. Chelsey felt his thighs tense as he pulled back on the reins and brought the racing stallion to a walk. Dropping the reins, he slid his hands over her arms and shoulders. "Did the bastards harm you?" he demanded. "If they did..."

"Oh, Alex, I thought you were dead!" She buried her face against his neck. "I saw them shoot you and you fell and I thought, oh God, I was so sure that—"

"Shh." His mouth whispered against her temple as his hands moved over her body, reassuring himself that she was not injured. "Everyone is safe and unharmed." Responding to the pressure of his thighs, the stallion turned toward the Roman ruins.

"I don't want to go back," Chelsey murmured against his skin. She wished they could stay like this forever, close in each other's arms, sheltered by the night and Alex's warm robes. She wished they could ride like the wind over the sand dunes and emerge into a world where they could be together always.

"We have to go back," he said as if he had read her mind. She heard pain equal to her own in his strained voice. Their time together was drawing to an end.

Alex rode with his arms tightly cradling her. Chelsey rested her head on his shoulder. Tears slipped from beneath her closed eyes.

Harry Sahok walked forward as the white stallion

pranced toward the low Roman wall. He stroked a hand down the stallion's arched neck, as if to prove to himself that the horse was real. He inspected Chelsey's chiffon and sequins.

"I don't understand one damned bit of this. Who the hell are you?" Sahok asked softly, staring hard at Alex.

"Not now," Chelsey interjected. "I'll explain everything tomorrow." Sahok deserved the truth. Maybe he would even believe it.

Sahok nodded slowly. "Porozzi, Achmed and Ish are in cuffs. We've got everything on tape."

Alex looked down at Sahok. "Go now. You have what you came for."

Harry Sahok hesitated, then raised his hand and gripped Alex's fingers in a hard shake. "We're going to need your rental car to help transport these people."

"Take the rental car," Alex said. Chelsey sensed the tension building where she leaned against his chest. His body was as hard as steel. She could almost feel the explosive forces working inside of him. She swallowed a sob and tightened her fingers on top of his hands, felt the horse shift beneath them. "Send a car back for Dr. Mallon," Alex said to Sahok.

Not for *us*. For *Dr. Mallon*. Chelsey ducked her head and closed her eyes. She was trembling all over. The time left to them had narrowed to minutes.

A dozen questions disturbed Harry Sahok's dark eyes. But he understood this was not the time. Chelsey waited atop the stallion, shaking in Alex's strong arms, watching as the cars departed.

The desert was never entirely silent. The earth whispered. Moonlight nested atop the Roman ruins and tinted the rustling sand silver. A warm, dry breeze caught the ends of the chiffon headdress and fluttered it across Chelsey's bare arms.

She wanted to scream and cry and hurl herself against onrushing time, wanted to hold it back. Pressing herself against Alex's warm, strong chest, Chelsey bit her lips and listened to her own mindless whisper. "No, no, no, no. Please no. Not yet. No."

When she opened her eyes, she saw a silken tent through her tears, lit by perfumed lamps. Inside, Chelsey could see gold pitchers and platters of figs and pears. Piles of silk cushions beckoned.

Alex dropped from the back of the stallion and lifted his hands to her. She slipped into his arms and clung to him. They stood together in a fierce embrace. "This is the end, isn't it?" she whispered.

"We have until dawn," he murmured against her hair, molding her body against his arousal. "No longer. Then you must use your wish or forfeit."

"I don't care about the last wish! I would forfeit it gladly if I could keep you here!"

He tilted her face up to him and gazed at her as if he strove to engrave her image on his memory. "You know I have to leave you," he whispered in a thick voice.

Chelsey leaned back in his arms, letting him support her weight. Her left leg was trembling and throbbing. She had landed hard when she was thrown from her abductor's horse. Her leg ached and burned deep within. She had no idea what had happened to her cane.

For the first time since she had been stricken by polio Chelsey realized that having one leg shorter than the other was not important. For over a decade she had fantasized about having two perfect legs, about having a body she could be proud of. She had fantasized about something that wasn't important. Loving and being loved—that was important. Her leg was not.

Clinging to Alex, holding him in silence, she wondered who she would have become if there had been no polio, if she had had two healthy, well-shaped legs of the same length? Would she have been a different person? Less strong and self-reliant? Less ambitious? Less driven to prove herself? Would she have been less sensitive to the pain of others?

"Come with me," Alex whispered against her hair. "Let me carry you to the tent and love you one last time." He bent to take her into his arms, but she flattened her palm on his chest and gently shook her head. A rush of tears blurred the outline of the silken tent.

"No," she said quietly. "It's time for the last wish."

Surprise flared in his eyes, followed by regret and the pain of rejection. Alex gazed deeply into her clear, steady eyes, then he stroked her hair, caressed her cheek with the back of his hand. He kissed her softly, tenderly—so tenderly that Chelsey's body ached with the bittersweetness of his mouth on hers.

Then his demeanor changed. He stepped backward and bowed deeply before her. "I am yours to command, mistress. I await your final wish."

"Goodbye," Chelsey whispered, closing her eyes. She fought to swallow the lump rising in her throat. "It was a lovely dream. For a while it seemed possible, and that was wonderful. I will always be grateful."

"Goodbye, my dearest. I'll never forget you, Chelsey. Never!"

"What?" She opened her eyes and clutched the front of his robe, afraid that he was leaving her. "Alex, I'm not saying goodbye to you. I'm saying goodbye to a fantasy that I've clung to for far, far too long. I'm letting it go."

"I don't understand," he said, frowning.

Chelsey almost laughed, feeling the excitement build deep inside and rush into her eyes. She was trembling all over. This had to work. Life would not be worth living if it didn't.

"I wish..."

The gold coin appeared in her fingers. Moonlight gleamed along the rim as it warmed against her skin.

Alex gazed deeply into her eyes and spoke rapidly. "Thank you for this time. Thank you for restoring my belief in the goodness of humanity, and thank you for sharing yourself with me," he said softly. "I will never forget you, Chelsey Mallon. I will dream you." His eyes flew over her face, memorizing her, making love to her.

"I wish..." She gulped a deep breath and hoped to heaven that she phrased this correctly. "I wish that Alexandre Duport be released from his sentence as a genie and that he be restored as a real man in the real world. I wish this to happen now."

"Chelsey, no." Alex stared. "Your leg!"

"I choose you," she said softly, loving him so much that she ached with the force and depth of it. "You told me once that given a choice between self-interest and love, I would choose self-interest. My dearest Alex, you were wrong."

For an instant Isabel's image wavered between them and then faded forever. True love was not selfish. A love that was strong and true soared beyond self. True love transcended flesh and bone.

"My leg is part of who and what I am, it's all tangled together. We're uneasy friends, my leg and I, but we can live together. But dearest Alex, I cannot live without you."

A low groan rumbled up from his chest. He closed his

eyes and clenched his fists. "With all my heart, I thank you for your generosity and your unselfishness. But, my noble mistress, I cannot grant your wish. Your wish must benefit you directly." The moonlight played tricks, making it seem that tears moistened his eyes. "That is the rule."

She held out the coin. "I love you, Alex. I'll never love another man but you. If you love me, too, and if you want to share my life and make it whole, then granting this wish will benefit me more than anything else in this world. Otherwise I will live my life alone and lonely." She held the coin between them and gazed directly into his damp, glistening eyes. "Whether you grant my wish or not depends on this. Do you love me, Alex? If you don't love me, then you're right. This wish brings no direct benefit to me and you cannot grant it. But if you love me, oh Alex, if you love me…then you must grant my wish and make my life complete."

"Oh my God," he whispered, staring at her face. "Do I love you? I love you with all my heart and mind and soul! I love your generosity of spirit, your quiet courage. I love your honesty and your laughter. I love the apple fragrance of you, the feel of your skin against mine. I love the way your eyes light and shine when you look at me and say my name. I love your goodness and integrity. I love you more than life itself!"

The coin sprang from Chelsey's fingers and shot upward above their heads where it burst into a white column of flame. Shimmers of strange color streaked the sudden wind that swirled around them, billowing Alex's robes and tearing at Chelsey's chiffon. The sand sang in their ears. Chelsey clung to him, staring in awe and fright at the flashing colors, listening to the clash of destiny within the wind and whirling sand.

When it finally ended, the abrupt silence was as shocking as the colored wind and the singing sands had been.

Slowly, holding on to each other, they raised their heads and stared around them. The stallion and the silken tent were gone. They were dressed in jeans and light jackets as they had been earlier in the evening.

Chelsey lifted shining eyes. She raised a trembling hand to his beloved face. "You love me," she whispered.

His hands tightened on her arms. "You gave me back my life!" Tears glittered in his eyes. Grabbing her by the waist, he lifted her and swung her in a circle. "I'm real, Chelsey! I'm alive! You did this, my darling, darling woman, my dearest love!"

When he set her on her feet, he kissed her, deeply and hungrily, pledging forever, promising with lips and hands what words could only hint. It was not until much later that they gazed toward the distant glow of Istanbul, impatient to return to their hotel and the passion of celebration.

"Do you suppose Harry forgot to send a car for us?" Chelsey asked, sitting on the low Roman wall. She didn't care. As long as she was with Alex, nothing else mattered. She couldn't take her eyes off him, couldn't stop touching him, reassuring herself that he was real and they were together.

"Shazam." A startled look lifted his eyebrows. He gave her a sheepish grin. "I forgot. The magic is gone." Sitting beside her, he took her hand. "We'll have to wait until Sahok remembers us."

"Alex," she said, turning to face him in the moonlight. A blush heated her cheeks, and she pressed her forehead against his shoulder, hiding her expression. "Will you do something for me?"

"I will move the earth for you, my beloved." He kissed

the top of her head and drew her into his arms. "But remember," he added gently, "I'm no longer magic."

"Will you…will you teach me to dance?"

He lifted her face and gazed into her eyes. Then he stood and bowed before her. "Would the most beautiful woman in creation honor me with this waltz?"

Shyly, she placed her hand in his and stood with a nervous wobble. She bit her lip. "Maybe…"

But his strong arm came around her waist. He held her close for a long moment, smiling into her eyes. Then he stepped forward on the sand. Chelsey stumbled and felt the heat flame in her cheeks. He paused, kissed her forehead, then stepped forward again. This time she followed and didn't stumble.

And suddenly she was dancing! Twirling around and around on the moonlit sand, floating to the strains of the waltz filling her imagination.

And it was fabulous, lovely, as exhilarating and wonderful as she had always dreamed it would be. In Alex's strong arms she felt graceful and poised, in exquisite harmony with herself and the world around her. She was loved, and she was waltzing.

She smiled into Alex's adoring eyes and leaned back in his arms, dancing, and her heart swelled with joy. Alex had not lost his magic.

To her this magnificent man would always be magic.

THE MISSING HEIR

by Leandra Logan

For my mother, Delores Leonard.
An extraordinary grandma, golfer and gambler—
and a whole lot more!

THE TELEPHONE'S RING pierced the dark silent bedroom, rousing Caron Carlisle from a deep sleep. She inched a long slender arm out from under the bedding, patting the nightstand in the search of her white trimline. It sounded off a bleating baker's dozen before she managed to draw the receiver down into her cocoon of covers and greet her caller with a husky hello.

"Good morning!"

For milkmen and vampires maybe. Caron groaned softly as she peeked over the hem of her sheet into the predawn darkness.

"Hello, hello, is anybody home?" a hearty male voice demanded.

Not recognizing the caller, Caron poised a trigger-happy thumb over the disconnect button. "Do we…"

"Well, we used to."

She slanted a brow warily. "When?"

"Ah, seems like yesterday."

Caron failed to swallow back a huge yawn. "I believe you have the wrong party."

"I'm looking for the Caron Carlisle who works for the law firm of snap, crackle, pop."

"Sharp, Krandell and Peterson," she croaked in correction, inching her shoulders up onto her pillows.

This night owl nut had the right number after all. Her unlisted number.

"Ah, Caron. I've found you, then."

The unknown caller's deep timbre sent a delicious tingle through her languid limbs. His voice held a familiar edge, as did his easy manner—a manner that somehow made arrogance an attribute. Caron rubbed her forehead in a foggy jumble. Who was this sweet-talkin' bozo?

"I hope you don't mind my calling at this hour," he continued conversationally. "I just couldn't wait another minute. In my line of work I often keep odd hours. Figured you do to."

"As a matter of fact, I don't," Caron differed cautiously, struggling in vain to place the man. As an associate of one of Denver's most prestigious law offices, it paid to be discreet. He could just be a client. Though most were on the stuffy side, a few live ones slipped in on occasion! And somehow, all the... unusual...cases ended up on her desk.

"Perry Mason puts you to shame, Caron. He's available at all hours of the day and night."

"Della Street was the available one," she automatically replied, a fan of the show herself. "The loyal secretary who forwarded only urgent calls to his *unlisted number.*"

"He's the only lawyer I've ever trusted, too," the calm male voice contended, not revealing how he had managed to get through to her. "Until now. Until this morning."

Morning? Caron sincerely doubted it. She grabbed the clock radio off the nightstand, drawing it up to her nearsighted eyes. The red letters glowed 4:49.

"Do you realize it's still nighttime to most of America?"

He heaved a depreciative sigh. "Still argue each and every point, I see."

"You can't *see* a thing on my end."

"*See* what I mean?"

Caron's heart stopped in her chest. Could it be *him*? No. Not after all these years. But he did like the "Perry Mason" show, even back then.... She cleared her throat, her mouth forming an O as she summoned the voice lost somewhere in her cottony throat. "Who? Who are you?"

"Well, I was hoping to soften you up a little first," he confessed with obvious amusement. "This is Rick Wyatt, Caron. From the class of '83. Truman High School."

"Hotshot!" Caron bolted upright to a seated position, the clock plopping into her lap.

A deep chuckle rippled across the line. "Yeah, Hotshot it is. Don't hang up on me now."

Hanging would be too good for him! Or was it just right? She toyed with the phone line, pinching several inches of it into a small noose. She squeezed it so hard that her fingers soon throbbed purple. It was no surprise that she still had some leftover emotion for this smooth-talking class rebel, this intelligent egomaniac who had taken fiendish pleasure in driving her to distraction at every turn. But the intensity of those feelings was indeed shocking to this savvy twenty-eight-year-old attorney who thought she knew herself inside out!

This run-in might be totally unexpected, but it was not beyond her control, she decided, straightening the wire with a determined jerk. Childhood neighbors, she and Hotshot had a history of niggling at each other's weak spots. Their relationship had heated up to explosive levels during their senior year when Rick had invaded her turf in the structured high school arena, taking his snappy show off the streets and into the student council chambers. Rick hadn't cared a whit about bettering the school. Toying with its policies from the revered president's chair had been nothing more than a game of skill to him. A chance to buck the system with a rally of loyal students in his wake.

Caron had eyed that president's seat with the longing of a dedicated student. After three years on the council, building up her support, she'd been defeated. President Hotshot went on to charm everyone. As vice president she found her more conservative policies were overruled over and over again.

But that was a long time ago, she reminded herself. They'd been out of touch for ten years, since graduation. He could no longer draw her into an emotional tizzy with a few words. Rick's attempt to bait her into a flare-up before even identifying himself, however, was vintage Hotshot behavior. Her rising to that bait was par for the well-traveled course of yesterday, too.

"Still up to your old tricks, I see," she eventually tossed back with forced smoothness. "Calling me now, knowing full well I'd still be in bed."

"Sorry about the hour. Please believe that I'd never stoop so low as to tease a woman in her most intimate spot. Not without permission anyway."

Caron held the receiver at arm's length for a moment so he wouldn't hear her quaking breath. His voice was still a masculine purr—French silk pie smooth. Caron was obsessed with sweets. Somewhere back in time, Rick's chocolate syrup eyes, full of mischief, mayhem and seductiveness, had been an irresistible treat to her. Instead she said sternly, "Does this nocturnal nonsense have a purpose?"

"All my moves have a purpose now. Though I still like to seize the moment, make it sizzle—"

"Well, don't expect me to hop into the frying pan with you!"

"I'm unavoidable when I want to be."

When he wanted to be. Rick Wyatt had dodged her for a decade. She focused on this hard nugget of truth as her insides began to cook, as if she were truly flat on her back in that pan.... "No need to explain your tactics to me. They're still legendary in my mind."

"There isn't time now for fond reminiscences, Caron. I'm calling about the baby."

Beds and babies. Dreaminess enveloped her groggy senses. Back in school, many a girl's fantasy had centered on Rick Wyatt and those very two things. Caron herself had often wondered what their child would look like, if it would have her thick chestnut hair and Rick's handsome features. "What are you talking about?" she managed to ask softly.

"The billon-dollar baby, of course! At least that's what you people are calling him."

His reply yanked her back to reality with a sharp, leashlike tug. "How do you know about the baby search? That's a confidential matter being handled by snap, crackle, pop!"

His chuckle crispened. "You haven't seen the morning headlines yet."

"Certainly not while asleep!" Energized with panic and fury she reached over to snap on the bedside lamp and grab her glasses, jamming them haphazardly on the bridge of her perfectly sloped nose. She blinked behind the lenses, primed for action. Then froze for a long aggravating moment, finding it difficult to acknowledge the embarrassingly obvious even to herself.

"Rick?"

"Yeah?"

"My copy of the *Denver Press* isn't due for an hour."

"Billion-Dollar Grandchild Sought By Douglas Ramsey," Rick dutifully recited for the paperless.

"Oh, no!" Caron reeled back, banging her head against the maple headboard. With effort she bit off a yelp as pain shot through her skull.

"You still there, Quick Draw? You okay?"

"Yes and yes!"

"So, you in on the case?"

"Most definitely." She massaged the bruise on her scalp through a tangle of mussed brown hair, wincing in pain over the new bump and her old nickname. The student body had tagged her Quick Draw because of her talent for sharp uptakes in class. Then and now the name sounded downright affectionate coming from Rick's mouth. How dare he, after dumping her so unceremoniously years ago?

"So give me the lowdown, Caron. What's this Ramsey guy's angle?"

Caron gripped the phone in a tight fist. This couldn't be happening to her all over again—Rick Wyatt entering her life in this upstaging way, on her most important case! It was even more humiliating to admit ignorance to this man. But what choice did she have?

"Rick, I don't know anything about the newspaper article."

"Hmm... You sure you have the skinny on this baby search?"

"I most certainly do! I'm in charge of it!"

"Really? You losing your Quick Draw touch or what?"

Fury boiled her blood at his challenge. She didn't like being caught by him this way: in bed and in the dark. "Maybe you could fill me in on the story," she requested with deliberate calmness.

"Glad to help you out," he merrily obliged with a rustle of paper. "It explains how Douglas Ramsey, founder of the Ramsey Department Store chain is searching for his alleged grandson. Alleged. That means he's not sure the kid exists, right?"

"Yes. In short, it means that we have no proof as of yet, that there is a grandson."

"Then it goes on, blah, blah, blah—"

"Fill in the blah blahs," Caron anxiously broke in, shoving her glasses farther up her nose.

"Oh. Well, it just gives some background on Ramsey, explaining how he has been estranged from his son, James, for much of the boy's life. That James died of cancer last year." There was a slight pause on the line. "You know about this stuff already, of course."

"Of course," Caron agreed, her brain ticking madly over the turn of events. Douglas Ramsey would be livid when he found out about this invasion of privacy. What if he blamed her? Trying to quell the trepidation mounting with every beat of her heart, she probed further. "I imagine it reports how James Ramsey spoke of a baby son before he passed away. That the elder man is desperately searching for his second-generation heir."

"Yep. According to the article, not only is the alleged grandson entitled to the Ramsey estate when he comes of age, but there is a finder's fee of a million at stake."

Caron gasped in shock. "*Douglas Ramsey* is offering a million dollars for information leading to the baby?"

"Right on."

"Then he's behind the article himself?" She knew her voice was a squeal of utter amazement, but she couldn't help it. The billionaire had obviously taken the reins of the baby search right out of her hands. It was downright irritating that he hadn't discussed this showy move with her. But it was totally unforgivable that he hadn't at least warned her as late as last night, giving her ammo to defuse Rick's guessing game. Oh, how satisfying that would've been.

"Maybe you better get together with this rich old guy and compare notes," Rick suggested.

"This is going to attract every baby bounty hunter in the state of Colorado!"

"Baby bounty hunter," he repeated slowly. "Say it fast three times, Quick Draw!" he urged excitedly. "Let's see if you've still got that rapid-fire delivery."

"I've still got it."

"Just testing the sharpness of your wit," he explained good-humoredly. "I have to be certain you're still as reliable as you were in school."

Such praise coming from a colleague at work would have delighted her to no end. Coming from the incorrigible Hotshot, it opened an unhealed wound deep within her heart where a shy, plump teenager still dwelled.

"You seem sort of dazed by all of this, Caron."

His observation was undeniably true. She was trying to digest the fact that Douglas Ramsey, the big man himself, had betrayed her big-time. After the great pains her law firm had taken to keep this baby search out of the limelight, he'd gone public on his own. She'd advised the billionaire against this tactic from the start, claiming people would go crazy if they thought they had a chance of plugging into the Ramsey empire by producing a baby boy heir.

And she had believed Douglas Ramsey had implicit faith in her judgment! Respect for her as a person. The elderly man had actually taken a fatherly interest in her, beyond attorney-client boundaries. Sure, he was an old grump accustomed to getting his own way. Sure, he was bossy to a fault. Perhaps he was incapable of trusting anyone completely. She certainly wouldn't trust *him* from now on!

"The paper says any inquiries concerning the baby should be made to your law firm," Rick went on to report amid the rustle of paper.

"Well, thank goodness the old goat did that much!"

"So, he is as difficult as they say," Rick deduced with a hint of triumph.

"Yes! No!" She stumbled for a fair assessment. "So, what's it to you anyhow, Rick?"

"I wish to inquire, of course."

Caron's brow furrowed in suspicion. "Is this one of your tricks?"

"No, Caron, honestly it isn't," he assured, sounding a bit hurt over the accusation. "If you still do your homework as diligently as you used to, you know that James lived here in the old neighborhood for the past few years."

Caron's brain began to tick faster. Of course James

had, not far from her parents' old place. Dare she ask Rick flat out? Obviously he still took great pleasure toying with her sensible side. She took a deep breath and asked, "Do you know the whereabouts of Douglas Ramsey's grandson, Rick?"

"What if I do?"

"Then you should be in my office today, that's what!"

"I'm calling you at home because I must insist upon anonymity. Caron, you are just the reliable go-between I need."

That word again. *Reliable.* Yuck! "A go-between isn't needed in a case like this. No one has broken the law. No one is in danger."

"You'd just be doing your job," he pointed out. "Under the covers so to speak."

"I like to play it by the book, Rick."

"Still the same philosophical, rule-hugging girl of yesterday," he judged in heaving disappointment.

"Still the class rebel intent on making his own rules," she tossed back. "Bound and determined to rub me the wrong way while doing it."

"Our last duel was sure a doozy," he recalled with suspect fondness. "Over that punch spill on your prom dress, remember?"

Caron found herself magically transported back to the humiliating moment a decade behind them. "I believe I called you a girl-mooching egomaniac who couldn't handle a punch."

"Quick to the draw," he concurred. "You know, it's kind of funny now."

"Is it?"

"Yeah. I operate a Laundromat and could remove that infamous stain in no time. My place is called Hotshots. You know, because of the shots of water in the washers, the air in the dryers. And of course my nickname.''

Caron already knew of his business venture, located a block off Fairfax Avenue near Truman High School. Apparently it was currently a neighborhood hangout as well as a place to clean clothes. She had no firsthand knowledge of the place, for she hadn't been back to those old stomping grounds in a long time. Not since her parents had moved to a trendy Denver suburb.

"Hey, I bet you don't want to help me because you're still stinging over old wounds," he chided.

His perception rankled her. "I have no time to bear grudges over fizzled romance and lost student council issues. I'm busy trying cases and saving people's butts."

"Then have mercy on one very special talcumpowdered butt, for old times' sake."

"Your butt or the baby's?"

"Cute, Quick Draw, real cute."

"Seriously, Rick, I'm doing everything I can to help this child attain his legacy."

"Maybe that favor isn't quite as simple as it seems. What if there are extenuating circumstances?"

"Such as?"

"Who's to say that the baby might not be better off in his current situation? You said yourself that Ramsey's a goat."

"But—"

"And money isn't everything, you know," he forged on. "I've got the feeling that if Ramsey finds this boy, he won't be willing to let go of him even if the setup doesn't suit the kid. If Ramsey is a genuine blackheart trying to control the whole show, the child could end up in a miserable existence."

"I would tell any prospective representative of the heir to keep in mind that the infant may never be affected by Douglas Ramsey himself. Considering his age…"

"The guy is only seventy-seven. He's still at the helm of his department store chain. He could be around for aeons."

"You really should step forward," she advised, trying to conceal her eagerness. "We'll start by putting together an affidavit."

"Can't you talk with me friend to friend?"

"We must go through the proper channels here, Rick."

"I get it. Law-and-order Quick Draw trying to keep the streets free of rebels like me. Just as you tried in the school council."

"I did not! I, ah, just thought I deserved to be in charge."

"Well, I still don't run by the stuffy rules of the world."

Caron huffed impatiently into the receiver. "Like it or not, this case is business. Billion-dollar big business. It would be much better handled in the office and out of the bedroom. At a decent hour!"

"I'm calling you to avoid all that!" Rather reluctantly, he added, "I hoped for a personal touch, Caron. You did so many little favors for me when we were young. It seems natural, us sitting down to iron out this heir's dilemma. There just happens to be a new Chinese place just down the street from here.…"

He was trying to remove her from her work setting. Wrap her around his… She gave her head a clearinghouse shake. "Rick, sitting in my office for a little chat is not going to turn you into a conservative toad. Let me pencil you in for nine today—"

"Put your damn pencil away!" he growled in defeat. "I only tangle with empty white collars. I clean 'em up and send 'em back."

"You still can't be bucking the system every inch of the way!" Caron cried in wonder.

"Whatever happened to us, Quick Draw?"

"A question I've asked myself many times," she admitted, matching his bewilderment.

"Look, this idea was a mistake," he said in a more tempered tone. "Never mind."

"But Rick—"

"Forget I called, Caron. If you care a whit about our history, neighborhood loyalty, whatever, you won't tell any of your white collars about me."

Before Caron could respond, the dial tone buzzed in her ear. She slammed down the telephone, slammed down the clock and was looking for something more to slam when her overhead light flicked on, brightly illuminating her mauve and gray bedroom. Caron squinted up to find Megan Gage, her lifelong friend and current roommate, standing in the doorway with her hand on the wall switch.

"What are you going on about?" Megan entered with a weary yet curious expression on her round, dimpled face. Just home from the night shift at Mercy Hospital, the petite blonde was wearing a crisp white nurse's uniform and identification badge. "Wrestling with a bad dream? The clock? The radio?"

"All of the above!" Caron swung her long slender legs over the side of the bed. "Men are the most maddening creatures!"

"You been wrestling with one of those, too?" Instant interest sparked her features. "I thought I heard you on the telephone when I walked in."

Caron hopped to her feet, peeling off her orange nightshirt as she charged the dresser for panties and bra. "I just got word that the billion-dollar baby deal has made the newspapers." Caron tugged on her underthings, then moved to the chair where last night's lavender jogging suit sat in a heap. "You know what this means, don't you?" she wailed. "I've lost control of the hunt for the missing heir. My precious chance to make a real mark at the firm! Oh, snap, crackle and pop will be livid."

"I've never heard you refer to Sharp, Krandell and Peterson that way before," Megan balked. "But I like it."

Caron winced in disgust. Rick's glib attitude was already affecting her!

"So, who is the madman who called about the news leak? Douglas Ramsey?"

Caron struggled with her sweatshirt, her head eventually popping through the crew neck. "Douglas Ramsey is the blasted leak. Spilled his guts without a word to me."

"So, who called?" Megan pressed. Always interested in her best friend's cases, she found this story of wealth, secret romance and potential heirs especially intriguing. "Who has you slamming things around and snapping like a wildcat?"

Caron sat down on the edge of the mattress to slip into her athletic shoes, deliberately drawing out the moment. She eventually peeked up from her laces with glinting green eyes full of passion and fury. "Hotshot."

Megan hooted in disbelief. "Get serious! That old high school tease line isn't amusing anymore. The days of our wishing for that magical call are long over."

"I mean it, Meg." Caron stood up, towering over her friend. "Who else could put me in fits without laying a hand on me?"

"Your mother for one," Megan promptly specified.

"Well, Rick Wyatt takes the prize this morning. Catches me in bed. Off guard. Uninformed. Leaves me feeling like an utter fool as he goes on to fill me in about my own case."

"So, Rick has an interest in the billionaire baby. Wonder if he knows that most of the girls in the class of '83 would consider a baby of his to be worth a billion?"

Caron snatched a brush from the dresser and gingerly styled her hair around the bruise on the back of her head. "With that monster ego of his? I'm sure he knows."

Megan rubbed her palms together with glee. "So, how'd he sound?"

"Like a cross between James Dean and Dracula."

"A rebel without a neck to bite?"

"A rebel without a Timex!" Caron dropped the brush with a clatter. "The jerk apparently keeps vampire hours at that Laundromat of his and gets the paper fresh off the press."

"Still cocky, eh?"

Caron rolled her eyes. "I'll say. Though there was something new running beneath his rebel savvy. A thread of vulnerability. As if this baby thing has gotten to him somehow."

Megan nodded. "Must've taken a lot of guts to call

here, considering the storms you two have ridden together. He must have one heck of a lead."

"Let's hope not. He blew up when I tried to get him
into the office. Insisted I forget about his call. My entire career hinges on tracking this heir and he ordered
me to secrecy concerning his potential part in it."

"Just think, your firm's spent a small fortune beating the bushes for this baby, and Rick Wyatt, the hotshot hunk of our old neighborhood, may hold the key
to it all."

Caron glared into space. "You know I could never
stand for Rick to know more about a subject than I did
in school. Now he's back, with the jump on me all
over again. Will I ever get the best of that man?"

Megan fluttered her pale lashes. "Intriguing challenge."

"And then there's that crafty bear, Douglas Ramsey," Caron sputtered. "He's gone behind my back
and offered a million-dollar reward for information
leading to his grandson."

Megan's small frame teetered with the weight of
the news. "Wow! That reward include you?"

Caron flashed her a look of loving exasperation.
"No, Meggy, I'm just the hired help."

"Oh, shucks. I could see us in new threads, on a
Club Med vacation." She thought hard, then brightened with a brainstorm. "Say, if Rick gets the dough,
maybe he'll take us on a sweet little trip."

Caron snorted. "We've been out of touch for ten
years. And the old baggage is there. He still wants to
bend all the rules, and you know it's not my nature to
bend."

"He's one to break a rule or two for," Megan recommended playfully, clutching her heart just below her nameplate. "I'll bet he's still gorgeous."

"A person can lose his looks without losing his nerve," Caron pointed out with a wicked curl to her mouth.

"A mere decade has passed."

"Appearances can change. Take me, for example," Caron invited without coquettishness.

"You're the siren you always aspired to be," Megan acknowledged, surveying Caron's coltish figure, tinted chestnut hair bobbed at the chin, and resculptured nose. "But I have a feeling Rick's still high octane."

"Probably," Caron grumpily relented. "But it's a fuel that doesn't burn me up anymore."

"I wonder if a girl can outgrow that kind of burn."

The pair shared a brief telepathic moment, honed to sharp clarity by their years of friendship. Inseparable since the sixth grade, they'd shared every secret, every dream with each other. It had been their ambition to earn their respective degrees, buy a town house, and live together as sisters until the right men came along—which is exactly what they were doing.

Potential husband material had moved in and out of their master plan with the passage of time, no one quite right to have and to hold forever. Caron found it heartbreakingly frustrating that she always ended up comparing her men to Rick. His delicious blend of street sense and good humor had delighted and tormented her through most of her girlhood. The memories grew more poignant with the passage of time. Most of them, anyway…

"Maybe you better send one of your fellow associates over to interview him," Megan suggested, her creamy brow furrowed in concern.

Caron released a ponderous sigh. "I don't think I can do that to him, even if he deserves it."

"This thing between you two is so emotion-packed," Megan murmured doubtfully. "So much about prom night remains unsettled. And you know it's churned and churned within you all these years."

"He already brought up our little tussle himself," Caron reported with a cringe, recalling her own retaliatory measures of the night. After Rick spilled the punch on her, she'd stuffed a sandwich into his scarlet cummerbund, popping a button on his white ruffled shirt as she'd grabbed a handful of fabric. The class would never forget that scene. Especially their poor respective dates. The abandoned pair had marched off in embarrassment and anger.

"Maybe I'll have a stroke of luck and someone will come in the office with a good solid lead in the right direction," she declared hopefully, "leaving Rick completely out of it."

"Yeah, then you could just forget all about his call," Megan proposed, a little heavy on the solicitude.

Caron flashed her a shrewd look. "Why, then I'd have to forget about our little wager, Meg."

Megan stared into Caron's dancing eyes and emitted a shriek. "You don't intend to cash in on that bet after all this time!"

"I sure do," Caron announced magnanimously, abruptly leaving the room.

"There must be a statute of limitations on bets made twelve years ago by a couple of dreamy teeny-boppers," Megan cried in mortification, trailing after Caron as she roamed the town house.

"You'd make me do it in a shot," Caron maintained, pausing at the kitchen counter to zip her purse shut.

"Of course I would," Megan agreed without shame. "But you're the humanitarian of the house. The one who became a lawyer to make the world a more just place to live."

Caron moved to the short staircase leading to the entryway, jingling her car keys. "On that cheery note, I'm off to buy my newspapers, to see if I can make this world a better place for one billionaire baby. If you'd like to go over our agreement," she added in afterthought, "it's still pressed between the pages of my '81 yearbook. Where it's been since the day we signed it."

"We're talkin' ancient history!" Megan howled, throwing her arms in the air as she ran for the shelves.

Caron clucked in suspect sympathy. "You'll see that we set no time limit, Meg. The first of us to get a call from Hotshot—whether it be about a homework assignment, a sock hop, or the temperature outside— is the true and real winner. You have to pay up."

Megan thumbed through the yearbooks in search of the right annual. "I could get arrested!"

"Not to worry. This humanitarian will represent you *pro bono*."

Something hit the door seconds later as Caron crossed the lawn to the driveway. Most likely *The Truman High School Memorandum, 1981.*

2

"'BILLIONAIRE BABY AT LARGE!'" Douglas Ramsey proudly read the headline of the *Denver Daily* before folding it in two and slapping it down on the conference table at Sharp, Krandell and Peterson.

Ensconced in one of the firm's large glass-walled offices with the billionaire and two of the partners, Caron noted that Ramsey, in his late seventies, was still an imposing figure. His gray flannel suit cut a smooth swath from his broad shoulders, his coarse hair properly covered his balding head and his blue eyes glittered hard with authority behind their bifocal barrier. He was a man to be reckoned with, one who often sought to maintain the upper hand by sheer intimidation.

Caron also realized that Ramsey was now searching their faces for shock value, for some dismay over his stunt. But of course it was too late. Hotshot had upstaged the unassuming billionaire with his early morning phone call. Caron had in turn immediately called her superiors after purchasing an armload of papers featuring the bad news. They had held a pow-wow before office hours to rethink their strategy. Ramsey had certainly muffed their plans to tread softly.

As Caron predicted, the partners were outraged. Up to this point, they'd been humoring the rich old client as little more than a courtesy, far more focused on the legal workings of the Ramsey Department Store chain. They considered the baby hunt a silly waste of time, called it Ramsey's Folly behind his back. It had been judged a job worthy of an associate only, and ultimately hoisted into Caron's lap. A lap that ironically had never held a real live baby. Caron had been considered the perfect underling for the job, not because of her skills as an attorney, but because Douglas Ramsey had taken such a shine to her during her two-year tenure at the firm. The strategy had been for Caron to put some steam into the search, just enough to satisfy Ramsey and his ninety-year-old spinster sister, Agatha. It was theorized that the baby most likely didn't exist and the search would die out. Naturally Caron resented this attitude and fervently hoped to find the baby heir, prove her worth to the company once and for all.

Unfortunately her month-long investigation had turned up precious little. There were no records, no gossipy biddies at James's former apartment building prepared to gleefully spill all. The entire riddle was based upon a deathbed statement James supposedly made to his Aunt Agatha. It was the general consensus of the partners that the ninety-year-old merely had fallen asleep at her nephew's bedside and dreamt the whole thing.

Of course there was no turning back now, not on the crest of Ramsey's publicity stunt. Not with the entire world on alert, waiting for the law firm of Sharp, Krandell and Peterson to come up with one billion-dollar baby. The lawyers all knew it was Douglas Ramsey's intention to get them searching more diligently. It had worked! Caron had to fight hard at the meeting to keep control of the case. In the end, the partners had conceded to her wishes.

"Yes," Ramsey crowed on in pride. "This is how you get action, fellows. And, miss," he added, shifting in his seat to glance warmly at his favorite associate, standing nearby in a flattering cream-colored gabardine suit and forest green blouse.

Two of the firm's partners, William Peterson and Lester Sharp, regarded Caron from their seats as well, expecting her to pick up the ball she'd fought so hard to keep in her court only one short hour ago. She had contended that no one in the firm knew better how to handle Douglas Ramsey than she. The claim went unchallenged. For the time being.

Caron figured his devotion to her stemmed from many small seeds. The complicated legal work she performed regularly for him. Her open expression of sympathy over the loss of his son. Her instant rapport with his elderly sister. The simple biological fact that she was a woman and would better understand his needs as a grandparent.

Ironically his assumptions concerning her motherly instinct were unfounded. An only child who had preferred to study while her peers baby-sat, she knew nothing about babies. Caring for anyone below the age of reason frightened her more than facing a potentially dangerous client behind prison walls. Having her own family was a far-off dream. At present she concentrated on nothing beyond the career she was carving out as the only female associate of the firm.

It was with her legal prowess that she hoped to impress the billionaire—and achieve her fondest wish, the partnership. True, they mixed business with pleasure on occasion, partaking in everything from hot-air ballooning to roaming the hills of Golden, Ramsey's hometown. He was lonely and confused, searching not only for his grandson, but for his roots, reexamining the early days when things were simple. The department store magnate was quite vigorous for his age and, despite his business dealings, always seemed to have time for Caron and a new excursion. Caron gave him as much attention as her busy day allowed, but was sometimes forced to decline his offers. He didn't like it.

Being forever the manipulator, he frequently tried to lure her away from the firm with job offers in his company. Caron consistently declined, not sure she could tolerate his blustery ways on a day-to-day basis, and not sure she could give up the drama of the courtroom. She'd worked so hard for the chance to stand center stage and sway people with articulate oration. The heavier her court schedule, the happier she was.

"Mr. Ramsey," she began, pacing round the room, "I thought we agreed this investigation would be left to our discretion."

"But you people were getting nowhere, Caron," he grumbled, his bushy gray brows slanting to the bridge of his blunt nose.

"Subtlety takes time."

"I expect this stuffy firm to be miffed by my bawdy offer. But some incentive was needed to beef up this search. Money is something everyone understands. They'll come to us now, rather than vice versa." He held up a large, halting palm as she opened her mouth. "I know you are going to remind me of the security angle. But I don't think babies will be snatched from their cribs and delivered to my doorstep. Without proof positive, I'd never accept a boy as my grandson."

"The huge reward is likely to bring out some enterprising charlatans though," Caron predicted in concern. "We're already getting outrageous calls."

"It won't be so bad, Caron. I whittled down the candidates by asking for a certain heirloom." Ramsey proudly gestured at the newspaper with the largest photograph of himself.

"Just what is this heirloom?" Lester Sharp demanded, twirling a pen in his hands.

"All you need to know is that it's a medal," Ramsey replied with a wily look. "To keep everybody honest, I'm going to keep the precise details to myself for now."

"Bah!" Sharp complained with a gesture of impatience.

"Root through the heap, Lester, and you may just find a nugget of information," Ramsey proclaimed. "A million-dollar nugget that would be worth a billion to a lucky little boy. You single out the prospects with a medal, and I'll speak with them. Here, by appointment. Easy enough."

"We were doing it the easy way, Douglas," William Peterson broke in huffily.

"Four weeks should have been ample time," Ramsey lectured sternly.

"James was a prosperous businessman in his own right," Caron pointed out, "with three print shops across the state. The list of his connections and acquaintances has proven endless."

"A good surgeon slices open his patient, makes the repairs, then sews him back up before the anesthetic wears off, before the patient bleeds to death. It's all in the timing," Ramsey bellowed, slicing the air with his hand. "A quick cut, then in and out."

Caron wandered over to the skyscraper window facing Lincoln Avenue, folding her arms across her chest with a pensive sigh. The removal of Ramsey's kidney last year was obviously still on his metaphoric mind. The perilous surgery followed by his son's death had forced Ramsey to confront mortality in spades. That was the reason for the search for the last Ramsey descendant.

Though impressed with Ramsey's quest to track down his heir, Caron had come to recognize his gruffness, his uncompromising nature, his reluctance to delegate duties. Why, his announcement to the papers was a prime example. He was determined to run everything, compulsively bullying employees and family members to the limit.

It was this very weakness that had gotten him into this jam in the first place. He'd suffered tremendously over the years because of his drive and forcefulness. His wife had passed away some time ago, long after their bitter divorce. His son, James, had sided with his mother, leaving father and son estranged right up until James's death. The notion that there might be another Ramsey floating around in the world was killing the old man.

More than once, however, she'd wondered what he'd do when he found his grandson. Things that were cut and dried in Ramsey's mind might not be so in reality. The child had a mother. Seemingly a mere detail to him. Perhaps the mother knew the score and she and her son were in hiding. Hiding from the glare of the public Ramsey life-style, the beady-eyed glare behind Douglas Ramsey's thick glasses. Did Caron have the right to yank them into the limelight? She found herself in a moral quandary over the possibilities. She found her trust in him wavering more today than it ever had during their two-year relationship.

And not because of Hotshot's soapbox lecture! Her own social conscience functioned quite well. Even though she followed the rules, it didn't mean she didn't question their value on occasion.

Peterson cleared his throat from his place at the long table, his small dark eyes telling her to soothe the savage beast. Poised to speak, she paused in uncertainty. This would be the precise moment to bring up Rick Wyatt and his claim, show she was on top of the leads flowing in. If she wanted to be a ruthless player who sought only results, she could give a full report and perhaps solve the mystery immediately. At worst they'd hit a blind alley. But could she betray a man she'd known since childhood? Despite their clashes, there was still the good stuff. Some of it had been really good stuff. Leave it to him to put her in a compromising position without getting physical!

With all eyes expectantly upon her, Caron took a seat at the table. "Mr. Ramsey," she began awkwardly, "I sincerely wish you hadn't taken matters into your own hands, but since you have... Since you have," she repeated in a stronger voice, making the gut decision to give Rick a temporary reprieve, "we have no choice than to adjust, to focus on the prospects who come to us."

"You believe he exists, don't you?" he quizzed sharply.

"I most certainly do," Caron immediately assured

so the partners wouldn't have to muster up false support.

"If only Agatha could give us more to go on," he said in regret.

"I've spoken to your sister a few times, sir, and her stories shift with the breeze." Caron tapped a round polished nail on the fat manila folder before her on the table. "I have scads of material here dating back to your childhood."

"Agatha's a dotty rambler," Ramsey rumbled in despair. "No doubt we could be blackmailed a hundred times over with the stuff you've compiled."

"Perhaps a good glitzy book of fiction could be gleaned." Caron's lilting laughter brought a glimmer to Ramsey's ruddy, glum features. "As I say," she went on with a note of levity, "there is too much embellishment for any real chronicle. We need hard facts."

"I know it's difficult to take Agatha's word alone on this," Ramsey conceded. "But that's all we've had all along—her insistence that James claimed to have fathered a baby boy. It's possible that she's just wishing. With her spinsterhood and my aloneness, perhaps it's a diversion to buffer the Ramsey pain. But I can't rest until I know for sure. And every fiber of my being tells me the baby's out there somewhere."

"Agatha is still often as sharp as a tack," Caron encouraged, giving his arm a pat. "She may have gotten the message just right."

"She took James's death hard," he confided, his voice quavering. "His lung cancer was a painful thing for both of us. Outliving one's descendant is a cruel twist of fate. Even near the end, when he agreed to see me, he was distant. And certainly said nothing about a baby. Probably was afraid I'd try to run the child's life as I did his." He drew his forearms on the table and hunched over briefly for a steadying breath.

"The first task is to find the child," Caron consoled. "Meet with the mother, see where all the pieces fit." To her annoyance, Ramsey's face clouded at the mere mention of the mother, just as it always did. Which was why she was giving Hotshot the benefit of the doubt for now. Maybe he was playing the role of the noble protector.

"That should settle things for now," he said in brusque farewell. "I'll forward all inquiries made at the house to your office." Straightening up, he beckoned to his chauffeur seated in the waiting area beyond the glass wall. The distinguished silver-haired man immediately entered the conference room to help the burly billionaire from his chair and into his coat. Everyone else stood up as well, forming a loose semicircle around him.

"By the way, Caron, are you free this Saturday night?" Ramsey asked. "I'm having a little party at my place here in Denver."

A smile twitched at her lips. A little party? It was a huge gala event for the social elite of the state!

"I'm certain she's free," Lester Sharp smoothly intervened.

"You privy to her social calendar?" Ramsey barked with his trademark glare.

"Why, no, of course not," Lester backtracked with a tight-lipped look.

"This is purely a personal invitation," he said in softer tones as he turned his attention back to Caron. "It won't mean your job if you can't come."

"I would love to attend," Caron accepted.

"Good enough!" He lumbered to the door, pausing briefly once more. "I'll send Franklin here to pick you up in one of the cars. About seven?"

"Perfect, sir."

"Bring along an escort," he added on his way out. "Can't have a lady like you out on the streets alone at night."

Once the door separated Ramsey and his man from the attorneys, the glass-walled room began to hum.

"If that old guy wasn't such an important client," Sharp muttered between clenched teeth.

"I'm beginning to think the whole gruff act is a charade to ensure his controlling hand," Caron speculated.

"Regardless, you certainly know how to smooth his feathers," William Peterson admitted. "Keep up the good work, Caron."

"If only he hadn't made that announcement to the press," Sharp complained. He'd wandered back to the table and was leafing through the file on Ramsey.

Caron shrugged. "He's accustomed to running the show. And the show wasn't big enough in his eyes."

"We've got to resolve this heir question one way or the other before this tops Barnum and Bailey," Peterson said. "The wily old coot's got us performing before a worldwide audience with his million-dollar challenge. Satisfy him, Caron, and in the words of a great book, 'you'll be put in charge of greater affairs.' Whatever you do, follow down each and every lead meticulously."

Caron closed her eyes with a satisfied grin. The message was music to her ears: clean up this crazy controversy and you'll move up in the firm. Her smile soon faded as Rick Wyatt's image floated into view behind her lids. Common sense told her that he never would've called without a concrete reason. Common sense told her that he was one heck of a lead. Why, oh why, did she always put so much stock in common sense?

"WHY ARE YOU SO LATE, Caron?" Megan complained at eight o'clock that evening upon her roommate's return to the town house. "I've been waiting for hours to hear about Hotshot."

Caron trudged across the kitchen linoleum, wrinkling her nose at her rambunctious pal seated at the table wolfing down a huge waffle. Their opposite working hours caused mealtime havoc. Caron occasionally joined Megan in her dinnertime breakfasts, Megan sometimes joined her in a more traditional meal. Ofttimes each fended for herself. This was going to be one of those independent nights for Caron. Her tense stomach was the size of a grape, sparing room for only a cup of coffee which she slid onto the table as she sank into a chair.

Megan frowned at Caron's wrinkled suit jacket. "Rick put ya in the spin cycle or what?"

"Very funny," Caron griped, gulping as the sweet smell of Megan's maple syrup invaded her nostrils. "Why don't you get a daytime job like everybody else? Eat a nice big hamburger at this time of night?"

"Because I'm not like anybody else." Megan hungrily sliced into the waffle.

Caron waited for Megan to stuff her mouth with food before telling her the news. "I didn't speak to Rick yet. Just didn't have the time."

Megan chomped hard and fast in an effort to swallow and speak. Caron took the opportunity to further excuse herself. "I spent the afternoon in court with my sexual discrimination suit and did some after-hours interviewing concerning the baby."

"Darn you, Caron!" Megan finally squawked with a gulp. "Don't you have any news?"

Caron sipped her coffee with a rueful grin. "Well, you wouldn't believe some of the heirlooms people brought in, trying to prove a link to the Ramsey clan."

"Just think, offering a million bucks for a relative," Megan marveled in disbelief. "I'd gladly give him one of mine at half the price."

"I've got a social-climbing mother to contribute myself," Caron tossed in. "Free of charge."

"None of the papers specified what the heirloom is, did they?"

"All I know is that it's a medal of some kind," Caron confided. "Confidential info, by the way."

"Sure, sure," Megan pooh-poohed with a wave of her fork. "So what did you see?"

"Along with tired, hungry babies of all shapes and sizes, I saw trophies, photographs, crystal—things that people pass along through generations. Some of the more notable efforts were a hood ornament from an old Thunderbird, a chunk of gold, a bronzed baby shoe, and my all-time favorite of the night, a suit of armor."

"What a bunch of hustlers," Megan uttered in awe.

Caron flashed her a lopsided grin. "Lots of wishful thinkers anyway. An unusual number of grandmothers brought in their grandsons. Babies they believed couldn't be the seed of certain disappointing males, I guess."

Megan giggled. "Desperate flights to cloud nine."

Caron laughed along. "A million dollars does tend to send the imagination soaring."

"So, after all your interviewing, are you any closer to an answer?"

"No, just more determined to speak to Rick."

"So, go get 'em, tiger!"

Caron squeezed her eyes shut, summoning inner strength. "What if I don't have what it takes to wrangle with him anymore?" she wondered just above a whisper.

"You wrangle for a living now, you idiot!" Megan said with her own brand of bolstering. "You are a *litigator*."

"It's still hard for me with him," Caron despaired, burying her face in her hands. "Can you believe it? One minute on the phone and I was a fat girl with the self-esteem of a peanut."

Megan clucked patiently, accustomed to soothing Caron's self-doubts. "You were never really fat. Just plump. And you have to face him," she insisted, prying Caron's fingers from her delicate features.

Caron rued her fate. "I'm going tonight. Going to see how they do their laundry on the wild side." She sighed wistfully. "Maybe I'll be the prettier one this time."

"Naw, that's too much to expect," Megan predicted. "I'll bet he's still muscle-rippling gorgeous. With that thick black hair, those long sweeping lashes."

"Megan?"

"Yeah?" she asked with a moony grin.

"I wouldn't make any more bets concerning Hotshot. You've yet to clear your tab as it is."

"Get out of town." Megan drained her milk glass and set it down with a thump.

"And I will be the prettier," Caron vowed with a feline grin. "After the jolt he gave me this morning, I figure it's only fair play to stun him out of his senses."

THERE WAS A GODDESS in his Laundromat.

Rick Wyatt had bolted out of the back room of Hotshots, freezing at the sight of the beautiful stranger near the front of the cluttered, machine-filled room. He'd been elbow deep in his own personal affairs, originally coming out to retrieve... What? His mind drew a blank slate as he gawked at her in amazement. The place occasionally held a straggler at this time of night, someone who hadn't timed their washload to coincide with his closing time of ten o'clock. But this babe had no laundry, unless she was carrying it inside the red clutch purse tucked under her arm.

A quick, sharp glance to the large-faced clock on the wall told him it was half-past ten now. Apparently he hadn't locked the door. Or had he? Maybe she was an apparition, one manifested by an imaginative man hungry for a good night's sleep.

"Baby, baby, baby," he uttered to himself, quaking in his Nikes. "Tonight's the night..."

Rick squinted for a better look, frustrated that the only bulb left burning was the small yellow nightlight over the front door. Flesh or smoke, she was something to see, a long cool beauty leaning a streamlined hip against dryer number seven. He drank in the small hat sitting atop her short cloud of chestnut hair, then skimmed on to her magnificent body, a striking reed in a red-and-blue blocked suit with yellow lapels. Rick, a self-proclaimed man of vanity and virility, was suddenly conscious of his own clothing: snug, tattered jeans and a faded green T-shirt.

What would she think?

Was she even for real?

Maybe his thrill-seeking libido had created her luscious shell. If so, he'd done a bang-up job!

With a deep fortifying breath, he spoke. "I, ah, didn't hear you come in."

She lifted a rich, sable brow. "I'm light on my feet."

He took a step forward, hands clasped behind his back. "We're closed. Have been since ten."

"The door was unlocked."

Was she or wasn't she? he wondered, raking shaky fingers through his hair. "I just don't get it. My bell didn't even ring. It always rings."

A small smile curved her cherry red lips. "Maybe your bell is broken."

"Yeah, maybe." With a burst of determination Rick strutted down the left aisle, past the pool table, past the pop machine, all the while watching her. He knew he'd be bursting the bubble of his own making if she vanished as mysteriously as she'd appeared, but he had to know for sure. He stepped up to the glass door, putting a power grip on the small brass knob. She was still leaning into old number seven, not dissolving into the scuffed tiled floor, not evaporating into the detergent-tinged air.

Hot damn! He was close to her now.

She was real all right. Further scrutiny under the single tubular bulb now centered over his head highlighted her curvy proportions in a golden hue. She was a three-dimensional babe with startling bone structure. Artistic cheeks and dirty dancing-honed hips. The package was wrapped in fabric that had never crossed his threshold empty or otherwise.

Downtown Hotshot meets Uptown Hot Babe. Determined to check the bell, he tugged the sticky door open with a single yank. Cool night air streamed inside to a merry jingle of welcome. Rick's system was jingling too, like a ribbon of sleigh bells. So how'd she get in without him hearing? He filled his lungs with invigorating night air, hoping to stabilize himself. It was a long moment before he shoved the door back into place with a slam and a clang.

"Losing your touch, Hotshot?"

Rick's head jerked back. There was an unmistakable familiarity in her taunt. An intimacy. He pensively rubbed his thin black mustache, not recalling ever being intimate with a goddess.

Rick rapped a knuckle on dryer number one and marched toward number seven, his eyes never once leaving her face as he counted off each machine. Her smile deepened the closer he approached, dimples miraculously forming in the hollows of those sculptured cheeks. It was impossible. Yet... "Caron?"

"As if you didn't know," she retorted, slapping her purse down on the dryer behind her.

Rick shook his head in undisguised awe. "It's been ten years, Caron."

"Why, you just talked to me this morning," she said, her voice slipping a notch.

"You happen to sound different in bed," he tossed back, his mouth curling mischievously. "Husky, croaky." He sauntered close, satisfaction warming his gut as she flushed over the innuendo. She deserved it after sneaking up on him this way. "I truly didn't recognize you until you called me Hotshot," he confessed on a more merciful note.

"Maybe it's because I've lost twenty pounds and replaced my glasses with contacts," she suggested, acutely aware of his heart-pounding proximity. Only inches shorter than Rick, she could face him squarely atop her high heels. She was determined to do so, just as she'd done without hesitation in the old days. Why did it seem more difficult now? Was it the sensuous gleam in his dark brown eyes, those arresting features, sharpened with age into flawless balance? His face was as beautiful as a macho man's could be. Good thing, considering his ego would no doubt accept nothing less.

"Ah yes, the Quick Draw wit," he acquiesced. "Sharpened to perfection on poor slugs like me, for the ultimate altruistic goal of saving butt after butt in court." Rick silently roved her face, mesmerized by the glitter of green in her eyes. Those sparklers, filled with vitality and promise, had led him on a merry chase throughout his boyhood. Now they were full of womanly knowledge. If she knew then what she no doubt knew now... He shuddered to think of the consequences.

"You are staring at me, Rick."

"You want me to."

"Flirty fool," she scoffed, blinking in disbelief as he raised a large hand to her face and began to trace his finger down the slope of her surgically perfected nose.

"This is new, too."

"Yes," she said breathlessly, acutely aware of the texture of his fingertip. His touch actually made her knees quake. If only she'd worn a longer skirt to hide in, she fretted, as his gaze fell to survey her from head to toe.

When his eyes lifted once again, they were penetrating and demanding. "Why are you here, Caron?"

"You called me." She kept her head high, knowing that the drop from his eye to his belt would be like falling from the frying pan they'd discussed earlier, straight into the flames. She'd already noticed that those ragged jeans of his still held the tightest rear end on the planet. "We have to talk about a certain baby," she stated. "A baby I think we both care about."

"Do you think we could possibly be on the same side of an issue for once?" he asked in mocking amazement.

Caron was aghast. "Of course we are! I want nothing more than for that sweet, defenseless boy to get what's coming to him."

Rick's mouth curved in a secret smile of satisfaction. "Right answer, counselor. You must really wow 'em in court with that delivery."

"I've had my moments," she agreed airily. "It's easier to get a point across without you there, contradicting my every word."

"Too bad I didn't follow you into the legal profession." He rubbed his square, stubbled chin. "We could've wallowed in continual debate and gotten paid for the pleasure."

She shook her head, her shiny brown cap of hair swinging around her face. "You are still the most exasperating boy I've ever known."

His deep, masculine chuckle echoed hollowly through the room. "Wrong answer, this time. This rebel's a man now."

3

OH, YES. RICK WYATT was a man now. Caron closed her eyes briefly against his smug smile, made more roguish these days by the black mustache now etched across his upper lip. She sought to still the quiver running the length of her before it visibly shook her in her high heels. A cool head was needed here. He'd seen right through her bid for attention. The moment would be his if she backed down even an inch. How many times in the past had he edged in close, dominating her with his sheer physical strength, his irresistible magnetism?

A million times.

Hotshot had turned her to putty whenever it suited him. Whenever he wanted something. Early on it had been the wheels from her buggy for his go-cart, nickels to round off his dollar. Later it was a cookie from her bag lunch, notes from literature class, hand-sewn seat covers for his old jalopy.

But the stakes were higher now. A billion times higher. With her precious job in the center of it all. If she botched this baby deal, she'd be out of a job, her reputation as a competent attorney at serious risk.

She was his putty only if she allowed herself to be.

Acknowledging his methods on an intellectual level didn't stop her fragile emotions from responding to him on a sexual plane. It was nearly impossible to reason with his sturdy broad-chested form hovering so very, very close. The fabric of his shirt was threadbare and pulled taut across his chest, enticingly outlining every muscle. A weightlifter's body. A young woman's dream. A precarious spot for a lady lawyer who relied so heavily on her powers of reason!

"Rick, you are invading my space," she accused.

"Caron, you are presently in my space," he differed. "Back on my turf of your own free will." He stepped closer, grunting in satisfaction as her bottom backed into old number seven, wedging her neatly between him and the dryer with a distinctive thump.

Caron's heart was beating a fierce tattoo now. Allowing him to corner her had been a mistake.

As his mouth curled into a lusty grin, she recalled its taste with sharp, surprising clarity. From where had the memory of their fledgling kisses materialized? They'd experimented with make-out techniques during the hot, sultry days of their fourteenth summer. Caron could still feel his lips, his tongue, the way his fingers raked her hair. It had been new, exciting, forbidden. Rick had been her friend, her wonderful, funny confidant during that summer of growth, that journey from child to teenager.

But once across the bridge, Rick had broken into a sprint. He'd gone on to experiment with every girl in reach. That bygone summer had drawn out their strong points, ultimately separating them because of their sharp contrasts. Puberty had brought Rick's virility and cocky indifference into sharp focus, as well as Caron's high IQ and knack for studies. Oh, how she'd wanted to tell the world she'd been in a three-month lip-lock with Rick Wyatt. But by the first snowfall, she was sure no one would believe her. She was the brain. The bookworm. The plump girl with the premature bustline. Rick Wyatt was…Hotshot. And he apparently didn't like the new her. Not enough to continue those kissing games…

"I had expected some sort of response from your end," he admitted silkily, grazing her arm with his as he propped a hand on number seven. "Something in the form of nipping legal hounds. Waited all day for them."

The naughty curl to her mouth confirmed she'd been sorely tempted to send in the cavalry. "I'm here because I think we can do better than that phone conversation. After all, our days of debating dress codes and dance bands and hall passes are long over. We are adults."

"I did call with high hopes, of course." Resting his hip on dryer six, he reached over to toy with her little yellow hat, shifting its angle on her head. "But we still debate with intensity from opposite poles."

In other words, he was still shaping the rules to suit him. Fiddling with her hat as he gave her the brush, too! His audacity on both fronts made her blood boil. "Just like that, eh?" she snapped, brushing aside his busy hands. "You involve yourself in a billion-dollar destiny and just say oops, not for me after all."

"My final decision was made with a little more effort than oops," he assured her. "I am more than brawn these days. Not nearly as brainy as you, but I get along."

If Caron didn't know better, she'd have thought there was a defensive edge to his tone. But it just couldn't be. To her knowledge, Rick hadn't had an uncertain moment in his entire childhood. And probably not in manhood, either.

Rick heaved a sigh of resignation. "Calling you was a regrettable mistake, Caron."

A mistake. That stung Caron deep. They'd been so close once. True, they'd never officially dated. He'd never even called her, not even once to cinch the bet with Megan. But their mental sparring over the years had been so intimate, so sexy, that she couldn't stand it that he didn't want her still. Not even with her new foxy look. "So much for old friends," she muttered in disappointment.

Rick reared back in surprise as she shifted the blame on him. "You wanted me to jump through your law-and-order hoops before you'd even talk to me. Treated me like a cocky kid who didn't know what was best for him."

Caron's mouth sagged open. "The last time we spoke you were a cocky kid, Rick."

Realization sheeted his face, defusing his temper. "Guess it has been that long. I will admit I was the terror of the neighborhood back then, the guy all mothers feared. Daughters were shoved into basements and under beds when I walked down the street." Humor twitched his jaw. "And I guess that's what made the challenge to win each and every one irresistible."

Caron's mother, Deborah, had been among those with one hand on her daughter and the other on the basement light switch. It hadn't stopped Caron, or any of the other girls, however, from flitting in and out of Rick's reach.

"A mature adult stands before you," he asserted passionately. "I'm continually working to prove myself worthy of this very neighborhood where I caused all the havoc. I love it here so much, Caron." His face lit up as he scanned his kingdom of a utility room with open fondness. "This is my investment in the good life, helping folks in need, befriending the local kids. It's especially satisfying to be here for the lonely ones who don't have the happy home life I had." Rick placed a hand on her shoulder. "Don't you think I'm making a difference, even if I'm not a stockbroker or a scientist?"

Expressing his importance, his purpose in life, seemed so urgent to him. Caron didn't know what to make of it. Since when was he unsure of his path? He'd glided along on good looks and savvy his whole life, hadn't he? "Rick, I'm sure you're a rousing success," she obliged.

His heavy brows arched in hope. "You really think so?"

All she could think about were his fingertips digging into the silky fabric of her color-blocked jacket, into the flesh of her shoulder. It sent streaks of heat through her body, driving all rational thought to the wayside. She twisted free of his trap with a breathless tug. "Don't, Rick."

"Maybe you should go, Caron," he suggested quietly. "I know now you can't help me."

"I just can't walk away," she explained in stubborn apology, her feet rooted to the floor. "You're... You happen to be..." She stumbled to express herself.

"Quick Draw lost for words?" he asked mockingly, looming over her willowy body, larger than life itself.

She pursed her lips in aggravated surrender. "You just happen to be my first solid lead."

"I am?"

"Well, you don't have to be so downright delighted about it," she bristled.

"I'm sorry," he offered in suspect sincerity. "You've always been so capable. Who'd have ever guessed you'd end up on my doorstep in need of anything!"

"We seem to need each other," she pointed out. "Obviously James Ramsey was part of this neighborhood family you are so fond of. I'll bet you were great pals who shared lots of confidences."

Rick rolled his eyes to the ceiling, as if about to surrender Valley Forge. "Okay, he was a good friend. We are still grieving his death around here."

"I am sorry for your loss," she offered softly. "Just give me a little more to go on, and I'll be out of here."

"One scoop in my arms and you'd be outta here too," he threatened.

Caron tried to ignore the storm growing in his manner. "What about the mother? At least tell me where she is."

"The mother is not an issue at this point."

"She should stand up and be counted immediately," Caron warned practically, "so Douglas Ramsey doesn't plow right over her."

"So he does live up to James's description," Rick muttered. "I won't allow him to treat the heir as a little possession straight from a cabbage patch with no history, no ties."

"The old man has a heart on some levels," Caron hastily assured. "He just needs to be shown the way. How to love unconditionally."

"I don't think he deserves an heir."

Caron could barely contain her amazement. Rick sure saw himself at the center of the controversy, pulling all the strings. But how like him with his ego, to fancy himself at the helm of this baby search. Adding him to the head count with Douglas Ramsey and herself, that brought the number of chiefs to three! She ached to probe on, find out just how this streetwise rebel ended up fighting this billion-dollar cause, but she checked herself promptly. If he blew up, he *would* scoop her up and deposit her on the street! With her luck, some old neighbor would be passing by in the dead of night and promptly call her mother!

As Caron stared into Rick's dark eyes full of emotion and strength, she recalled Megan's earlier remark about the guts it must've taken for him to call her at all. There had to be some tremendous intent behind it. She thought back to how he'd approached her, before the bantering got heated. "You said you were looking for someone reliable," she ventured, trying not to grit her teeth over the description. "I still am, Rick. Always will be."

Rick rubbed his chin, studying the floor. "Well, I had this plan.... Maybe I just hoped you'd be complacent—like many of the other women I know."

Caron erupted in a surprised laugh. "No, I guess I'm still not the pliable sort you've always desired most."

Rick appeared ready to argue, then thought better of it. "If it were to be carried out, it would have to be done so immediately. The closer Ramsey gets, the quicker the clock ticks."

"Huh?"

"Never mind that for now," he directed. "What I originally had in mind was to use your position to get me into Ramsey territory. I planned to personally check out this billionaire grandfather, make sure he wouldn't disrupt the boy's life."

Caron gasped in disbelief. "You really intended to take that powerful man for a test spin?"

"Why not?" Rick folded his arms across his chest, as still and sturdy as a mighty tree trunk. "He plans to take the potential heir for one, doesn't he?"

"Perhaps, in a way," Caron conceded, fingering her hat. Rick still had an uncanny insight concerning people. Persons other than herself, anyway. "It would be impossible to get close to a man like him without arousing his suspicion."

"It would've looked natural if you'd introduced me as your old school pal, as James's laundryman."

Rick's voice was casual, but his idea held a well-thought-out ring to Caron, someone who weighed her words in court down to the ounce. "He has built a department store empire on gut and instinct, something you understand quite well, Rick. It would be tough to hoodwink him."

"People see what they want to see, especially when they're desperate. It's the delivery that counts the most sometimes. Right, counselor?"

"Touché for courtroom tactics," she relented, rankled that he could still bring her down on the verbal mat with a sound smack, despite their maturity.

"So, those *would have* been my terms," he said expectantly."

"What was I to gain?" she demanded.

His gaze clouded. "I can't tell you yet, not exactly."

"My job would be on the line and you can't confide your motives?"

Rick threw up his hands in a flare of temper. "I knew we couldn't get it together! The whole damn state is looking for this kid and you're not sure you can risk letting downtown Wyatt here mingle with the upper crust." He seized her upper arms, giving her a gentle shake. "Let go and trust me, Caron. I can breeze in and out for the facts, before he knows what hit him." He searched her stoic features for any signs of a meltdown.

Caron struggled to hold her cool. "This search is my responsibility. My big chance for bigger things."

"Take a chance on me. The beginning of the tunnel is dark, but it is a shortcut for you. You see, Caron, no matter how many avenues you search, they all lead back here to Fairfax. Back to me."

His arrogance scalded her. "Really, Rick? Surely there must be a detour around the mighty you! Someone else in this business district, for instance, must know the whereabouts of that child!"

He rubbed the back of his neck with a weary sigh. "Like it or not we are joined at the hip on this one. I've got the info you need. You've got the influence with Douglas Ramsey I need. I'm smart enough to know he wouldn't buy my arriving at the stately manor one day just to chat about his son. He'd check me out, probe into things that are none of his business. The kid could never get away once the old guy knew his identity. That's what seems so unfair."

"Why must I wait for your information?"

"Because it's better for you," he said to her surprise. "If everything were to blow, you'd have an honest ticket out. Ignorance."

Everything could blow? Why oh why did Rick's life always seem larger than life itself? And how in the world had he managed to make his selfish offer sound downright gallant? "So you want my blind trust? The chance to run loose in my life?"

He shrugged, his angled jaw twitching. "Well, yeah. We trusted each other as kids, didn't we? Shared everything. Especially in the early days."

Caron's hand stole to her mouth, causing him to chuckle knowingly. He knew she was remembering the kissing games. She reddened, instantly dropping her fingertips from her lips as though they were red-hot to the touch.

Rick's lips proved even hotter than hers. With a finger hooked under her chin, he was impulsively kissing her, hot, hard and deep. He was experimenting as he used to, but with a whole lot more expertise.

And it felt so good. Her body liquefied in her shoes as she drank from his taste, his scent. No other male had ever made her insides quiver in a simple lip-lock. With a single feather-light crook to her chin he was thoroughly ravaging her mouth with driving force. She knew he was making a deliberate point, showing her just how profound their chemistry was.

She needed no such reminder.

He'd spoiled every simple smooch for every man after him a long time ago.

She finally broke the union, stumbling out to the aisle. "I just can't go along with you blindly," she whispered on a steadying breath.

"You just did."

Rick's triumphant grin convinced Caron that while he may be a special friend to many a kid in the neighborhood, he was certainly no humble Father Flannagan. She busily collected her purse, and her hat, which had somehow ended up on the floor. "This search is serious, Rick."

"You are still just too serious in general, Quick Draw. I was trying to show you that."

"My terms are simple enough," she stated briskly. "Give me something to believe in, or I'm out of here."

"Believe in me."

If Caron could only believe in those eyes, suddenly haunted with some secret yearning. That mouth, wavering the line between compassion and resentment. But Rick had let her down once with a crushing blow that still pained her at times. She just couldn't surrender without something. Anything. "You were right," she conceded quietly. "This conversation has nowhere to go. So, I'll just be going."

"It doesn't all come from books," Rick called after her retreating figure. "Just remember who taught you how to kiss."

Caron froze on her heel near the door, whirling back in fury. "Just remember who taught you right back. Who gave you the experience to go on and confidently kiss every girl in sight." She was gone then. Out the door with a slam and a clang.

"YOU HAVE GROWN into one major distraction, Bobber."

Up in his apartment above the Laundromat five minutes later, Rick regarded his companion with a tsk and a sigh. With capable hands he lifted the drowsy baby from its molded infant seat, gently resting him against his chest. He sat down in the rocker near the picture window facing the street, shifting the child in his arms so he could talk with him face-to-face. "My bell rang down there in the shop and for the first time in four years, I didn't hear it. How can you have me so hypnotized?"

Bobber's white moon-shaped face brightened at the playful timbre of Rick's voice, his lopsided grin of exasperation. "Anyway, thanks for not letting out a war whoop from the stockroom. I would've made the proper introductions. But as it was, buddy, she was absolutely too sassy to deserve it. Still, I gotta confess," he relented in a sigh, "seeing her in the flesh after all these years set the old heart to thumpin'."

The baby jammed a fat fist in his mouth, his blue saucer eyes wide and inquisitive. As Rick rambled on, the baby sucked on, drool rolling down between the folds of his double chin.

"I know what you're thinking, Bobber. Yesterday I said I could pull her into the caper with no trouble at all, if she had the guts to come within smooching range. Well, I did it. Kissed her, I mean. But there is obviously a limit to the hotshot magic. Male arrogance is the culprit here, my boy. Avoid letting it run your life once your drooling days are over."

Rick sighed again, running his thumbs through the baby's fine red hair. "No matter what, the law firm will be zooming in on this street within days, considering all the time James spent around here. That's why I've got you stashed away, isn't it, buddy? Of course, Ramsey's million-dollar reward is going to accelerate the law firm's investigation. That's what finally gave me the courage to call Caron this morning. A call I've been putting off for a week. She was my only hope of getting a sneak peek at Ramsey before he gets one of us."

Rick stared off into space for a moment, reliving their kiss, chock-full of unfulfilled passions and promises. Their mutual needs would remain in ungratified limbo it seemed. Though the static was still there, aged to high voltage. The air was thick with it, before they touched. Before they even spoke! he realized in retrospect.

Their desires were a ticking ten-year time bomb bound to explode before the heir controversy was settled once and for all. It was a certainty, because she would be back. Not right away, of course. She'd turn over every leaf in the neighborhood, drill every potential heir who marched into her office with a claim. Her pride would keep her sniffing out every clue around him. But she would ultimately return. He hoped it would be in time to still go ahead with his plan.

Bobber released a contented coo as Rick drew him back to his shoulder and rocked to and fro in the creaky old chair. "Sure, I would've liked nothing better than to take her into my confidence, Bob. Back in the really old kissing-game days I told her everything. But that was before she blossomed into a young woman, an articulate scholar. Of course, there were some high times after that, when I thought maybe I could match wits with her, regain the special bond we once had. But even taking on the student council presidency didn't give me enough mental prowess to overtake her for anything lasting. Even the prom ended badly. My last chance with the only girl who'd ever challenged me a whit. I walked away with a sandwich in my cummerbund. That's class, Bob. With a capital C."

Rick grinned as Bobber gurgled in an effort to join in. "You're right, man. I have to concentrate on our billion-dollar mission. Our news is big, Bob. And it can't be hushed up again once out of the bag. We owe it to James to follow his instructions. No matter how hot a babe is, a man's loyalty to a dying wish is top priority.

"Ah, you should've known her back then," Rick murmured, growing groggy himself from the motion of the chair. "She had a unique round beauty in the old days. A verbal pistol, but somehow warm and humane, too. I don't understand why she went and took such a stuffy job. Or why she had that silly nose job. There was something quite nice about it the way it was...."

THE SILHOUETTE OF MAN and baby in the apartment window, gently rocking together in a bath of yellow lamplight, made a moving picture on the street below. Caron stared at the red brick building for the longest time, finding it difficult to tear herself away from the touching scene.

She'd been sitting behind the wheel of her blue Saturn collecting her thoughts, when a light had flicked on in the picture window above the Laundromat. Caron hadn't known it was Rick's apartment until he moved into view, seating himself in the rocker with the baby. She'd drawn the key away from the ignition, frozen at the wheel.

So much for faith! The wily lout had the baby in his possession the whole time. Even though she'd pleaded for some gesture of good will, he'd remained silent through it all!

Yet, the sight of the pair nipped at her heart. Rick still had the power to send her, all right. She watched his head move in animation, no doubt conversing with the child. A lullaby perhaps? A fairy tale? The baby eventually fell against the wide breadth of his shoulder like a rag doll, at home in the cradle of his sinewy arms.

But that baby wasn't at home at all, she reminded herself, shaking out of her reverie. She was willing to bet her hard-earned sheepskin on it. No wonder Rick didn't want Ramsey to start investigating his personal life. Rick had all the evidence needed to seal the case. A good twenty-five pounds' worth!

"OH CARON!"

Caron halted in the courthouse hallway Thursday morning at her mother's shrill voice. A cursory look around convinced her there was no time to slip behind one of the marble pillars. No time to meld into the bustle of the lunchtime crowd. Deborah Carlisle had her trapped, cornered for the sort of confrontation she called conversation.

"At last!" Deborah, handsomely decked out in a smart beige suit, her dark blond hair cropped and stiff with spray, skidded to a smooth stop before her daughter.

"Hello, Mom," Caron greeted, unconsciously clenching her teeth. Mother and daughter suffered from nature's curse of opposing personalities. Caron's wealth of feelings and her keen sensitivity for her fellow man hovered just beneath the surface. Deborah's nerves of steel and shallow values were buried beneath a buffer of extremely thick skin.

Deborah raised a clutch purse to her small, slightly heaving chest. "Didn't you see me? Didn't you hear me? I was right behind you."

Caron shrugged helplessly, forcing brightness into her tone. "Did you sit in on the trial today?"

"Yes, darling. What a wonderful speech you gave

at the end," Deborah enthused, clasping her hands together. "Not one complaint from the other side."

Caron smiled wryly. "Objections aren't permitted during the final argument."

"Of course, of course," Deborah conceded in airy dismissal. "I must say that I'm surprised you didn't notice me in there. You usually do."

Indeed Caron did! Her keen internal defenses usually announced Mother Carlisle's courtroom appearances by drawing to attention the little hairs on the back of Caron's neck. Had since the fraud case where Deborah had stood up to voice an objection to something the judge said. It took some fast talking to avoid a fine that time. Deborah stayed away from court for three blissful weeks.

"It seems to me that asking for thousands of dollars for sexual harassment is a little greedy though, dear," Deborah chided, patting her golden shell of hair.

Caron summoned patience from the depths of her soul. "Mother, if we'd have asked for a quarter, they may have given us just a nickel. Understand?"

Deborah rolled her attractive hazel eyes, sabotaged with a heavy layer of mascara and green shadow. "Heaven knows I try. But the fuss seems so inflated for the crime."

"Mother, my client is in therapy. She's truly suffering." Caron drew a breath as if to continue, then clamped her mouth shut again. Deborah was in true form today and nothing would sway her. She'd never held a job outside the home, but still felt she could put a price tag on the serious charge of harassment in the workplace. But why not? Caron mused sourly. Deborah compulsively put a price tag on everything.

Measured all situations by her own set of narrow-minded values and personal value of a dollar.

"Let's talk about something fun," Deborah suggested, raising a finger to Caron's face to fluff the strands of brown hair curving her cheek.

Caron shifted her purse and briefcase from one hand to another in a fidgety movement. She'd been planning to stop by Hotshots while the jury deliberated. Knowing that the baby was there was driving her crazy. But it was the last thing she cared to confide to her mother, who still indulged in negative reminiscences about Hotshot himself. Deborah never forgave him for breezing into Truman High politics with bulging muscles and a flawless face, usurping Caron from the president's position on the student council. "Never cracked a book but always had a charming crack," Mother Carlisle said at the time. She'd spent the year trying to unseat Rick through the faculty to no avail.

Of course, there was the prom incident to cap off the year. Her gentle father had been distressed over the time she'd eventually arrived home. Her mother went wild over the stain on her sateen gown. The price tag had been outrageous, on the dress and on the evening itself. Deborah had ranted to the neighbors afterward, proclaiming it the crowning touch of Rick's high school antics. Caron had crawled into her summer job at the library during the sultry months of controversy. Deborah had milked it for all it was worth, one last hurrah before the class of '83 dispersed into adulthood. Deborah's friendship with Eleanor Wyatt, often on shaky ground because of the children, was utterly destroyed by it. Considering the feud with the Wyatts still stood firm to this day, Caron hoped to keep Rick's connection to the billionaire baby a secret.

"I see you took advantage of the sale at Brooks," Deborah was chirping as she scanned Caron's blue wool blazer and gray A-line skirt, oblivious to Caron's rattled state of mind.

"Yes, I bought this suit and two others."

Deborah lifted a carefully plucked brow. "Something a little jazzy too, I hope."

"You know I need separate outfits for court," she fired back in timeworn explanation. "I did buy something more colorful, though, something I spotted in Reed's window. A bold color-block jacket with a matching miniskirt."

"The one with the yellow lapels?" Deborah asked, cringing her face for the worst.

"Yes, Mom!"

"Yellow doesn't suit you, dear," she said in crisp judgment. "You have a winter complexion."

"This is a lemon yellow, not a gold one."

"Yellows can be tremendously tricky," she maintained dubiously.

"Bought a matching hat, too," Caron confided with a smirk. "Little felt cloche."

"Yellow?"

"Lemony lemon," she confided in exaggerated urgency.

"Oh, my stars." Deborah clapped her own cheeks for effect, careful not to disturb her makeup.

Caron pushed back the sleeve of her blazer and stole a glance at her watch.

Deborah's thin brows arched in discontent. "In a hurry, are you?"

"It is lunchtime," Caron attempted.

"I'd skip a few lunches here and there if you want to wear that block suit well," she advised on the QT, as if masking a family scandal.

"I am in control of my own body," Caron objected in a clear voice. "And skipping meals is no way to stay healthy."

"My daughter the lawyer thinks she's a doctor now!" Deborah lamented. "I've kept this figure for thirty years by munching on lettuce leaves at lunch."

"Nice chatting with you, Mom."

Deborah caught her arm as Caron began to edge into the crowd. She pulled her back with a yank. "You don't even know why I'm here," she chided. "I spent the entire morning thinking of you."

"Mom—"

"It just so happens I bought you a gift," she tempted in singsong. "For Saturday night's affair…"

Caron whirled back, her eyes boring into her mother's. "What affair?"

"I know all about your invitation to the Ramsey estate," she returned, pursing her lips smugly. "I stopped by your office this morning looking for you and that nice Mr. Peterson told me all about it."

Caron took delight in mentally placing the talkative partner over a pit of zealous prosecutors.

"This is *the* social gala, my dear daughter," Deborah gushed with reverence. "I overheard a couple of women discussing it at the spa last week. Oh, if only I'd known then that my daughter was going! I'd have told 'em a thing or two!" She paused to scowl. "Of course if your father had better connections at the bank, we'd have our own invitation. He has the salary now, but none of the clout."

"Father is wonderful just the way he is," Caron automatically asserted.

"I'm sure you and the partners have some sort of prearrangement," Deborah said pitifully. "No extra tickets, I suppose."

Tickets? Caron grimaced. It wasn't a production of *Hamlet* at the Denver Center of Performing Arts! Of course, to Deborah such an event would be a stage performance. "By invitation only, Mom," she calmly voiced aloud. "You know how social etiquette works."

"Especially for the cream of society. So hard to break in."

Caron had grown accustomed to her mother's thirst for a sip of that cream. When Deborah left the Truman High neighborhood for Raspberry Hills Village, she had high hopes of joining the ranks of the elite. She had managed to finagle and harangue her way up the social ladder a rung or two, but that was all. She was still trying.

"This really is a business affair for the law firm, Mom," she firmly explained. "Douglas Ramsey is a client."

"I read all about that billionaire baby in the papers yesterday," she forged on with a pouty look. "Of course I never figured you to be involved, until Mr. Peterson told me."

"It's been confidential to this point," she protested in excuse.

"But this connection could be priceless to us— you—socially," Deborah chided in excitement. "Caron, you might find the missing baby yourself. To think that you might be the little mite's savior!"

Deborah would explode if she knew that Hotshot

had his hands on the baby, that he wished to be master of the boy's fate. Caron suppressed a smirk as she pondered the possibilities. What if Rick ended up with a cool million because he happened to befriend James Ramsey, gain the late man's trust? What if her mother eventually came to the ironic realization that she herself could've made the Ramsey family social connection through James, had she not fled her old neighborhood for the fancy suburbs?

Leaving Deborah to watch the facts unfold in the newspaper in days to come, to sort out the shoulda-beens and coulda-beens all on her own, seemed like the most satisfying and self-preserving thing to do.

"I really must dash now," Caron said.

"All right. You can walk me to my car, feast your eyes on the most exquisite dress ever. You'll never guess the color. Not in a hundred years."

Caron bit her lip. "Rose?"

"Yes, my darling, yes. We'll get it right this time round," her mother assured. "Finally, another night at the ball, my Cinderella. With no padded hips and no permanent punch stains. No Hotshot!" Her rejoicing laughter echoed through the high-ceilinged hallway, causing heads to turn. "Mr. Peterson said you had no date," she mumbled on the downbeat as they approached the elevator.

Caron rolled her eyes. "It's fine with me. I consider it more of a business event than anything else."

"How about that Paul Drake?"

Caron froze in her tracks. "Who, Mother?"

"The pleasant young man who called me the other night looking for your unlisted telephone number."

Caron drew an astonished breath. "So *you* gave it out!"

"He did call at a hideous hour, but such a charming man. And considering it was concerning a high school reunion..." she trailed off, as if giving an adequate excuse.

A reunion for two, anyhow! Caron bit her lip hard, swallowing back the laughter. Rick must've called her mother right before he called her.

"Oh, he sounds just delicious," Deborah chattered on, as they stepped into the elevator. "Said he's single and runs his own detective agency in California."

"Certainly a scrumptious catch," Caron concurred wryly. Despite his proclamations of charitable intentions, Rick certainly still had a rebellious streak in him. Imagine, getting her number in the most daring way possible. Pushing Deb's buttons with promises of a reunion to show off Caron's achievements. Intimating his availability as a single professional man. The most mischievous part of the stunt, of course, was introducing himself as Paul Drake, prosperous private detective, knowing full well that Deb would make an utter fool of herself the moment she tried to brag about him to anyone else. Unlike the majority of Americans, her mother had little time for television or mystery novels, so therefore wouldn't recognize the name of Perry Mason's fictional sidekick.

This was just the sort of scam that made Rick shine. He knew it would make her laugh. He was so clever, so street smart. Oh, how anxious she was to get back to his place. Because of the baby, of course!

4

IT WAS NEARLY four o'clock that afternoon when Caron finally pulled her Saturn into an angled parking slot in front of Hotshots. She sat back for a moment to catch her breath, to think back on the times when she'd been among the teenagers on the sidewalk lining the strip of storefronts.

The area looked older in the stark sunlight, older than it had during her school days, older than it had under last night's cover of darkness. Still, the shops were well kept. Rick's Laundromat was positioned between an ancient music store whose window was still plastered with posters featuring the latest trends in tunes, and Marshall's Market, the mom and pop headquarters for after-school snacks and milk on the run. Rick's building had originally housed a shoe store patronized by the elderly. Clever Hotshot certainly had had a vision when he transformed it into a thriving business, catering to all ages, judging by those entering and exiting.

Some things had changed, some things had not.

Despite the fact that the jury had deliberated only two short hours over her sexual harassment case, delivering a very favorable verdict on behalf of her client, despite the fact that she was dressed in one of her power suits, Caron still felt every bit as insecure as the students now passing by her windshield no doubt did.

Rick Wyatt made her feel that way! she inwardly lamented, rapping the dashboard with disgust. His insensitive treatment of yesterday, along with her mother's callous insistence that she was never good enough, were the seeds that made her the insecure woman she was today.

But she was pretty enough! Logic told her so over and over again. Megan told her so as well.

Caron had no illusions of ever being able to straighten out her mother. But Rick was another matter entirely. Enticing him into pursuit, solid proof of her desirability, would be the ultimate triumph. She'd tossed and turned the night away analyzing her own motives and feelings. The slinky suit had been—though rather unconsciously—the first move in a strategy for seduction. She wanted to reach Hotshot on a purely animal level. Prove to both of them that she was too beautiful for him to resist. In her mind, this would cancel out his rejection years ago. She was getting to him already. It seemed to be on a purely angry level, but at least he was thinking about her....

Caron's frivolous mission was completely out of her sensible character. But the notion of blowing him out of the water had escalated steadily in her mind since his call. She wanted to down him so badly her ears nearly rang from the pressure. If she finally managed to make herself his obsession, she'd never feel unattractive again. She'd have conquered the best.

But there was the baby to consider first and foremost. With effort, she turned her thoughts back to the business at hand. An innocent boy's future depended upon her.

Caron eluded the heat of the October sunshine by ducking under Rick's brown-fringed awning. The large canvas cover, obviously fashioned for the cowhide look, had apparently been folded up last night, escaping her attention. Suddenly it occurred to her that the inside of the place was nothing but a dark, murky memory of machines and shadows. Blending in with a cluster of giggly girls, she tried to peek through the front windowpane. Wooden slat blinds tilted shut made it impossible, however. Just desserts, considering that her energies had been funneled into being the scenery, not absorbing it. Summoning courage on a deep breath, Caron turned the knob and gave the sticky wooden door a shove.

The bell didn't jingle into an intimate, quiet room this time. Her entrance was lost in the hubbub of bright lights, laughter-laced chatter and grinding machines.

She certainly wouldn't be striking a provocative pose on dryer number seven again, she thought with a look at the machine. It was currently being stuffed full of undershirts by a potbellied man with more hair in his ears than on his head.

So this was Rick's wonderland during visitor's hours. She rotated on her heel, drinking in the western motif. Who'd have ever imagined Hotshot to be a closet cowboy beneath his old leather jacket and streetwise lingo? Yet, in the light of day, there was no denying the Colorado country theme of the huge carnival of a room. The walls of knotty pine served as the backdrop for an elk's head, prairie sketches and a variety of wood and stone bric-a-brac. The slow twang of a Willie Nelson ballad erupted from ceiling speakers, crackling along with the tuneless drone of the machines.

Had she ever really known him? The uncertainty made this moment even tougher. Caron liked predictability. She prepared all of her moves as she did for her cases, with meticulous caution.

Caron soon realized that Rick had meant it when he said that he controlled all the moves on his turf. He was standing near the washers, enchanting the socks—and Lord only knew what else—off a tight circle of females. Duded up in black jeans, a red-and-black plaid shirt and scuffed black boots, he was definitely dressed for show. No matter how strong his detergent, how amusing his roomful of games, Hotshot himself was the major attraction. It reminded her of the way he'd held court in the Truman High halls. Hip and sexy, spouting all the right lines. As his rich laughter floated up into the soap-scented air, Caron wondered if anyone ever really changed under the skin. Could he be the sensitive, caring man he claimed?

"Still have your girls, I see."

Rick's head snapped up as he caught her teasing salvo above the din. He regarded her with a measure of surprise over the top of a fiftyish blonde. Something crossed his chocolate brown eyes beneath those luxuriant black lashes. Hope? Anticipation?

"Just demonstrating how a spritz of hair spray can remove ink from cotton," he announced. He turned back to his women to add, "Blot with a towel and add it to your load."

"Aren't you Deb's daughter?" a feminine voice abruptly exclaimed.

Caron turned to find her former next-door neighbor standing behind her. "How are you, Mrs. Bernside?" she asked, delightedly clasping the older woman's hand.

"Just fine, Caron. My, my, you've turned out lovely," she said after a head-to-toe inspection. "Simply lovely."

"Thank you," Caron murmured, a warm tug at her heart. This was a woman who had on many occasions listened to her dreams, her fears, fulfilling the patient caretaking role her own mother never could quite master. "How's Sharon?" she asked, inquiring after Mrs. Bernside's daughter.

"She and Dean have given me two darling grandchildren," Judy proudly reported.

Caron began to pick out other familiar faces in the circle of stain students. They were the mothers of her former classmates, the same women who had disliked and feared Rick, who had made every attempt to shield their precious daughters from him. Now they were patronizing his place, hanging out right along with the new generation of kids! Perhaps he had truly turned over a new leaf. Or perhaps this was the challenge of a lifetime for an amorous con artist with a chip on his shoulder.

"Hey, Rick, you gotta get this babe!" a skinny teenage boy with yellow hair called out from the air hockey table against the back wall. "Can't ruin your record, man."

"He'll come through," his small, dark competitor chimed in, giving the blonde a high five above the table.

Caron folded her arms across her chest, lifting her chin as Rick swaggered her way with group approval. Ever so slowly he rolled up one plaid sleeve, then the other, over his thick forearms. He was peeling back power, sinewy muscle under taut, hair-dusted skin.

This wasn't going at all as she'd planned it. He was already calling the shots again, as he had with their kiss last night. Hoping to escape, she jerked her eyes up to his face. Another trap, she realized with heart-stopping fright as they locked into a single intense beam of his 'n' hers.

His eyes were full of surprise most of all. Naturally he hadn't expected her back so soon. But what disturbed her was the mischief twinkling in their chocolate depths. He was up to something that was going to leave her putty once more.

"Rick..." she trailed off in hushed warning.

"Relax," he murmured under his breath. "Trust is a two-way street. If I'm gonna give some, I'm gonna get some, too." He paused for a beat, giving her a chance to dart for the exit if she wished. When she stood her ground, he turned to the boys. "Hit it!"

One of the hockey players in back dropped a quarter in the jukebox and to Caron's amazement, streams of a lively fiddle number crackled through speakers overhead.

Rick grasped Caron by the hand and yanked her to his body. She stopped short against his solid torso with a thud.

"What are you trying to pull?" she squeaked for his ears only.

"Back off a little, Caron," he chided good-humoredly, wrapping an arm around her waist over the bulk of her wool blazer. "You're too anxious."

"Anxious? Me?" Caron was fuming, steeping like a little teapot about to blow its delicate porcelain top.

This was ridiculous! She hadn't come to give a show. She was about to set him straight, when his mouth slanted in a roguish grin. He already knew she hated this display. Just as sure as he was a closet cowboy!

"This is the two-step tradition here at Hotshots," he explained calmly. "The Hotshot himself is expected to dance with each and every new lady customer."

"What if I say no?"

"Then you will be the first."

The crowd was cheering them now. Rick took the initiative, swiftly sweeping her into motion, steering down the front aisle lined with dryers.

"Still all fun and games," she griped, following his lead the best she could. A jumble of sensations surged through her, pumping her heart all the harder. Everyone had stepped back to provide a path, even the man at dryer number seven. They clapped to the beat as Rick whisked her along, forcing her to draw her feet up and down off the floor with his. As they passed by the boys in back, the dark-haired one set a worn straw cowboy hat on Rick's head.

"Whimsy is as necessary to humans as water and air," he chided in her ear. "All those years in school and you still haven't learned that simple lesson."

Caron's cry of rebuttal was lost in her throat as Rick whirled her around smartly. Hoots and howls rewarded the tricky maneuver.

"See, Caron, everybody loves a good show," he claimed proudly between breaths. She was puffing a bit herself, taken aback by the absurdity of the moment, the physical demands of the dance and Rick's downright earthy mystique.

In spite of her determination and well-tuned cardiovascular system, Caron lost her footing as they sa-shayed around the counter holding the cash register. Her heel accidentally landed on his instep, and she toppled into him in a breathless heap. He stopped short with a grunt of pain, his hands closing at her waist to right her.

"I didn't mean it," she said as they stood motion-less to the closing strains of the song. "Really, I didn't."

A burst of applause exploded from the crowd, and everyone began to drift back to their own business. Everyone but Caron and Rick. He still had a grip on her waist and had no intention of letting go.

"I bet you trample 'em in court in those heels," he eventually muttered, his eyes slits under the brim of his hat.

Caron raised her eyes from the mat of dense black hair sprouting from his open-necked shirt. "I'm proud of my performance. Though my show doesn't compare with yours, cowboy."

"You could do just as well with the right partner," he proposed silkily in her ear. "I'll come dance on your turf sometime soon and prove it. We'll really give a jury something to deliberate."

Caron peeled his hands from her body with ur-gency. "You will always be a wise ass."

"You came back for more."

"Maybe I'm a customer."

"Maybe I'm not sellin' any," he growled back in surprise.

"The customer's always right."

He pushed up the brim of his hat, drawing his face to hers. "The customer got the brush yesterday."

"Still too slick, Rick."

"Still too mouthy, Caron."

"I know about that baby, you oversexed rebel," she ground out.

Rick drew short. "You think I'm too sexy?"

"I think you're just plain too much!" she shot back in exasperation.

A high-pitched squall pierced the air all of a sudden, paralyzing them both. A teenage girl with frizzy blond hair, dressed in a hot pink jumpsuit, shuffled forward with a carrot-topped bundle squirming in her arms. "Hey, Rick, you didn't say anything about fixing leaks."

"Give him to me, Hayley," Rick directed in resignation, opening his arms to receive the fussy child. He set him in the crook of his arm to examine the large wet spot darkening the inside leg of his blue-and-white striped suit. "Ask the hired help to do you a favor…" He nuzzled his mustache into the baby's tear-stained cheek, favoring the teen with a disgruntled look.

Hayley shrugged. "Sorry, man. Pay me a plumber's wage and I'll fix all the leaks you want."

"Get back to your broom." Setting his hat on her head, he shooed her off.

Caron favored him with a smug look. "I saw you holding him in the window last night."

"Guess the jig's up, Bobber," he surrendered with a sigh. "Caught by a peeping Tom."

"Short for Robert?" Caron quizzed in hope.

"Short for Thomas, I'd say."

"You're impossible!"

"Your nose is too short now," he complained. "I want you to know that, Caron."

"Oh, for Pete's sake!" she lamented, throwing her

hands in the air. "Listen to me, Rick. This baby changes everything. He's the best little offer I've got right now."

Rick stared at her for a long, calculating moment. "Let's settle this in the back. While I change the Bobber."

The storeroom was piled high with crates of detergent and fabric softener. A workbench and a weight bench dominated the back wall near an old wooden staircase, which Caron guessed led to Rick's overhead apartment. A freestanding sink was on the left, and beside it a worn changing table piled high with rattles and disposable diapers. Rick shut the door behind them, muffling some of the noise. "Hold onto him while I run upstairs for another suit," he directed suddenly.

Before Caron could protest, Rick thrust the fussy bundle of flesh into her arms. She handled the baby awkwardly, attempting to brace his back with one hand, pushing his head against her lapel with the other. Already uncomfortable and ornery, he sensed her inexperience and let out a yowl. "Now, now, Bobber. Do you want the world to know that I'm at a loss with miniatures like you?" She pressed her lips against his temple, finding his wispy head of red hair soft and mildly fragrant. Under calmer circumstances, holding him might be a treasured moment, a chance to learn the finer points of the task. As it was, he writhed and kicked with all his might, preferring to lunge into the unknown rather than tolerate her.

"Tormenting another generation of males, I see," Rick mocked upon his return. With easy movements he set the whimpering baby on the table and peeled off his wet clothing.

Caron paced around the cramped room. Just like the front, this stock area was cluttered. "You know, if you put things in order, worked out some sort of system, you'd have a lot more space to move about. It would really increase your efficiency."

"As it happens, I believe things here are extremely efficient," Rick countered. "I make a good profit. My customers are delighted with the atmosphere. In short, I am a rousing success. This rebel soared beyond the neighborhood's expectations and made good. On my own terms," he added with emphasis.

"That's the only way you could ever do it," Caron relented.

"Being inventive has given me a lot of satisfaction," he boasted eagerly. "There are thousands of orderly Laundromats all over the country that follow your expectations. But this place is more than just a place to wash clothes. It's a second home to a lot of nice people. We watch all the big games on my wide screen television. We have pool tournaments. We even have the occasional karaoke contest."

"Don't forget your dances," Caron added wryly. "With each and every new babe."

"It's all in fun," Rick said. "Get me one of those wipes from the blue box on the windowsill."

Caron peeled a moist cloth out of the plastic container and brought it to the changing table. "Rick, I can't help but wonder if you're carrying this king-of-the-neighborhood thing too far. No matter how noble the gesture, hiding an infant from his relatives without cause can land you in deep trouble."

"I never said Bobber was the Ramsey baby," he cautioned. "File that fact away in your orderly noggin." He folded the soaked diaper in two and handed that to her. "And file this in the basket over there, please."

Caron reluctantly obliged, stopping to wash her hands at the sink. "So, where is his mother?"

Rick shrugged, swabbing the Bobber's behind. "She, ah, had to get away for a while. Needed time to regroup."

"Because the love of her life died," Caron swiftly speculated.

He turned to her with a flick of annoyance. "I never said the mother was in love with James Ramsey."

"Oh, you're as slippery as ever!"

"And you're still marching to your own conservative drummer," he accused reaching for a fresh diaper. "Still trying to fit in with people who don't know squat about the real joys."

Caron wandered over to finger the baby's eiderdown curls. "You've never had to concern yourself with fitting in, have you? You always managed to slide along as the big man, dazzling them with your charm. I've had to work harder for my place."

"I doubt it," he differed mildly. "What do you think a rebel does once the diplomas are handed out and the spotlight dims?"

"I wouldn't know," Caron promptly admitted. "I went on to school with a full scholarship and worked my tail off."

"I took the less scenic route and climbed up off the street," Rick assured, busily clothing the baby with fresh things. "My journey was a little different, Caron, but I've been knocked around by life like everyone else. I too have the customary dues statement stamped paid in full—for this decade, anyhow." He turned to regard her with a forthright expression.

"How can we ever reach a compromise in this jam we're in? One minute in my arms and you step on my foot."

Caron closed her eyes briefly to veil her uncertainty. How could she tell him she tripped because being in his proximity still turned her to Jell-O? That grazing his body had left her a stumbling, bumbling idiot? She wanted to be the alluring one this time!

"Your feelings for me are shading your sense," he accused.

Though the statement was true, Rick had no concept of her feelings for him. Never had. And much to her own bewilderment, Hotshot was one subject she couldn't pin down in definitive terms. He cluttered her heart and her mind in much the same way junk cluttered his shop. No rhyme, no reason. No cure.

"Caron, we are down to the wire here. Your own detectives will find out about me soon. You're either with me all the way, or out there with them."

Caron stared mutely at the thumb he was tilting toward the street. The thought of being left out of his world devastated her. She already knew it to be the coldest, loneliest place on earth. She raised her thumb and finger an inch apart. "Give me something, Rick," she requested in a small voice. "Something to convince me that we won't land up in federal prison on kidnapping charges."

"I happen to be carrying out James Ramsey's last wishes," he confessed, raw emotion fanning lines around his eyes. "At least I'm trying to. You see, James began to regret telling his Aunt Agatha about the baby. He knew if she spilled the beans to Douglas, there would be inquiries. He didn't want his child to deal with the old man if it just wasn't right. Get it?"

"Why you, Rick?" she asked, struggling to understand this complicated man's sense of loyalty.

"James and I were close," he said softly, cuddling the baby possessively. "He was a beloved member of this tight-knit family neighborhood."

"It's such an awesome responsibility!" Caron exclaimed, trying to ignore the tug at her heart as Rick planted a kiss on Bobber's head. To be loved so thoroughly by Rick must be heaven on earth. "You are at the helm of the heir's destiny for cryin' out loud."

Rick's jaw settled into a grumpy line. "That's the way James wanted it, I tell you. Is it so hard to believe that he could entrust me with such an important task?"

It was! And she knew it was written all over her face.

"I was hoping you'd take my word for it, help me on faith. But that obviously isn't meant to be." Rick gave her the baby once again and withdrew his wallet from his back pocket.

Caron drew a heart-pounding breath, causing the sober baby to glare up at her suspiciously. Did he have the Ramsey medal in there?

But it was a folded sheet of paper he extracted from the credit card holder. "It just so happens that James put his wishes in writing. I guess he sensed the end was near, that he might never see me again." Rick blinked long black lashes. "He didn't."

Caron traded the baby for the paper. Unfolding it under his scrutiny made her feel like a heel. She couldn't lower her eyes to the page.

"C'mon, read it, satisfy your doubts." When she continued to focus on him, he growled in anger. "Let me start you out. 'Dear Rick...'" Caron's gaze dropped to the letter as Rick began to recite it word for word.

It is with sincere affection that I write this note of goodbye. It is up to you to decide upon the inheritance. I would have done so myself, had I been stronger at the end. You, young man, must be my strength. Check out my stonehhearted father, Douglas. If he doesn't meet your standards, back off! I trust you to do what's best.

Love, James

"He even signed it with love, Caron. This is family. This is commitment."

Caron refolded the letter and carefully stuffed it in his shirt pocket, giving Bobber's bottom an awkward pat. "It's so hard for me to improvise...." She trailed off under his strained features, again searching for words that wouldn't hurt him any further.

"I respect your standards, Caron," he said quietly, swaying in place to soothe the baby.

"You most certainly do not!" she cried in awe.

"Okay, I don't," he confessed, with the pout of a boy caught playing hooky. "I think you're being difficult when you could be easy, just like always. At least you gotta admit I've shown you some good faith here. I've laid out a big-time ace, shared with you an extremely personal note that no one else will ever see. Still you hesitate!"

"If I could just talk to the mother. Maybe she has the proper heirloom. That would seal up the doubts for everyone."

Rick pinched her lips closed with his fingers.

"Leave her out of this for now, okay? James asked me to set it right."

Caron pushed his hand away. She wanted to be fair. And she certainly had the right claim. The letter proved it beyond a doubt. If only she could let her guard down with Rick. But she knew better than to risk her heart with the Hotshot.

"You should understand James's doubts about Ramsey," he continued on. "You know the old guy is pretty crusty at times."

"I guess I could give you one chance at him," she relented wearily. "I'm invited to a party at his place Saturday night. He said I should bring an escort."

"That shindig reported in the papers?" he asked in delight. "Sounds perfect!"

"I'll pick you up around seven-fifteen," she told him, turning on her heel to leave.

"Yes! My record's complete!"

She whirled back in fury to find him twirling Bobber in the air like a pudgy, squeaky, red-nosed missile. "What do you mean?"

"You are the last girl in the class of '83 to officially date the Hotshot," he teased. "All eighty-one are now accounted for."

"What bunk!" Caron scoffed suspiciously.

"I swear it's true," Rick insisted with an indolent shrug.

"Take my roommate, Megan Gage, for instance," she quickly challenged.

"I did." Rick's grin was infuriating as he turned the baby in his arms to face her. "Tell her to go home and ask, Bobber."

"Eat dirt, Wyatt!"

"See ya Saturday, Quick Draw."

Caron marched full tilt through the front and out the door, nearly colliding with Judy Bernside on the sidewalk outside. The elder woman's arms were full of folded blankets.

"Let me help you," Caron offered breathlessly as the stack began to tumble.

"Thanks, dear. I'm parked right over here." Mrs. Bernside circled a burgundy sedan, opening the back door on the driver's side. She proceeded to stack the blankets on the seat, two at a time.

"Looks like you're sprucing up the bedding," Caron observed.

"Rick's large capacity machines sure come in handy during my fall and spring cleaning sprees," she explained, closing the door with a satisfied thud. "So nice to see you again, Caron," she said, digging her car keys out of her purse. She paused and scrutinized Caron with a sigh. "I still can't get over it. You looking so striking. Your mother must be proud...."

"In her own way perhaps," Caron replied with a wan smile.

Judy Bernside nodded in understanding. "You were one of Sharon's nicest friends back in school. I knew you'd do well."

"I suppose you're wondering what I'm doing here today," Caron ventured.

"Doing at a Laundromat with no laundry?" Judy's blue eyes lit up merrily, her voice betraying her curiosity. "Rick does get a lot of visitors from your class. It's sort of a watering hole for those old pals who wish to keep in touch." Her tongue clicked as she realized her blunder.

Caron made light of it with a laugh. "I never was part of that crowd. Rick and I were sparring partners, nothing more. I was here today—" She checked herself in midsentence, realizing she could no longer tell this woman everything with teenage impulsiveness. "Actually, Rick has a legal matter that needs attention."

"Well, he couldn't be in more capable hands, I'm sure," she said, squeezing Caron's hand. "Did him good to face a woman who didn't melt in his arms."

"That dance gimmick must get him a lot of mileage," Caron wagered.

"Mmm, yes. All in all, it is a positive thing. So many people like the romantic nonsense of it all. Still," she said with a smirk, "it was a lark to see no swoon in your step."

Caron bit her lip. No simple swoon for her. She'd clumsily plunged into his arms with a painful stomp!

"Well, don't let him give you a run for that retainer," Judy advised in farewell.

"I won't," Caron promised warmly. "The baby certainly is cute," she ventured casually.

"Bob? Bobby?" Judy laughed. "Doll baby, that one."

"He belong to a neighbor?"

Judy paused in thought. "Why, I don't know. It's just like Rick to help out someone in need, though. He's as generous as the day is long. Mind you, he still has that smooth, wily streak in him. Just as always. Some of the old biddies round here think he's reborn, that it was their stern attention years ago that turned him around." She hooted at the idea. "Rick's parents raised him and the three others just fine without any interference. Sure they were a ragtag bunch of kids. Sort of spoiled perhaps because the mister and missus were so grateful to have adopted so many."

The Wyatt children were adopted? What an intriguing revelation. But what a practical explanation! Rick's own circumstance was most likely fueling his emotions concerning Bobber, driving him on to find the baby's rightful place. "I didn't realize Rick was adopted."

Judy nodded in understanding. "Hard to believe, considering how well they all blended. Most folks didn't know. The Wyatts moved in with the four of them already in tow. I suppose Eleanor was fearful her kids would be set apart from the others if the news leaked out. Of course it doesn't matter now that they're all grown. But Rick," she said, shifting gears, "he was a charmer from the word go. Nothing those ladies did or did not do fazed him any. It's wonderful that he's managed to polish his charm and funnel his skills into something useful."

"Still the same under the skin, however," Caron ventured in judgment.

"Yes, that's just the way it is," she agreed with a jingle of her keys. "Once a hotshot, always a hotshot."

5

"LIFT THAT LEG just a little higher. Let it pull just a bit farther than last time...."

Caron groaned in unison with the other leotard-clad women lying on the exercise-room floor at the Ladies Only Fitness Club. Along with Megan, she was a regular on Thursday nights from six-thirty to eight-thirty.

With a fresh law degree and a grinding determination to be a lean, mean litigator, Caron had enrolled in the club's complete program of diet and exercise. And how it had worked! Since then this workout of aerobics and calisthenics had become a religious ritual, a spiritual as well as a physical exercise. The heart pumped and the soul vented. The most noble of quests for personal caretaking.

So why in the world was she thinking of Rick Wyatt with every hip roll, every leg lift? All of their differences slid to the background as she invited his sexy image into her mental comfort zone. He was luring her to carnal thoughts with his flashing dark eyes and luscious-looking mouth. It was as if he were right there. Almost.

She moved her right leg up and down, trying to kick the fantasy away to the beat of a popular Janet Jackson song. But the ploy didn't work. The more she kicked, the clearer he became, stretched out before her, face-to-face on the floor.

Eventually she abandoned the battle. With lids hooded to shield her naughty thoughts, she indulged in some personal exercise erotica, allowing Rick to possess her every pore. To claim her like a man on fire. Soon she was aflame, lost in her own imagination.

The music eventually stopped with shattering abruptness, leaving her alone and untouched. Caron snapped her eyes open and ankles shut at the same moment, scanning her fellow huffers for any reaction. It was a ridiculous feeling, suspecting that someone might be privy to her private pleasures. No one could read her mind.

Jennifer, the group's lanky blond leader, bounced to her feet at the mirrored wall up front, motioning them all to follow suit. "Great job, ladies. Especially you, Caron," she marveled. "You really got into the workout. It helps to let yourself go. To give in so totally."

With a small self-conscious smile Caron shifted from one foot to another, pulling her creeping red leotard back over the curve of her bottom. If one only dared do it in real life.

As Jennifer rummaged through her box of cassettes, a tardy Megan Gage entered the room with a sheepish grin on her pert face. She paused at the bench against the side wall to peel off her jeans and sloppy sweatshirt down to the pink leotard and tights underneath. She skipped into her regular spot beside her roommate, fingering her head of mussy golden curls.

"I must look a fright," she gasped to Caron. "I ran

over to Talbot Center to do some shopping this afternoon and lost track of the time. Did I miss anything?"

"It seems not," Caron retorted, simmering over Rick's claim to have once made it with this trusted friend.

Megan looked puzzled. "What's the matter with you? You lose your case today?"

"No, I won."

"Then it must be Rick," she rattled on, doing some quick arm stretches. "Did you confront him about the baby? Tell him you caught him in the window?"

"I did," Caron affirmed tightly. "And he told me something. About the two of you."

Megan froze, her face draining of color. "He told you about me?"

"Just a teaser," Caron uttered under her breath. "Maybe you could supply the details."

"I will," she promised defensively with a toss of her head. "Later."

Later couldn't come soon enough for Caron. When the roommates made their usual stop at the club's snack bar after class, the mood was far from festive. They sat stoically at one of the small round tables in the ice-cream parlor atmosphere, sipping on apple spice iced tea, glaring over the rims of their tall, cool glasses.

"Can't you see what you're doing to yourself, Caron?" Megan lamented. "You're falling into the same old pattern with Rick."

"Hey, I'm mad at you," Caron fired back. "Don't try to pull that exasperated buddy stuff on me."

Megan shook her head, keeping rein on the conversation. "I never would've encouraged you to check him out, had I known you'd crumble into a million pieces all over again. I thought it would be a lark for you to face the ghost of prom past, wallop him with your charms."

"I believe Rick may still have the same potent effect on me as chocolate fudge cake," Caron philosophized remorsefully. "Both have proven far easier to resist when separated from my senses."

Megan rolled her expressive blue eyes. "You and your penchant for sweets. For Rick." She fidgeted with her glass on the tabletop under Caron's expectant gaze. "What did Rick tell you about me?"

"He said he had you," Caron supplied, her anger flushing her cheeks.

"*Had* me!" Megan squealed, causing heads to turn. "In the historical saga sense?" she asked in a hush.

"Tell me about it, Megan," Caron ordered.

"Well, it was at the beginning of senior year," Megan reluctantly began. "We, ah, went to the mini golf course, then sorta made out in front of my house in his old Chevy. But believe me, Caron, we didn't get far. You know how my father was about my dating at that age. He had the yard light on within five minutes. The one we used for nighttime volleyball games," she clarified for impact.

"He claims he had every girl in the class except me," Caron flared in pain.

"He always did love to bring a gasp to your lips, didn't he?" Megan reasoned.

"But what a thing to say, if it isn't fact," Caron challenged in mortification.

"It sounds like a silly joke," Megan consoled, giving her hand a pat. "Face it, you are far more straightforward than the average person, far more precise. While it makes you a great attorney, it leaves you gnawing over some things that should be taken lightly. Many people indulge in teasing exaggeration just for fun. Rick is a master at it.''

Caron's voice remained steeped in betrayal. ''We've always shared everything as the closest of sisters would. I have no secrets from you, have I?''

''I intended to confess the next day,'' Megan claimed in good humor. ''Boy, oh, boy, I couldn't wait to tell you. Figured I had the bet snagged.''

Curiosity quelled some of Caron's anger. ''Well, didn't you?''

''The snake never did officially call me on the telephone, before or afterward. I obviously eventually backed out of telling you. You were serving on the student council with him and so wound up about it all.... The whole thing seemed better off buried.''

''I see,'' Caron conceded with effort.

''Really, Caron?'' Megan asked hopefully.

Caron nodded with fervor. ''I've been downright ridiculous.''

''We've always been the truest of friends,'' Megan assured her. ''No man has ever come between us. Not ever.''

''There was that pianist at Sonny's Grill,'' Caron reminded her.

''So there was,'' Megan relented. ''But we tickled his ivories when we caught on to his game!''

They sipped their tea between giggles.

''Caron, don't let Rick slide you into a vulnerable position,'' Megan advised hesitantly. ''Not with your job at stake.''

''He won't,'' she assured defiantly. ''He can't.''

''He still can,'' Megan differed softly. ''You nearly

cracked up when you thought he'd taken on every girl in class."

"It was silly of me to get so upset," she scoffed with a wave.

"So possessive," Megan countered with compassion. "He didn't understand the depth of your feelings for him the last time around, and I suspect he still doesn't."

Caron rubbed her temples with a sigh. "Don't tell me to back away, because I can't. Not only is he harboring a baby under suspicious circumstances, he's got a letter from James Ramsey, instructing him to act on behalf of the heir." Caron paused as Megan gasped. "He's insisted upon my discretion. And here I am, trapped into conducting useless interviews to shield him."

"Did he show you a medal?" Megan asked in a hush.

"No."

"Maybe he has the wrong baby, Caron."

Caron shook her head forcefully. "Oh, no. I recognized James's handwriting in the letter. I figure Rick doesn't trust me enough to cough the medal up yet. Figures he can always burn the note, return the baby to its mother, and claim it was all a mistake if he wants to. But if I see the medal, I can identify it for Douglas Ramsey. Rick could never escape then."

"You're considering turning him in?"

"Yes."

"So, what did you do in the end?" Megan demanded.

"I asked him on a date, of course!"

"Seriously, Caron."

Caron flushed in embarrassment. "Douglas Ramsey asked me to his bash on Saturday and I invited Rick along."

Megan's rich, husky laughter shook her tiny body. "Only you, Caron, could end up in this mess with Rick Wyatt. Just keep in mind that he really is a lot like chocolate to you—a sweet treat that goes straight to the hips. *Straight* to the hips."

"I NEVER THOUGHT I'D SEE this gorilla in a monkey suit ever again," Kyle Wyatt crowed, strolling into the storage room of Hotshots early Saturday evening.

"Just hoped to outshine you for once," Rick jeered, scanning Kyle's brown suit and striped tie. Kyle often toiled away weekends at his accounting firm, donning a suit nearly round-the-clock. Despite the fact that he almost lived in conservative attire, Rick could see him as nothing more than a gangly goof-off.

Rick was the indisputable lady-killer of the family, no matter what he wore. Tonight he was drop-dead chic, his broad-shouldered figure draped in an elegant black tuxedo with a crisp white shirt and crimson cummerbund. Seated in a battered swivel chair, his thick hair was being attended to by Hayley. The teenage Hotshots employee was not sparing the spray as she brushed his black coils back off his face to a thick ducktail cascade.

"So, when was your last formal affair, Ricky? Prom?" Kyle's question was rhetorical, the sort of dig an older brother takes at a sibling. A year younger than Kyle, Rick had always been the brunt of his brother's humor. Rick, in turn, retaliated by pestering his two little sisters, Angie and Erin, to distraction. The four of them were still on close terms, even though the girls had left the neighborhood to raise children of their own.

"Maybe if you shaved the overtime once in a while and put on a suit just for the fun of it, you'd snag a date for yourself," Rick suggested. "C-P-A meets G-A-L."

"According to the grapevine, it sounds as though you did some fancy steppin' to get this G-A-L," Kyle fired back. He watched Rick fumble with the black silk tie at his neck for a moment or two, then stepped up to the chair to slide it into a smooth bow.

"It's a little tight," Rick croaked playfully, stuffing a finger in the starched collar of his dress shirt.

"I don't doubt it," Kyle snorted. "Considering the size of your head."

"Hey, lay off the Hotshot," Hayley sniped as she spritzed and brushed with the flair of a temperamental artist. "He's on a mission."

"Yes, little lass, it was I who put Rick on to Caron Carlisle's connection with Sharp, Krandell and Peterson," Kyle smoothly accredited himself. He dropped into a wooden chair beside the changing table, stretching his long legs out on the concrete floor. With a small cowlick at the back of his sandy head and the mischievous twinkle in his hazel eyes, the twenty-nine-year-old looked more like an overgrown teenager than a businessman.

"Only a louse would've kept her bombshell looks a secret, though," Rick growled, spinning in the chair to confront his brother.

Kyle chuckled. "Hotshot on the hot seat. How sweet it is." He gazed at Rick's brooding expression with some surprise. "Hey, you aren't falling for her, are you?"

"Nothing so foolish," Rick denied, knowing better than to ever deliberately give his tormentor ammunition. His feelings for Caron at the moment were best described as ticklish—something big brother would have a field day with! Rick just didn't understand what Caron was trying to do to him. She was so flirtatious, then so guarded. So hot, then so cold. If she was responding to his behavior, he was lost, totally bewildered. Sometimes she seemed geared up in the present, and other times she would slip back to some fretful place in the past. Was she specifically disappointed in him? Was she stewing about their old duels?

"Yo, Ricky," Kyle broke in, snapping his fingers. "You sure Caron doesn't have you by the nose?"

"I'm just intrigued with the new shell on the old engine," he claimed evasively. With an angry squeal Hayley dashed his face with sticky spray.

"That's no way to talk about a girl!"

Rick winced in apology, wiping his sticky brows. "Forgot about you, kid. Sometimes you seem too young to know."

"Remember when you were sixteen, Rick," Kyle began. "Why—"

"Never mind," Rick cut in sharply, reaching out in an effort to cup Hayley's ears. She twisted away, not about to miss anything. "Just cut the chatter about my past, brother," he ordered, settling back in the chair.

Kyle raised his hands, pleading no contest. "Don't let me get you all riled up over Caron Carlisle."

"I am not riled!"

"He was like thunder when she was here the other day," Hayley reported. "Almost tossed her out."

Rick shot her a dirty look. "I am fine now. She's graciously giving me what I want. A chance to question Ramsey."

"And that's all you're after from that scrumptious creature." Kyle regarded him in doleful amusement.

"Considering the circumstances of James's last request and my duty to carry it out, I would think you'd ease up. I don't find it amusing either, that you kept her transformation from me. She put me on the spot!"

"I heard she was gorgeous," Kyle relented, raising his shoulders a fraction. "But you know I only listen to rumors for the vicarious pleasure of it. I leave the spreading of them to Ma."

"I owe you," Rick warned with a stabbing finger.

"With the tangled web you're weaving, you won't have time for me," Kyle predicted, stretching his arms above his head.

Hayley paused with brush in hand. "That web stuff is really deep, Kyle, ya know?"

"Ah, if you were a mite older, Hayley," he said with a sigh of resignation, "I'd—"

"Do her taxes," Rick cut in snidely.

Kyle sniffed in annoyance. "Ha, ha. If you seriously wanted to pump up my love life, you'd hook me up with Caron's roommate."

"Megan Gage?"

"I hear she's a nurse now," Kyle said. "I had a crush on her all the way through school."

Rick grinned. "I might do it. She and I were golfing buddies way back when...."

The jingle of the entrance bell echoed to the back.

"Since I'm officially on laundry duty tonight, I'll check it out," Kyle announced, popping out of his chair. He leaned his lanky body against the doorjamb, peering out front. "Evenin', Ma!"

Rick grinned from his chair with a knowing nod. Of course Eleanor Wyatt had to see him in his tuxedo. His parents still lived only three blocks from Fairfax in the family's green stucco rambler. She popped in often, to gossip with her friends and do an occasional load of laundry to support his business.

"Evenin', Mrs. Foley," Kyle called out in a second greeting, turning back to measure Rick's look of growing consternation.

"Evenin', Mrs. Monahan," Kyle greeted for a third round, nearly laughing out loud as Rick slapped a hand to his eyes. "Look who's here to see you off, Ricky," he reported with feigned guilelessness. "Ma. And Ma's dearest friends."

The terrible trio. At one time it had been the fearful foursome, when Caron's mother had been part of things. But between Deborah Carlisle's thirst for the big time, and the prom incident, the friendship had given way under the strain.

To Rick's relief only his mother breezed into the back room.

"Hi, Ma. How's the Bobber doing?"

"Papa's having the time of his life looking after him," Eleanor said, her round, wind-flushed face beaming. "Such a treasure."

"Sure you don't mind having him all night?" Rick asked.

"We expect you to share him," she chided, a trifle hurt.

"So, you just in the neighborhood, Ma?" Rick asked as she unbuttoned her gray cloth coat.

"I live here, remember?" she said defensively, busily tugging the knit gloves off her plump hands. She looked up suddenly, surprised to find Rick's chocolate eyes dancing in merriment. "Oh, you tease!"

"You're always welcome here, of course." Rick looked off into space, his angled jawline twitching. "What's your pleasure tonight? A quick game of pool? A little air hockey?"

"Such nonsense, Ricky!" she chided with the click of her tongue.

"You come to check me out in my threads, then?"

"Why, of course not," she scoffed. "Just came from supper at the new Chinese place, just passing by on the way to the movies."

"I see. How's the food over there?"

"Dandy and economical." She paused expectantly, then blurted out, "So stand up and let me get a look at you! You know the early show starts in fifteen minutes!"

Rick eased out of the stuffed vinyl chair. He patiently towered over the stout, gray-haired woman now circling him with the lint brush she'd slipped out of her purse. "So you were just passing by, huh?" he couldn't resist goading as she brushed at the immaculate fabric.

"I'm always out on Saturday night. Papa has his cards and I have the girls." Eventually satisfied that the lint was licked, she straightened up to face him with a clucking sigh. "Lean over, your tie is a mess."

Rick complied, grasping the lint brush thrust at him.

"Hey, I fixed that tie," Kyle objected.

She tossed her fair-haired son a look of pity. "No surprise to your mother." She turned back to Rick in earnest. "Now Ricky, be on your best tonight."

"I will shine," he promised magnanimously.

"Whatever they serve, you eat it."

"I will eat everything on my plate, Ma."

"Whatever you do, don't fight with that Mr. Ramsey."

"I will eat everything on my plate, Ma."

Eleanor Wyatt snapped the tie into a bow, glaring up at her son. "You could blow this whole thing with your attitude."

Rick drew a breath and turned to Hayley. "Go out front and hold down the fort, will ya?"

"Yeah, sure, boss," Hayley replied. With a pop of her gum, she was gone.

Rick turned back to address his mother. "I am determined to check out Douglas Ramsey to my satisfaction. Whatever it takes."

"Just don't antagonize him," she stubbornly persisted.

Rick's square jaw tightened. "If he was the warm fuzzy type, none of this would be necessary."

"Sometimes you have to work with people, like those ambassadors do."

"An ambassador I ain't," Rick snorted.

"Watch out or you may land on your rump," she cautioned.

"A place I've been many a time," he good-humoredly finished her thought. "Besides, I have Caron to pave the way if I go too far. She knows just what to say and how to say it."

"She didn't grow up hoity-toity like the mother, did she?" Without waiting for an answer, she forged on. "You know Deborah never thought much of the folks around here. Thought she was better even when she lived two blocks over from us. I'm telling you when the mister used to get the morning paper off his stoop, his pajamas were nothing special. Mrs. Hines saw him lots of times while walking her poodle."

He closed his eyes for a moment, images of Quick Draw's soft green eyes and gently curving mouth setting him aflame. "Caron's an angel, Ma. A livin', breathin' angel."

"Well, I heard she's prettier now...." she trailed off wistfully.

"Does everybody know that?" Rick demanded.

"I imagine so." Eleanor pried her brush from his clenched hand and stuffed it back in her purse. She proceeded to dig around in the roomy bag, ultimately extracting her wallet.

"Now, Ma—"

"Just settle down." She opened her wallet and fished a folded ten-dollar bill out from behind a photograph. "Can't have those Carlisles thinking you can't put on a fine date. Can't have it ending like the last time...."

"I don't want your money, Ma." Rick started a dancing dodge around the short, quickstepping woman who had tirelessly tried to keep rein on him during his childhood. "I'm going to the Ramsey mansion for Pete's sake! He's loaded."

"This is for a soda or something afterward. And Papa would say you should have it. Just call him up right now and ask him," she dared in time-worn persuasion. "Heaven knows you can't be walking around with a pocketful of coins from those machines out front," she reasoned, trying to stuff the bill into his breast pocket. "Your tuxedo trousers will sag from the weight. You'll be lopsided and Mr. Ramsey won't even talk to you."

"How many times have I told you, Ma, Rick doesn't spend all that change he makes," Kyle protested, grasping her arm with laughing eyes. "He has real bills of his own, just like you and me."

"Your little brother doesn't make the kind of money you earn at that fancy office," Eleanor scolded under her breath, tapping Kyle's hand away. "It's change."

"Rick is a successful entrepreneur," Kyle insisted, stopping short when he caught Rick's warning look. The brothers had traveled this territory before and Rick just didn't have the time tonight.

"Thanks for the dough, Ma," Rick pleaded no contest, leaving the folded bill in place behind his white handkerchief.

"So, hadn't you better get going?" Eleanor asked with a quick glance at her watch.

"What about your movie?" he queried.

"I've got another minute to see you off."

"I'm waiting for Caron," he confessed reluctantly. "She's picking me up."

Eleanor's ample bosom heaved in loving exasperation. "Is your pickup truck broken again, Ricky?"

"No, Ma, Caron insisted upon doing things this way. And she did invite me out. I didn't want to argue the point. I'm trying to win her over, remember? Minimize the bickering ways of our youth."

In response, Eleanor opened up her wallet again. "A little gas money is in order. Papa would say so."

"Cut this out, Ma!" Rick closed her wallet and returned it to her purse. "The money, the tux, none of it is going to mellow me out!" He zippered the sack and thrust it back into her arms. "I am what I am!"

"A rebel through and through," she relented in exasperation. "Always trying to prove yourself. Why, even as a toddler, you'd draw a chalk line for the mailman to cross. He had to do it to reach our mailbox, but you made such a production out of it, pretending he was a bully primed for a rumble."

"Why bring that up now?" he grilled impatiently.

"Because I want you to acknowledge that you still have an attitude beneath all this razzle-dazzle," Eleanor replied, not the least bit put off by the stormy expression on his handsome face. "You could spoil this opportunity."

"My customers love me," he insisted, angry that any female could slip beneath his skin, even the one who knew him best.

Eleanor wagged a chiding finger at him. "You still draw invisible chalk lines each and every day! You're about to slouch your way into Ramsey's fancy place with a chip on your shoulder."

Rick held firm under her unrelenting gaze. "Well, James had faith in me, didn't he? And it's all falling into place. The coincidence of having Caron positioned at the law firm just gives me the feeling that it'll be all right."

Eleanor raised a brow in speculation. "How much have you told Caron?"

"Just enough to satisfy her." Rick drew air through his teeth, trying to control his racing pulse. The thought of really satisfying Caron was sending lightning bolts of desire through him. She was so hot now, with her sophisticated air and streamlined body. But so damn controlled. What a confining prison for such a burnin' babe!

If only... He had no idea what it would be like to be on her side on any issue. Still, making his cause her cause just seemed like the ultimate strategy. The unattainable dream of yesterday rekindled in the form of this heir business.

Caron was still intellectually out of his reach, but irresistible just the same. The last thing he'd expected to feel was the familiar sexual pull. But the pure chemistry that had fueled their verbal duels in school still lingered between them after all these years. A cruel trick of nature, but undeniably true. The flame had flared as cleanly as a match struck to sandpaper. He couldn't stop thinking of her in that little yellow hat. Dressed in nothing but the teeny tiny hat.

"Careful, son," Eleanor was rambling on. "Caron's a shrewd one."

He smiled wanly. "Hopefully not as shrewd as you, Ma."

"At least not on the subject of you, let's pray."

Hayley popped her frizzy blond head into the room. "There's an old man out on the sidewalk in a uniform, Rick. He's driving a limo and looking for a guy dressed posh enough to ride in one."

Eleanor raised a hand to her heart. "Those Carlisles have really made the big time!"

"Not that big, Ma," Rick scoffed, glancing in the small mirror on the wall on his way to the door.

"Then she sent it on purpose, just to show us up," Eleanor assumed in affront.

Rick raised a dubious brow. "Caron?"

"*Deborah*, you sweet, ignorant child!" Eleanor brushed her sons aside and marched through the place to join her friends at the huge window facing the street.

Rick trailed after her with Kyle at his heels. "Good

night, Ma," he said, planting a kiss on the top of her head.

"He is parked right at the bus stop!" Eleanor cried, jabbing an accusatory finger. "The seven-twenty will be here anytime now. Then Deborah will get a ticket!" Her prediction sent a ripple of laughter through the group of window peepers. "We'll see who has the clout around here."

"Hold her back, Kyle," Rick instructed under his breath as their mother touched the zipper of her purse with an itchy trigger finger. "I feel an extra limo allowance coming on."

Sure enough, she and Kyle were soon tangling with the purse.

Eleanor raised her head to deliver a parting shot as Rick darted for the door. "Whatever you do, Ricky, don't let that girl stuff anything down your cummerbund again!"

He touched his forehead in a small salute. "Don't worry, Ma. Every thread's insured this time."

6

RICK CLIMBED INTO the plush interior of the limousine to find Caron perched on the rear bench, a delicate red rose on a bed of gray velvet. He swooped down beside her, cozily grazing her thigh with his trouser leg. His gabardine against her sateen scraped noisily in the hushed vastness of the enormous vehicle, causing them mutual pause, bringing home memories of prom night. Together again in the very same colors. In the very same electrified state of mind.

Rick gazed deeply into her gem green eyes, wondering just what she was thinking, wondering if he should say something, anything about the aura of déjà vu. He decided against it for the time being. He couldn't afford to lose his cool. Checking out Ramsey with a clear head was crucial.

"This is one hell of a back seat," he remarked abruptly in boyish wonder, shifting his interest to the massive automobile. "Not cramped like my old green Chevy. Remember that car I had in school, Quick Draw?"

"Yes, of course," she replied. "Have you ever stopped to think about how many people have never once sat in the back seat of their own cars?"

"Do you realize how many hot-blooded teenagers have?" he challenged with a good-natured wink.

"Perhaps you would've been well served with this

sort of divider," she proposed, gesturing to a sheet of tinted glass separating them from the front seat. "I'm sure, given the chance, the neighborhood mothers would've purchased one for your Chevy. And the fathers would've gladly installed it for you."

Rick's eyes grew warm and guileless. "Think it would've stopped me?"

"It is bulletproof and soundproof. Yet..." She trailed off with heavy doubt in her tone.

Rick slanted her a knowing look. "Sounds as though this isn't your first ride."

She gasped in disbelief. "In a back seat?"

"In here, dope!"

"No, as a matter of fact, it isn't," Caron replied with a trace of pride. "Mr. Ramsey often provides me with luxury transportation. I can tell you it soon spoils a person."

Rick lifted a lofty brow. "Well, if this is a blatant ploy to lure Bobber to your side with a taste of the good life, you're wasting your time."

Caron slanted him a wary look. "He's not corruptible?"

"He's not home."

Caron couldn't help but laugh. "Perhaps I'll swing by again tomorrow. If he hasn't flown the coop permanently, that is."

Her querying statement brought a wry curl to his mouth. "Bobber won't be disappearing just yet. My folks have him for an overnight visit is all. I'll tell him you were asking after him."

Caron frowned in confusion. "Why, wasn't that your mother at the window?"

"Yeah. Pa's got sole custody for a few hours. At this very minute he's probably holding both Bobber and an inside straight close to the chest with glee." A tender note deepened Rick's voice as he reported his family affairs.

"Eleanor looked a bit disturbed," Caron openly fretted, raising a hand to her chin-length fluff of auburn hair.

Rick realized with pleasant surprise that it was a nervous gesture, for her glossy strands were styled as deliberately as his own. She was one tempting package top to bottom in her rose-shaded dress with spaghetti straps and filmy matching shawl, her exposed shoulders and legs now lusciously lean beneath satin-smooth skin. Knowing she still had a tender underside beneath the new look, that she still cared about his mother on any level, warmed him like a camp fire.

"Don't worry about Ma," he placated with a twinkle in his eye. "She's just a trifle disturbed over your wheels."

Caron's carefully made-up face grew stricken. "Surely she doesn't think I rolled through my old neighborhood in this monstrosity to rub the good life in your faces!"

He shook his head. "Naw."

Her sigh of relief was audible. "That's good."

"She thinks your mother sent you through the neighborhood in this monstrosity to rub the good life in our faces."

"Mr. Ramsey insisted upon sending it," she defended herself.

"I figured as much, Caron," he comforted, reaching over to catch her hand in his. Bypassing the sexy little thighs pressed together beneath the creeping hem of her dress took an enormous surge of willpower. But he couldn't take the chance of misreading her signals.

If he made a move and she shoved him aside, he'd die, just as sure as if he lay down in the street in front of this moving limo. Losing her the last time had almost done him in. And he'd had youth and resiliency on his side.

Well, he'd grown up, clearing away a lot of that adolescent confusion. It was time to settle down, have a pack of kids. Rick wasn't sure if Caron wanted the works: the vine-covered cottage, the babies, the clutter those things brought into life. She certainly wasn't comfortable handling the Bobber. She was a tigress while fighting for the heir on principle, but the hands-on handling of a real live baby seemed to scare her. Of course that could be cured if it was just inexperience. If it was preference, that would be a major obstacle.

No matter what her preferences, Rick was currently head-over-heels in love with her all over again. He wanted to edge in closer, find out if it was possible to stake his claim and make it stick. But her behavior was too erratic. If she said no, the bouncing back would be impossible. The old heart just didn't hold the same buoyancy it had ten years ago.

"Did you explain it to your mother?" Caron broke in anxiously.

"No—"

"Damn you, Hotshot!" she cried, snatching her hand from his.

"I didn't have time, Quick Draw. The seven-twenty bus was due any second and Ramsey's man—"

"Franklin," Caron supplied.

"Franklin was in the loading zone."

"Oh," she said with pause. "Well, I imagine he doesn't deal with such restrictions very often."

"Don't worry about a thing. I'll tell Ma tomorrow

that your mother didn't hire this stretch to yank her chain."

"Thanks." The snap in her reply was diminished by the fleeting softness in her eyes. She averted her gaze as he turned on her with unabashed curiosity.

"It's always been your nature to care for people," Rick pointed out gently. "I'm glad some things weren't altered along with your nose."

"Are you knocking my snoot or my mother's snooty attitude?" she wondered guardedly.

"Maybe both. Each seems a little too perfect."

"Mother really let some of her old cronies have it years back with her determination to make it in the big time—whatever that may be," she conceded wistfully. "I imagine your mom wasn't too thrilled with the idea of our reunion, no matter how businesslike."

"Their feud is their problem," Rick objected. "Our fathers never even entered into it!"

"Oh, yes, our duels are separate from the rest," Caron acquiesced without hesitation. "But our silly prom night clash did finally give them an incident to pin all of their silly differences on. An excuse to part company for good."

"Food fight is what they still call it in the neighborhood," he differed with a flash of white teeth.

Caron's small jaw dropped. "They still talk about it?"

"Yeah. Probably because no one's topped it. And this new date has fanned the old fires. Ma got to reminiscing about your hands in my cummerbund—"

"I hope you quelled her fears," Caron huffed, flushing in the dim light.

"Better yet, I got insurance on this number," he reported proudly, patting his lapels.

"You didn't!"

"Mr. Linden wouldn't let me leave the formal-wear shop without it," he claimed under her mortified look. "Not after he heard on the grapevine that I was tangling with you again."

"You spilled punch on me first!" she attempted to reason. "They all should remember that!"

"They do. Guess it's part of the reason they think we're a combustible combination. Face it, baby, together we're TNT."

"Well, be sure to respect this dress," she advised saucily. "*She* picked it out again."

He reared back on the seat in surprise. "Still making choices for you?"

"Still trying," Caron huffed.

"You tell her about us?"

"I merely told her that the nice young man who called her about the class reunion was accompanying me to the party. She assumed it was Paul Drake, of course."

His mouth curled mockingly. "It's naughty to lie."

"Advice from the master to the apprentice!" she accused. "Paul Drake indeed. What if she'd recognized the name?"

"There must be a few in the phone book," he reasoned calmly. "Besides, I consider the character an alter ego, so that minimizes the untruthfulness of it."

Caron offered no dispute. "I appreciated the easy out in this case. I believe you deserve a chance at Douglas Ramsey and it has nothing to do with her whatsoever. Though I don't like subterfuge of any kind, the less I tell Deborah the better."

"Sorry you didn't have the sort of childhood I had," he returned in understanding intimacy. "But

I've always suspected Deborah loves you in her own way. Taught you how to fight for what you want, anyhow."

Caron's smile turned briefly brittle. "Yes, weaponry and strategy are her strengths. Her weakness lies in choosing the worthwhile battles. Money and position are her ideal, the gateway to happiness."

"Pretty sad, really," Rick said quietly.

"Pathetic!" Caron promptly chimed in. "And isn't Douglas Ramsey the prime example of shallow wealth? He's lived his life in an emotional limbo, focused only on getting to the top of the heap. Now, in the twilight of his years, he's realized what's been missing—the human factor. Despite his desire to change, he doesn't seem to know how to handle relationships. Happiness is an internal affair within each of us."

"So, you gotta boyfriend?"

"What kind of a question is that?"

"Can't blame me for being a little curious," he said easily, picking up on the dismay in her tone. "You were invited to this fancy ball, Cinderella, complete with the coach, the slippers and the flashy dress. Seems you had everything lined up but the prince."

"Mr. Ramsey asked me at the last minute, if you must know." In a motion of self-preservation, she pulled her thin shawl over her breasts. The filmy fabric only increased her appeal, drawing an enticing curtain of mystery over the mounds of soft flesh pushed up at her sweetheart neckline.

If he didn't know her so very well, he'd have sworn she'd done it purposely. But she hadn't. Her defensive shield was genuine. It was so Quick Draw.

"I don't have a steady, either," he confessed simply, making the obvious assumption on her status.

"Oh, you still think you know it all," she fumed, gazing out of the smoky window at the city lights.

"Give me a break! No guy in his right mind would set you free to roam the night in a billionaire's limo. Especially not with the Hotshot in the back seat. Fully insured till noon tomorrow."

Caron's face sheeted in astonishment. "Is that an invitation of some kind?"

"It's just a fact. Do with it as you will."

As each considered the possibilities, the car rolled along the highway like a magic carpet, heading for the outskirts of Denver. Eventually they approached the massive electronic gate built into the stone wall surrounding the Ramsey property. When they wound their way through the well-kept grounds spotted with mighty oaks and shrubbery, Caron reached over to the side seat and collected her black woolen coat and small black purse.

"Caron, why did you bring a coat if you're not going to wear it?" he wondered in bewilderment.

"I don't want to get mushed beforehand, that's why," she answered distractedly, gazing past him as they rolled to a stop under the massive stone arch at the entrance of the house.

Rick hid a smile behind his sleeve, totally convinced that Caron had absolutely no idea of just how lethally gorgeous she was tonight. He knew she'd been deliberately vamping him all week, but she was obviously unaware of her profound effect on him, naive as to just how much he wanted to plunge deep inside her. She didn't believe she had that sort of power over the male species in general. After all these years, she was still unsure of her beauty.

It was nothing short of a crime.

Crimebuster Rick to the rescue—if and when she found herself ready and willing to mush that spectacular dress.

A uniformed doorman was on hand to promptly open the door and assist them. Rick bypassed his arm with a fluid motion, stepping aside so that Caron could take the man's arm. Once her feet were firmly on the walkway, Rick took over as her escort.

The people milling at the entrance to the huge stone home turned to stare down the broad staircase at the unknown couple, most likely to see if they were celebrities. Rick enjoyed the attention, even if he and Caron lacked the proper notoriety. He'd never looked better or had better company on his arm. With an assuring pat in the region between her fanny and waist, he ushered her up the bank of steps.

"So, what do they do at this sort of bash?" Rick queried under his breath. "Dance, eat, play parlor games?"

"This sort of bash can be described as a high-priced schmooze session," Caron replied frankly. "People mingle, brag, and make connections both business and social. An orchestra will supply the music, which few will probably dance to. Buffet tables of food will be set out. Drinks will be served by uniformed help. Empty glasses will be whisked away promptly and efficiently."

"Faster than you can say baby bobber buggy bumpers?"

Caron's groan was audible as they joined the crowd streaming inside. "I imagine it's something like your Laundromat, but on a much bigger scale. Without the pool table and detergent.

"Good evening, Mr. Ramsey." Caron greeted their host warmly in the huge, crowded foyer moments later. He'd swiftly dismissed the trio of men he'd been speaking with at the sight of Caron.

"So pleased you could make it," he said with delight, his eyes bright behind his thick, wire-rimmed glasses.

She drew Rick forward. "This is the man I was telling you about this morning, sir. Richard Wyatt."

"I've looked forward to meeting you all day," Ramsey said, shrewdly surveying Rick as he pumped his hand.

"The feeling is mutual," Rick returned smoothly, meeting his gaze directly.

Ramsey's brows rose to a bushy V, his booming voice expressing a measure of bemusement. "So you are a classmate of Caron's. It's certainly a coincidence, you having contact with my late son and my attorney."

"Yes, Caron and I have been grand old friends since childhood." He smiled guilelessly. "Served on the student council together, that sort of thing."

"I was in the middle of a crisis at my anchor store in Boulder when her call came through," Ramsey reported without apology. "Naturally I didn't have much time to confer with her."

No time to discuss his late son's friend? Rick didn't care for the sound of it. But he could feel Caron's shoulder nudging his arm in warning. He decided to take heed for the moment.

"What did you actually say, Caron?" Ramsey

paused in recollection. "That James patronized Mr. Wyatt's Laundromat?"

"Yes," Caron affirmed. "And he—"

"Odd stroke of fate," Ramsey mused.

"We marveled over the coincidence, didn't we, hon?" Rick wrapped a possessive arm around her shoulders. It felt so good to hold her, even if her body stiffened at his touch. She was undoubtedly bristling because he was setting a false precedence of their current "friendship." One chance and he would make it real enough.

"We marveled all right." Caron's response was bright, but delivered through clenched teeth.

"Caron and I have always been big debaters," Rick forged on, rubbing his hand down the length of her back. "Talk over everything. As it happens, we were discussing your article in the newspaper. I told her I happened to know James, that he lived not far from my shop."

"So you know nothing of a baby?"

"Not a thing," Rick confirmed without hesitation. "Was Caron right in assuming you'd care to meet with me anyhow?"

"Of course I'm glad she thought of bringing you," Ramsey said, his voice thick with emotion. "I—I'm sure you have many things to share, Richard." He took a cursory glance around the busy room. "Let's find some privacy for a nice chat, shall we?"

"My friends call me Rick," he told Ramsey in invitation a short time later as Ramsey beckoned them into a room in the back of the house. The trio had marched through a maze of corridors in silence, their feet pounding carpets, tiles and hardwood along the way. Ramsey turned on the wall switch and shut the heavy door after them with a thud.

"Why, look, Caron. Mr. Ramsey has a pool table after all," Rick swiftly noted with approval, his eyes sweeping through the oak-paneled room. "I have one at my Laundromat, you see," he revealed under the perplexed look of his billionaire host. "Though mine is a little less ornate," he added, stepping up to admire the table of carved teak.

"So you enjoy billiards, eh?" Ramsey's large face lit up over the prospect.

"Oh, yes, sir," Rick affirmed, wandering over to the rack of sticks on the wall. "We call it pool over on my turf."

"When the table's teak and the balls are ivory, it's billiards," Douglas Ramsey heartily maintained. "Brandies all around?" When he received double nods of acceptance, Ramsey headed for the bar in the back corner. "Yes, we play games here at the big house too, Caron," he said conversationally.

"I was attempting to draw comparisons between your party and one of Rick's gatherings at his Laundromat," Caron responded as she slipped into a butter-soft leather chair. "Hotshots is kind of a local hot spot."

"You see, I have to have most of my fun at work," Rick explained. "The business keeps me very tied down. I have some hired help, but I'm pretty much on my own." He wandered over to the bar and took the two stout snifters offered him by his host. He served Caron chairside, leaning against the wall of polished panel behind her. "I'm a self-made man without much use for regulations and fancy trappings."

Was Rick trying to pick a fight? Caron wondered in

awe. How on earth would challenging Ramsey's luxurious life-style serve Bobber's interests? She twisted around to frown at him warningly. He rewarded her with a trademark rebel scowl.

"We have the self-made image in common, Rick," Ramsey assured him without rancor. "But you already know that I am immersed in regulations and fancy trappings. Though the reputation I have around Denver, around the blasted world as a matter of fact, is a little harsh. I'm more than a hard-edged businessman who worships the dollar. I'm a human being who is searching for answers, just like everyone else."

"I've heard you referred to as an old goat," Rick confessed. "But I don't take much stock in rumors and innuendo. I believe only what I check out for myself."

"Old goat, eh?" Ramsey chuckled with genuine amusement. "Imagine that, Caron."

"I can't," she murmured, shifting on the smooth leather at the echo of her own words. This rebel had a death wish.

Ramsey lifted his snifter to his lips. "Your Laundromat sounds like a creative business venture. An interesting concept, taking the boredom out of a decidedly bleak chore. Seems I'm not the only one here who can turn a buck," he added graciously, further groundwork for an amiable chat.

"But my people are top priority," Rick shot back.

Ramsey scowled, but kept his tone even. "As you may have gathered from Caron and the papers, I'm still struggling with the personal side of my life. I'm trying to mend my ways with the people close to me, give my grandson what he deserves. This search is of monumental importance to me. The fact that you knew James is of monumental importance to me."

"Yes, maybe we do have some common ground," Rick said quietly. He set his glass on an end table beside Caron and sauntered back to the pool table. "Yes, sir. The toys may be fancier, but it's still the same game, isn't it?"

Ramsey hesitated only moments before nodding firmly. "Rack 'em up." He rounded the bar and joined Rick to select a stick off the rack, sparing Caron a brief look. "Caron, perhaps you'd like to go upstairs and look in on Agatha now. She's been anticipating your visit."

"Why, certainly." Caron recognized an order from a powerful client when she heard one. She drained her glass with great reluctance and set it on the table beside Rick's. She hadn't intended to leave them alone for a minute! Both on a probing mission. Both difficult men. Rick the rebel versus Douglas the goat.

"You'll find her private elevator at the end of the hall, m'dear," Ramsey directed, sizing up his stick. "It'll take you directly up to her suites. Her staff is expecting you."

Caron paused at the door. Rick turned suddenly, as if smelling her fear. He tossed her a cavalier wink behind the old boy's back. Would he have the good sense to temper his questions? He'd never shown restraint in his youth, even over the most mundane school issues. What would the grown-up rebel do, with a genuine cause to fight for this time?

Agatha Ramsey was indeed waiting for her. In the hallway with open arms. "Franklin called the moment you arrived at the gate!" she greeted, enveloping Caron in her frail arms.

Agatha was a tall, lithe woman, a font of timeless beauty and infinite knowledge—knowledge that unfortunately had to be challenged for accuracy on occasion. With teasing eyes and yellowed hair cut short and feathered around her small, delicate features, she couldn't be a more delightful companion for a lively chat. There was certainly no harm to her aimless reminiscences, as long as one wasn't conducting an investigation on the basis of her claims—as the law firm of Sharp, Krandell and Peterson happened to be doing. Caron hoped to continue their friendship long after the baby mystery was put to rest.

"We'll just have ourselves a little party in my parlor," she announced enthusiastically.

Caron followed the elderly woman into a cozy lamp-lit room filled with mismatched pieces of furniture and antiques, ranging from Art Nouveau to Italian Deco to Victorian.

"I thought perhaps you'd be downstairs tonight, Agatha."

"Oh, I could be," she asserted airily. "Douglas tells people I'm too frail to attend this or that." Her voice dropped to a conspiratorial octave. "Even that gruff old bulldog brother of mine doesn't have the guts to admit to his guests that I hate stuffy affairs, even at my stuffy age!

"I like my peace, my possessions," she rambled dreamily, gesturing for Caron to sit on a mahogany parlor sofa with sloping dolphin arms. "This room especially. It's off-limits to the staff. My personal maid is allowed in here once a week for light cleaning, under my supervision." She brushed her thin, veined hands together with glee. "Let's have a sherry, shall we, Carrie?"

"Let me serve you, Agatha," she proposed, half rising from her seat.

"No, I can still serve drinks." Agatha flitted off to a gilded walnut cabinet, which Caron guessed to be eighteenth century. "I hope you don't mind my calling you Carrie." She turned to Caron for approval, gripping the neck of a stout bottle of amber liquid in her fingers. "You've never told me if you like it."

"It's different, but I like it." Caron held her breath as Agatha splashed two sherry glasses full to the brim. Amazingly, she spilled not a drop.

"I had a close friend for many years named Carrie," she confided meditatively. "We modeled together all over the world, making our fortunes. She's gone now."

"Deceased?" Caron asked, taking the glass offered her.

Agatha plopped herself on the sofa beside Caron, taking a healthy gulp of wine. "No, just lost her mind is all. I hope my body stops ticking before my brain does."

"Me too," Caron agreed.

"You're such a pleasure," Agatha chirped. "I suppose you've come to talk about James again, and his baby. I'd like that."

"Mr. Ramsey shocked us all at the firm by advertising for the child," Caron intimated, twirling the stem of her glass in her fingers.

"I told him to tell you first," she was swift to clarify. "Though he's genuinely fond of you, dear, he does like to fancy himself in charge of everyone in sight." Her mouth lifted in what Caron recognized as her secret smile. "I was the one who came up with the idea of the medal hand-me-down, you know."

Caron stiffened. "What do you mean, Agatha?"

"Near the end, when James was fretting about Douglas and the baby, what to do about proof of parentage, I gave the medal to James to pass along to his son. Then, if the mother ever wished to enter the lion's den, she would have the entrance fee."

"Clever," Caron said.

Agatha tittered nearly to tears. "Just the right price, an appropriate entrée to the Ramsey dynasty. A simple silver dollar in a circular setting. It's a symbol of the first dollar Douglas cleared on his first department store fifty years ago. He wore it on a chain around his neck to the grand openings of Ramsey Department Stores for years and years. He was originally grumpy when he learned I nicked it and gave it to James." She paused for a breath. "But I was right to do so. Now he's grateful for the link to the child."

Caron's mouth curved fondly. "Mr. Ramsey didn't want any of us at the firm to know the precise specifications of the medal."

"But true, true friends share secrets," Agatha gushed with another sip of wine.

Caron gave her hand a brief squeeze. "Almost done with business," she promised. "Just how often did you see James during the years he lived on Fairfax Avenue?"

"Only occasionally," Agatha replied. "He'd never come here to the house, of course. Might run into his father. We'd meet in restaurants or galleries. You see, he shared my interest in art. Did I tell you that before?"

"No."

"Oh, yes, James had a gentility about him that roughshod Douglas never could have accepted." She paused with a wistful sigh. "I think James was better off keeping his distance from his father. They would've clashed constantly. James was a sensitive man, as was his mother. Had he lived, he never would've been equipped to run the Ramsey stores. It would've been nothing but sorrow."

It made sense. Only a sensitive man would've sent Rick on such a delicate mission, Caron mused. He'd obviously sensed Rick's own streetwise toughness and figured he was a worthy match for the old man. In this silent deliberation, she raised the sherry to her mouth. Her eyes widened as she realized the finely etched crystal in her hands did not have the same meticulous care given the glistening brandy snifters downstairs. A fine coat of dust lined the inside of the glass, partially dissolved at the wine line. Agatha really meant it when she said this room was left to her discretion! It was a wise reminder that this grand old lady had her frailties despite her bravado.

"You like the sherry, don't you, Carrie?" Agatha's hands fluttered fussily over Caron's hesitation and she drained her own glass in a final slurp.

"It's fine," Caron assured her. "I just had a drink downstairs and want to pace myself." She took one polite sip before setting it on the table before them. Oh, the things her own mother would be surprised to learn about the upper classes. Deborah had such an unvarnished image of how the rich folk lived, unaware that pain and tangled relationships plagued them along with everyone else.

"You had expressed interest in our family albums," Agatha ventured in open eagerness. "Would you like to see them now?"

"Very much so." As much as she wanted to trust

Rick and his methods, she was determined to continue the investigation on her own, in a parallel, more detached manner. Rick was too fired up, too evasive to be trusted completely. A photograph of a Ramsey resembling the Bobber would be a valuable find. Something she could hold on to, even if Rick let go on his end.

"You'll find them in there," Agatha chirped, gesturing to a bookcase with beveled glass doors.

Caron retrieved the albums and brought them to the coffee table. "I'm looking for anything that could help me identify the baby if I see him," Caron explained, settling back on the settee with a book in her lap.

"Ah, identifying markings, eh?" Agatha nodded with a shrewd glint in her eye. "Have you had a lot of claims?"

"Too many," Caron replied dourly. "Some of them quite outlandish. Any solid leads would help tremendously."

"I'd like to see pictures of the babies," Agatha requested. "I believe I'd know a Ramsey if I saw one."

"I'll send over a batch for your perusal," she promised, impressed with Agatha's self-assurance and dedication. The knowledge that Bobber's photograph couldn't be included in the bunch stung her conscience a little, but the more she learned, the more she was sure James had good reason to put the heir's fate in Rick's hands. Agatha would understand her deception in the end.

Behaving so unconventionally was tough on Caron, so job jeopardizing as well! Rick certainly had honed his manipulating ways to perfection—crowding her into this jam! She wasn't sure which had a more profound effect on her, his verbal flimflam or his tantalizing touch. His massaging fingers on her shawled shoulders and bare back tonight right under Ramsey's nose came back to haunt her, titillate her; but most importantly, to warn her. A hand that could rock a cradle and her senses with the same deftness was one to be wary of!

An hour of thumbing through pages and pages of the Ramseys' pictorial history brought Caron no further clues. "I believe I'd better be joining my date downstairs," she announced, gauging the growing fatigue in Agatha's face.

"I would've enjoyed meeting your fellow," Agatha told her with a disappointed sniff.

"I'll bring him up one day soon," Caron promised as she returned the albums to their proper place in the case.

"We'll have a bit of a party then," Agatha rallied in merriment, flitting to Caron's side in slippered feet. "Just the three of us."

"I couldn't help noticing there are no professional modeling shots of you in the albums," Caron said with regret, arranging the books in the order she found them.

"Douglas didn't think it ladylike to include them in the family archives," she huffed. "Not many women worked and lived on their own in the old days, you know. As it is, my best work is on canvas." Agatha took several steps to the wall, drawing back a tapestry curtain. Rather than the expected window, there was an oil painting on display in a huge scalloped frame.

Caron drew an astonished breath. It was a portrait of Agatha. Circa 1920s by Caron's estimation, judging from Agatha's youthful face and figure and the silver-plated mesh purse in her hand. Save for the purse and a fox fur at her throat, she was totally in the nude. With masses and masses of the brightest red hair Caron had ever seen, tumbling over her ivory shoulders.

_____ **7** _____

THE MOMENT CARON CLOSED the door to Douglas Ramsey's den, Rick turned back to the table to arrange the colorful striped and spotted balls in a pyramid on the green felt surface. "Eight ball okay, sir?"

"Fine. I know them all, Rick." Ramsey carefully chalked his cue. "I must warn you, I'm a serious player. I can concentrate on a business deal and the game with admirable dexterity."

"I'm good too," Rick flatly asserted. "I often whip someone's pants while washing someone else's."

"Your table get a lot of play?"

"Constant," he reported, skimming the lavish teak surface with covetous eyes. "Especially when kids are free to roam. You know, summer, after school, weekends."

"No child has ever touched this masterpiece," Ramsey confirmed the obvious.

"I like to lure the kids off the street," Rick explained, setting the white cue ball in position for the break. "They need something to do more than anything else. I know I always did."

"No experience with them, myself," Ramsey readily admitted. "You break. You're the guest."

Resting his stick in the crook of his thumb, Rick took careful aim at the cue ball. With a sharp crack it hit the triangle of colored balls, scattering them in all directions. The red one rolled into the left side pocket. "No experience, you say. But raring to jump into parenting with full force." Rick sized up his options while waiting for Ramsey's response. As important as the man's answer was, Rick was taking some pleasure in playing on the deluxe table, too. He could do absolutely anything while playing the game. Anything mental, anyway. With fluid grace he leaned over, poised his stick, and shot the cue ball into his blue one, sending it across the fine felt surface into a corner pocket.

By his expression, Ramsey appeared disgruntled by the questions and Rick's prowess in the game. "I'm willing to take the chance on the child."

Rick found Ramsey's autocratic outlook extremely irritating and took pleasure in sinking another ball. "Kids can't be returned like Ramsey Department Store merchandise," he informed him, pausing to chalk his cue.

"I know that!" Ramsey barked, his complexion reddening. "And maybe it won't be a successful union. But it's every man's right to know his grandson. If I step in now, while he's young, he'll accept me as a fact of life. Without his father's tainted opinion," he added with resolve.

"You gonna take total custody of him or what?" Ramsey balked at his nerve. "Why do you ask?"

"Because I'm curious, I guess." Rick forced calmness into his demeanor, slightly shrugging his broad shoulders under his elegant jacket. "I imagine the entire state is curious. You opened the door when you put it in the papers. Frankly, I'm fascinated by you, sir. Because you're Caron's client. Because you're James's father."

"Yes, I thought we were going to discuss James," Ramsey complained.

"I didn't mean to offend you, sir. If you are uncomfortable with the issue of the heir himself—"

"I am not!" With large, weathered hands propped on the edge of the table, he leaned over with a glint in his eye. "I will tell you and anybody else this, young fella. If that child is living in a two-room apartment with an irresponsible mother, I'll take over in a wink. I'll sue for custody and make certain that boy has every advantage."

Rick bit his lip. Every advantage or every disadvantage? He couldn't debate Ramsey's negative effect on James's childhood, not without arousing the suspicion that he knew James much better than as a casual customer. That would get Ramsey fired up and digging around. The billionaire would trace the heir right to Hotshots in no time.

"I have many things to offer the baby," Ramsey continued as Rick bulleted his yellow ball into a corner pocket. "I want the kid to be happy. Your curiosity satisfied?"

"I wish you well in your hunt, sir." Rick raised his head from the table and flashed him a wide smile.

Ramsey shot him a wary look. "Just how well did you know my son?"

Rick held his gaze with a set jaw, quelling the emotions threatening to swallow him. "He was a regular customer."

"You engage in a lot of talk?"

"My place is a carnival of activity," Rick hedged, setting up his next shot. "People can come in for companionship, entertainment. I have the sports channel on my wide screen television. He sat in on a game now and then with the guys."

"James liked sports?"

Rick flashed him a pathetic smile. The old crust didn't even know that! Even with all of his recent probing! "Football, basketball. Seems he always wanted someone to toss a ball around with when he was a kid."

Ramsey nodded. "I was so busy when he was young. Then, before I knew it, he'd turned against me. The divorce split everything wide open and they both cut me off!" Ramsey growled. "His mother wouldn't take financial help. She felt that the money would become a bartering chip in our relationship. She wanted a clean break and got one."

Rick could read the frustration in the old man's eyes, the hunger to set the record straight with somebody. This was his chance to probe further. "Would this grandson ever see a game?" he asked quietly.

"Yes, yes, whatever he wanted." Ramsey paced the length of the table as Rick sank another ball. "You liked my son, didn't you?"

"Very much. I like most of my customers. All of my regulars."

"Is there anything you can tell me, Rick, anything that would help me out?" he asked, his forceful voice laced with desperation.

Rick shrugged uneasily in his tuxedo, uncomfortable in the clothing and the company. "I can tell you James was a good guy. If it makes you feel any better, I think he was satisfied with his life, with the decisions he made."

"Caron intimated that you were fairly close to him," Ramsey said unexpectedly.

"She did?" he asked mildly, concealing his annoyance. Caron had only spoken to Ramsey for a minute this morning and she'd managed to let that slip. Quick Draw was still true to her name.

"Did he have a special lady friend, someone he might have brought to your Laundromat?" Ramsey prodded.

"No, he washed his clothes all by himself, sir." Rick flared over the billionaire's glowering interrogation. His own mother certainly knew him well! But he couldn't stop himself. Like Ramsey, he would have to use intimidation in an effort to keep the upper hand.

"If he fathered a child, he must've mentioned it at some point," Ramsey snapped, his eyes turning hard. "Maybe during one of those male bonding sports broadcasts."

"All those games were, and still are, watched by a crowd of howling, backslapping, food-snacking guys intent on blowing off some steam and rooting for the home teams. No girls allowed, no babies allowed." Rick went about the business of sinking the rest of his balls with precision, taking the game without giving Ramsey one shot.

Ramsey leveled a beefy finger at him. "If you're hoodwinking me about the baby, I'm going to find out."

"What would my motive be?" Rick asked.

"I don't know," Ramsey bellowed bitterly. "Maybe you're after the reward. Maybe you thought I'd give you something just because you knew James."

"I don't want your money, man!"

Ramsey grunted. "It's difficult to believe you came here in an altruistic gesture!"

"That's your loss, sir. Not everyone is trying to

jump aboard your gravy train.'' Rick's comeback was a quiet counterpoint to the old man's blast. But Rick realized it was too late to smooth talk his way back into the old man's good graces. If only he'd kept his cool from the start. Breezed in and out of this place without hassle. But in his zeal he'd been as demanding as Ramsey himself. Digging into his emotional well for the questions instead of his cache of common sense. If Ramsey sensed the depth of his feeling for James, he'd soon be digging into everything. And there was nothing he could do to stop him.

Well, all things considered, the trouble he'd taken to get inside the big house had not been wasted. This guy was one lousy grandpa candidate. Few questions remained in his mind at this point. What Rick would do when he ultimately got caught in his charade, and how he was going to hang onto Caron's job for her, however, were both on the top of the list. Though she was an honest woman, he was going to have to convince her to lie, say she had no idea what he'd been up to. And that was a half truth in itself. She had gotten him in here on false pretenses, but she really didn't know what was going on. He'd make the law firm understand if he had to.

"It's obvious you don't appreciate my visit, after all," he eventually muttered.

"I'm not accustomed to back talk from youngsters like you," Ramsey told him, his blunt nose reddening from equal doses of brandy and aggravation.

"Perhaps because they are employees in fear of unemployment," Rick shot back in anger. "I've avoided such groveling predicaments by building my own little empire. Where I come from, respect grows out of proving your stamina and grit. And showing some heart," he couldn't resist adding.

Ramsey sputtered for a response. "Why are you so angry? I should be mad over this skunking. I play to win. Always."

Winning at any cost. Rick received the message loud and clear. Grandpa of the year! "Thank you for the game, sir," Rick said, replacing his stick in the rack.

"I didn't have a chance here at all," Ramsey blustered. "Not in the game, not in this conversation. You came with a chip on your shoulder, didn't you?" When Rick didn't deny it, he sighed heavily. "Perhaps it's because I'm rich and James was not. Perhaps you just wanted to see what was denied him."

"There's many kinds of rich, Mr. Ramsey," Rick protested, eyeing the edge of his mother's ten-dollar bill in his breast pocket behind his handkerchief. "James had enough to get by. So do I."

Ramsey released a bushel of air from his large chest. "Well, then explain to me how we ended up in a squabble," he invited, "if you don't want my money and you're not fighting a battle for my late son."

Rick shoved his hands into the pockets of his baggy trousers and rocked on his heels. "There's a logical explanation, sir, one I know Caron would back up in a minute."

"YOU TOLD MY BILLIONAIRE client that you're a hotshot?" Caron gaped at Rick across the table in the bustling restaurant. "He wondered why you're argumentative and insolent, and your answer was that it's simply your nature?"

Rick nodded, rather humbled by Caron's scolding.

The Ramsey party was two hours behind them and they were seated in the new Chinese restaurant near his Laundromat, polishing off lemon chicken and fried rice. He'd successfully dodged the subject of the pool game until now, by claiming that memories of James had welled up inside and he needed quiet time to deal with it. Certainly the truth as far as it went. He'd also sensed it would be easier to tell her here on his turf, where the walls were paneled with pressed wood and water came straight from the faucet.

"So, will I be getting an angry call tomorrow?" she asked, pulling the cloth napkin from her lap to dab her mouth.

"Depends whether he's a tattletale or not. Besides, it's Sunday. A day of rest for all of us hopefully."

"Douglas Ramsey's stores are open on the seventh day," Caron assured him dryly. "Isn't your place?"

"Not very often," Rick replied. He smiled in half-hearted hope. "Maybe he'll leave me alone. Eventually give up the hunt."

Caron shook her head. "I don't intend to second-guess him, not after his announcement to the press."

"Yeah, the old guy is a loose cannon all right," Rick grumbled.

"How could you let it go so wrong, Rick, after you worked so hard to get there?" Caron chided in confusion.

He leveled his fork at her. "It was your fault!"

Caron, sipping water from her glass, nearly spouted like a fountain at the accusation. "Me?"

"You went and told him that I was close to James."

"What should I have said?"

"That I knew *of* James," Rick scolded. "That he was just a customer."

"Douglas Ramsey wouldn't have left his guests for a private chat about his son's laundry," Caron sputtered.

"Well, he had a game plan of his own. Wanted to ask me all the questions. The nerve of the guy! Insinuating that I had ulterior motives."

"The inevitable is starting to happen," Caron cautioned. "He's grasping at any straw. And there's more," she added sympathetically. "I discovered tonight that Agatha had red hair in her youth. One look at Bobber and they're going to go bonkers."

"We'll see," he said quietly, pushing aside his half-empty plate.

"Oh, Rick," she confided in a rush, "I'm so disappointed that we didn't have a happy ending tonight. I had hoped that you and Mr. Ramsey would come to terms. That you'd have felt comfortable telling him about the baby."

Rick smiled indulgently over her romantic notion. "He has a problem with control, Caron. And I have a problem with his problem."

"There's always tomorrow," she said on an upbeat note.

Not with Ramsey there wasn't. But he didn't have the heart to tell her. "I'm still working on tonight," he protested good-humoredly, tossing some bills on top of the check. "Don't forget, I left my jokemeister brother Kyle in charge of my livelihood."

Her lilting laughter was refreshing. "Oh, that's right. Shall we go see if he's done any damage to that sudsy pickup joint of yours?"

They strolled leisurely down the sidewalk past the dimly lit storefronts, loosely holding hands. It was after midnight and the street was nearly deserted, save for an intermittent pedestrian or headlight beam. They stopped in front of the Laundromat, and Rick fished his keys out of his pocket. He opened the door, then ushered her inside the dimly lit place.

"First we must neutralize," he announced.

"You sound like a captain out of 'Star Trek,'" she teased.

"Just a shopkeep with an alarm system." He opened a gray box above the light switch and punched in the proper code on the numbered buttons. "Safe and secure."

"In your universe," Caron finished neatly.

Rick paused to lock the door once more, then scanned the room with a nod of satisfaction. "Yep, it looks like everything is in order."

Caron wandered around, a trifle lost in the obscurity of the dark, deserted room and in the confines of her own uncertain heart. "Kyle help out often?" she ventured in conversation. "Somehow I can't imagine him tinkering with all the gadgets in here."

Rick broke into an easy grin. "He doesn't have a mechanical bone in his body. I shudder to think of what would happen if a hose burst or a machine shorted while he was in command."

"Figures still his specialty?"

Rick thrust his hands into his pockets, leaning a shoulder into the pop machine. "Juggling numbers and eating junk food by the pound remain his passions. Though he'd like to include a certain little nurse in that buffoon act of his...." he trailed off.

Caron blinked in surprise. "Megan?"

"Yeah, it seems he's always admired her from afar. Wants me to fix him up."

"Really?"

"Just told me so tonight."

Caron's breathing quavered as she stood near the row of dryers, recalling her last late-night visit. The place held the same intimate ambiance, with the single bulb glowing over the door, the machines gleaming white in the shadows. She fingered the collar of her black woolen coat, wondering where this uneasy moment was going to lead.

Rick passed her by, reaching over the dryers to tilt the wooden blinds shut against the front pane. Caron's eyes traveled with him, a quiver racing the length of her body. The air around him was heavy with tension and detergent, and a recently consumed pizza. She had never wanted a man so badly. Never wanted so desperately to be touched. Even if it meant there was no tomorrow attached to the proposition.

"What are you thinking about, Caron?" he asked as he fussed at the windows.

Caron stared longingly at his back. "Just that, by golly, you got through the night without spilling a thing on me."

"So, what are my chances?" he asked huskily, spinning on his heel to confront her with the most raw expression she'd ever seen on a man.

Her heart leaped up to her throat, making speech nearly impossible. "What did you say?"

"Does it seem right to fix Kyle up with Megan? I have to be sure of success, you see. Can't set up my own brother for a fall."

"I think it would be a chance worth taking," she murmured, her face warming to a pink over her misunderstanding of his intent. "It just so happens my people are important to me, too. I wouldn't want anybody to end up with a broken heart."

"She sure was an attractive little gal," Rick went on, fumbling for conversation. "Lots of fun, too."

"Yes, she confirmed your date," Caron said crossly.

Rick wondered suddenly if Caron could be feeling territorial about him. What a titillating thought! "I just meant that Kyle would probably do well by looking her up," he sought to explain.

Caron's eyes never left him as she drew open her coat and placed her hands on her hips.

Rick quaked with desire as he drank in the heaving breasts spilling out of her neckline, the way her fingers pressed into her curves, pulling her dress taut over her belly. Was it a deliberate ploy? "Why, Caron Carlisle, I swear you are trying to seduce me every time I come into range."

"Not every time!" she cried in affront.

"You were the first time."

"Which first time?"

"The most recent first time." He moved in closer.

Caron nearly melted as he caught her chin in his finger again. "I just want you to see that I'm attractive, Rick."

"Of course you are!" He dipped his mouth to hers hungrily.

Caron absorbed the impact of his crushing kiss, of his powerful body crowding her back against the dryers. He'd held her by the chin only the briefest moment this time, proceeding to use both hands to strip her coat away. Soon he was caressing her with at least a hundred fingers in a thousand places. But something troubled her. The white enamel surface of the dryer was shockingly hot, heating her bottom right through the fabric of her dress.

"It's burning," she squeaked urgently.

"Yeah, baby," he growled against her lips.

"I mean the dryer."

With a moan of reluctance, Rick pulled his mouth from hers and reached around her to set his palm on machine number four.

"Is it an electrical short in the wiring or something?" she wondered in panic, her fingers curled around his lapels.

If this interruption had been instigated by a woman other than Quick Draw, he'd have seriously doubted her true and genuine interest in making love. Considering her penchant for prudence, however, his doubts about her were only marginal. Caron simply worried about the practical things by nature. A most cautious babe always. But somehow he had to figure out just where he stood with her.

More than anything in the world Rick wanted Caron to want him. But he had to know for sure before she sent him over the edge.

"Can't you see that the sparks flying from me right now are far more dangerous than any old machine could be?" he demanded incredulously.

"But what does it mean, Rick?"

"Only that Kyle was treating his number friends from the office to some highjinx laundry service," he soothed with a crooked grin. "He can really make this place rock with a pocketful of change." There was a moment of silence between them, Caron staring up into his eyes, hands still clutching his lapels.

"You still make 'em rock, Hotshot?"

The question was soft, full of a quiet desperation. This was it! The final reassurance he'd been longing for, the necessary benediction.

"You bet I still rock," he drawled, fingering the

shimmery shawl knotted at her chest. He removed the delicate strip of fabric with care, drawing it across the length of her shoulders, grazing her bare skin with its stiffness. She shivered openly over the small erotic gesture.

"Last time..." Her voice trailed off fearfully, back into the distant past.

Rick grasped her trembling hands in his. "The last time was just an adolescent appetizer which has left me starving, Caron. Think you can handle this hungry man, back for more after a ten-year fast?"

8

CARON COULDN'T BELIEVE her ears. He'd been pining for her for the last decade? It didn't make any sense. He'd unceremoniously dumped her after they'd made love in his Chevy on prom night—on the very seat covers she'd sewn for him! The one and only time they'd really ever been intimate after the kissing games of their childhood and he let her drop out of his hands forever. To this day the class of '83 didn't know that the couple's fiery encounter at the dance had led to the ultimate adult act. Her sharp mother had instantly figured it out upon her arrival home, in a different car, her dress and hairdo in a state. That was the real reason for the rift between her and Mrs. Wyatt. Caron was sure no one else knew other than Megan. After all, Rick immediately chose to make it past history by not returning for her the following day as promised. Just another conquest for him.

What on earth was Rick trying to do to her now, insinuating they should pick up right where they left off? On so many levels she wanted to do just that! Every nerve ending in her body was alive, crackling in electric anticipation. But some sort of explanation was in order. He'd said a lot of things the first time round and she'd blindly believed in him, without her characteristic reserve. Could she afford another one-night stand with the only guy she'd ever really loved, just for the sheer physical pleasure of it?

"You all right?" he asked.

"Very all right," she murmured, winding her arms around his neck. She would not think about the last letdown. He wanted her and that was all she needed for the night.

With a ravenous growl he sucked at the hollow of her throat, leaving a wet trail of kisses along her creamy shoulders. She tilted back as he nuzzled his face in the peaks of her uplifted breasts, delving his tongue down between the cushy mounds. Heat spiraled down her spine along with her zipper as Rick opened her dress with a single fluid tug. The spaghetti straps were no anchor for the small, gaping garment. It ended up a crimson heap at her feet.

Rick's eyes grew slitted and predatory as he moved back a step to absorb the erotic goddess of his dreams—all grown up in a strapless bra, garter-belted stockings and high-heeled shoes.

Her supreme primitive fantasy was unfolding before her eyes. Rick's stiffened body was nearly vibrating over his concupiscence for the new her. He seemed primed to swallow her whole.

The darkness of the room and the headiness of their carnal reunion gave her the courage to play the vamp of his dreams. She nudged the toe of her shoe up his trouser leg and spoke in sultry tones new to her tongue. "I've never stood before a tuxedoed gentleman like this before. Natty down to the bow tie."

"I'm not feeling like much of a gentleman," he murmured, chuckling without apology, his hand eagerly stealing to his throat.

"Let me start you off." She shimmied closer.

"You did this last time, too," he recalled huskily.

Caron's fingers stiffened at his starched collar as vivid memories of their youthful sexual encounter swept over her like a tidal wave, making her once more feel like a plump, insecure virgin. "You still remember it all?" she asked bleakly, frozen in time, in spirit.

"I remember everything," he revealed proudly. "Women are flattered when a man remembers, right?" he asked, puzzled over her sudden distress.

"I was hoping that once you saw the new me, you'd forget the other time," she confessed, avoiding his eyes as she loosened his tie and unbuttoned his collar.

"Forget one of the most precious moments of my life?" His voice was thick with shock as he gently kneaded her arm.

"You don't mean that!" she snapped angrily, wrenching free. "Not any more than you meant forever back then. Look," she placated, blinking back the tears. "I understand now why teenage boys whisper promises in dark cars to get what they want. But you have no right to continue to pretend you meant the things you said back then. It certainly won't make me more receptive now. That chubby kid with only her wits to feed from, still lives deep within my heart, Rick. I can accept starting anew. Good grief, I can hardly keep my hands off you—the chemistry is still that strong. But don't pretend you cared before. I won't let you."

A mask of hurt pulled his features tight. "I've always cared in my own way, Caron," he assured. "You've never been less than a real beauty to me."

"Not true!" she cried out. "You would've settled for me from the start. Returned my love!"

"You *loved me?*"

"Oh, shut up!" she squealed, pushing at his chest. "Of course I did! And how do you think I felt way, way back when you kissed the daylights out of me for a whole summer, then went on to all the other girls? How do you think I felt when I toiled three years for the student council presidency only to have you zoom in and snatch it away? You couldn't leave me alone, Rick. You just had to keep stepping on my heart until it was crushed flat."

Rick shook his head in mystification, as if trying to translate her words to another language. "Caron, you must try and understand. Your beauty was never an issue. It was there, it was natural. It was a joyful sight to a hot-blooded kid." She tried to protest, but he pressed his fingers to her lips. "I simply could not handle your smarts. The older we got, the more evident it became that your wit far surpassed mine. I liked the limelight, being on top, and it killed me to accept that you had the brains to best me. You didn't drive me away. My own fears of being second-best did."

Caron felt chilly, standing before him in next to nothing, feeling chubby even though she was not. He must have sensed her inhibitions, for he drew her against the solid expanse of his chest.

"Oh baby, I was trying to prove myself a man with all of those girls. Teenage boys do that. But I joined the council to get your sole attention, prove I could survive on your turf. I was too dense to figure out why it made you mad. I thought you'd admire me for it. And you did seem to enjoy our verbal battles...."

"I've been fighting my whole adult life to be the sort of woman men find attractive," she quavered. "I never wanted to feel like a rejected little girl again."

"There was never anything wrong with you." He raised his thumbs to the twin teardrops rolling down her hollow cheeks. "Your shape was just a little curvy. I loved it! I even loved your old bumpy nose."

"You don't deserve all the blame. I was an insecure mess even without you," Caron admitted with a sniff. "My mother raised me to believe I could never be perfect enough for the right man, and she keeps reiterating the fact in her own little ways."

"She's doing you a grave injustice," Rick agreed.

"But so did you, you know," she told him brokenly, making an admission she swore she would never make. "You built up my esteem, my hopes, that night you made love to me. Then you took it all away when you didn't show up the next day—as you promised you would!"

Rick splayed his hands across her bare back, finding it so, so silky. "Caron, we have to talk about that particular morning-after. And we will—soon," he hastily vowed under her belligerent look. "But we must choose a time when we're calm, understand? This is a charged-up moment for us already. All this other stuff, it's getting in the way of—for lack of a better word—the climax of our evening. It's up to you to decide if we stop here or if we—" he grinned rakishly "—go on ahead."

Caron noted that his hands were moving along her gartered bottom now, trying to sway her decision with skin-tingling persuasion. "I can't back off now, Rick," she moaned heavily. "Tonight is all that matters for us. Your eyes are still as addictive to me as a barrel of Hershey's syrup. I just want to dive in and wallow all night long."

The admission jarred him. "But what I mean is—"

"Don't bother with the pillow talk."

"Caron!"

She knew she was unraveling before his eyes. Her long, thin fingers moved over his face, skimming inside the curve of his ears. Her eyes roamed his fully clothed body with serious intent.

"Caron, I don't know what sort of man you think I am," he said incredulously. "But I want you to know that I do have an explanation to offer. I want you to enjoy our lovemaking with that understanding. I want you to have a little more blind faith in me."

"I don't know what to believe right now," she confessed on an impatient wail. "You've asked for so much of my unquestioning trust as it is."

Rick shut his eyes for a brief moment. "I know. I can't help it."

"I just know sex has never seemed more right," she coaxed. "Let's go for the best, outdo the last time."

"Caron, I don't know if we can do it any better than the last time," he entreated in earnest, his hands gliding along the slope of her hips.

Her eyes darted up to his, nonplussed by the admission. He meant it.

"Let's just build up a slow steam and let things escalate naturally," he suggested huskily. "We'll build on our sweet adolescent encounter, let it enhance our adult passions...."

"Let's just forget," she pleaded.

"Let's remember," he insisted, pressing her fingers to his mouth. "You took off my tux then. Do it again, Caron."

The slight pressure of Caron's delicate hands working the buttons on his stiff white shirt caused Rick to shudder openly. His pleasure gave Caron incentive to forge on, pushing his jacket over his shoulders. "You needn't be so cautious," he murmured. "I'm insured, remember?"

Caron laughed in comic relief, eagerly peeling him bare, layer by layer. Standing before her in nude magnificence, Rick took her very breath away. She sank her fingers into the forest of black hair on his chest, moaning. "Where are we going to do this, Rick?"

"Why, the hottest spot in the place," he said, slapping a palm on the dryers.

"On top?"

"Yep."

"Won't it be awkward?"

He grinned boyishly. "I don't know. It'll be an experiment for both of us." Rick dug into his jacket pocket for change and stuffed the coins into several of the dryers clear down to number seven. He set the timers and they hummed to life, tumbling hollowly with heat.

Knowing that Rick had never done this with any other woman gave Caron a feeling of comfort and lunacy at the same time. "Maybe I should take off my things before we—"

"Don't touch that stuff!" he cautioned. "It stays, it's mine."

"Even the shoes?"

"Especially the shoes," he growled, pinching her chin. "I too have several fantasies yet unfulfilled. Have had them since you leaned against number seven in your little yellow hat."

Caron wove her arms around Rick's neck as he

drew her close to his sinewy length. His shaft grazed her lacy garter belt once, twice, undulating for entry to the nylon barrier housing her femininity. Clasping his lean buttocks in her long fingers, she picked up his rhythm, lavishing in the burning friction they were creating.

With a sudden sweep she was in his arms, gently deposited on the humming beds of warm steel. Her heels clanked against the top of number four as she stretched out on her back.

Rick stood over her in the shadows, feasting upon her reclining form with hungry eyes. Ever so gently he skimmed the inner bow of her thigh with the tips of his fingers, along her stocking, then over the top to her exposed skin. With a sharp breath he slipped underneath the garter belt crushing her nest of curls. When she groaned in satisfaction, he lifted her leg, drawing it over his shoulder. Caron shuddered in open delight as his touch invaded her tender moist folds, exploring, searing her sensitive nerve endings. Eyes glazed and gleaming in the dimness, he weaved his magic on her, unabashedly watching his own moves and her responses. Heat seared up through her abdomen, a red-hot coil about to spring into flames. A clenched hand on his thick, muscled arm, she soon reached climactic heights.

Rick eased her leg down, climbing atop the machinery in one leap to hold her quaking, shuddering body. "Oh, how I love you," he moaned into her hair.

"Don't say it, Rick," she choked out in huffs, clamping her shaky hands on his rock-solid shoulders.

"I mean it and will say it." Rick pushed himself to a prone position, his features stormy with ache.

"Having you back again. It's all I ever wanted. It's never been as sweet with anyone else."

"Just believe in the moment, Rick." Caron licked the circle of her lips, inviting him for a taste. "I'm your baby tonight."

Rick's mouth was on hers with relish. Caron invaded his mouth with her tongue, savoring the taste of him, the same bittersweet taste of the first time.

"I want you inside of me, Rick," she cajoled huskily.

"I've waited so long—" He broke off, choked with a labored passion.

Caron drew him down, arching her back into the solid warmth of his body, fusing it with hers. His hair-dusted legs rubbing into hers caused delicious sensations to shimmer clear through her stockings. She wound her legs around his waist, her high-heeled shoes grazing his back. "Shall I take them off now?"

"No!" His order was a ragged utterance as he poised overhead for one last look into her sweet face. When her legs nudged into his waist, he plunged inside her with an urgent thrust. He drove into her over and over again to the tune of her enticing urgings, soaring on the mounting thunder in his ears. When her cries grew reedy with need, he exploded inside her.

With a moan of victory, Rick lightly collapsed on her length. They huffed together in a sweat-slicked heap for a long while. "We topped the first time," he rumbled deeply. "Who'd have thought it possible?"

Caron placed her hand on his rapidly beating heart. "It all seems like a dream. A dream I don't want to awaken from."

"Then you shall spend the night up at my place,"

Rick proposed, tweaking her nose. "When you awaken, you'll know it's real."

Caron struggled to sit up, her stockings and garter belt askew. "Do you think that's proper?"

Rick regarded her wickedly. Propriety hardly seemed an issue worth debating in that outfit of hers. "I know that I don't have enough coins to spend the night on these blasted dryers," he teased.

"What does that bed of yours run on?" she asked.

Rick rolled off the machines, hoisting her over his shoulder. "I rock that one without so much as a nickel!"

THE FRONT DOOR BUZZER of Rick's apartment sounded at eight o'clock the next morning.

"Where's that coming from?" Caron asked sleepily from the kitchen doorway.

Rick, standing at the coffeemaker near the fridge dressed only in a pair of baggy gray sweatpants, spun around at the sound of her voice. Picking up twin mugs of steaming coffee from the counter, he paused to leisurely peruse the tossed-over kitten rubbing her sleep-heavy eyes. "Guess we really mushed that dress of yours, didn't we?" he asked in gentle teasing.

Caron cast a look over at the rosy garment hanging in wrinkles on her form. "I'll cover it with my coat," she decided in the throes of a yawn.

Rick delivered a mug to her at the doorjamb where she was nesting, impulsively kissing her cheek. He didn't have the heart to tell her about the detergent stain. He'd discovered it a half hour earlier when he'd gone down to retrieve their clothing from the Laundromat floor. Must've happened when he backed her up against the dryers. He'd wrecked another fancy dress. Wait till Deborah found out!

The buzzer sounded off again, as sharp as the sun slanting through the square window above the sink. Oh, how he hated this interlude to end! Pretty soon the whole world was going to close in on him, and he just might lose Caron because of it. He needed more time alone with her. More time to join them at the hip with Krazy Glue bonding. As it was, her faith in him was shaky at best. She wanted to believe in his convictions and was doing quite well with the ones she understood. But the big quake hadn't hit them yet. Rick wanted to have the sturdiest foundation possible when it did.

One thing was certain. He would never let her go again. They'd reconnected last night as if there hadn't been any lapse in their relationship. And once he explained about the first time, she would give it a prized spot in her memory, savor it in the manner it deserved.

"Rick, the door," Caron prodded.

"It's just reality calling us back," he conceded regretfully into her short cloud of mussed hair.

"Might be too important to ignore," she reasoned.

"Don't worry." He inhaled one last gulp of her fragrance before pulling back. "No one's ever backed off from me without a fight." Rick set his coffee on the counter and headed across the living room to the door. His mother, in the company of the Bobber, was on the other side.

"What on earth, Ricky," she chided, bustling past him. Rick stepped out of her path as the bulky diaper bag slung over her shoulder bumped his rib cage. "I was beginning to think you were still spinning around in Deborah's limousine." She thrust the cheery baby into his arms. "I think you should go put on a shirt. No one ever knows who may be calling—" She stopped.

"Caron's calling at the moment, Ma," he said, adding a necessary look of warning to the needless announcement.

"You did it again, didn't you, Rick!" Her loud, sudden lament caused Bobber's face to crumple against Rick's bare chest.

"Ma, we are consenting adults," Rick stated, nuzzling his bristly chin into the baby's bright red hair.

"Together one night," she scolded in awe. "And you did it again!"

"Mrs. Wyatt, please—" Caron interceded, jolted awake by all the commotion.

"Shame on the two of you for doing this to me!" Eleanor dumped the diaper bag and her purse on the kitchen table.

"Ma!"

"Just look at her dress, Richard Wyatt," Eleanor challenged with a jabbing finger. "Deborah will expect us to pay for it again. I will refuse this time too, I tell you!"

"My mother will not charge you a cent," Caron objected, openly suppressing a smile.

"Did she purchase it, Caron?" Eleanor demanded, standing her ground on the kitchen linoleum, a short, round thundercloud in her gray coat, a white scarf tied under her chin.

"Yes, she did," Caron admitted. "But—"

"You two children deserve each other!" Mrs. Wyatt threw her hands into the air.

"You are absolutely right, Ma." Rick moved up behind his mother with a stricken-looking baby in his arm. "Now tell Bobber you didn't mean to yell."

Eleanor gently patted the baby's cheek. "Don't you dare grow up like this rebel, baby boy."

"Ma, don't brainwash the Bobber."

"I should've known something was afoot when I couldn't get you on the phone," she clucked. "Then to be roused by Douglas Ramsey!" She shook her head in disgust.

"Mr. Ramsey called you?" Rick asked sharply.

"He said he got no answer at your Laundromat last night or this morning. Caron's roommate gave him your home number and he claims it's been busy for hours."

"That persistent old—"

"Goat?" Caron supplied glumly.

"Exactly!" Rick agreed.

"Look over here," Eleanor huffed, stomping to the shelf holding the telephone. "The receiver is off the hook."

"Incredible," Rick mocked, puckering as Bobber fingered his mustache.

"So it's no accident, then." Eleanor replaced the receiver with a thump. "So, you did manage to antagonize that rich man out of his senses."

"He certainly did," Caron affirmed in disapproval.

"No wonder you're incognito," his mother scolded. "Hiding out to lick your wounds after defeat. What would the neighborhood kids think of their hero?"

"They'd think I was a fallible human being," Rick ground out fiercely. "Wrung through the spin cycle by the Ramsey family disaster. I tried to be kind, to make my points politely, but the old guy wouldn't have it."

"And now he's no doubt turning the tables, checking up on you." Eleanor sized up her son with an insightful eye. "Ricky, you're in too deep. As much as I liked James, he wouldn't want this to take its toll on you."

Rick prowled the room with the thumb-sucking baby contentedly riding on his arm. "No, I can't give up. I thought so last night, for a while. But having Caron back in my life has shown me miracles are possible, if you want them badly enough. It isn't fair to brush Ramsey off after one clash. If people had done the same to me, I'd a been sunk by now."

"So, what's next, Rick? You want to meet with Ramsey today?" Caron asked hopefully.

"No, not yet."

"But Rick, the world's crashing in on us, on your scheme, on my job...."

"More than you know, honey," he agreed dolefully. "That's why we need some time to recharge. How does a night in the mountains sound? No telephones, no parents, no Granddaddy Bigbucks."

She gaped at him in amazement. "Just take off?"

"Right! We'll take Bobber to the Rockies, to one of those fishing resorts in the foothills," he proposed with new zeal. "We can leave now and easily return later on tomorrow. How does your Monday look?"

"I have a fairly light schedule ahead," she said after a moment of thought. "I planned to concentrate on the baby search."

"Ain't life ironic?" he crowed. "You can focus on the baby face-to-face."

"How will I ever explain my duplicity to the Ramseys?" she wondered in despair. "To my bosses?"

"I'll eventually take those blows for the both of us," Rick insisted. "You and I will never be on opposing sides of anything again, I promise you."

"Oh, you think you can conquer the entire world with those bulging muscles," Eleanor chided, skimming the toast crumbs off the counter with a dishrag.

"I intend to use brainpower this time," Rick informed her with a thrust of his chin.

"The very bulging muscle which gives you the most trouble," Eleanor rejoined.

"I feel funny about running off when this powder keg is about to explode," Caron protested.

"This girl makes sense," Eleanor chimed in.

"It can't explode without the three of us, now can it?" Rick reasoned, stepping closer to Caron. Bobber, true to his name, was bobbing into his chest like an animated doll, unaware of the controversy surrounding him. "We need time together before we face the world. I have things I want to say to you," he said on an intimate note. "I want to clear up your doubts about me. We have to learn to trust each other before outside interference threatens to blow us to smithereens again."

"Again?" she repeated in bleak confusion, smiling as the baby fingered her cloud of hair.

"I'll explain in my own time," he promised quietly.

"You'll be yammering on in explanation for the next century before this thing is through," Eleanor predicted, on tiptoe behind him so as not to be forgotten.

Rick turned in impatience. "May Caron and I yammer on into oblivion together. We've lost enough precious time as it is!"

"I never had anything against you, dear," Eleanor told Caron with effort, determined to budge into their circle.

"There was a time when you and my mother were good friends, Eleanor," Caron reminded her softly.

Eleanor raised her chin high. "But things happened."

"Ma, soon everybody will know everything."

"Heaven help us all!" Eleanor cried in exasperation. "But, if I can be of any help…"

"Take my tuxedo back to the cleaners, will ya?" he asked, tugging at the scarf knotted under her chin.

"How'd it fair? Will I be embarrassed out of my mind this time?"

"Not unless you dump something on it yourself," Rick reported with an eye roll.

"Then the insurance was a waste," she huffed. "Money down the drain."

"Speaking of money, please take your sawbuck out of the top pocket of the jacket. Caron didn't charge me a cent for the ride, the party, or the Chinese afterward." Rick beamed in victory when Eleanor, after failing to find a worthy retort, was forced to keep her mouth clamped shut.

"BELIEVE ME, I'M NOT offended by your mother's attempt last night to push money on you. It's kind of sweet the way she clucks over you." Caron chuckled as she dug through her evening bag on her front stoop twenty minutes later. "What I don't like, is that for some reason, the issue of money—the haves and have nots—seems to surround us from all corners."

"How so?" Rick asked, shifting Bobber, cozy in a quilted jacket with a hood tied close to his white moon face, from one arm to another.

"My mother believes wealth is the key to importance as a human being. Your mother believes cash is the weapon to handle us Carlisles. Ramsey obsesses with money and the power it brings."

"That's not everybody."

Caron gripped the doorknob, shoving her key in the lock. "Just wait till Megan gets her hands on you."

"Why?" he asked incredulously.

"The million-dollar reward for leading Ramsey to the baby." Caron pushed open the door, beckoning them into the tiled foyer of the split-entry town house. "Megan believes I deserve part of it for my role in the search. I've tried to explain that I am just the hired help, but—"

"But she isn't having any of it," Megan interrupted, hanging over the wrought-iron railing above them. "If it ain't old Hotshot," she oozed in greeting.

Rick regarded the pert blonde with amusement. "I plan to make sure Caron is rewarded for her efforts."

"Don't forget about the best friend behind the woman," she saucily directed.

"Unlikely, Megan," he conceded, "since you've obviously kept your gutsy wits about you. How've you been?"

"Worried sick about my best friend," she tossed back, her round blue eyes sheeted with relief. "I was afraid she drowned in a vat of rich, syrupy chocolate."

"Megan!" Caron squawked in embarrassment, zipping up five stairs leading to the living area of the house. "He knows."

"You addicted to anything, Meg?" Rick asked, following with the baby.

"I'll never tell," Megan purred. She turned her attention to Caron, now seated on the sofa, in the process of slipping off her high heels. "By the looks of your scuffed shoes, I'd swear you walked to Ramsey's."

Caron reddened. "Quite the opposite as you well know."

"And your dress looks like you crawled there," she pressed the issue with gaiety. "Just wait until your mother sees what's left of her Paul Drake dreams. A stain the size of Utah on your butt. And..." She turned her attention back to Rick in unspoken significance.

"Rick Wyatt playing the role of the dashing detective, Drake," he finished neatly with a slight bow at the waist. Bobber thought his movement was a game and squealed for more.

"Isn't he a lamb!" Megan gasped in delight, taking him from Rick's arms. "It's so nice to hold a baby with no health troubles for a change," she cooed. She sat down in an armchair with him, loosening his hood. "So nice to hold a billionaire," she chirped, bouncing him on her knee. "Ooo, your cologne is divine. What do they call it? Oil de bottom?" Bobber sat contented in her lap with a huge grin, obviously enjoying her animation. "So, are you betrothed yet, baby? I'm still free as a bird."

"My brother, Kyle, was asking after you," Rick said, strolling around the sun-drenched room. "He's not rich, but he's trained in many of the niceties that are still beyond Bobber."

"Just because Caron is sold on a Wyatt, doesn't

mean I'm as foolish. You guys never knew when to quit—nearly turned the school upside down!"

"I don't appreciate you discussing my love life," Caron put in.

"She's just guessing about the upside-down part," Rick assured. "Go get ready before your mother storms in and upsets my stomach."

"She's called several times already," Megan reported. "Starting at eight o'clock last night."

"What did you say?" Caron demanded.

"Well, the first time I claimed I didn't see your date at all, because you rolled off to fetch him in Ramsey's limo. Boy, did that tickle her! She didn't call back for four hours." At Caron's coaxing gesture, she continued. "The next time I said you were still out. Then this morning I said you were in the shower. Then you were sleeping soundly. The last call was about twenty minutes ago."

"I had better get going," Caron conceded hastily, popping up from the sofa with new energy. "I still have to contact my secretary as well," she murmured half to herself as she moved across the carpet. "Let her know I may not be in till late tomorrow."

"If at all," Rick called out as she disappeared into her bedroom.

"Where are you taking her?" Megan questioned bluntly.

"Maybe it would be easier if you didn't know," he suggested.

"After all the lies I've told in the last twelve hours, I think I can be trusted."

The contradiction of her statement may have escaped her, but Rick couldn't resist chuckling over it.

"We're going to the mountains for the night," Caron called out through the doorway, pulling a lime green sweater over her head before disappearing from view again.

"I'll take good care of her," Rick insisted defensively under Megan's suspicious glare.

Megan scrutinized him over the baby's bright red head. "How can I be sure, Hotshot?"

He balked at her nerve. "Why should I care if you are?"

"Look, Caron is like a sister to me," she explained in quiet reprimand, tossing a look to her bedroom to make certain Caron wasn't in listening range. "I picked up the pieces last time, and though I'd do it again, I'd rather not."

Rick eased down on the arm of her chair, speaking in low tones beneath Bobber's gurgles of glee. "I didn't realize until last night that Caron ever deeply cared for me."

"Well, you can be a lout," she accused.

"What else did I do?" he asked bleakly.

"You told her about our date, for one thing. It really hurt her, Rick, even after all these years."

"Well, she aggravated me to the limit that day," he said in excuse.

"She's liable to do so a lot of the time," Megan cautioned, rocking Bobber from one knee to another as he squirmed for action.

Rick drew a breath of patience. "I was only kidding."

"Well, you sound sincere," Megan relented somewhat dubiously.

"I *am* sincere!"

"It isn't enough on its own," Megan persisted.

"This relationship will only work if you understand the Caron psyche."

"I don't follow you," Rick muttered.

Megan shrugged uncomfortably. "What I'm trying to say is that she's normally not impulsive concerning men. She's not into casual flings. Her weakness for you is strictly out of character."

"You make her interest in me sound like a disease," he complained.

"Well, you are accustomed to heating girls into a fever," she teased.

Rick grinned. "You can rest easy over my feelings for Caron."

"They are..." she trailed off expectantly.

"They are private and personal for now," he maintained. "If you're looking for thrills of your own, look up Kyle."

"But you're the Wyatt I can't seem to shake from my mind at the moment," she said with sardonic sweetness.

His black brows arrowed suspiciously. "Why?"

"Because of a little wager between two best friends," she snorted rudely. "If it weren't for you I wouldn't be in the jam I'm in with Caron. At the very least, you should consider sending me on an itsy bitsy vacation with some of your reward money." Her lips puckered pitifully. "I will need lots of time to recuperate from the pain and humiliation I am about to suffer at your hands, mister!"

9

"So, DO YOU THINK you managed to keep the hounds at bay for the next twenty-four hours?" Rick asked Caron a short time later. They were nestled in the cab of his white pickup truck, rolling away from the city. Bobber sat between them, strapped securely to his car seat, gnawing on a teething cookie.

Caron turned her attention from the two-lane road to favor him with a smile. "I left word at my office that I'd be unreachable."

"Unreachable, eh?" Rick winced in pain. "Sounds like an indescribable loss."

Caron's sweet, light laughter filled the cab, causing Bobber to roll his head her way, his round face beaming.

"I think you've got a second fellow falling under your spell," Rick observed fondly.

"I hope so," she said, stroking the baby's velvety cheek. He allowed it from the comfort of Rick's care, favoring her with a small purr. It hurt Caron on a new unexplored level that Bobber was still nervous with her, still often regarded her with guarded eyes. She knew darn well that he didn't even know what he was doing, whom he was rejecting or why. But winning the child's approval had become supremely important to her. It would prove that she could manage babies in general.

Since the beginning of the heir hunt, Caron's mothering instincts had gradually awakened with a niggle here and there. She found herself glancing at babies on the street, wondering if any of them was Douglas Ramsey's grandson. She soon began to notice the differences in them—size, temperament and coloring. Babies became a subject of study. The arrival of Bobber on the scene had taken her from casual interest to hands-on participation. He was her answer to the baby riddle and an important part of Rick's life.

Apparently her time had come to think about raising a family of her own. She understood why her instincts for motherhood had lain dormant until now; with no siblings she had concentrated on the single professional life, gradually distancing herself from married friends with maternal duties. But she couldn't help wondering if it just wasn't in the cards for her. If she failed to befriend this particular baby, how could kid-crazy Rick ever entrust her to bear his children? Would she even have the courage to risk her own baby's rejection? What if, in the end, Rick ended up with Bobber himself and the baby couldn't tolerate her? Would Rick's vow never to let her go again be broken as his prom night one had been?

Her throat was tight with apprehension, but she forced herself to speak. "Rick, is it possible that you could end up with Bobber? Raising him, I mean?"

"It's true that someday I could end up with custody of the Bobber," he theorized with carefully chosen words. "But I highly doubt it's going to happen. Besides, I'm looking forward to fathering children of my own."

Caron gulped under his intent look. "How many?"

Rick released a carefree chuckle. "I'd be bound and

determined to keep on going until I land one with a bumpy nose and a fiery quick-draw wit."

Caron returned his easy grin with as much pleasure as she could muster. He was telling her that he wanted her children and expected her to be pleased. If only she had some guarantee that she could be that kind of nurturing caregiver.

They continued on their mountain trek, the Rockies a hazy outline on the horizon as they headed west on 66. The scenery was rustic, farmhouses with smoke curling from their chimneys, combines rolling over the flat farmland, planting winter wheat. They passed through several quaint, small towns, stopping once for a forty-five-cent cup of ice-cold apple cider, and later on for a lunch of trout, delivered fresh to their plates from a mountain stream.

"Estes Park, gateway to the Rocky Mountain National Park," Caron read on a sign as they rolled up to a guardhouse leading into the sprawling property. Rick handed the man behind the window five dollars and they continued through the gate.

"Have you been to the Rockies lately?" Rick asked softly over Bobber's dozing form.

"Not in ages," Caron confessed. "But one never forgets the splendor." They continued on the twisting road, wending upward into the majestic mountains. "Do we have a destination?" she asked a short time later. "It's one thing to be impetuous at our age, but we do have the baby along...."

Rick's profile remained glued to the winding road, but the laugh lines around his eyes and mouth crinkled. "Don't worry so much. We have reservations at Pine Cone Cottages, a small resort about twenty minutes from here. It's a getaway of mine, just right for some fishing and relaxation." He paused for a sober moment, as if preparing to say something important to her. "I want you to know I appreciate all of this, Caron."

"What do you mean, Rick?"

"Your willingness to escape on this outing, when you know damn well we're on the hot plate at home. Your blind faith in me and the Bobber. You've been just great since the start. The loyal pal I could always count on years ago. To me, that's every bit as important as the loving."

"Rick, I am anxious to settle that prom issue," she admitted, toying with the handle of her purse.

"We will," he promised.

The sensual quality of his voice made her knees squeeze together in anticipation. Rick always could make everything turn out right. Once Rick decided how he was going to handle Ramsey, they could concentrate on their own personal dreams and ambitions. Whether she had a job at that point was a question that lingered in her mind. A lot. "Rick, you read about the missing heirloom in the paper, didn't you?"

"Yeah, sure."

Rick's angular profile remained steady on the road. "It seemed like a subject best left alone. I imagine it would be impossible for you to continue the search, if you discovered the heirloom in the possession of a certain guy, wouldn't it?" he wagered.

"It would be concrete evidence," she admitted. The last piece to the puzzle—and ruin any chance of returning to the office with a reasonably clear conscience.

The last thing she wanted to see today was that silver dollar!

As it was, the end of the line was coming soon enough. They both knew it.

"You've been doing your job to the best of your ability," he insisted steadfastly.

Not true! If it had been anybody but Rick, she'd have hauled him in to the powers that be on the basis of James's note and the portrait of the nude redhead. They might have laughed her out of the office, but she would've followed through as expected with her trademark methodical investigating and definitive deduction. Rick had a way of twisting her and the issues around his little finger, until she wasn't capable of any rational thought!

Midafternoon they arrived at the resort. It was a small, quaint place sprinkled with ponderosa pines and lush meadowland. Log cabins sat in a crooked line, banking the edge of a meandering stream. Rick continued down the narrow private road to the larger log home sitting at the end of the row. It sported a wide porch across the front. A wooden sign carved with Pine Cone Office hung from the dormer, flapping with every gust of wind.

As Rick popped out of the truck to register, Bobber stirred to life again. The sight of Rick's retreating figure greatly distressed the baby. His moon face quickly reddened and his lower lip quivered in discontent.

"It's all right, Bobber," Caron consoled on a nervous note. "I'm still here."

Bobber, having apparently forgotten about Caron, rolled his head to the right to place the voice. Fear and fury flashed in his china blue eyes as he sized up his situation.

Caron's own lip shook slightly along with her arms

as she fumbled with the straps confining him. "Now, little baby," she crooned, "let's be happy together, you and I. After all, I'm all that's standing between you and a cool billion."

He hesitated in uncertainty as she knelt on the seat and awkwardly grasped him under his arms to haul him out of the molded car seat. "Not a whimper now," she pleaded, easing him up and over.

Bobber didn't whimper. He wailed. Squalled at the top of his lungs the second his bottom hit her lap.

Rick emerged from the office minutes later to discover the truck cab empty. His gaze skated the area to find Caron off near a cluster of pines with Bobber in her arms, strolling and singing an off-key tune into the wind. An odd sensation crept through his system at the sight of Caron struggling to win over his little guy, moving him far more profoundly than any of her sexy flirting had. Of course as a novice, she was trying too hard to win the baby over. She was a bundle of nerves and Bobber had been irritated with her all along for that very reason. But she was working on him with passionate resolve.

No wonder she asked if Rick had intentions of raising Bobber. She obviously wanted to be prepared!

Rick realized with sudden certainty that he could never love another human being as much as he loved her at that moment. All her attempts to please—just because he'd asked her to—culminated in a huge knot of emotion, reaching to every fiber of his insides, clear down to the toes of his black boots. He hadn't felt this vulnerable, this frightened, since... Since Caron climbed into the back seat of his Chevy in 1983!

"You pinch that kid or what?" he called out as he crossed the span of gravel. The moment Caron whirled on him, her moist eyes mirroring the Bobber's, he realized he'd been too flippant.

"It isn't funny that babies don't like me," she wailed desperately, depositing Bobber in Rick's arms.

"My mistake," Rick conceded, shifting the baby to his shoulder. "I wanted to help you laugh it off."

"Ha, ha." Caron glared at him, all the more angry as the creases in his cheeks deepened in his effort to suppress his smile. "Just a joke, is it? Watch the spectacle. Watch the fumbling woman pinch the baby? Watch the—"

"Watch the most delightful, most endearing sight I've ever seen," Rick quietly interrupted.

"What?" she cried in confusion, wiping her cheeks with the back of her hand.

"With all you've conquered in your life, you're crushed that this baby doesn't warm to you."

"How can I have babies of my own if they're going to cry the moment I touch them?" she wondered bleakly.

"Aw, c'mere, Quick Draw," he murmured in invitation, drawing her close to make it a threesome. Bobber's sniffles filled her ear as he rested his forehead against her hair. "You went to school for a zillion years to become an attorney, exerting an enormous amount of patience and energy, I'm sure. You have to give this child care thing a chance with at least a fraction of that zest."

Caron rested her head on his chest in exhaustion. "What if I can't do this?"

"You can," he asserted. "Your desire is the main thing. Bobber can sense you're nervous, that's all. And I think he misses his mother," he added in honesty. "As it happens, she will be coming around tomorrow to rescue him."

"Oh, Rick." Caron released a breath of relief, burrowing her cheek into the denim of his jacket.

"In the meantime we're going to enjoy our day. By the time we head back, I can guarantee Bobber will be your best buddy." When she lifted a dubious brow, he set the baby back in her arms. Bobber's head spun at Rick in betrayal. "This is your call, man," he said, ruffling his red hair. "The hottest babe in the woods wants you. Don't blow it."

Bobber accepted his fate, just as long as he could keep an eye on Rick. Caron made certain he could, trailing Rick back to the truck as he retrieved their suitcases.

Their log cabin proved to be a warm, two-room affair with braided rugs, a wood-burning stove, a kitchenette, a double bed and a miniscule bathroom.

While the baby slept off his exhaustion in his portable crib in the kitchen, Rick settled down on the creaky steel-framed bed in the bedroom.

"Shouldn't we be doing something else?" Caron asked halfheartedly as Rick pulled her against his length.

"Like what?" he rumbled in discontent.

"I don't know," Caron murmured, nipping his shoulder through his T-shirt. "Unpack or something. It *is* the afternoon."

"Take a page from Bobber's book," Rick suggested, twirling a lock of her silky hair around his finger. "When he's tired, he conks out."

"And when he's angry, he bellers," Caron added meditatively, running a finger along Rick's mustache.

"Maybe there is something to be said for expressing one's feelings more openly, as a baby does naturally."

"I love you, baby," Rick groaned contentedly, squeezing her close. "And I can't stop the urge to show you how much. Especially on this nice, cozy bed..."

"All I've ever wanted was to be a part of everything you are," she said softly, nipping at his ear.

Rick couldn't help but notice, however, that there was something quite wicked dancing in her gem green eyes. "What's going on in that pretty little noggin?" he asked.

"I was just thinking, Rick. For the first time in this girl's memory, you look like a desperate teen!"

"You put that look there, lady," he growled wolfishly. "You'll have to wipe it away. Over and over again, I hope."

"Sounds like a long-term job," she huffed in exasperation.

"Sounds like a marriage proposal," he corrected, moving his thumb across her chin.

She gaped in amazement. "You're asking, right now?"

"I can't think of a better time, considering I've already asked you to have my baby."

"Oh, you mean the bumpy-nosed one with the quick wit?" she sought to clarify with feigned innocence.

"I do. And any others that may turn up."

"How can I refuse such a romantic offer?" Caron dropped her lips back to his, melding her limbs into his length.

"Oh, Caron," he rasped, tearing his lips from her mouth. "I've missed you in my life."

"Why didn't you call me before now?" she asked, desperate to understand.

He frowned thoughtfully. "Because I didn't want to be turned down, I guess. Didn't want to find out you weren't that angel I remembered. Then the heir situation came along and Kyle told me you worked at snap, crackle, pop. The coincidence seemed too incredible not to be fateful. It seemed like a second chance for us."

"You didn't sound too interested on the telephone," she recalled dryly.

"I always come on too smart. Especially when I'm scared. Believe me, calling you was one of the most courageous things I've ever done. I was hoping for instant harmony. All I got was your instant suspicion. True to nature I blew a fuse. Couldn't handle the bickering with my heart split in two over James and everything."

"And then I showed up at your place."

"Something I never expected you to do!"

"I couldn't leave it alone," she admitted.

"Not you!" he agreed in dour adamancy, tweaking her nose. "I just expected the cops, or the bar association, or the Mounties, or Ramsey himself. But you charged at me in person. Set me up for the fall in your snug, racy suit and little yellow hat." He rolled his eyes with an unsteady sigh. "You've always been a singeing heat in some very uncomfortable places inside of me."

"Good."

Rick's heart began to pound harder as Caron sat up to straddle him, digging her jean-clad thighs into his rib cage. She took the initiative by pulling off his T-shirt and gently clawing through his dense chest hair with her tiny fingernails. He pulsed with anticipation as she slowly, slowly raked upward to his nipples, beading them with rapid little scrapes. With a lazy-eyed look she drew her mouth to the small dark circles to lavish them with long wet sucks, her hands again roaming free on his pink, sensitized skin.

Just when he thought the hair on his chest was going to ignite into a forest blaze, she ever so slowly uncurled on his length. Soon she was pressing her pelvis into his arousal, stimulating his lower body to an equally aching madness through their layers of confining clothing. With frenzied frustration he ran his large hands down her spine, pushing up her lime green sweater, kneading the gentle curve of her bottom deeper and deeper into him.

Caron's breath came in hard, fast puffs as his arousal grew beneath her.

"I'm not a man who likes restraints," he complained heavily, unclasping her bra, reaching up to peel it and her sweater off with one fluid motion.

"Mmm..." With a heady moan of need, Caron arched her back so he could unbuckle and unsnap the lower barriers between them. Since the urgency was his this time, Rick first slid his pants off, kicking them aside with amazing dexterity. He then reached back down to unfasten her zipper, tugging the layers of fabric down over her hips to reveal creamy, satin skin.

Heat as intense as the sun beating down on the roof burned them as they ever so slowly ignited in afternoon lovemaking. Unlike the last time on the dryers in the dead of night, or the first time in the back seat of Rick's car, they were on brilliant display for daytime exploration.

Caron was like a pliable kitten as she rolled off him, tucking herself underneath his body for a long, liquid kiss. Rick slowly tasted the recesses of her mouth, his hands cupping her face. When he started to shift position on the bed, he felt her hands pressing him back down on her. He would've thought it was his skin-grazing appeal, if not for the flash of uncertainty in her eyes.

"What's the matter, honey?" he asked gently, teasing her lower lip with his thumb.

Caron rolled her head on the pillow, blinking to avoid his eyes. "Nothing. Just love me, Rick. Like this. Right now."

"You're still self-conscious about your body," he second-guessed in awe.

"Only without clothes!" she confessed in a squeak.

"But we made unbridled love last night," he chided.

"But it was dark...." she stumbled in explanation.

Rick gaped in disbelief. "My sweet, innocent darling. If you had any idea just how attractive you really are...you'd really be dangerous!" Deaf to her murmurs of protest, Rick rolled off her. With one arm propped under him, he took leisurely perusal of her lanky nude form, stretched out in ivory splendor before him on the worn blue sheet.

"Rick—"

"Hush, now," he crooned, evading her swatting hand to stroke the curve of her thigh. His touch traveled up to the juncture of her womanhood, caressing the wispy V in the breadth of his huge palm. Satisfied with her sigh of pleasure, he continued his leisurely trip to her navel, then on to her slightly rounded breasts.

"Thank goodness she didn't tamper with you two beauties," he said, kissing the small fleshy mounds with a grateful smack. When she released a relaxed laugh, he kissed them again and again, tantalizing her nerve endings to the breaking point. "You can trust me all the way, my love," he assured hoarsely. "My beautiful, beautiful love."

In the midst of his sweet torment, she moved her hand to his arousal, skimming his solid shaft with light-hard pressure. When he stopped for a breath, she exploited his vulnerability, tipping him over on the mattress.

"Wench!" he growled, reeling back on the bank of pillows. She followed his fall, landing on his chest with a thud, locking her lips on his before he could regroup. After a dizzying kiss, she sat up again on his abdomen, guiding him deeply inside her. He smiled. Her new belief in her beauty was the cause of his incredible happiness. Or at least the second reason.

"This what you had in mind?" she asked, tipping her head back with new abandon.

"Give it to me," he ordered thickly.

With hands gripping his massive shoulders, Caron moved over him. Fevered impulsion soon brought them to a heart-hammering climax. They collapsed together in the soft, cushy mattress.

"Now this is what I call an afternoon nap," Rick groaned in pleasure, gently stroking her back.

Bobber's cry suddenly bounced off the walls of the cabin.

"Nap time's over," Caron declared on a sigh, slowly raising herself from the bed, scanning the floor for her clothing.

"I dearly love that kid, but in some ways I will be

extremely glad when his mom comes back for him," Rick grumbled, swinging his legs over the side of the bed. "Coming, you little siren!" he called out.

"Our own children will no doubt be a bit of an inconvenience on occasion," she predicted, tossing him his rumpled briefs and jeans.

"Yeah," he conceded, impatiently tangling with the clothing as Bobber squalled all the louder. "But at least I'll have the pleasurable memory of making them myself!"

AFTER TREATING BOBBER to a snack of applesauce and a diaper change, the trio took a walk along the stream running behind the cabins. Bobber rode in an infant carrier on Rick's back, his round blue eyes glowing as brightly as the azure skies above them. Caron had had the foresight to bring along her camera. With Bobber's hand-clapping approval, she began to take candid shots of the boys and the scenery.

"When we get back to the cabins, we'll have to ask the owner to take a few group shots of the three of us," Rick proposed. "It'll give us something to remember this crazy little triangle of ours."

Caron could read the regret in his eyes. Whatever was in store tomorrow concerning Bobber, Rick was seeing it as a loss. It was understandable. He was just wild about the child. To have a child with him…

"So, tell me more about this bet between you and Megan," Rick prompted in a change of subject, taking careful steps on the dirt trail.

"I was wondering when you were going to bring it up," she said in a knowing tone, matching his effort to be lighthearted.

"She sure was in a huff about it."

"Well, you don't have to look so smug over her misfortune," Caron chided, the dimples deepening in her cheeks.

Rick shrugged his broad shoulders. "Guess I just can't help myself."

"Then you don't deserve to know the details," she proclaimed, turning on the heels of her hiking shoes, trotting farther up the dirt trail winding into the hills.

Rick caught up in a few easy strides, trapping Caron from behind in a bear hug. "You'll talk, missy," he muttered in mock menace against her fragrant fluff of hair. "We have our ways, don't we, Bobber?"

Caron twisted out of his arms, turning to face a pair of laughing faces. "If this innocent only knew of the things you involve him in," she cooed.

"He's just one of the guys," he retorted, reaching back to tug at the visor on the baby's bonnet-style cap.

"All right," Caron surrendered. "Megan and I made a pact back in school. Foolishly, of course," she added.

"Let us be the judge," he directed, arms folded across his chest.

Caron stared off into the horizon at the looming mountains with a reminiscent grin. "Well, we made a wager over which one of us would get a phone call from you first."

"You did?" he asked in boyish delight.

"Of course we thought the chances of it occurring faded years ago," she assured him in a downplaying tone. "I just happened to have kept the signed agreement stuffed away inside my yearbook."

"Held out for me all this time," he boasted.

"It was forgotten there, Rick," she insisted.

"Sure, sure," he agreed with a wave of dismissal.

"Pressed into the pages with my old activity pass!"

"Hope you're listening to this, Bobber," he advised under his breath. "This is the same kind of stuff that is going to happen to you, man."

Caron sighed in exasperation at the sight of Bobber focused on a scampering chipmunk. "He couldn't care less, Rick."

"Babies are a wonder of miracles," Rick retorted. "He may remember my advice when he really needs it."

"Heaven help him!" Caron lamented, throwing her hands in the air.

"Hey, for the class rebel, I haven't done so bad, have I?" he challenged, cuffing her chin. "I've got a great business. Lots of family and friends. And now the circle is complete with the girl of my dreams. The Bobber could do worse."

He guided her mouth to his for a leisurely kiss. Caron closed her eyes, savoring the sweetness of his lips, all the while aware of the added attraction of a fat little finger exploring the curve of her ear.

"So what does the loser of the bet have to do?" Rick asked, releasing her lips with a smack.

Caron gazed at him with twinkling green eyes. "It would spoil the fun to tell in advance."

"Not fair!"

"You're the one double-dealing," she argued. "You've been running up an enormous credit line on trust. I want to hear about the prom, Hotshot, right now! Why didn't you come for me?" Caron knew the pain she was feeling was expressed vividly on her torn-up face. But he wouldn't dodge the issue any longer. "It won't affect our future, if that's what you're afraid of," she added to soften her flare-up.

"As I told you, I understand about teenage boys now—"

"Well, you don't understand about me, Caron," he cut in. "And in this case, I think the pain was spread out pretty equally." Despite her noises of confusion, he kept his silence as he grasped her elbow, guiding her to the grassy ground banking the stream. "Let's sit here for a little while. Watch the water roll."

Caron obligingly sat beside him on the hard ground, reaching over to dab Bobber's runny nose with a tissue. "It's not like you to be at a loss for words," she prodded in complaint.

"I know the words. Expressing them is the problem." Rick kept his eyes on the rushing waters sparkling in the sunshine for a long, pensive moment. He eventually turned to her, his dark eyes steady and warm. "You see, Caron, it just so happens that you won that bet of yours ten years ago."

"What!"

"To tell you the truth, it's still painful for me to remember. And I've never told another living soul," he confided with difficulty. "Except Ma."

Caron placed her hand on his raised knee, peering at him expectantly. "You called me?"

"Just like I promised. Got the brush-off from your mother. She said you were sleeping or something."

"So you gave up?"

"So I came over," he quickly corrected. "Tangled with Deborah in person."

"Why didn't you tell me this sooner?" she gasped in dismay.

"And let her wreck all the good stuff?" he demanded in endearing indignation. "Not on your life! Nope, I figured there was no rush."

"And what if I had hesitated as you hauled me up on the dryers?" she asked wryly.

"I don't know! Guess I just hoped—and rightly so—that you'd be too turned on to ask questions. I knew this moment would come soon enough, if everything worked out."

Caron thought about the revelation, anger surging through her system. "My mother's interference knows no bounds! I'd like to get my hands on her this very minute."

"Which is one reason why I've chosen to tell you miles away from the city," he explained. "We have to settle this between ourselves. Drawing her into it is only secondary in importance."

"If you did care, Rick, why didn't you come back the next day or the next?" she persisted, her heart constricting in pain.

Rick sighed deeply, covering the hand on his knee before she could snatch it away. "Caron, your mother was as rude and mean as she could be about it—"

"The rebel succumbs to Deborah's tirade," she interrupted in disappointment.

"Worse," he confessed. "Deb shot some points home that I simply couldn't argue."

"Like what, Rick?"

"Emotionally, I was set to fight for you, Caron," he declared fiercely. "You did crazy things to my heart and I cherished you as I did no one else. But your mother wounded me with the truth. I had an attitude problem. I took what I wanted. You, on the other hand, were extremely mature, directed. Then she pinned me down about the future." Rick shot Caron a helpless look. "My intentions didn't extend past the weekend. I'd always gotten by on the seat of my pants."

"Your rejection shattered me completely!" she cried woundedly.

"I didn't know!" Rick maintained defensively. "It never occurred to me back then. You just seemed to have your act so together. She was very persuasive on that count. Said I'd only be an anchor in your life, that you were a brilliant girl with a full scholarship to Harvard. Harvard! You never told anybody about that, Caron."

"I was already known as the bookworm of the student council," Caron said in defense, "while you were regarded as the shining rebel knight fighting for student rights. I couldn't have stood the extra heckling."

"Well, Deb did a full number on me about messing with your future," Rick went on. "Said you were destined for great things. Hell, she was pushing all my buttons. She knew if you'd given me your virginity, you'd give me a whole lot more. I was slapped down properly. Figured she was right. I didn't have what it takes to handle a bundle of brains like you."

"How awful for you," Caron conceded in sympathy.

Rick shook his head dazedly. "Then she moved in for the kill. Insisted that my glory days were over the minute I grabbed my diploma. That the popular rebels like me who floated through high school with charm and arrogance never grew up, that we were the burger flippers and floor scrubbers. She said wallflower scholars like you made the world go round and would eventually shine as responsible adults. By the time I walked away from your house, I wasn't sure I had the skills to direct my feet home."

"She never said a word," Caron whispered numbly. "She knew how I cried. Pretended it didn't matter." Caron put her fists to her eyes to blot out the memory.

"She thought it was the right thing to do," Rick offered in fairness. "But I've never understood why she didn't appreciate your beauty as well as your brains. What a tragedy."

"She has dwelled on my unattractiveness since childhood," Caron admitted. "I've never been able to shake that feeling of physical inadequacy."

"You've always been the most desirable creature on earth to me," he murmured huskily.

"Oh, how her lecture must have hurt."

"It was a hell of a graduation present," he confirmed soberly, "learning you're a has-been at eighteen. Though it wasn't her intention, it turned out to be just the jump start I needed. I wasn't about to give up the respect of my peers—my own self-respect."

"So you went out and earned the admiration of the entire neighborhood," Caron finished with a smug nod.

Rick grinned. "Eventually. I enrolled in vocational school, pooled my mechanical abilities with some training. I worked at a car dealership for a couple years, saving my money for a business of my own. The building housing the shoe store came up for sale and the rest is history."

"The neighborhood really needed a Laundromat," Caron agreed. "And a place to socialize. Hotshots is a very inventive combination."

"Don't pass the word about our rendezvous atop

the dryers," he cautioned in teasing sternness. "If the sideline were to catch on, I'd have the vice squad after me!"

Caron's eyes slitted naughtily. "Don't worry, darling. The only person I'd like to lure to the dryers is my mother. A nice hot tumble inside number seven might be just the thing to shake her to her senses!"

Rick sighed wistfully. "I've often wondered what would have happened if you had opened the door on that day so long ago."

"What if?" She squeezed his hand. "All we can do now is move on together, grateful for the second chance."

"Yep. And speaking of second chances, I want you to help me unharness this critter from his upper deck seat," Rick said, reaching around to playfully poke Bobber in the tummy. "He's in extremely good spirits right now, making it your perfect time for some intensive Bobber bonding."

When Caron reached for the baby this time, it was with a far steadier grip. To their relief, Bobber took the transfer like a trooper, pressing his hands into Caron's cheeks. She promptly rewarded him with a kiss.

"Whoa, there, partner," Rick cautioned in a teasing voice. "You got a lip-lock on my babe." When they nuzzled and giggled on, paying no attention to his complaint, Rick did the only thing he could think of. He snapped some pictures of them. About a dozen or so.

10

"I DON'T LIKE THIS, Rick." Caron's tone was ominous as she and Bobber stood beside him on the sidewalk in front of Hotshots late Monday afternoon. They'd just returned from their trip to the Rockies and a Closed sign hung in the front window, wedged between the glass and the tilted wooden blinds. Rick had no intention of changing his mind about his master plan, either. No amount of cajoling from Caron would sway him.

"Stay here, troops," he directed, popping inside for a brief look around. Satisfied that everything was undisturbed, he joined them back on the sidewalk, moving toward the street door leading directly to his second-floor apartment. Caron was right on his heels, Bobber resting in the hollow of her hip, a huge diaper bag swinging from her shoulder.

"Figure it this way," she proposed anxiously, "if they were meant to be a lifelong item, fate would've brought them back together, too."

Rick set the portable crib against the brick building and turned to plant a kiss on her perfectly pert nose. "Fate is sort of forcing them together, Quick Draw. Wily old Cupid plans to make them in-laws."

They took on the steep staircase with all of Bobber's belongings, debating the parent issue all the way. Bobber, now content in a newfound friendship with

Caron, leaned comfortably into her torso, a thumb planted firmly in his mouth. His trust had become immensely important to her, making it all the more important that he have just the right future—with or without Douglas Ramsey.

"Set him in his high chair," Rick requested, moving through the small apartment, switching on lights. "We'll heat up his grub and get those prizefighters over here for the final face-off."

"What if one won't come?" Caron asked doubtfully, securing a bib around the baby's neck. "After we've invited the other," she added for effect.

Rick paused in the center of his kitchen, clutching a baby bottle and a jar of strained carrots. "Just which one do you think would turn down the opportunity to sound off to this audience?" he wondered incredulously.

"Which indeed?" Caron laughed in surrender. "You don't even know what's funny, Bobber," she added in a teasing note as he mimicked her.

"You call Deb the debutante first," he suggested, moving to the microwave. "She can probably run faster than my ma, but she has more miles to cover."

Eleanor Wyatt was the first to arrive about a half hour later, her round, cheery face set in uncharacteristic discontent. "Deb wouldn't dare show up here," she proclaimed as she crossed the threshold. "No offense to you, Caron," she added with a small nod in the younger woman's direction. She peeled off her woolen coat, swiftly settling into Rick's wooden rocker with Bobber and a book of fairy tales.

"Now Ma—" Rick began, only to be interrupted by the front buzzer. Caron moved to the door to find her mother on the other side.

"Caron!" Deborah exclaimed. Despite her warrior stance, her shell of stiff gold hair was slightly mussed and her kelly green suit a trifle rumpled. "I don't understand any of this," she hissed in her daughter's ear. "I've been in constant touch with Megan since Saturday night, begging for news of you. Then you call with this preposterous summons. What on earth could Richard Wyatt have to do with you? Is he up on charges or something? Does he need an attorney?"

"Rick isn't in any trouble," Caron said under her breath, casting a quick glance back into the apartment to see if the Wyatts could hear their exchange. By the set of Rick's shoulders in the kitchen doorway, she was sure he could. "We spent last night together in the Rockies."

"But what of the charming Paul Drake?" she desperately demanded.

"There is no Paul Drake, Mother. Rick is the one who called you for my number."

"That's fraud!"

"That's entertainment," Rick corrected with a cutting, mirthful edge.

"You didn't take *him* to the Ramsey affair, did you?" Deborah demanded in despair with the thrust of a manicured finger. "No wonder Megan's been giving me the brush-off! How can you be falling for him again, Caron? Your professional reputation will be tarnished!"

"It most certainly will not," Caron scoffed hotly. "Rick is a reputable businessman. And even if he weren't, I'd still want him just because."

"Come away with me now," Deborah urged.

Caron held firm as Deborah attempted to pull her

out on the landing. "You won't pull us apart again, Mother. I love him. Still love him," she corrected.

Deborah released her with a bleak cry. "Why him? Why now, after all these years?"

"Come in and find out," Caron invited with a sweeping hand.

"Seems I have no choice!" Deborah shot past her daughter into the living room, a well-dressed locomotive of fury.

"Hello, Deborah," Eleanor greeted flatly.

Deborah slowly drank in the sight of Eleanor, seated in the rocking chair with the baby in her lap, and the array of baby things scattered around the apartment. She whirled back on Caron on the verge of explosion.

Rick sauntered closer, his arms folded across his expansive chest. Clad in a white T-shirt and faded blue jeans, with his dark eyes burning and his mouth curled sardonically, he was an older version of the rebel she knew and resented.

Deborah eyed him warily. "Indulged in some free-lance fatherhood I see, Richard."

"Ricky did no such thing," Eleanor countered in indignation. "He—"

"Ma, please," Rick cut in, extending a stifling hand. "The Bobber's legit, Deborah," he informed her easily. "Legit by even your standards."

"I imagine you told Caron everything," Deborah deduced on a plainly unapologetic note as her gaze shifted from Caron's granite expression to Rick's smug one.

"I am so disappointed in you, Mother," Caron said tersely.

"I did what I thought best," Deborah staunchly maintained.

Caron shook her head in pity. "You've always tried to control me."

"You were a child back then, Caron," Deborah fired back. "I did what I thought should be done to ensure your future. You've always had a quick wit, a brilliant mind. You needed to nourish your intellect, not your libido."

Her mother's blunt remark scalded her to the core, but she sought to control her temper. This was a fight she could win hands down, by just being in the right. "You should've trusted my brilliance then, Mother. Trusted me to decide my own fate."

"A young girl infatuated with the class hunk?" she spat in disbelief.

Rick drew a huge cynical smile. "Thank you for the compliment. As you know, good looks are essential in the race for social supremacy."

"Shut up, son," Eleanor intervened.

He murmured a suspect apology, stepping closer to Caron in support. The last thing he wanted was a face-off between the Wyatts and the Carlisles. Caron was on his team. Permanently.

Deborah attempted to put her arms around her daughter's stiff body. "I love you with all my heart and wanted you to have every opportunity to succeed," she babbled in justification. "I couldn't let you throw it all away for some passionate affair."

"You don't know that I would have," Caron urged, using her elbow as a buffer between them.

Deborah's face crumpled as if fancying herself the injured party. "But I couldn't take the chance, don't you see? Yes, perhaps Rick Wyatt was momentarily interested. But what if he became bored with what you had to offer? Boys that age only appreciate a fancy wrapping. They—"

"She did have a fancy wrapping!" Rick cut in again sharply. "You're the one who's held her back, Deborah, always insinuating that she had only brains to see her through life. That she was plain and could only aspire to beauty."

"Stay out of it, Ricky!" Eleanor scolded. "We all can see Caron's never been prettier."

Rick's patience evaporated. "Forget it, Ma! Caron needs my assurances until she learns that she's a lovely woman inside and out. Until Deborah stops pressing her own image of beauty on Caron."

"Why, I never!" Deborah blurted out in instant denial.

"For heaven sakes, Deb," Eleanor huffed, ignoring her own advice against interference, "has any one of us ever met your standards?"

"I only strive for the best," Deborah maintained, studying her flawless nails.

"Always strived for something better, you mean," Eleanor corrected. "You've been blind to the best. It's been under your very nose all these years. A wonderful husband, a devoted daughter. And a group of true friends—whom you chose to abandon," she added with a wounded look.

"Well," Deborah said with a sniff, "I've always felt that our break would have been a clean one had the children not fought the night of the prom."

"Hey, don't you dare blame us for your problems," Caron swiftly interceded.

"Your girl is right," Eleanor admitted. "We used

them as an excuse. So, have you found better friends in your new neighborhood?''

"Not better," Deborah confessed. "But I do like change, Elly. You and the girls have always been content with staying close to home, hanging around this neighborhood. 'Tisn't enough for me."

"Mother, I fear you will never have enough of anything," Caron told her sadly. "I know I certainly will never please you."

Deborah reared back in shock. "Why, Caron, is this the way you really feel?''

Caron nodded with difficulty. "You always push things too far, Mom. You believe in me only to a point, even now."

"But I'm so proud of you, dear."

"You are *almost* pleased, *almost* proud. Perfection, to you, is always just around the corner."

"You have an attitude problem, Deborah," Rick informed her. "Take it from the attitude expert."

Deborah's face contorted in fury. "How dare you invade my life this way?''

"I dare because I intend to take you on as my mother-in-law," he announced, baring a row of white teeth under his slash of a black mustache.

Deborah clutched her heart as though shot point-blank. "You don't mean it!"

"We're taking the vows, all right," Rick affirmed, glowing under her mortified look. "To love, honor and banter with the best of 'em for the rest of our days."

"But you've been out of touch for ten years," Deborah sputtered. "How can you possibly be sure it's right?''

"Because we took that long journey separately,

Mother," Caron promptly informed her with pride. "We've known others and no one quite compares."

"Ditto for me, Mother Deborah," Rick agreed.

She shot him a lethal look. "Don't ever call me that! What about your career, Caron?" she attempted to reason. "Your social connections to people like the Ramseys?"

"I don't plan to fall into a dark hole after the wedding," Caron retorted, embarrassed by her mother. "I love my work and I will continue practicing law."

"Are you still so concerned with the cream of the crop?" Eleanor challenged. She rose from the rocker with Bobber, gently depositing him in his playpen. "Of course you must be, sending a limousine into the neighborhood to pick up my son."

Deborah blinked in confusion.

"Don't play innocent with me," Eleanor scolded, hands on her ample hips. "Caron picked Ricky up Saturday night in a stretch limo. It reeks of your highfalutin ways!"

"If I had a limousine, I'd have ridden past your place myself," Deborah snapped back.

"Probably honking the horn to the tune of 'Yankee Doodle Dandy,'" Eleanor snorted.

"A job for my chauffeur," Deborah corrected.

"You two are having the time of your lives ripping into each other," Caron observed in horror.

"Who can make a better job of it than two ex-friends?" Deborah reasoned with a satisfied nod.

"Or two future in-laws?" Eleanor chimed in, to Deborah's chagrin. "I managed to live with all of your airs before you moved away," she acknowledged graciously. "I imagine I can adjust once again."

"Well, my style was okay when you wanted help

choosing a wallpaper pattern or a new dress," Deborah reminded her.

"Yes, you do have a certain flair," Eleanor relented. "But it doesn't mean you know everything."

"I know you could look ten years younger if you tinted your gray hair brown and wore heels rather than those rubber soles," Deborah observed with sharp inspection.

"Lots of the movie stars have gone completely gray," Eleanor maintained with a sniff. "And I have weak arches. You know about my arches, Deborah."

"And scarves are out as headwear," Deborah added, spying the plaid one tossed over Eleanor's coat on the sofa. "O-U-T!"

"Why—You are O-U-T!" Eleanor frothed, pointing to the door. "As of right now."

"Very well." Deborah stepped rapidly to the door. "But this isn't over yet."

"I won't be turned away this time, Deb," Rick warned, winding a thick protective arm around Caron. "I've got nothing but pride in myself now. I'm quite worthy of being the son-in-law of the illustrious Deborah Carlisle."

Caron turned to him as the door slammed shut after her. "What have we done to her, Hotshot?" she wailed in worry.

"Given her a dose of real life," Eleanor piped up. "Don't you fret, Deb will come around." She leaned over to stroke Bobber's head with a loving hand. "Perhaps not in time for the wedding, but certainly in time for the first birth. Not even that dragon could resist a precious one like you," she cooed at the child.

"Ma!" Rick protested. "Let me get a ring on her finger first." But he was pleased over the prospect of his mother fussing over his baby sometime in the future. Caron could see it in those delicious dark eyes of his.

CARON ARRIVED at the office Tuesday morning to find it a hubbub of activity. She paused at her secretary's desk just as the pleasant, middle-aged woman was setting the telephone back in its cradle.

"Good morning, Glenny," Caron said cheerily, edging her hip against Glenda Bain's desk to examine the telephone messages thrust into her hands. "I see half of these are from Mr. Ramsey," she noted, thumbing through the yellow squares of paper.

"The other half are from his sister, Agatha," Glenda reported, picking up the telephone as it buzzed again. "Sharp, Krandell and Peterson," she rattled off. "Oh, yes, Mr. Ramsey," she said, her eyes rising to her immediate superior for on-the-spot direction.

Caron raised a finger to her lips, then reached for the open appointment book on Glenda's desk to scan her schedule.

"Yes, sir, I can assure you that she's expected in today," the secretary efficiently hedged. "She hasn't reached her desk yet, however...."

Caron set the book back down on the cluttered desktop, pointing to the open space at one o'clock. Glenda swiftly relayed the message and hung up.

"He didn't like the delay," Glenda said with a cringe. "He was already chomping at the bit yesterday, along with the sister."

"He's current with all of the claims of last week," Caron complained. "But," she relented, "the man is accustomed to snapping his fingers for immediate action. So, how did the interviewing go without me yesterday?" she asked brightly, forcing herself to keep up the pretense of the search. She hoped by day's end Bobber's mother would be back and things would be settled.

Glenda nodded with a smile. "I put that sharp paralegal in charge of the interviews just as you instructed. He filled out the questionnaires according to your specifications. I must say, there are a few possibilities," Glenda informed her hopefully, rolling back in her chair to retrieve them from the bottom drawer of the file cabinet behind her. "You'll find a couple possibilities in there," she said quietly, setting the folders in Caron's outstretched arms. "Medals, I mean. It sure would help if we knew exactly what sort we were looking for."

"Mr. Ramsey's simply trying to protect himself from any flimflam," Caron offered in excuse. She hadn't told a soul at the firm that she knew the medal to be a silver dollar, fearing Douglas would be angry with Agatha for spilling the beans. At the rate the secrets were mounting, Caron feared she would soon burst. "Can't trust anybody these days with a billion at stake," she said with a laugh. "Not even one's lawyer."

"He's got the best in you, Caron," Glenda proclaimed.

Caron shot her a crooked grin. "I guess we can allow him some slack under the circumstances just the same. We all have a confidence or two we believe is best kept."

"Let me know if you wanna trade a few," Glenda teased, twirling a pencil in her hand.

Caron stopped short by the door to her office with a sudden afterthought. "By the way, keep on the lookout for my personal photos. I left them at the one-hour place downstairs and they'll be sending them up."

"Will do," Glenda promised, reaching again for the ever-ringing telephone.

Caron spent the morning going through the motions of examining the claims. Like last week's batch, yesterday's ranged from outrageous to pathetic to downright hilarious. Douglas Ramsey would be demanding answers from Rick and her in short order. The idea of snowing a man like Ramsey had been insane since its inception. How could Rick have been so arrogant? So infuriating? So damn stubborn?

He was born to it, that's how! Rick Wyatt had been a rebel with one cause or another since they were kids. Of course this time the cause hadn't been a self-serving exercise in wit, but fought in the name of another. Rick had done it for James Ramsey. He'd acted altruistically out of loyalty, out of friendship.

Caron propped her chin in her hands, closing her eyes with a soulful sigh. Is that how she would explain it, when the whole scam blew? Would Ramsey have empathy for Rick's allegiance to James? For her allegiance to Rick? Maybe her career at the firm would be over. Maybe she'd have to brush up on her two-step and look at dryers three through seven as a business commodity rather than a hotbed of lust.

When Caron returned from her quick lunch at the café downstairs, the Ramseys were already comfortably ensconced in her office. Ramsey was pacing about; Agatha sat on the small sofa opposite her desk.

"No one outside so we just came in," Ramsey explained.

"Hope you don't mind, Caron," Agatha chirped,

eyes twinkling behind wired reading glasses. Her small feet were up on the cushions, case files heaped around her. "We just couldn't wait to see this latest slew of contestants."

"Contestants, sister?" Ramsey's bushy gray brows lifted over the rims of his glasses. "This is not 'The Dating Game.'"

"No, it's like 'The Match Game,'" Agatha tittered, sparing Caron a wink as she goaded him on. "Match up the itsy bitsy baby with the right medal, then match up the old grouchy billionaire with the baby."

"A fool at ninety," Ramsey muttered.

"A crusty buzzard at seventy-seven," she tossed back gaily.

"Any prospects in this batch?" Caron asked dutifully.

"Not yet," Ramsey replied in a bark, wandering over to the windows with his meaty hands clasped behind his back.

Caron set her purse on the desktop, doing a double take as Agatha's thin, veined hands shifted through the files atop the cushion. Lodged in the stack was a large colorful envelope. An envelope from Rapid One Hour Photo on the main floor of the building.

"Why, what on earth is this?" Agatha squeaked in girlish curiosity. With surprisingly nimble fingers, she pulled open the sticky flap of the envelope.

Her pictures! Bobber's photograph was inside that envelope! Caron's heart hammered in her chest as she thought back to the nude portrait of Agatha, to her milky white skin, her reams of brilliant red hair. The resemblance might mean nothing to the elderly woman, or it might just be the key.

"Those are personal pictures of mine," Caron said

cheerily, rounding the desk as fast as her beige heels and tight brown skirt would allow. "A friend and I took a trip to the Rockies over the weekend and—"

"So that's where you were yesterday," Ramsey charged with the noises of an irate parent.

"Why, yes. But believe me, the search moved on efficiently." Caron reached for the envelope in Agatha's hand, but failed to take firm hold of the flap. The pictures spilled forth, spreading over the carpeting. Agatha swiftly swung her small legs over the side of the sofa to help with the retrieval.

"Oh, my stars!" Agatha's half glasses slipped to the tip of her nose as she took one of the pictures featuring the threesome.

"The owner of the resort took it," Caron ventured awkwardly—and uselessly, she soon realized. Agatha was caught up in her own thoughts. Specifically distressing thoughts, for the old woman's complexion was growing pasty under the rouge splashes on her cheeks, and her eyes were welling with tears.

"Look, Douglas," she gasped hoarsely, motioning to her brother with a jerky, bejeweled hand.

Douglas Ramsey strode swiftly to her side. "Why, I see nothing, woman," he rumbled impatiently, after raising the photograph to his face for a good look. "Except that Rick Wyatt was with you, Caron. No wonder I couldn't track him down! What's this? There's a baby riding on his shoulder in some sort of sack." The old man's look was sharp and suspicious. "Where the blazes did he come from? He's mine, isn't he?"

"His name is Bobber and he isn't yours, Mr. Ramsey," she scoffed, again put off by his autocratic attitude. "You cannot lay claim to a baby as if he were a piece of property." She knew she was being disrespectful to the firm's biggest client, but she didn't care. Bobber deserved better.

Slender teardrops slipped out of Agatha's eyes, magnified behind her thick lenses. "I cannot believe it. After all these years. I just cannot." With a cry she collapsed on the file-strewn cushions.

"Agatha!" Caron rushed to her side, dropping down to the sofa to steady her while Ramsey reached for the telephone. With a huge, shaky finger he punched in the number of his physician's office.

"I must speak to Doctor Norwood this instant, young lady!" he was roaring into the telephone after apparently being brushed off. "I don't care if he's conferring with Doctor Spock, Doctor Kildare, or Doctor Dolittle! Yes, I do realize he's busy. I've known him forty years and pay for a chunk of that fancy suite your bottom is perched in. You tell him Douglas Ramsey is on the line. Never mind how it's spelled!"

Caron pressed her fingers against Agatha's wrist to find her pulse steady and strong. "Has she eaten anything lately?" she asked anxiously.

Ramsey shook his head. "Should've stopped, I suppose. It's my—" He broke off to turn his attention back to the telephone. "Agatha's collapsed, Fred. No, we're just around the corner at the lawyers. Right. Fifth floor, Caron Carlisle's office." He slammed down the phone. "He's coming to us."

Caron nodded in relief. "Summon my secretary, tell her to get some water in here."

Ramsey balked for a brief, surprised moment.

"Hurry up," Caron prodded, massaging Agatha's wrists.

"Yes, yes," he relented, swinging open the door and bellowing for water.

By the time the doctor arrived, Agatha was coming around. She blinked several times, struggling to take in her surroundings. Caron's heart lurched in compassion at the sight of the normally spritely woman in a vulnerable, woozy condition.

"There now, old girl," Fred Norwood said cheerily, patting Agatha's shallow cheek. The dapper man with a head of thick white hair and bright gray eyes was amazingly calm and pleasant considering the summons he'd received. "Shame on you for giving Douglas such a scare."

Agatha smiled wanly. "Where am I, Doctor?"

"Why at your attorney's, m'dear. Cutting your crabby brother out of the will, I hope." He tucked his stethoscope back into his black bag and rose from the sofa. Though nearly Ramsey's age, he was about half his size. This didn't stop him from standing up to the billionaire in doleful disgust. "This delicate flower needs constant care, fool," he chastised under his breath.

"I know it," Douglas Ramsey grumbled, stroking his chin nervously. "She all right?"

"Yes, for a frail, elderly woman who's obviously been traumatized, she's tip-top."

Ramsey rubbed the back of his neck. "She had it in her head to be here today. The baby search means so much to her. I take the blame, however. Sometimes I forget just how old the spunky gal is."

"Get her something to eat," the doctor advised. "And get her home."

"Not yet," Agatha protested feebly, struggling to sit up.

"We'll take good care of her, Doctor," Caron promised. "We've sent for some hot sandwiches and cold drinks."

"Thank you for coming, Fred," he said, seeing him to the door.

"Stop by my office soon, Douglas," the doctor directed.

"I'm in perfect health," Ramsey protested in surprise.

"You certainly are," Fred Norwood retorted, jerking open the door. "Fit enough to give my receptionist a well-deserved apology."

"Oh, give her a raise instead," he blustered in dismissal.

"Money doesn't buy everything," the doctor chided. "Maybe this baby grandson you're so intent on finding will teach you some compassion. Heaven knows none of us have had any luck."

Ramsey tried to shoot off a proper response, but his old friend was off with an airy wave.

Caron could feel Ramsey's eyes upon her as they sat around her desk a short while later, eating their take-out food. To her relief, he had the sensitivity not to probe about the photograph. Still trying to recover from her fainting spell, Agatha was eating in slow, labored bites, sipping on soda pop from one of Caron's ceramic mugs.

"Feeling better, Agatha?" Ramsey inquired gently.

"Much," she replied with a bit of her old spark.

"Excellent. Franklin will take you home then."

Agatha eyed him in sharp suspicion. "What are you planning to do in the meantime?"

"Caron is going to take me to the Wyatt boy's Laundromat. He's had my baby all this time! And he was close to James, just as I figured," he reasoned in a growl. "I knew something was burning in that man's gut the night of the party."

"Yes, but you don't understand the cir—"

"Just hold on right there," he ordered Caron sternly.

Caron clamped her mouth shut, the recipient of his wrath for the first time. Their relationship had been so congenial until now.

"I wish to be a part of this confrontation at the laundry place," Agatha insisted.

"That is impossible." He reached across the desk and gave her frail hand a squeeze. "I'm no fool, Agatha. I've got the picture now—no pun intended. That baby has your red hair, the roundness of your youth. It's enough for me, coupled with Wyatt's probing investigation at the house." Agatha tried to speak, but he held up a meaty hand. "I didn't tell you about our clash the night of the party, I know. Actually, it makes your identification all the more spontaneous, doesn't it?"

"Yes, Douglas." She threw up her hands in abdication.

"Come along then," he said, helping her to her feet. "Franklin is right outside. You two may as well start off now."

"Very well," she agreed with surprising meekness.

"Knew all along, didn't you?" Ramsey chastised as Caron pulled her Saturn out of the downtown parking lot fifteen minutes later.

Despite the intensity of the situation, Caron had to suppress a nervous giggle at the sight of the hulky billionaire stuffed into the passenger seat of her car, fingers gripped to the dashboard. She wondered how long it had been since he'd been in a regular-size vehicle.

"I don't know anything for sure, sir," she replied honestly, braking for a yellow light. "I can only say that Rick had some sort of agreement with your son, James. He asked for my assistance and I couldn't refuse."

"Some good-humor man, this Richard Wyatt," he snorted in bitterness. "In cahoots with James. With you. I don't know him from Adam and he's manipulating me like a puppet on a string."

"You didn't exactly fall prey to his game, though, did you?" she pointed out.

"I offer a million dollars for information leading to my grandson and this guy harbors the child and penetrates my defenses for a closer look—through my trusted attorney!"

Caron was glad the light turned green and she could concentrate on driving the car.

"He have the medal?" he barked.

"I haven't seen it," Caron replied. "And Rick has never admitted that the baby is the right one. Not yet, he hasn't."

"Why not?" he asked in surprise.

"I don't think he wanted to put me in that tight of a spot," she explained in Rick's defense. "I believe he was trying to keep me in the dark for my own good. So I wouldn't feel obligated to turn Bobber in."

"So, he believes you do have a shred of loyalty toward your client," Ramsey snapped sarcastically.

"Believe it or not, I have been looking out for your interests, too, sir," she assured him. "You wouldn't be happy if the baby wasn't where he really belonged. Rick just wanted to make sure of where that was."

"What did he promise you?" Ramsey wondered incredulously. "Fortune?"

"Love," Caron replied just above a whisper, keeping her eyes on the road. "Rick and I do go a long way back, Mr. Ramsey. He came to me because of our link, for help in honoring your son's last request."

"What request?"

"He wished for Rick to decide upon the fate of your grandchild."

"The arrogance!" Ramsey exploded in rage. "He's nothing more than a—a—"

"Rebel?"

"Exactly!"

"Last requests are important, sir," Caron reasoned. "Rick was closer to James than he let on and took his death extremely hard. He's been riding on emotion ever since. I believe fulfilling James's last wish is part of his grieving process. He desperately wants to do the right thing for the heir. Without jeopardizing my job, by the way."

"Foolish girl!" he muttered in disbelief. "I could have your job with the snap of a finger."

"I know," Caron agreed. "But I'd do it again. For Rick. For James. Please try to see this as a happy ending to your quest, sir," she pleaded. "Rick assured me the child's mother was due back today."

Ramsey's face beamed in satisfaction. "Ah, now we're getting somewhere."

11

"WHY, THE PLACE IS buttoned up tight. In the middle of the afternoon!"

Caron was expressing her surprise to Douglas Ramsey as they stood on the sidewalk outside Hotshots a short time later, staring at the Closed sign in the shuttered windowpane. Her heart pounded in her ears as she imagined the worst. What if Rick flew the coop with the baby, leaving her with the consequences?

"Maybe he's inside." Caron moved toward the door, trying to keep up a calm front.

"He's probably harboring the baby's mother in there," Ramsey theorized in anger. Edging past her, he raised a large fist to the door. "C'mon, c'mon," he bellowed. "Open up I say!"

Miraculously, a rattle soon signified that someone was working the locks from the inside.

Rick swung the door open wide, drilling the man with a penetrating look. "Open up or what, sir? You going to blow my house in?"

"I just might!"

Rick stepped into the doorway, completely filling it with his wide, solid form. He easily kept them at bay by bracing his powerful arms on either side of the wooden jamb.

Caron watched him metamorphose into the Hotshot with three simple actions: the lift of his square chin, the slit of his eyelids, the slouch of the left shoulder. An inherent warrior stance, honed to perfection by years and years of rebellion. To an authority figure like Douglas Ramsey, the act was utter arrogance, calculated defiance. But Caron could read the real story behind the shield these days. Rick was arming himself against an internal attack more than anything else, determined not to give in to his own frailties.

"The time has come, Rick," she said in soft counterpoint.

Rick looked at her for a long, stubborn moment. What was he waiting for? she wondered, gazing into the depths of his troubled eyes. Ramsey had the goods on him and that was that. "Rick, you really have nothing more to lose at this point," she stated quietly.

"I hope you're right." With a resigned sigh, he stepped aside, allowing them to enter.

"I know everything, young man," Ramsey charged impatiently.

"I doubt it," Rick retorted. "But do come in. I prefer to clean all dirty linen behind closed doors around here."

Rick fiddled with the blinds as they stepped inside, allowing daylight to flood the place. He did keep the Closed sign in place, however.

Caron scanned the place to find one surprising visitor on hand in the stuffy silence. Agatha, alert and rejuvenated, was seated in one of the red vinyl chairs beside the pop machine.

"What are you doing here, Agatha?" Ramsey demanded in amazement. "The doctor said—"

"Never mind what Fred said to do," she cut in, her voice and eyes bright. "I'm back in form. As good as it gets these days, anyway."

"Where is the limousine? Where is Franklin?" Douglas Ramsey blustered.

"I sent him for a luncheon break," Agatha replied saucily. "He won't be back for an hour."

"Why, I'll have his head!"

"You most certainly will not," she chided. "I was bound to get here one way or the other. Franklin's wise enough to know when he's licked. Which is more than I can say for you!"

"But why are you here, m'dear?" he asked in a softer tone of total bewilderment.

Agatha's catlike eyes gleamed. "Because I have some answers and want more."

"I know it all now," Ramsey informed her. "Caron has filled me in on this man's connection to James, to the baby in the picture. Wyatt here will not deny us our heir any longer. If he tries, I shall have him up on charges."

"Now, Mr. Ramsey," Caron swiftly interceded, "surely we can calmly sort this thing out." To her frustration, Caron realized that Ramsey wasn't paying the least bit of attention to her, but looking at something over her shoulder. She whirled to find Rick's sister emerging from the storage room with Bobber in her arms. "Erin?" she ventured in surprise.

"Yes. Hello, Caron." Erin punctuated her greeting with a sunny smile as she tossed a curtain of blond hair out of Bobber's reach. "It's been a long time."

"Years," Caron clarified, taking in the younger woman's tanned skin and slender form set to advantage in a springy floral dress. "You look wonderful, as if you've just stepped off the beach."

"Well, you're close," Erin admitted. "My husband, Ben, and I just got back from Mexico."

"I would like to hold the boy if I may," Ramsey requested in brusque impatience.

Erin shot her big brother a questioning glance.

Rick nodded solemnly, his black lashes fanning his sharp cheekbones. "Let him hold the baby. He won't drop him."

Bobber went willingly to Ramsey, inquisitively fingering the golden clip clasping his maroon tie to his snowy white shirt. "You'll be wearing one of those on your ties some day," Ramsey told him in singsong pleasure.

"So, Mr. Ramsey, just what about Bobber tipped you off?" Rick asked with new suspect civility in his tone.

"Nothing!" Ramsey replied bluntly. "I imagine Agatha has explained about the photographs of your mountain trip. Her memory was jogged, not mine. Imagine the nerve of this upstart thinking he'll decide if I'm fit to be your grandpapa!" he told Bobber, bouncing him in his arms.

"Douglas," Agatha warned.

"Ah, what?" he asked, tearing his eyes from the child.

"Don't you wonder just how I identified the heir?"

"The red hair, round face, I see it all now. Don't worry, Agatha. If you're on hand to pave the way, you have nothing to fret about. If the medal isn't here, we'll just have to wait for the blood tests for positive proof."

Agatha opened her curled hand to reveal the silver dollar medallion on its original chain.

Ramsey moved forth with Bobber to get a closer look. "By George, it's the one!" He looked over at Rick in accusation. "So you did have it all along."

"James gave it to me, along with his note asking for help," Rick explained.

"Douglas, there is something I wish to explain," Agatha again tried to intercede."

"What? That Rick Wyatt deserves the reward for finding the heir?"

"Rick does deserve the reward," Agatha agreed with a cagey grin.

"So be it," Ramsey conceded. "I have what I want."

Agatha's lined face narrowed in disgust. "You don't even know what you have!"

"Of course I do. I have James's baby in my arms. What I don't have, however, is the mother. She will have to be dealt with. And Caron promised me she'd be here today."

"Calm down and listen to me," Agatha directed with unexpected force. "The heir is the spittin' image of James's first love. Her name is Julia. I spotted the resemblance immediately. It's truly uncanny."

Ramsey's head spun in all directions. "How can she be his first? Where is this woman? I wish to speak to her right now."

"She doesn't wish to mix with any of us, Douglas."

"You are talking utter nonsense, woman. You haven't fully recovered from your fainting episode."

Caron blinked in shock. Was Agatha confused? As confused as Caron was herself?

Erin made the next move, stepping up to take Bobber from Ramsey's arms. Caron watched as the infant curled into Erin, content as a babe in his mother's arms. And why not? she slowly speculated, as the pair joyously engaged in a flurry of tickles and giggles.

The baby was in his mother's arms.

Erin was Bobber's mother!

And she had appeared on schedule, just as Rick had predicted. Just as Rick had known she would—probably well in advance. Bobber's father was no doubt Erin's husband Ben, a former classmate of theirs. Ben with the bright red hair.

This led to one certain deduction: Bobber was not the Ramsey heir. Caron's analytical brain ticked crazily over the puzzle pieces, sorting them, fitting them into one larger picture. The entire thing reeked of a setup.

As for the mysterious Julia, old flame to James, she had to be a little too old to bear anyone's child. And she wanted nothing to do with the Ramseys, according to Agatha.

One long look into Agatha's clear eyes convinced Caron that the woman knew exactly what she was saying.

With that decision made, she shifted her gaze to Rick. Their eyes locked for a long, startling moment. And the answer to the riddle was finally clear.

"I never said Bobber was the one," he reminded her.

Caron felt her hackles rise as she thought back on all the trust she'd offered him. All the detours he'd taken from the simple truth. "Quit beating around the bush, Rick. I deserve to hear it all from you."

"The Bobber is my nephew," Rick confessed. "I've been caring for him while Erin and her husband took a well-deserved vacation."

"Don't be so modest, Rick," Erin urged, turning to Caron. "The trip was his idea. He even helped with the arrangements."

"And insisted upon caring for the Bobber," Caron deduced.

Erin nodded with a laugh. "I wish you'd all stop calling my baby by that ridiculous nickname. Rick made it up for him because his round head resembles a fishing bobber, red on top and white on the bottom. His real name is Ricky, after his generous uncle."

"Wily is right!" Caron seethed between her teeth.

"I want my heir, dammit," Ramsey bellowed. "Everyone is talking riddles."

"There's your heir, sir," Caron proclaimed with bitter force, in a grand sweeping gesture toward Rick. "Agatha claims to have recognized him in the photograph, and I know it's not me."

"But, but—". Ramsey gaped in befuddlement. "James told Agatha he had a baby. You are a grown man, Richard."

"Many parents regard their children in those terms," Rick pointed out. "Especially at sentimental moments. He knew his life was draining away when he confided in Agatha."

"Don't you faint on me now," Agatha cautioned her brother moments later as Caron and Rick eased him into a chair beside her.

"This is preposterous," Ramsey mumbled, looking lost for the first time in Caron's memory. "I am so confused."

"It's simple really," Rick ventured to explain. "I am your grandson, sir. I've known so for a few years now. James simply walked in here one day to announce that he was my natural father. I've known my whole life that I'm an adopted child, as are Erin and my two other siblings. Our brood is a patchwork of genes, but it hasn't stopped us from being a tight-knit family."

"Why'd he wait so long to claim you?" Ramsey asked. "And he thought I was a neglectful father...."

Rick jumped to his natural father's defense with lightning speed. "James had just learned that he'd fathered a child. My natural mother had an attack of conscience when she heard his health was failing and contacted him. He immediately investigated and tracked me down."

"Oh, I see," Ramsey mumbled, removing his glasses to rub his eyes. "It seems I've missed the real facts all along by jumping to conclusions."

Rick took pleasure in affirming it. "James was heartsick over the years we lost. But we made the most of our time together by nurturing a close friendship." He paused to get a grip on his emotions. "He wasn't sure I should ever take the risk of contacting you, fearful that you'd intrude on my happiness. But, in the end, he ultimately felt I should have the option. All he asked, was that I wait until after his passing. I wasn't sure we could make a go of it, so I brought the Bobber in as a decoy and contacted Caron." He cast her a look of apology, yearning for a glimmer of understanding, of forgiveness in her eyes. But only the pain of his betrayal reflected back at him, shooting daggers into his heart. "Caron didn't want to deceive you," he assured Ramsey, unable to face her any longer. "I persuaded her, tricked her."

"I had more faith in your abilities as an attorney," Ramsey chastised her in disappointment.

"I am still a good attorney!" she hastened to interject. "Just a foolish lover."

Rick's gaze tore to her again, his muscled body frozen in anguish. He couldn't argue such a personal issue in front of these people. He wanted nothing more than to throw her over his shoulder and run for the hills. Force the empty look out of her eyes with ardent lovemaking and passionate promises. But he owed the Ramseys something, after the hullabaloo he'd caused.

"I didn't mean anyone any harm, sir," he assured. "I thought I was clever enough to check you out without any fuss. But what did we do but end up in an instant flare-up. I walked away the night of your party with no intention of ever seeing you again. But you were clever enough to see there was more to my story than met the eye. Inherent stubbornness and determination kept us in the same arena."

"So you thought you'd put off the inevitable by whisking me off to the mountains!" Caron lashed out. "Hide out as long as you could!"

"For Pete's sake, Caron, we were only gone one night!" he reasoned.

"But it was enough to get me where you wanted me."

"Yes, in a marrying mood!" he admitted, causing the Ramseys to gasp. "Sorry, folks. But I'm not going to let this woman get away a second time." He whirled back to her. "Caron, I knew the charade was crumbling and I wanted to solidify our relationship beforehand. I love you, honey," he declared passionately. "You have to believe that."

"I can't believe any of this!" she wailed, all professional poise thrown to the wind, despite the importance of the client on hand. "How silly I must've looked, hot on the trail of the red-hair link between Agatha and the baby."

"The red hair turned out to be a welcome red herring," Rick conceded, biting back a twitching smile. "It's just an accident that Erin's husband is a carrot top."

"None of this erases your part in this deception, Miss Carlisle," Ramsey chastised. "You should've reported Rick's scheme to me immediately."

"Yes, sir," Caron readily agreed, twisting the handles of her purse in trembling fingers. "It would have simplified things for all of us."

"She had the heir's best interest in mind," Rick broke in forcefully. "Even though she didn't know I was the heir in question. And it was the way James wanted it, too!"

"I expect utter loyalty from anyone in my employ," Ramsey insisted, lowering his fist to the arm of his chair.

"Oh, hush up, you big bully," Agatha scoffed. "Carrie did the best she could. She will always be my good friend. And yours too."

"I believe this is a good time for me to leave," Caron said with a shaky sigh. "I'm expected back at work."

"I can't lose you again, Caron," Rick pleaded. He knew the moment she walked out the door, the spell between them would be broken. If he could make her understand now while the wound was fresh. It would swiftly heal.

Caron's face crumpled in anguish. "Total trust you said! And I believed you!"

"I was trying to shield you!"

"You used me."

"I never thought it would go this far." Rick stared at her bleakly. "Please believe that I'm out of secrets."

"I'm out of faith, Rick," she choked out. She blinked several times in an effort to check the tears in her eyes, hoping she wouldn't break down in public.

"Please don't be upset, Carrie," Agatha chirped beseechingly.

"Don't go, Caron," Rick pleaded, grabbing for her arm.

"You've already made me look like a total incompetent in front of these clients," she snapped in his ear. "Let me leave with the last shred of dignity I possess."

Rick dropped his hand from her arm, unable to argue her point. With a final apology to the Ramseys, she made her exit.

"Well, at least everything is out in the open now," Agatha murmured, looking up to Rick with loving, misty eyes. "I, for one, am delighted that our heir is long out of diapers. We can begin to build a memorable relationship right away. Right, Douglas?"

"I was expecting a bouncy baby who wouldn't talk back," Ramsey grumbled. "Who'd offer a little unconditional love to a poor old man."

"You would try to force a miracle," Rick grumbled, eyes darting to the window as Caron's Saturn rolled off down the street. "Unconditional love doesn't exist, man. You can't even buy it with all your dough."

"How can you say such things?" Agatha scoffed. "You of all people, Rick Wyatt, know that Carrie's love for you has been unconditional. And as for miracles—" her sparkling eyes wandered to her brother "—you've brought this crusty old dog a second chance. A red-herring stunt second only to the parting of the Red Sea."

Rick drove his hands through his hair with a mighty groan. He'd lost the best thing that had ever happened to him for a second time. Hoping James would forgive his flare of regret, he fervently wished with all his heart that he'd left well enough alone with the Ramseys. He shouldn't have needed such a monumental excuse to contact Caron in the first place. He should've called her last week in honor of the new Chinese place opening down the street.

"Give me those cupcakes this instant, Caron!" Megan ordered, chasing Caron around their kitchen table. The nurse had awakened around dinnertime the same day to find her roommate wolfing down bakery cakes smothered in rich chocolate frosting.

"Let me eat myself into oblivion," Caron cried with a full mouth, dodging the small blonde in the striped jammies.

"I can't. Nurses are dedicated to saving lives." With a grunt, she jerked the box from Caron's hands. "Now," she said, her eyes narrowing in professional interrogation, "just how many of these have you taken in the last hour?"

Caron glared at her, a huge chocolate ring around

her belligerently set mouth. "Not enough to numb the pain."

"Oh, you've had enough, all right," Megan deduced as she counted the frosting smudges in the box.

"If you don't give me those back, I'll just get them somewhere else," Caron threatened with a shaking fist.

"Let's just calm down," Megan placated, pulling out two chairs at the table.

"I don't want to," Caron said with a defiant lift to her chin.

"Sit!" Megan ordered, shoving her into a chair.

Already limp from the events of the day, Caron sank down at the table like a rag doll, resting her head in her arms. Megan set the box on the counter and sat down beside her. "Now, we're dealing with something big," she calculated. "Really, really big."

Caron nodded from the shelter of her arms.

"Your mother flipped out at the Laundromat," Megan guessed. "She found out about your second stained dress and—" She abruptly stopped in mid-theory as the back of Caron's brown head rocked back and forth.

"It's Rick," she croaked hollowly.

"Rick broke up with you," Megan proposed, only to receive another negative head rock. "No? Then Ramsey found out that Rick's harboring his fugitive grandson. Bingo!" She snapped her fingers. "The whole thing came tumbling down around your ears."

"Yes."

"Bobber is now the happy recipient of a cool billion," Megan murmured, shaking her head in wonder.

"No."

"Yes, no," Megan squawked in frustration. "Where have I gone wrong?"

"Rick is the billionaire baby!" she told her in a muffle.

"Come again!" Megan shrieked, pulling Caron up in her seat.

Caron nodded numbly, fresh tears springing to her eyes. "It's true, Meggy. He was the real heir all along. Bobber is his sister Erin's boy. He used him as a decoy and me as a go-between chump. Wanted to see if the Ramsey scene was for him before committing himself."

"He borrowed the baby to throw the scent off his trail while he mingled in the thick of things?"

"Exactly."

Megan gaped. "Gee, the guy's pretty smart."

"Too smart for the likes of me," Caron said languishingly. "I fell for his charms again. At my age!"

Megan reached across the table to squeeze her hand. "I thought he loved you."

"He says he does, but who can believe him after the stunt he's pulled?"

"Couldn't you try?" Megan coaxed.

Caron pursed her mouth stubbornly. "I can't think of one reason."

Megan balked. "I can think of a billion of 'em."

"Megan, the man, not the money, is at issue here."

"Your mother would be ashamed of such talk," Megan teased. "But you are right, of course. Shall I go and defend your honor?" she suggested fiendishly. "Pummel that bad boy's chest in your name?"

"Thanks for the offer, but I think it will be best to put Rick behind us for good."

Megan lowered her small fist on the table with determination. "Consider him completely forgotten."

Caron nodded numbly with a sniff. "Right after you fulfill the bet, he'll be history."

Megan's face fell. "Rats. Thought I had ya there."

12

"YOU ARE THIRTY MINUTES late!" Rick whirled on Kyle in fury as he entered Hotshots Friday afternoon. "I can't go out to lunch with you anymore. Ma has to leave. She has a dental appointment."

"Ah, Rick, it can't be that late." Kyle slowly sauntered inside. Dressed in a conservative dark suit, with an open bag of potato chips in his hand and a mischievous grin on his face, he was a mass of contradictions in himself. He followed Rick's jabbing finger up at the large round school clock on the wall. "Gee, I did lose track of time," he yielded in genuine surprise. "I've got to get back to the office myself pretty soon."

Rick glared at him. "Where the hell have you been?"

Kyle's face glowed. "It was the craziest thing, Rick. I was passing by Marshall's Market next door. Around noon, right on schedule," he hastened to add in his own defense.

"You trip outside and hit your head on the curb?" Rick asked, his black brows arching in menace.

"Whew, aren't you the touchy billionaire baby today," Kyle grumbled. "They say all really rich people are miserable inside. Must be true."

"Only poor people say so," Rick snorted. "And I'm not sittin' on a billion, not yet."

"It's only a matter of time, really, until you and Grandpa Ramsey come to terms—of endearment." Kyle sank into one of the red vinyl chairs against the wall, dipping a long-fingered hand into his bag of potato chips. "In the meantime, you have a million to tide you over."

"I deserved the reward money. Led the old man right to the heir, just as he wanted." Rick leaned over Kyle, resting his hands on the chrome armrests of his chair. "Tell me why, Kyle," he invited in false cheeriness. "Tell me why I asked Ma to cover for me during the lunch hour, only to have you waste her time and mine."

"Where is Ma?" Kyle wondered, sand-colored hair falling into his eyes as he anxiously scanned the room. "Ma?" he called out.

"She won't protect you this time," Rick warned, his hands locking Kyle's wrists to the chrome arms of the chair, nearly crushing his chip bag.

"She likes to, makes her feel young. Ma!" he hollered.

Eleanor emerged from the back room with an armload of mini detergent boxes. "Oh, hello, Kyle. Finally got here, did you?"

"I was just going to tell Rick about my dream girl, Ma. Thought you might want to hear about it."

"I'm all ears," Eleanor said brightly, scooting up the aisle. "Ricky's certainly interested," she noted, beaming over the brotherly scene. "Hunched over you like an eager cat."

"Yeah, right." Kyle gulped down the chips in his mouth, smiling under his brother's glare. "Anyway, I was passing by the market, and I noticed the place was stuffed with people. A cheering throng. I got to figuring they must be giving something away in there."

"So are they, Kyle?" Eleanor dumped the detergent boxes on a washing machine in preparation for a hasty exit.

"Slow down, Ma. It wasn't anything like that at all. Megan Gage was roller-skating through the aisles of the store, dressed in her old gym suit, singing our old high school fight song.

"'Cheer, cheer for Truman High,'" he sang out, catching Rick by the arm before he could bolt off. "Slow down, brother," he advised under his breath. "They're not giving any of that away, either. Caron was the first to leave the scene."

"Why didn't you come get me, brother?" Rick demanded. The fact that she'd been in his territory for the last half hour was more than he could bear. No matter how he'd tried during the last few days to trap her for a second round, she'd managed to evade him. The firm had given her the week off as a reward for solving the billionaire heir mystery. She used the time to scatter herself to the winds.

Oh, the satisfaction she must've felt hanging around right under his nose.... Rick's fists opened and closed reflexively, as desire and desperation surged through his system.

"I was literally trapped inside the store," Kyle was telling him in genuine sympathy, greedily digging in the bag for chips now that his hands were again free of Rick's vise-grip. "You know how uncertain mob behavior can be. We were packed in there like sardines and old Pop Marshall was trying to transform spectators into customers. Can't blame him, I suppose, considering that the stunt was costing him plenty. You see, Megan may have been a roller queen at one time, but her balance isn't very good anymore. Rammed into a display of canned corn and toppled into a freezer full of frozen dinners. Cans rolled and crushed boxes flew, boy."

"Why would a grown woman do such a thing?" Eleanor clucked in astonishment.

Kyle tipped his head with a pensive sigh. "It's not for us to reason why. In those short shorts, keep a rollin' by."

Eleanor shot her elder son a sour look that he blithely ignored. "It's hard to believe that level-headed Caron would associate with a flake like her," she mused in disapproval.

"Megan has not lost her marbles," Rick announced with great reluctance. "She did it on account of me, I'm sure." The news drew the same sort of moans and groans his rebel antics of old used to.

"You haven't stirred up this kind of fuss since high school," Eleanor clucked in confusion.

"Well, it is leftover high school stuff, really," he explained, with a dismissing wave. "She was fulfilling the terms of a bet she and Caron made years ago. The first one to get a phone call from me was the winner. The loser…" He paused, rolling his eyes to the ceiling. "The loser obviously had to skate through Marshall's Market on skates in her gym suit singing the school fight song."

"I imagine at the time it seemed like a frivolous debt, but now with the passing of years, I suppose it was an excruciating experience," Kyle wagered with a hearty chuckle.

Rick nodded in new empathy. "It sure explains why she's been so annoyed with me since my initial call to Caron concerning Ramsey."

"And explains the messages written on her white sweatshirt," Kyle added in further deduction. "The front said, Hotshot Is A Billionaire Bum. The back said, A Cruise Can't Cost That Much. I just figured she was speaking for Caron, so I wasn't going to tell you."

"I think each of them took her best shot at this Hotshot," Rick wagered with a mournful shake of his head.

"You still know how to get the girls goin'," Kyle marveled, drawing a frown from Rick.

"Hadn't you better get back to your job, Kyle?" Eleanor pointed out.

"Well, I wouldn't have to worry about it if I were a billionaire," Kyle grumbled, extending his long legs in the aisle as if no longer in such a hurry. "Say, maybe my blood kin has a wad, too," he pondered in sudden inspiration.

"A wad of something," Rick gibed, knowing full well that Kyle, like many adoptees, had no interest in searching for his natural parents.

"So, now all of a sudden being a Wyatt isn't good enough for my boys," Eleanor scolded with an edge of panic.

"Oh, c'mon, Ma," Rick scoffed, his tone softening with his features. "I've told you a hundred times since James popped into my life, that you and Pa are the only folks I want."

"Yes," she agreed with a sniff. "James made it easy for all of us by accepting you on your terms—moving into the neighborhood, nurturing a friendship with no strings attached. But his father wants so much more. He wants you heart and soul."

"He's an old man looking for a second chance," Rick relented quietly. "I've had more patience for his position since accepting that." Rick had done a lot of thinking during the past few days. As he longed for mercy from Caron for the underhanded stunt he'd pulled, the more mercy he offered to the billionaire in search of absolution. "I stopped by his barn of a house last night. We talked. Hell, we argued!" he corrected. "We both have a history of being a bit difficult, but I think we can come to some sort of a truce, maybe even some common ground. For instance, we both agree that Caron's role in my deception should be kept from the law firm. But we fought over who treated her with more understanding. The old goat really has a soft spot for her underneath it all!"

"And you know I was only teasing you, Ma," Kyle chimed in, laboriously rising to his feet with his crumpled bag of chips to envelop Eleanor in a bear hug. "We've always been rich in our own way."

"Certainly what I've taught you!" she huffed with a shadow of a smile. "No one would put up with you boys, anyway, not the way I do."

"Could you do me a favor?" Kyle asked, cupping her face in his hands.

"I'll try," she ventured, brushing some salt from his chin.

"Tell Ricky to fix me up with Megan, will ya, huh?"

"Are you sure she's your type?" Eleanor wondered dubiously.

"She's a nurse," Kyle promptly reported, bringing a shine of approval to his mother's face.

"You work something out, Ricky," Eleanor directed. "Arrange something nice for your brother and this roller skater."

"Hey, I don't even have a girl anymore," Rick exploded incredulously, aiming a thumb at his expansive chest.

"Oh, yes, you do," she huffed with a sigh. "You help Kyle."

"Megan does deserve a cruise, I guess...." he mused, stroking his square chin. "Do I dare further torment her by sending you along on the same ship?"

"Sounds like the perfect setup," Kyle agreed excitedly. "Make it first class for both of us."

"Make it separate cabins for each of them," Eleanor automatically inserted. "Now, I'm afraid I must be off to my beauty parlor appointment," she said with a glance to her watch.

"I thought you were going to the dentist," Rick recalled in confusion.

Eleanor's round cheeks grew pink. "Well, I was going to surprise you, but I am really going to have my hair tinted."

"Because of what Deborah Carlisle said?" Rick demanded.

"Yes and no," Eleanor replied. "You see, Deborah can be a real pain, but she does know a lot about color and style. I have faith in her advice, no matter how rudely it happens to be delivered."

Rick growled in frustration. "She doesn't deserve a friend like you, Ma."

"She'll be back just the same," Eleanor predicted with a twinkle. "Ironically enough, she'd never let the son-in-law catch of the century get away—now that he is the catch of the century." Eleanor kissed Rick's pained face with a smack. "You must learn to laugh over the irony of Deborah's shallowness. It's hard to say that even in time, she will ever acquire any depth. I give Caron credit for accepting this and working around it."

"I really don't think we will have to concern ourselves with Caron or her mother ever again," Rick complained.

"Well, life does hold a surprise or two, does it not?" Eleanor pointed out wistfully.

Rick shook his head. "Caron thinks I betrayed her trust."

"She has a right to be angry. But in your defense, you didn't deliberately hurt her."

"Wouldn't have shamelessly used her, if you'd known it would destroy her," Kyle helpfully appended.

"How was I to know I'd fall apart at the mere sight of her after all these years?" Rick challenged to no one in particular. "That we were both an amorous accident just waiting to collide? I tried to back off, but she wouldn't let me. We just tumbled deeper and deeper into ourselves, into this missing heir thing. I thought I had control, but I never did, not really."

He paused with a resigned sigh, closing his eyes to find Caron there. He shook the vision away, just as he'd done a thousand times during the past few days. "Maybe I just don't deserve her."

"Let her be the judge, Ricky," Eleanor advised. "It will be good for your rebel soul to show a little humility this once."

"Yeah," Kyle added, rubbing his hands together in greedy anticipation. "Having the chance to kick you around after all these years should give her a little satisfaction."

Rick's annoyance with Kyle uncorked in a burst of laughter. "Shut up, big brother, or I'll book you on a budget cruise—aboard *Jaws*."

Kyle pointed at his mother as she prepared to speak. "Don't say it, Ma. Don't tell him separate sharks."

"PINCH ME AND TELL ME it's real."

"Pinch you, Caron?" Megan turned away from the ticket counter at Stapleton International Airport, a validated pass in her hand. "I'm the one going on the cruise."

It was an overcast day in late November, shortly after dawn. Megan was decked out in a royal blue outfit fit for Princess Diana. Caron looked like little more than a peddler in her faded jeans and worn fringed suede jacket.

"I know you're going on the trip," Caron agreed with a smirk. "But as you wing off to connect with your ship in Miami, I'll be zipping back to the town house for a nice long breakfast before work. Bound and determined to make all sorts of noises I can't make while you're sleeping."

"What a clown!" Megan hooted. Then, tipping her

curly blond head in afterthought she added, "After that roller-skating fiasco a few weeks ago, maybe I should be the one pinching you."

"It wasn't as much fun as I thought it would be," Caron wistfully confessed as they sank down into molded chairs, Megan's belongings scattered at their feet. "Winning the bet, I mean."

"I think it would've been a lot more fun for both of us ten years ago," Megan mused, patting Caron's knee in consolation.

Caron appreciated Megan's unyielding support since her breakup with Rick. She would miss her desperately during the next two weeks. She hadn't felt this alone in years.

"I guess we can't go back and heal those old adolescent wounds, can we?" Caron eventually theorized softly, thinking of how that decade-late call had changed her life so profoundly. And that of Rick's as well. He was in line to inherit a fortune! Megan's dues had been paid out in the open with a simple spin through the market, over in a matter of minutes. Caron knew she'd be working through her dues with an aching heart for a long, long time.

Megan released a meditative sigh. "No, we can't truly go back. We've grown up too much. Even if we could somehow return in a time warp, it would be through new, wiser eyes."

"I sure don't feel any smarter," Caron grumbled, shoving her hands into the pockets of her jacket. "And trying to recapture a lost passion was a stupid stunt."

"But what you had with Rick was far more than a stab at nostalgia," Megan protested.

"Maybe I don't deserve anything more than a lesson out of this," Caron philosophized. "I went after him with the express purpose of landing on top of him."

"Well, I imagine you accomplished that." Megan fluttered long, innocent lashes.

"Very funny," Caron retorted, unamused by the earthy pun.

"Well, I personally have a very soft spot for Rick these days," Megan airily admitted. "After all, he did come through with this trip."

"Yes, a prince of a rebel," Caron snapped tartly. She was perplexed by his good deed. She'd spent the days after their blowup convincing herself he was still nothing more than a wolf, preying on the female population for his own amusement. Then he'd come across with this surprise for Megan....

"Wipe that suspicious scowl off your face," Megan chided. "He said he felt remorseful over the leftover bet, and my subsequent humiliating roller ride."

"If he's such a generous benefactor, where is my trip?" Caron demanded. "I'm the one he drew into the thick of his crazy scheme. The one he drew undercover. I nearly lost my job over this! If Mr. Ramsey hadn't kept quiet about my part in things, the partners would've had me for lunch."

"Concrete proof that there must be a merciful streak in the Ramsey clan," Megan maintained.

Caron rolled her eyes. "Oh, sure."

"Maybe Rick has different plans for you," Megan blurted out, bringing a cloud to her friend's face. "I mean, maybe he's going to pay you back some other way."

The boarding call for first-class passengers crackled over the speakers as they each silently mulled the thought.

"Well, this is it, kid." Caron stood up with her antsy friend, giving Megan a fierce hug.

"Take care, Caron." Megan gathered together her baggage and with a final peck to Caron's cheek, joined the passengers streaming into the boarding area.

Caron waited until Megan disappeared out of sight, then with a glance at her watch, moved out of the gate area into the crowded terminal corridor.

"You look absolutely naked without a baby in your arms."

Caron halted at the sound of the rich voice in her ear, spinning around to collide with chocolate eyes and a mile-wide chest.

"You!" she lashed out, instantly breaking the promise she'd made to herself to handle their next encounter coolly. But she couldn't help herself. This rebel always managed to catch her heart off guard. Always had the edge, the power to reduce her to a fragile schoolgirl. Undoubtedly she'd never outgrow his effect on her.

"You without Bobber..." He rubbed his mustache as he took full inventory of her. "You look so empty-handed somehow."

"You've described me to a T," she returned evenly, hoping to disguise the shudder rippling down her shoulders. "Empty-handed."

"You did cut your teeth on him, so to speak," he wistfully continued. "Learned everything you ever wanted to know about Bobbers, but were afraid to ask."

"Yes, I'll never forget him," she promised.

"Lucky guy."

What on earth was he doing here? she wondered.

"So, is Megan aboard the plane already?" he asked conversationally as if reading her thoughts.

"Yes. You are a funny guy, Hotshot," Caron blurted out in mystification, knowing she should avoid the lure of banter, and scamper. But she couldn't let it lie. After all she'd been through, she had to have her say one last time. "You send me over the moon with your crummy scheme, jeopardize my job—then you turn around and give Megan a vacation for roller-skating through a market. And come to see her off!" she added, obviously disbelieving the final affront the most.

Rick absorbed the verbal blow with a tilt to his chin. "Is that what you really think, Quick Draw?" he chided.

"The facts stack up only one way. Even Perry Mason would agree."

"Jealous?"

Caron reared back huffily. "Of which part?"

He was completely dominating her space despite the foot traffic around them. "I wasn't about to send you off on a romantic cruise without the Hotshot here as escort. And I couldn't get away. Besides," he added on an injured note, "you've been a hard woman to pin down, for an invitation of any kind."

Caron raised her chin, avoiding his eyes. "Well, you stopped trying."

"I'm a hothead."

"So I get no reward for all my mental anguish," she sought to confirm in surprise.

"You get me," he offered.

"What an egotistical offer, after scrambling out here to see Megan off."

Rick tipped his black head in the direction of the gate. "I'm here seeing Kyle off," he corrected.

"He's taking Megan's trip?" she asked softly, her heart alight with the news.

"Why, you didn't think I was interested in Megan—then or now, did you?" he hooted in amazement.

"Not ever!" she lied.

"I told you Kyle was the one who—"

"I know, I know," she cut in, a hot flush heating her skin.

"You just want me all for yourself," he teased.

She did.

It took all Caron's willpower not to melt into the folds of his shiny leather jacket, not to stand on tiptoe and nuzzle the morning stubble on his chin. His scent was drawing her in, making her woozy with yearning, with the need to be cuddled and reassured as only Rick could. But he couldn't just swoop back and make her swoon. He needed to prove his intentions. And it would be a tough sale after this last stunt of his.

"Yeah, Kyle's sailing the love boat," Rick replied, obviously unaware of her quivering insides. "He deserves the trip, too. He's always around when I need him." Rick winced, then laughed. "Man, will it be a nice break not to have him around when I don't need him for a change."

"Just how intimate is this dating-game prize?" she demanded with a sudden urge to play mother hen.

"Not very. They're seated on the plane together, but their cabins are separate aboard ship. You can ask Ma," he added under her narrowed look. "She made the arrangements."

"Megan barely remembers him," Caron scoffed.

"Maybe it will be to his advantage," Rick wagered in good humor. "Unlike myself, Kyle had to struggle for the girls way back when."

Caron's back stiffened under her pink sweatshirt. "Megan thinks you're quite the knight, supplying her with this trip just for the asking."

He stroked his jaw with a contemplative groan. "Handling Kyle could be a bogus price to pay. Gee, I hope she didn't think this was a completely free ride on the Hotshot here."

Caron's tight-lipped nod solemnized the occasion. "The end of innocence for Megan as well."

"Hey, don't lay her innocence on me, too—make me the ogre who toppled both class beauties. I take only responsibility for you, sweet thing."

"Always handy with the right line—when you want to be."

"Hey, I'm trying to prove that I'm a good guy," he asserted, anger flashing in his eyes. "That I've grown up with the sensitivity to understand the bet, and the embarrassment it's caused. Had I just called Megan after our date, called many others as well, I'd have been a better young man back then."

"Then I would've been skating through the market!" Caron argued ruefully, deliberately twisting the issue to buy time. Time to steady her quaking limbs.

Time to grow a protective shell against his heady sensuality. Being angry with Rick didn't diminish his masculinity, or his attraction.

"Skating through there with Pop Marshall on your tail would've done you good back then," he taunted, grinning devilishly over her indignant gasp. "Would've given you a chance to laugh at yourself, see all of us as bungling kids. You were so serious, Caron. I thought we'd cured you of that, but—"

"Damn you, Rick!" she yelled, glancing around the bustling terminal. "This is no place to have a scene."

"This is the perfect place," he argued, capturing her flailing wrists in his hands. "Everyone gets emotional in airports."

"Over the departure of a loved one, maybe."

"You've flown off from me, haven't ya?" he reasoned, his deep husky voice catching slightly. He pushed her back out of the mainstream, crowding her into a wall of rental lockers.

"Rick, you used me to get what you wanted," Caron accused in open pain.

"Caron, you came at me for one big, fat, sex-charged payback. Now, was that very nice?"

"Well, it turned out pretty nice," she popped back with forced flair.

"Forget it, honey," he said in a rough little whisper. "You can barely pull off the power trip stuffed inside one of your armor suits, with your hair glued together in a crash helmet and your face painted in a glossy mask." His eyes gleamed in triumph. "I've lucked out. Got you cornered here in nothin' at all."

Her eyes widened. "I'm dressed."

He took a handful of the soft brown hair cupping

her chin. "You're pretty much stripped down to the real girl here, the emotions ripe on your bare baby face."

"How dare you?" She tipped her chin high, but couldn't escape the heat of his breath on her scrubbed complexion, the spicy scent of his soap in her nostrils, the pressure of his hands on her shoulders. When he grazed her cheek with his thumb, she couldn't suppress the shudder of desire.

"See what I mean?"

"Okay, so we're physically attracted to each other," she conceded, as if pleading no contest to a charge of disorderly conduct.

"Together we are an inferno, babe," he uttered into her hair, his hands slipping into her jacket, kneading her waist through her soft sweatshirt.

"Well, it isn't enough," she argued.

"How about that I've always loved you and you're the only woman for me?" he persisted forcefully. His mouth curved in wicked glee. "How about that I have a rich grandpa?"

"Can I ever learn to trust you?" she wondered in exasperation.

"You've always trusted me, Quick Draw," he pointed out matter-of-factly. "Trusted me in the back seat of my Chevy, on top of my dryers, up in the mountains."

"Sex isn't everything!"

"That's sadly true," he relented in feigned remorse, pinching her chin as she tried to avert his gaze in a huff of disgust. "Listen, Caron, you never would've gone along with my scheme to check out Ramsey if you didn't believe in me. Deep inside you trusted my ability to make it right. Believed in my strength as a protector."

"I suppose," she begrudgingly agreed, giving in to the feeling of surrendering self-discovery.

"And I never would've let anyone blame you, hurt you," he asserted. "Your instincts about me have always been right, honey. I've always wanted only what was best for you. When I let you go the first time, it was the first totally unselfish act of my life."

"My romantic heart still wishes you would've come for me," she said in a broken little voice.

"I've come for you now," he proclaimed fiercely, obviously on the edge of losing it. "Caron, I love you so much. And after all the dodging you did for me and the Bob, it's my honor to announce that you've replaced Perry Mason as my favorite mouthpiece."

"Now there's something," she acknowledged with a sniff.

"Darn tootin' it is! Marry me, honey," he coaxed in desperation, cradling her face in his huge hands. "Just as we planned on the mountain trip. We'll have a half-dozen Bobbers. Pester your mother into behaving like a person. Air out that musty place of Ramsey's."

"But we'll fight," she protested. "We always have."

"A good debate heats the blood," he scoffed in dismissal. "Actually," he confided with a roguish slant to his mustache, "I'm sorta looking forward to it. Even to losing a skirmish once in a while on pure technicality. To the winner go the spoils, baby," he uttered huskily in her ear.

"Well, what about the Laundromat?" she persevered in doubt.

"It'll go on as always, of course," he replied in surprise.

"But Mr. Ramsey told me you're going to be dipping into his business affairs. I don't want you to change into your grandfather, Rick."

"Fat chance! Though I am going to spend some apprentice time at his headquarters, I will always be the owner and operator of Hotshots. I have plenty of family backup, more with you at my side. Why, it's a neighborhood monument!" he charged on passionately. "The place of my comeback. The place of your yellow-hatted entrance. The place we rediscovered... Well, face it, the old Chevy is long gone."

"Oh, Rick." She curled her arms around his neck burying her face in his jacket.

"Oh, Rick, what?" he asked in gentle persistence, his hands slipping beneath the back of her sweatshirt to the silkiness of her back. "You've always been so good with words, Quick Draw."

"You know."

A throat cleared in disgruntlement behind Rick, causing him to whirl on his heel.

"You are in my way," a stocky woman in a tan trench coat chortled.

"This is a private moment, madam," Rick asserted in curt dismissal.

"You two happen to be leaning against my locker, you rebellious young man!" she said, gesturing behind Caron. "Certainly no place to elicit a declaration from this woman."

"She has a point," he told Caron with dignity. "This is best settled at home atop the dryers."

"Yes, my darling," Caron yielded meekly. "With the Closed sign in the window, I trust."

Rick nodded firmly. "Of course. You have any pressing appointments today?"

"I'm due at jail this afternoon. What of your day?"

"The limo is picking me up later on...." he trailed off loftily. "Franklin could drop you off at the prison afterward."

"Sounds perfect," Caron purred.

With a nod to the dumbfounded woman, Rick took Caron by the arm and guided her into the ever-moving mass of people in the terminal.

"I still do, you know," she murmured in his ear.

He hung an arm over her shoulders in adolescent carelessness, regarding her with the pure delight reserved for youngsters and lovers. "You do?"

Feeling like a girl out of school, Caron impetuously kissed his whisker-roughened cheek in the sea of strangers. "I've loved you long and hard, Hotshot. Yesterday and today."

He flashed her a raffish grin. "Tonight, baby, don't forget about tonight."